W9-BYA-539

ALSO BY PHILIP NORMAN

FICTION
*Slip on a Fat Lady*
*Plumridge*
*Wild Thing*
*The Skaters' Waltz*
*Words of Love*

BIOGRAPHY AND JOURNALISM
*Shout: The True Story of the Beatles*
*The Stones*
*The Road Goes On for Ever*
*Tilt the Hourglass and Begin Again*
*The Age of Parody*
*Your Walrus Hurt the One You Love*
*Awful Moments*
*Pieces of Hate*
*The Life and Good Times of the Rolling Stones*
*Days in the Life: John Lennon Remembered*
*Elton*

PLAYS
*The Man That Got Away*
*Words of Love*

# EVERYONE'S GONE TO THE MOON

# Everyone's Gone to the Moon

## Philip Norman

RANDOM HOUSE
NEW YORK

Library of Congress Cataloging-in-Publication Data

Norman, Philip
Everyone's gone to the moon/Philip Norman.
p.    cm.
ISBN 0-679-44831-4
I. Title.
PR6064.075E85    1996
823'.914—dc20       95-47975

Printed in the United States of America on acid-free paper

24689753

FIRST U.S. EDITION

*Book design by Carole Lowenstein*

*To Sue, Who Was Always Right,*
*in Love and Gratitude*

# SECTION ONE

# News

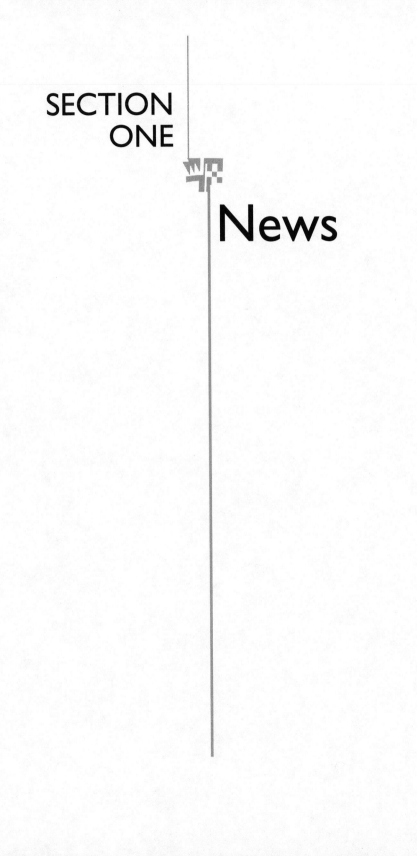

I

Your Worships," the prosecuting police sergeant began with his mis-
leadingly gentle and compassionate County Durham lilt, "the facts are
as follows. At approximately ten-thirty P.M. on Saturday the fourth of
January, 1966, P.C.'s 71 James and 206 Carswell were on motor patrol
duty in Market Street, Stockton. They observed the accused come out of
the Grapes public house and commit a nuisance into the gutter."

The accused was a ragged heap whose mainly outdoor life had reduced his clothes and skin to almost identical shades of moleskin grey.
He slumped in the central dock, bleary-eyed and uncomprehending, as
the majesty of the law took its course.

"His gait was unsteady and his speech was slurred, and the officers
formed the opinion that he was drunk. When told he would be arrested
he said . . ." The sergeant consulted the charge-sheet and winced. "He
said . . . pardon me, Your Worships . . . 'Can't a man have a peaceful
piss?' "

In the crowded press box, Louis Brennan of the Stockton Evening
Telegraph cupped his chin soulfully in one hand. But he was not following the case. He was watching the female probation officer who sat in
the pew directly below his, awaiting her turn to give evidence. At thir-
tyish, maybe even more, she certainly qualified for his fantasy of being
seduced by an older woman. On the debit side were pointed elbows,
short, greasy hair and a brown floral dress of which not one but two
rear hooks had come accidentally unfastened. Strange how lust-
quenching rather than the opposite was that knobby bare back, traversed by a mangy tightrope of black brassière-strap.

Louis was twenty-two years old, 5'11", pale-skinned and faintly
chubby, with prominent blue-grey eyes and a mole to the right of his
mouth in exactly the place where a Regency courtesan would have

drawn a beauty spot. His wispy fair hair was parted near the centre, hopefully emulating Steve Marriott of the Small Faces. For a reporter in Stockton-on-Tees, earning the union minimum, his clothes were fashionable, even elegant: dark blue blazer, grey herringbone hipster trousers, gunmetal-blue tab-collared shirt (39s 11d from Stockton Co-op) and thin dark brown leather tie. His shoes were by Dolcis, laceless with elasticated sides. Beside him, leaning against the red plush bench, was a tightly rolled City gent's umbrella.

Turning to a fresh slip of dun-coloured copy paper, he began writing with his Osmiroid italic fountain pen. But it was not about the nuisance committed into the gutter of Market Street, nor anything to be found in the Evening Telegraph's circulation area.

"London is undergoing yet another of its new kaleidoscopic shifts of fashion. The 'in' people are deserting Carnaby Street and are returning to that original crucible of style, the King's Road . . ."

The chairman of the magistrates glared at the still-silent and motionless grey heap in the dock. "Wanting to go to the toilet is no excuse. You have behaved in a disgusting fashion. You will be fined ten pounds."

"Do you wish time to pay?" asked the Clerk of the Court, peering malevolently over gilt half-glasses.

"What did he say?" the chairman demanded.

"He said, 'It's a poor world when a man can't have a peaceful piss,' Your Worship."

". . . The Mod vogue of last year is now rated strictly for the birds," Louis wrote. "The cognoscenti . . ."

"You what?" a voice whispered satirically in his ear. His friend Mike Finnis, the other half of today's Evening Telegraph court-reporting team, leaned over for a closer look, breathing out fumes of Kit-Kat.

"The word is 'cognoscenti.' "

Mike pulled a goggle-eyed face, as if the word was a solid object lodged in his windpipe.

"We prefer simple English here oop north."

"You stink of chocolate, Finnis."

The Clerk broke off from ascertaining the prisoner's disposable assets to give them a homicidal glare. Louis and Mike both hastily assumed the studiously meek attitudes of medieval calligrapher monks.

". . . The cognoscenti favour a more classical style—jackets high-buttoned and waisted with an additional ticket pocket. Suede is also in, in military-style jackets with high collars and epaulets . . ."

Here inspiration faltered for the moment. Louis reached down to the briefcase at his feet and, with the court reporter's furtive smoothness, brought out yesterday's Sunday Dispatch colour supplement. Glancing through it for the sixth or seventh time, his prominent eyes assumed a familiar look of mingled admiration, envy, desire and hopelessness.

The front cover was as visually ravishing as always. Its title ran across the very top—"SUNDAY DISPATCH" in dignified Roman capitals, befitting Britain's oldest quality Sunday paper, then *"magazine"* in fancy italic lower case, symbolising youthful urgency and irreverence. Below was an image from the brand-new (and still far from fully explained) war in Vietnam. A huge American army sergeant, bullnecked and crop-headed, chewed a huge cigar and flourished a multi-gripped black machine gun. No coverline or caption spoiled the effect, which was sophisticated amusement at the plethora of medals and insignia on the sergeant's olive fatigues, the so-typical American superfluity of a name badge on his breast, and the name printed on it: "McDaniels."

Inside were twelve continuous colour pages of Vietnam War, followed by six of even more glamorous fashion. Stick-like girls with cropped hair, sculpted white faces, flesh-pale lipstick and fish-shaped black eyes modelled one-piece trousered garments and dresses and skirts that broke amazingly a good two inches above the knee. Some girls had hair dyed vermilion, platinum white or bluish grey. Some wore apache berets or domed caps with peaks like masters of foxhounds. Some were shown headless, leaning half out of frame: as disembodied torsos, arms, necklines or silver-booted legs.

Interspersed among war and short skirts were the advertisements for which The Sunday Dispatch colour supplement was famous or notorious, according to your point of view. Men in black velvet jackets and ringleted women in Empire-line dresses sat at candlelit dinner-tables, passing around After Eight wafer-thin chocolate mints. Fluffy white Persian kittens romped on matching acres of Kosset carpet. James Bond–like figures in ski-suits and sunglasses toasted each other orgiastically in Cinzano Bianco. On one page, a Vietnamese baby covered in leprous burns crouched in a doctor's arms. Opposite, cream was being poured from a height over a thick wedge of piecrust and scarlet fruit. "MMM!" the caption said. "CREAM MAKES SIMPLE THINGS SUPER!"

Next to the court building was a small café with blistered white paintwork and a weatherbeaten fascia displaying the incomplete bas-relief legend "NACK BAR." Situated as it was at the heart of judicial Stockton, the clientele to be found behind its steamy front window were almost exclusively policemen, accused persons and reporters.

"Watched your chap Shildrick on telly last night," said Ken Blight of the Billingham Mercury. The Mercury and Evening Telegraph shared a table, comparing notes on the morning's cases. Information, even whole phrases were freely exchanged among the supposed deadly rivals. Not for nothing is a reporter's handiwork known as "copy."

"What's Shildrick been on now?" Guy Simpson, the Mercury's Jimmy Tarbuck lookalike, asked Louis.

"Granada TV . . . *What the Papers Say.*"

"Great stuff! How'd it go?"

"Tremendously well. Didn't you think so, Ken?"

"Aye, he looked very composed."

"It's bloody good going, isn't it?" Mike Finnis said with almost evangelical pride.

Neither of the Mercury men looked disposed to argue.

"Granada's *What the Papers Say,* networked all over the country . . . one week, presented by Charles Wintour, Editor of the Evening Standard . . . next week, Michael Frayn, columnist on The Observer . . . next week, Jack Shildrick, Editor of the Stockton Evening Telegraph. The only editor from the provinces who's ever been asked to do it! What do you call that if not bloody good going?"

"I don't know how he keeps the pace up," Louis said. "That's two telly appearances this week. He was on *Look North* on Monday as well, talking about the Prudhoe pit lay-off."

"And he's been buzzing round the office like a blue-arsed fly since he got back from the seductive Orient," said Mike. "Another complete design rejig. Two or three new campaigns. A technology page . . ."

While his colleagues synchronised magisterial comments on a case of indecent exposure, Louis reopened the Sunday Dispatch colour supplement. Beyond the blue-helmeted girls, the burned Vietnamese babies and the "After Eight" dinner party was a picture of Tom Jones in his familiar get-up of ruffled blouse, tight leather trousers and eighteenth-century pigtail, reclining horizontally over most of a double-page spread. Underneath him an ostentatiously small black headline read "TOMFOOLERY, by Evelyn Strachey, photograph by David Bailey."

"Still readin' that load of cods?" Ken Blight asked.

"Yes—only it's not a load of cods."

"That's just exactly what it is. A load of bloody cods."

"Great picture by Bailey, though," Guy Simpson said.

"Aye—if you want to see Tom Jones bursting his britches over your Sunday morning bacon and eggs."

"It isn't Tom Jones who bursts his britches. It's P. J. Proby."

Unmindful of the distinction, Ken Blight began to read over Louis's shoulder, masticating cheese roll noisily within his gold-tinted Viking

beard. "I told you, it's cods, man!" he exploded "Who is this . . . Evelyn
Strachey?"

"An ace writer," said Louis.

" 'Ace writer' be boogered! I canna make head nor tail of what he's
on about. Is it a he, by the way?"

"Yes. At least, I think so."

"All right, so what does this mean? 'Jones made an ineffably camp
gesture that gave him a fleeting look of Gertrude Stein . . .' "

"Sick," Mike Finnis murmured, renewing the argument that Louis
and he conducted sotto voce at courts, inquests, council meetings and
planning inquiries. "It's a totally unreal world, man. Colour supplement heaven! And sick, sick sick."

"What's sick about it?"

"What's sick about it? Pictures of starving famine victims on one
page and ads for double cream and Drambuie on the next. What do you
call that if not sick?"

"They do some brilliant things sometimes, though," Guy Simpson
said. "Did you see the pictures of them old men in Russia the other
weekend? They live on nothing but sour milk and herbs, and they're
still riding horses and topping out their wives at the age of about a hundred and fifteen."

It was one o'clock, the critical time of day for an evening paper: all
the more reason, therefore, to dawdle over another round of milky cof-
fees at the Nack Bar. Mike Finnis went to the jukebox and put on the
Animals' "We Gotta Get Out of This Place." Guy Simpson produced
World's Press News with its meagre two pages of job advertisements.
Eric Burdon's guttural rasp spoke for everyone present, and all other
provincial reporters throughout the land: "We gotta get out of this
place . . . if it's the last thing we ever do . . ."

"OK, lads . . . anyone fancy subbing the farming page of the Yorkshire Post? Or being production editor for Spastics News?"

"Nothing on any of the nationals?" Mike Finnis asked.

"Not a thing. The nearest to Fleet Street, I'd say, is the Hornsey Journal. 'Courts and municipal, shorthand essential, above rate for right
man.' "

"I keep on telling you young 'uns," Ken Blight said, with his air of
patriarchal wisdom. "Jobs on nationals are almost never advertised. It's
all done on the inside . . . wheels within wheels."

"So what are you saying?" Mike Finnis demanded. "That us poor
boogers out in the sticks don't stand a chance of getting to Fleet Street?"

"You could do. But it's a matter of catching someone's eye down
there. That's not so easy from two hundred miles away."

"Unless you're Jack Shildrick," Louis said.

As always, mention of Shildrick brightened the atmosphere. Even the two Mercury men shared in the thrill of the Evening Telegraph Editor's sure and superpowered rise to glory.

"Aye, Shildrick'll get to Fleet Street. He's gone about it in a really clever way, you see. Getting himself on a show like *What the Papers Say* . . . running these crusades that the nationals latch on to."

"He's supposed to have had any number of offers already," Mike Finnis said. "After his killer prams campaign was picked up by the *Today* programme, both the Mirror and the Sunday Express were after him. The word is that he's holding out for the job he really wants."

"What's that?"

"Editor of the Guardian. Or he could go into television. Apparently they love him down at Granada. They say he's a natural in front of the camera."

"I just wonder if he can keep on going at this rate," Guy Simpson said. "What is he now—thirty-seven? By the time he's forty, if he's not careful, he could have burnt himself out."

As Louis and Mike took their seats at their facing desks, Bob Feetham, the Municipal Correspondent, leaned across the aisle with a copy of the Evening Telegraph's midday edition.

"Look at the Nibs," he advised them in a choking voice.

Down the extreme right of the front page ran the Nibs or News in Brief column containing items of national and international rather than Teesside and County Durham interest: Federation of Bakery Workers threatens all-out strike . . . U.D.I. talks to resume between Wilson and Ian Smith . . . Crash of third U.S. Starfighter jet in West Germany.

"Look at the dropped caps," Bob Feetham urged.

Every item began with a black "dropped" capital letter grafted into the body type. The first word of each had been so chosen that the dropped caps formed a spaced-out acrostic:

**F**

**U**

**C**

**K**

**S**

**I**

**Z**

**E**

**R**

"My God," Mike whispered raptly. "That's brilliant. Who did it?"

"Colin Fry, I think."

Colin Fry was the most creative of the Evening Telegraph's younger sub-editors, the only one conceivably resourceful enough to devise something beginning with a letter z from among today's news agency stories: "Zoo officials in London confirmed today that panda Chi-Chi is pregnant . . ."

"Hasn't Sizer noticed it?"

"No . . . he doesn't read the paper. What do you want? He's only the News Editor."

A letter in a dark blue envelope had been pushed under Louis's type-writer bar. He ripped it open and glanced impatiently through the four sheets of wavy-edged Basildon Bond, all filled on both sides with pains-taking, oversized words in Quink Radiant Blue:

> . . . Both the dogs are well. Merrylegs is now a huge fat lump, so that you'd never even think she was Melody's daughter. Mummy and I took them in the paddock this afternoon and Melody found a rats' nest as usual. Ugh, I hate their little naked pink tails!!! The Rawlinson girls are coming over tomorrow and we are probably all going to the point-to-point . . .

"Did you ever see a correspondent so ardent?" Bob Feetham said with a wink at Mike Finnis.

"I know. A letter every single day."

"And does he write religiously back to her?"

"Does he heck! He's too busy ogling the crumpet in Classified Ads."

"Mist-er Brennan!" a nasal voice shouted. Bob Feetham hastily resumed typing. Louis sighed and leaned outward from his desk. "Yes, you. The distinguished gentleman from down south. Could I trouble you to step over here for a minute?"

Sizer sat midway in the high-ceilinged, white-tiled room, facing his reporters like a schoolmaster. Beyond him, at the sub-editors' horseshoe-shaped table, several figures could be seen in writhing con-vulsions over the News in Brief.

The Evening Telegraph's News Editor was a dark, simian-looking Yorkshireman with arms whose length would not have shamed an orangutan. It was said that he could pick up a used dog-end from the gutter without having to bend. Paradoxically his nails were short and well kept and he emitted an odour of antiseptic cleanliness.

"Busy, Mr. Brennan?" he enquired with elaborate sarcasm. All Louis's absurd overproductivity could not dispel Sizer's belief that any-one born south of Doncaster must by definition be an effete malingerer.

"What are you on? And I don't mean artsy-fartsy byline stuff. Stories of interest to a Durham readership."

"I've got the overnights from Stockton bench. The miners' lodge meeting at Crook. And the man who refused to let his wife be buried in the cemetery."

"Is she in his back garden?" Sizer demanded.

"We don't know yet. The public health people are digging it up tomorrow."

"Aye, right. Well I've got you down for an inquest at the Swing Bridge first thing. Then a leek show in Bishop Auckland, results to be phoned in full for first edition. And do a bit on these." He tossed over a set of multi-coloured minutes from the Borough Health Executive and a handout from the Gas Council. Louis gathered them up without a word. He made it a point of pride to offer no demur, whatever the mountains of work dumped on him.

"Oh, yes," Sizer added, "and I've a small query on your expenses." He beckoned Louis round to look at the expense sheet over his shoulder. His clean, antiseptic smell was especially strong today. Presumably he had a wife and children who loved him and to whom he was gentle and kind.

"Here . . . you've put 'Bus fare: Bank Top–office, threepence.' "

"Yes?"

"No!" Sizer crossed the line through with a flourish. "If it was only a threepenny fare, you should have walked."

"I hate him!" Mike Finnis chanted into his typewriter roller. "I bloody hate him! Hate, hate hate!"

"He's just a bureaucrat," Bob Feetham said. "News Editor? He wouldn't recognise a piece of news if it jumped up and bit him on the arse."

"Why does Jack Shildrick tolerate him in that job?" Louis asked.

"Because he's just what Shildrick needs."

"But he's such a useless tool."

"Exactly. If you're a whizzkid like Shildrick, you don't want a deputy who's . . . Hey up!" Mike broke off in an urgent whisper. For Shildrick himself was now visible at the far end of the room.

As always he appeared with dramatic suddenness, as if he had sprung up through a trap-door rather than darting from his office across the passage. And as always the effect was galvanising. Figures that had formerly slumped over ramshackle typewriters or burrowed in mounds of paper now sat tinglingly upright and alert. Even old Willie Pittuck, who could only be trusted to type out the prices from South Shields fish-market and whose trousers were sewn at the crotch with white thread, seemed to scent the infinite excitement and promise.

The backdrop of the subs' table brought out the huge contrast between Shildrick and his balding, overweight and Bri-Nylon-clad elder subordinates. Boyishly slim and slight, he resembled some studious school prefect appointed to read a Latin oration on prize day. His pointed, rather feminine face was framed by horn-rimmed glasses with slight bifocal lenses. His dark hair was cut in a fashionable but unostentatious flat-top. He was dressed, as if already a television star, in a navy blue suit, a dark blue shirt and pale gold tie. Most unusually, for industrial Teesside in January, he sported an exotic suntan. His multitudinous recent activities had included an extended trip through the Far East under an Institute of Journalists' scheme whereby senior British journalists went as missionaries among the poor benighted souls attempting to run papers in Hong Kong or Thailand. He had returned only last week, to write a series of characteristically vivid and no-nonsense reports for the feature page as well as crusading leaders on the reunification of Korea, Indonesian overpopulation, press censorship in Malaysia and the evils of child prostitution in Bangkok.

"He's at it again," Mike Finnis said with a chuckle. Shildrick could now be seen talking urgently to Bill Amos, the Chief Sub, and a doubtful-looking Sizer. They were joined by Harold Pearce, the brown-overalled Head Printer, his normally obdurate face wearing the look of an exasperated but indulgent parent.

"We plate up for the Late City Final at half-past," the Head Printer said. "If you're going to rejig the front, you'll have to move like greased lightning on skates."

Smiles were exchanged around the subs' table behind them. Shildrick was never known to move like anything else.

"Jack . . ." Sizer broke in with wheedling despair. "Are ye quite sure?"

"I'm quite sure," Shildrick replied. "In the same Victorian sense that a corpse is quite dead." He had the faintest of Lancashire accents, clipped and educated, though it was well-known he'd been born a collier's son in darkest Accrington. Even at moments of highest deadline panic, there was usually something to be learned from him about grammar or etymology.

He seized an Evening Telegraph from the new pile just brought up from the works. "That splash you stuck on the Midday wouldn't wake up an insomniac asleep on a bed of nails. 'Gyratory Traffic Plan for Chester-Le-Street'! What kind of a word is 'gyratory' for a page-one lead? You can't even pronounce it, let alone understand it. And surely we can find something more dynamic for an illustration than a bloody blueprint from the Ministry of Transport."

"It's just a bit of a slow news day . . ."

"No day's a slow news day," Shildrick said, "unless you want it to be." He turned away from Sizer with a peremptoriness that gladdened the heart of every onlooker. "What else is in the tray?" he asked the Chief Sub.

"Nothing that adds up to a hill o' beans. Lord Robens to address North-East Development Association. Hard of Hearing conference in Newton Aycliffe. Plan to eradicate bird-droppings from city monuments. Report on smoke emission from Teesside industries."

"Show me that," Shildrick said. He seized the weighty blue-bound report and began quickly turning its pages. The Chief Sub and Sizer looked on like U.S. Cavalrymen, with mounted Comanches on every skyline, waiting for John Wayne to think of something.

"Bingo!" Shildrick stabbed at an open page with his finger. "Look at that! How could you not see it? It's a bloody gift wrapped up in cellophane and tied with a pink ribbon. 'With current levels of smoke pollution, every resident of the Teesside conurbation can be reckoned to smoke the equivalent of ten cigarettes a week!' "

"Yes?" Sizer and the Chief Sub looked blankly at each other.

"That means every man, right? Every woman, right? And every child! The lungs of young kiddies—clean, young lungs—befouled and polluted by the greed of industrial giants! Ten cigarettes a week! That is totally disgraceful. It shames this city. It shames this county. It shames every one of us with any pretensions to be a caring parent."

Shildrick took the pen from the Chief Sub's hand, bent over the table and began drawing feverishly on a layout sheet. "Do a banner right across the top, 'Your Chainsmoking Children.' Put two people on it, Hurwitz and another quick worker, and run it down for setting folio by folio. Kill all this Chester-le-Street dross—and the Nibs. I'll do a Page One Comment to run along the basement."

He turned to rush away, then spun around, light-footed as a dancer. " 'Chainsmoking' one word, not hyphenated. Also . . . get on to the children's ward at Stockton Memorial and see what the figures are for asthma sufferers. And ring Charles Westburg and see if he'll put down a question in Parliament. This is a national, not just a parochial problem. We should keep it going as a campaign—'Let's Speak Out for Pure Air.' "

Half-way to the door, he spun round again. "Here's a question for you. You're a history of Fleet Street buff, aren't you?" With a start Louis realised that the question was directed at him.

"Do you know what Lord Northcliffe used to call the great Edwardian reporter Hannen Swaffer? 'Poet,' Northcliffe called him. And that's what I'm going to call you because you use words like one."

He rushed back down the aisle, brandishing the clipped-together copy Louis had left in his tray only that morning.

"This piece you've written on kite-flying is excellent. Just what I need to liven up the Home Page on Saturday. I love the metaphor about university senior wranglers. You've got a delectable, light touch. And you can be byzantinely funny."

"Thank you," Louis said, blushing to the roots of his unnaturally parted hair.

"Don't thank me. I should thank you for putting things like this into my hands. I want you to do a series of others like this . . . four or five, foot-of-page sort of style, about twelve inches each." Without waiting for a reply, Shildrick darted off again. "We'll make a special block for it," he called over his shoulder. "White-on-black . . . something like 'Louis Brennan Looks at Life.' All right?"

" 'Byzantinely funny' eh?" Mike Finnis said with a repetition of the word-stuck-in-windpipe face. And I thought you were just a Southern wise-arse."

"Chuffed with you, wasn't he?" Bob Feetham marvelled from across the aisle.

Louis watched the dapper, sunburned figure disappear to write a leader that had to be marked up and in the compositor's hands inside fifteen minutes. No one in his whole career—his whole life—had ever excited, inspirited and praised him like this. Then his heart sank, down to his Dolcis shoes, remembering what had been said this morning at the Nack Bar: about the Mirror, the Sunday Express, the Guardian, Granada Television . . . He had found Shildrick against odds of ten million to one, and it was terrible to think of losing him again.

---

Louis's digs were ten minutes' walk from Stockton city centre, in a rambling Victorian house overlooking Jubilee Park. An iron fire-escape led to the nest of first-floor bedsits where he dwelt between a washing-machine demonstrator and a sexagenerian clerk at Middlesborough Assizes.

His room had a sloped ceiling and a leaded window looking out on paths, grass and Stockton City Council's coat-of-arms outlined in night-flowering stocks. There was a saggy double bed with a crimson cover, a Baby Belling cooker and a meter-operated wall gas-fire. On a table below the window were a green Olympia typewriter, a pile of office copy paper and a black plastic-covered cuttings book. Under the table in two thick piles were back issues of the Sunday Dispatch colour supplement.

It was the only evening this week when covering City Council committee meetings, then going on to review the star cabaret in some opulent workingmen's club, would not keep him at work until 1 A.M. or later. As he ate his paper-bag supper of bacon-and-egg pie, two saveloys and a plain chocolate Bounty, he leafed wistfully through "SUFFOLK RE-VEALED," a Sunday Dispatch colour supplement's cover story now almost six months old. Page after sumptuous page presented the East Anglian landscape in images of eerie beauty. Lone white windmills caught the sun on limitless plains of waving wheat. Haycarts loomed, ghostly, in dawn-misted lanes. Gnarled old men sat over dominoes in pub inglenooks as if chosen, composed and highlighted by Rembrandt. You knew, of course, that Suffolk had always been there, looking much like that. The colour supplement's special magic was to make even timeless English counties seem suddenly novel, exotic and relevant.

With the second half of his Bounty, he turned to his own cuttings—the features, columns and think-pieces written for the Stockton Evening Telegraph these past four months on everything from electric guitars and umbrellas to Victorian lemonade bottles, the Greyfriars school stories, cross-country running, Bob Dylan's lyrics and the pleasures of spring. Also preserved inside the thick Perspex pages were congratulatory memos from the Editor, "Shildrick's Herograms," as they were known: "I thought your piece on the Whyton pools winner was excellent today . . ." "Good solid work for News Focus on telephone-box vandalism . . ." "A delightful essay on the outsize spring onion . . ."

He was not unique in being so praised. Anyone who turned in good copy, be it the straightest court or planning inquiry report, could expect a Shildrick Herogram pushed under his or her typewriter before the ink on the edition was dry. It explained why, as well as functioning at a peak of enthusiasm and exhilaration, the Evening Telegraph was almost devoid of envy and backstabbing.

A creak of the loose floorboard outside his door was followed by a diffident tap. Thinking it was his neighbour, the washing-machine demonstrator, soliciting coins for her electricity meter, Louis threw the door open with a look of humorous long-suffering. Standing there, clutching a wine-collared corduroy windcheater around her throat, was a very tall girl with short, fringed blond hair that gave her the faint look of a disillusioned Roman emperor. Her name was Rosemary Boyfield, though among Louis's circle at the Nack Bar she was known as Agrippa. This derived, not from her Caesarish aspect, but from Ken Blight's speculation that in bed she must be "a gripper."

She stared at him with very much the look that Caesar once gave Brutus at the end of a trying day. "How could you do it?" she demanded.

"I'm sorry. I thought it was the kindest way."

Agrippa gave a mirthless laugh. "Kind? What, a note just left in the copy-tray? You didn't even bother putting my name on it. Suppose Les Nobbs had opened it, thinking it was for him?"

Les Nobbs was the hairless and shelf-bottomed chief reporter of the Stockton and Teesdale Journal, the Telegraph's weekly stablemate, on whose staff Agrippa worked as a graduate trainee. Louis's mind grappled briefly with the vision of a lovelorn Nobbs assimilating his decision that their brief fling must end, and his hope that they might still remain good friends.

Agrippa advanced into the room, still clutching her windcheater defensively around her. "Don't worry, I'm not going to stay. I wouldn't dream of interrupting his high-and-mightiness."

This was tremendously cheering news. With luck, he could still be first into the communal bathroom, and then quickly under the bed-clothes, listening to Radio Caroline on his Philips "3-Transistor" radio. To his intense disappointment, however, Agrippa slid off her coat, revealing a floppy-necked pink mohair sweater and navy blue ski-pants. "I just don't understand," she said. "What did you mean, there are the things I don't know about you that if I did would change my mind?"

"I just can't tell you, Rosemary." Perfectly true, since it had been pure literary invention, a clever touch hinting at a turbulent, perhaps even criminal past, so that his decision to chuck her had a glamorous as well as virtuous and unselfish aura.

Unfortunately, now that she was actually here in person, bugger and blast, its effect was to suggest there might be scope for further discussion. Going from bad to worse, she sank down into the little chintz-covered armchair beside the gas-fire and gave a long, shuddering sigh. "I made no demands on you. You told me you'd got a serious girl-friend down in Cambridge, who looks like Miss Scandinavia. I knew it was no strings, have a good time, see how it crumbled cookie-wise . . . ." With a grimace—of physical rather than emotional anguish—Agrippa felt about underneath herself for a moment, then held up a small grey pointed object. "What's this?"

"Oh, sorry . . . it's the stopper from my Old Spice bottle. It's terribly easy to lose it in that chintzy pattern."

A stray copy of the Sunday Dispatch colour supplement was lying near the gas-tap. On its cover was a female figure of almost unearthly thinness, crop-headed and hollow-faced, with a chest as flat as a boy's and white-stockinged legs like articulated pipecleaners. Clutching a scrap of piebald fur around her, she stared forth with huge, blackened eyes that seemed aware of the world's incredulous derision. The coverline read "TWIGGY GETS INTO FUN FUR." Agrippa picked it up, unwillingly fascinated. "Ugh! How can anyone think she's attractive? She looks like some kind of famine victim."

"There are some incredible pictures by Duffy inside." He had a sudden happy inspiration. "Would you like to take it with you?"

"No, I would not, thank you very much," Agrippa replied with a wince. She gazed listlessly at the back-cover advertisement—a group of men and women in evening dress, drinking White Horse Scotch whisky from crystal tumblers around a real live white horse—and shook her senatorial head. "I've tried my darnedest to understand you . . . sitting next to you in court and at City Council all those times . . . I kept looking into those great big eyes and wondering, 'What's he thinking?' "

Good point, what *was* he thinking? About Chelsea boots, like the Beatles wore, with elasticated panels, reaching half-way up the shin. About whether "California Dreamin' " by the Mamas and the Papas would be number one in the New Musical Express chart this week. About how he pined for her to go with such intensity, it must almost be visible, like ectoplasm wreathing from the mouth and ears of a psychic at a séance.

Then Agrippa shifted her ski-trousered legs, showing the slim shapeliness inside the perma-crease, and Louis suddenly forgot about Radio Caroline. Kneeling down, he pushed her coat off her shoulders, slipping his right hand under her mohair jumper and inside her waistband and knicker-elastic. With a resigned sigh, like an industrial chimney he'd once seen artfully dynamited, she toppled backwards, closing her eyes and opening her mouth.

In no time they had assumed their usual posture in the undersized chair, Louis snogging Agrippa from above, straddling one of her legs, his thick herringbone tweed grinding with ever greater agitation against her unyieldingly gusseted Dacron. As always, she opened her jaws to their fullest extent, making him feel at some moments like an animal-trainer with his head in the lion's mouth, at others like Jonah shining a lantern up at wet, overarching ribs inside the whale. His right hand, meanwhile, moved up her knobby back to her brassière-hooks, and down to the surprising coolness of her upper bottom.

After thirty-five minutes or so, she pulled her mouth free. In the gas-firelight, her cheeks were flayed raw by his unshaven chin. "Louis . . ." she murmured despairingly. "What do you want from me?"

She herself unconsciously answered this question by starting to work her hand down behind the oversized metal buckle of his hipster belt. Louis grew tense, contemplating at the same moment the great enterprise and daring of this act in a female, and the many obstacles with which the hand must contend before reaching its objective. Having negotiated the barely passable aperture between the buckle and his drawn-in stomach, the hipsters' shallow rise afforded it manoeuvrability about on a par with a St. Bernard trapped in the burrow of a fieldmouse. Much—indeed, all—depended on whether it slid straight on down inside his underpants-elastic or took the marginally easier outside route, then making a tight right-angled turn to seek its quarry through the Y of the Y-front.

Tonight, unfortunately, it chose this latter alternative. For, as so often happened, what seemed the simplest inverted Y-shaped aperture for workaday purposes now became a labyrinth of a complexity that would have daunted Beowulf. And, as always, the protracted blind-mole fumbling, burrowing and plucking to reach the quarry and draw it through the hole had a catastrophic effect on mood, reducing the quarry from an engorged and lurking monster to something as tiny, soft and pliant as the tail of a little piggy on its way to market.

Louis's usual way of restoring himself at such moments was to think the phrase "big, cruel nurse." The picture that flashed into his mind, however, was of a shirt-collar held down at each point with buttons in the style until recently only encountered in imported American TV detective dramas. Suddenly, the closing paragraphs of the unfinished King's Road fashion article began tumbling out of his subconscious: "Out go Mod penny-rounds and pin-collars à la Searchers and Kinks. Onward advance the conquering hordes of gingham tab-collars and buttondowns, their mitred cuffs sometimes featuring two or three buttons of stylish . . ."

With no attempt at finesse he detached his piggy from the wiggling, crawled over to his desk and groped for what should have figured least in this transaction: The Pocket Oxford Dictionary. "Sorry," he said absently over his shoulder. "I just want to check whether 'iridescence' has one r or two."

2

Though long unaware of it, Louis had always possessed three qualities essential to a journalist. He was rootless. He was accustomed to low life. And he breathed the damp reek of failure as his natural element.

Few backgrounds could have been more ideally designed to promote the fatalistic adaptability and stoic unfeelingness that make the successful reporter. His father was a former R.A.F. officer, of genteel airs but feckless and nomadic disposition, who mysteriously believed that dropping propaganda leaflets from Blenheim bombers over Germany was adequate preparation for a post-war career as a publican, restaurateur and impresario. Born in 1943 above a London gin palace, Louis had almost immediately found himself transplanted to a Georgian coaching inn in sleepy rural Bedfordshire. The years between five and eighteen he had spent on the Isle of Wight, watching his father attempt a succession of quasi–show business ventures from penny-in-slot machines and tea dances to self-service cafés and roller-skating rinks.

Low life and failure were there in equally generous measure, along with an ever-dwindling sense of origin or identity. His antecedents were London Cockney, yet his father spoke nostalgically of squadron messnights and fly-fishing on the Bedfordshire Ouse, and his family's business was fleecing holidaymakers on Seaview Pier. The question Louis found difficult to answer even then was "Where do you come from?"

Education at a fifth-rate but pretentious private school nurtured his resigned predisposition to failure in his turn. His only talents, of no discernible use at the time, were mimicry and English composition. Even when knowing little or nothing about a subject, he could still turn out an essay interesting enough to read aloud to the whole class. The first hint of his vocation came in the fourth form, after he had enlivened an account of silk manufacture in the Scottish Central Lowlands with colourful digressions about Paisley ties and dressing-gowns. "Have you ever thought of becoming a journalist?" the geography master asked with faint disgust, flinging his exercise book back at him.

At school-leaving time, with nothing else but seaside catering in prospect, Louis finally did think of it. He probably would have got no further but for an atypical stroke of luck. His parents had long since divorced and his mother—herself now thankfully rootless—worked as a beautician, giving facials on a circuit of department stores throughout East Anglia. Among her clients was a Mrs. Langhorn, whose husband owned a dozen weekly papers circulating between Peterborough and Norwich. Wheels were set to work within wheels as mudpacks set and nail-polish dried. Two days after his eighteenth birthday Louis left the Isle of Wight to become an "editorial trainee" on the Whittlesey Advertiser, 160 miles away in the heart of the Cambridgeshire Fens.

Like most local newspapers, the Advertiser prospered by printing what was not new. Column after column of village paragraphs described the same whist-drives and charity tombolas featuring the same participants, year in year out. "Stories" in the form of untoward happenings were actively discouraged. "Nothing for us, is there?" the Chief Reporter said hopefully each Monday when he telephoned the police, ambulance service and fire brigade. The paper was printed on a flatbed press, little advanced from Caxton's time, and proofread hurriedly, if at all. These were the days before finding misprints and hapless double-entendres in newspapers became a national sport. When the Whittlesey Advertiser said in the obituary of a flower-arranging socialite that "some of the most important balls in the county will miss her touch," or that the Lady Mayoress of Soham had "whanked" rather than thanked a visiting dignitary, or that a much-loved district nurse on her retirement had been presented with "an electric cock," or that a local R.A.F. station had been visited by "Her Majesty the Queer," there ensued only strangulated silence, such as might follow a bride's accidental emission of wind on her wedding night.

The duties prescribed for Louis as an editorial trainee were not stimulating. They included making tea for the whole reporters' room, filing, stapling photographs to cork boards in the front window, and fetching a tube of ointment from Boots each Friday for the Editor's haemorrhoids.

During his second week, the lowly assignments tossed at him included talking to a local woman who was about to celebrate her 100th birthday. Later that day, the Editor appeared holding his copy and brusquely asked, "Do you spell your surname with one *n* or two?"

"Two," Louis replied, struck through with sudden panic. Had the Editor already decided he was unsatisfactory and that his indentures must be cancelled forthwith?

"Why do you think Mr. Newton wants to know that?" he quavered to the senior reporter who'd been detailed to show him the ropes.

"You're probably going to get a byline."

"What's a byline?" Louis asked innocently.

That Thursday, on the Advertiser's archaic front page, he saw his name in type for the first time. Twelve small black capital letters made him what he'd least dreamed of ever becoming: a celebrity. Walking down Whittlesey High Street later, he felt sure people must be pointing him out to one another behind his back.

No drug was ever so instantaneous in its effect. The next week Louis got another byline, for a feature about a village church with two pulpits instead of one. The week after, he got another for an interview with a farmer who still ploughed with Shire horses instead of tractors. The week after that he got two in the same issue, for a report on a Red Cross cheese-and-wine party and a lengthy review of the Whittlesey Methodist Drama Society's performance of *Mr. Pym Passes By*.

He had already made up his mind that he would never reach Fleet Street. Everything he heard about it, and that he read and saw in films and on television, convinced him he would survive no longer than minutes amid "the Street's" frenetic speed, its wild panic, its shrieking anger, its brutal sarcasm and pitiless impromptu sackings. The bylines one saw in national dailies—weird, exotic names like Fenton Bresler, Sefton Delmer, Chapman Pincher, René McColl—seemed barely of the same species as the dowdy, unhurried Bobs and Daves who staffed the Advertiser. The self-effacing fatalism of Louis's childhood still had a long course to run. Better not even to try than be instantly unmasked as a feeble impostor.

But Fleet Street, like so much else in Britain, was changing. Nowhere was that change more startlingly illustrated than in The Sunday Dispatch, grey bastion of Tory politics and typographical propriety, which in the year of Louis's A-levels was bought by the Scots lumber magnate Fulton McIntyre. Among radical innovations announced by McIntyre was a full-colour "magazine section" on the pattern long familiar in America and Canada.

At the beginning it was an unmitigated disaster, barren of advertisements, so expensive to print and distribute that each elevenpenny copy of The Sunday Dispatch was reckoned to be costing Fulton McIntyre two shillings and threepence. Delivery boys across the land complained of the weight which the new supplement added to the Dispatch, and the difficulty of pushing its swollen bulk through customers' letterboxes.

The print industry dubbed it "McIntyre's Folly"; rival press barons shook their heads over it in delighted anticipation; David Frost and Co. satirised it on *That Was the Week That Was*. But McIntyre remained oblivious to the taunts and predictions of imminent ruin, and continued to pour resources into his haemorrhaging brainchild.

Louis, meanwhile, was learning everything the Whittlesey Advertiser could teach. He learned the difference between a Rural District Council and an Urban District Council, and between a Parish Council and a Parochial Church Council. He learned how to spell "fuchsia," "tulle," "suffragen," "ancillary," "dais" and "*Lohengrin*"; the meaning of "sub judice," "*sine die*," "font," "stet" and "overmatter"; and the printable terms for the variegated sexual offences which Cambridgeshire Fendwellers famously committed with their mothers, children, sheep, pigs, chickens and goats. He resigned himself to deep unpopularity among his Advertiser colleagues, to whom his bylined features meant only that he was working harder than he needed to, an activity in the worst possible taste. For two years, his only friends were his typewriter and his ever-expanding cuttings scrapbook.

In his third year, he started going steady with a girl named Portia Bolton-Phelps, whom he had met at a Young Farmers dance. Portia belonged to the "county set" of millionaire landowners, Lord Lieutenants and High Sheriffs whom the Advertiser served as faithful vassal and mouthpiece. She had straw-blond hair, secured by a pink Alice band, and eyes of Nordic pale blue. More attractive to Louis was the enormous house named Bottisham Park where she lived. When staying there overnight, he slept in a heavenly small oak-panelled room, lined with books from floor to ceiling. Portia's mother was small, nut-brown and smiley. As time went on, and puppy love waned, he found his lust for Mrs. Bolton-Phelps growing well-nigh uncontrollable.

This was the year 1965, when so many marvellous things were happening somewhere else. The Beatles had soared to uncharted heights for an out-of-town pop group, appearing in the Royal Command Variety show, conquering America, becoming Members of the Most Excellent Order of the British Empire, even presenting their own special edition of *Juke-Box Jury*. Each week brought a wonderful new single, if not by them then by the Rolling Stones, the Animals, the Hollies, Billy J. Kramer, Manfred Mann, Herman's Hermits, the Walker Brothers, the Righteous Brothers, the Animals, Unit Four Plus Two, Dave Dee, Dozy, Beaky, Mick and Tich. Female fashion daily became more close-cropped, angular and monochrome, and male fashion more Beatle-ishly and Beau Brummelly extravagant and colourful. As in the Top 20, extraordinary changes were happening in films, in theatre, in interior design, in travel, in cookery, in language. Beatle-like fame was descending on young men and women only a little further into their twenties than Louis and, in many cases, of the once-submerged "working class": fashion models like Jean Shrimpton, Penelope Tree and the extraordinary Twiggy, photographers like David Bailey and Terence Donovan, fashion designers like Mary Quant and Barbara Hulanicki, actors like Peter O'Toole and David Warner, painters like David Hockney and Peter Blake, "pirate" radio disc jockeys like Simon Dee and Tony Blackburn.

Longing and frustration boiled over each weekend as he opened the Sunday Dispatch with its Review section, fronted by the memoirs of ex–Prime Ministers or great soldiers; its Close-up investigations into scandals, frauds and disasters; its colour supplement, offering such epoch-making photo-features as "What Is Pop Art?" "A Baby's First Year of Life," "Behind the Closed Doors of London's Clubland" or "Ballooning over Uzbekistan." For "McIntyre's Folly" was now the marvel of Fleet Street, a commercial gold-mine built on the unlikely foundations of quality, daring and extravagance. It had made the Dispatch the top-selling Sunday "heavy" with unprecedented sales of 1.6 million, and earned the prescient McIntyre one of the life peerages that rained like confetti from Harold Wilson's new Socialist government. Though all the other quality Sundays now had started rival supplements, none could equal Lord McIntyre of Ludgate Hill's creation as the mirror and chronicler of suddenly stylish, affluent, double cream–gorging, "swinging" Britain. Whether one sought enlightenment on the economic future of Ecuador, the potential of a new Cabinet minister, the direction of Parisian couture, the filming of the latest James Bond story, the durability of a French copper cooking pot, the most pristine shade of white emulsion paint, the authentication and true nature of any of the thousand-and-one new "trends" which materialised each week, there was only one possible authority.

The Dispatch colour supplement's principal feature writer Evelyn Strachey represented everything Louis most longed for as a journalist. He wanted not to be covering Great Gransden Road Safety Committee but to be writing Strachey's elegantly deadpan interviews with pop stars like Tom Jones and actors like Albert Finney, and humorous essays on "Conspicuous Thrift," "Parkinson's Law," transvestite clubs and gang warfare in Liverpool. He wanted to be published, not in smudgy newsprint "pars" but in the colour supplement's lovely chaste type, in book-length paragraphs set in double measure, with dropped capitals and starred copybreaks. He wished with all his heart to change places with Evelyn Strachey, even though he knew nothing whatever about his journalistic exemplar, not even whether "Evelyn" was feminine, as in Home, or masculine, as in Waugh.

Yet here he was, twenty-one years old and still nowhere. Underlining the low expectations of his future, he now had to pay frequent visits to Cambridge, where Portia was studying to become a secretary. How different things might be if he were an undergraduate, with rooms in some ravishing ivy-covered college court and three years to do nothing but read, enjoy himself and be admired. For anyone who aspired to a paper like the Sunday Dispatch, this—or Oxford—was the only place to be. He heard with despair how the Dispatch and other quality Sundays periodically sent teams down from London to snap up the cream of the university's journalistic talent.

Towards the end of 1965, he realised he was scheduled to attend weddings of friends of Portia's on four successive weekends. He perceived that, as in gundog-training, he was patiently being shown again and again the way to do it.

The following Friday, he bought a copy of World's Press News. A month later, he had uprooted himself again and was heading north.

---

"Come on in, Poet," Jack Shildrick called before Louis had a chance to tap on his half-open door. "I've got people playing merry hell about you."

Shildrick's office was an archaically wide and lofty apartment with a single large window overlooking the chimneys of the city bottle works. Around the wood-panelled walls hung portraits in oils of past Evening Telegraph Editors, men uniformly lacking flair and energy, under whose stewardship the paper had plodded along barely changed for almost a century. Below their dull white collars and envious-looking faces hung framed newsbills from Shildrick's most notable campaigns—"LET'S SPEAK OUT FOR CLEAN AIR"; "SAVE THIS SCHOOL"; "THE SPENNYMOOR MARTYRS"—and newspaper design awards that the Evening Telegraph nowadays often carried off against bigger and technologically superior competitors like the Manchester Evening News and Birmingham Post.

The desk, where Shildrick sat in a padded black leather chair, was of ultramodern Swedish design. A white Anglepoise lamp shone, day and night, on a wild mêlée of copy, proofs, reference books and the portable typewriter with which he might be hammering out anything from a full-page feature on North-eastern population growth to a stand-in television review.

As Louis entered, Shildrick tilted his chair forward and swivelled it round the far end of his desk. High-speed castors allowed him to propel himself to filing cabinets, layout-board or conference table with the least possible disturbance to his flow of ideas, and with the velocity of a squash ball.

"I should give you more theatre crits to do, shouldn't I?" he called over his shoulder. "Brings out the beast in you."

Seizing a piece of paper from the conference table, he spun the chair around and shot himself back behind his desk.

"The Hon. Sec. of the Stockton Masque Players takes grave exception to the piece you did about them the other night." He tossed Louis the letter, a sheet of superfine bond with the kind of royal blue engraved address that would have made any other editor of a provincial paper instantly assume a Muslim prayer position on the carpet.

"Ruth will give you a copy of the letter I've dictated back. I've said I see nothing wrong with our critic saying the first-night audience was noisy and that two shillings is too expensive for a souvenir programme."

This was Shildrick as everyone on the Evening Telegraph knew him, from the Chief Reporter to the Angling Correspondent. So long as accuracy, honesty and fairness were maintained, he would back any member of his staff to the death.

"Hasn't Barry Theakston made a superb job of these?" He motioned Louis to a set of photographic prints, so fresh from the dark-room that they were still damp. They showed various aspects of a pit village on the main road from Stockton to Newcastle.

"Crofton, isn't it?" Louis asked.

"Aye. And it's being literally shaken to pieces by juggernaut lorries. People can't even walk along the main street. They have to dodge from doorway to doorway like Maquisards in Occupied France. Those big side-mirrors can literally lop someone's head off. We're going to run a piece on page one every day—schoolkids in peril, church foundations subsiding, babies breathing noxious fumes—until the Min. of Transport sees sense and builds them a bypass. Incidentally, this piece of yours on shirt-collars is . . . delightful." Shildrick held up the copy Louis had left in his tray only the previous evening.

"Alpha-plus work. I've one query. What's this word?"

"It's 'Yicch,' " Louis said.

"Yicch?"

"Yes. To convey how horrible drip-dry material is."

"That's your one trouble, you see. You're inclined to go all obscure. Something like that just brings the reader up short. I'm drinking vintage champagne, and it suddenly turns into cooking sherry."

Shildrick crossed through the offending word. Otherwise the copy marked up for setting bore no alterations. "I'm thinking of making you John Blunt, you know," he added casually.

Louis felt his stomach lurch downward like a runaway lift. John Blunt was the Evening Telegraph's diary feature, occupying the lower half of the editorial page for five days out of six every week. Its author, though pseudonymous, was the paper's only full-time feature writer, freed from Newsdesk drudgery to go virtually where he pleased and cover what he liked. There was no more enjoyable or prestigious job on the North-east's whole journalistic horizon.

"Joe Cain says he needs a change," Shildrick went on calmly. "He's done it for three years . . . wonderfully well too. Now he wants to move over to politics. Or maybe go into our London office, writing colour stuff for the whole group. I think you'd be a splendid choice to take the page over from him. It's a key job . . . well, you know that. And wonderfully varied. One day you could be in a nunnery in Redcar, the next you could be in West Germany, interviewing men of the Durham Light Infantry . . ."

"But . . ." Louis gasped. "Do you really think I could do it?"

"Of course you could. You've got a delicious style, you're a tremendous worker, you can turn it out under pressure. It'd suit you to a T."

Suddenly, with a kind of inward pole vault, Louis realised just how much it *would* suit him to a T. A whole lifetime resigned to under-achievement had been cancelled by this boyish figure in its leather chair. Every day that passed with Shildrick convinced him more that there was nothing he couldn't do if he tried.

"Oh, golly, I'd just love it," he said dreamily.

A look that was almost anxious flitted across Shildrick's face. Louis had a sudden sense of powerful engines being thrown into reverse. "Don't think it's a *fait accompli.* Joe hasn't told me when he wants to hand in his seals of office, and I've not fully made up my mind yet. There'll be other candidates as good as you. Maybe even better than you. I've got one chap in mind, very good, from the Newcastle Chronicle. You can see his cuttings if you like."

"I'd just do anything for the chance," Louis said.

"Just leave it with me for two or three weeks. I'm not saying you will . . . but you might just get a surprise . . ." Shildrick took off his glasses and polished them, revealing the surprising fragility and femininity of his face. Behind the bifocals were hooded, almost sultry eyes, like those of some rebellious young Victorian woman bent on flouting the conventions of her time. He smiled at Louis—the quick, indulgent, admiring smile that would make anyone on the Evening Telegraph go through hell on a pushbike for him.

"Meanwhile, keep up the good work. You're lobbing me some marvellous stuff at the moment."

———————

There was just time to tell Mike Finnis as they clattered down the Evening Telegraph's winding staircase, which, bizarrely, was inset with arbours of heraldic stained glass. Louis's first job this Monday morning was to attend an inquest into an erotic suicide; Mike's to witness the paying-in of a charity cheque at the Yorkshire Bank by a chimpanzee.

"I can't believe it! Nobody as young as me has ever done John Blunt before. Joe Cain must be at least thirty."

"He's over thirty," Mike said pityingly.

They crossed the front vestibule, like an old-fashioned banking hall with its polished counter where people could hand in small-ads or choose verses for In Memoriam notices like "The trumpeter sounded / St. Peter said 'Come' / The Pearly Gates opened / And in walked Mum."

"Do you realise what it means? I'd be off the diary—no more Sizer. And I'd go into conference with all the bigshots every morning."

"I just wouldn't count on it too much," Mike said. "You know what Jack can be like . . . flinging off ideas all over the place. Remember that time I was convinced he'd promised me I could be Education Correspondent? Then I found he'd offered it to about five other people at the same time."

At the Coroner's Court, Louis found himself with the Billingham Mercury's Guy Simpson on one side of him and Agrippa on the other. She wore a mustard-coloured sweater with the points of a red shirt-collar sticking up through its crew neck. As he sat down and unscrewed his Osmiroid, she pushed her open notebook into his sightline. Written in it was a Pitman's shorthand outline of hook *h*, upward *l* curve and dot vowel *o:*

"Hello!"

"Hello," he replied with an identical outline, then leaned forward in an exaggerated pose of studious attention. The subject of the inquest was a Baptist lay preacher who had jumped from the Swing Bridge wearing nothing but a transparent plastic raincoat, a pair of women's panties and the self-garotting thongs around his wrists and throat. Still alive when recovered by the River Patrol, he had expired a few hours later from the too-powerful cocktail of riverborne chemical pollutants.

While a police pathologist gave gruesome anatomical particulars,

Agrippa scribbled more shorthand and swivelled her notebook around to Louis. Vowel *I* . . . curve *m* with *s* loop . . . "miss" . . . vowel *u*. Simultaneously he felt a nudge from the other side. "Posted off your entry yet?" Guy Simpson whispered.

"Entry for what?"

"Didn't you see the Dispatch colour supplement yesterday?"

"No. Why?" It had been the one Sunday in months that Louis's paper shop had sold out of Sunday Dispatches. He'd been forced to spend a day of lower-grade envy and yearning with The Observer.

"They announced a competition for young writers. Just up your alley, I'd have thought it was."

"You're not serious!"

"No, I'm not serious. Yes, I'm serious."

Louis came as close as was possible to grabbing a colleague's jacket lapels during a Coroner's summing-up. "What else did it say? Tell me, damn you!"

Guy smoothed his Jimmy Tarbuck fringe apologetically. "All I remember is that it's for young writers . . . it's being judged by their Editor . . . and some London publisher . . . If I were you, I'd roust out a copy pretty damned quick . . ."

On the table to Louis's right, a still more complex passage of shorthand had now appeared in Agrippa's notebook. *D* stroke, *u* vowel . . . "do you" . . . hooked *r* stroke . . . "remember the" . . . hard *th* curve . . . "other" . . . *n* stroke, vowel *i* . . . "night"?

He turned to her with a smile intended to be both reassuring and noncommittal, and outlined an emphatic hook *y*, circle *s*, "Yes."

Agrippa gave him a bleak, stabbed-Caesar stare, then abruptly rose, gathered up her notebook, grabbed her cream shortie duffle coat and strode from the room. Never a brilliant shorthand student, and much too excited at this moment to differentiate between lateral and upward strokes, he had confused the outlines for "remember" and "regret."

---

No newsagent in the whole of central Stockton could supply a day-old copy of The Sunday Dispatch colour supplement. Louis and Mike Finnis even went to the railway station, to see if any unsold bundles were being put on the train back to London. Finally they ran a copy to earth in a Chinese chippie in Turbine Street. Its cover showed Danny La Rue, the female impersonator, photographed with sumptuous irony by David Bailey. The owner refused to let them have it unless one half-wrapped a portion of rock salmon, the other an order of sweet-and-sour prawns.

"Here you are!" Mike shouted, brandishing a vinegary page. " 'The Sunday Dispatch Magazine Under-Twenty-three Writers' Competition. First prize—two hundred and fifty pounds.' And . . . bloody hell, how about this, boy! 'The winner will also receive an overseas assignment for The Sunday Dispatch Magazine.' "

"What's the bloody subject, though?"

"Don't get stroppy. Have a prawn."

"I don't want a sodding prawn."

"Here we are. 'Entrants must write a profile of no more than two thousand words . . . of anybody living.' "

The whole formula had a dismaying, alien sound. On local papers, length is calculated in inches, columns or half-columns. And Louis had only the haziest idea what "profile" meant. "Two thousand words. How long do you think that is?"

"A bloody lot," Mike said. "Maybe almost as long as one of your theatre crits."

"Drop dead, Finnis. What else does it say?"

"The judges will be Toby Godwin, Editor of The Sunday Dispatch Magazine . . . Arden Sinclair, one of London's most exciting young publishers . . . Entrants must be under the age of twenty-three on March first, 1966. So you're OK then." Louis's twenty-third birthday was in mid-April.

"You've got to go in for it, Brennan. It's tailor-made for someone like you."

A wave of his former, pre-Shildrick self surged through Louis. With a sinking heart, he imagined the announcement being read yesterday by all the handsome, God-gifted young men at Cambridge and Oxford universities. "What's the point? I wouldn't stand a chance."

"You'd stand as much chance as anyone. You've got to go in for it. You will, won't you?"

"But who would I write about?" He thought of a recent lesson imparted by Jack Shildrick. "I mean 'whom'?"

"There's lots of fascinating characters up here. Why not one of these new Labour whizzkids in Newcastle? T. Dan Smith . . . or Andrew Cunningham."

"I don't think I can get steamed up enough about the North-East's Development Plan."

"You're off tomorrow and the next day. You've got time to think of a good person and get most of the writing done."

"Some hopes," Louis said glumly. "You know where I've got to go."

"Cambridgeshire?"

"Yes, bugger it! Bugger it! Bugger it!"

Mike made his face a solemn rictus. "I really think you'll have to do the decent thing this time, you know," he said, ducking a swipe before Louis could even aim it. "The least you can do is slip a little ring on her finger."

At 5 A.M. the next morning Louis was already on the motorway south, right foot pressed entreatingly on the accelerator of his battered white Austin Mini. At Ferrybridge's four giant cooling towers, where County Durham unequivocally became the North Riding of Yorkshire, he stopped for double buck rarebit at his usual transport café. The jukebox was playing the Beatles' new single, "We Can Work It Out," with its almost churchy harmonium effect. When John Lennon sang "Life is very short," the whole thing slowed into what seemed like an eerie fairground waltz. You seriously wondered if they hadn't gone too far this time.

He reached Hedloe Manor Farm just after ten o'clock. His mother was in the kitchen, carving a large ham on the immense scrubbed wooden table. Her professional cosmetician's valise stood open at her elbow. As she advanced to kiss Louis, he saw her eyes flicker above his and then to the right. "What's the matter?" he sighed.

"I only wonder," she drawled in her salon voice, "if it's quite wise to part your hair at that funny angle."

"Where are you working this week?"

"Benton's in Peterborough, then Corman and Hadley's in Bury St. Edmunds. I've got Mrs. Langhorn coming in to have her face waxed on Thursday. She always wants to know how you're getting on."

"Where's Aubrey?"

"On the tractor, drilling cabbage. He'll be in for his elevenses soon."

Louis filled the electric kettle to make coffee. Water came from the farm's own subterranean well, drawn by a pump in the sink. "Heard from Gran lately?" he asked.

"I talked to her on the phone the other night. Apparently there's a lot more trouble over Grandad's legs. Roehampton say he's too old for the full-length ones now. They're going to give him little short ones with rockers instead of feet, to stop him going backwards if he has a fall."

The sound of a banging latch was followed by footsteps along the side path, and a snatch of curious song: "Fee-ee de-leedle-i-de-doo-doo-WUH!" A tall, distinguished-looking man with a Roman nose stooped at the doorway to remove his soil-encrusted shoes. He wore his usual tractor-driving ensemble of filthy grey trousers, powder-blue sweater, Tattersall-checked shirt and Old Harrovian tie. He entered the kitchen weaving to and fro and rotating his flattened hands like a Mexican chorus in a Carmen Miranda film. After him romped a black Labrador, as slim, glossy and playful as a seal.

"Come here, come *here,* Hercky!" shrieked the man to the dog. "Grr, I'll give him such a lacing. All right, old boy?" This last in a sidelong manner to Louis, who nodded obliquely by way of reply.

"What time did you set off?"

"Four-thirty."

"Well done!" rapped Aubrey, and to cover their mutual unease broke into one of the extempore songs he sang to himself during hours alone on tractors amid acres of cabbage or Brussels sprouts. "They call you Mis-ter Poo. De-doo-de-doo. The furry foxweasel—is out to get you-WUH."

They had coffee in the brocaded drawing-room with its view of the large garden's ivy-covered walk. In the corner stood a lacquered radiogram, disused since the mid-fifties, when Aubrey's departing wife had sawn the mechanism out of it.

"So what do you think of these Beatles now, old boy?" Aubrey asked.

"I still think they're wonderful."

"Wonderful? Wonderful, old boy? With their nasty long hair and their nasty little leather jackets?"

"They don't wear leather jackets any more," Louis said patiently.

"I don't care a bugger about that. They're still nasty little things who need a damned good haircut. And you do as well, old boy, if I may make so bold. Come on, Mister Furry Foxweasel," Aubrey said to the Labrador, rising abruptly. "We must get back to work."

"Are you still doing drumhead cabbages?" asked Louis's mother in a voice which now unaccountably assumed an East Anglian agricultural tinge.

"No. Pea. The pernicious pea," Aubrey replied. "Nasty little things," he added, possibly meaning the Beatles, possibly a plural version of Louis. He led the dog from the room, pumping his elbows in his Carmen Miranda dance and singing "Nas-ty lit-tle things" to the tune of "Help!"

"He's still as mad as a hatter," Louis's mother commented placidly.

"Those trousers look pretty far gone."

"Don't tell me! They stink! And we can't even wash his underpants. Mrs. Pavitt has to put them straight into the furnace."

Louis picked up the broadsheet Daily Mail and glanced through it. On the editorial page was a learnedly hilarious piece by Bernard Levin about reaching one's thirty-third birthday. Despite that grotesquely advanced age, what utter bliss to be Bernard Levin! "You'll be going over to Portia's, of course," his mother said.

"Yes," Louis replied wearily.

"Dulcie Bolton-Phelps is very upset, you know."

"Why should she be upset?"

"She says she was convinced you were going to announce your engagement at that New Year's Eve dance of theirs. Apparently they're already making plans to convert some rooms above the stables into a flat for you both."

"It's nothing to do with me if people get the wrong idea."

"But it was a bit off, the way you just disappeared up north like that."

"It was for work. My career."

"So you said. But . . . I don't know. You're almost twenty-three. All the successful young people in London seem to be your age, or even younger."

He absorbed this routine example of maternal encouragement almost without flinching. "I could be getting an important new job on the paper. This marvellous man I told you about, Jack Shildrick, has as good as promised it to me."

"Don't jump down my throat for what I'm going to say . . . but it's still not too late to make a change, you know."

"I don't want to make a change."

"Gordon Venables, who's in charge of our toiletries for men division, takes a couple of trainees every year, and he's told me he'd seriously consider your application. If you did well at sales, he says, you might have a chance of moving over into public relations . . ."

Louis gaped at her, momentarily winded by this vision of himself.

"If you wanted to get engaged to Portia, you'd be able to afford it," his mother went on hastily. "And you'd have a wonderful time . . . go to lots of cocktail parties. The last one they gave us up at the London salon had our new fragrance, Mémoire de Paris, coming out of a fountain in the middle of the room . . ."

---

If he had ever doubted it was all over with Portia, he realised it when he saw her waiting for him at the main gate of Bottisham Park. Following Paul McCartney's look on the *Rubber Soul* album-cover, he wore the gunmetal-blue shirt with its tab-collar open and a new black rayon polo-neck underneath. To Portia and her circle the only reason why one should wear a sweater under a shirt was having a stiff neck. "What's the matter?" she asked as he got out of the car to greet her. "Have you been sitting in a draught?"

They went straight off for a walk with Mrs. Bolton-Phelps's two black Labradors in the paddocks that surrounded the house. Portia wore a sheepskin-lined suede car-coat and thick socks tucked into rubber boots. Underneath, he knew, would be purple bloomers, a Chilprufe vest and a roll-on corset. As she unlatched a gate, golden hair streamed away from the pale nape of her neck. He remembered sadly applicable words from a recent hit by the Walker Brothers: "Girl, I know it's been tough on you. But through it all, you've been so true . . ."

The fiction somehow staggered on that Louis had gone up north only to make his way, so that he and Portia could all the sooner—in his opaque words—be "properly together."

"If I get the John Blunt job, my career will really be starting to move . . . I didn't think I could do it at first, but Jack Shildrick makes it sound so easy. You know, I read about a conductor, I think it was Sir Thomas Beecham, who had the ability to make his musicians play better than they really could. That's what Shildrick does. And he's so incredibly down-to-earth and friendly. If you're walking to the office and Shildrick comes along in that big Humber of his, he'll always stop and give you a lift. Remember what a stuck-up twit old Newton on the Advertiser was, and he hadn't got a hundredth of Shildrick's flair . . ."

"Will you be coming down for Tricia Marks's wedding on the twenty-fifth?" Portia asked.

"I don't know. I may be working."

An enormous tear formed in Portia's right eye and began trickling down her cheek.

"With a newspaper diary, you just can't think ahead that much," he said tetchily. "I thought you understood by now."

The tear dropped on to her shoulder, zigzagged down her suede sleeve and fell heavily off the edge of her sheepskin cuff.

"I do. I do understand by now."

After lunch he found himself alone with Mrs. Bolton-Phelps in one of the house's two huge stone-flagged pantries. She was wearing a dark green suit, its skirt quite short, and sling-back patent shoes. Her legs were quite a good bit nicer than Portia's.

"We think your hair's gone awfully funny," she told him in her forthright way. "What's your idea in parting it so near the middle like that?" She looked up at Louis with her brown, slightly puggy face held coquettishly on one side. He wondered what it would be like to bend her back and enjoy her against the marble shelf with its bowls of peeled potatoes and carrots. He visualised her laughing tolerantly as he did so.

"Couldn't you drive in to Cambridge this afternoon and have a little trim?" she pleaded. "You looked so much nicer without those long side-boards. Portia says they're like a big sausage on each side of your head."

He spent the evening alone with Portia in the "den," a remote room provided with sagging, dog-hairy armchairs and a television set. The Billy Cotton show featured a guest appearance by the Beatles, performing "We Can Work It Out." John Lennon had discarded his Rickenbacker "short arm" guitar to sit at the flat electronic organ that every other group would seize on now. "He's got such a cheeky face, hasn't he?" Portia said, and Louis, despite everything, felt a surge of possessive jealousy.

Then an old gangster film came on, starring George Raft and James Cagney. Portia took off her pink sweater and Chilprufe vest and undid her brassière at the back. The ensuing fumble was the limit of their amatory adventures, a ritual by now as formalised as Japanese theatre. An early, wise instinct had warned Louis that to proceed further would be an almost guaranteed one-way ticket to a converted flat over the stables. And, with almost psychic clarity, he could imagine her forgiving smile afterwards.

As he toyed with the small but respectable breasts, his eye was caught by a back copy of The Sunday Dispatch colour supplement protruding from a wooden rack near the fireplace. It was among the most arresting of recent front covers—a picture of Bobby Moore on a turf-green background, framed as by a Victorian cigarette-card. Aligned with Moore's portrait was the card in reverse, detailing England's chances under his captaincy in the forthcoming World Cup. Every period detail was right, down to the heading "Famous English Footballers, one of a set of 52, issued by W.D. and H.O. Wills Ltd." Louis remembered how, in that moment, the dusty, unregarded impedimenta of the Victorian age had suddenly seemed piquant and amusing. It was the feeling you got every Sunday morning, ransacking the grey newsprint pages for their glossy colour treasure. The whole world was being discovered anew.

What could he possibly write in tune with that stunning originality and smartness—and sustain over the huge span of 2,000 words? Twiddling a roseate nipple abstractedly, he re-examined Mike Finnis's suggestion of T. Dan Smith, the North-east's entrepreneurial whizzkid. Or maybe Frank Harris, the City Manager just appointed by Newcastle Council at an epoch-making £10,000 per annum.

"Anyone living," the rules specified, so it need not necessarily even be someone famous. It could be an interesting member of one's own acquaintanceship, even family. As Louis dutifully sighed and bent his head there suddenly popped into his mind the conversation he'd had this morning with his mother about artificial legs. He pictured the one solitary figure in his recent lineage who had come anywhere near fame or public distinction. He remembered colourful stories familiar to him since childhood; bizarre souvenirs that were part of the furniture. And all at once, a huge happiness shone in his heart.

Turning away, he fumbled in his jacket for his notebook and unscrewed his Osmiroid. Portia shrank back on the sofa, covering herself with her forearms. "Sorry," he said perfunctorily, and began to write: "On Grand National Day, 1912, my grandfather hid in a pile of straw which, unknown to him, was heavily impregnated with horse-manure . . ."

3

Is this all true?" Mike Finnis asked through a mouthful of toast.

"Yes, it is. And please don't get buttery fingermarks all over it."

"Your grandfather really wrecked the 1927 Test Match?"

"You can look it up in cuttings if you like. Hobbs and Wally Hammond were batting. Play had to be stopped for about four hours while they cleared the barrage balloons off the pitch."

It was the following Wednesday afternoon, back in Louis's Stockton bedsit. Mike and he both being on "morning and evening" shift, there was leisure to ape the university tea-time of his dreams. Mike sat in front of the gas-fire, holding a piece of toast in one hand and the finished competition entry in the other. Behind him his girlfriend, Carol Constantine, reclined across the chintz armchair in a cascade of frilly petticoats, tutting over pictures of Twiggy in the Sunday Dispatch colour supplement.

"You're such a bloody worker," Mike sighed mournfully as he resumed reading. "It's just not on."

"It's not on, Louis," Carol agreed with a soulful glance at him above Mike's head. A severe-looking girl with beautifully brushed long hair, she was front-of-house manager at Stockton Civic Theatre. While never objecting to their frequent threesome, she often spoke of "finding someone" for Louis, in a businesslike tone that made him suspect the person she had chiefly in mind might be herself.

"Is this your grandfather?" Carol stretched out a slender arm and picked up the ancient postcard photograph propped beside Louis's typewriter. A sepia-coloured young man with heavy-lidded eyes like his, but wearing a top-hat and morning coat, stood beside a motion-picture camera as big and unwieldly as a tripod-mounted tea chest. In the background stood a van of 1920s vintage bearing the emblazoned legend "GAUMONT-BRITISH NEWS."

"That's him. Pincher Bassill."

"Pincher Bassill?"

"All those old cinema newsreels, you see, were in ferocious competition with each other. One of them would buy exclusive rights to film a major sporting event, like the Grand National, and the others would go to amazing lengths to smuggle in a cameraman and steal shots of it. My grandad and his sound man Tommy Scales were the past masters of pinching."

"Incredible nerve they must have had," Mike said. "Makes Fleet Street seem pretty tame by comparison."

"Nerve? I'll say! To go and balls-up Jack Hobbs's innings . . ."

"How did they balls it up?" Carol asked.

"God, how didn't they? Movietone, who were Gaumont-British's deadly rivals, had bought the rights to the twenty-seven Test Match and put guards on every door, so my grandad hired an open-cockpit plane and filmed it from the air. To stop him, Movietone put up barrage balloons. Grandad disguised himself as an ice-cream seller on a tricycle, got into Lord's and cut all the cables. But, for some reason, the balloons didn't fly away; they came flopping straight down onto the wicket."

"It's a great story," Mike said, tossing the copy onto the bed.

Louis mopped his brow and took a gulp of lukewarm tea. "Do you really think so?"

"Best thing you've done. Byzantinely funny, as Jack Shildrick would say. I love the bit after him almost suffocating in the horseshit at Aintree. And all that stuff about impersonating the Duke of Windsor in the South of France."

"I've tried to do it the way Evelyn Strachey would."

"Who?" Carol demanded.

"Evelyn Strachey . . . Louis's pin-up boy on the Dispatch colour supplement."

"Or girl," Louis said.

"Or girl." Mike reached for the copy again. "It's very touching, too. How amazing to lose both legs at such a great age, and then have the courage to learn to walk with artificial ones."

"Shoot from the hip, Cisco. Do you think I've got a hope in hell?"

Mike gave his already loosened tie a discomfited yank.

"I think it's a very nice piece . . ."

"But?"

"I've no idea what kind of thing you'll be up against. They're bound to have thousands of entries. Lots of smart Oxford and Cambridge types. I mean, two hundred and fifty quid and an overseas assignment. Who could resist having a go?" He grinned apologetically up at Carol. "Except me."

"But you think I ought to have gone for someone famous? T. Dan Smith or somebody."

"I honestly don't know, mate."

"I don't know either. Perhaps I shouldn't even bother to send it in."

"Are you loco? Of course send it now that you've done it. What have you got to lose? Only a stamp."

---

But later, as he counted the words one final time to make absolutely sure there were "no more than 2,000," hopelessness swooped down on Louis again. In his whole life, he had never won anything: no book on school Speech Day, no silver cup for sporting prowess, no sweepstake, raffle nor Premium Bond prize. Even in competitions for things marginally desirable—a plastic conker with a face from Eagle comic, a holiday in the Scilly Isles, a year's supply of Oxydol—his automatic assumption had always been of standing no earthly chance. What chance then for this one, heavenly beyond his dreams?

None the less, he took the manila envelope of special café-au-lait creaminess he had bought for the purpose, slipped his six immaculately typed quarto sheets inside it and carefully printed: WRITERS' COMPETITION, THE SUNDAY DISPATCH MAGAZINE, MCINTYRE HOUSE, 150 FARRINGDON ROAD, LONDON E.C.4. Rather than stuff it disfiguringly into his corner pillar-box, he drove into town to send it Recorded Delivery from the central Post Office. As he tucked the receipt into his wallet, he had an odd sense of preserving something more than just a temporary proof of payment. Looking down at his shortie tweed overcoat and bronze Saxone shoes, he framed a thought so far-fetched it wasn't worth even finishing. "This moment could be the . . . in my whole . . ."

Apart from Mike and Carol, the only person he told about the competition was Portia. It was one way of filling the chasms of reproachful silence on the telephone line from Bottisham Park.

"I've written all about the terrible battles they used to have on racecourses . . . flashing mirrors in one another's eyes and shaking each other's camera-gantries . . . and about the Great War, when my grandad's car was cut in two by a shell . . . It's funny, I've known about these things for so long, and never thought of writing them down. Once I started, the whole thing just seemed to fall off the end of my arm . . . God, wouldn't it be wonderful to win two hundred and fifty pounds? I could buy you something really great," he found himself babbling on. "Like a mink stole. You'd like a mink stole, wouldn't you?"

The sudden switch from culpable absence to mink took Portia audibly aback.

"Of course . . . that would be a wonderful present," she faltered. "But, you know, you shouldn't bank on winning."

"I know. But if it did happen," he said, confident he was spinning purest make-believe, "the first thing I'd do would be to buy you a mink stole."

Arriving for his shift next morning, he found a small crowd huddled round Mike Finnis's desk—Bob Feetham, Colin Fry, Gillian Barfield, the Woman's Page Editor, Harry Wyse from the Bishop Auckland branch office. Mike greeted him with a grimace of tragic stoicism. "Heard the news? Jack Shildrick's going."

With numb deliberation, Louis propped his umbrella against the radiator. In his mind's eye the John Blunt column, and every wonderful thing associated with writing it, exploded with the ghastly slow motion of a nuclear mushroom cloud. "Going where?" he heard himself say.

"The Sunday Dispatch!"

"What's this?" Peter Fearn, the Sports Editor, came up with Enoch from the teletype room.

"Jack's leaving."

". . . to go to the Sunday Dispatch."

"Well, booger my Aunt Ada through her long johns."

"They've had their eye on him for a long time by all accounts," Bob Feetham said, "and last week they called him down and offered him a dream job. Personal assistant to the Editor."

"Well, we all knew it had to happen," Peter Fearn said through billows of custardy pipe-smoke. "The North-east was never going to be big enough for Jack. We were just a stepping-stone."

"What do you mean?" Mike demanded. "He's put his heart and soul into this bloody paper."

"I don't say he hasn't. Good luck to him. He's put Stockton and Teesside on the map . . . given all you kids a wonderful run. I'm surprised it's turned out to be The Sunday Dispatch, though. It's such a bloody stuck-up outfit. All Oxbridge double-starred firsts there, boy. Most unlike them to pick up a young northern meritocrat."

"Who is Editor of the Dispatch?" Louis asked. In 1966 Fleet Street editors were shadowy deities, little known outside their immediate environment.

"Dudley Mowforth, isn't it?" Mike said.

"Aye." Peter Fearn nodded. "A strange booger by all accounts. But he's certainly done some champion things with the paper."

"Mowforth's been in the chair for a good few years—since before

McIntyre bought the Dispatch," Bob Feetham said. "He must be starting to think about retiring fairly soon. The word is that Jack's going to
be groomed to take over from him."

Louis had often heard this word "groomed" used about people destined for greatness, serving out their time on Newsdesks or in Features
departments. Pleasant it must be to stand there, having your coat
brushed glossy. With Shildrick gone out of his life, would anyone else
ever think him worth grooming?

At that moment, Shildrick himself darted into the room with a pile of
cuttings for follow-ups to drop on Sizer's desk. He was wearing a pale
grey suit and a dark blue shirt that already seemed part of some more
rarified journalistic sphere. His staff broke into applause. "Good on
you!" Colin Fry shouted.

Shildrick turned and gave his boyish grin. "Thanks, mate."

"When are you off?"

"End of the month. I'm supposed to give half a year's notice, but the
Board are very decently letting me go sooner. Got to think about finding
somewhere to live down in the wicked Smoke."

"Do you know what you'll be doing on the Dispatch?" Bob Feetham
asked.

"Panicking, probably," Shildrick said. He took off his glasses, revealing those surprising sultry Victorian-girl eyes. "Wishing I was back,
having a Friday-night jar with you ugly bunch at the Spotted Frog . . ."
As he spoke there was a catch in his voice and he wiped at one eye with
a little finger. The thought of leaving them all at the Evening Telegraph,
even for a new job like this, seemed to bring him close to tears.

For days afterwards, there was talk of nothing else throughout the
Teesside journalistic community. From every colloquy in the Evening
Telegraph's canteen, every strident group in the Spotted Frog and other
favoured watering-holes, could be heard the name "Shildrick" or
"Jack" and those magic words which soft, unenvious North-eastern ac-
cents pronounced "Soon-dea Dispatch."

"Apparently he's going to have a wide-ranging brief," Bob Feetham
reported. "News . . . features . . . Review section . . . the Close-up team."

"And the colour supplement?" Louis asked.

"Not that, no. It's got its own separate, independent editor. Jack'll be
busy enough as it is, anyroad. I can't wait to see what he'll do with
Close-up."

"His missus is none too chuffed about it by all accounts," said Bill
Amos, the Chief Sub.

Louis knew, of course, that Shildrick was married, with a wife who
preferred to stay clear of journalistic life, seldom even coming into the

office. But it was terrible to think of such a future being hampered by domestic constraints.

"You can imagine, it's a big upheaval for the family . . . they've got two bairns at school up here. And Jean Shildrick's involved in a lot of good works . . . educational therapist, J.P. and all that . . ."

The more immediately relevant question of who would succeed Shildrick at the Evening Telegraph was debated with a curious apathy. Six years before, the paper's cautious, parsimonious Board of Directors had made a choice of brilliant adventurousness. No one imagined for a minute that could happen a second time. "The job's not even being advertised around the group," Mike Finnis told the after-Court gathering at the Nack Bar. "So it's got to be someone from inside."

"It couldn't be Sizer, could it?" Louis asked.

Ken Blight laughed with a spray of doughnut crumbs. "Not likely! Even they aren't that bliddy desperate."

Two days later, the appointment appeared on the Newsroom notice board. It was Maurice Pratt, the Industrial Editor, a bald, skeletal man of fifty, universally agreed to justify his surname in every possible way. As a mollification, Sizer was promoted to Deputy Editor and given a glass cubicle with a sliding hatch, a television set and a company executive diary.

For a time, however, the excitement surrounding Shildrick's departure staved off the awful thought of what would be coming after him. Stockton Council passed a motion of gratitude for his contribution to the public life of the city and its image nationwide. There were tributes from all the region's M.P.'s, from Teesside's Chief Constable and across the political spectrum from the National Union of Miners to the Northeastern Association of Conservative Agents. Tyne-Tees Television made a half-hour programme recalling the highlights of his editorship—the campaign to save Newton Aycliff Primary School from closure, the coffee-and-sandwich airlift to South Durham villages cut off in the blizzard of '63, the fight for a bypass to Spennymoor, which was even now about to be granted by the Ministry of Transport. Shildrick was then interviewed, motionless for once in his high-speed office chair, cool and relaxed at the threshold of his dazzling future.

"Will you be sad to leave the North-east?" the off-camera interviewer asked.

" 'Sad' hardly does it justice," Shildrick replied. "I've had six wonderful years up here. I've had the inestimable luck to work with tremendous people and to have the support of enlightened and courageous proprietors. No editor can ask more than that." He took off his glasses, revealing that the hooded Victorian eyes were once again shiny with tears.

"I don't want to be too pious about this," he continued, "but I know that wherever I go I'll always carry the memory of the generosity and good fellowship that this wonderful Geordie-land of yours has given to an Accrington lad." He dabbed at one eye, voice fading with emotion. "This is a . . . kindly place."

His send-off from the Evening Telegraph was like none ever seen or remembered there before. After putting his last Late City Final to bed, he was "banged out" with the valedictory hammering salute of compositors' mallets on metal trolleys, an honour as a rule only given to brother printers. The entire staff—editorial, advertising, switchboard, dark-room, canteen, even balers and van-drivers—then assembled in the Newsroom to see the company Chairman, J. G. Talbot, present him with an inscribed barometer. Every face was a study of pride and sadness. Several of the women around Louis dabbed at their eyes.

"Thank you for this," Shildrick said, holding up his cumbersome brassy gift like some stylish modern jazz instrument. "Whenever the needle points to 'Stormy,' I'll think of Harold Pearce here, when I've told him I want to rejig page one at ten minutes to edition time." Amid an appreciative titter, he laid the barometer on the subs' table.

"These have been six marvellous years," he continued. "I've had the inestimable luck to work with tremendous people and, if I can say so in front of Mr. Talbot, the support of an enlightened and courageous management. No editor can ask for more. I don't want to sound too pious about it all. But I know that wherever I go, I'll carry with me the memory of the generosity and friendship that this wonderful Geordie-land gave to a lad from Accrington . . ."

He took off his glasses, dabbing at a now familiar gleam of manly tears, his voice faltering as before at the thought of Geordie-land's preeminent virtue. "This is a . . . kindly place . . ."

Behind Louis, Florrie the canteen cook gave a rending sniff. "Oh, Mr. Amos," she whispered, "I'll worry about him down there in London. He looks such a boy."

---

Three weeks later, on the day after his twenty-third birthday, Louis received a curious communication. It was a black-and-white postcard of Soho Square, a place which, although born a Londoner, he had never visited. On the reverse were half a dozen lines of unfamiliar and barely decipherable scrawl.

Dear Mr. Brennan,
    I am delighted that we preferred literature to [something] If you have not yet turned your attention to [something] can I urge you to

do so? You have a funny and [something] and quirky eye and it is a novelist's one. I should be delighted to have you on my [something]

Yours, Argl Suclr.

"Can you read this signature?" he asked Mike Finnis, tossing the card across.

"Looks like 'Argl Suclr.' "

"But who is Argl Suclr? And why's he sent me a postcard of Soho Square?"

"Maybe he's a film censor."

"What are you on about?"

"That's all I know about Soho Square. It's the headquarters of the British Board of Film Censors."

Next morning on his typewriter was a creamy foolscap envelope with incisive electric typeface and the franking "London EC4." Unfolding the single sheet of white bond inside and incredulously glimpsing its black engraved "SUNDAY DISPATCH" letterhead, his first thought was that it might be from Jack Shildrick, throwing him the crumb of some "stringer's" assignment like covering a case at Newcastle Assizes.

Dear Mr. Brennan,
    I am delighted to tell you that you have won our Writers' Contest. The cheque will follow in a few days.
    Will you please telephone my colleague, Mrs. Freya Broadbent, reversing the charges, so that we can find out something about you before making the announcement?
    Many congratulations.

    Yours sincerely,
    Toby Godwin
    Editor
    Sunday Dispatch Magazine

"What is it?" Mike demanded.

Louis held out the letter dumbly.

"Bad news?"

Louis shook his head.

"What then? You look like a dying duck in a thunderstorm." Mike snatched the letter, read it, then let out a whistle. "Ee, you jammy boo-ger!"

"What's the trouble?" asked Bob Feetham, looking up from his City Council minutes.

"This jammy booger's just won the Dispatch Writers' Contest. Two hundred and fifty jimmy o'goblins!"

"I'd forgotten all about it," Louis stammered. "I didn't think I had a chance . . ." He read the letter again, half expecting the words to evaporate.

"Good for you, lad," Bob Feetham said. "When do you collect the crinkly?"

"It says 'the cheque will follow in a few days.' "

The telephone buzzed. Mike answered "Newsroom," then held it out to Louis. "Call from London for you."

"Mr. Brennan?" said a silky upper-class voice. "This is Arden Sinclair, of Arden Sinclair Books. I just wanted you to know I was for you right from the beginning. Your piece was so obviously the only candidate. As soon as one started to read it, one knew it was quite out of the ordinary. I couldn't decide what it most reminded me of—a smiling Joyce Cary or a more sombre P. G. Wodehouse."

Light slowly began to filter into Louis's brain. "Oh . . . you were one of the judges."

"Yes. I sent you a postcard. Did you get it?"

"Yes. Thank you."

"You are writing a novel, aren't you?"

"No, I'm not."

"You must. You absolutely must. That piece is the work of a born novelist. I see you as a combination of Thurber, Salinger and Evelyn Waugh. With, maybe, a soupçon of Gogol. Have you read *Dead Souls?*"

"No."

"I'll send you a copy. Look, I know I'm jumping the gun, and Toby Godwin will probably have my guts for garters . . . but I must publish you. You can come and see me and talk turkey whenever you like."

A small crowd had by now collected around Louis's desk. "Well done, lad," Bill Amos said, holding out his hand.

"Cigars all round, is it?" asked Colin Fry.

"I always knew he had a bit of polish about him. Didn't I say to you, Colin . . . ?"

"Who was that?" Mike Finnis asked.

"Arden Sinclair. He's a publisher. He wants me to write a novel."

"Well, you'd best get on with it," Bob Feetham said.

"Anybody know who Joyce Cary is?"

"Who?"

"Joyce Cary. I'm supposed to write like her."

"Why, aye . . . she was in that picture. With Trevor Howard, wasn't it?"

"What's this—a street accident?" Sizer came up, his metal-banded shirt-sleeves perilously close to brushing the floor.

"Me laddo here has covered us all with glory," Bill Amos said.

"He's won the Dispatch talent contest," Mike Finnis explained.

"Oh aye?" The Deputy Editor gave a grimace both scornful and pained, like a victim of acid indigestion in the Settlers advertisement.

"Well, come on!" Amos said. "Ye could shake his hand, you miserable old . . ." At that moment the phone buzzed again.

"Someone else from London," Mike Finnis said, passing it over.

"Louis Brennan?" A female voice this time, also upper-class but seductively husky.

"Yes."

"This is Val Lewis. I'm Picture Editor at the Dispatch Magazine. Look, we're starting to think about your foreign assignment. Was there anything you specially wanted to do?"

"No, not really," Louis said.

"Bailey's just off to Latin America for us. We thought of maybe pairing you up with him. Or there's this other idea of re-creating life on the Mississippi for our big American issues in the autumn. Would you mind terribly much if we sent you to the States?"

"Oh . . . no."

"OK. We'll all have a think and I'll be in touch again. The Seychelles, for a fashion-shoot, is another possibility—or Corsica. We're trying to get a writer and photographer into a gang of bandits for a month . . . Just make sure your passport and inoculations are up to date."

———

That lunch-time at the Spotted Frog was an expensive one for Louis. Afterwards he walked twice around the block, crunched half a packet of fruit Polos, shut himself in the Newsroom telephone-box and dialled the magic number at the top of Toby Godwin's letter, FLE 1000. Even the ringing-tone sounded luxuriously brand-new.

It had time to ring only once. "McIntyre House," said a woman's voice with a heavenly London accent.

"Um . . . could I speak to Mrs. Freda Broadbent?"

"On the Colour Mag?"

"Yes, please."

"One moment." He resisted the urge to slam the receiver down and run. Curious how stupendous triumph felt little different from waiting outside a headmaster's study for six of the best.

"Hallo."

The most upper-class voice so far. Definitely "Hallo," not "Hello."

"Is that Mrs. Freda Broadbent?"

"Freya Broadbent, yes."

"This is Louis Brennan."

"Oh . . . hallo." The voice became crisply alert. "You're our prizewinner."

So he was! He really was!

"Thank you for ringing, Mr. Brennan. Many, many congratulations. And may I say there was never any doubt in my mind . . . the quality absolutely jumped off the page. To me, it read like a spikier Compton Mackenzie. Or perhaps a jollier Günter Grass. We're probably going to run it in the Magazine, you know."

Louis's stomach turned over. "Will that be next Sunday?"

An attractively musical laugh. "Oh, no. But soon. Soon for us, anyway. The thing is, Mr. Brennan, our Editor, Toby Godwin, would very much like you to come down and see him. Could you possibly do that?"

"Yes, I could," Louis said.

"When would suit you? Needless to say, we'll be happy to reimburse your travel expenses."

"Next week one day?"

"How about Thursday?"

"Yes."

"Shall we pencil in three o'clock here at McIntyre House? I'll meet you in reception myself. I'm the magazine's Chief Researcher, by the by. Oh, and one more thing. Could I just get a few biographical details, for when we announce you as our winner? You're from Stockton . . . that's County Durham, isn't it?"

"I only work in Stockton," Louis said. "I wasn't born here."

"Right. Where were you born?"

"In London."

"So, we'll say 'Louis Brennan of London . . .' "

"But actually I was brought up on the Isle of Wight."

"OK. . . . 'Louis Brennan of the Isle of Wight . . .' "

"Only, I haven't lived there for a long time . . ."

"Shall we compromise on your parents' present address, then?"

"Well, my father lives in Berkshire . . ."

"Berkshire? Fine."

"But my mother's in East Anglia. I've spent quite a long time there, too."

"So where should we say you're from, Mr. Brennan?"

"Oh . . . put 'Stockton,' " said Louis.

4

No true-born Londoner ever really belongs anywhere else. The next Wednesday when Louis got off his train at King's Cross, it was not with a visitor's excitement but with the homecomer's deep sigh of relief. Everything at long last was in rightful proportion—whitish buildings, grey pigeons, red buses, the muted roar of a city with nothing to prove. From the posters for Myer's Stout and Phillips' Stick-a-sole Heels to the Finlay's tobacconist, from the shoe-cleaning Chelsea Pensioner to the circular Underground sign, all that he saw instantly resolved the puzzle of his origin and identity.

He wore his only suit, a charcoal-grey Maenson Duo bought from Arthur Sheperd's in Cambridge (at the cost of an anguished moment when the assistant opened a credit ledger and enquired, "Which college, sir?"). His long-collared blue shirt and dull gold tie had been chosen in hopeful imitation of Jack Shildrick. Though the day was sunny he carried his umbrella, meticulously rolled, to ward off any suspicions of provincialism.

The first black taxi on the rank was driven by a man in a raincoat and flat cap, with a voice that Louis recognised as of his true forebears. "Yus, guv?"

"The Sunday Dispatch, please."

"McIntyre 'ouse." The driver nodded, twisting down the flag on his meter.

The odour of the taxi's ribbed brown leather seat conjured up theatre lights along Shaftesbury Avenue, neon signs for Schweppes tonic water and Wrigley's chewing gum, News theatres, oyster-bars, paperboys' foghorn cries, foreign restaurants, hot chestnut braziers and mink coats; the whole metropolis to which Louis had never ceased to feel umbilically connected, whether marooned on seaside piers, fogbound fens or far northern industrial estates. As his taxi weaved among spirit-warming red double-decker buses, he leaned forward to read the matchlessly romantic names of his mislaid heritage: Pentonville, Aldgate, Cheapside, Shoreditch, Camberwell . . . Faces in the bus windows gazed impassively down at him, little dreaming how he envied each and every one of them for being clever enough to live here all the time.

"McIntyre 'ouse," the driver announced over his shoulder, but Louis had already spotted it. In the colourless vista of Farringdon Road, indeed, one could hardly miss it. Eight floors high, ultramodern in design, it occupied an island site between two side streets, stretching for a hundred yards on palisades of opaque silver-tinted glass. Its upper windows jutted out at an acute angle to form seemingly overlapping rows, each row alternated with a cladding of burnished copper. As Louis leaned from his taxi window, sunlight glinted off these numerous copper panels, momentarily dazzling him.

The taxi stopped beside a white portico with "THE SUNDAY DISPATCH" etched on it in lustrous royal blue. Through the panoramic window to the right could be seen dozens of female figures at desks talking animatedly into telephonists' headsets. Yet another lucrative McIntyre innovation had been to restyle his female classified advertising staff "Mack's Tele-Ad Birds," thereby giving even the Dispatch's Property and Situations Vacant columns a touch of Carnaby Street, Sandie Shaw and *Ready Steady Go.*

When Louis offered the price shown on the meter, his driver stared blankly at him. "Ain't this on account?"

"No."

"Sure?" The driver shook his head wonderingly. "First time I've ever brought anyone 'ere, I fink, who didn't say, 'Put it on the Dispatch's account.' "

Automatic glass doors opened noiselessly on to a wide foyer walled in hessian, carpeted in nubbly beige, furnished with black leather couches slung on chromium frames. Two commissionaires, red-sashed and bemedalled, tended a black-lacquered reception desk. Above their heads were grainy blow-ups of recent powerful news pictures in The Sunday Dispatch—a Vietnamese woman keening over her incinerated village; Twiggy in her white fun fur and stockings; the funeral of the three Metropolitan Police officers recently gunned down by bank robbers in broad daylight; Eric Burdon of the Animals.

Louis approached the kindlier-looking of the two commissionaires. "My name's Brennan. I'm here to see Freya Broadbent."

The commissionaire consulted a directory, then spoke inaudibly on a grey telephone. "She'll be straight down. Just take a seat over there."

He sank down on one of the squashy black leather couches, settling his umbrella awkwardly beside him. To his right, three steps led up to a bank of salmon-coloured lifts and, beyond, some kind of delivery counter, very busy and noisy. Over the partition behind him floated the wheedling cacophony of Mack's Tele-Ad Birds. Out in the street he could see taxis constantly arriving, then driving off without any money seeming to change hands. Through the automatic doors came a constant stream of men in fashionably thin suits and girls in short dresses, passing the quiescent commissionaires with the wonderful nonchalance of belonging to this paradisical place.

On the glass coffee-table lay the previous Sunday's colour supplement, its cover a dark sepia photograph of women in long skirts and button-sided boots, decorously waving miniature Union Jacks. "Armistice, 1918," the caption said. Even so dustily perennial a subject as the Great War suddenly seemed new, modish and surprising.

"Mr. Brennan? I'm Freya Broadbent."

Before him stood a woman in her mid-thirties, petitely built, with short black hair neatly framing her face. She wore a high-necked grey wool dress and black patent high-heeled shoes. He struggled to his feet and shook a cool hand tipped by flawless red nails. "Hallo," she said in her crisp voice. "So nice to meet our prizewinner at last. Did you have a good journey up?"

"Down. Yes, thanks."

Mrs. Broadbent looked puzzled. "Down? Haven't you come from the Isle of Wight today?"

"No. Teesside."

"Oh, yes, of course." She gave her attractive laugh. "I remember now. Anyhow, let me take you to Toby Godwin."

Following her up the three steps to the lift area, Louis had time to note that the Chief Researcher's wool dress broke above the knee and that her legs were prettily shaped. "By the way," she added, "please let me know what your travel expenses are. We should be able to pay you in cash before you leave. That's what I hope, anyway."

"It's just my train fare," Louis said.

"You travelled First, I hope." She pressed the lift button and moved one point of her bobbed hair away from her mouth. She had prominent eyes and a nose just short of bulbous, but was still unaccountably desirable.

The lift was walled with copper-coloured mirrors. Louis struggled to look at none of his and Mrs. Broadbent's many burnished reflections. "By the way, we're definitely going to be running your piece," she said.

"Oh." He still could barely grasp the thought. "Do you know when?"

"July, I think is the plan."

"July?" That was still almost two months away.

"Don't be too disappointed. Remember, we have a minimum five-week lead time. We're already working on our June issues now."

---

They stepped out at the fourth floor, into an atmosphere that Louis found deeply strange. He was used to practising his craft amid frenetic and ceaseless noise. Here reigned the quiet and calm of some Benedictine cloister. From somewhere near came laughter, followed by what sounded like a popping cork.

He followed Mrs. Broadbent through some swing doors into a wide concourse which, though crowded, still seemed serene and leisurely. Telephones rang on a low, discreet note, and a single typewriter pecked. They turned sharp right into a glass-walled office where a girl in a Suzy Wong dress and tortoiseshell spectacles was standing at an open filing cabinet.

"Louis Brennan," Mrs. Broadbent murmured, and the girl smiled in concurrence that he was well-known and eagerly awaited. "Of course. Go straight in."

The name "Toby Godwin," together with his neat italic signature, had suggested someone elegantly saturnine and slender. Instead, in the inner office, Louis found himself shaking hands with one of the fattest men he'd ever seen. But for a pink shirt and thin floral tie, indeed, Toby Godwin could convincingly have understudied Friar Tuck or Gessler in *William Tell.* His stupendous girth hung inches over the tormented waistband of his grey trousers and bore so heavily against his shirt's modish front pleat that, by the fourth button, the pleat zigzagged as crazily as a dynamited railway-line. He had straggly pepper-and-salt hair framing a nearly bald pate, muff-like sideburns and an amiable, squashy-nosed face.

"Hullo, welcome," he said in a booming but mellifluous voice. "Many, many congratulations. Do sit down. Now, first things first. Can I offer you a glass of vino?"

Louis took the shallow black leather armchair which Godwin had indicated. Luxuriously red-carpeted, the office had a magnificent view through its slanted casement across London to the new G.P.O. Tower. Pasted on the long inner wall were covers of the magazine in backward sequence, including Danny La Rue, the Bobby Moore cigarette-card and American top sergeant McDaniels. Below on the black polished worktop stood a row of thick red leather volumes, each with "THE SUNDAY DISPATCH MAGAZINE" lettered on its tooled spine in gold.

"Right . . . let's see what we've got." With the effortful grunt inevitable to one of his physique, the Editor stooped below the work-top and opened a refrigerator. Inside were about a dozen horizontal bottles as well as boxed French cheeses, tins of pâté, anchovies and Bath Oliver biscuits, jars of stuffed olives, family-size bars of Toblerone and a glass compartment packed with fruit and salad. "I can do you a 'sixty-three Pouilly Fumé . . . a Muscadet that's drinking rather well . . . Dopf Perle d'Alsace . . . some rather nice cheesy Chablis?"

"Chablis, please."

"Excellent choice. I think I will, too." He poured and handed Louis a fluted goblet, filled almost to the brim.

"Thank you, Mr. Godwin."

"Cheers. And do call me God. Everybody does. Would you care for a cigar?"

"Oh . . . no, thanks."

Godwin settled himself behind a desk on whose polished top could be seen no trace of journalistic activity. Reaching to a multi-coloured box, he selected a cigar as long as a flintlock pistol, sniffed it, rolled it appreciatively close to his right ear, snipped the end with a leather-handled cutter and lit it painstakingly. Curling blue smoke wafted the smell of Christmases Louis had never known.

"It was an absolutely super piece. I loved the bit about your grandfather stopping the Test Match. And hiding in the horse-droppings at Aintree. You've got an absolutely distinctive style. Pointilliste, I think is the word. Like a more knockabout H. G. Wells. Or perhaps a kindlier Thorne Smith."

"Thank you."

"And very touching, too, the sequence about him losing his legs and having to learn to walk with artificial ones."

"Thank you."

Godwin tilted his pink avoirdupois back in his chair and gave Louis an attentive beam. "Well, now . . ." he said. "What are your plans?"

This was the dream moment, and Louis grasped it with both hands. "I want to work for the Sunday Dispatch."

The Editor guffawed, an explosive "Hooh hooh!" that, mixed with his cigar smoke, ended in red-faced spluttering. "No bones about that then, hooh hooh hooh! Straight from the shoulder, eh? Hooh hooh hooh! Urghh! You young rip!" He coughed extensively, then recovered himself with a gulp of wine. "Well, strictly speaking a job wasn't among the prizes we offered but, of course, we now have your former editor, Jack Shildrick, down here with us, and he says you were one of his most able and hard-working young feature writers—a really bright lad. So all in all I think you'd better come and join us, don't you?"

"Yes," Louis said.

"Generally speaking, hiring staff writers isn't our bag. The bulk of our pieces are commissioned from freelances. Until now, the only permanent person we've had in that capacity has been Evelyn Strachey."

"Who's my absolute idol," Louis said.

"Yes, he's wonderful, isn't he?" So the mystery of Strachey's gender was solved at last. "And incidentally I'm sure Evelyn will be delighted with your success. He's always been very keen on encouraging young writers."

With what seemed almost paternal pride, Godwin beamed at Louis again. "My suggestion is that we take you on as a writer for, say, a six-month trial period. At the end of that time, if we still like each other, you'll be offered a staff appointment. Does that sound OK?"

"Yes."

"How much notice do you have to give at your present paper?"

"A month," Louis said.

"So you could start with us . . . when? Beginning of July?"

"Yes."

Godwin slid back a hatch beside him. "Dear heart," he said to the bespectacled girl, "could you ask Terry B. to come in for a moment?" It occurred to Louis how he could spoil this moment in a split second that would torture him for the rest of his life. He had only to jump up and dash his wine over Toby Godwin . . . attack the huge pleated shirt-front with his fists . . . drop his trousers, yank down his Y-fronts and start rummaging among the hairs in his anus . . . He gripped the stem of his glass in conscious self-restraint.

"Terry Bracegirdle is my deputy here, the person you'll be working to, a marvellous Features Editor and an absolutely super bloke," Godwin continued. "He hails from the Durham area as well, so as two northern lads you should get on famously."

"I'm not actually from the North," said Louis.

Godwin looked puzzled. "Haven't we got you down as Louis Brennan of Stockton?"

"I grew up on the Isle of Wight."

"Ah . . . right." As the Editor made a note in his meticulous hand, a man of about thirty looked round the door. He had a handsome, aquiline face set off by square black Michael Caine glasses. He, too, wore a pink shirt, but what Louis chiefly, and enviously, noticed were trousers in large, multi-stranded brown-and-black check that until recently had been the exclusive province of Rupert Bear. "Hullo, dear boy," Godwin greeted him. "This is our young prizewinner, who, I'm delighted to say, I've persuaded to join us. Louis Brennan—Terry Bracegirdle."

"Con-grat-you-lations," Bracegirdle said with the familiarly gentle and friendly north-eastern lilt. Louis could tell at once how extraordinarily nice he was and how pleasant and rewarding it would be to work under his direction.

"We haven't even broached the subject of money yet," Godwin said. "What do you think would be a fair shake, Terry?"

"Twenty-five a week?" Bracegirdle suggested.

"Is twenty-five adequate?"

Louis gave a dazzled nod. The hatch beside Godwin slid back to reveal the bespectacled girl. "When you've finished with Mr. Brennan," she said, "Jack Shildrick would like to see him."

"Why don't you go up to Jack now?" Godwin said. "Then Freya can collect you and get you photographed. Later, I hope you can join me for dinner at Chez Victor and meet some of your new colleagues. It'll be too late for you to get back up north tonight, so we'd better book him an hotel, hadn't we, sweetie? See if you can get him in at the Great Northern; if not, you'd better try the Savoy."

―――――――

"Come on in, Poet," Shildrick said, as if the hiatus of the past six weeks had never been. He was wearing a snugly fitted dark grey suit that gave him an almost vicarish look as he leaned at a broad lectern covered with page-proofs. The office was noticeably smaller than his old one at the Evening Telegraph, though it had the same impressive view across London as Toby Godwin's, one floor below.

He shook Louis's hand, gave him a light congratulatory punch on the shoulder and steered him across to the lectern. "They've agreed to let me give the Review section a complete new look—Books and Arts . . . Fashion . . . Motoring . . . It was all a bloody hodgepodge, between you and me. What's the good of having the finest critics in Britain if you have to read them with a magnifying-glass? I told them, 'I don't want to change anything, just clean the windows . . .' " See what a difference some column rules and a bit of white space make? And isn't that a stunning picture of Gielgud?"

"I just don't know how to thank you . . ." Louis stammered.

"Don't thank me," Shildrick said. "It was your talent . . . and enterprise." He took off his glasses, which were of a more modern design than formerly, with smoky grey frames. Hero-worship, as always, made Louis not quite like to look into the fragile, feminine face.

"But I'm told you put in a fantastic good word for me."

"I only said what was true. 'He's a marvellous writer. He always carries a rolled umbrella. And he looks a bit like Byron.' "

A middle-aged secretary entered with a tray bearing a rose-decorated teapot, a milk jug and two matching dainty cups. "Oh, bless you,

Pippa," Shildrick said. "You'll have a cup of tea with me, won't you, Poet?"

"Thank you." For all Shildrick's flair for democracy, this had never happened in his time on the Evening Telegraph. As the tea was poured, he nudged Louis and pulled an expressive face.

"See what a lovely life it is down here. Tea out of bone china cups. Earl Grey . . . not that dishwater Florrie used to brew up. Lemon instead of milk if you like."

They sat with their cups on a cream sofa littered with galley-proofs. The middle-aged secretary came across and handed Shildrick a phial of saccharin tablets. In these few weeks she had clearly become as indulgently devoted to him as everyone back in Stockton had been.

"So . . . Toby Godwin's taken you on, has he?"

"Yes. I'm still pinching myself. If I could have chosen any job in the world, this would have been it."

A flicker of doubt crossed Shildrick's face. "Aye, you'll have an interesting time. Though I wonder if the Colour Mag will be able to keep someone as hard-working as you busy enough. My plan was always that you should join us up here on the paper."

So all along Shildrick had been making plans to bring him here from Stockton. Louis felt a momentary twinge of guilt at having upset whatever that wise and judicious strategy had been.

"I think you'd fit into the Features department wonderfully well," Shildrick added. "And you've got that lovely humorous touch. I still quote that line of yours comparing kite-flyers to university senior wranglers. What you really ought to think about is the Cicero column."

At this Louis could only goggle. The Dispatch's "Cicero" was the most glamorous as well as illustrious gossip column in the quality Sunday field. Occupying half a page in the Review section, it ranged with complete freewill from politics and the arts to whatever freaks of fashion or human eccentricity caught Cicero's sardonic oratorial fancy. Its past authors were figures of eminence beyond the merely journalistic; persons who had gone on to write best-selling spy thrillers or present film review programmes on BBC2.

"But . . ." he quavered, "what about Hugo Kennie?" Kennie's name had signed a column of eccentric brilliance ever since Louis had been composing village paragraphs for the Whittlesey Advertiser.

Shildrick put down his cup and looked around him as though wary of eavesdroppers. "Keep this to yourself . . . but Hugo may be giving up the column fairly soon. He's got a contract to write a book, and he's doing a new TV show with Desmond Morris . . . Come Christmas we could be wanting a new Cicero to address the Senate."

"And you really think I could do it?"

"Yes, I do," Shildrick said tersely. "Keep it under your hat for the present and we'll talk about it more after you come down."

"Right." Dizzily Louis breathed in warm air from his empty teacup. How many more dream jobs would fall into his lap today?

"So where'll you be staying?" Shildrick asked.

"I haven't thought yet. Probably with my grandparents—to begin with anyway."

"Where do they live?"

"Clapham. Where do you?"

"Hampstead," Shildrick said. "The wife likes the intellectual life. And the Heath's lovely. You must come and have a meal with us . . ." At this moment Freya Broadbent put her neat dark head round the door.

"Sorry," she said, "I have to take our prizewinner away to be photographed now."

As Louis followed her out, Shildrick called, "How much are the Colour Mag paying you?"

"Twenty-five pounds a week."

"Are you happy with that?"

"Yes, very."

"What . . . only four pounds above the N.U.J.'s London minimum? They could try a bit harder than that. I'll have a word with Toby Godwin and see if I can't get it up to thirty."

---

He was given a lift to the restaurant by Godwin's deputy Terry Bracegirdle in Bracegirdle's custard-yellow E-Type Jaguar. With them travelled a girl with long red hair who, in the E-Type's cramped black leather cockpit, was obliged to sit on Louis's lap. Flaming tresses tumbled fragrantly close to his face, a braceleted hand rested close to the prickling hairs on his neck; an orange tweed skirt rode up high from knees of flawless smoothness. Bracegirdle, studiously dashing in hornrims and his Rupert Bear hipsters, gunned the long yellow bonnet through Bloomsbury streets as sunnily peaceful as those of some small market town. Ahead loomed the G.P.O. Tower, a huge silver mace above the Victorian house-tops, its studded summit winking and sparkling like a mirage. "Oh, boy!" was all he kept thinking. "Oh, boy, oh, boy, oh, boy, oh, boy, oh, boy, oh, boy!"

The restaurant, on the fringes of Soho, was painted bright pillar-box red. At the name "Mr. Godwin," dour French faces melted into welcoming smiles; they were shown straight through to a semi-private rear portion where a long table waited next to a wall-sized gilt mirror. Toby Godwin was already at the head of it, mountainously pink-shirted, buttering bread and sipping white wine, surrounded by a colloquy of stripe-jerseyed waiters. His uproarious "Hooh hooh hooh!" had been audible from the street.

"Ah, there you are, dear boy," he boomed. "Well met, well met. Come and sit here by me. Now, I want you to meet two more of your new colleagues. Jessamyn O'Shaughnessy, our Fashion and Beauty Editor . . . Cedric Scurr, Art Director and my right hand. Would you say that's an apt description, Cedric? Hooh hooh!"

Louis had seen the exotic byline "Jessamyn O'Shaughnessy" many times over the colour supplement's breathtaking fashion spreads. He had always thought such a personage could have no choice but be as rangily beautiful, cool and elegant as the model girls she described. Instead he beheld a sturdily built woman approaching middle age, with lank ash-blond hair and the fleshy, rosy-cheeked face of a cook in some Edwardian advertisement for Oxo. Fashion and beauty did not get going until her neck and arms, which were girlishly framed by a shift dress as light and diaphanous as stitched-together spring flowers.

"Art Director," however, was a term as mysterious as it was portentous. He wondered what might be the indispensable function of this short, swarthy, black-haired man, slightly bald on top, wearing tortoiseshell bifocal glasses, a lemon needlecord jacket and a houndstooth Top Dog shirt. Shaking Cedric Scurr's hairy hand, he prepared himself for the now familiar experience of congratulation and praise. But none came. The bifocals regarded him with the fathomless opacity of some tarn in the Himalayan foothills.

"Will Evelyn Strachey be coming?" he asked Godwin.

"Alas, dear boy, I believe he's out of the country at present. Evelyn is away on a job, isn't he, Terry?"

Bracegirdle was at the opposite end of the table, the red-headed girl close beside him. "Yes," he nodded. "In Geneva."

"Seeing Brando . . . of course. Ah, here's Freya! Will you sit here next to our prizewinner, darling? Now, is Bollinger all right for everyone *comme apéritif? Monsieur le sommelier, s'il vous plaît! Nous désirons le Bollinger. Deux bouteilles . . . non, trois bouteilles. Pour commencer.*"

Jessamyn O'Shaughnessy took a packet of Gitanes from her shoulder-bag, lit one and blew acrid smoke across the table into Louis's face. "So you're another of these gritty, thrusting northern lads, are you?" she asked in a languid drawl.

"I don't actually come from the North . . ."

"Louis was on the same paper as Jack Shildrick," Mrs. Broadbent told her.

"Oh!" Jessamyn said with an eloquent roll of her rather bloodshot eyes.

"We were all absolutely bereft when he came down here to join you," Louis said. "He's such a brilliant journalist. And an incredibly nice man as well."

Surprisingly, his new colleagues did not unite in the expected paean of praise to Shildrick. Across the table, Jessamyn and Scurr exchanged an expressive glance, and beside him Mrs. Broadbent tapped her scarlet nails on a tin ash-tray marked "Ricard." Even Godwin's squashy, amiable face could summon up no more than the faintest of wry smiles. "Yes . . . he's certainly been a breath of . . . ahem . . ."

"Is he involved in anything you're doing on the colour supplement?"

"Oh, please!" Jessamyn exclaimed with an anguished wince.

"We try, despite its ubiquity, to discourage this term 'colour supplement,' " Godwin told him. "Since our advertisement revenues support the paper, we prefer to think of them as a supplement to us."

"We call them the Steam Section," Mrs. Broadbent put in. "Rather rudely, I always think."

"But aptly," said Terry Bracegirdle.

"The arrangement is, we don't interfere with them and they don't interfere with us," Godwin said. "On editorial matters, I'm answerable only to our proprietor."

Three waiters began pouring champagne from white-necked bottles. Toby Godwin handed Louis a tall glass and raised his own. "Here's health, dear boy. May you give us many more pieces like your tour de force about your grandfather. OK, you young rips, let's decide what we're going to nosh. *Huîtres? Petites fritures? Pâté de Strasbourg?* Remember, one and all, that oysters is amorous. Hooh hooh hooh!"

The rest of the evening was a blur to Louis. Looking back later, it seemed to have passed in a flash, although there were moments when its excitement, glamour and wonder seemed to stretch out into eternity. The food was the richest and most expensive he had ever eaten—liver pâté circled by a thick yellow butter crust, wafer-thin veal swimming in Madeira wine, dark chocolate profiteroles obliterated by squirted frills of whipped cream. As well as the champagne there was Châteauneuf du Pape or Pouilly Fumé, both of which, he saw from the wine list, cost over £5 per bottle. The main part of the restaurant thronged with celebrities of whom he had heard or half heard—Tony Richardson, Harry Salzman, Donyale Luna, George Weidenfeld, Alan Clarke of the Hollies. "Ooh, look!" Jessamyn cried at one point, "there's Twiggy. And Justin. I must ask them how the session with Terry Donovan went. Coo-ee!"

Louis tried not to gawp at the white-faced, coal-eyed waif, familiar from innumerable magazine covers, television programmes and cinema newsreels. Her hair was cropped to a silvery scalp, as shiny-smooth and round as the knob on a Victorian bedstand. She wore a tiny shift of imitation chain mail suspended from a silver collar that might have been filched from the tomb of Tutankhamen or the champion bull at a fatstock show. With the cigarette legs and frightened-doe face went a robust, no-nonsense Cockney voice. "Don't send me back to that studio again," she pleaded as she hugged Jessamyn. "Talk about primitive! He practically 'ad me pissing in a bucket."

"Twiggy, darling, this is Louis Brennan. Our newest young writer . . ."

" 'ello," she said with a friendly nod.

". . . and her manager, Justin de Villeneuve." Louis shook hands with a long-nosed, velvet-suited youth about his own age, whose eyes moved continually from side to side like beads computing on an abacus. "Won't you both join us, Justin, dear boy?"

"No, ta," de Villeneuve replied in a voice as unlike a nineteenth-century French admiral's as it was possible to conceive. "We're off to the Ad Lib. Ringo's 'avin' a little do. Should be a good scene . . ."

Glancing across the squadrons of scarlet and green bottles to his reflection in the mirror, Louis tried to arrest runaway time by deliberately noting every detail of the assembly. On his right, Toby Godwin was looking with a lover's devotion at a newly arrived portion of coq au vin. On his left, sitting up straight like a virtuous schoolgirl, Freya Broadbent was eating a lamb chop with her fingers. During the afternoon he had become intensely aware of her prettily shaped legs, set off to perfection by the short grey wool dress and black patent shoes. He wondered if his new life was to make the seduced-by-older-woman fantasy come true at last. He imagined Mrs. Broadbent's snub face with its curves of dark hair at first avoiding his kisses, then greedily returning them.

He realised he was happy in the total, unqualified way that people usually were only in films and plays. His only regret was in not being closer to Terry Bracegirdle, the handsome, agreeable, enviably trousered Deputy Editor, to discuss what assignments he might undertake when he joined the colour supp . . . the Magazine. Time enough for that, however. With the North-east as well as love of trousers in common, how could they get on other than well?

Opposite him, Jessamyn O'Shaughnessy had already pushed her lamb chops away and was lighting another Gitane. Next to her, Cedric Scurr bent over a plate of pigeon, bifocalled eyes still swimmingly opaque. Realising his napkin had fallen to the floor, Louis bent to retrieve it. The split second below table-level was enough for him to see

Jessamyn's forearm resting on Scurr's hip, her jewelled fingers clenched and moving in a gentle but firm pump-action.

He turned hastily back to Toby Godwin. "This is a wonderful dinner. A bit different from my usual diet."

"And what is your usual diet, dear boy?"

"Bacon-and-egg pies. Cadbury's Smash. Saveloys."

"Saveloys?"

"I've got this overcoat with a big inside poacher pocket, where I always keep a couple. Just what you need late at night after writing up an erotic suicide."

"Hooh hooh hooh!" roared Godwin. "Saveloys! Poacher pockets! Hoooh hoooh hooooh! Erotic suicides! You young rip!" Not the least wonderful part of this evening was how almost everything he said—and almost everything anyone else said—caused his new Editor to explode into delighted guffaws. He thought of the bilious and irascible tyrants he had always pictured holding positions of authority in national journalism. Who could ever have dreamed a Fleet Street executive could be thus, overflowingly jolly and all-providing, so much like Leech's illustration of the Ghost of Christmas Present that one wanted to creep under his generous cloak and, like Tiny Tim, hide one's head in his quivering, sheltering girth?

With the coffee and double cream came brandy, Armagnac, Calvados and Drambuie. Godwin clapped his pudgy hands, summoning the head waiter with an open casket of cigars in many sizes. "A nice Montecristo, I think, for our young prizewinner. If there's one piece of wisdom I can pass on to you, dear boy, it's this. Never smoke any cigars but Havanas. Every one is rolled by hand on the thigh of a young Cuban girl. And the very best ones sometimes have a pubic hair rolled in with the leaf."

"God!" Mrs. Broadbent said mock-severely. "What sort of advice is that for someone about to join your staff?"

"I can think of better, actually. You'll find it more or less sums up our philosophy on the Magazine. If a thing's worth doing . . ." Godwin paused and looked fondly down the white causeway of crumpled napkins, chocolate-smeared plates and empty bottles. ". . . If a thing's worth doing, it's worth doing to absolute bloody excess! Hooh hooh hooh hooh!"

# 5

He pressed the front door-bell that made a "Brring!" as old-fashioned as the 1950s, then stooped and poked in the stiff steel flap of the letter-box. There was the familiar spotless hallway with the red carpet and terracotta-coloured lino, the steep ascent of dark polished banisters. There was the mirrored coat-stand with its umbrellas, known as "gamps," its pin-pierced hats, its wheeled shopping bag covered in Black Watch tartan. As he had since the age of eleven, Louis held his breath for the moment it took the glass-paned kitchen door to open and Grandma Bassill to approach with her tripping, purposeful step.

At four in the afternoon she was, as always, immaculately dressed and made up. With her pale blue twinset and flowered apron, she wore a double-strand imitation pearl necklace and matching earrings. Her scanty hair was freshly dyed dark henna red. He bent and kissed her decorously, knowing her dislike for "too much sloppy stuff."

"We wondered where you'd got to," she said in the voice that was both politely refined and as Cockney as stewed eels and mash.

"I went wrong on that big new road along the Embankment. Couldn't turn round until I got to Wandsworth Common."

"Your Mummy's been on the blower to see if you'd arrived safely. So's your ladylove. What's 'er name?"

"Portia."

"That's it. I met her, didn't I? Nice sort of a girl with fair 'air. She says can you give her a tinkle back when you've settled in."

"Right," Louis said, instantly dismissing the thought from his mind.

He followed Grandma Bassill down the hall, with its unchanging smell of Mansion polish and cake mixture, and into the narrow kitchen-cum–living room. Grandad was seated in his wheelchair at the table, a game of Patience spread before him on the green baize cloth. But for his snowy mop of hair, he seemed little changed from that lean young man behind the big-eared movie camera. "Hello, boy," he said, twisting round to shake hands. His quirked-down mouth and fleeting wink conveyed more to his grandson than the most extravagant Sicilian hug.

In the great days with Gaumont-British News, he had taken his tiny, peppery spouse to Lord's, Wimbledon and Royal Ascot and on annual sea cruises to Madeira. Now, in her late seventies, she repaid the favour by caring for him, without any state help, sixteen hours a day, still somehow finding time to put on make-up and pearls. The only weakness in her five-foot-nothing tower of strength was sometimes appearing to think the surgeons had also removed his comprehension.

"You're famous now," she reminded him. "Lou's written an article all about you. And taken first prize."

"I know," Grandad said tolerantly.

"Why don't you show him your new legs?"

"Sure. It's the new big idea from the boffins over at Roehampton. They've decided to turn me into a rocking-horse." Grandad propelled himself backwards, clear of the table. The grey chalk-stripe trousers he wore—relic of some twenty-year-old business suit—had been cut down to half their proper length. From each reoriented turn-up protruded a stout black metal rod, ending in a curved flipper.

"Can't fall backwards, you see, with all that extra support behind. Need it when I play your Gran at shove-ha'penny!"

Carrying his bags upstairs, Louis met Nancy, whose husband rented the first-floor rooms his grandparents could no longer use. A mountainous Irishwoman—and, providentially, a nurse—she had a thick County Sligo brogue whose sorest test always seemed to be her landlady's surname.

"Remember I told you, he won that prize for writing?" Grandma Bassill said from the hallway below. "Now the paper've give him a job. He's starting there tomorrow."

"Will ye look at that now," Nancy said. "Ye must be main proud of him, Mithossoth Bothosol."

He unpacked in the small green top-floor room where he had so often slept as a child. The single window looked down on to a confluence of back gardens in which some neighbours grew prize roses and others kept cast-off baths and kitchen sinks. Above the green-counterpaned bed hung a photograph of Grandad Bassill, pith-helmeted, with his dismantled movie camera, on the howdah of an Indian elephant. On the dressing table stood one of him in a top-hat, photographing the 1924 Wembley Exhibition. The wardrobe was full of artificial legs, superseded as stumps changed shape and the years advanced. One of them still wore a brown mudguard shoe and maroon ankle sock.

High tea was baked beans on three rounds of toast, followed by tinned pears and a Wall's ice-cream wafer. Afterwards Louis sat in his old place beside the iron hearth whose mantel of framed photographs made his family seem almost normal. On his parents' wedding picture Grandma Bassill had made loyal reparation to his wronged mother by wedging a snapshot in the frame to obliterate his father's face.

"I've been so amazingly lucky," he said as Grandad spread out the cards in rows again. "If I hadn't gone north, I wouldn't have met this marvellous man, Jack Shildrick, who's encouraged and helped me so much. The Dispatch would never have taken me on if it hadn't been for him. They say he'll end up as Editor there before long. He's a ball of fire and energy, and he makes everyone who works for him feel excited and . . . exhilarated. He's a terrific chap."

"You're lucky if you can work for someone like that," Grandad nodded. "We had an Editor much the same at Gaumont—Castleton Knight, his name was. Always up to tricks, he was, to nobble the opposition and get the film home first. Kidnapping Charlie Chaplin was his biggest stunt. And hanging cards reading 'Gaumont-British News' round the necks of the St. Neots Quads at their christening. Eisenhower's supposed to have planned the D-Day landings to give the best camera-angles to Castleton Knight."

Grandma Bassill came through from the scullery. " 'ow much did they give you as a prize for writing about Grandad?" she asked.

"Two hundred and fifty pounds."

"All that time he sat there telling you things, you were storing it all up." She aimed a playful cuff at his head. "Artful little devil!"

"Ready for a shove, Mum?" Grandad said.

As she went to the dresser, a loud, drawn-out "frrrppp-put-put-put," like a sluggish outboard motor, issued from the region of her apron-knot. Long tradition demanded that no one should remark on or even appear to notice this. She returned with the mahogany shove-ha'penny board and the cardboard box of smooth brass discs. "Why don't you have the first game with Lou?"

"Fair enough." Humming softly, Grandad got down from his wheelchair onto the new rockers, supporting himself on two specially shortened sticks. The height of a small boy above the table, he positioned the first disc at the edge of the board, and squinted along it in preparation for his shot. "I warn everyone," he said. "I'm in championship form tonight."

---

At 8 o'clock next morning Louis was already on the tube from Clapham South to Farringdon. Shampooed and twice-shaven, he looked as smart as he knew how in the Air Force–blue double-breasted Jaeger suit, cream button-down shirt and black knitted silk tie which had been the first investment of his prize money. The train was hot and fitful and crowded with West German football supporters, here to see their national team play England in the imminent World Cup final. Most of their fellow passengers glared darkly at their pale raincoats and little macintosh hats, clearly pining to open the bomb-bays over Dresden once again. But Louis felt only beatific love for all mankind as he sat on the familiarly warm red-and-blue upholstery, inhaling the gritty air like a Sahara traveller gulping frozen beer.

Eight forty-five found him already pacing up and down outside the copper-faced grandeur of his new office. At 9 o'clock, when the front doors of McIntyre House still showed no sign of opening, he walked down to Ludgate Circus and half-way across Blackfriars Bridge. Looking up river to St. Paul's and the Tower, he once again felt the deep peace of knowing exactly where he came from and belonged. From a nearby sandwich bar he could hear the Hollies singing "Bus Stop." It reminded him how keenly he looked forward to working with Terry Bracegirdle. To underline their kinship, perhaps he should talk to Bracegirdle with a slight North-eastern tinge. He beguiled another fifteen minutes by dropping bits of paper into the Thames and practising his Durham accent on the lyric to "Bus Stop." "Al' the pipple stared as if we wor boath quite inseane . . ."

When he returned to McIntyre House at 9:30, the front doors had been opened and the two commissionaires were on duty in the hessian and black leather vestibule. "Sir?" the friendlier-looking one said with a glimmer of recognition.

"Louis Brennan. I'm starting on the Magazine today."

"I doubt if there'll be anyone there yet. But go on up."

He took the lift to the fourth floor and followed the memory of Mrs. Broadbent's legs through the swing doors, into the concourse he had only glimpsed on that first visit. It was wide and light, and completely deserted. Down the right-hand side was a row of glass partitioned executive offices; on the left was a long, glassed-in space furnished with architects' desks and white Anglepoise lamps. The door to Toby Godwin's office stood open on its scarlet carpet, polished work-top and red leather-bound volumes. After a moment, a cleaner came out with an armful of empty wine bottles and dropped them noisily into a wheeled rubbish skip.

On a desk-top half-way down the concourse, a telephone began ringing. With the reflex of the Newsroom Louis walked over and picked it up. "Hello," he said, and for the first time, thrillingly: "Sunday Dispatch Magazine."

"Hello." It was a woman's voice, curiously halting and croaky.

"Can I help you?"

"I'm phoning about the recipe . . . in your supplement yesterday."

"The recipe? Ah, well, I'm afraid . . ."

"I've never heard of stuffing lemons with . . . sardines . . . and . . . I'm sure the quantities were wrong. You couldn't possibly have meant a pint of double cream . . ."

"I'm sorry, I don't . . ."

"My whole family's been sick all night," the voice croaked. "I'm only just able to come to the phone even now . . . A whole pint couldn't have been right . . . not with avocadoes . . . and sardines. We're all horribly ill, thanks to you . . . the dog worst of all . . . My husband says that if you don't publish an apology in your next issue, he's . . ."

"I'm afraid this is my first day here," Louis said. "All I can do is take your number and ask someone to call you back." But with an exclamation, that could have been retching, the line went dead.

At 10:20, someone finally arrived in one of the glass-walled side offices. It was a grey-suited, orange-shirted man in his early forties, with peaked black hair and champagne-bottle shoulders. Louis waited politely in his doorway while he prodded a cigarette at his mouth and patted his bulging pockets for a match. "Er . . . morning. I'm Louis Brennan."

The man removed his cigarette and proffered a dry hand. "Jim Deaves."

"I wonder if you could tell me where to sit?"

"Sit?"

"I'm joining you today."

"Are you?" Jim Deaves said blankly. Behind Louis, a young woman in pink had also arrived and was unpacking a briefcase at a block of three desks midway in the concourse. "Margaret!" Deaves called.

She raised a broad, high-cheekboned face between two swinging points of dark brown hair.

"This is Louis Brennan, who's joining us today. Did you know about it?"

"Of course I did," the young woman said coolly.

"Well, I had no idea."

"Didn't anyone tell you?"

"Of course not. Why would anyone tell me? I'm only the Business Manager. Of what possible concern could it be to me that God's put yet another person on the payroll?"

The words were spoken feelingly but without resentment. Deaves shovelled back his cigarette as if afraid his mouth might be growing lonely. "All right . . . where are we going to put him?"

"There's a place free here, between Freya and me."

"Take this desk then, Louis, for the time being anyway," Deaves said. "By the way, this is Margaret Cole, our Chief Sub."

"Chief and only Sub," she amended with a smile. Just then Cedric Scurr walked through the concourse, wearing an ice-blue shortie raincoat and carrying a large black portfolio. Ignoring Louis, he went in to the adjacent glassed area, slammed down his portfolio and switched on a lamp.

In 1966, the concept of a female sub-editor was still a deeply exotic one. Margaret Cole was about twenty-eight, tall and slender, in a pale pink dress whose Nehru collar gave her a somewhat clinical look. "I liked your prizewinning piece," she said. "In fact, I've got it here, waiting to go in." In a wire basket Louis glimpsed the white pages he had posted three months ago, with hope below zero.

"Do you know when that'll be?"

"It's scheduled for August, I think. Gilda, from the Art Department, was wondering what we could do for an illustration."

Louis glanced at his watch: it was now 10:35. At Stockton Petty Sessions, they would have gone through half the list by now, and be breaking for coffee.

"What time does Terry Bracegirdle usually get in? I'm supposed to report directly to him."

"About eleven . . . eleven-fifteen. Depends what he was up to last night."

"How about Toby Godwin?"

"Not till lunch-time. At least."

By 10:50, the concourse was definitely coming to something resembling life. Secretaries had appeared in the outlying offices; telephones were ringing and, now and then, being answered. In an alcove festooned with posters and glossy prints a crop-haired woman was peering at transparencies spread on a garishly lit white table. Scurr, in his parallel glass sanctum, had been joined by a dark-haired girl in a blue dress with a white Colette collar. Other than Margaret Cole no one spoke to Louis, or even seemed to notice him sitting there.

At just after 11 o'clock, Jessamyn O'Shaughnessy and Freya Broadbent came in together. The Fashion and Beauty Editor's face was blearily devoid of make-up and her ash-blond hair scraped back in a ponytail tied with an elastic band. Mrs. Broadbent, too, was somewhat different from the figure who had been co-starring with Jane Fonda in Louis's fantasies. She wore a coloured headscarf, knotted under her chin, and carried two full shopping bags. The effect was not so much siren as vicar's wife en route to a sale of work.

"Ah, our young prizewinner!" she said with her staccato briskness. "How are you liking it so far?" She dumped her bags behind the third desk in the block and began to unpick the knot of her scarf.

"Apparently no one knew he was supposed to be starting today," Margaret said.

"But, honey, that's utterly ridiculous."

"Well, no one had told Jim Deaves, anyway. So there's no desk for him. Not even a typewriter."

"In that case, he'll just have to muck in here with us," Mrs. Broadbent said. "You won't mind that, will you, Louis?"

"Not at all."

"If I make too much noise on the telephone, you must promise to tell me. I honestly shan't be offended." She took off her pink coat to reveal a turquoise paisley dress, with a little-girl collar and puffed sleeves, ending some five inches above her knees.

"Nice dress, Freya," Margaret said.

"Do you really like it?"

"Yes, it's super."

"I hae ma doots," said Mrs. Broadbent. "Thirty-nine may be a bit too old for Biba. And Tarquin complains that when I sit down, he can see my pussy."

At that moment Terry Bracegirdle came through the concourse from the inner end, and went into the office between Jessamyn's and Jim Deaves's. Already ensconced there was the red-haired girl who'd sat on Louis's knee on the journey to the restaurant. With an inward sigh of relief, he straightened his black knitted tie, buttoned his jacket and walked across to Bracegirdle's open door.

The Deputy Editor looked even more dashingly handsome and likeable than at their first encounter. He wore a pale green shirt and the same greenish tweed hipster trousers that Louis himself had recently almost bought at Jaeger. The red-haired girl stood beside him intimately close, her arm not quite encircling his shoulder. "Hi," Louis greeted him with a bright, ready-for-anything smile.

Bracegirdle's aquiline face looked up, momentarily baffled, then cleared as if reminded of something not very important. "Oh . . . hi," he said distantly.

"Got here a bit early, I'm afraid."

"Sorry?" The soft Durham voice, in which Louis had sensed such instant rapport, was coolly formal.

"This morning . . . 'fraid I was a bit early. Too keen for the off."

"Sorry?" Bracegirdle said.

"Too keen to be off and running."

"Oh."

Louis fought against a feeling that every word he uttered had to be translated from Mandarin Chinese. "Did you get my letter?"

"Letter?"

"I wrote to you from Stockton. With some story ideas."

"When did you send it?"

"About three weeks ago."

"I don't think I saw it . . ."

"It's in your top basket," the red-headed girl told him.

"Oh . . . right." With a grimace of being harassed beyond endurance, Bracegirdle grabbed up the letter and glanced through it, pushing back his boyish quiff of hair with a mitre-shaped shirt-cuff. He grimaced again and drew in air noisily through his teeth.

"Ah doan't think any of these are quite right for us . . . not reelly . . ." His North-eastern accent intensified in softness and mildness. " 'Proa-file of Albert Finney,' we've already done . . . 'lady racing drivers,' noah . . . 'allotment keepers,' noah . . . 'the faces behind *The Archers*,' noah . . . 'Mecca Old Tyme Dancing,' Noah . . . 'John Stephen, King of Car-naby Street,' noah."

He gave Louis a smile of almost brotherly sympathy and handed the letter back.

"Sorry about that. Keep trying, though."

Riven with self-disgust, Louis returned to the concourse. Godwin's bespectacled secretary, Tessa Burland, was there, chatting to Margaret and Mrs. Broadbent. With her hair coiled in a bun and her over-long tweed skirt, she looked more severely efficient than ever. But she, at least, seemed neither surprised nor disconcerted by his presence.

"Ah, Louis . . . I'm afraid God's running a bit late this morning, but he's just rung in with a message for you. He's sorry he wasn't here to welcome you personally when you arrived, but he hopes you've settled in all right, and that you can come to his Ideas Lunch today. It's at one o'clock in his office."

―――――――――

"Ah, come in dear boy! Welcome!" Toby Godwin, in a tent-like beige corduroy suit, was winding the cork from a bottle of red wine pinioned between his knees. The hair that overhung his yellow shirt-collar was still wet from shower or shampoo.

Behind him, the formerly pristine black work-top was covered by an expanse of food difficult to take in at one glance. There was a whole cold salmon, elaborately decorated; a joint of beef, a ham and a tall, sculpted game pie. There were silver platters of salad in variegated colours, avocado halves, chicken mayonnaise and giant prawns, half a Stilton, a whole Brie, celery, French loaves, cheese biscuits, strawberries, raspberries, peaches and bunches of pink grapes. Tessa was taking white-topped wine bottles out of the refrigerator to add to the half-dozen red-topped ones already drawn up.

"Chablis, dear boy? Or Côtes du Rhône?"

"Chablis, please," Louis said.

Godwin handed him a brimming goblet. "There you are. And don't go around saying you were treated shabbily, hooh hooh! Now . . . you know everyone, I think . . . Cedric . . . Jim . . . Terry B. . . . Val Lewis, our resourceful and very charming Picture Editor."

Louis smiled at the crop-haired woman who had been glancing at him with complete indifference out in the concourse for most of the morning. She had a suntanned skin, baggy eyes, a turned-up nose and a turned-up mouth. She was at the same moment quite ugly and quite sexy. "We spoke on the phone, didn't we?" he said.

"Yes. I meant to get back to you," Val Lewis said. "Unfortunately, the Corsican bandit idea didn't pan out."

"And Evelyn! Come in and meet our newest young recruit."

In the doorway stood a man of about forty with a large balding head and the close-set eyes and drooping mouth of some inbred minor prince in a family group around Queen Victoria. But for some traces of beard on cheeks and jaw, his skin had the marbly pallor of unripe Stilton cheese. He wore unfashionable charcoal trousers, pulled high around his bulky waist, and a white short-sleeved shirt of some archaic porous Aertex-like material. His right hand was turned palm downward, holding a lit cigarette. His left rested on his hip.

"Are you . . . Evelyn Strachey?" Louis stammered.

"Yes," the man admitted shyly.

"I've read everything you've ever written . . . Tom Jones . . . Simone de Beauvoir . . . The Jack Spot Gang . . . Danny La Rue. You're the writer who's most inspired and influenced me . . ."

"Thank you," Strachey said with a kind of little bridling curtsey.

"Evelyn, dear boy, come and dig in . . . Tessa has decided we're all in danger of getting constipated, hooh hooh, so we've chucked the spuds and Yorkshire pud from Simpson's and tried out this new Islington place, Nick's Diner. Plenty of roughage, you see, hooh hooh! There's walnut, celery-and-apple salad, three-bean salad, carrot-and-cheese salad, pilau rice salad—and what's this yummy-looking stuff, dear heart?"

"Chicken breasts with mayonnaise, dill and white grapes."

"Oh, what ho, what ho, what ho! Now dig in, everyone!"

Louis held back politely while his new colleagues piled up multi-coloured plates and annexed the ring of low-slung black leather arm-chairs around Godwin's desk. Terry Bracegirdle's was evidently the most favoured place, so close to his chief that he, too, could use the desk as a table. Tessa sat on a high stool beside the work-top, pen and thick shorthand pad at the ready. When all was clear, Louis helped himself to salmon and celery salad and took the hard upright chair behind Jim Deaves.

Conversation was at first desultory, between uninhibited eating and drinking; most of it far above his head. "How was your trip to Milan with Lord M.?" Bracegirdle asked Godwin.

"An absolute breeze."

"Was he a pet as usual?" Jessamyn asked.

"Oh, an undiluted pet. I took the precaution of getting a pile of new thrillers from the Literary Department, and he spent most of the time happily immersed in Len Deighton and Rex Stout. The only catastrophe was when we couldn't get any Daz at the airport."

"Daz?" echoed Jessamyn.

"Eccentricities of the mighty, darling. Our proprietor and Chairman prefers to wash his own smalls by hand, hooh hooh hooh!"

Godwin's spoon and fork propelled a prawn-filled avocado shell around his plate with the zest of a Ben-Hur charioteer. He filled his mouth again, chuckling contentedly.

"Lord M., I'm delighted to say, is as happy as Larry with all of us. Ad bookings for this quarter are up twenty-five percent on the last, and almost thirty percent on the corresponding period for 1965."

Cedric Scurr's fish-eye glasses looked up from a wedge of game pie. "I've had Tim Mandeville on to me again about Tesco," he said. "Now apparently they're offering two and a half times our regular colour-page rate."

"But you told him the answer's still no," Toby Godwin said.

"Yes—and he went pretty spare." Scurr's flat classless voice produced a surprisingly good imitation of hoarsely patrician outrage. " 'Is this the only bloody magazine in the world that turns ads down . . . ?' "

"Does Lord M. really not mind losing all those spondulics?" Bracegirdle asked, leaning to refill Godwin's glass.

"Lord M.—bless you, dear boy—shares our view that we have a product of a certain standard and that cut-price supermarket offers could only dilute it, whatever the short-term gain. You'll remember he supported us in exactly the same way when Woolworth's wanted to do that big ad at Christmas."

"Oh, but I love Woolworth's!" Evelyn Strachey exclaimed, clasping his hands winsomely together. Amid appreciative laughter, he got up, took his plate to the work-top and returned, pale naked arms balanced to the rhythm of a sashaying gait. Louis did his best not to reflect how appropriate had been that long uncertainty over Strachey's gender. This, after all, was London, where incalculably different values applied to everything. Surely someone who presented so overt an appearance of being, in Stockton Evening Telegraph parlance, "as queer as a nine-bob note" could not really be so?

Not until the Brie had disappeared and the Stilton been reduced to a scooped-out brown husk did Tessa unflap her shorthand notebook and Godwin call the meeting to order.

"OK, you young rips." He popped a grape into his mouth, his dump-ling face abruptly serious. "There's something in the nature of a slight emergency. I've been going over our editorial costs with Jim there . . . and I'm afraid to say we show every sign of finishing the year quite a bit under budget. Don't we, Jim?"

Deaves nodded through an exhalation of cigarette-smoke. "Yes, we do. Despite the best endeavours of all of you on your expenses . . ."

"And God's at the Terrazza," put in Bracegirdle.

"—and the Savoy Grill," added Val Lewis.

"—and Carrier's."

"—and the White Elephant."

"—and Chez Victor."

"Hooh hooh hooh!" Godwin bellowed. "Cheeky young devils! Seri-ously, though, kids, we mustn't end up under budget or it'll only make the accountants worry that they're giving us too much."

"What sort of sum do we have in hand?" Bracegirdle asked.

"It looks like about forty thousand," Jim Deaves said.

"So we must try to get in some really big foreign trips before the end of the year," Godwin said. "I've asked Terry here to tell all our big-name writers—Mailer, Capote, Tony Burgess—they can go and do a piece anywhere they like . . . just stick a pin in the map."

"James Cameron's agreed to go back to Vietnam," Bracegirdle said. "He wants to know if he should fly from there to Manila to do corrup-tion under the Marcos regime?"

"Absolutely, dear boy. Once you get that far round the world, it's just as easy to go on as turn round and come back. What else can we think of?"

"I've got my Ungaro shoot in Acapulco," said Jessamyn.

"Well, why don't you travel back from there via L.A. and New York? There's bound to be a good fashion story in one or the other. Who could we get over there to shoot it, Val darling?"

"Carl Fischer was good on the Hell of Harlem. Or Art Kane's very keen to do something for us."

"Fine. Either would be super. Now . . . who'd like a cigar?" Godwin selected a brown musket-barrel and passed the coloured box over to Scurr, who took one and passed it to Jessamyn, who took one also.

The Editor tilted back in his chair and blew a blissful blue smoke-ring. "Oh, by the by, how did it all go down in the East End with Mama Kray?"

"Great!" Bracegirdle exclaimed. He looked across at Evelyn Strachey with bright-eyed adoration. "Evelyn's done a smashing piece. Bailey's going down there to shoot a cover on Friday."

"The twins as well?" Godwin asked.

Strachey nodded. "I've even persuaded Ronnie to bring his boa-constrictor."

"Super. Now, as you all know, our prizewinner, young Louis there, started with us today as a feature writer. He's obviously raring to go and, in fact, with energy that does him credit, has already sent me a profile idea."

Godwin flipped open an orange folder and took out the other letter that had been euphorically typed in the Evening Telegraph's Newsroom, what now seemed a lifetime ago. " 'I'd like to do a piece about Paul McCartney at the crossroads,' " he read in his patrician boom. " 'For months, rumours have been circulating that the Beatles cannot much longer stand the huge pressure of their fame. McCartney, in particular, has huge potential as an individual performer, as his solo recording of "Yesterday" on the *Help!* album showed. He is also hugely intelligent, witty and unpretentious and, I'm sure, would repay an in-depth interview.' "

There was a brief silence. Then Strachey gave a loud, deliberate belch. "Oh! pardon me!" he said unapologetically.

"OK . . . Paul McCartney. What do we all think?"

Bracegirdle grimaced, sucking in air through his teeth. "Ah doan't think it's reelly for us. The Beatles have been done to death since they got their M.B.E.'s. Everybody noahs everything there is to noah. In any case, ah think it's too soon after Evelyn's Tom Jones piece."

"What do you think, Evelyn?" Godwin asked.

Louis looked hopefully at Strachey, remembering his reputation as an encourager of young writers, and because the Paul McCartney piece had been conceived to be written just as Evelyn Strachey would do it.

The encourager's heavy Saxe-Coburg face had wrinkled in distaste. "I think McCartney's pretty boring actually," he said with a petulant twist of his shoulders. "Ringo Starr's much the most interesting one of the four because he's so transcendentally uninteresting. Ringo's sort of

Brechtian in a way, while McCartney's just Mabel Lucie Attwell. It's up to you, of course. But I must say I'm not very keen."

Godwin smiled ruefully down the room at Louis. "Sorry, dear boy. These are my two infallible sounding-boards. If both of them are agin, I fear it's 'no.' "

He picked up another sheet from the folder. "Now—here's an idea from Jack Shildrick, the Steam Section's new northern whizzkid. After the Review, Books and Arts and Close-up, he's now turning his galvanic attention to the sports pages. And he's come across a geezer called . . ." Godwin peered closer in amusement. ". . . called Singapore Charlie Small, hooh hooh, who's about to set out on the first solo circumnavigation of the world."

"First what?" Cedric Scurr asked in disgust.

"First solo circumnavigation of the world. The idea is to follow the routes of the old tea clippers around Cape Horn to Australia. According to Shildrick, this Singapore Charlie client is e'en now preparing his boat, the *Lady Patricia*, for proving trials down on the Solent. The Steam Section has negotiated to pay him a smallish sum to receive reports by wireless from him during the voyage. 'I think it could make a real bang-up piece for you,' Shildrick writes, 'with lots of scrummy colour pictures . . .' "

Deflated as he felt, Louis could not help smiling at the familiar note of Jack Shildrick enthusiasm. The response of his new colleagues, by contrast, was a satirical, Lancashire-accented murmur.

"Eh, by goom!"

"Eh, by the 'eck!"

"Eh, by the drop o' York!" Cedric Scurr said, sounding uncomfortably like Shildrick. "Mash us a pot o' tea and pass t' black pudding."

Godwin drew on his cigar, evidently in deep thought.

"I grant that, as a rule, suggestions from the Steam Section are profoundly unwelcome. But this one conceivably might not be too bad. We haven't done much about boating before. Could you see it, Cedric? A nice double-page spread of pristine bows cleaving the waves . . . fearless figure in oilskins at the helm . . . one man alone against the oceans of the world . . ." Scurr nodded grudgingly. Bracegirdle said nothing; Strachey was picking his teeth with the prongs of a fork. "OK, then, I don't see why we shouldn't give it a run up the mizzen mast, or is it mainmast, hooh hooh!"

With a start, Louis realised that the Editor's eye was fixed squarely on him.

"What do you all think? Might this be something for our young prizewinner to get his teeth into?"

"But . . ." he faltered, "I don't know anything about sailing . . ."

"Didn't you tell me you grew up on the Isle of Wight?"

"Yes, but . . ."

"You must have spent your whole life in boats then, dear boy. And as this Singapore whatsisname is doing his sea-trials in the Solent, you'll be back on home territory." Godwin turned to Tessa and said firmly, "Put it on the list, darling. Louis to profile lone yachtsman. As for you, dear boy, you'd better go straight up to Shildrick now and see what background he can give you. All right, kids, that winds it up, I think. Thank you."

As the executives rose, Tessa murmured something to Godwin, who held up a pudgy hand. "One more thing. Does anyone want to see the World Cup Final at Wembley on Saturday? A pair of tickets have drifted deciduously down to us from Lord M.'s secretariat."

"It's two seats in the V.I.P. Stand," Tessa said, "and an invite to the Prime Minister's after-match reception at the Royal Garden."

"So . . . you can see England doubtless get thrashed by the krauts, and hobnob with H. Wilson afterwards. Any takers?"

Strachey gave a heartfelt groan. "Oh, God! I'm so bored by the World Cup!"

"I'll be in Crete," Bracegirdle said.

"Jim?"

"I'd love to, but we've got Heather's parents coming."

"Cedric? Oh, he's already gone. Jessamyn? No? How about you, Louis, dear boy?"

"Yes . . . please. If you're really sure no one else wants them?"

"You'll need an advance in expenses," Jim Deaves added as they emerged into the concourse together. He beckoned Louis into his office, where he stubbed out his cigarette, lit another, then stooped to a drawer and produced a pink form.

"This," he said, "is probably the most important acquaintanceship you'll make today. It is called, for obvious reasons, a pink slip. You fill in the amount you want here, get God, Terry B. or myself to countersign it, then take it down to Cashiers on the second floor. It's best to avoid the period just before lunch, when there tends to be rather a rush. Now . . . how much do you think you'll need to go and interview this yachting person? Forty? Fifty? Sixty? Oh, to hell with it, let's call it seventy-five." Deaves scribbled in the amount and added a chaotic signature. "We've got to use up the bloody stuff somehow."

---

Shildrick was to be found in a considerably larger office than four weeks earlier, carpeted in nubbly beige and with two square cream-coloured armchairs as well as a much-elongated sofa. The familiar cluttered desk now enjoyed a corner view of Ludgate Circus and the G.P.O. Tower. Standing with him at the proof-covered lectern was a young man in a purple shirt, with the kind of thinly good-looking face Louis had seen many times among the privileged Cambridge crowd.

"Face him down!" Shildrick was saying. "Legal managers are there to be bloody argued with!" He beckoned unceremoniously to Louis. "Come in, Poet . . . OK, I'll run it through the typewriter one last time. You get on to Foxcroft in Bonn and tell him to make sure every one of those names will stand up even if you whack it about on a marble slab."

He punched Louis lightly on the upper arm and drew him closer to the lectern. He was wearing one of the pale grey suits designed for Hepworths by Hardy Amies, his navy blue tie matched by a two-pointed handkerchief in the breast pocket. On the lectern was a layout sheet, empty but for a dramatically large photograph of the West German soccer eleven.

"Poet, this is Nick Fenton, who runs the Close-up team," Shildrick said. "Nick, this is Louis Brennan, who's just joined the Colour Mag and, I'm hoping, is soon going to pitch in with us on the paper, maybe to write Cicero. I'd give him to you, only he's such a bloody stylist. I couldn't bear to see one of his prose poems chopped down to a fat caption."

"Hi," Fenton said curtly. He turned back to Shildrick. "And, if need be, I can shoot Wakefield out to Cape Town tonight, can I?"

"Aye, if you must. Only tell him not to antagonise our regular man there . . . and I'd best have another gander at that stuff from the Securities and Exchange Commission."

"OK. Will do."

As Fenton left the room, Shildrick gripped Louis's arm, glancing round cautiously as if for eavesdroppers. "It's a bloody wonderful yarn, this," he murmured. "We're on the way to proving that a major international investment fund has systematically defrauded millions of small savers and that one of the most pukka names in the City is so twisted that he could hide behind a spiral staircase and never be spotted. If we can just get it past the lawyers, I'll tell you, the financial institutions of this country will never be the same again. So how are you keeping?"

"Fine."

"I'm glad you're doing my lone yachtsman. Can you imagine? The sports people were originally just going to do the plans of his boat, cropped down to about the size of a bloody postage stamp! I told them, you're mad! This is a great story, gift-wrapped in cellophane with a pink ribbon around it! One man in his little cockleshell, circumnavigating the globe. It's Sir Francis Drake and Raleigh all over again . . . a new Elizabethan spirit of adventure. If we handle it right, it could be the biggest thing since Hunt and Tensing conquered Everest!"

Louis grimaced and sucked in his breath, the way he had seen Terry Bracegirdle do. "It's just that . . . I know nothing about boats and sailing."

"You? I thought you grew up by the sea."

"By the sea, yes. Never *on* it."

"I don't see that matters a bit," Shildrick said. "Just write it as you see it, with all your marvellous eye for detail. You've got tremendous material. He's quite a character, is Singapore Charlie . . . a real old sea-dog, you know . . . knocked around the world all his life from 'Frisco to the Barbary Coast. Wife's a bit of a tartar, but I know you'll handle her with your usual consummate tact. I told Toby Godwin when he rang up just now, 'I can't wait to read what our Poet does with this one.' "

For Louis, as ever, the Shildrick magic had worked instantaneously. He felt there was nothing in the world he couldn't do.

"I'm sorry," he said. "I just felt a bit all at sea."

"Aye, that's just the way to feel," Shildrick grinned, nudging him. "Just remember this. Life on a national's really no different. You just write 'in London yesterday' instead of 'in Stockton.' And you work in conditions infinitely more gracious. Just don't get rattled, take everything as it comes, and I know you'll do brilliantly. And remember, if you need me, I'm always here for a chat. We northern lads must stick together, mustn't we?"

# 6

Louis was the only one of his old school gang not to have gone straight from the Isle of Wight to a job, shared flat and life of bliss in London. These past three years, he would willingly have changed places with any of them. Even the one who ran the transport fleet for Bird's-Eye frozen foods. Even the one who travelled for the Initial Towel Supply Company.

That afternoon at his new desk, he picked up the modern grey phone that was for his exclusive use. Dialling 9 brought an instant ultramodern dial-tone. No more clicks and whiny Durham voices saying, "Sorry, there's noah outside lines . . ." No more looking over his shoulder for fear Sizer might suspect it was a non-business call. Praise the Lord, no more Sizer!

"Good afternoon. Debenham, Tewson and Chinnocks."

"Mike Hunt, please."

"Hello?"

"Is that My Cunt?" Louis asked—a joke dating back to the third form, but still as appealing as ever.

"Brennan! You out-of-condition beast! Where are you?"

"Here! In London!"

"What . . . on holiday from the frozen North?"

"No, working. I'm on The Sunday Dispatch." Saying so produced a thrill that was almost sexual. No, totally sexual.

"Poor old Sunday Dispatch!"

"Rude monkey! Look, we must meet and take wassail together—you, me and Paul. You two are still sharing a flat, are you?"

"Yes, horrible experience though it is. Had we moved to Redcliffe Gardens when I last saw you?"

"How are his socks these days?"

"Not too bad. As long as we hang them out of the window in a poly-thene bag overnight."

"So can we get together? What about tonight?"

"OK. Do you know the Feathers off High Street Ken?"

Louis smiled for sheer joy at the words "High Street Ken."

He was almost bursting with triumph that evening as he drove from Clapham down through Battersea and out under the galleon-crested pillars of Chelsea Bridge. On the Mini's back ledge, his Philips "3-Transistor" was playing a brand-new Rolling Stones song called "Under My Thumb" with an eerie offkey descant of single guitar strings and xylophone. He remembered interviewing three of them backstage at the Middlesborough ABC: Mick Jagger in a white fisherman's sweater; Brian Jones, lispingly innocent; Charlie Watts, by far the nicest one, who'd drawn a little decorative scroll around their autographs in his notebook.

Across the river, West London was like an island, ringed by trees, creamily brilliant in the inexhaustible sunshine. "Under ma thumb . . . a gurl . . ." Louis sang along with Jagger's exultant sneer. He felt a sudden pang of anxiety, lest Chelsea, Kensington and Fulham should have been catacombed to capacity by pleasure-seeking youth all this time that he'd been messing around in the provinces. Was there, even at such a late stage, still some room left for him?

"Hello, Lou. You're looking very preposterous this evening."

Mike Hunt was standing with Paul Rich in a corner of the—yes, it actually was!—Dickensian saloon bar. Nearby, a barman in a dark suit was ladling portions of sausages and baked beans onto newfangled oval-shaped plates. It was a part of the wondrous new Britain that pubs now served hot meals instead of (as at Louis's father's former establishment) merely crisps, biscuits and grudging slices of cold veal-and-ham pie. A sign in curly mock-Victorian writing described the sausages as "Prime Hot Porkas."

Mike Hunt was an Isle of Wight farmer's son, burly, straw-haired, and good-humouredly resigned to the long-time homophonous rendering of his name. Paul Rich's depleted eyebrows and scarred lower lip testified to regular rugby-playing and periodic accidents with small boats in the Solent. Louis had nothing in common with either of them except school, that bond equivalent to surviving Colditz together.

"A writers' competition!" My Cunt exclaimed. "Can't have had many other entries, can it, Paul?" He set down his empty pint glass and belched, turning the gaseous sound into "Uxbridge."

"Either that or he slept with one of the judges."

"How could I sleep with one of the judges, you tool? Anyway, they were all men."

"That shouldn't stop you, ducky. Oh . . . Uxbridge!"

"Well, I'm sorry I shan't be able to follow your glories," Paul said. "I never read the Sunday Dispatch."

"No, the News of the World is more your mark, Rich. Or else Razzle."

"Sometimes that supplement's really terrible," My Cunt said. "And sometimes it's brilliant. I liked the thing the other week about erotic Indian statues."

"That was The Observer, dildo!"

"So what's happened to your blond and blue-eyed, long-leggity beastie?" Paul asked.

Louis writhed with embarrassment at this long-redundant description of Portia.

"The last time I saw you, you were almost married. You told me you hadn't any idea how you were going to get out of it . . ."

In the adjacent bar hidden by a carved mahogany partition, an actorish voice became ringingly audible. ". . . I have never seen such a crowd of boorish, ill-bred, misbegotten apologies for . . ."

"Good God!" Louis said. "Is that who I think it is?"

He hopped up on the bar-rail and looked round the partition. At the next counter stood a young man of his age, wearing a wide-brimmed plantation owner's hat with a red-and-green ribbon. The babyish face beneath was suffused with heat and indignation.

"Pushing and shoving in that yahoo manner makes me absolutely . . ."

"Brenda Brown!"

The young man glanced round with an expression of slightly moderated disgust. "Well, tickle my arse with a feather," he said.

"I will if you come round here and have a jar."

"Oh God! What did you want to ask him for?" My Cunt said in a voice calculated to carry.

"He is an old school-mate. And I'm feeling terribly sentimental today."

"But he's such a poncy, prancy, prissy, posy little prat."

The description did not seem ill founded. Brenda Brown was dressed with the fastidious care that had earned him his feminine sobriquet as a ten-year-old: black, high-buttoned suit, embroidered waistcoat with taut gold watch-chain, silk hunting-stock secured by pearl-headed pin. With agility born of riding to hounds, he hoisted himself to sit on the bar counter, and took off his wide-brimmed hat. At twenty-three, he had gone completely bald but for some pale fuzz that gleamed like golden cobwebs between his long, wiry sideburns.

"What do you think, Mike?" Paul Rich said. "Isn't there even less on top than there was before?"

"Yes, I do believe you're right. And get the outfit."

"I know. Looks like a cross between Simon Legree and Sir Kreemy Knut."

"Why don't you go and piss down your own leg and play with the steam?" Brenda said calmly. He lit a gold-tipped black Sobranie cigarette and looked at Louis with prominent, double-lashed eyes.

"As a matter of fact, I was wondering when I was going to see you. Unlike both of these remnants of a diseased afterbirth, I happened to know about your success in competition. My lady mother sent me the cutting about it from the Isle of Wight County Press. It was nothing less than I expected of you."

Louis was staring in fascination at Brenda's black boots. Cuban-heeled and pointed, they had elasticated side-panels not foreshortened below an expanse of sock and white leg, but soaring to infinity inside his knife-creased trousers.

"God, those bloodyfucking boots! I've got to have some. Where did you buy them?"

"These? A place called A Load of Cobblers in Carnaby Street."

"Anyway, how are you, Brenda? Still pretending to be in the antiques business?" Brenda Brown worked for Crichton's, a Knightsbridge auction house, not as grand as Sotheby's or Bonhams but sufficient to maintain his pose of existing in the first rather than this second half of the twentieth century.

"Didn't you know I'd been in hospital?" he asked, offering Louis a black leather cheroot-case.

"No. What was up?"

"Complete nervous exhaustion."

"Don't believe him, Louis," Paul Rich said. "He went into hospital to be circumcised."

"If you are going to be disgustingly and intrusively personal, Rich . . ."

"Personal! Look who's talking! Who told that nice, inoffensive little Penny Twelftree that the scarf she was wearing made her look like she'd been sick over her dress?"

"Yes, and the best half of you ran down your mother's leg as well."

As always, the moment had come when Brenda's invective transcended the harmless abusiveness of old school-friends. Paul Rich put down his pint of draught Guinness and grasped one lapel of the high-buttoning suit. "One more crack like that, Brown, and I'll take you outside," he said almost pensively.

"Absolutely whenever you're ready . . ."

"Hey, hey, come on, lads," Louis broke in. "Peace treaty. Treace peaty. Remember it's my first day in the wicked Smoke." As he uttered the phrase he remembered Jack Shildrick using it three months ago.

"Let's have another round, one of those nice black gaspers of Brenda's, and maybe a prime hot porka. Then I'm relying on you to take me into the proximity of women."

———————

Half an hour later he was in the front of Brenda's open-topped M.G.B., racing up the steep hill off High Street Ken, past a garish red-and-gold boutique called Bus Stop and Biba's garish black-and-gold one. On the opposite pavement, a barefoot girl in a skimpy wasp-striped dress and a floppy-brimmed hat spread her arms rhetorically before the window of Irvine Sellars Modern Menswear. "What a lot of boring shirts!" Louis heard her say in a ringing patrician voice.

"Have you seriously got tickets for the World Cup?" Brenda shouted against the headwind.

"Yes. Feel like coming?"

"I always feel like coming."

"All right, I'll make a deal with you. Take me to where you got those boots and I'll take you to see our brave boys go down fighting against the Wehrmacht."

Approaching a zebra crossing, Brenda double-declutched ruthlessly hard. Two foreign-looking nuns with their forefingers stuck in guide-books leapt for their lives.

"What's the name of this street, Brenda?"

"Kensington Church Street."

"And this one at the top?"

"Christ's thorns, what ignorance! Bayswater Road. On your right is the Russian Consulate, on your left coming up is Orme Court, home of Spike Milligan. Whom you can see in the park most days, restoring the figures on the Pixie Oak."

To allow Brenda to change from his working clothes, they stopped off in a street somewhere just off Hyde Park. Getting out of the M.G.B., Louis felt a sensation of being sheltered and comforted, as if the double terrace of pilastered early Victorian houses were leaning out to form a protective arch over his head.

They entered the grey-carpeted hallway of a first-floor flat. Through a half-open door on the right, Louis glimpsed drawn-curtain twilight and a quick, alarmed movement under crumpled bedsheets. "Oh," Brenda remarked nonchalantly. "Peter and Melanie must be fucking."

Brenda's room was a cramped, narrow cubbyhole determinedly got up to resemble a country squire's den from Surtees' Jorrocks. On the wall hung a series of foxhunting prints with titles like "View Halloo" and "Gone Home." A meagre bookcase, lined with leather-bound ad-

ventures of the equestrian grocer and his dog Mr. Sponge, also displayed a brass horn and an ivory-handled riding crop. Next to the
lumpy single bed stood a pair of tall boots in brass-ringed wooden trees.

While Brenda substituted a clerical grey pinstripe suit for his black
one, Louis lounged on the bed, leafing through the stack of Playboy
magazines that stood behind a more ostentatious one of Horse and
Hound.

"I like her," he said, letting a centrefold drop to its full length. "Why
can't I write things like this? 'June's Playmate appealingly combines little-girl charm with big-girl proportions.' "

Brenda turned from the full-length mirror, his hunting-stock half
tied. "You know, don't you, that I've always regarded you as one of
those people who make the wheels of life turn a little easier? What
would you say to our taking chambers together? We're obviously
highly compatible. Both of us should have been born fifty years earlier."

"What's the matter with here? Looks perfectly all right."

Brenda wrinkled his retroussé nose. "Too many pockets of filth. And
not very nice goings-on sometimes, as you might expect from people
brought up in Shanklin. They did an abortion with a knitting-needle in
the bathroom last month. Hardly the most cheerful thing to think on of
a morning while you're standing there, slapping on the Max Factor
Lazy Shave."

"Well, I've got to find somewhere," Louis said. "I can't impose on my
poor little Gran indefinitely. And Clapham's not really an address to
mention in smart society, is it?"

"Precisely so. So why don't I keep an eye out in the Evening News
and the Standard for a nice little bijou somewhere central?"

At 10 o'clock the sky was still light, with an aureole of deep pink
framing the attics, chimneypots and twisted TV aerials of the bedsitter
subcontinent. In the South Ken street where Brenda parked, every
house seemed to have its big first-floor windows thrown open on music,
clinking and hubbub, and at the top of balustraded steps every front
door seemed to stand invitingly open.

"This is us—number seventy-two, flat six."

"Who's giving it?" Louis asked.

"Good God, man, I don't know. If we don't like this one, there's another in Pelham Crescent, which I seem to recollect is not many leagues
distant. And there are further possibilities in Campden Hill and just off
the Goldhawk Road."

"But shouldn't we at least be bringing a bottle?"

"I never bring a bottle. I prefer, if possible, to take one away."

Going up the narrow stairs, they passed a room where girls' floppy

hats and shoulder-bags and boys' Lenin caps and striped Mod jackets
had been heaped on a bed. "I'm boiling," Louis said. "I think I'll stick
my jacket in here."

"That would be extremely ill-advised," Brenda told him.

"Why?"

"There are disagreeable people who make a career of thieving from
coats and handbags left on beds at parties. Whole teams of them do it
scientifically, street by street."

In a second-floor room lacking any feature but an iron grate and
lights swathed in red crêpe paper, a sweating crowd danced the Shake
and Hully-gully to The Kinks' "You Really Got Me." Among them was
My Cunt performing an old-fashioned foxtrot with a tiny, black-haired
girl who, even in the olfactory confusion, emitted body odour like a
smell of cottage pie wafted from school kitchens.

"This is Poupette," he screamed above the searing mayhem of Dave
Davis's guitar break.

"She's hideous," Brenda shrieked back.

"Who cares? As long as she's on the Pill . . ."

In the adjacent strip-lit kitchen, a Formica-topped table was covered
with pints of bitter, bottles of red wine whose labels vouchsafed little
more than the words "red wine" and a glass bowl of scarlet liquid
thickly sedimented with sliced apple and orange. Louis spooned some
into a paper cup and followed Brenda back out into the front hall. Seeing two girls approaching, he politely stood aside for them. One was tall
and dark, the other small and curly-haired. Both were wearing skinny
knitted tops and pale corduroy miniskirts with low-slung hipster belts.
"Are you and Jason coming on to Guys and Dolls?" the dark girl was
asking as they passed.

"No," her friend replied. "We're going to bed." She smoothed down
her hipstered hips in a purposeful way. "Honestly, I'm feeling so randy
tonight . . ."

He felt a cold twitch deep in the Y-fronts, astonished even more than
excited to think a girl could be capable of saying something like that.

---

The Sunday Dispatch's reference library was a vaulted, wood-panelled
room, more luxurious in its appointments than the office of the Stockton Evening Telegraph company's managing director. Together with
the cuttings envelope marked "SMALL—Singapore Charlie, single-
handed yachtsman," Louis was surprised to be handed another marked
"SMALL—Charles E. W., aviator." This second, much older brown
packet bore the rubber-stamped word "DEAD," crossed through repeat-

edly with the ballpoint frenzy of a librarian compelled to acknowledge error. Idly Louis wondered in what previous incarnation the putative circumnavigator of the world had been connected with aeroplanes and managed both to die and to be resurrected.

As he tipped the file envelopes onto his new desk, Margaret Cole smiled up at him from the copy she was subbing and hooked one curtain of brown hair behind her ear. At the third desk in the block, Mrs. Broadbent was speaking on her telephone in a voice like a series of short, sharp hammer blows.

"... You did not, Tarquin! No, you did not, Tarquin! In any case, you know you're strictly forbidden ever to touch my private things ..."

"There was a call for you," Margaret said. "Someone called Portia. I've written her number down."

"... Tarquin, you did not! No, you did not, Tarquin! The bottle was not two-thirds empty! That is a complete and utter falsehood ...!"

The Magazine concourse, although today full of people, still had the profoundly calm and safe air of a monastery cloister. Across the aisle from Louis, Val Lewis, the Picture Editor, was poring over cardboard-mounted colour transparencies—or, as he now knew they were called, "trannies"—spread on the garish white neon surface he now knew was called a light-box. Behind the adjacent glass office wall, Terry Bracegirdle could be seen talking in urgent dumb show into his telephone, shielding his other ear the better to hear the connection with distant and exotic foreign parts. The Deputy Editor wore yet another Jaeger shirt that Louis himself had almost chosen, tab-collared and dull sherbet pink, perfectly blending with his pink-and-purple floral tie and plum-dark hipsters. As he talked, a quiff of newly shampooed hair flopped over his brow. He pushed it back with a gesture of boyish enthusiasm.

Behind Mrs. Broadbent, through the Art Department's partition, Cedric Scurr stood at his long bench, smouldering cheroot in mouth, cropping photographs with a paper guillotine and switching them around on layout sheets with contemptuous sleight of hand, like someone demonstrating "Find the Lady." After each two-page sheet had received its glued-down images and galley-type, it was brought out to Margaret for final checking by Scurr's assistant Gilda, a dark-haired girl in her mid-twenties, wearing a white-collared navy minidress and thick-heeled, gilt-buckled shoes. The Magazine's colour printers were at Welwyn Garden City, sixty miles away; copy and layouts were sent and glossy page roughs returned by couriers in an atmosphere of diplomatic top secrecy reflecting what treasure they contained and what fortunes any other Sunday magazine would give for the briefest glimpse of them.

Otherwise you could look at almost any part of the concourse and have
no idea that anything journalistic was going forward.

After years under the slave-whip of news editors and chief subs,
Louis found this tranquillity deeply strange. No one made any attempt
to monitor his comings and goings, give him any more work or even
enquire how the work he already had was progressing. Terry Bracegirdle, his supposed immediate superior, had again made only the most
cursory and reluctant acknowledgement of his existence. Having given
him the lone yachtsman story, Toby Godwin seemed quite uncon-
cerned about his progress on it—and, indeed, with everything else that
was or wasn't going on. Beyond his distant partition-glass, the Editor's
noble head could be seen above an unencumbered desk, smoking a
cigar and contentedly scanning the day's newspapers. From time to
time, when Scurr or Bracegirdle went in to see him, an uproarious
"Hooh hooh hooh!" would echo down the concourse.

Louis sifted through the Library cuttings on Singapore Charlie Small,
making notes in one of the magnificent spiral-bound stenographer's
pads freely available from the stationery cupboard. The cuttings under
this name were few, describing the participation in various solo long-
distance yacht races of a mariner whose age in so testing a milieu became progressively more remarkable—fifty-eight, fifty-nine, sixty,
sixty-one. The longest piece, from the Dispatch's own sports pages, outlined Singapore Charlie's heroic and romantic, not to say suicidal, plan
now, at the age of sixty-four, to girdle the earth's oceans in the wake of
the nineteenth-century tea and grain clippers like the *Cutty Sark* and
*Thermopylae.* The piece described his long struggle to raise the money
for a boat capable of making so incredible a voyage, and his search for
backers to equip and provision it for its almost nine months afloat. As
well as the Dispatch, three other commercial sponsors were involved:
Kilcrankie Scottish knitwear, Meux beer and a maritime processing
company named Ocean-Dredged Aggregates.

The packet for Charles E. W. Small, aviator, was considerably bulk-
ier. It revealed that in the late twenties and early thirties, before taking
to the ocean, Singapore Charlie had been a solo pilot, attempting pio-
neer flights in competition with Lindbergh and Amy Johnson, but with
little of the same success. A crumbling yellow half-page from the Daily
Herald for 21 March 1929 described how he had narrowly escaped
death after crashing his Avro biplane at Croydon aerodrome when taking off for a projected non-stop solo flight over the North Pole. His nick-
name, suggesting a career of piratical forays up and down the Malay
coast, actually derived from an ill-judged landing at Singapore in 1931
when he had almost incinerated himself by colliding with oil flares on

the runway. The most spectacular mishap had occurred in 1933 when, looking down to wave at people seeing him off from Osaka, Japan, he'd flown his Tiger Moth straight into some telegraph wires and been hurled back onto the ground like a stone from a catapult.

"Are you Louis Brennan?"

At his elbow stood a man of about forty in a three-piece pinstripe suit, a pink shirt with a white stiff collar and a dark blue tie zigzagged with scarlet. In defiance of all modernity, his hair was combed straight back from a sloping forehead and shiny with archaic oils. His long nose quivered as if at a faint scent of ordure. He held up the buff-coloured galley-proof where Louis's prizewinning words had at last, really and truly, been rendered in the Magazine's chastely beautiful typeface.

"McRory—Legal Department," he said in a voice of almost levitating hauteur. "I've been looking through this piece of yours on Grandad for possible libel-risk."

The stress put on the word "Grandad" had already raised Louis's hackles like a dog with an invisible ghost in the room. "Yes?" he said coldly.

The lawyer glanced down the proof, which was heavily annotated in red ink. "Is this really all true?"

"Yes, it is."

"There really was a newsreel cameraman named Terry Cotter?"

"Yes."

"And what is your source for so alleging?"

"I've met him," Louis replied.

"And this . . . Castleton Knight . . . was that really his name?"

Louis reddened. "Yes."

". . . really procured the deliberate disruption of a Test Match?"

"Yes."

". . . hired racecourse touts to throw potatoes studded with razor-blades at his business rivals?"

"Absolutely."

". . . exploited children for commercial gain?"

Louis nodded.

". . . was responsible for covering a member of the Royal Family in whitewash?"

"Right."

"Isn't he going to object to our saying all this?"

"I don't think so," Louis said. "He's been dead for twenty years."

"Don't worry about Angus," Margaret said sympathetically as the pinstriped figure resumed its place at a spare desk across the way. "Our lawyers have to be obstreperous. It's their only consolation for having almost everything they say totally disregarded."

"I think he's a bit of a pervert actually," Mrs. Broadbent said. "The only query marks he ever makes on my proofs are beside references to knickers or bras. And he once offered, in an extremely odd fashion, to take me to dinner at the Cavalry Club."

"His father's a judge who happens to be a friend of Lord M.'s. Otherwise he'd probably be starving in some seedy little chambers in Lincoln's Inn."

This reminded Louis of the most glaring omission in his Sunday Dispatch career so far. "I still haven't met Lord McIntyre. Does he come round the Magazine very much?"

Margaret smiled as Scurr's assistant, Gilda, brought another completed layout over to her desk. "When was the last time we saw Lord M. around here, Gil?"

"I know . . . it was last Christmas," Mrs. Broadbent said, "when he came to congratulate us on our first hundred-and-seventy-page issue. I remember thinking how strange it was that so rich and influential a man could smell so strongly of pepper."

"It's those awful suits he wears," Margaret said. "I don't think he's bought any clothes since his demob from the Canadian Mounties."

"I thought he took a direct personal interest in the Magazine," said Louis.

"He does. The advertising flat-plan is couriered to him religiously every week."

"Wherever in the world he happens to be," Mrs. Broadbent added.

"Sometimes he'll even send a note to Tim Mandeville, the Advertising Director, saying something like 'the half-page colour for White Horse whisky is an excellent read.' "

"Actually, I don't believe all that stuff about Lord M. only reading the ads," Mrs. Broadbent said. "God always says he's as editorially astute as Beaverbrook or Rothermere."

"He and God have a good relationship, do they?" Louis asked. As if in reply, another happy bellow came from the direction of Godwin's office.

"Like Sonny and Cher," Margaret nodded. "God used to be McIntyre's personal assistant, before they dreamed up the Magazine. He was thin in those days—comparatively so, anyway. They say there's only one chair in London more secure, and that's in the Throne Room at Buckingham Palace."

---

"You didn't tell me it was going to be the Royal Box," Brenda said.

Louis shifted luxuriantly—though, alas, not comfortably—in his red velour seat. Far below on the striped greensward, a Royal Marine band spread out like a game of toy soldiers was playing barely audible selections from Gilbert and Sullivan. The huge, clamorous oval with its segmented Union Jacks and red, black and yellow West German tricolours was strangely devoid of perspective, as if one could reach and touch the two marzipan-green Moorish towers at its furthermost end. The noise of 88,000 voices at fever pitch seemed to come from far off, like sea-sucked shingle.

Their tickets had brought them, unbelievably, to Wembley Stadium's V.I.P. Stand, commanding a view bettered only by the television cameras that were to broadcast England's inevitable defeat in her first-ever World Cup Final to every other technological nation. Barely half a dozen rows below them were the seats where the Queen and the Duke of Edinburgh would presently join other distinguished spectators on this day of inevitable disappointment. Louis could clearly see the grey head of Harold Wilson, and the greying one of Edward Heath resolutely turned in the opposite direction. He could even see Heath's plump thumbs, twiddling round each other like irritable little pink diplodoci.

Already this Saturday had been a heady one. From the morning session at the Feathers, Brenda had driven him to Carnaby Street, that mythic place about which he had written so many articles for the Stockton Evening Telegraph without once so much as setting eyes on it. Now at last he had breathed the air of the surprisingly short and narrow thoroughfare, behind Liberty's department store, where every shop sold clothes or shoes under sleek male Christian names—John Stephen, John Michael, Lord John, Just Paul—and almost everything on display was a Stockton Magistrates Court daydream come true. He had bought a wide-lapelled jacket in grey herringbone, two Ben Sherman button-down shirts, one cream, one daringly pink, and—at last, at last!—the black, square-toed Chelsea, or Beatle, boots with elasticated side-panels reaching half-way to his knees.

He looked fondly down at them yet again, trying to ignore their crushing constriction of his toes and the band of fiery agony across each instep. His shoe size was 8 and the shop had only a pair in size 7. After a prolonged struggle to get them on, involving Brenda and two assistants—and breaking an ivory shoehorn which the elder assistant had owned for twenty-five years—he'd taken them anyway. The shop's hand-on-heart assurance was that they would "stretch with wearing."

Wembley Stadium's shingle noise suddenly increased, as if an extra-large wave were breaking all round it. Barely twenty feet away, Louis saw the Queen climbing the grandstand stairs, accompanied by Prince Philip and a bevy of tail-coated officials. He had never beheld his sovereign in the flesh before, and was struck equally by her tiny stature and the almost fluorescent pinkness of her coat and petal hat. The wavery little wrist seemed too fragile to support its large white patent handbag. The wanly pretty face, as familiar to Louis as the coins in his pocket, seemed to nod and smile directly at him.

Between the aisle and him was a single empty seat which, in these final moments before kick-off, suddenly became occupied. A tall, white-haired man in an old-fashioned black suit sat down with a thankful grunt and laid a shooting-stick on the red carpet beside him.

"Let me see if I've got this quite straight," Brenda said, lighting a Balkan Sobranie. "The Sunday Dispatch have put you in the Royal enclosure at the World Cup Final . . . but they don't expect you to write anything."

"We're a colour magazine, you see. The earliest we could publish anything would be in five weeks."

"I see, so you just enjoy yourself with all the nobs, and then go on and guzzle champagne with Wilson and our brave, unlucky boys. God, you couldn't have a much nicer job, could you?"

"Did I understand your friend to say that you work for The Sunday Dispatch?" the white-haired man asked. Louis found himself looking into a ruddy-cheeked face whose eyes were the blue of washed-out denim. The faint intonation could have been either American or Scots.

"Yes," he replied. "The Magazine."

"Ah. Very good."

"You enjoy it, do you?" Louis asked grandly.

"A great deal, yes. And do you?"

"Oh, it's wonderful," Louis said devoutly.

"I think something's happening," Brenda interrupted. Down on the pitch, the Royal Marine band were marching from their original configuration to form a hollow square facing the Royal Box. Bubbling with euphoria, Louis turned back to his new acquaintance.

"It's an absolutely lovely life. You see, we've got this marvellous proprietor who never interferes . . . and doesn't care how much money we spend."

The white-haired man inclined his head attentively. "You don't say so. That must be exceedingly agreeable."

"Yes, it's amazing. I mean . . . there's more money around than people know what to do with. All you have to do is push a bit of pink paper through a window, and someone hands you out a great wad of five-pound notes . . ."

"England!" Brenda cried as a file of white-clad figures came capering out of the players' tunnel, amid roars that already seemed tinged with commiseration.

They drove back into Central London in a jubilantly horn-honking cavalcade of cars and charabancs. On the pavements of Willesden and Kilburn, people were dancing and hugging one another. It was like the stories Louis had heard from his father of V.E. Night in 1945.

At traffic lights on Edgware Road, a taxi-driver pushed down his offside window, leaned over and shouted, "Is it true? We beat 'em?"

"Four–two," Brenda shouted back.

"I thought it was supposed to have been two–all at full time."

"We scored twice in extra time."

"Cor! Bloody marvellous!"

A cheering crowd had already assembled in Kensington High Street below the sidelong wedge of the Royal Garden Hotel. West German supporters were there in equal number, accepting defeat as stoically as their team had on the field, despite the questionable nature of the first goal in extra time. Groups of rival fans could be seen earnestly discussing it, as a rule ending up by exchanging scarves and shaking hands.

Louis's gold-embossed invitation spirited him and Brenda through well-defended glass doors and up to a second-floor reception room with panoramic views over Kensington Gardens and Knightsbridge. The stars of the conquering team were already there, close-barbered and college-blazered: Bobby Moore, Bobby Charlton, Geoff Hurst, still glowing from the miracle of his hat-trick. With them stood the Prime Minister, his snub face as complacent as if the victory had originated in a Cabinet memorandum. Surprisingly, he was not smoking his usual honest burgher's pipe, but a cigar of a size and richness that Toby Godwin might have envied.

As Louis took a glass of champagne from a waitress's silver tray, he caught the eye of a small man with Brylcreemed hair who was nibbling a sausage on a stick. The brotherhood of print is always unmistakable.

"Ramsden Greig—Evening Standard," the man said. "You are a scribe, too, aren't you?"

"Yes. Louis Brennan . . . Sunday Dispatch Magazine." Would he ever get over the indescribable bliss of saying that?

Greig pulled an impressed face, then nodded at the elaborate buffet. "To think two years ago our paper ran a leader warning that Socialist government would bring back the age of meat-rationing. It's more like the last days of bloody Nero."

Across the room, Harold Wilson was being cajoled to join the England team acknowledging cheers out on the balcony. He drew deeply on his cigar, laid it in an ash-tray, then stepped through the French windows, taking his briar pipe from an inside pocket and putting it into his mouth in that familiar solid, unpretentious and trustworthy way.

"Good old Harold," Ramsden Greig chuckled. "Would you think he's got Rhodesia, a dock strike and a sterling crisis on his hands? He's like Alfred E. Neuman on the cover of Mad magazine. 'What, me worry?' "

Brenda suddenly nudged Louis. "Look! Isn't that your boy-friend from the match?"

"Where?"

"Over by the door. Talking to Alf Ramsey."

It was, indeed, the big white-haired man who'd spoken to Louis at Wembley. Their acquaintanceship had ripened no further: at half-time the white-haired man had left his seat, never to return. Under the hotel chandeliers, his black suit looked even more dusty and archaic. Still holding his shooting-stick, he sipped orange juice and nodded gravely at what the England team manager was telling him.

"Who do you suppose he is?" Louis said.

"Search me. Some lonely old plutocrat. You should have kept in with him. He might have set you up in a nice little hat shop."

A few minutes later, they found themselves near the panoramic window overlooking Kensington Gardens. A deep pink sky drenched the spike of the Albert Memorial, guaranteeing yet another wonderful day tomorrow. A few feet away stood a group consisting of Bobby Moore, Lord Robens, Wynford Vaughan Thomas and the Prime Minister, reunited with his cigar and holding forth in his familiar nose-pinched accent, though not, as customarily, about the need to tighten belts, pull together and forge a new Britain in the white heat of the technological revolution.

"You should come to one of our get-togethers at Number Ten," he was saying. "They're done very much like the ones Jack Kennedy used to give in Washington. All sorts and conditions of men are there . . . Archbishop Makarios of Cyprus . . . John Kenneth Galbraith . . . Morecambe and Wise . . ."

He paused as the white-haired man appeared at his elbow. "Good night, P.M.," Louis heard the faint Scottish—or was it Canadian?— voice say. "I'm afraid it's already past my bedtime."

A photographer bobbed forward to catch them shaking hands. It seemed to Louis that Mr. Wilson's smile had an almost audible whirr of machinery behind it.

The picture taken, the Prime Ministerial smile abruptly vanished. "That was an uncalled-for editorial about me in your paper last Sunday," he said. "Admit it, now. It was quite uncalled-for."

The white-haired man continued smiling blandly. "You know I have nothing to do with editorials, P.M. My Editor, Mr. Mowforth, pursues his own line."

"But with your backing."

"With my backing to think and write as he sees fit."

"So, tell me, or I'll have to go and ask the Oracle at Delphi. What do I have to do to win the approval of the mighty Sunday Dispatch?"

"Thank you for my invite, P.M. It's been a wonderful day . . . and a wonderful victory."

Turning away, the white-haired man met Louis's mesmerised gaze. Into the washed-out blue eyes came something like a twinkle. "Good night, young man," he murmured as he went by. "Keep on spending those fivers."

Only now, in the little breeze caused by his passing, did Louis catch a faint but unmistakable smell of pepper.

# 7

Starting the day at Grandma Bassill's was a complicated procedure. The ground floor was out of bounds until she had got Grandad out of bed and into his wheelchair, put his legs on and installed him at the kitchen table to wash and shave. The bathroom and lavatory were both in the first-floor domain of their lodgers, Nancy and Dermot, and a Catholic abundance of noisy small children. Before about 9 o'clock the lavatory was almost continually occupied, its ground-glass panes silhouetting the occupant in disconcerting detail.

Louis was awoken by childish cries and unintelligible parental imprecations, combined this morning with fiery streaks of pain from both insteps. To accelerate the promised "stretching" of his new Chelsea boots, he had slept in them. He was beginning to understand what broken-footed maidens in Imperial China used to endure for fashion's sake.

He was hobbling back from the bathroom in boots and pyjamas when a loud "brring!" came from the front door. Grandma trotted to answer it in the blue dressing-gown and hairnet she did not discard until Grandad's ablutions were complete. "Lou!" she called warblingly up the stairs. "There's somebody 'ere for you."

On the doorstep stood a man of about twenty-eight whose sunburned, beaky face and fringed hair gave him a marked resemblance to Ray Ennis from the Swinging Blue Jeans. He wore white hipster trousers, a grey satin puff-sleeved shirt split open on a hairy chest, and high-heeled cowboy boots. Round his neck hung two Nikon cameras, their hooded lenses of almost phallic length. He smiled, showing very white teeth. "Hey," he said. "Louis? I'm Patrick Prince."

"I'll be right with you," Louis said.

"Okay. Groovy."

Grandad was in his wheelchair in pyjama jacket and braces, with shaving-brush, mug of hot water, mirror and old-fashioned cut-throat razor neatly set out for him on the kitchen table. "Well, I'm off," Louis said. "Wish me well on my first assignment."

Grandad held up a slender hand over his shoulder. "Good luck, boy. Last job I did in the Solent was the Coronation Fleet Review, 1937. Nice expenses on that one, you know. 'Hire of high-speed launch' . . . 'Laundering clothes damaged by sea water' . . . 'Gratuity to Admiral of Fleet for bringing battleships closer into shot.' "

Louis had never been in a Lotus Elan before. He lay back almost horizontally as South London flicked by in dumb show, powered by a metallic roar somewhere behind his head. The built-in radio blasted out Wilson Pickett's "Land of 1,000 Dances": "Na nana na na nana na na na na na na na na. Nana na na . . ."

"Na . . . nice car!" he screamed above the chicken-sax solo.

"Huh?"

"Very nice car."

"Oh . . . yeah. Not much room, that's the only drag." His new colleague turned and grinned with a pearly gleam. "I'm seeing this great chick at the moment . . . dancer at the Talk of the Town, who gives the most fantastic blowjobs. But the car's nowheresville for that scene, man. Only way we can manage it is if I bring along a special spanner to take off the steering-wheel."

The Elan hurtled up a long hill, past a signboard reading "ROEHAMPTON HOSPITAL." Louis felt both his legs tingle in sympathy with the ones removed from Grandad there. "So what are we doing today?" Patrick shouted above Lee Dorsey's "Workin' in a Coalmine."

"Didn't Val Lewis tell you?"

"She just said it was some guy going to sail round the world, and shoot Kodachrome, maybe for a cover."

"His name's Singapore Charlie Small."

"Singapore how much?"

". . . Charlie Small. He's planning to follow the routes of the old tea clippers—you know, round Cape Horn and everything. The paper's financing him in return for exclusive radio reports while he's at sea."

"So it's all just one big plug, is it?" Patrick said.

The thought hadn't even occurred to Louis. "Have you done many yachting stories before?" he asked.

Patrick flashed him a disbelieving look. "You're joking."

As the Elan roared past Woking, then Guildford, Louis feverishly reread the Library cuttings on Singapore Charlie and a manual of basic seamanship borrowed from Paul Rich. But it was hard to feel too anxious on such a day, hurtling to an assignment for The Sunday Dispatch like a scene from TV's *Route 66*, his ankles elastic-sided—albeit throttlingly—and his wallet stuffed with five-pound notes. To add further piquancy, this was the same road he used to take a couple of years earlier, from Isle of Wight weekends back to the dreary solitude of Whittlesey. Who would ever dream that life could get so much better?

From time to time he glanced curiously at Patrick Prince, in whom the Elan's phenomenal powers of acceleration seemed to introduce an excitement bordering on the erotic. Plunging in and out between heavy lorries on the hairpin bends around Haslemere, Patrick's eyes grew strangely bright, his cheeks flushed, his breath audibly stertorous. On the twisting hill down from the Hog's Back, they came up behind a dilapidated green van toiling along with smoke belching from a chimney on its roof. With a couple of hundred yards before a totally blind curve, Patrick slammed one pointed toe to the floor. The Elan took the wagon, dodging back into lane just as a vast, flat-nosed motor-coach lunged round the bend ahead. Slowing to 70 again, Patrick let out a long, satiated sigh. On the tight frontal bulge of his white hipsters there appeared a little spreading path of damp.

In less than forty minutes, they spotted the first A.A. sign to "Newman's Hard Marina," crested by the silhouette of a yacht. "I'd love to stop and have a joint before we get there," Patrick said. Louis made no reply, puzzled that on such a hot morning anyone could possibly be thinking about a roast lunch.

---

Newman's Hard Marina was a perfect composition of expensive new boats and expensive old thatched cottages, restaurants, chandlers' shops and pubs. A stone's throw from the forest of masts, the New Forest stretched to right and left along the tranquil Hamble River. Shaggy wild ponies wandered unconcernedly among the Land Rovers and dinghy-trailers or reclined with their spindle-legged colts on the waterside outcrops of bright yellow furze.

"There you go," Patrick Prince said. "The *Lady Patricia*."

The name was lettered on a sleek silver hull berthed broadside to the quay. Down on its cluttered deck, a man in a dark blue baseball cap was stooping and rummaging in an open cardboard box. "Mr. Small?" Louis shouted.

The man glanced up. "Speaking."

"We're from the Sunday Dispatch."

"Oh, lumme . . . I wasn't expecting you till next week."

"I'm sorry. We were definitely told today."

"Oh, well, not to worry. Come you aboard."

Louis descended the rope-railed companionway on sweating and fiery feet. Even to his untutored eye, the *Lady Patricia* was evidently brand spanking new, her deckboards pristine, her brasswork brilliant, her furled sails flawless, her coiled ropes pure white. All around the narrow foredeck stood piles of cardboard cartons, some prised open to reveal bottles of wine, jars of salad cream, tins of soup, tomatoes, baked beans and condensed milk, canisters of olive oil and pots of honey.

Singapore Charlie Small was a wirily built pensioner with an innocent-looking face clasped between bushy white side-whiskers. Beside him—towering over him—was a curly-haired woman wearing a yellow oilskin and the navy blue rope-soled shoes of the yachting aristocracy. "My wife, Bunty," Singapore Charlie said.

Louis stretched out his hand and Mrs. Small put a printed sheet of paper into it. "Can I give you that to be going on with?" she said in a clipped lady-of-the-manor voice. "I always think it saves an awful lot of time and unnecessary questions to have the facts set out in black and white."

Louis glanced at the sheet. "Angela 'Bunty' Small was born in Karachi in 1912 . . ." he read. "Educated at Benenden and the King Edward High School for Girls, Islamabad, she always maintains she did not really get going in the Great University of Life until 1939, when chance and fortunes of war brought about her enlistment in the celebrated ANYS (Auxiliary Nursing Yeomanry) . . ."

Behind the flush-built cabin, three men were reclining around the creamy padded cockpit bench. All were in their late thirties, wore immaculate yachting apparel and regarded each other with the inscrutable hostility of patients in a doctor's waiting-room.

"Can I introduce Mr. Leslie Brendan of the Dispatch supplement, who's doing the write-up on me," Singapore Charlie said. "This is Michael Truswell, Publicity Director for Meux beer, Peter Hackforth, Press Officer for Kilcrankie knitwear, and Simon Gilkes from the P.R. department at Ocean-Dredged Aggregates. Meux have given me a wonderful supply of pressurised bitter for the voyage. And I'm wearing the cap, you see, Peter," he added, smiling at the second man and tilting his head for Louis to see. Above the peak were the words "Pure new wool by Kilcrankie."

As Louis climbed painfully down into the cockpit, the third P.R. man plucked at his sleeve with an ingratiating smile. "You will emphasise, won't you, that Ocean-Dredged Aggregates are also important sponsors of Mr. Small, even though we may not have an instantly identifiable

product to display. We're the world's biggest dredgers of marine aggregates, processing an average of five billion tons per annum. Give me a
ring back in London and I'll let you have all the figures."

"You must be sure and mention the automatic steering gear," Mrs.
Small said. She pinched Louis's elbow and pointed to the stern, where
an airborne blade swung gently to and fro like a windsock. "Write
down, please, that it was specially designed for us by the famous Atlantic yachtsman Pixie Thelwall. That's 'Pixie,' as in Arthur Rackham,
then T.H.E.L.W.A.L.L."

They crowded into the Perspex-roofed, green-carpeted cabin: Singapore Charlie, Louis, Mrs. Small, Patrick Prince with his Nikons, flash-
gun and camera-bag, and the three edgy-looking public relations men.
Mrs. Small provided the commentary in the tones of a duchess reluctantly showing day-trippers round her stately home.

"On your left, sleeping area . . . short-wave radio . . . compass . . . automatic steering gauge . . . Verey pistol . . . binoculars . . . On your right,
galley . . . gimbaled chair and tray unit . . . chart-table."

"And a rather splendid new kind of loudhailer," Singapore Charlie
added. He reached for the striped instrument, clipped above the chart-
table. The clip, however, refused to unclip. Singapore Charlie sighed in
exasperation and struggled with it. There was a loud snap.

"Oh, lumme . . ."

"Charles, please leave that," Mrs. Small commanded.

"Dearest, I was only . . ."

"Charles, *leave* it!" She turned abruptly back to Louis. "Please write
down that the gimbaled table and chair were specially designed by Mrs.
Angela 'Bunty' Small to give complete stability in all weathers."

Louis's notebook was still resolutely in his jacket pocket. "Are you a
good cook?" he asked Singapore Charlie.

"Oh, lumme, no. A good fry-up's about my limit. Or the odd . . ."

". . . Primus stove with special bread-baking compartment," Mrs.
Small continued. "Since, as I'm sure you know, my husband is a vegetarian, please write down that we also carry supplies of wheat-germ
and have facilities for growing mustard and cress . . ."

"Is this the beer?" Patrick asked. In an alcove near the floor was a
coloured bar-dispenser with a pewter mug underneath it.

The Meux P.R. man shouldered proudly forward. "Our special Directors' Gold Medal Final Section. Guaranteed to stay in peak condition in
any hemisphere."

"You know what would be really endsville-groovy? If I could shoot
Charlie here, pulling himself a half."

The compliant mariner allowed himself to be photographed kneeling and drawing off a tankard of bitter, raising it to the camera and taking a deep draught. Between shots, the Kilkrankie knitwear man solicitously rearranged the baseball cap to show its logo to best advantage. As Louis pressed back against the bunk, the P.R. for Ocean-Dredged Aggregates again plucked at his sleeve.

"If it's at all possible," he murmured, "I'd love your man to get some shots featuring our name somehow or other. What would you say to my getting one of our silt lorries out there on the quayside? Or I think I could even lay on a mobile decompression-chamber . . ."

---

"This is more like it," Patrick said two hours later, stretching out opposite Louis in the padded cockpit. *Lady Patricia* had put ashore all but the two of them and Singapore Charlie. Overhead, two brand-new creamy sails bore them across the Hamble estuary, towards the choppy waters of the Solent.

"Yeah! Yeah! Give it to me, baby!" Patrick leaned up against the deckhouse with levelled Nikon, twisting its phallic lens into focus. Away in the prow stood an heroic figure, brown arms gripping the rail, brown face under wind-whipped baseball cap seeming already to picture the horizonless ocean wastes ahead.

"Isn't that old lady of his the utter living endsville?" Patrick grinned as he snapped.

"I know." It had taken all Louis's persuasion to convince Mrs. Small that the interview should continue during *Lady Patricia*'s first full sea-trials.

"Some of the things she said to you, I didn't know whether to crease up or cry. Like 'I always try to sort out all my husband's screws before a voyage.' "

"And what about when she told me he had the body of a thirty-year-old?"

"Yeah, I felt like saying, 'Where does he keep it? In a cupboard under the stairs?' "

Singapore Charlie approached hand over hand and dropped into the cockpit beside Louis. He looked above and around him with watery grey eyes, twitching his cap-brim straight. "I've just been doing my sums," he said. "*Thermopylae* on her maiden voyage out of Liverpool in 1844 did Melbourne, New South Wales, Shanghai and home in one hundred and seventy-nine days. To match that average speed with a hull an eighth of her length means making landfall in Sydney in one hundred days, in other words a daily average distance of one hundred and thirty-seven point five miles."

"And *Thermopylae* had a crew of how many?"

"Forty. Most of 'em trained topmen."

"Charlie!" a voice cried from above them. "Could you look up here please, babe?" Tight trousers and cowboy boots notwithstanding, Patrick had climbed the footholds to the top of the mainmast.

"That photographer of yours is very intrepid," Singapore Charlie smiled.

"Would that be a fair description of you?" Louis asked.

"Oh, lumme, no. Scared stiff of all kinds of things."

"Such as?"

"Oh, piles of things. Being washed overboard. Hunger. Thirst. Sharks. Having to put on that damned wetsuit if the steering gear goes on the blink."

"And loneliness?"

"No, not that," Singapore Charlie replied tersely. "Whoops—time to go about. Remember to tuck in your tuppenny when you hear 'Watch the boom.' "

As *Lady Patricia* came about, Louis gazed with curiously dull emotions at the Isle of Wight's long misty silhouette. He could see Seaview's church spire and, below, the dark clump where the pier came slantwise out to sea. How had he managed to spend his whole childhood there without ever once setting foot in a sailing boat, or even learning to swim?

Patrick emerged from the cabin where he'd been reloading and flopped down on the opposite bench. "Where's our boy?" he asked.

"Gone upfront again."

"Here—want a puff?" Patrick held out a cigarette loosely rolled in yellowish paper. Its lit end smouldered doggedly, despite the stiff sea breeze.

"Thanks, I don't smoke," Louis said.

"You don't?"

"Only the occasional small cigar."

"Why not try? It'll really sort your head out."

"No, honestly, thanks."

Patrick took a deep drag, sucking the smoke noisily through his teeth. "I suppose I'd better not offer our skipper a puff, had I?" he grinned.

Louis was puzzled afresh by this metropolitan habit of passing a single cigarette around rather than offering the full packet. "I don't think he smokes."

"I'll bet he doesn't." Patrick sat up and glanced round, puzzled. "Where is he, by the way?"

They looked both ways along the tilted ridge of white sail, polished woodwork and bright chromium. From the prow with its raked observation rail to the stern with its gently swinging airborne rudder blade, there was no sign of Singapore Charlie.

"Hello!" Patrick bellowed into cupped hands.

Nothing could be heard but the swish of the waves, the thud of creamy ropes against pristine masts, the self-absorbed click of the automatic steering gear.

"Oh, mother," Patrick murmured.

"You don't think he . . ."

"I dunno, man."

"But surely we would have . . ."

"I'm going to have a look," Patrick said.

Louis followed him up from the cockpit and along the left-hand walkway, clinging for dear life to its immaculate rope rail. A couple of feet below the sea sped past, boiling and fuming like blue-black ink. One slip of a Cuban heel and it would be the end. He imagined himself hitting the water, one final glimpse of a cold-moulded silver laminate hull, a last twinge of agony from the new boots before choking green death closed over him.

Beyond the mainmast, invisible from astern, was the compartment holding *Lady Patricia*'s two emergency life-rafts. From its open hatchway protruded a pair of blue-trousered, feebly waving legs.

Patrick dropped to his knees on the heaving deck while Louis wrapped both arms around the mast. "Charlie! Is there some problem?"

"I'm stuck," a muffled voice replied.

Teetering like high-wire artists, they managed to grasp a leg each and haul the mariner to freedom. His white-whiskered face had turned a rich bilberry colour. "Oh, lumme," he panted.

"What happened?" Patrick asked.

Singapore Charlie struggled to his feet. His confinement upside-down seemed to have aged him by about twenty years. "Thought I saw a tear in one of the life-rafts. Trouble is with those things, if you lean in too far you lose the purchase to pull yourself out again. Thought I was going to asphyxiate . . ." He hung on a virginal rope, gulping in draughts of air. "Oh, dear . . . oh, dear, oh, Lord, oh, lumme . . ."

By the time they returned to harbour under auxiliary motor-power, the grey afternoon had changed to rose-coloured evening. Recovered from his mishap, once more composed, gritty and taciturn, Singapore Charlie lounged on the cockpit cushions, nursing an outsize pink gin. As the headlands of the Hamble estuary slipped by, he raised his glass to Louis and Patrick and winked.

"Here's to a pair of good shipmates," he said. "By the by, no need to mention that business with the life-raft coaming to my wife. She argues, but I always say I never feel quite comfortable with a new boat until something's gone wrong. Happy days!"

The masts, thatched roofs and shaggy ponies of Newman's Hard grew nearer and nearer. Patrick shot off a final roll of Singapore Charlie standing at his prow-rail like a Viking jarl, safe home after victory and plunder.

Suddenly, with a deep groan, *Lady Patricia* heeled over and came to a dead stop.

"Oh, lumme . . ."

"I don't believe this guy," Patrick gurgled, peering over the side. "He's only run the bloody thing aground."

A further hour and a half passed before the misfortune was noticed on shore and a launch could be dispatched to tow *Lady Patricia* off the sandbar. Louis watched the rescue craft approach—anxious P.R. men and marooned sailor's wife also aboard it—through mint-fresh Zeiss binoculars. Focusing on Mrs. Small's face, he gained some inkling of what would motivate a man to spend nine months at sea in utter solitude, and how tempests, killer whales and Cape Horn's ninety-foot waves might conceivably be a slightly softer option.

---

He wrote the copy in a single evening in Grandma Bassill's unfrequented "best" sitting room, at times glancing up for inspiration at the china cabinet of orange Lustreware, the hand-tinted photographs of wartime wedding groups, the 1930s cocktail cabinet and the Magicoal electric fire.

It came out longer than "Pincher Bassill": eight and a half of The Sunday Dispatch's thick white bond quarto sheets, each retyped as many as five times to eliminate every last mistake and smudged letter *e* or *a*. At dawn the next morning he awoke to a terrible premonition that he'd written "spankerboom" when he meant "spinnaker," and couldn't rest until he had crept downstairs to redo that whole page.

He left the top copy on Toby Godwin's deserted, pristine desk, then took the better of the two carbon copies round to Terry Bracegirdle. Resplendent in a thickly red, pink and orange striped shirt, the Deputy Editor was scanning a pile of American magazines including Time, Life, Look and the Saturday Evening Post. He glanced up, mystified, as Louis proudly laid the faultlessly typed paged before him.

"What's this?"

"The round-the-world yachtsman."

"Already?"

A disbelieving—was it perhaps even admiring?—grin split the handsome bespectacled face. "Ye can take more time on things than this, ye noah. You're not on the Stockton Evening whatsit now."

At just before 11:30, his telephone buzzed. "Louis," said Tessa Burland's calm voice. "Could you come in and see God, please?"

"Extremely enjoyable, dear boy," Godwin boomed as he appeared in the doorway. "Absolutely first-class work. I'm delighted."

The red-carpeted office smelled like a Kardomah coffee house. On the long work-top were baskets of croissants, brioches, Danish pastries, apricots, nectarines and peaches. Perched among them, sipping coffee, was a ruddy-faced man in a navy-blue pinstripe suit with a gold watch-chain threaded from a lapel into his breast pocket.

Godwin lounged contentedly back from his desk, the pristine surface of which bore only Louis's manuscript, an outsize French coffee cup and a peach cut into scarlet-hearted halves. His pepper-and-salt tonsure, as usual at this time of day, was spiky and damp with hurried, too-recent showering. His violet-shirted girth swelled up from its tortured waistband like the breast of a prize goose, ready for Bob Cratchit to plunge the carvers in.

"I don't think you've met Tim Mandeville, our Advertising Director," he added. The oily-haired man smiled with a face of unmitigated evil. "Tim . . . this is the winner of our Young Writers' Competition who's now with us permanently and has turned in an absolute tour de force about this lone yachtsman, Barbary Jack . . . er . . ."

"Singapore Charlie Small."

"Exactly." Godwin popped a quarter of a peach into his mouth and glanced back through the copy with a reflective chuckle. " 'Got the body of a thirty-year-old man . . .' hooh hooh. Impertinent young scallywag. Now then, Val's sent a lensman to shoot this Barbary Small cove, has she?"

"Yes, Patrick Prince."

"So we're poised and ready to go down the slipway. Excellent, excellent. Help yourself to coffee, dear boy. And there's Fortnum's croissants and brioches . . . or do you prefer *petit pain au chocolat?*"

For the rest of the morning Louis sat at his desk in a daze of euphoria, covertly belching pastry-fat and waiting for Terry Bracegirdle's corroborative praise. It still had not come by lunch-time, when the Deputy Editor went off in a guffawing group with Scurr, Jessamyn and Evelyn Strachey. Creeping into the empty office, Louis saw his copy still in the wire basket, now half obscured by Time, Newsweek and Look magazines.

He spent the afternoon similarly on tenterhooks, writing a long, sub-tly boastful letter to Mike Finnis and Bob Feetham in Stockton, now and again glancing at Bracegirdle beyond the glass partition, dictating to his red-haired secretary, laughing with Strachey or Scurr or engaged in visually dramatic long-distance telephone calls. The weather being hot-ter than ever, Toby Godwin treated the whole office to ice creams. On a nearby stationery cabinet stood a cardboard box, filled with melting choc ices, Orange Maids and raspberry Mivvies.

"Louis!" Val Lewis called across to him just after 4 P.M. "The lone yachtsman pictures are in."

He hurried across to the Picture Desk, where twenty or so trannies, each stamped "PHOTO: PATRICK PRINCE," were spread on the light-box. Val handed him the viewing glass he had heard called a "loupe," and he bent and peered at the various lit and magnified images: Singapore Charlie with wife on the quay at Newman's Hard; drawing a half-pint of bitter in the cabin; raising his tankard in a toast; gazing from under his cap-brim into *Lady Patricia*'s rigging, gnarled and omniscient about winds and tides. There was also a mischievous rear view of him just after *Lady Patricia* had run aground, hanging over the rope rail and gaz-ing down in evident stupefaction.

"What do you think?" Louis asked.

"Oh . . . they're fine," Val replied.

At 6 o'clock, having still heard nothing from Bracegirdle, he started for the lift, then on impulse turned and looked into the Deputy Editor's office. Bracegirdle was on the telephone, tilted back in his chair, comb-ing his boyish quiff with his fingers and talking in an agitated under-tone. "All right, Stephanie . . . I said all right, Stephanie, just doan't go on any more. Ah've toald you I'll be there. About half-six, all right? OK, 'bye."

He hung up and gave Louis a glance of only hazy recognition.

"Sorry . . . I just wondered if you'd had a chance to read it yet?"

"Read what?"

"My profile of Singapore Charlie."

"Oh . . . yes," Bracegirdle said abstractedly. "It's fine."

---

"I've had the most peculiar letter from Portia," Louis's mother said.

She was spending a week in London for a refresher course at the Bond Street salon and, as usual, earning her board by giving her mother a full facial. Before her sat Grandma Bassill, wrapped in a bath-towel and shiny-faced with deep-cleansing cream. In his wheelchair at the kitchen table, Grandad scooped up his last game of Patience and began dealing himself another hand. On the television by the scullery door Reginald Bosanquet was reading the ITN 6 O'Clock News.

"What do you mean 'peculiar'?" Louis asked.

His mother drew on a Pall Mall Kingsize, then resumed slapping Velvatone foundation on to Grandma's upturned face. "Oh—that she's terribly worried about you, she thinks you may be having a nervous breakdown."

"Me?"

"She says she's been in London almost three weeks, but still hasn't seen you . . . you never answer her letters or return her phone calls."

"I've just been rather busy, that's all."

"You could be a bit nicer to her, especially after all she's gone through to be up here with you. Our training course isn't easy, you know."

"I know," Louis said, half watching an ITN sequence of Frank Cousins leaving T.U.C. headquarters.

"We only accept about a dozen girls a year at the school. And I happen to know Portia worked like stink to get through all the courses in two months instead of six, just so she could come to London at the same time as you."

"I know," Louis repeated sullenly.

"As a matter of fact they're delighted with her on our counter at Fenwick's. Mrs. Delaport, the Head Consultant, reckons she'll end up running her own treatment room."

Hearing the word "Beatles," Louis turned to the 6 O'Clock News again. The four of them were shown descending an aircraft-staircase somewhere in America. These days, they no longer wore matching neat fringes, suits and shortie raincoats, but a miscellany of jerkins, T-shirts and sunglasses. The crowd, shown pressed against a chicken-wire fence, also had greatly changed—no longer screaming and weeping in adoration but shouting, grimacing and catcalling. One grimly serious girl brandished a placard which read "JESUS DIED TO SAVE YOU TOO, JOHN."

A later sequence showed them seated at a long table behind a battery of television microphones while John Lennon recanted yet again in a weary—but still, somehow, entertaining—monotone. "What I originally said was in confidence to a friend . . . It was just my view of things . . . the way I express it. When I said it, I didn't mean Jesus as a person or a thing or whatever . . . but I shouldn't have said it, and I'm sorry . . ."

"Silly chap," remarked Grandma Bassill, who now wore the first of a pair of black eyebrows that would have done credit to Cruella DeVil. "Saying he was more famous than Jesus."

"He didn't," Louis said. "And anyway, it's sort of true."

His mother stood back and regarded her handiwork critically. "Have you heard from your father since you won the prize?"

"I phoned Hungerford to tell him."

"And what did he say?"

"He was out mending a jukebox. Olwen took a message."

"Hasn't he written to congratulate you?"

"Not so far."

She glared at the framed photograph of herself as a wartime bride beside the uniformed figure whose face had been loyally obliterated by a modern snapshot of Grandad.

"You know what he is, don't you?" she muttered, licking her eyebrow pencil and bending over her mother once more.

"No," Louis said. "What?"

"Bloody speechless with jealousy, that's what. Because you're not ballsing your life up the way he's totally ballsed up his. Mum . . . do try to hold still."

---

With a heavy heart he summoned the recollection that Portia was sharing a flat with her school-friend Penny in Pembridge Villas, just off Notting Hill Gate. Arriving there just before 8 P.M., he got no answer at the basement front door and was thankfully turning to leave when Portia and Penny appeared at the top of the area steps. Portia's face smiled wanly, under its new professional layer of lipstick and orangey powder. He was struck by how sad her arms looked, cradling a bag of bananas, and her fingers, plucking the silver top of a pint of milk.

Awaiting his opportunity, he sat on a kitchen stool as they put things away, and did his best to be bright and interesting. Into his mind, and quickly out again, floated a spectre of the mink stole he'd once recklessly promised to buy Portia if things should ever turn out as they now had. Thank God, she'd never mentioned it again.

". . . Just the ordinary copy paper's this wonderful ivory-white bond. And you can have notebooks, pens, headed stationery, even cuttings albums absolutely ad lib. Remember how on the E.T. I couldn't get a new biro unless I handed in the old one to prove it was really used . . ."

Portia, it turned out, resented his neglect much less than Penny did on her behalf. As Louis was recounting his recent adventure afloat with Singapore Charlie Small, Penny scribbled something on a "Don't Forget" kitchen-pad, tore off the sheet and thrust it pointedly into his hand. An itinerary for making amends, it read:

Finch's pub, Portobello Road
London Steak House or

The Ark, Ken Church St.
Le Kilt discothèque

In the event he was required to do no more than walk Portia round a neighbouring garden square. Children chased each other on the protected grass and a radio somewhere was playing the Easybeats' "Friday on My Mind." "Gonna have fun in the city . . ." his mind couldn't help blissfully echoing.

"Look at that extraordinary car. It's a Jensen Interceptor, isn't it?"

"Is it?" Portia said tonelessly.

". . . be with my girl, she's so prid-ee . . ."

He stopped and gave an anguished sigh. "Look, you know what I'm going to say, don't you?"

"Yes," Portia said.

"I need some time to think . . . to sort myself out . . . be on my own. I'm just starting this new job with The Sunday Dispatch . . . I don't know where I'm going to be or what I'll be doing . . . it's not fair to you to go on pretending . . . in a few weeks, it could all be different . . . but at the moment, my head's just in a whirl . . . I feel I might even have a nervous breakdown unless we can get this sorted out . . . Anyway, you've got a new job . . . lots of exciting things ahead of you, too . . . and, you know, perhaps in a few weeks . . ."

A sudden terrible thought struck him. In the Singapore Charlie copy, had he *meant* "spankerboom," not "spinnaker"?

Portia had bowed her Alice-banded head. "Oh . . . Louis!" she murmured.

"I'll tell you what I'm going to do. I'm just going to walk away now . . . right now, this minute . . . and you do it, too . . . a clean break's much the best way for both our sakes OK? I'm going now. I'll ring you."

"Will you?"

"I promise. OK—I'm going, and you go. It's easier on us both this way. 'Bye. I'll be in touch, I promise. 'Bye."

Head lowered like a scaffold-bound prisoner, too-tight boots lending extra gravity to his step, Louis walked towards the turning at the top of the square. Glancing back, he saw Portia still standing beside the Jensen Interceptor. He rounded the corner and—boot-agony or not—leapt joyfully high into the air.

An hour later he was safe amid the blessed maleness, unreproachfulness and crudity of old school-friends, drinking red wine by the glass after the new pub fashion and receiving tips for survival as a single agent—whoopee!—in the metropolis.

"One thing to remember," My Cunt said, "is never, if you can possibly help it, wear a white shirt to work. I had a brand-new Tern on the other morning when we were surveying down by Brompton Oratory and by half-ten, I'm not kidding, the inside of the collar and the cuffs were jet-black. Oh . . . Uxbridge!"

"My advice," Paul Rich said, "is always keep a hundred quid in a special emergency abortion fund. You never know when some daft bint's going to get herself up the stick."

"I thought they all took this new contraceptive Pill," Louis said.

"That may be—but most of them forget about it half the time. If they miss just one night, you can end up in Shit Street."

"If you want any pot," My Cunt said, "there's a guy I can send you to in Cornwall Gardens."

"Pot?" Louis repeated.

"Oh, Gawd! OK . . . scrub round that."

By 10 o'clock, the world seemed to be wrapped in Beaujolais-coloured cotton wool. He became aware that My Cunt was shaking his arm.

"Wake up there, will you, Brennan! I said, 'Do you want a woman?'"

"The thing is, you see, neither of us can bear the awesome disgrace of your having been in London nearly a fortnight without flinging your spindly little leg across."

"He obviously needs a bit of help to get the old spindly airborne. Tell you what, Paul. Shall we ring up Stubbington?"

"Yeah, let's get him Stubbington."

Cloudily he watched My Cunt cross the crowded bar to the callbox beside the Gents'. Within what seemed only seconds, a girl was seated on a bar-stool among them, drinking draught cider, smoking a Café Crème cheroot and throwing back her head to roar with laughter, like a bluff, brawny musketeer, at everything that any of them said. She had old-fashioned back-combed, flicked-up hair and chiselled features that reminded Louis of someone he knew well, though he couldn't quite think whom. She wore a short skirt and jacket of viscous nubbly yellow material. Her voice was the brisk contralto of a Roedean hockey-mistress.

Then, like scenes changing in a film, Paul and My Cunt had retreated along the bar and Louis and Stubbington, whose first name he either had not heard or had forgotten, were sitting on closely adjacent stools, she laughing her hip-smiting musketeer's laugh because he seemed to possess almost psychic power to know what she was going to say, and was finishing every one of her sentences before she could. He had realized by now why her prominent nose, indrawn mouth and thrusting jaw seemed so familiar. It was as if Harris Tweed, the bungling detective from Eagle comics of his childhood, had taken to false eyelashes and Carmen rollers. But the dark-stockinged knees on the bar-stool were small and shapely, and between the nubbly jacket lapels he detected a cavernous wobble.

After that, the scenes became more blurred and random. He remembered being helped up a shabby staircase and through a hallway with a bicycle standing in it. He remembered watching Stubbington unhook her bra, and two huge boulders bounding towards him like an Alpine avalanche. He remembered the bright overhead light they had neglected to turn off; a soapy dive which in his drunken state was almost devoid of feeling; and surprising Roedean-accented exclamations of "Ooh, what a lovely purple-headed bed-snake"; "Ram it into me till it comes out of my mouth, you dirty sod!"; and "Christ, I want to lick your balls!"

Less abandoned, at another moment, was the shrill yelp of "Youch!"

"Sorry . . ."

"Good God! . . . You haven't still got your boots on!"

"Sorry . . . I've been told it's the only way I'll stretch them . . ."

He left just after 7 A.M. the next morning, declining Stubbington's offer of breakfast. She held the plasterboard front door open for him, picking at a false eyelash left precariously intact like a window-shutter in the wake of a hurricane. "Are you sure you wouldn't like an egg?" she asked.

He debated inwardly which kind was less appealing under the circumstances. The kind advertised by Bernard Miles and stamped with a little lion. Or the kind waiting to be fertilised by valiant little tadpoles, leaping and curveting upriver.

"No, really . . . Thanks all the same."

"Give me a ring, then."

"OK. Sure. 'Bye."

# 8

That morning it was surprisingly easy not to arrive at McIntyre House until almost 10:15. On his way from the lift Louis saw Evelyn Strachey coming towards him, pale forearms balancing as delicately as a high-wire artist above Niagara Falls.

Pounding head and parrot's-cage mouth notwithstanding, he stopped and groped for suitable words. He must if possible make friends with this supreme practitioner of his trade, whose mannerisms and clothes doubtless were of a high fashion beyond his ken, who could teach him so much that he desperately wanted to learn, and whose interest and unselfish pleasure in up-and-coming young writers was reiterated on every side.

"Evelyn . . . I just want to say . . . your profile of David Warner last Sunday was wonderful!"

"Oh . . . thanks," Strachey replied with a simpering smile and the just perceptible rotation of the hip which, Louis still resolutely told himself, must have an explanation other than the obvious one. It was surely just impenetrable upper-classness, trendiness, Londonness. Doubtless Strachey talked and walked in exactly the same way when escorting strings of glamorous girl-friends.

"I loved all that about playing Hamlet with an American accent . . . And the story of the girl at the party."

"Thanks ever so much."

"I've finished my lone sailor piece," Louis went on. "It's with Terry Bracegirdle now."

"Yes, I know," Strachey said in an admiring tone. "I've seen it."

"You have?"

"Yes. Terry likes me to look through all the pieces."

"And . . . can I ask what you . . . thought of it?"

"I thought it was fine."

Louis walked into the Magazine concourse, his hangover forgotten. It was as if the clouds had parted and Zeus had reached down from Olympus to pat him on the head.

"Something arrived for you by special messenger," Mrs. Broadbent said, indicating a bulky envelope on his typewriter. Inside he found an expensively printed book detailing the worldwide operations of Ocean-Dredged Aggregates, and a visiting card inscribed "Simon C. Gilkes."

"Do you know yet which Sunday the Singapore Charlie piece will run?" he asked Margaret. "I suppose the best time would be a week or two before he sets off, in case any other papers get on to it. He's supposed to be sailing on August fifteenth, which is a Tuesday. I was wondering if there's any chance of doing it on the thirteenth?"

Margaret glanced across at Mrs. Broadbent. "Hasn't anyone told you?"

"Told me what?"

"It isn't going in."

Louis gaped from her back to Margaret. "Not going in? Why?"

"Cedric didn't like the pictures."

"He said he didn't see why we should give a plug to a stunt by the Steam Section that no one was going to care about anyway," Mrs. Broadbent added.

"But . . . it was all arranged with God . . . and Jack Shildrick . . ."

Margaret smiled ruefully. "There's a fact of life here that you'd better learn if you want to save yourself a lot of tears. Cedric's the one who controls the visuals and budgets space on the flat-plan. So Cedric's the one with ultimate yea or nay. If he takes against something, no matter whether it's all been fixed beforehand by St. Peter and the Archangel Gabriel—it's out."

For a moment Louis considered going into Scurr's department and arguing with the jokey deference that had sometimes been known to sway crusty Evening Telegraph subs. But a glance at the Art Director's distant cross-combed pate warned him it would be hopeless.

"Surely if the pictures weren't good enough, they could be redone?"

"It wasn't just the pictures," Margaret said. "Terry B. didn't like your piece much either."

"But . . . he told me he thought it was fine."

"Ah," Margaret nodded. "That dreaded word. Remember in future that if anyone round here says your copy's 'fine,' it's roughly the same as a kiss on the cheek from a Sicilian mafioso."

"Terry shows everything to Evelyn Strachey, you see," Mrs. Broadbent added. "Evelyn said that no one was interested in yachting pieces, and Singapore Charlie sounded just a boring little man . . ."

Louis gazed incredulously through the open door of Jessamyn O'Shaughnessy's office. Strachey was seated daintily on the edge of a desk, leafing through a copy of Woman's Wear Daily. From unseen quarters came the pop of a champagne cork. "Then I'll go straight to God about it . . ."

"It'll be a waste of time," Margaret said.

"But he had me in yesterday and told me it was the greatest thing since . . . I told you what he said."

"Doesn't matter. Not if Cedric, Terry and Evelyn have given it the thumbs-down."

"And anyway, you won't see God around for a bit," Mrs. Broadbent said. "Not while the Test Match is on at Lords."

Margaret gave him a sympathetic smile, hooking a strand of hair behind her ear. "Come on, don't look so woebegone. At least you've got your prizewinning piece about Grandad in on Sunday. We get first colour proofs from the printer this afternoon. I'll try to find one good enough for you to take home tonight."

———————

At 6:30 that evening he hobbled disconsolately to the lift, carrying his page-proof in an opulent orange cardboard folder. As he waited for a down lift, an upward-bound one stopped unbidden and its salmon-coloured doors clattered open. Inside stood Jack Shildrick and his newspaper henchman, the superior-looking Nick Fenton.

"Come on in, Poet," Shildrick said, beckoning. "You can ride up with us, then down again. You've met Nick, from Close-up, haven't you?" He turned back to Fenton. "The nub of the whole thing is that bloody identity parade. Hanratty swore he was in South Wales, and could even produce witnesses to back him up, yet Valerie Storey positively identified him as the killer, even though it was pitch-dark in that field and the car had no interior light. Hey up, I'll tell you what! They've got Hanratty down at Madame Tussaud's, haven't they?"

"I suppose so," Fenton said. "In the Chamber of Horrors."

"Get someone to give 'em a ring. Ask if they'll loan him to us. We'll re-create the identity parade with the waxwork in the middle. Not to traduce that poor girl's evidence—just to show how easy it can be to confuse one face with another." Shildrick turned abruptly back to Louis. "Why so sad and palely loitering, Poet?"

"The Magazine aren't going to use the lone yachtsman piece," he said dully.

"Not going to use it! Whyever not?"

"Oh . . . some problem over the pictures. And they don't seem to think Singapore Charlie is all that interesting."

"That's rubbish," Shildrick almost snapped. "He's an extraordinary man, embarking on a stupendous adventure. And a first-class writer was sent to talk to him."

The lift doors opened. Instead of remaining to travel down again, Louis found himself being pulled by the elbow out onto the noisy, bustling newspaper floor. "I'll get right onto Tussaud's, shall I?" Nick Fenton said.

"Aye—tell 'em we'll pay for delivery, take out special insurance, anything. It really is a good yarn, is it, Poet?"

"Oh, yes. Terrific."

"Well, if the Mag are silly enough to pass on it, maybe I can have it for my Review front . . . Oh, and another thing, Nick!" Shildrick called after Fenton's retreating back. "See if you can recruit a few of the thuggier types from the Newsroom to make up the identity parade. The subs' table ought to give you a few promising candidates."

Louis's heart, meanwhile, had turned a breath-stopped back somersault. Even his grandiose daydreams had never aspired to the Dispatch's Weekly Review front, with its serialised-for-a-fortune memoirs of politicians and field marshals, its extended essays by the likes of James Morris and Malcolm Muggeridge.

"But . . ." he stammered, "it's terribly long . . ."

"An average Review front's twenty-five hundred words. For a really good read we can always find more space inside."

"And the photographer only did colour pictures."

"A colour slide'd convert to black-and-white. Don't worry your head about any of that. Just booger off downstairs and get the copy."

Ten minutes later he was sitting on the cream-coloured executive sofa whose nubbly pile was already stained by proof-ink and eroded by constant meetings. Shildrick leaned against his newspaper-lectern, reading the second, inferior carbon of the Singapore Charlie profile. The nine sheets took him less than eight minutes.

"OK, Poet, come over here." Louis joined him against the lectern, on which was spread a page-sized layout sheet with the Review section's dignified small masthead shaded on it in pencil. Beneath was a roughed-out banner headline, "CRISIS IN CABINET."

"You're a wizard, aren't you?" Shildrick said.

His tone implied that Louis's wizardry was also a kind of impertinence. He leaned on the spread-out sheets, pushing up his glasses to rub the side of his nose. There was a glimpse of the hooded eyes and delicate features that reminded one obscurely of crinolines and bustles and writing-desks in rectory bedrooms.

"All I'd say is, you need to work on the beginning a bit. For these first three pars you're all over the place. I don't think you need any of this about the clipper-routes and cargoes . . . This is where you hit your stride, here where you describe the harbour. That's a lovely line about 'foals the colour of liqueur honey.' "

As always with Shildrick, Louis was torn between self-disgust at his own woolly-mindedness and exhilaration at beholding the broadly signposted highway to perfection.

"I see what to do . . ." He grabbed a loose pencil. "I can cut this whole par . . . go straight from the intro to the ponies. Cape Horn in winter, then the Hamble in summer . . ."

Shildrick joined thumb and forefinger in a gastronome's O of approval. "Perfect. And here, where you've written 'spankerboom' I think you mean 'spinnaker.' We'd best get it right, or we'll have yachtsmen all over the country writing in."

"You mean you're going to use it?" Louis quavered.

"Too true I am!"

"This weekend?"

"Too right! Iain Macleod's memoirs'll keep for a week. They're pickled in bloody boredom and complacency anyway. This is just what I need as a counterpoint to Close-up on the Hanratty affair."

"Does it matter that Singapore Charlie isn't setting off till the end of the month?"

"No, not a bit. If we run it now, it'll stake our claim to the story, start the interest in him really cooking, maybe even encourage other sponsors to come forward. Get him some thermal long johns to go with all those cardigans, or a keg of lager to put alongside the bitter."

A further obstacle occurred to Louis and he voiced it reluctantly. "But it was written for the Magazine. Will they mind it being taken for the paper?"

"Leave that to me," said Shildrick. "I know there's some funny convention about the Colour Mag being an ivory tower and having no truck with us proles on the fifth floor. But if they're passing up something as good as this, I can't think that Toby Godwin'll play dog in the manger. I'll give him a ring now, directly I've spoken to Dudley Mowforth about dropping the Macleod stuff."

Louis said nothing. He felt as if an invisible sun were shining straight into his eyes.

"One thing, though," Shildrick added. "We'll have to lose the bit about running aground."

"Oh, no. Really?"

"And the stuff about him writing off planes all over the world in the thirties."

"But it's so funny. Looking down to wave at the crowd and twanging into telegraph wires . . ."

"I know, it's rib-tickling stuff. But we're presenting this man as a modern Francis Drake. We can't turn round in the next breath and say he's a blithering incompetent."

---

So there it was the next Sunday morning, forced with difficulty under the stiff letterbox flap to scatter into component parts on Grandma Bassill's tufted doormat. His wildest dream in double measure, and more.

A Sunday Dispatch Weekly Review front bearing all the hallmarks of Shildrick drama and style. A four-column photograph of Singapore Charlie's small face, under baseball cap-brim and Kilcrankie knitwear logo, smiling with an old sea-dog's knowingness (which in Patrick Prince's original colour transparency had been directed not at far horizons, but at a tankard of Meux draught bitter). Underneath, a banner headline and strapline in Ultra Bodoni italic, reminiscent of auction posters for the slaves the clippers also carried: "ONE MAN AGAINST THE OCEANS OF THE WORLD. Louis Brennan meets a Francis Drake for the Sixties."

And in the Magazine—at the very back, two pages sandwiched between "Erica Kirkham's Year of Good Cooking" and Polyphemus' Crossword—"PINCHER BASSILL by Louis Brennan, Sunday Dispatch Magazine Young Writer of the Year." The picture of that top-hatted young man and his big-eared movie camera, made the more romantically Edwardian by an extra, luxuriant sepia wash. Really and truly, his words in the elegant serified type he now knew to be Plantin 9 point:

"On Grand National Day, 1912, my grandfather hid in a pile of straw which, unknown to him . . ."

Was it because of having seen it at several proof stages beforehand that the dream come true felt so oddly flat and disappointing?

# SECTION TWO

# Business

9

The tail-coated trainee footman lowered a bowl of pale green soup tremblingly past Louis's left shoulder, into the space between two broad rows of silver cutlery. "Thank you," he said, glancing at the face above the stiff shirt-front and bow-tie. Smeared with adolescent blemishes and sweating profusely, it wore an expression of hypnotised terror like that of the vampire's helpless victim in some Hammer horror film.

"We serve with the right hand, our left hand behind our back," intoned Mr. Frederick as a second pupil commenced delivery of a similarly unsteady red-and-gold plate to him. "The fingers of our left hand, not crudely clenched but spread to their full extent, the thumb in alignment with the fifth or sixth vertebra . . ."

He broke off to watch his soup's final descent with the unforgiving vigilance of an international ice-skating judge. He was about sixty-five, pale, skeletally thin, goggle-eyed and veinily bald save for a few strands of reddish hair combed vertically around large, flat ears. He wore a sky-blue silk shirt with matching trousers, an aquamarine cravat, a pair of rimless spectacles suspended on a gold chain, and monogrammed black velvet slippers.

"Careful, careful, don't spill it!" he shouted in sudden fury. The trainee shied in terror, causing soup to engulf his kid-gloved thumb, then surge the other way over the plate-rim and onto the polished table top.

"Ugh, maladroit," Mr. Frederick sighed. "No, leave it, *leave* it!" he hissed as his scarlet, sweating pupil mopped at the puddle with a damask napkin. "Away! Go! Out of my sight!"

Louis took a cautious spoonful of the soup, which was cold, as he had suspected, and faintly prawny in taste. The little dining room had French windows open on a garden, where a further group of trainees, also in Victorian full dress, were drilling with cake-stands and hot-water jugs under the eye of a stripe-waistcoated butler. Through open windows above floated the voices of other instructors in Mr. Frederick's academy.

". . . a mild solution of water and methylated spirits will remove the stains from most silverware . . ."

". . . Remember that a butler never knocks before entering ground-floor reception rooms. Only at the doors of bedrooms and boudoirs . . ."

". . . the correct garnish for a Pimm's Number One is lemon and cucumber with fresh mint or borage, if available . . ."

The third or fourth butler Louis had encountered that morning re-filled his glass from a napkin-ringed bottle of Chablis. He put down his soup spoon and opened his spiral-bound notebook.

"So," he resumed, "you teach them everything."

"Everything," Mr. Frederick said faintly, as if the burden was almost too great to bear. "Buttling. Pantling. You probably didn't know that a pantry is so-called because one used to find a pantler in it."

"No, I didn't."

"Here at Mr. Frederick's we combine what I believe is a unique education in the domestic arts with a full service to those still interested in the more gracious side of life. Our graduates can be found in most of England's great houses as well as throughout the world. On a freelance basis, we can provide staff for anything from a full City liverymen's banquet to a candlelit dinner for two."

He bent his veiny, flat-eared skull over his soup bowl and drank with a loud slurp. "Tell me again what this article of yours for the Dispatch supplement is about."

"It's an enquiry into whether domestic service survives in the egalitarian sixties. Can the master-servant relationship have any place in an era where socialism rules and class barriers seem to be tumbling?"

"Ah, well, of course, it isn't what it was," Mr. Frederick sighed. "When I started as under-footman to the Duke of Saxmundham, the servants' hall numbered almost a hundred. People these days, you see, are afraid to practise the niceties the way they used to. Lord Ardmore, to whom I was personal gentleman's gentleman before the war, refused to have loose change in his pocket unless it had been washed in eau-de-cologne. One would never dream of putting a newspaper on a breakfast tray without running a warm iron over it first. The late Marchioness of Whitby—a wonderful old lady—insisted on both her coachmen being exactly the same height. If one was shorter than the other, he'd have to sit on a pile of cushions."

An imperious ring on a Delft china bell brought the two sweating trainees from the sideboard to clear the soup-plates. Louis became aware that Mr. Frederick was studying him intently, smoothing strands of reddish hair down over one large, pink ear.

"Perhaps what we should do is send you out to a function with one of our teams so that you can get a flavour of it." He nodded at the butler. "I'll put you in the charge of Mr. Loynes there, who's one of my most experienced executives. He'd be all right with you, wouldn't he, Mr. Loynes?"

The butler—whose accent, surprisingly, was faint Cockney—smiled with a flash of half-frame glasses. "Oh yes. We'll take good care of him."

"We can loan you a footman's suit," Mr. Frederick continued as a trembling white-gloved hand reached down past him. He gave Louis another bulgy-eyed smile, stroking his left ear reflectively. "You can change in my room . . ."

In another frenzy of annoyance, he jerked his head around to upbraid his luckless pupil once again. As he did so, the ear he had been fondling suddenly detached itself and fell into the ascending soup bowl. Exposed between reddish strands was a hole in a trimmed-away stump about the size of a teacup handle. The footman's eyes bulged in his dewy face at the pale pink prosthesis lying like a stranded whale among the green soup dregs.

"Oops!" said Mr. Loynes with reassuring joviality, interposing himself between the stricken trainee and the plate. In a few deft seconds, following evidently well-rehearsed procedure, the ear had been retrieved, wiped off with a napkin and clamped back in position, and Mr. Loynes was pouring red wine from a decanter.

"Shall I serve the lamb now?" he asked.

---

As well as Mr. Frederick, Louis had interviewed a housekeeper in South Kensington, a gardener in Fulham, a nanny in Belgravia, a chauffeur in New Cross and the principals of three domestic service agencies, filling two spiral-bound notebooks and twenty typed sheets with their diverse views on the role of servants in the Sixties. Despite the richness of the subject matter and his growing involvement, it was hard not to feel like an army conscript, set to some all-absorbing but ultimately pointless task like eating jelly with knitting-needles or whitewashing coal.

Since his double triumph five weeks ago, he had not managed to get another word into The Sunday Dispatch Magazine. Nor was anything he had written or was engaged in writing to be found on even the most distant of its forward schedules. Positioned though he might be at its very hub, a daily witness to its conception, composition and production, there were moments when it seemed almost as unreachable as from the press box at Stockton Magistrates Court.

It was not that he lacked for things to do. There was scarcely an Ideas Lunch when another seeming plum of a project did not come his way, wreathed in cigar-smoke and Toby Godwin's indulgent guffaw. "How about this one for our young prizewinner there? . . . Trickle along and see what you make of it, dear boy . . . I regard you as Candide, exploring the world on our behalf, hooh hooh hooh . . ."

So, as well as working on "Whither the Sixties Servant?" he had been to Birmingham to profile Peter Watkins, director of *The War Game*; to a mansion flat off Baker Street to interview a Japanese woman who was making an avant-garde art film about bottoms; and to Oxford to see a professor whose elvish fantasies were a cult sensation among American college students. From each he had returned alight with enthusiasm to hammer out his copy at daily-deadline speed. For all three perfectly typed pieces the outcome had been the same—lavish public praise from Godwin, then the cold plunge into the fathomless indifference of Cedric Scurr's bifocals; the sink without trace into the Grimpen Mire of Terry Bracegirdle's pending file.

He had come to understand that the munificent picnics in Godwin's office every Wednesday had little or no connection with what appeared in the Magazine. Their purpose was simply to eat, drink and exchange the multifarious gossip of McIntyre House, with special stress always on the underprivileged oafishness of the newspaper, or Steam Section. "Ideas" featured simply as a kind of cabaret over dessert when, cigar in hand, Godwin would read aloud from the thick file of suggestions received from freelance writers and photographers or their agents. These were almost always shouted down, usually amid howls of derisive laughter.

The constituents of each issue were actually decided by Terry Bracegirdle and the Art Director, Cedric Scurr, leaning over Scurr's "flatplan" of miniature rectangles showing the proportion of editorial pages to advertisements. Shortage of the Magazine's precious space was ostensibly why Louis's work could not be used; the irresistible prior claim of such brilliant late-summer features as "Norman Mailer's Cuba," "Inside Broadmoor," "Human Torches of Phnom Penh," "Soul Food for Beginners" and "Is This Chimp Really Smiling?" Yet he could not help but notice how wonderfully elastic and accommodating was that same space to both his senior writing colleagues, whose working days were largely spent in a huddle around Scurr and his all-powerful felt-tip marker. Jessamyn O'Shaughnessy's fashion pieces, though seldom lon-

ger than 500 words (and invariably rewritten by Margaret Cole, the
Magazine's solitary Sub-Editor), had been the cover story three Sundays out of the past five. And for Evelyn Strachey, on the rare occasions
he bestirred himself to profile the newest French film director or Soho
drag artist, all existing schedules dissolved; huge tracts of space magically opened up; not infrequently, ways even were found of circum-
venting the five-week production schedule, to rush the sanctified copy
into print as soon as possible.

The lobbying stratagems that Louis had often used with effect on the
Whittlesey Advertiser and Stockton Evening Telegraph all proved useless here. To warn, for example, that some rival publication might think
of doing the same story if it were not printed quickly could have only
disastrous results. Major features in the very latest production stages
were routinely dropped at the faintest whisper that a rival magazine,
The Observer's or Daily Telegraph's, might be contemplating something even glancingly similar. There had been the recent occasion
when The Sunday Times Magazine's cover had featured a starving Indian child almost identical with the one then running through the Dispatch Magazine's presses. The entire run had been cancelled and the
cover replaced, all at a cost that would have kept the famine-hit state of
Bihar in milk powder for a month.

Even more useless to suggest that a feature on Professor J.R.R. Tolkien's Hobbit books might conceivably interest a Sunday Dispatch Magazine reader at least as much as Evelyn Strachey's recent profile of a
Japanese poet who had posed for photographs wearing nothing but a
jockstrap, a Nazi officer's cap and motor-cyclist's gauntlets. On Louis's
previous papers, readers had been an ever-present and dangerous force,
not only writing and telephoning but frequently appearing in person to
dissent, cajole, even threaten bodily harm if something you had written
did not please them. But here, readers were of no interest, save in multi-
ples of millions or as new-style marketing hieroglyphics denoting their
social status and spending power, AB, AB1 and so on. The occasional
telephone caller who penetrated the McIntyre House switchboard got
no further than a secretary with an upper-class accent soaked in ennui.
Letters of complaint were ignored, unless their gaucherie or philistinism merited reading aloud, amid more guffaws, at the Ideas Lunch. To
all went the same curt photocopied reply:

Dear———
   I am sorry you did not like our feature on [the Ad-Lib Club, Saigon's Bar Girls, the Bihar Famine, Cooking with Calvados, Understanding the Pre-Raphaelites, Glasgow's Razor Gangs, Wagner's

Women, The Hell That Is Bogotá, Fabergé's Lost Masterpiece, The World's Highest Railway, Abortion Tokyo-style].

Yours sincerely,
Toby Godwin, Editor, Sunday Dispatch Magazine.

Louis was of course no stranger to office politics, and he knew exactly how his problem could be solved. He must strike up the happy working relationship with his Features Editor that was so obvious and natural, even though it had thus far mysteriously refused to kindle. He himself was probably to blame for being too eager and over-friendly, not thinking ideas through sufficiently before firing them off. To attune his thoughts to Bracegirdle's, he spent hours in the Library looking through back issues at features bearing the stamp of the Deputy Editor's modish northernness—"Andy Capp Goes Home"; "Wearside's Mister Big"; "The World of the Whippet." He tried to think of ideas either with a gritty, newsy edge or from the world of camp show business where Evelyn Strachey had scored so many triumphs. But all in vain. Each multi-clause memo he dispatched the thirty feet to Bracegirdle's office came inexorably back, punctured by curt handwritten annotations: "No," "Not for us," "Done it," "Boring," "Think modern." His attempts at friendly overtures to enquire about his three unused pieces were met by the same faintly mystified stare through Michael Caine glasses that caused him first to babble stupidly, then founder in tongue-tied embarrassment.

None of this diminished his admiration—and, paradoxically, his liking—for the debonair figure at the centre of all the Magazine's most vital projects, in ever-changing striped shirts and pastel hipsters, telephoning, telexing, holding meetings (to which Louis was never invited), orating to rapt listeners in his passionate yet mild Geordie accent, pushing aside freshly shampooed hair in that familiar gesture of boyish enthusiasm. He developed almost an obsession with Bracegirdle, piecing together snippets of information about his house in Twickenham, his pretty young wife, Stephanie, his three-year-old son, Ringo, his pet bassett hound, Bogart, his passion for strenuous outdoor sports like hiking and rock-climbing. His glamour in Louis's eyes increased still further with the discovery that he and his red-headed secretary, Venetia, were having an affair and that every Thursday night, under the alibi of "working late," he stayed with her at her flat in Shepherd's Bush. As a result, Venetia's Magazine career was flourishing in a way that threw Louis's failure into even starker relief: she received regular bylines as a researcher in the same type-size as eminent writers and photographers, and latterly had been encouraged by Bracegirdle to try her hand at composing captions, headlines, "standfirsts," even fully-fledged short features. Only too clearly, for those whom Bracegirdle thought worth encouraging the sky was the limit.

Sunday mornings in the pub for Louis were times of yearning shame as he watched his friends, and people all around, studying Sunday Dispatch Magazines containing nothing by him, just as his mother and Aubrey would be doing, not to mention Mike Finnis, Ken Blight and all his old colleagues up on Teesside. His excuses were growing lame and hateful to his own ears: "I've got several things in the pipeline . . . but a colour magazine works so long ahead . . . it takes months for things to work through the system . . ."

Despite the wonderful privilege, freewill and riches of his new job, there were times when he felt almost nostalgic for local newspaper life, where at least you always knew how much you were needed. Sometimes, with unrequited energy at boiling-point, but nothing left to do, he would sit at his desk and type gibberish, just for the sake of feeling occupied. "Now then, the first thing to do I would suggest is one of the following . . . Alternatively, in the reverse case, I can only recommend you to consider . . ."

Jack Shildrick was there of course, one floor above, to lend a sympathetic ear, buoy up his spirits and put things into northern common-sensical proportion. But for Shildrick, too, as hot summer turned to mellow autumn, things had not been going exactly swimmingly.

It was clear that, despite his manifold activities around the paper, he had staked much in personal reputation as well as Lord McIntyre's money on Singapore Charlie Small's solo world-circumnavigation. And not even so devout a supporter as Louis could pretend this was beginning auspiciously. Emerging from the Hamble estuary on August 15th, Singapore Charlie had mistakenly turned right instead of left, quickly sighting the steel-smelting chimneys of Fawley rather than Spithead and the open sea. Extensive megaphone instructions from the accompanying pilot-launch had been needed to turn *Lady Patricia* around and point her in the right general direction for Australia. The daily press had naturally had a field day—"A PROPER CHARLIE!" (Daily Mirror); "WHAT A CHARLIE!" (Daily Sketch); "LEFT FOOT DOWN A BIT!" (Daily Mail).

The story since then had taxed even Shildrick's big-drum editorial gifts to the limit. Finding his way successfully around the Bay of Biscay and into the South Atlantic, Singapore Charlie had been met by unbroken fine weather and almost continuous flat calm. While this boded well for his target of reaching Sydney in 100 days, it did not make his exclusive reports to the Sunday Dispatch very dramatic, or even interesting. The weekly front-page column "signals from a Sea-Dog" that Shildrick had fought to obtain for his protégé was already showing definite signs of strain. Week one had been a diverting enough account of Singapore Charlie's life on board, his navigational observances, his vegetarian cookery, his daily sea-water bath, his solitary feasts of nut cutlets and claret in a pre-war velvet smoking jacket. In week two, he described flying fish, porpoises and a distant school of basking sharks. In week three, he described slipping over on deck and breaking the crown of a front tooth. In week four—significantly demoted to an inside column on page 2—he had little to report, save that an exhausted homing pigeon had flopped down out of nowhere into his arms, and had to be revived with cream crackers and Meux special premium bitter.

Shildrick had turned his office into the voyage's operations centre, installing the short-wave radio by which contact with Singapore Charlie was maintained, and an additional telephone line for the equally constant and pressing task of informing, reassuring and placating Mrs. Angela "Bunty" Small. Though taking down and rewriting the radioed messages was the duty of the Dispatch Newsdesk, Louis's original interview kept him anchored to the story's periphery. He would often drop in to see how things were going and remember that wonderful Friday when he and Shildrick had fielded galleys of his Review front piece, still damp from the composing room.

It was in Shildrick's office that he finally met Dudley Mowforth, the Dispatch's Editor-in-Chief and a figure, if possible, even more surprising and disappointing in the flesh than Evelyn Strachey. Aged about sixty, with chiselled features and a military moustache, he seemed to belong to the thirties or forties far more than the hectic decade his newspaper had so defined and shaped. For all his power and eminence, he appeared withdrawn, even shy, shaking Louis's hand with just the tips of his fingers, then glancing quickly down at his stubby, old-fashioned brogues. How anyone seemingly so devoid of personality could have created the Dispatch's many-hued brilliance was mystifying. Still, this was the man who'd spotted Shildrick's qualities from 200 miles distant, so there had to be something to him.

Another time while Louis was there, an elegant man in his mid-forties strolled through Shildrick's ever-open door. He wore a grey double-breasted suit, a white shirt and a tie whose silly pale pink stripes clearly represented something of the gravest distinction. "Jack," he said in a lazy drawl, "I'm 'fraid I may have to borrow back your man's spot on page one. Jacobson is filing awfully well from the Lusaka conference."

Shildrick looked up from rewriting Singapore Charlie's log with an uncharacteristic harassed sigh.

"You can't," he replied curtly. "Dudley guaranteed that space to me for at least six weeks. We've got a big investment in this story. We've got to sell it as hard as we can."

The visitor chose a cigarette from a silver case, glancing amusedly round at the maps and charts on the walls, the transmitter and microphone on their steel table, the still-unreturned Madame Tussaud's waxwork of James Hanratty.

"Jack," he said with affected kindliness, "I know you're enjoying all this ham radio stuff tremendously. But don't you think we should be using the front for something a bit better than a sort of mid-Atlantic I-Spy Club?"

From the omniscient Margaret Cole, Louis learned this had been James Way, Deputy and Foreign Editor of the Steam Section, and an unsuspected obstacle to Shildrick's supposedly irresistible upward path. "He's always been seen as Dudley Mowforth's heir-apparent, just because of having the perfect credentials . . . you know, Eton, Balliol, the Foreign Office, married to the daughter of a viscount. Apparently he was always against bringing Shildrick down from the North, and does everything he possibly can to make his life difficult. If he gets the paper, as everyone expects him to when Dudley retires, I think your friend might be needing a subscription to World's Press News."

---

Louis arrived back at McIntyre House just before 3 P.M., paying off his cab from the thick clump of £5 notes in his hip pocket. For each of his three previous unused stories as well as "Whither the Sixties Servant?," he had drawn advance expenses of between £50 and £75. Even after clothes-shopping expeditions to Carnaby Street, pub sessions, bistro dinners and taking taxis everywhere, he still carried a cash float of around £100. Drawing his £30 weekly retainer in addition was almost a troublesome chore. He remembered George Harrison saying somewhere the nice thing about nowadays was that people were always pressing fresh amounts of money on you before you'd quite spent what they'd pressed on you last time.

The Magazine, wrapped in post–Ideas Lunch tranquillity, was as hushed and still as some sleepy little town square in old Mexico. With seigneurial largesse, the feast's leftovers—silver platters of dog-eared lettuce and spoiled rice, stumps of French bread, odds and ends of fruit—had been left on a steel cupboard in the main concourse for secretaries and other lower-grade staff to plunder. As usual, the only person visibly at work was Margaret in her pink Nehru dress, mousy hair hooked behind one ear as she typed out a version of some copy whose muddle was too extreme for mere blue-pencilling. Indispensable as she was to the Magazine, she belonged to what Toby Godwin jovially called the "Second Eleven" of ordinary workers, not invited to Ideas Lunches nor allowed expense accounts. At night, when her colleagues went home in company cars, minicabs or taxis, Margaret took the 171 bus back to a bed-sitting room in Finsbury Park. But at least her assiduity left her well-placed whenever crumbs fell thus from the First Eleven's table. Beside her, still untasted, lay a silver-wrapped portion of Camembert, the heel of a baguette, an apple and a banana.

Freya Broadbent was sorting through the Magazine's usual huge daily cache of P.R. handouts, free gifts and engraved, gold-bordered invitation cards. As Chief Researcher her life was a ceaseless social whirl of film previews, theatrical first nights, book-launching parties and meals, receptions and junkets held for the promotion of new products. In the past week alone, she had been entertained to lunch by the directors of Veuve Clicquot champagne, taken by special train to Manchester for the launch of Len Deighton's latest spy thriller and flown to Paris for the inauguration of a range of Dunhill men's toiletries. If ever approached to do any of the mundane background digging and double-checking her office implied, she claimed to be already busy almost beyond endurance.

Louis was no longer sure whether or not he hoped to be seduced by Mrs. Broadbent. At times, her neat behind and attractive musical laugh would rouse him to intense attention under his desk. Then she would arrive in her vicar's wife headscarf, carrying two full shopping bags, and his secret erection would shrivel like a garden slug drenched with beer. She herself was obsessively interested in all branches of sex, discussing "knee tremblers" and "going down on people" with Margaret as loudly and briskly as if they were items on a sale-of-work stall. Though almost forty, she made no bones about taking the Pill (kept in a box marked "pills" so as not to offend her Irish cleaning lady) nor about the modest but memorable niche she occupied in modern English fiction. She was the estranged wife of the novelist Festus Broadbent, who had remained married to her long enough to beget a son, Tarquin, before decamping to a bachelor existence in Morocco. Margaret had pointed Louis to the relevant passage in *Runs Deep the Cam*, volume one of Broadbent's Drumbeat at Dusk trilogy.*

Pushed under the bar of his typewriter was an inter-office memoran-

---

*"Later that night on the towpath near Magdalene, Hodgkin found his manhood vigorously seized by the Girton girl's impatient little fingers. 'I say,' she remarked, 'I hope you don't mind my mentioning it, but your goolies are ice-cold . . .'" Chapter IV, p. 138.

dum. He pulled it out, confident it would not contain toilsome or worrying news. On The Sunday Dispatch Magazine, memos were seldom other than calls to some kind of jollification.

From: God
To: Cedric, Terry, Jessamyn, Evelyn, Val, Jim, Louis

By way of ringing the changes, I am holding an Ideas Breakfast on Tuesday Sept 21st at the Connaught Hotel, Carlos Place, London W.1. David K. has agreed to come along and outline his ideas for the New Eve issue.
I do hope you will be able to join us at 8:45 A.M.

As usual no one asked where he had been, how he was getting on with his piece or when—or, indeed, if—he thought he would finish it. He typed up his notes on Mr. Frederick, omitting the fall of the ear, then did a fresh set of expenses and took them into Jim Deaves's office. A new secretary was there alone, looking rather forlorn behind the steel desk where all expense sheets met. She had long honey-blond hair and a peaky, white-lipped face, ridged by false eyelashes as dense as gummed-on centipedes.

"Hello," Louis said with a condescending smile.

"Morning," she answered respectfully.

"Jim around?"

"He's just popped out to get some cigarettes." Her voice was clear and educated, with just the faintest softening of the r's.

"Would you ask him to sign these for me when he's got a minute?" Louis dropped the three typed sheets into a wire basket, on top of a similar production marked "Freya Broadbent." A random entry caught his eye: "Taxi to Hampstead to look at fossilised fish."

"You're Louis Brennan, aren't you?" the new secretary said as he turned to go.

"Yes."

"You won that competition. I remember your picture in the magazine. And your piece about your grandfather. It was so-o lovely."

Louis looked at her with kindling interest. Her honey hair tumbled round the shoulders of an orange shirt-dress with a long collar. On one wrist she wore a filmy gold chain. He wondered with unaccountable resentment whether it was a present from a boy-friend or fiancé.

"Have they made you a full-time writer here now?" she asked.

"Yes."

"Allowed to do anything you like?"

"Mm-hm."

She frowned in mock balefulness. "Ooh, you are lucky! I'd give anything for a job like that."

Below the desk-rim was an abbreviated hemline and the beginning of slim, smooth legs. He made a lightning switch from aloof maestro to democratic sympathy and understanding. "So you write then, do you?"

She grimaced, wrinkling her snub nose. "I try. Nothing like in your league, though."

"Oh, I don't know," Louis protested, though she was indubitably right. "You might be very good. What kind of things do you do?"

"Stories. Articles. Even the odd poem."

Her legs were definitely nice. Young maestro found it in himself to be kindlier still. "You should bring some of them in. I could look through them for you."

The forlorn black eyes gazed at him in awe. "Would you?"

"Of course."

"I mean, I wouldn't want to presume . . ."

"No, honestly. I'd like to." Looking at her bowed golden head, with the back-combed rise behind its centre parting, Louis suddenly pictured everything about this girl. Her neat little flat. Her tidy wardrobe and well-ordered shelves. Her bedside table and luminous-dial travelling clock. Her neat, well-meant but hopeless little writings, her sweet, humble and blameless little world. To receive her grateful worship for one or two evenings might be just what his bruised ego needed. And when he tired of her, he'd let her down gently.

"Perhaps we could discuss it over a drink," he suggested.

The blackened eyes steadily returned his gaze. "That would be lovely."

"Or dinner?"

"That would be lovelier still."

"I'm sorry . . . I don't even know your name."

"It's Fran," she said. "Fran Dyson."

---

Shildrick's office door, unusually, was shut. Before Louis had time to knock, it was pulled open brusquely from inside. A dully-dressed woman with a sunburned face and a luxuriant crop of short grey hair glanced uninterestedly at him, then said over her shoulder: "So I take it that's your last word on the subject?"

Her voice was genteel-accented Durham, with the frigid clarity of a headmistress or magistrate. Shildrick had appeared beside her in shirt-sleeved royal blue and speaking in a ventriloquial undertone so that his secretary wouldn't hear. "Look, Jean, I'm just sick and tired . . ." Seeing Louis, he checked himself and smiled a little glassily. " 'Ullo there, Poet."

"I'm sorry," Louis said. "I didn't mean to intrude."

"You're not intruding." There was no mistaking the sincerity in Shildrick's words. "I don't think you've ever met my wife, have you? Jean— this is Louis Brennan, who I've been raving so much to you about."

"No . . . How do you do?" Louis proffered a hand, blanking the amazement out of his face. From all that used to be said about Mrs. Shildrick back in Stockton—her job as an educational therapist, her many charitable works, most of all her steadfast refusal to appear with her husband at public functions or even come into the office if she could help it—he had always expected someone on the severe and forbidding side. But never this steel-haired matron who, although not unattractive in a weatherbeaten Katharine Hepburn kind of way, seemed less like wife than mother (or, perhaps more accurately, mother-in-law) to the slim, boyish figure beside her.

"Hello," Jean Shildrick responded without enthusiasm, groping inside a handbag-cum-purse of the same design that Grandma Bassill favoured.

"Hold on a minute, love." Shildrick's manner had returned to its usual quick-thinking composure. "I can phone down for a car to take you . . ."

"Please don't trouble," his wife said curtly.

"But how'll you get there otherwise?"

"I'll manage."

They exchanged a few more words inaudibly in the corridor. Then Shildrick came back into the room and shut the door. Meeting Louis's eye, he blew out his cheeks with an ostentatious "phew." "Not married, are you, Poet?"

"Me? No."

"Stay that way as long as you possibly can. A journalist with a family—I mean a serious journalist, like you are—can only ever hope to be an all-round disappointment. Home too late for the dinner party . . . never there for the kids' school sports or Nativity plays. Take my advice and spare yourself the sight of all those crestfallen faces."

He beckoned Louis across to the black-and-white wall chart of the world's continents and oceans where Singapore Charlie Small's downward progress past Spain and Africa was denoted by a thick arrowed line. Shorter arrows at transverse angles represented the currents which were proving so irritatingly helpful and the trade winds which remained so disappointingly unassertive.

"So . . . day thirty-three, and on course for the Cape of Good Hope, still in perfect sailing weather. Thus far, in this epic voyage of a latter-day Raleigh, the biggest cliffhanger is whether Australian dentists recognise the English National Health. And whether our hero will have enough vitamins to sprinkle on his cornflakes. Better tune in and see what the non-news is today."

He bent to the radio transmitter and twiddled its black central knob, muttering instructions to himself. After a moment, a crackling sound punctuated by Morse pips came over the amplifier. Shildrick sat down at the table and picked up the thumb-operated hand microphone. Louis came and stood listening behind him.

"Dispatch calling *Lady Patricia.* Dispatch calling *Lady Patricia,*" Shildrick repeated in a zombie monotone. "Are you receiving me? Over. Dispatch calling *Lady Patricia.* Are you receiving me? Over."

There was an expansion of the crackling, then a familiar voice became fragmentedly audible. "*Lady Patricia* to Dispatch. Receiving you. Over."

"Charlie!" Shildrick said in his normal tone. "How are things? Over."

"Hello, Jack," Singapore Charlie's voice replied. "You're very faint. I can hardly hear you. Over."

"I'm sorry. I'll talk as loud as I can. Is this any better? Over."

"Sorry. Didn't hear that. Over."

"I said, 'I'll talk as loud as I can,' " Shildrick almost bellowed. "Is this any better? Over?"

"Yes, a little. Over."

"So what's the weather like today? Over."

"Sorry, I didn't get that. Over."

"What's the WEATHER like today? Over."

"Did you say 'the weather'? Over."

"Yes. Over."

"Pretty good. Been sunbathing most of the day. Over."

"How's the tooth? Over."

"Sorry? Over."

"The TOOTH! Over."

"Oh . . . the tooth. Not too bad. I stuck a bit of Polyfilla around it, which seems to be . . . *crackle, crackle* . . . Over."

"You'll just have to lay off the treacle toffee until you can get it seen to in Sydney. Over."

"What? Over."

"I said . . . I said any thoughts yet about this Sunday's column? Over."

"Oh, lumme, no, not really. Not a lot's happened since the last one. Over."

"Have any ships passed you? Over."

"Nope. Over."

"Sighted any interesting marine life? Over."

"Nope. Sorry. Over."

Shildrick gave a visible sigh. "All right, don't worry. The Newsdesk will come on to you later this afternoon to go through your week's . . ."

"Oh, lumme, no!" Singapore Charlie's voice interjected.

"What is it? Charlie? Over."

"Oh, Lord lumme . . ."

"Hello, *Lady Patricia*," Shildrick said urgently. "Are you receiving me? Is anything wrong, *Lady Patricia*? Over."

After a moment, Singapore Charlie's voice re-emerged from the static. ". . . that bloody pigeon! It's done nothing for the past ten days but squitter all over the place. Now it's done it on my bloody chart-table . . . Wish I'd wrung its neck as soon as I set eyes on it . . ."

Shildrick sighed again. "All right, Charlie, we'd best sign off I think. The Newsdesk will call you in about an hour. And we're getting a list of health food shops in Sydney, so you'll not run out of wheat-germ. Good-bye, captain, and good sailing! Dispatch out." He switched off the transmitter and slumped dispiritedly back, tapping his delicate fingers on the steel table top.

"For a moment I thought it was at least a typhoon," Louis said.

"Aye, I know. Or a giant whale, or Lorelei sitting on her rock. But only pigeon-shit on the chart-table. Will that make a gripping lead for Sunday, do you think?"

Shildrick suddenly sat bolt upright and grasped Louis's hand. His touch was surprisingly cold. "Wait a bit! What's that poem about the sailor and the bird? You know . . . 'Water, water everywhere. And not a drop to drink.' "

"You mean *The Rime of the Ancient Mariner?*"

"That's just what we've got here, isn't it? Modern ancient mariner, befriended by feathered orphan of the storm. I know there's been no storm . . . we'll have to scrub round that bit."

"But in the poem the bird's an albatross, not a pigeon. And the mariner kills it and is cursed for ever."

Shildrick batted the objection away. "Same difference. There's nothing the great British newspaper-reading public loves as much as a nice tug-at-the-heartstrings story about an animal . . . or bird. Remember Goldie the eagle in Hyde Park? We've had a Goldie here all the time and I'm that blind, I couldn't see it." He bounded from his chair, once again firing on every cylinder. "Come on, Poet, we're in business! Stop arguing how many angels can dance on a pin-head, and get behind that bloody typewriter!"

With a little thrill Louis sat down in Shildrick's black leather chair at
the proof-littered desk with its ever-burning Anglepoise light. Beneath
him, the chair's high-speed castors trembled like racing skates. He
threaded a sheet of copy paper into the unassuming, overworked portable typewriter.

"Ready?" Shildrick paced to and fro for a moment, rubbing his
hands. "Right, this is it . . . Out of the trackless wastes of the South Atlantic, comma . . ."

"Yup," Louis said, hammering.

". . . a small, comma, bedraggled shape . . ."

" 'Bedraggled shape'?"

"Yep . . . has brought companionship and cheer to a lonely mariner
. . . no, seafarer, one word, point. New para. A lost homing pigeon . . .
hold up, we'd best think of a name for it. One a bit nicer than what
Singapore Charlie's probably been calling it."

"Persephone?" Louis suggested.

Shildrick winced. "Too precious. We want to get kiddies interested as
well, if we can." He stood and reflected, pushing up his glasses to rub
the tail of his left eye. Once again Louis tried but failed to imagine him
leading a home life at all, let alone one with the grey-haired, stoutly
shod woman earlier present.

"All right, got it!" Shildrick said, clapping his hands. "Make that second par begin . . . Singapore Charlie Small . . ."

"Yup."

"And cap P, Pidgy the pigeon . . ."

"Pidgy the pigeon?"

"Aye. No harm in being a bit obvious . . . have become inseparable
shipmates on this epic, round, hyphen, world voyage, comma, reported
exclusively to the Sunday Dispatch . . ."

# 10

Six weeks on, Louis was still occupying the top back bedroom at Grandma Bassill's with its lace-curtained view of back gardens and out-side toilets, and the wardrobe full of Grandad's cast-off false legs. Though Brenda Brown and he often talked desultorily about sharing a flat there always seemed to be too much afoot, like drinking and clothes-buying, to get down to a serious search. It was another reason he felt apart from his new colleagues: they living in smart areas like St. John's Wood, Pimlico or Dulwich, he taking the Northern Line each night, back to the long, windy escalator at Clapham South station and that irredeemably unglamorous view of the Common and South Side. If anyone asked, he said he was staying in "Clap-ham," humorously stressing the second syllable like Peter Sellers's "Bal-ham, Gateway to the South."

Life with Grandma Bassill was never dull, as he realised afresh when he came downstairs on the morning of the Connaught Hotel Ideas Breakfast. His first bewildered thought on opening the kitchen door was that she'd decided to amuse him with an impersonation of the Duchess in *Alice in Wonderland* or Marley's Ghost from *A Christmas Carol*. Bal-anced on her vermilion coiffure was a pillar of cotton wool five or six inches high, held in place by a strip of bandage tied in an outsize bow under her chin. The room was in uncharacteristic disarray, with towels and empty cotton-wool packets everywhere, and Grandad in his wheel-chair not yet combed, washed or shaved.

"I've had an accident, Lou," she announced tersely. "Grandad's had to get Nancy down here to see to me. Good job we took in a nurse for a lodger, isn't it?"

"Gran . . . whatever have you been doing?"

"Fell off that little footstool when I was unbolting the scullery door—

straight backwards onto me 'ead. I must have put it on the slippery lino, I suppose, instead of the mat."

No hint of this early-morning drama had reached Louis at the top of the house. Grandad's face, still aghast above a buttoned pyjama collar, gave some inkling of what he had slept through.

"Are you serious? You fell backwards off a stool! Onto your head!"

For answer, she ducked the cotton-wool pylon, showing him the crust of red at its base. Grandad sighed dazedly, combing his forehead with tremulous fingers. "I'm always telling her, make sure it's on the mat, 'cos if it's on that shiny parquet, it'll run away from under you. Same as I used to tell her not to stand stepladders in the bath if there's ice on the bottom. But will she ever listen?"

"I told you when you married me—I was born rash," his spouse retorted. "I can't 'elp it. It's the way me mother put me 'at on."

Louis put an arm around her, aghast but also fighting an urge to smile. "You know, you really must take more care . . ."

She shook him off briskly. "Oh, rats! I'm all right."

"I've told her, she's being too flippant about it," Grandad said. "A purler like that . . . she'd only got to hit herself on the base of the skull . . ."

"Oh, do stop goin' on about bases of blooming skulls, Dad," Grandma snapped. "It's probably done me good. Got rid of some of my mad blood."

<hr />

The Connaught Hotel's vestibule was small and intricately wood-panelled like the cosier type of Tudor palace. As Louis came up the steps from the revolving door, Toby Godwin was checking in a briefcase at the cloakroom counter. Beside him, talking volubly, stood a brown-suited, yellow-shirted man of almost identical dodgem-car girth. But whereas Godwin was greying and straggly, the stranger was dark and straggly with fiercely staring brown eyes and a short but voluminous black beard. He looked somewhat like an overfed pirate and more than somewhat like Bluto, the malevolent giant in the Popeye cartoons.

"Hullo, dear boy," Godwin's voice boomed through the 8:30 quiet. "Punctual to the minute, as always. I hope you're good and hungry, as the brekker here is absolutely first-rate. By the way, I don't think you've met David Kausman yet, have you? David is our Fine Arts Editor and consultant on diverse topics—how should I encompass them, dear boy? Everything from Magritte to Merseybeat, hooh hooh hooh!"

The black-bearded man glanced at Louis without interest, then resumed what he had been saying. His voice was no Bluto boom, but as grave and exquisitely modulated as that of an archdeacon in a pulpit. "Notice how the whole thing is made up of conditionals, 'I *may* go out tomorrow, *if* I can borrow a coat to wear . . .' And the shivering pathos of that central image . . . Simon Smith and his dancing bear . . . It must represent the ultimate point of nihilism in a pop lyric . . .''

The Ideas Breakfast got off to a bumpy start. While not turning a hair at Louis's scarlet polo-neck or Evelyn Strachey's short-sleeved Aertex shirt, the Connaught refused to allow Jessamyn O'Shaughnessy's pale blue trouser-suit into its dining room.

"Are you joking?" she exploded. "Chanel hasn't even shown this in London yet."

"I'm so sorry, madame," the Italian maître d' murmured. "It's the rule of the management. Ladies are asked to wear skirts."

"Right!" Jessamyn thrust her bag into Louis's arms, unflapped her white belt and stepped neatly out of the suit's wide-cut bellbottoms. Its remaining tunic, though barely covering the dark summit of her tights, was beyond doubt technically describable as a skirt. "OK now?" she demanded. The dazed maître d' opened his mouth, closed it again, then sighed and ticked their reservation.

Chuckling, Godwin led the way through the panelled dining room to a round table with an outsize bowl of pink hyacinths in the centre. Nearby stood a special private buffet bearing a row of engraved silver chafing dishes, assorted cereals, bowls of prunes, baskets of rolls and croissants, peaches and fresh figs. Waiters moved forward to greet them, offering trays of Bucks Fizz and Black Velvet.

"Now . . . dig in, boys and girls. Here's scrambled eggs, fried eggs, poached eggs, boiled eggs . . . bacon, mushrooms, kidney, sausage . . . and is this Cumberland sausage, waiter? Excellent! There's porridge with fresh cream if anyone would like it. Kippers. Ah, and kedgeree . . . otherwise it wouldn't be the Connaught, would it. Hooh hooh! Evelyn, dear boy, don't hang back. What can I tempt you to?"

Strachey surveyed the chafing munificence, then fluttered his hands indecisively. "I think I just want an Oolong tea and a yoghurt."

At the buffet Louis found himself next to the brown-suited bulk of David Kausman, now talking intensely to Val Lewis between feeding his black beard lumps of torn-apart croissant. After taking scrambled eggs, Louis helpfully turned the spoon round to Kausman, who grabbed it up without acknowledgement. ". . . It was originally a truth serum. Used by the Americans on prisoners in the Korean War. Now every hip kid at Berkeley is taking it—'turning on,' they call it. You can see the same graffiti all over the campus, 'Turn On, Tune In, Drop Out . . .' "

Toby Godwin settled down contentedly behind a plate tiered with egg, bacon, mushroom, sausage, kidney and sauté potato. On his right, a waiter poured coffee; on his left hovered one with a bottle of Veuve Clicquot.

"May I say on behalf of you all what a pleasure it is to have David here back from his summer in New England academe and, I can vouch, raring to go on all sorts of wondrous projects for the winter. You remember we had the idea of a special issue entitled The New Eve for one of the hundred-and-twenty-eight-pagers the ad boys need us to fill during November? Well, since Terry B. will be busy on 'What Is Scotland?' and Jessamyn has two autumn fashion supplements to fill, I've asked David to think how it might be put together. The floor is all yours, dear boy."

Kausman pushed aside a barely tasted plate of eggs, lit a flat yellow cigarette and drew on it deeply.

"How has the female form evolved in twenty thousand years?" he reflected in his precise, ecclesiastical voice. "Looking down the sweep of history from the Cycladic fertility goddess to Twiggy, what has changed—and what remained unchanged? Today, the perfect female form is straight up and down. But in the Middle Ages, a large abdomen was the sine qua non of female allure. Or take the breast. The Two Venuses of Tamrit, one of the masterpieces of North African cave art, shows us that prehistoric man preferred the breast to be conical and pendulous. Compare that with the cantilevered Regency bawd . . . the whaleboned Victorian lady . . . Jayne Mansfield . . ."

"Can you see it, Cedric?" Godwin asked a little anxiously.

Scurr gave an uncharacteristic decisive nod. "Historical guff over a few mixed spreads. Plenty of pendulous, comical tits."

"I think David said 'conical.' "

"Whatever," Scurr shrugged. "The cover could be a bit of a problem, though."

Kausman glanced round at him without enthusiasm. "There are infinite possibilities in art. Think of Rubens, Goya, Giorgione, Ingres, Lautrec, Augustus John, Picasso, Bonnard, Edward Hopper, the Surrealists . . ."

"We had a Goya as a cover for 'The Curse Through the Ages,' " Val Lewis objected.

Terry Bracegirdle sat forward, sweeping the boyish quiff off his forehead with a multi-green-striped cuff. "Ah doan't think we should get too bogged down with the past," he said. "Let's think modern. Surely we should have a spread of the heavenly bodies of 'sixty-six. Raquel Welch . . . Julie Ege . . . Ursula Andress . . ."

"But it's about manipulation, too, isn't it?" Jessamyn said. "How we poor birds have had to shrink or swell up according to what you boys fancy at the time. There should be an element of that."

"So if the manipulators of the past were the Rubenses and the Goyas, who are the manipulators of today?" Godwin asked.

"Clothes designers," Jessamyn replied. "Fashion editors . . . photographers."

"Hey, I know what would be smashing," Bracegirdle said. "Get the same dolly-bird shot by three different photographers . . . three different fantasies in one heavenly silhouette."

"Who would we use?" Val Lewis asked.

"I don't know . . . Shrimpton? Donyale Luna?"

Sensing no advantage for him in the discussion, Louis got up unobtrusively to replenish his plate at the buffet. As he squeezed behind Kausman's chair, his felt his free hand suddenly gripped. "One thing I do insist," Kausman said. "This issue has got to have something in it written by Louis Brennan."

He turned and gave Louis what in other circumstances would have seemed a furiously hostile glare. "That piece of yours about your grandfather made me laugh so much, I almost shit myself."

---

"How would I describe David Kausman?" Margaret studied the brown suit that was distantly visible in Toby Godwin's office, striding up and down in impassioned oration. "As a blessed genius. And a bloody menace. Wouldn't you say so, Freya?"

"Yes, I think that's fair comment," Mrs. Broadbent nodded. "There are some times when you want to kiss him and others when you want to wrap him in newspaper and flush him down the loo."

"If he wanted, he could be this country's leading modern art critic," Margaret said. "There's no one big in that world he doesn't know. He goes and stays with Chagall in Provence . . . drinks with Francis Bacon and Lucian Freud at the Colony. He practically lived with Hockney in the States this past summer. One day, if you're lucky, he may invite you back to his house in Putney. The Picassos, Bonnards and Legers will make you fall over."

"He's a Renaissance man, really," Mrs. Broadbent said. "I always picture him in some sixteenth-century Florentine palazzo, enfolding innocent young girls inside his cloak."

"He's the most extraordinary compendium of useless and arcane information," Margaret said. "Doesn't matter what you want to know, David can always tell you. The names of the England Test team of 1929 . . . the arrangement of oars on a Roman trireme . . . the Uruguayan electoral system . . . how to drive from Greenwich Village to Central Park in New York . . ."

"Is he a good writer?" Louis asked.

"Impeccable," Margaret said, "but so agonisingly slow, his publishers call him the Stone Cutter. He's supposed to have been writing the definitive book on Matisse for about the past fifteen years. God tells the story of having lunch with him at the Terrazza one day, when David suddenly went white and dived underneath the table. 'That's my publisher over there,' he said. 'I'm terrified he's going to make me give back the advance.' "

"He's broken even God's record for coming back late from lunch," Mrs. Broadbent said. "Six-fifteen wasn't it one day, Mags?"

"God's line about him was the best of all. 'The price of Kausman is eternal vigilance.' "

Kausman had by now left Godwin's office and was approaching down the concourse on scuffed and squeaky desert boots, arguing with a perplexed-looking Jim Deaves. ". . . David, I love you dearly," Deaves protested as they came into earshot, "but even our accounts people will do their conkers over this. You were supposed to fly direct . . . London–Paris–London."

"Is it my fault that the Magazine pressed me into service when I was supposed to be hanging the Lowry exhibition?" Kausman's voice had the sorrowful dignity of an early Christian martyr.

"Be that as it may, David. I can't see how we can justify a first-class air-ticket from London to Paris via Chicago . . ."

Kausman stopped abruptly and hoisted his brown-and-yellow immensity onto the edge of Louis's desk. "For the New Eve issue I'd like you to go and talk to some leading fashion designers," he said. "Ask them what kind of shape they picture when they first sit down with their charcoal. You should definitely see Mary Quant at Bazaar . . . and Barbara Hulanicki of Biba. I know both of them quite well. I'll tell them to expect your call."

"Right." Louis reached thankfully for a telephone directory. Kausman turned to Mrs. Broadbent, in front of whom lay a toppling pile of ancient Library envelopes. "Are you available to do some research for me on this?" he asked.

She looked up with the alarm of a runaway convict in the bayous who hears bloodhounds baying. "Not anything very long-term, David. I'm going to be immersed in a major project of my own for the next few weeks."

"What project?" Kausman demanded.

"It's fascinating, actually. Did you know that, when General de

Gaulle fled from France in 1940, he didn't go straight to London to or-
ganise the Free French? For a few months, he and his wife lived in a
place called Petts Wood, down in Kent. God's agreed that I can do a
day-by-day reconstruction of their life there."

Kausman appeared not to have heard her. "I want to include a
spread on Eve as the essential image of womanhood. Could you ring a
few leading historians—Alan Taylor, Hugh Trevor-Roper at Oxford—
and ask them what they think Eve looked like? You can offer them up to
forty guineas per quote."

As Louis wrote down Biba's telephone number in Kensington
Church Street, Gilda from the Art Department draped another freshly
pasted-down layout sheet on Margaret's desk. She was as usual sleekly
smart in her Black Watch tartan minidress and heavy buckled shoes.
But something in the face under the dark fringe suggested caution,
even apprehensiveness, as if she felt a little scared of all the leg she was
showing. "Here's the colour spread for 'Death in a Saigon Street,' " she
said. "I'll start on the mono pages this afternoon."

David Kausman stared after her, bearded mouth agape. "Who's
that?"

Margaret glanced round, puzzled. "You mean Cedric's assistant?"

"She's exactly what we need for the New Eve issue. Pretty but not too
pretty. The archetypal average dolly-bird. A blank canvas for men to
write their dreams on. That uptight, slightly haunted look is perfect!"

He continued to gaze in fascination as Gilda climbed back on her
stool, pulled down her miniskirt and began ruling lines on a new layout
sheet. From afar, her voice could be heard diffidently humming Bob
Dylan's "I Want You."

"It should be the centrepiece of the whole thing . . . the same girl shot
by three photographers, each as a different fantasy object. I'll get Bailey
to put her in Victorian crinolines . . . Terry Donovan to do her as a Rossetti wood nymph . . . Patrick Prince to dress her up as a whorehouse
madame . . ."

"David, you must be joking!" Margaret protested.

"What do you mean?"

"She's as pure as the driven snow."

"This is nothing filthy," Kausman added with dignity. "It's a serious
anthropological study."

"It's sexy pictures dressed up as a serious anthropological study,"
Margaret corrected. "And Gilda's far too shy and proper to let her picture appear in the Mag, let alone strip off for it. She's a devout Christian
and a Sunday School teacher. She spends her spare time organising
tea-parties for under-eights. You'd never persuade her."

---

"I've looked at one or two places in South Ken and Earl's Court," Brenda Brown's voice shouted against the thunder of the Four Tops' "Reach Out, I'll Be There." "But they were mostly sink-holes of filth, with tins of bearded mandarin oranges or bloodsoaked socks left under the bed. Either that or a quite extortionate sum was being demanded for fixtures and fittings."

"Mm," Louis replied abstractedly from inside the Lord John changing cubicle. He stuffed his mauve shirt into the bottle-green hipsters and picked up a corduroy jacket, pale brown and double-breasted, with military-style epaulets and lapels whose broad lower points curved slightly upward. Thanks to the flimsiness of the corduroy, they also curled slightly outward. Two of the eight frontal buttons already seemed less than secure. But in return for looking like Paul McCartney on the *Rubber Soul* album, he could live with that.

". . . Of course, it would help if we knew exactly where we wanted to live," Brenda shouted—now over Georgie Fame singing "Getaway." "Then we could buy the Evening Standard as soon as it comes out, and be round on the doorstep like a dose of shakes."

Smoothing his sweaty fringe across his forehead, Louis stepped out through the cubicle's frontier saloon-style swing doors. Brenda, bald and pinstripily immaculate, was flicking through a revolving rack of short cloaks hitherto favoured only by stage magicians and troopers of the Household Cavalry. Nearby, oblivious of their presence, a teenage assistant dressed like an extra from *The Pirates of Penzance* sang and danced with the music blasting from speakers in the eggbox grotto walls.

Louis struggled through the racks of Beau Brummel collars and chained and padlocked suede coats to a vestigial strip of mirror. "Well? What do you think?"

"Quite nice." Brenda brushed at the jacket and pressed its curling lapels flat with his thumbs. "Especially if you're just going to join the relief column to Mafeking."

"Looks great on you," the assistant said, pirouetting past.

"The trousers are much too long, of course."

"Get those altered for you in ten minutes."

The jacket and trousers, a custard-coloured shirt with a thin black check and a broad purple kipper tie came to £19.17s. Louis paid for them with the clump of Sunday Dispatch five-pound notes from his hip pocket. The trousers came back from the alterations tailor in eight minutes, one bell-bottom leg lopped noticeably higher than the other. But he could live with that.

In Great Marlborough Street, one of the new traffic wardens was diffidently slipping a parking summons under the wipers of the M.G.B.
"Piss off," Brenda shouted. "You neo-Fascist ex-army bastard!" He
threw away the summons, vaulted behind the wheel and put on a black
velour hat with a massively wide and bendy brim. "Where to now? Portobello Road to buy a second-hand nose irrigation set?"

"I can't. I've got to interview the woman who runs the Biba boutique."

With a reproachful "tut" Brenda leaned over and flattened the lapels
of the new cord battledress jacket, which were starting to curl upwards
again like crusts on a British Railways sandwich. "See you at Finch's
afterwards then."

Louis shook his head with a sigh. "In a rash moment, I promised this
little secretary from the office I'd take her out to dinner and advise her
about getting into journalism. But I really don't know if I can face it
after all."

"Where are you meeting her?" Brenda asked.

"Bistro du Vin in Fulham Road."

"The thing to do, I suggest, is get there a bit late and have a shufty at
her from the door. If it's no go, see you at about nine in Finch's back
bar."

---

"Come on. You can't put it off any longer. Let's have a read."

Fran Dyson winced as if in physical pain. "Honestly . . . you don't
have to . . ."

Louis held out a hand in mock severity. "Come on. Give."

With a sigh, she unzipped the shoulder-bag on the bench beside her
and passed an orange cardboard folder around the guttering candle
flame. He peered at the first of the typewritten sheets inside—a poem
headed "Solitude."

                    I am alone . . .

"You don't have to tell me. I know it's terrible."

"Ssh, and let me read."

                    Far off I see
                    A distant factory chimney
                    Belching red
                    I am alone . . .

While affecting to study the lines with the objective dedication of a
G.C.E. examiner, Louis stole another covert look at Fran. This evening

she was immeasurably more attractive than he remembered her in the office, her honey-coloured hair tumbling onto the shoulders of a pink dress, vaguely fluffy in texture, its hem barely enough to form a lap under the table-rim. Then there was the contrast between the Cleopatra-cruel black of her eyes and her air of forlornness and pessimism. She seemed pathetically grateful for being taken out by him, perhaps even sensing the quick once-over she'd been given before he joined her at the table.

> ... Outside my room
> The street-lamp dies with a
> Click
> I am alone ...

He nodded as if quietly moved, and turned to a two-page short story apparently about Eskimos:

> "How shall I find this thing?" Erenek asked the old man.
> "It lies many leagues distant," the sage replied. "And there is much of danger on the ice ..."

There were further short stories, all unfinished, mainly about knights setting forth on heroic quests in mythical kingdoms. Some, Louis noticed, had been written on the same office typewriter that produced Jim Deaves's periodic pleas for expenses over £100 to be accompanied by at least one receipt. An attempt at a more conventional epic style, which petered out after three pages, began "My mother died before I was born ..."

"You don't have to tell me," Fran said. "They're hopeless, aren't they?"

She smiled, showing tiny dimples in her chin and both cheeks that made the pale, sad face suddenly look almost diabolically mischievous. For some reason it made Louis think how miraculously smooth the skin at the very top of her thighs must be, and imagine his hand exploring there.

"Not at all," he said fervently. "I find them really ... interesting ..."

The dimples vanished as she stared at him in something like wonderment. "Do you?"

"Yes. They've got ... life ... good expression ... a nice sense of humour. That Eskimo one looks particularly good."

The black centipede eyes seemed to mist over with relief and gratitude. "You mean they're not completely hopeless?"

"Not at all. You shouldn't run yourself down."

"Thank you so much. You've no idea what that means, coming from someone like you."

"And are you alone?" His words were engulfed by a bray of laughter from the table a few inches to their left.

"Sorry?"

"Are you alone? Like your poem said."

She lit a Rothmans Kingsize with one of the new French disposable lighters, and inhaled in a world-weary way. "I've been alone. Growing up with masses of people around you doesn't necessarily mean you aren't lonely. In fact, it's sometimes possible to be lonely in the midst of a crowd."

"Of course." He nodded wisely, starting to frame a speech about his own essential loneliness, prodigious talents and eminence notwithstanding. But she carried straight on, picking shards of wax from the candle with tapering, well-kept fingers. "Even as a little girl, I used to feel I didn't belong to this world, do you know what I mean? I had to go to quiet places and be by myself. They used to say, 'Francesca, come to your party, come and be with your friends.' I could never make them understand that I wasn't being funny. I just needed that solitude . . ."

When they'd started dinner, Louis had been lolling back in his seat with an air of slightly abstracted kindliness. But in the past two hours, as Fran's allure had grown, he'd found himself pulled further and further forward, his head nodding like a dog on the rear ledge of a Ford Cortina. His face was beginning to ache slightly from its rictus of sympathetic understanding.

"So," he found himself continuing, "how did you come to be working for Jim Deaves?"

Fran shrugged, blowing smoke directly into his face. "It was on the noticeboard at college. I thought 'God, Sunday Dispatch, better get in there. Even if it's just as a grotty little secretary, typing memos and filing expense sheets.' "

"But you want to move on to do . . . what? Research? Writing?"

"Anything." The centipede eyes narrowed balefully. "I bet I could be at least as good as that Jessamyn O'Shaughnessy. I mean, how does she get to be Fashion Editor looking the dog's breakfast she does?"

Louis nodded feelingly. He had often wondered much the same.

"She can't spell, let alone write. And Jesus, she gets away with murder. You should have seen the expenses she put in after that fashion shoot in Morocco. 'Coca-Cola for brushing my teeth . . . Money to make beggars to go away.' They all spend like maniacs, you know."

"I know."

"Jim showed me the Overmatter file yesterday—you know, the pieces they've commissioned but know they'll never use. Toby Godwin's got dozens in there. Do you know how much Jim thinks the whole lot are worth? A hundred thousand quid!"

Overmatter was a subject Louis had no desire to think about. He picked up the menu, which was of stain-resistant plastic and decorated with humorous quasi-Gallic drawings. A fat woman with breasts spilling out of her bodice was captioned 'Courgettes farcies.'

"Would you like something else?"

Fran shook her head, grinding out her half-smoked cigarette in the liquid candle grease.

"No, really. I'm full."

"No trifle?"

"No."

"Profiteroles?"

"Uh-uh. Just coffee."

"And you must have a brandy as well."

The coffee and brandy were a perfect way of tilting the conversational balance back to his own brilliance and kindliness. He made a big thing of pouring cream into her coffee over an inverted spoon, just as in the best colour-supplement ads. As he savoured the (non-existent) bouquet from his small balloon glass, an even better wheeze occurred to Louis. Before Fran could sip, he took her glass and held one side of it, then the other, against the candle flame that still guttered stubbornly between them. He cradled the glass lingeringly between both hands— conveying how nothing less than perfection satisfied him—then handed it back to her. For understated suavity, James Bond could hardly have done better.

He raised his own glass. "I'd just like to say one thing."

The black centipedes were fixed back on him with irreproachably worshipful attention.

"Those pieces of yours are really . . . really interesting. And I'm sure you're going to make it."

She hung her head. "Really?"

"Yep." Sensing the moment to be just right, he reached across and stroked her downcast right cheek. "Really. You've got to believe in yourself. Say to yourself, 'There's nothing I can't do if I really want to.' "

"You're so nice to me." She raised her face slowly and demurely, making Louis's heart turn over, although not in quite the way that was intended. The cheek he'd been fondling now bore a long, dark smear. Instinctively glancing at his hands, he saw that both were blackened from the soot he'd inadvertently streaked round her brandy glass while warming it at the candle flame. In some things, James Bond still clearly had the edge.

---

Outside, the Earl's Court Road was nearly as busy at midnight as at midday. An open Mini-Moke zoomed among the black taxis, packed with floppy-hatted figures, female and male. From the Australian buzz in a nearby pub came a twangle of Indian sitars and John Lennon's voice, lazily contemptuous: "Turn off your mind, relax and float downstream . . ."

The horror had passed without a word being said on either side. Fran's black mark had disappeared during an absence in the Ladies', giving Louis time to inspect his own slightly sooty nose in a knife-blade and scrub it frenziedly clean with the spit-wetted end of his kipper tie. Subsequent masterful behaviour with the £3.16s bill had brought his opinion of himself almost back to par.

As they walked along Scarsdale Villas towards the lights of St. Mary Abbots Hospital, he racked his brain for some witty or insightful comment about English literature, journalism, food, the Beatles or the prevalence of Australians in London. All he could think was how desperately he didn't want to end the evening, find his Mini and go back over Chelsea Bridge and through Battersea to where Grandad's legs would now be standing neatly by the pre-war fridge and Grandma would be seated at the kitchen table in a blue flannelette dressing-gown, tying up her scarlet coiffure in spills of the Evening News.

"This is me," Fran said, suddenly stopping and turning to him. They had reached a peeling portico entrance with black-and-white-checkered steps. Beside the glass-paned front door was a clotted mass of entry buzzers and name-cards, printed and handwritten.

To his excitement, she did not attempt to say good-night here, but groped in her bag, found a key and pushed open the front door as if she expected him to follow. The cavernous front hall had a polished side table with a mass of letters and circulars jumbled on it. Fran picked up an envelope, glanced at it and stuffed it into a coat pocket. He felt a surge of frantic jealousy. Who was having the effrontery to write to her?

"I'm afraid there's no lift," she said.

Louis followed her up a staircase, along a passage, then up a second staircase. "Where are you . . . exactly?"

"Right at the top, I'm afraid."

He had taken no regular exercise since leaving school, five years before. In addition, he had spent the last few months on an unbroken diet of cream, red wine, pastry, garlic, Havana cigars, lemon tea and chocolate. By the third staircase his mouth tasted of rotting cabbage leaves and his heart was wagging as if loose from its moorings under his close-fitted shirt.

"Are you OK?" Fran asked over her shoulder.

Somehow Louis smothered the frantic wheezes of an okapi pursued by a pack of cheetah. "Mm-hm."

"Not much further now."

On the fifth flight, thank God, the balustrade of the topmost hallway came into view. It had a mass of dresses, skirts and coats thrown over it, like jumble put out for collection. As they climbed nearer, he noticed the orange shirt-dress she'd been wearing when he first spoke to her. He realised this wasn't jumble but her wardrobe, in both senses of the word.

The top of the house was a flat without the benefit of its own front door. From the landing extended a narrow hall with closed doors all along it.

"This is all very nice," Louis said insincerely. "Do you have it to yourself?"

"No."

"Who do you share with?"

"Just some friends," she said with that barely perceptible softening of the r. He divined that it would be bad form to enquire any further.

She threw open the first door down the hall, revealing a sitting room whose anonymous drabness proclaimed it to be shared by several people, all of whom cared equally little about it. On one wall, above a saggy brown sofa, hung an immense pink paper dragonfly. The only light came from the large globe of white paper overhead. "Do sit down, won't you?" she said formally.

He subsided into the sofa whose pile bore luminous greasy highlights along its back and arms. She took the shallow-backed armchair opposite, pulling her fluffy pink dress to within about eight inches of her knees.

"Would you like another coffee?"

"No, really, thanks."

"Whew, that's a relief. Because I'd rather not go into the kitchen just at present."

"Why?"

"I'm a domestic slut, that's why."

Deliberately Louis got up, crossed and knelt down next to her. The black centipedes watched in amusement as his face neared hers, closing just before the moment of contact. Despite the garlic in their food, the wine, coffee and cigarettes, her mouth felt as cool and transparent as mist. After a moment, he sat back on his boot-heels and smiled, still with a touch of seigneurial kindness.

"I'd like to see you again. Would that be a good idea, do you think?"

"You'll see me tomorrow."

"I don't mean there. I mean . . . you know what I mean."

She stretched out a hand to flatten a lapel on his new corduroy battledress jacket that was curling upward again. "Yes," she said shyly.

"Yes, I can see you again? Or yes, you know what I mean?"

In a single, economical movement, he had pushed her—or was it that she pulled him?—back into the armchair. The first shy melting probe expanded to a full-dress mouth struggler, with tongues jostling for precedence and finally even teeth pressing together. He could see nothing but her closed eyelids, whose blackness was streaked with silvery green like the wings of flies. His left hand disbelievingly traced a bra-line under the fluffy pink dress. After a moment he took his mouth away, half fearful that she'd refuse his kiss next time. But she didn't. And she didn't, and didn't.

With a disbelieving gasp, he nuzzled her forehead near the seam of honey hair, then buried his face in an adjacent cushion, inhaling a long-stored aroma of cosmetics and cooking.

"Do you mind if I make a confession?" her voice said, rather briskly in his ear.

"What?"

"It's rather unromantic."

"That's OK."

"I'm starving!"

He sat back on his heels again and stared at her. She lay there with the fluffy pink dress hitched up to unimaginable regions, as coolly as if on a poolside sun-bed. The dimply-devilish smile peeped out again. "It's terrible, isn't it?"

"Not at all. I tried to persuade you to have a dessert . . ."

"Shall I tell you what I'd really love now?"

"Crème caramel?" he suggested. "Profiteroles?"

"No, a marmalade sandwich. Made with Robertson's Golden Shred. You know . . . Gollyberry. Only I just can't face going into that kitchen."

The kitchen was immediately across the hall, its light operated by a string just inside the door. After a moment, with a flickering buzz, a neon tube glared into life overhead. Fran had not exaggerated the condition of things. The sink was full of dirty washing-up, evidently dating back several meals; pots and saucepans as well as plates, immersed in water with an iridescent scummy crust. On the blue Formica table stood a mug half-full of congealed tea, an empty shell in a Peter Rabbit eggcup and what Louis at first took to be a dead mouse but was in fact a dehydrated and discoloured teabag still nestling in the spoon that had dunked it.

Opening a wall cupboard on a scene of hellish asymmetry, he found a Sunblest loaf and—after squalid probings among half-used stock cubes and whiskery Ski yoghurts—located the jar of Golden Shred marmalade. The cutout golliwog you could save up for an enamel badge was still stuck to the underside of the lid. It wore cricketing pads and flourished a bat over one shoulder.

Returning after a few minutes, he found the sitting room empty. Fran's black corduroy coat lay where she had dropped it near the clothes-laden banister-rail. Her shoulder-bag, her shoes—low, with gilt bands around the heels—and her fluffy pink minidress formed a trail down the passage. "Where are you?" he called.

"Last door on the right," her voice replied.

"And . . . erm . . . would that, by any chance, be the bedroom?"

"Yes, it is."

"So . . ." May as well have this quite clear, he thought. "You want your marmalade sandwich in the bedroom?"

"Yes. Please."

"All right. Just hold on a moment."

Rapid thinking was called for. Louis now had an erection which, inside his shallow hipster crotch, felt as huge and volatile as the R101 airship; he also was keen to urinate. The hope that erotic excitement might cancel this out was dashed by remembering how much house red, brandy and coffee he'd drunk tonight. Merely thinking about it made the insidious contrary pressure inside the trouser-borne dirigible suddenly mount to bursting-point. He put down the plate containing the marmalade sandwich and pushed open the only possible door. With relief his groping fingers found another string-operated light switch.

The bathroom was, if anything, even worse than the kitchen. A clotted mass of pointed nail varnish bottles, lacquer spray-cans, rusty nail-scissors and denuded emery boards filled the shelf above the basin, overflowing onto the floor around its base. On the rim of a multi-ringed bath stood another mug of cold tea dregs and a safety razor with a switch of hair still clinging to it. In the lavatory pan was a cylindrical white object, the application of which Louis comprehended only vaguely. Almost elegantly slantwise it lay, like some Great War battleship at anchor in a secret fjord.

He lifted the dingy pink plastic seat and tilted it back against the cistern. With a loud clatter it fell forward again. The phenomenon was a common one in households where peeing was not done from a standing posture, and would not have mattered much but for two additional complications. The first was Louis's erection; the second, that tonight, for the very first time, he happened to be wearing the new daringly brief underpants called "Skants" which dispensed with the frontal fly hole he had relied on since going into long trousers. Almost balletic dexterity and coordination were needed to hold the reluctant lavatory seat upright and pull the bursting R101 safely clear of the Skants' tight waistband, at the same time arching backward as far as humanly possible so that its fitful, spasmodic jet would fall into the fjord rather than squirting horizontally at the wall.

"What are you doing?" Fran's voice called with an edge of acerbity.

"Sorry. I'm right with you."

Flourishing the marmalade sandwich like a Connaught waiter, he pushed open the last door along the passage. The room was in darkness. He could faintly distinguish a low-lying bed, and the spread pallor of her hair.

"Gollyberry!" he said, holding out the plate.

"I told you I was a slut, didn't I?" she said.

"You've retired for the night, have you?"

"Mm. I'm shattered."

"And do you want me to join you?"

"If you like."

He walked over to the spread hair, put down the plate on a bedside locker and drew back the sheet. She had put on a long nightdress, the sort grannies used to wear, with embroidery down the front and a circle of lace round its neck.

He took off his jacket, shirt, kipper tie, trousers and socks in virtually a single movement and, wearing only the Skants, slipped in beside her.

"You are a nice person, aren't you?" she said in a small voice, perhaps more accurately described as a wee voice.

"Yes, I think so," he said perfunctorily, moving in. But the manoeuvre, somehow, was not successful. He ended up with her head on his shoulder, her knees clamped tightly together and turned away, his free hand able to reach barely half-way down her thickly-protected back.

"You're not a Bad Man, are you?" she went on, stressing the A. A. Milne–ish capitals.

"No," he sighed, realising that, damn and blast, it was true.

"Just cuddle me then," she murmured. "Be like my big brother."

11

Even for the Magazine, David Kausman's terms of employment were highly unconventional. He worked as Fine Arts Editor only six months of each year, the other six being spent lecturing at American universities, organising international art exhibitions or excavating another sentence or two for his biography of Matisse. Despite his prestige, he had no office nor even desk of his own. Instead, he commandeered one end of Cedric Scurr's Art Department, removed Scurr's blow-ups of Buster Keaton and self-incinerating Cambodian monks, and substituted his own gallery of Walker Evans, Andy Warhol, Turner and Atkinson Grimshaw. He seldom appeared in the office before early afternoon but would frequently still be there at one or two the following morning, to the consternation of McIntyre House's under-exercised security men. Although married, with numerous children, he seemed little encumbered by domesticity and, indeed, was seldom to be seen unaccompanied by a beautiful young girl who was either acting as his temporary, unpaid assistant or writing a thesis about him.

His expense account, even more than Toby Godwin's, was the stuff of legend. He was renowned for going into pernickety detail on one line ("Sellotape from John Lewis, Never Knowingly Undersold, to repair mount of Patrick Procktor print") and on the next lapsing into epic vagueness ("Dinner for Royal Society"). A recurrent usage, often quoted by Jim Deaves, was "Taxi There. And Back." As a writer, he was paid the top word-rate of £70 per thousand, and further lengthened his marble-sculpting composition process by a parsimonious pride in using only the very shortest words. By further unique arrangement with The Sunday Dispatch's ever-obliging cashiers, his earnings were paid directly to a firm of wine merchants in St. James's.

David Kausman was the very last person Louis would have expected to become an ally, encourager and bulwark against the hostility of Bracegirdle, Strachey and Scurr. Indeed, such was Kausman's piratical fierceness and brusqueness, it took some little time to realise he liked and approved of Louis with the same mysterious intensity that others disliked and disapproved of him.

"I've read your piece on the designers," he announced in his arch-deaconly voice the following Monday morning, hoisting his brown-suited bulk on to the corner of Mrs. Broadbent's desk. "And I'm not putting it into the New Eve issue."

Louis's stomach gave the familiar downward tilt. "No?"

"No. It's too good."

"I'm sorry?"

"It's far too good to use for what I intended, which was just a set of quotes illustrating an anthropological thesis." Kausman struck at the first page with a stubby forefinger. "These are wonderfully vivid portraits of Swinging London. Is it really true that Mary Quant's husband cuts her pubic hair into a heart shape?"

"That's what she said."

"And the Barbara Hulanicki sequence is heaven on a tricycle. I'd no idea she had that childhood in Palestine. The story of how her father's death inspired Biba's brown chalk-stripe dress is riveting. I'm going to tell God right now that I'm pulling this from the New Eve scheme, and it must go in on its own, with at least two colour spreads."

Despite the intoxication of the praise, Louis felt his spirits sink. At least the New Eve issue was tied to a date on Cedric Scurr's forward schedule. Better to have something appear, however squeezed and emasculated, than his usual nothing at all. "Couldn't you find space for it?" he pleaded. "I've got so many other pieces waiting around at the moment."

"What pieces?" Kausman demanded.

"One on Professor Tolkien . . ."

"You interviewed Tolkien!"

Louis nodded gloomily, thinking of the manuscript gathering dust somewhere in Bracegirdle's office.

"My students at Yale this summer were demented about *The Lord of the Rings.* They've all renamed their dogs Frodo and Bilbo . . . the campus coffee house is called Gandalf's Garden . . . the new Culture Center, which everyone hates, has 'Another Bit of Mordor' chalked on it. But I haven't seen a half-way decent profile of him yet. Who else have you done?"

"Yoko Ono."

"Ah!" Kausman said.

"Do you know her?"

"More than I'd like. I met her in Greenwich Village, when she was with the John Cage crowd. And I was involved in helping her wrap the Trafalgar Square lions in white last year. Did you know she's been trying to knock off John Lennon?"

"John Lennon!"

"The guy who runs the Indica Gallery, where she shows, is a great friend of mine. Lennon of course, as one can tell, has always been an artist manqué. Apparently they met at her Unfinished Objects exhibition last summer. She got him to pay fifty pounds for a Granny Smith apple, and he was . . . fascinated! But I can't believe the Magazine has pieces like this and is just sitting on them."

"I keep trying to get Terry Bracegirdle to put them in," Louis said.

"Never mind Terry Bracegirdle. Go straight to God."

"I have. But he always says there's this huge shortage of space."

"Shortage of space!" Kausman exclaimed. "There was enough space for that pretentious and self-indulgent profile of Françoise Dorléac that Evelyn Strachey wrote between jerk-offs!"

As the Fine Arts Editor barrelled off on his squeaking desert boots, Mrs. Broadbent leaned over to Margaret Cole with an incredulous smile. "Is it true that David's persuaded Gilda to be his modern Eve?"

Margaret glanced up from her subbing and nodded.

"You're not serious! How on earth did he manage it?" They both looked towards the Art Department where the neat, dark head of Cedric Scurr's assistant could be seen, as usual, studiously bent over photostats and layout sheets.

"Heaven knows," Margaret replied with a shrug. "He was in there talking to her most of the other afternoon, mesmerising her with those great tragic brown eyes of his. By the time he'd finished, the poor girl had a dazed look like a rabbit caught in the headlights of a car."

"It was probably bribery," Mrs. Broadbent said. "I expect he promised to take her to one of Hockney's parties. Or to Paris to have lunch with Magritte."

"We'll never know," Margaret said, "but it seems to have worked a treat. Bailey's already photographed her as a Rossetti wood nymph. And Donovan's renting a room in Soho to do her all in moody black and white à la Bill Brandt. According to Val, the Bailey pictures are wonderful."

"After all, she's a very pretty girl," Mrs. Broadbent conceded. "Modelling for all these top photographers will probably be the making of her."

"That's just what I'm worried about," said Margaret.

Covertly Louis watched Fran Dyson approach down the concourse, distributing a pile of memos from Jim Deaves. She was wearing a pale blue minidress with a matching headband, and the same tumbled-over suede boots as on Saturday. But of the various surprising personae revealed to him then—the relentless solitude-seeker, the writer of medieval romances, the scathing critic of Jessamyn O'Shaughnessy—there was now not the faintest sign. The honey-gold head was once again respectfully bowed. The black centipede eyes looked from right to left, warily shy.

"Thank you," he said with studied neutrality, receiving a memo from her pile.

"That's OK," she replied with what he interpreted as equally deliberate lack of emotion.

"That dress is almost indecent, isn't it?" Margaret commented as Fran moved out of earshot.

"I know," Mrs. Broadbent agreed. "But you have to admit she's got the legs for it. Not a bruise, a lump or horrid blue vein anywhere."

"She's a real little mouse, isn't she? I don't even know her name."

"I do. It's Francesca."

"Oh . . . Francesca!"

"Jim says she's absolutely super at her job. The Overmatter's never been so beautifully organised."

"I wonder why she looks so terribly miserable all the time."

Over at the Picture Desk, Val Lewis was talking to a familiar figure with centre-parted hair, a beaky, sunburned face and pearly-white smile. Since their Singapore Charlie assignment, and its failure to reach the Magazine, Louis had rather dreaded meeting Patrick Prince again. But after finishing his discussion with Val, he hurried over, beaming, accompanied by a man with a head of tight, greying curls and the face of an older, fatter Bob Dylan.

"Hey, hoss! How ya doin'? And . . . hey!" Patrick held out his arms extravagantly to Mrs. Broadbent. "It's that Freya! My fave chick! How you doin', babe?"

"Hallo, Patrick," Mrs. Broadbent said, colouring demurely.

"You haven't met my new assistant." Patrick indicated the curly-haired man. "This is Joe."

"Hi." The new assistant's voice was quietly American.

"Joe's from New York," Patrick said. "You'll never guess what he was until a week ago. Go on, man, tell them."

"I was a cop," said Joe.

"No kidding," Patrick grinned. "He was a New York cop! Now he's into hipsters and snakeskin boots. He reads the *I Ching* . . . smokes charge. This is the way it's all going, man. Turn on, tune in, drop out!"

"I'm really sorry about your pictures of Singapore Charlie," Louis said. "I thought they were terrific. I couldn't understand why they didn't get in."

Patrick waved the apology away. "No sweat. You win some, lose some. Now they've got me on this New Eve caper, whatever the fuck that's supposed to be."

"It's a theme issue, edited by David Kausman. Tracing the evolution of the female form from cave-paintings to Twiggy."

Patrick rolled his eyes at Joe. "Sounds like mothers' day in hell. And who's this Gilda chick?"

"Gilda? Cedric Scurr's assistant?"

"Oh, her! The one who keeps her arms crossed over her tits all the time as if she's afraid she's gonna lose 'em!"

"Are you photographing her, too?" Louis asked.

"Supposed to be, yeah. As my ultimate fantasy." He grinned at Joe. "That one's gonna take some work, eh man?"

"Patrick!" Jim Deaves had appeared at his office door, lighting a fresh cigarette from the butt of his last one. "How very nice to see you."

Patrick stiffened, rolled his eyes at Louis and mimed a heartfelt "Shit!" as Deaves ambled over in a miasma of Senior Service smoke.

"Patrick—I'm extremely sorry to raise what is a distressing subject for everyone. But I'm duty-bound to remind you that, while your cash advances on account of assignment expenses now total . . . what would you estimate they total?"

Patrick shut his eyes in agonised mental arithmetic. "About four grand?" he hazarded.

"Let's say four grand, though I have a dire premonition the amount may be nearer five or even six grand. And what even our infinitely tolerant accounts people are biting their nails to know is this: Might there be a chance of your submitting an account in the foreseeable future?"

"Look, I'm sorry, man," Patrick said. "You know how hard it is when you're lammin' about all over the world . . ."

"I do know how hard it is," Deaves agreed mildly. "So here's what I suggest. Why don't I lend you my secretary for a day or two to go through your receipts and type the whole thing out in nice tabulated columns? Then you can start again with a completely clean sheet."

Patrick sighed and shrugged. "OK, that's cool. As long as she doesn't get in my hair when I'm trying to shoot pictures."

"She won't," Deaves assured him. "She's an extremely quiet and discreet girl, as well as highly capable. Her name is Fran."

"There's the most tremendous power struggle being waged among our friends up on the Steam Section," Toby Godwin chuckled, popping a grape into his mouth. "Poor old Jamie Way is going around in a state of crimson fury . . ."

"Why?" Terry Bracegirdle asked, cutting a deep wedge of Blue Vinney and adding it to the red Leicester and Brie already on his plate.

"Loss of birthright, dear boy. Jamie's spent the last ten years waiting in the wings for Dudley Mowforth either to retire or become Director General of the BBC. But there seems now to be at least a modicum of doubt that he'll just be handed the paper on a plate."

"You're joking." Jessamyn pushed away her figs and cream half-eaten and reached for a Gitane. "Who'd get it if Jamie didn't?"

"Jack Shildrick."

"What?" yelled Jessamyn, Scurr and Bracegirdle together. In his hard upright chair behind Jim Deaves, Louis craned forward, listening eagerly.

Godwin poured himself more port and passed the decanter across his desk. "This lone yachtsman caper of Shildrick's, which we rather hastily brushed aside, is turning out to be the most terrific success."

"But it's so boring!" Evelyn Strachey lamented, cuddling his naked arms.

"Boring or not, dear boy, it's whacking on new readers for the Steam Section—another seventeen thousand this last Sunday when Malay Pete, or whatever his name is, fed the pigeon sherry through an eyedropper. All the dailies are now trying to get in on the act, which they can't since Shildrick has signed Frisco Joe to us exclusively. Lord M. is absolutely cock-a-hoop. There are going to be special new ads and even a TV promotion . . ."

"Tim Mandeville's shown me the roughs," Cedric Scurr interjected. "You've never seen anything so tacky. A picture of a globe, a compass and a baseball cap. And underneath, 'Oceans of excitement each week with The Sunday Dispatch.' "

Godwin looked mystified "Why a baseball cap?"

"It's Singapore Charlie's trademark," Louis said. "Even when he fell over the side trying to do rudder repairs, his baseball cap was still on his head when he came up again."

Evelyn Strachey turned round with contemptuous heavy-lidded eyes. "Thank you so much for telling us," he said in a voice devoid of gratitude.

Godwin chuckled again, snipping the end from a Romeo y Julieta. "Well, he's certainly man of the moment upstairs, is Mighty Jack. And by way of consolation, he's been good enough to send me a note, expounding how he thinks we on the Magazine are getting everything wrong."

"What?" several incredulous voices yelled.

Godwin pulled open a desk drawer and took out a densely typed memorandum covering two clipped-together foolscap pages. At the end, Louis could see the hastily scrawled Christian name that had signed so many heart-lifting communications to him.

"Right, kids, pin back your lug'oles. Here beginneth the *pensées* of Mighty Jack."

Godwin began to read aloud in booming parody of Shildrick's accent: " 'My basic thought is that you're wasting too mooch space on things that the ordinary reader doesn't oonderstand or can't identify with. I think you should spent mooch less time coovering unwearable fashions, remote foreign countries and obskewer Continental film directors, and shift the emphasis to matters of everyday concern to us all . . . home-making, leisure, pets, holidays and health . . .' "

"You're joking!" Jessamyn wailed.

"He's *so* provincial!" Strachey shuddered.

"Ee, by goom!" Scurr muttered in far more effective parody. "Eh, by the 'eck. That's a belter, that is."

Godwin rapidly scanned the memo's numerous remaining paragraphs. "I don't think I need weary us all with any more of this. Suffice it to say that, whatever his strengths in the black-and-white area, Mighty Jack has no more idea what makes a good magazine—to quote Dwight Eisenhower—than a pig knows about Sunday."

"Is there really a chance he may get the paper instead of Jamie?" Jim Deaves asked.

Godwin shook his leonine head. "Anything can happen in this life, dear boy, as you well know. But whatever convulsions for the Steam Section lie ahead, I have our Chairman's assurance that our editorial independence is sacrosanct."

He handed Shildrick's memo to Tessa on her stool. "Angel-girl, be kind enough to compose a detailed, reasoned and vibrantly appreciative answer, of which the underlying sentiment is 'Piss off.' "

———————

"Hello. Jim Deaves's office."

"Hello," Louis said in a nicely judged new mixture of amusement and kindliness.

"Hello." The efficient voice throttled down at once to awestruck softness. Through the partition of Deaves's office he glimpsed the blue band as Fran bent her head. In all fairness, he couldn't keep her on tenterhooks any longer.

"This is just to say again how much I enjoyed the other night."

"Did you?" she murmured.

"Tremendously."

"Thank you."

"And I've been wondering if we can please, please, please do the whole thing all over again?"

"If you like," she almost whispered.

"I was thinking about tomorrow night. After I've finished being a footman."

"Finished being a what?"

"It's for a piece I'm doing on domestic service in the sixties. A man with a false ear is sending me out to be a footman at a society cocktail party."

He felt her smile against his ear.

". . . But that only lasts from six to about eight-thirty. So could we meet and do something afterwards?"

"Oh, Louis, I'd love to," she said, exciting him with this first use of his name. "But I'm still supposed to be helping Patrick Prince sort out his expenses. I'll probably be at his studio till quite late."

"Well, let me pick you up from there. If you're not ready, Patrick won't mind my sitting and waiting for you."

"All right."

"And I promise I won't be wearing a white wig and breeches."

Fran gave a little laugh that was just the right mixture of admiration, indulgence and caress. Really, the whole thing couldn't be going better.

---

He travelled down in the lift with a group of executives from the newspaper's Business Section, all wearing pinstripe suits, smelling of lunchtime gravy and loudly discussing the virtues of United Jockstraps over Consolidated Jam Tarts. At the ground floor, a commissionaire politely stopped them descending into a front lobby bathed in harsh white light. Near the glass doors, a television team were setting up in a confusion of cables, metal cases and arc-lamps. Before the waiting camera, having a microphone threaded through his shirt-front, was Jack Shildrick.

Spotting Louis among the spectators, he jerked his head and mouthed an impatient, "Coom 'ere." A girl in white Courrèges boots stepped forward to flick a powder-puff around his face, which already bore a thick mask of brown make-up.

"Not bad, eh, Poet?" Shildrick murmured as the powder-puff dabbed his hairline. "Main item on BBC News tonight. Reggie Bosanquet and an ITN crew waiting their turn outside . . ." He nodded at a black leather sofa, where a row of men and women sat clutching notebooks and cassette recorders. "The Mail . . . the Standard . . . the Telegraph. Everybody wants Singapore Charlie now and nobody can have him, except through us."

Louis smiled at this typically modest northern use of the royal "we."

"It's a great story. You always knew it was."

"You did your part, writing that marvellous piece for the Review," Shildrick said.

"And Pidgy helped, of course."

"I know. Thank God Singapore Charlie's a vegetarian, or Pidgy mightn't have lived to see the Cape of Good Hope. Anyroad, that was just the bait on the hook. As I'm going to say in a minute, if I can remember my notes, this is a good old-fashioned yarn of pluck and fortitude at a time when the country desperately needs heroes who aren't called John, Paul, George and Ringo. The spirit of Drake and Raleigh lives on in an O.A.P. in a baseball cap."

He gave Louis an exhilarated punch on the upper arm. "We're going to make Lord M. a fortune on syndication, text and pics. Hey, and did I tell you? I've done a wonderful deal with George Weidenfeld for our old salt's memoirs, hardcover and paperback, the Dispatch on one-third royalties. I don't suppose he can write his way out of a wet paper bag, so I'm getting Nick Fenton to ghost it for him."

Before the disappointment had fully hit home, Shildrick was already well-advanced on making it better. "I know you really ought to have been offered the job as you know him already, but I knew you'd understand it was a bit difficult for me politically. The Newsroom had been processing his pieces and, anyway, there's this bit of needle against the Colour Mag on the fifth floor—which I know is silly, but there you go.

"Anyway," he went on hurriedly as the light intensified and the television people began shouting harsh, panic-stricken commands, "ghostwriting's not really your mark, is it? The Cicero column is what we've always agreed you should be doing . . . and that may be in my gift sooner than you think. Hey up, you'd better skedaddle, Poet. I think they're ready for me."

---

"I'm sending you to a cocktail party given by a wonderful couple," Mr. Frederick said, leading the way up a winding staircase into ever more ominously private and unfrequented regions of the house. "He's the Vicomte d'Alvaro-Escasany, head of one of the oldest Spanish champagne houses. She used to be Jonquil Parry, the television personality. Do you remember Crumpet the Cart-horse?"

Both had been household names back in the primeval days of early-fifties television. As a six-year-old, Louis had possessed a string puppet facsimile of the latter and nurtured a preternatural lust for the former.

"Not Jonquil Parry! I used to love her on 'Children's Hour.' "

"Delightful woman," Mr. Frederick murmured. "A friend, I like to think, as well as a valued client." He led the way along a winding passage and threw open the door of a small attic bedroom. "Here we are. Welcome to my abode."

The room was furnished with a single bed, an antique bureau and a dimly burning pink table-lamp. On one wall was an old photograph of butlers, footmen, coachmen, maids and gardeners drawn up in three lines outside a porticoed front door.

"Here are your toggoes." Mr. Frederick unzipped the suit container he was carrying and tenderly laid a footman's braided tail-coat and trousers, a striped waistcoat, white dress-shirt and starched ruff on the bed. "You shouldn't have any problems. It's really no different from putting on an evening suit."

"Thank you," Louis said, slipping off his cord jacket and starting to unloosen his tie. Mr. Frederick, however, still lingered by the door, smiling and fingering a right ear which, for a mercy, seemed securely anchored tonight. "Do give me a shout if you need any help . . . with buttons or anything."

"I will. Thank you."

Left alone, Louis changed clothes at Olympic speed, somehow managing the waistcoat-buckles, even the minuscule hook fastening of the starched ruff, not removing his chocolate-coloured flares but slipping the roomy serge footman's trousers on over them. Putting a hand into one pocket, he discovered a wired champagne cork, several empty pistachio nut shells and an ancient Ritz cracker.

Half an hour later, resplendent and double-trousered, he sat knee to knee with three other footmen and two waitresses in a white van being driven by the butler Mr. Loynes through duskily grand Mayfair streets. Round his feet were cartons of glasses; on his lap he supported a foil-wrapped tray of mixed canapés. The smoked salmon odour recalled Toby Godwin and, by extension, how important tonight was to "Whither the Sixties Servant?," which still had no narrative shape or obvious intro. "A few incurious eyes . . ." he thought. "A few indifferent eyes . . . A few indifferent faces were turned to the plain white Ford . . ."

"Ever done this sort of thing before?" Mr. Loynes asked as the van skirted Grosvenor Square. Outside the vast new American Embassy, a few anti-Vietnam demonstrators stood with placards under the tolerant eye of a solitary policeman.

"I used to work as a waiter in my father's ballroom," Louis replied.

"Ah, you know the drill then."

"Yes, I know the drill."

They pulled up at the rear of a creamy-pillared mansion, and carried cartons and platters in procession into a cavernous kitchen where white boxes of the Vicomte d'Alvaro-Escasany's eponymous champagne stood waist-high on all sides. Mr. Loynes took out a gold-swathed bottle, opened it in three rapid twists, poured a glassful, tasted and gave a faint but eloquent grimace. "OK, all, the sooner we get through this, the sooner we'll all be home and tucked up in bed, I'm not saying who with! Girls, start polishing glasses and setting out nibbles without picking your noses if possible. Lads, follow me."

The house was evidently well-known to Mr. Loynes. He led the way along a stone-floored passage, up a dark staircase and through a baize door into a front hallway with a huge glass chandelier and a long curved staircase. Half-way up it was a column supporting the bright-coloured ceramic torso of a top-hatted, banjo-playing black man.

As Mr. Loynes shepherded Louis and his three colleagues into line, a dyed-blond woman approached, uneasily smoothing down the hips of a floral evening dress. The hawkish profile showed just a trace of she who had excited Louis's six-year-old libido, playing the piano for Crumpet the Cart-horse to do his inept stringy dance.

The transmogrified Vicomtesse d'Alvaro-Escasany glanced cursorily over the footmen, taking a cigarette from a silver box. "Well, they look very beautiful as always, Mr. Loynes."

The butler bowed, exuding servility in a visible pink glow. "So kind, Your Grace."

"I must say I'm a bit nervous. It's the first time we've ever had the Press here."

A shaft of panic transfixed the third footman in the line. Had his subterfuge already been exposed? Had the Observer or Telegraph magazine somehow got wind of his idea and decided to muscle in on it?

"Yes . . . Jennifer of Queen has agreed to drop in," the Vicomtesse added. "So we'll all be in Jennifer's Diary next month, which will be rather super . . ."

Those long summer ordeals in his father's employ on Seaview Pier served Louis well tonight. His post was at the top of the curved staircase, just above the ceramic black minstrel torso. As each new arrival reached the summit, he bowed and offered his silver tray of tall champagne glasses. It was amazing how easily deference and self-abasement came back.

The guests were mainly people of the Vicomtesse's age and theatrical has-been status—women with their hair in wispy topknots and Empire-line minidresses showing mummified cleavages; cross-combed men wearing velvet smoking jackets or silk Nehru coats. From Louis, they passed into a first-floor drawing-room to be greeted by their hostess and the Vicomte, a glazed-bald creature wearing a scarlet ceremonial sash. The staircase continued to an upper landing, where two small children in night clothes could be glimpsed peeping resignedly between the banisters.

Up from the front hall now climbed a stiffly bouffanted woman in almost homicidally brilliant pink—obviously Jennifer of Queen—closely followed by a man of about thirty whom, before respectfully averting his eyes, Louis fancied he recognised.

"Thank you," Jennifer said in a crusty contralto, taking a glass from his tray. The man, however, hesitated, then asked, "Do you think I could possibly have a Scotch?"

The last time Louis had heard that steady, cultured voice it had been at a press conference on ITN News, declaring he would refund every dollar of the Beatles' American concert earnings rather than let them run any risk from those outraged by John Lennon's religious views.

It took much willpower not to stare at the snub face with its short wavy hair and rather shy, uncertain brown eyes. "If you'll just hold on, sir, I'll see if I can get you one."

He went through the drawing-room crowd to the long table where the waitresses came to replenish their canapé plates and Mr. Loynes stood opening and pouring champagne.

"Excuse me, Mr. Loynes . . ."

"Excuse you or squeeze you?"

"Someone's just asked me for a Scotch."

The butler gave a long-suffering sigh. "Oh, yes . . . there's always the odd one or two awkward buggers like that. The best thing when it happens is pretend you don't speak English. Then they nearly always take what you give 'em and like it."

"He knows I speak English. It's Brian Epstein."

Mr. Loynes's expression thawed. "Oh, well, why not?" He reached under the table and produced a bottle of Johnnie Walker. "I always did go a bundle on Cilla Black."

Bearing only the cut-glass tumbler on his tray, Louis sighted Epstein talking to the Vicomtesse and a man dressed like a Salvation Army officer in high-collared one-piece black. He approached and waited respectfully to be noticed.

"Poor Brian," the Vicomtesse was saying. "Whatever will you do?"

"I know!" Epstein agreed with theatrical dolefulness. "Perhaps I'd better go back to school and learn something different."

"Is it definite?" the man in black asked.

"Absolutely. They came to me in a deputation after their Candlestick Park concert and said, that's it, Brian. That's the finish. And I've since had it in writing from both John and Paul . . ." Seeing Louis, he picked up his whisky with a friendly nod.

"What will they do now?" the Vicomtesse asked.

"Well, of course, they won't stop making music. They're doing some things in the studio at the moment that are quite wonderful. But definitely no more tours. I'm signing on the dole, first thing on Monday morning . . ."

As Louis moved on, ears still straining, the man in black flicked a spent match onto the empty silver tray. "Bring me a Scotch, too, will you?" he said.

---

Patrick Prince's studio was a deconsecrated Baptist chapel near Primrose Hill. Though every stained-glass window bloomed with light, Louis had to knock repeatedly at its ironbound Gothic door before being admitted by Joe, the former New York policeman. "Hi," he said amiably, drawing on a loosely rolled green joint.

"I'm here to pick up Fran."

"Sure." Joe stood aside, holding out the joint. "Wanna turn on?"

"Er, no thanks."

Inside, pews, pulpit and altar had been replaced by a white, pine-floored space littered with tripods, umbrellas and silver camera cases. Wooden steps led to a modern gallery with a sleeping-cum-office area where Fran's honey-coloured head was just visible, studiously bent over a desk.

Below, in front of an outsize grey paper screen, Scurr's assistant Gilda sat in a carved wooden chair that might have been looted from sixteenth-century Florence. Her neat black hair was rumpled, her eyes had been elongated by smears of purple; she wore nothing but a khaki shirt with epaulets, sergeant's chevrons and the blue star insignia of the U.S. Army. On the floor beside her was a champagne bottle and a half-empty glass. Patrick, in puff-sleeved yellow shirt and white jeans, knelt before her, Nikon aimed but not firing.

"Aw, come on, babe," he pleaded. "You can do it if you try. Come on now, pussycat . . ." Gilda shrank into the chair's opposite corner, clutching the shirt round her throat as if an Arctic blizzard were blowing.

Beside Louis, Joe inhaled noisily and chuckled. "You know how lawng he's been woiking on her? Tree hours!"

Patrick rose, wiped his brow, took the joint from his assistant and grimaced a welcome at Louis. "Hey, Capitaine. To what do we owe this honneur?"

"I've come to pick up Fran," Louis said.

"She's still upstairs, sortin' out my tangled finances. Just hang out for a bit, OK?"

Patrick jerked his head at the still huddled and shrinking Gilda.

"What are we're gonna do with this bird, eh? At it since half-six, and not even one decent roll shot yet. I keep telling her, this could be the most beautiful experience, you know? Like the poet said, when we break through the paper walls of everyday circumstance and discover our sufficient beauty beneath . . ."

"You can say what you like, Patrick," Gilda replied. "I'm not taking it off."

"Aw come on, don't be like that, flower. Pour her another drink, Jojo? Or have some of this grass, which'll like really blow your mind."

"No, thank you," Gilda said with a shudder. Patrick rolled his eyes and handed the joint to Louis who, after weeks of virtuous refusal, suddenly thought, "Why not?," placed the damp communal end between his lips and took a cautious puff. It felt like inhaling Paxo sage-and-onion stuffing. Since that puff seemed to have no effect, he took another, then another.

"Excuse me, Patrick," a clear voice interrupted, slightly softening the r. Fran had appeared at the gallery balustrade, holding a slip of paper. She was wearing a clerical-looking white blouse fastened at the neck. Patrick raised a hand as if appealing for virginal innocence to be respected.

"Yes, darling?"

Fran, for her part, seemed unconscious of the tableau underneath her. "There's this Diner's Club receipt from the Hilton Hotel, Bangkok, for four hundred dollars. Have you any idea what it might have been for?"

Patrick scratched his head and frowned. "Oh . . . yeah. It was a fashion job for Jessamyn. She wanted the models to have real beggars around them. I had to buy a couple of rickshaws."

"Shall I put it down as 'miscellaneous hospitalities' then?"

"Yeah. Right. Groovy."

"Thank you." She withdrew out of sight again.

"OK," Patrick said, "let's have one last try. Jojo, get some sounds on the go, will you, man? See if that makes us feel any groovier?" Joe went to a silver hi-fi at the wall and put on Wilson Pickett's "Mustang Sally." Louis, feeling suddenly overwhelmed, sank down into a canvas director's chair. It was a feeling far slighter and subtler than drunkenness, as if his senses were toy building bricks, toppling sideways in slow motion.

In this benignly detached frame of mind, he watched Patrick and the former New York policeman both break into the kind of dance as a rule only performed by girl backing groups on *Ready Steady Go*, Patrick in addition staring and pouting like Mick Jagger and unbuttoning his yellow shirt onto a chest as pale and hairless as an oven-ready chicken. "Aw, come on, babe! Live a little! Haven't you seen *Blow-Up*? Come on, Jojo. Let's see how they do it in Vegas!" With his Dylanesque smile, Joe began to unflap the heavy belt of his matelot-striped hipsters. "Get 'em off, Louis!" Patrick urged. "Show her there's nothing wrong . . . we're all beautiful. Let's make it a love-in!"

A disbelieving smile twitched the tight corners of Gilda's mouth. "Yeah!" Patrick cheered, weaving his hands around her and taking the opportunity to tweak the khaki shirt off her left shoulder. But, with a furious hiss of "No!," she pulled it back and shrank inside the chair, crossing her legs tightly enough to crush a Brazil nut.

The record stopped. Patrick gave a deep sigh and laid his Nikon on the floor. "OK, sweetie, you win. Get your drag back on. I'll just have to tell Cedric . . ." He glanced upward, and his voice tailed off.

With a leisurely panning motion, Louis allowed his eyes to join the direction of the others'. Half-way down the pine steps from the gallery, Fran was standing in the attitude of a child roused from sleep by grown-up noise. It took his toppling senses a surprisingly long time to register the detail added to the tumbled honey hair, the waif-white face and centipede-lashed eyes, which was that she was naked.

For what seemed like months, but in reality was probably no more than a couple of weeks, his eyes travelled to her every compass-point. She had slightly square shoulders and breasts which, although not large, were high-set and erect, with nipples covering their whole tips in two thick, strawberry-coloured cones. The flawless concave stomach had a tiny budded navel, the kind that goes out rather than in. With strangely heightened vision, he saw a line of golden fluff running to the dark triangle beneath. Why were those always dark, he wondered, whatever the colouring elsewhere?

The seemingly endless pause was finally broken by Patrick. "Was it another query on the expenses?" he asked.

Fran did not reply. She continued down, lightly but carefully, her bare feet slightly squeaking the polished surface of each step. At the bottom she stopped, flicked her hair down her back, then crossed her arms over her breasts in a vulnerable, almost sacrificial gesture that still did not quite shut away those two warm, moist-looking strawberry cones.

It was as if she was completely alone in the spotlight, staring with shy obliqueness, but also quiet satisfaction, at some private vision on the inside of her half-closed lashes.

Without taking his gaze off her, Patrick dropped to one knee, fingers groping for the Nikon he'd just set down.

"Hold it like that," he murmured. "Don't even breathe."

# 12

Today, Terry Bracegirdle's shirt had broad vertical black, brown and navy-blue stripes, a long collar with the very latest rounded ends, and two sets of two buttons along each mitre cuff. He leaned back in his chair, swept away his boyish quiff and grimaced with the teeth-gritted anguish that Louis's ideas—if it were not Louis's physical presence—always seemed to cause him.

"I doan't think it's for us. Not reelly." The pleasant Geordie voice was almost caressingly regretful. "And anyway, you're not a hundred percent certain it's true, are you?"

Behind him, a claret-coloured four-button jacket was carefully arranged on a polished wooden hanger. Taped beside him on the wall were colour snapshots of wife Stephanie, son Ringo and bassett hound Bogart at home in Twickenham. As usual in this office, Louis found himself blushing and stammering out twice as many words as necessary.

"Epstein definitely said no more tours. Everyone's thought . . . I mean, it's been on the cards since their albums were burned by the Ku Klux Klan in America. But no one's officially . . ."

"A bit of chat overheard at a cocktail party isn't 'officially,' " Bracegirdle interrupted. "And even if it is true, it's not reelly a magazine story."

"Does that matter? They're the biggest thing in pop since Elvis Presley . . . and no one's going to see them on stage any more." Passion loosened the knots around Louis's tongue. "What happens to the four of them now? And to their relationship with Epstein? Lennon's supposed to be getting into avant-garde art . . . McCartney's writing film music . . . Harrison's having sitar lessons from Ravi Shankar. How can they fly off in all these different directions and still . . ."

The Deputy Editor's attention had become distracted by a mark on the front of his maroon kipper tie. He scratched at it with a thumbnail, sucking in air exasperatedly through his teeth.

"Couldn't I at least go and talk to Epstein?" Louis pleaded.

Bracegirdle shook his head commiseratingly. "Sorry. The Beatles have been done to death. For my money there's lots more interestin' things going on in pop at the moment. Like Crispian St. Peters or the Nashville Teens . . ."

He broke off to grin at Cedric Scurr, who had come up silently beside Louis on lace-up rubberised boots. The Art Director's paisley shirt-sleeves were rolled half-way along his ape-hairy forearms, a sign of high aesthetic stimulation. "I've had 'em blown up if you want to come and see," he said.

"How do they look?"

"Pretty good."

Without a further glance at Louis, Bracegirdle rose and tipped his jacket off its hanger. ". . . And she actually works here?"

"Yeah," Scurr replied. "She's Jim's secretary."

"Ah've never even noaticed her . . ."

"No. Nobody has . . ."

Louis followed them across to the Art Department, where a small crowd had already collected around Scurr's place at the long work-bench. Spread out there were half a dozen photographic photostats of Fran as she had walked down Patrick Prince's stairs last night, some full-length, others in close-up.

Bracegirdle scanned the selection with the rosy-faced wonderment of a Bisto Kid scenting a casserole. "Ah've never noaticed her before," he repeated. "Have you, Freya?"

"Yes, of course," Mrs. Broadbent replied crisply.

". . . Have you, Margaret?"

"Only because she always looks so incredibly miserable."

"And what's her name?"

"Fran."

"Fran Dyson."

Scurr pulled aside a three-quarter-length shot in which tumbling hair obscured one side of Fran's downcast face and her crossed arms pillowed the tip-tilted cones in something very like—and something very unlike—virginal modesty.

"Here's our cover."

"Are you kidding?" Jessamyn exclaimed.

"It says everything the issue's supposed to be about . . . The New Eve . . . Bird 'Sixty-six . . ."

"Hey, I've got a great idea for a coverline!" Bracegirdle exulted. "What about, 'Hello, Dolly-bird'?"

Jessamyn studied the print, brushing away an ash smear from her ever-smouldering Gitane. "I'm afraid that in your enthusiasm, you boys are overlooking one major point. Or rather two. These are tits."

"Partially concealed tits," Scurr amended.

"Pristinely innocent tits," Bracegirdle added.

"Whatever . . . they're tits. Are you seriously proposing to show tits in the Sunday Dispatch?"

Scurr shrugged. "We've had them in the Magazine before."

"When?"

"Horst Munzig's pictures of the rain forest pigmies."

"Ah, but they were black tits," Mrs. Broadbent said. "Everyone knows that black tits don't count."

"Aw, come on, Freya, think modern," Bracegirdle urged her, sweeping his quiff off his eyes. "This is what we're all about. Breakin' down the barriers of repression and inhibition. Pacesetters in the new aesthetic."

"You mean making sure a lot of chaps get a nice stiffie on a Sunday morning."

"Aw, doan't be so borin'," Bracegirdle winced.

"What about Bailey's pictures of Gilda?" Val Lewis asked.

"Writeoff," Scurr replied. He gave Gilda, beside him, an unaffectionate chuck under the chin. "There you go, kid. You're off the hook with your Bible class."

"Bailey'll probably come after you with a sawn-off shotgun."

"Take him to lunch at the Mirabelle. Offer him an air-ticket anywhere in the world he wants to go. He needn't even shoot anything if he doesn't want to."

"What do you think God will say?" Jessamyn asked.

Scurr's reply was a sardonic smile and one of his uncannily accurate impersonations: "Absolutely first class, dear boy. Hooh hooh hooh."

The ensuing day passed in a series of small but telling dramas—or, as Mrs. Broadbent called them, "vignettes."

The first occurred when Fran herself emerged from Jim Deaves's office with two coffee mugs, on her hitherto unremarked mid-morning journey to rinse them out in the Ladies'. The effect on the whole concourse was galvanising. Conversations ceased in mid-word, elbows dug into ribs, eyes swivelled round on stalks. She was wearing her orange shirt-dress and looked as shy and uncertain as ever. But something about the lowered black eyes hinted that she was aware of the attention, and not particularly upset by it.

Louis had not spoken to her since before last night's dénouement. When he'd left the studio at midnight, fuddled with champagne and grass, she had still been nude, and seemingly beyond any communication as Patrick Prince shot roll after roll of film. But just as he was getting up to follow her, Terry Bracegirdle emerged from the Art Department and walked rapidly in the direction of the Ladies'. Fran was absent long enough to have rinsed a gross of coffee mugs. Presently, laughter floated over the corridor partition, mingled with a clipped and nose-pinched version of Bracegirdle's voice.

> Plots have I laid, inductions dangerous,
> By drunken prophecies, libels and dreams,
> To set my brother Clarence and the king
> In deadly hate, the one against the other . . .

Margaret smiled drily at Mrs. Broadbent. "Hear that? He's giving her the Olivier–as–Richard III routine."

The next vignette, barely half an hour later, was an animated discussion in dumb show between Bracegirdle and his secretary and "personal researcher," the flame-haired Venetia. Its conclusion was Venetia's exit from the office, her face even redder than her shoulder-length tresses. She, too, was bound for the Ladies', where Toby Godwin's secretary, Tessa, and Val Lewis's assistant, Carol, subsequently joined her. To straining ears in the concourse, the word "bastard" was repeatedly audible. Some time later, Tessa went into Bracegirdle's office and brought out Venetia's coat, headscarf and handbag, and Venetia left—as it would prove, never to be seen again.

Shortly before lunch, Toby Godwin came out of his office, clad in a bursting lilac shirt and holding the cover mock-up that had been passed through to him a few minutes earlier. His pudgy face wore the indulgently lopsided smile of a parent inured to any devilment by his offspring. "Tell me," he said, "who is this most scrumptious girl?"

"She's Jim's secretary," Jessamyn told him.

"And her name?"

"Fran Dyson."

"Remarkable," Godwin mused.

"So what do you reckon to it as a cover?" Scurr asked.

"Absolutely first class, dear boy."

"Do you think there'll be any hassle from upstairs, though?"

Godwin laid the mock-up on Scurr's work-bench and studied it at length. The picture of Fran had been cropped to end just below her folded arms and tipped-up breasts. The famous Roman/italic masthead ran behind her back-combed crown. To the lower right, in festive typeface, were the words "HELLO, DOLLY-BIRD!"

"I can't in all honesty see why there should be. It's an extremely artistic and tasteful study of the modern female form, which is what we're about here. Granted, it goes a little further than we have in the past. But this, after all, is 1966."

"Do you think Lord M. will feel that way?" asked Jessamyn.

"Lord M., I'm quite sure, can be persuaded to the view that someone was going to do this sooner or later, and it may as well be us. The advertisement potential, of course, will not be lost on him."

Scurr grinned. "Playtex should want to be involved, for one."

"Yes, I think they very well may. Living colour on one spread, the living bra on the other! What an extremely uplifting idea! Hooh hooh hooh!"

"So we can go ahead, can we?" Scurr said, with a fleeting wink at his coterie.

"Absolutely, dear boy. Leave Lord M. and the geezers upstairs to me."

The climactic vignette came at around 4:30 that afternoon. There was first an inaudible and progressively heated discussion in Jim Deaves's office between Deaves and Terry Bracegirdle. Bracegirdle then abruptly walked out and back into his own office, followed by a smoke-wreathed and protesting Deaves.

"It's not on, Terry," he said. "You can't just ride roughshod over people like this . . ."

"Oh, doan't keep wittering on about it," Bracegirdle snapped. "Ah've spoaken to Personnel. They say they'll get you a temp by first thing tomorrow morning."

"But it takes weeks to train a new girl properly. And she's half-way through sorting out a gigantic expenses deficit for Patrick Prince . . ."

"That's what I mean about wasting resources. She's obviously much too bright to be sitting there, typing out photographers' expenses . . ."

"If you won't see reason, I'll have to go to God . . ."

"Ah've already cleared it with God, so doan't waste your time."

After a few minutes more, Deaves stumped angrily back into his own office and spoke at some length to Fran, who listened in nun-like stillness, honey head meekly bowed. She then rose, pulled her lime-green coat from the stand, picked up her shoulder-bag and one or two personal effects, went along to Bracegirdle's office and sat down behind Venetia's empty desk.

Louis didn't have a chance to speak to her until almost the end of the day, when Bracegirdle was closeted in Godwin's office with Strachey and Jessamyn. Pretending to be purposefully en route to the lifts but then struck by a spontaneous impulse, he retraced his steps and looked through Bracegirdle's open door. Fran was seated sidelong at her new desk, changing from tumbled-over suede boots to a pair of flat-heeled shoes.

"Hello," he said, gathering into the word every possible nuance of sophisticated quizzicality.

She glanced up, flicking the second shoe around her heel. Honey hair half-curtained her face, as in the cover mock-up. Louis felt his heart do a double back-flip.

"So . . ." He looked round the office with an ironic air of being deeply impressed. "You're working for Terry now."

"Yes."

The word had a faint, challenging query after it. But Louis still plunged on in his former role of great man taking kindly interest.

"I'm delighted. It's a much better job for you. You'll meet interesting people . . . Probably do some bits of research . . . and I'm sure you'll get on well with Terry . . ."

He became conscious of a great and aching lack in the encounter so far. Whatever had happened to "Thank you"?

"I was wondering . . . when we could . . . when I could see you again?"

"I'm afraid I'm busy all this week."

The cold hostility in her voice almost took his breath away.

"Oh . . . That's a shame. How about next week?"

"Same next week." Her tone had changed to uninterested condescension. "Sorry."

In a deep-freeze so palpable he could almost see the $CO_2$ vapour and hanging carcasses, Louis twisted his face into a smile and strove for a graceful exit-line. "All right . . . but I refuse to be disheartened. I'm definitely going to ask you again. OK?"

"All right," Fran said, glancing down at something on her desk.

Stunned with disappointment and self-disgust, he took the lift down and stood outside on the pavement, intending to hail one of the taxis that always passed McIntyre House in flotillas. But this evening, in corroboration of his repulsiveness, every one had its "For Hire" light switched off. As he still waited twenty minutes later, the automatic glass doors slid apart and Terry Bracegirdle and Fran came out together. Bracegirdle was leading her by both hands and talking animatedly as if to reassure her that where they were going was both magically exciting and perfectly safe. Ignoring Louis, they crossed the road and disappeared in the direction of Ludgate Circus.

"Over here, Poet!"

He turned to see a maroon Ford Zephyr parked at the kerb a few yards from the entrance to the newsprint delivery bay. Behind the wheel sat an editorial driver with the thick neck and Teddy-boy haircut peculiar to his station. Signalling from the wound-down rear window was Jack Shildrick.

"What's up with you this fine evening, young man? You look as if you've lost a guinea and found sixpence."

Louis coerced his features into a nonchalant grin. "I'm fine. Just a bit tired."

"Working you hard down there, are they?" Before he could answer, Shildrick went on: "More than me at the moment, as it happens. I've actually got an evening with the Missus for a change. Can I drop you anywhere?"

"A Northern Line station?"

"Right. Get in." Shildrick leaned forward to his driver, who turned with the look of devoted indulgence common to all who worked for him. "Les . . . where's the nearest Northern Line station from here?"

"Camden Town. Or Chalk Farm."

"Could you bear to drop Mr. Brennan here on our way?"

"Sure. Then it's 'Ampstead, is it?"

"Yes, Hampstead," Shildrick agreed with a noticeable drop in enthusiasm-level.

He was wearing the pale grey "Hardy Amies at Hepworths" suit whose quasi-Guardee line, on anyone less neat and compact, would now be slightly out of date. As the car headed up Farringdon Road, he detached a galley-proof from the thick sheaf on his knee and thrust it at Louis. "Here you are. Have a read of the jokes in Cicero this Sunday."

The galley contained the humorous single paragraphs that were sprinkled among the longer pieces on Cicero's weekly half-page. After the final one was a bold italic signature, "Hugo Kennie." Louis gazed at it with more envy and longing than could be put into a single thought.

"Nice, aren't they?" Shildrick said, taking the galley back.

"Yes. I love the one about Kenneth Kaunda's trousers."

"And how about the world's shortest books? 'Italian War Heroes . . .' 'Integrity' by Harold Wilson. Hugo's on form this week."

"He's got a wonderful light touch," Louis said wistfully.

"So could you have. In fact, I thought of you when he did that piece on Guy the gorilla at London Zoo, putting it all from the gorilla's view-point. I thought, 'That's just the kind of thing our Poet would have picked up and run with.' "

Louis turned to him, dazzled with unutterable hope all over again. But Shildrick was staring out at Regent's Park, his small fingers drumming on the beige leather arm-rest.

"By heck, what a week!" he sighed. "Dudley's away in Washington. James Way's editing the paper. Conferences, conferences every five minutes. And bugger all going on anywhere. Unemployment may climb to half a million. Mrs. Gandhi calls a conference of nonaligned nations. G.P.O. to introduce post-codes, whatever the thump they are."

"What's Singapore Charlie doing?"

Shildrick gave his curiously feminine smile. "Aye, there's always Singapore Charlie hits the Roaring Forties. Did I tell you a group of M.P.'s are lobbying for him to be knighted when he gets back? I've said it ought to be done on Plymouth Hoe, where Raleigh sighted the Armada."

To their right appeared the maroon-tilted frontage of Camden Town Underground station. As Louis groped for the door-handle, he felt a restraining hand on his arm.

"Do you fancy coming and having a meal with us, Poet? Or have you got plans afoot with your trendy friends?"

He pictured the kitchen in Clapham South, Grandad with the umpteenth game of Patience spread out while Grandma watched William Tell on ITV, shouting, "Watch out, Bill!" whenever danger threatened from behind.

"No. Not at all."

"Then come home with me. I've been meaning to ask you for ages. It may not be anything fancy, like they do in the Colour Mag, but I know you're down-to-earth. You'll take us as you find us."

"But it's your evening off. I wouldn't want to intrude . . ."

"You won't," Shildrick replied tersely. "In fact, between ourselves, I'll be glad of a bit of moral support."

They stopped half-way in an uphill, tree-lined street of substantial Victorian houses sculpted from cheerless dark red brick. "Thanks so much, Les," Shildrick said, as if his driver had brought him safely over the polar ice-cap.

"Want me to 'ang about?" Les enquired.

"No . . . I don't think there'll be any alarms or diversions tonight." There was no mistaking the note of regret in Shildrick's voice.

"OK. Well, you know where to reach me if you needs me."

All the houses had a slightly gloomy air, but Shildrick's was so much more so than its neighbours that a passer-by might have wondered if anyone actually lived there. The front hedge was ragged, the grass behind it long uncut, the paintwork a dull institutional green. Neither of the large ground-floor bay windows showed any sign of life.

"Come in, Poet," Shildrick said, unlocking a heavy front door panelled with multicoloured stained glass. Louis could not help noticing the slightly cautious way he entered his house, like the drunk in the ritualised seaside postcard who suspects a curl-papered spouse may be waiting with a rolling-pin.

The front hall was drably cavernous, its only furniture a coat-stand of unmistakable northern baroqueness, messily heaped with garments exclusively female or juvenile. Along both walls hung framed photographs of Shildrick surrounded by groups of men, some in shirt-sleeves, some in blazers and suits, some black, Asian or Oriental, all plainly fellow journalists according him welcome, farewell, congratulation or homage.

Shildrick set his proofs on top of an antiquated radiator, where some opened mail was already strewn, and joined Louis before this informal museum to himself. "Accrington Courant, 'forty-seven . . . I was the youngest Chief Reporter they ever had . . . Getting my Hannen Swaffer Award for all-round excellence . . . With the back bench at the Bangkok Post on my I.O.J. Travelling Fellowship. You've never known a climate like out there, Poet . . . buckets of rain every afternoon . . . Now, these faces you know, at the old Stockton E.T. . . . That was when I was guest of honour at the Teesside industrial correspondents."

He broke off and glanced up the uncarpeted wooden stairs. At the summit of the first flight stood a girl of about three, wearing a shapeless floral garment almost down to her ankles.

"Hello, Dozzie!" Shildrick ran and scooped her up, revealing she was also barefoot. "This is my daughter, Rosalind," he announced. "Where's your shoesies gone, darling?"

For answer the girl removed a piece of green matter from her left nostril, inspected it with fascination as if it were some exotic canapé, then ate it.

"Don't do that, Dozzie," Shildrick said, gently prising her forefinger from her mouth. "Where's Mummy? Downstairs, is she?"

With Rosalind clinging to him, he led the way down a pitch-dark, winding staircase, into a basement living room wallpapered with outsize lozenges of garish browny-orange. Down the middle ran a wooden table with a big old-fashioned wheelback chair at one end and flimsy modern ones distributed down either side. Through a doorway to the right Mrs. Shildrick could be seen, stirring something on a gas stove. From the same quarter issued a savoury but not quite pleasant smell.

" 'Ullo, love," Shildrick called out, with what seemed rather resolute cheeriness. His wife turned round, astonishing Louis all over again with her iron-grey hair, weatherbeaten skin and almost judicial severity of expression. Her face seemed permanently set in a look that said, "I know what you're up to, my lad, and I'm not having any of it." She was wearing the same clothes as on that day at McIntyre House, or else others similarly eschewing fashionable colour, shape or length.

"You remember Louis, don't you?" Shildrick said. "One of my brightest and best on the E.T. Now a rising star of the world-renowned Colour Mag."

Mrs. Shildrick regarded him steadily, as if she knew what he was up to but wasn't having any of it. "Yes, I remember Louis," she conceded.

"He was at a bit of a loose end tonight, so I brought him back for a bite with us."

The news did not fill Mrs. Shildrick with unadulterated joy, as she demonstrated by turning sharply on her sensibly brogued heel and resuming her work at the stove. "Sit down, Poet," Shildrick murmured with an apologetic grimace, motioning Louis to the wheelback chair, then joining his wife just out of sight, Rosalind still clasped in his arms. Louis was keenly reminded of occasions in childhood when schoolfriends had taken him home to tea without asking their mothers first. There was a murmur of voices, Shildrick's inaudible and conciliatory, Jean Shildrick's repeating, with that unforgettable northern doggedness, "It's not fair . . . It's joost not fair . . ." Shildrick remonstrated with her again, there was a short silence, then frozen peas could be heard showering from a family-sized bag into a saucepan with the furious rattle of a machine-gun fusillade.

Louis continued to ponder the mystery of Jean Shildrick over supper, which was comprised of pieces of batter-encased meat, he wasn't sure what kind, vaguely warm on the outside, pink and cool as sorbet within. The most likely explanation was that she'd once been young-looking and attractive, but that an unkind trick of Nature had greyed her hair and leathered her skin with prematureness all the more cruel in contrast with her spouse's unchanging boyishness. Or maybe she'd always looked much like this, raising the greater puzzle of why Shildrick should deliberately have married someone who evermore would be mistaken for his mother or maiden aunt. In the upward gallop of his career, temptations to stray must have been numerous. Yet, in London as up north, Louis had heard no murmur about his private life, other than that he was "happily married" and "a devoted father."

A father he indubitably was, not only to Rosalind but also two boys,

eleven-year-old Warwick and nine-year-old Seth, both of whom sat on
Louis's left, their energies divided between overtly attacking and abus-
ing each other and covertly taunting and torturing their little sister.
With the meat and Bird's Eye peas came boiled potatoes whose hard-
ness, given their tiny size, was little short of miraculous. No wine was
offered, only a choice between tap-water and Robinson's lemon barley.
Shildrick and Mrs. Shildrick sat at opposite ends of the table, which separated them by a considerable distance, she pushing bits of lukewarm
batter into Rosalind's mouth, he lounging in the big wheelback chair
with some of the same young-tycoon elegance as in his high-speed
black leather one at the Dispatch. Not since leaving the orbit of his own
father had Louis been at a meal-table where dissension was snatched so
suddenly out of thin air.

"Very nice, Jean," Shildrick said, pushing aside his barely half-
finished plate.

Mrs. Shildrick, whose mouth happened to be full, greeted this seemingly uncontroversial statement with a spluttering sound and wildly
rolling eyes. "You're doing it again! You know I hate it!"

Her husband looked almost as startled as Louis felt. "What? What
have I said?"

"Calling me by my name like that. 'So-and so this, Jean' and 'so-and-
so that, Jean.' I know I'm called Jean! I've been called Jean for thirty-
nine years! I don't need to be told so every five seconds!"

"I'm sorry, love," Shildrick said pacifically. "I don't realise I'm doing
it."

"I know, that's the trouble. You're so far set in this chirpy chipper
northern chappie routine, it's getting . . ."

She was interrupted by a blood-curdling shriek from Rosalind. Warwick and Seth both shrank away in the opposite direction, giving exaggerated study to the food on their plates.

"Seth, you pinched her again, didn't you?"

"I didn't, Moom, honest," the boy replied in unreconstructed Teesside. "It were Warwick!"

"No, it weren't!" Warwick protested in the same north country
pseudo-subjunctive. Louis took advantage of the distraction to pack as
much of his chilly, pink meat as possible under his flattened knife.
Amazing how much like school this evening was turning out to be.

Rosalind was continuing to howl like a soul in purgatory, the entire
lower half of her face stained with tomato ketchup and studded with
batter-fragments. "Pick her up, love," Shildrick urged.

"You pick her up!" Mrs. Shildrick suggested. "She sees little enough
of you!"

"I told you before, Warwick. You're not to pinch your sister. She's only a little girl."

"Perhaps if you were around a bit more to discipline them, they'd not be turning into little yahoos."

"It weren't me, Dad. It were Warwick!"

"Ooh, you lousy cow! You know it were you!"

"You say it were me again, Warwick, and I'll bash your brains in."

"I'll punch you in the balls."

"I'll punch you in the balls twice."

"All right, all right. If you want to have this out, we do it in the proper way . . . in the garden, with the boxing gloves on."

"Oh, yes," Mrs. Shildrick agreed with reverberant irony. "Getting them clubbing one another senseless when you've only been home five minutes. That's very nice, isn't it? I don't think."

After tinned fruit cocktail topped by pink Instant Whip, Louis asked for the bathroom and was directed to the second door on the right at the top of the stairs. Up here hung further photographs of Shildrick being honoured by groups of journalists. Through an open door could be seen an unmade bed with perhaps fifteen shirts, his familiar pale and mid-blue ones, evidently just washed but not ironed and cavalierly thrown in a heap by there-could-no-prizes-for-guessing-whom.

The bathroom was somehow the biggest surprise of all with its dingy white enamel, veined green lino, stained lavatory pan and detached bath-plug. Louis glanced at himself in the mirror above a mug of crusted toothpaste tubes and splayed brushes. Impossible to imagine Shildrick standing here first thing every morning, his face a mask of shaving soap—or did he use electric?—as he plotted the Dispatch's latest coup, with Warwick, Seth and Rosalind all doubtless beating a tattoo on the door. Somewhere below, a telephone pealed and was answered at the second ring.

As he came downstairs again, the Shildricks were talking in the front hall just out of view.

"It can't be helped, love . . ."

"No, of course it can't," Mrs. Shildrick said bitterly. "It never can be, can it?"

"Look, Jean . . ."

"Oh, no! There you go again!"

"I'm sorry . . . it just slipped out."

"Well, we've had half an evening of your company. I suppose we should all get down on our knees and . . ."

She broke off to give Louis a hard stare. Shildrick turned round with an expression that Louis had not seen on his face these past two and a half hours.

"Sorry, Poet . . . we're going to have to cut it short. That was Nick Fenton on the blower. I'm wanted urgently back at the shop."

"What's happened?"

"A slag-heap's collapsed and buried half a pit village in South Wales. From what's come over on the wire, it looks pretty nasty. I've phoned for Les; we can drop you off at a tube station on our way."

He was like a man freshly awoken from a coma, ravenous and raring to go.

# 13

Mrs. Atyeo leaned from her armchair, baring teeth like the bleached ribs of some wrecked schooner half-buried in yellow sand. "Now," she said, "perhaps to begin with you could tell me exactly what it is that you want."

Louis, seated on her right, exchanged a glance with Brenda Brown, cradling his knee on a tapestried stool before the fireplace. They were used to this curiously annoying kick-off question in interviews with prospective landlords and landladies, and had often discussed which among the various pressing answers would be the most counter-productive. "We want a place we can fill up with mud and watch one-legged midgets being buggered by donkeys . . ." "We want to see the flat you advertised in the midday Standard, what do you think we want, you stupid old fart?"

Mrs. Atyeo was a tall, scarf-swathed lady in the early seventies with grey hair scraped into a bun and a nervous, gobbling voice. They were being received in the front sitting room of her house in a hilly Victorian terrace a few yards off High Street Ken. It was the kind of room Louis often looked into enviously after dark: ceiling-high white bookcases, gold-shaded lamps, oil paintings around the walls. Over the mantel-piece hung a portrait of a cravat-wearing and Brylcreemed late husband whose expression gave some clue to his widow's distracted, apprehensive manner. The accommodation on offer was the basement directly beneath them.

Brenda twitched his hunting-stock, smoothed his bald pate and cleared his throat. "Basically, we're a couple of busy professionals who need a central London pied-à-terre that's civilised and comfortable without breaking the bank, if you know what I mean."

The prospective landlady studied him, turkey-wattles quivering above the folds of her silk scarf. "And . . . Mr. Brown, umph, isn't it? . . . you work at Crichton's?"

"Mm, that's right."

She turned to Louis. "And Mr. Brennan, you're with the Sunday Dispatch."

"Yes. The Magazine." Even after all this time, to say so was still thrilling.

"My son-in-law's a journalist on the BBC—Edwin Wiltshire. You've probably seen him on *Panorama*."

Among ruthlessly horn-rimmed political interviewers the name was almost as distinguished as Robin Day's or Robert McKenzie's. "Yes, of course," Louis agreed reverently.

"Well," Mrs. Atyeo continued, "it's a veddy, veddy pretty little garden flat, just recently redecorated. Since the paper came out, you can imagine, umph, the telephone has hardly stopped ringing. A couple of the foreign embassies in Phillimore Gardens are offering to take it sight unseen." She rolled back her upper lip from the schooner's yellowed bones again. "But I think perhaps I'd sooner have two nice young Englishmen."

Striving to express by every movement and gesture how absolutely that description fitted them, Louis and Brenda followed her down a dark back-stairs to a stone-flagged basement passage. At the rear was a single large bedroom with French windows leading to the tiny, dark, barren rectangle that legitimised the term "garden flat." The front living room, which gave directly onto the area steps, was carpeted in musty beige and distempered in pus-pale yellow. On the left, through a Spanish-style arch, was a surprisingly modern kitchenette. The black-and-white-floored bathroom extended under the road outside, with a separate W.C. beyond it. There was an odour of mummified cooking fat and leaking gas.

Mrs. Atyeo looked about her with unabashed ecstasy. "It's twenty-seven-ten a week, as the advertisement says. And we'd have to discuss the matter of a deposit to cover, umph, breakages."

Brenda smoothed his bald head again and gave her a smile of devastating nice young Englishman charm. "We were hoping that in the circumstances you might possibly agree to waive that."

"Well, you know, that is the usual practice where, umph, furnished properties are concerned. Not that I think for a moment you'd deliberately go round, umph, umph, breaking things. But accidents do happen."

Brenda nodded and also shook his head to show the extent of his sympathy to her point of view. "But working in an international auction house, as I do, one does have some cognisance of handling precious things with care . . ."

She considered for a moment, plucking at the brooch which secured her scarf.

"All right, we'll waive the deposit. As long as it's understood that any breakage or damage must be made good."

Brenda tapped the wall next to the kitchen arch. "I've got quite a lot of pictures and prints. I suppose there'd be no objection to my putting some of them up?"

Mrs. Atyeo clutched her brooch in alarm. "But if you do any damage to the wall, you will make it good, won't you?"

"I wouldn't do any damage. Just a screw-hole here, here and perhaps here."

"But if you make a hole, umph, umph, umph, you'll have to make it good."

The two nice young Englishmen withdrew into the bedroom for private discussion.

"I think it's all right, don't you?" Brenda said.

Louis looked sceptically around him. "Only this one bedroom, though."

"But does that really matter? One or other of us is nearly always away. And I don't imagine I'm going to wake up and find you bumming me."

"Just hope you don't wake up and find *her* bumming you."

Brenda gobbled like a turkey, shaking imaginary wattles. " 'If you make a hole, umph, umph, you'll have to make it good.' Does that mean make it a nice big hole?"

"Yes . . . and you and your 'cognisance of handling things with care.' I hope she never finds out how many M.G.B.'s you've written off."

Back upstairs, Mrs. Atyeo poured two affrontingly small sweet sherries to seal the bargain. Brenda had phoned his office to check on his messages so, for the sake of image, Louis thought he'd better, too. In reality he could be away from McIntyre House a month and no one would inquire where he was.

"Magazine," said Margaret Cole's quiet voice.

"Hello, it's Louis. Nothing happening, is there?"

"Where are you?"

"High Street Ken. Looks like we've found a flat at last."

"You'd better get back," Margaret said. "There seems to be something pretty big in the wind. A meeting of the whole paper has been called for four-thirty. The word is that Lord M. himself may be going to speak to us."

The meeting was in the Dispatch's big open-plan Newsroom. It was the first time Louis had seen the whole staff of the paper before: perhaps two hundred people, seated on the reporters' desks that were not fully occupied until Thursday each week, or leaning against the archipelago of grey steel filing cabinets. For every half-familiar face from Business News or Close-up there were scores he could not identify from Foreign, Parliamentary, Sport, Literary, Travel, Letters. The Magazine contingent, grouped around Toby Godwin, stood out as vividly as West Indians in a Lord's Test stand.

"Come on, God," Jessamyn whispered with her customary after-lunch slur. "Don't hold out on us. What's the scuttlebutt?"

"It's about the editorship, isn't it?" Cedric Scurr said.

Godwin gave an indifferent shrug. "Your guess is as good as mine, dear boy."

Silence fell as the swing doors opened from the executive corridor. First came Lord McIntyre with Dudley Mowforth beside him, then James Way, then Shildrick. He was wearing the navy single-breasted suit, royal blue shirt and slim gold tie which, though still pristinely neat and glossy, now rather strongly evoked the distant days of 1965. In one hand he carried a galley which he handed to Nick Fenton with a brief instruction before darting to join the other V.I.P.'s in front of the Newsdesk.

The proprietor's attire of musty-looking black double-breasted suit appeared no different from when Louis had confided in him at Wembley, back in the summer. He shuffled some rough notes and looked benignly around the huge congregation of his employees. If he was speculating how many of his fivers had just been lavished on restaurants throughout central London, the faded blue eyes gave no hint of it.

"Well, thank you all very much for coming this afternoon, ladies and gentlemen," he said with his faintly transatlantic brogue. "This is a sad occasion, but one which I trust you will also think a happy occasion. To deal with the sad aspect first, I must tell you that Mr. Dudley Mowforth has announced his intention of retiring as Editor of The Sunday Dispatch."

There was a rustling exclamation. Lord McIntyre turned to Mowforth, whose short military moustache was grimacing with what seemed almost agoraphobic shyness.

"I know I speak for you all in paying tribute to Mr. Mowforth as an inspirational Editor as well as the innovator of most of the features which have made The Sunday Dispatch the success it is today. Without him, we wouldn't have Close-up; we wouldn't have Business News or the Review; we wouldn't have the Colour Magazine, at least not in its present form. He's been the initiator—shall I say 'midwife,' Dudley?—of virtually everything these past few years that's got the Dispatch talked about, written about, broadcast about, but, above all, read by almost fifty percent more people than any other quality Sunday paper."

"Hear hear!" several voices shouted, Toby Godwin's among them.

"This coming weekend's paper, therefore, will be the last edited by Mr. Mowforth. However, I'm delighted to say that he won't be leaving us altogether. He has agreed to retain a part-time post with McIntyre Newspapers as Special Advisory Editor."

Lord McIntyre paused and looked around, the rosy face more alert than it had previously appeared.

"I don't have to tell you that these are changing times, and that a title like ours must always guard against complacency if it's to maintain its lead in a highly competitive market. In choosing Mr. Mowforth's successor, I've borne in mind the Dispatch's duty to its existing readership, but also its need to strike out in new areas—especially that of campaigning and investigative journalism."

He turned to James Way, who was perched on the edge of the Newsdesk, a loungingly elegant composition of pale grey suit, cream shirt and silly-striped tie.

"Mr. James Way has been a loyal deputy to Mr. Mowforth for nine years, and a Foreign and Diplomatic Editor of great distinction. It is with his full understanding and support that I have invited Mr. Jack Shildrick to take over the chair."

There was a loud gasp, impossible to decipher either as approbation or horror. As Louis's heart soared with pride, he saw Scurr turn to Terry Bracegirdle and pull a face of disbelieving agony.

". . . Mr. Shildrick, in the few months since he joined us here, has shown himself an editorial executive of great brilliance. I have only to mention the A-Six Murder reconstruction, the inquiry into dangerous vacuum flasks and the exposure of the Golden Salamander insurance fraud. With the round-the-world voyage of Singapore Charlie Small, he's given us a world exclusive. Nor need I remind anyone of the paper's brilliant coverage of the Aberfan tragedy last month, which he masterminded on the spot. You may like to know that the National Coal Board has confirmed this week that, thanks to our Close-up investigation, the procedure for ensuring the safety of slurry-tips in proximity to mining villages is to be drastically overhauled."

James Way turned and shook Shildrick's hand, a picture of graceful sportsmanship in everything but his eyes, which were almost incandescent with hatred.

"Mr. Shildrick," Lord McIntyre continued, "becomes Executive Editor, with Mr. Way as his Deputy, responsible for all departments of the newspaper. The Colour Magazine will remain under my personal supervision as before, with Mr. Mowforth providing liaison where necessary with its Editor, Mr. Godwin, and me."

Shildrick stepped forward, looking almost ludicrously boyish and slight. "This is a wonderful moment and a great honour," he said. "I'll do my utmost to live up to it. Those of you I don't know yet I hope to get to know. I hope you'll come to me with your ideas, with your problems, your comments on what I'm doing with the paper. My door will always be open."

Lord McIntyre drifted off, accompanied by Mowforth and Way. A crowd of well-wishers surged around Shildrick, among them Louis, torn between desire to congratulate and reluctance to appear a sycophant. But seeing him, Shildrick reached past others to shake his hand, then used it to draw him a little apart from the crush.

"Poet . . . don't think I've forgotten what we discussed vis-à-vis your triumphal advent to the paper. But things are going to be a bit hectic to begin with. You understand?"

"Of course," Louis said.

"Jack . . ." Nick Fenton interrupted. "We need a decision on Hanoi."

"OK." As Shildrick allowed himself to be ushered away, he winked conspiratorially at Louis. "Just give me a couple of weeks. All right?"

"Right," Louis nodded, with eyes shining.

There was a meeting in Toby Godwin's office immediately afterwards, over Earl Grey tea and Richoux fresh strawberry tarts, coffee éclairs, meringues, cream slices and pecan-nut Danish pastries.

"So we're still all right then, are we?" Scurr said, poking sugar lumps past the lemon-slice in his cup.

"Of course we are, dear boy. You heard what the Chairman said just now. And he's reiterated it to me again in private. Our editorial independence is guaranteed."

"But Mighty Jack Shildrick's not going to like it much, is he?" Terry Bracegirdle said. "After all, it means he's not really Editor of the whole paper."

"He's obviously a bloody lethal operator," Scurr added. "Look at the way he shafted Jamie Way. Isn't it just a matter of time before he starts trying to get his hands on us as well?"

"And you know he wants to," Jessamyn said. "Remember that ghastly memo about dropping foreign stories and doing gardening and knitting?"

Godwin shook his head tolerantly, fork jabbing at a defenceless éclair. "He can like it, or he can do the other thing. Nothing changes the reality of the situation, which is that our advertising revenues are the cornerstone of McIntyre Newspapers. Lord M., thank goodness, is canny enough to know that if you own a Golden Goose, you keep it nice and snugly under your jacket. Put your minds at rest that we shall not be interfered with in any way by Mighty Jack Shildrick."

He slid another éclair and a strawberry tart onto his plate and flipped open the file in front of him.

"Now, to move on to more germane matters, I want to ask you young tearaways a question. Who is, beyond any doubt, the world's most beautiful woman?"

Bracegirdle visibly cudgelled his brains. "Sophia Loren?" he suggested.

"Ursula Andress?" said Jim Deaves.

"Danny La Rue?" offered Evelyn Strachey, sashaying to the work-top to refill his cup.

Godwin smiled tolerantly amid the shriek of merriment. "It's Elizabeth Taylor, of course. And what a subject for a cover story! Child star to Hollywood goddess! The five husbands! The millions of bucks that were poured down the drain on *Cleopatra*! The love affair with Richard Burton! The two-million-pound diamond!"

"Could we get her?" Bracegirdle asked.

"We've got her, dear boy. I wrote to her people some time ago, and a 'yes' has just now come back. We're being given full access. Absolute co-operation. Every door open."

"Burton, too?" Jessamyn asked.

Godwin nodded. "Burton too, naturally. The idea is that I fly out to talk to them at their home in the South of France, and you kids get busy on background interviews, her family, friends, film producers, business associates. Her lawyer has supplied a full list which, Tessa darling, you'd better give to Terry. We're talking about a profile of six, maybe seven thousand words."

Hope of some small peripheral task outweighing either embarrassment or heartache, Louis joined the subsequent council of war in Terry Bracegirdle's office. Strachey, who had been about to shut the door, opened it again for him with a flirtatious smile. Fran was sitting there in silky blue-grey with huge leg o'mutton sleeves, her honey head humbly bowed in the presence of so many deities.

Bracegirdle swept back his shampoo-floppy quiff with a satirical grin. "Well, we noah what always happens, doan't we, when God decides to write a proafile? Remember Simone Signoret? And Bertrand Russell?

And President Nkrumah of Ghana? He flies all over the world . . . stays in the best hotels . . . eats in the most expensive restaurants . . . we feed him mountains of background interviews, which he sits on like a great big broody hen till the Art Department is screamin' for the copy . . ."

"And then decides he can't face writing it after all," Jessamyn said.

"Exactly. So, Evelyn, you'd better stand by as usual to rescue this Liz Taylor extravaganza with your puissant pen."

Strachey nodded. "Right."

"And, Jessamyn, get yourself off to L.A. as soon as you can. There's a whole bunch of these background interviews to do in Hollywood." Bracegirdle took the list from Fran and studied it. "Roddy McDowall, her co-star in *Lassie* . . . Bennie Thau, the former head of M.G.M. studios . . . Pandro S. Berman, producer of *National Velvet*, which I can remember seeing with me mam in the ninepennies at the Essoldo Picture-drome, North Shields."

This last was clearly for the benefit of Fran, whose blackened eyes had become earnestly fixed both on him and the list in his hand.

"Ah thought, if you agree, Ah'd let Fran here do some of the London ones," he continued, sweeping back his quiff again. "She's a reelly first-class researcher. We should be putting her to better use than just sitting in an office, answering phones."

Jessamyn exchanged a brief smirk with Strachey. "OK, why not? Let her have a go."

Bracegirdle turned back to Fran, his face stiffened into a mask of schoolmasterly formality. "This Pandro Berman's going to be in London next week, staying at the Connaught. You'd better take him out to lunch. I'll tell you the sort of questions to ask. Remember, we're just looking for quotes to drop into God's piece."

She bowed her head. "Yes. Thank you."

"Is there something I could do?" Louis asked.

"I think we're all right, thanks," Bracegirdle replied with too-elaborate gratitude. "What Jessamyn and Evelyn can't handle, I'm going to get done by reelly reliable freelances."

Louis gave no sign of feeling the nettle slap. And, glancing through the list again, Bracegirdle seemed to relent. "There's her mother, Mrs. Sara Taylor, who's also in England at the moment. Unless . . . You didn't want to interview the mother, did you, Evelyn?"

"No, thanks," Strachey replied with a little shudder.

"All right, I'll put you down for Mrs. Taylor. Fran will give you the address."

"Fourteen South Drive, St. George's Hill, Weybridge," Fran said, glancing up at Louis with blackened eyes devoid of all recognition.

He took the last of his clothes from the wire hangers over the serried artificial legs, and closed the wardrobe door with a little pang. After almost three months, it would seem strange not to awaken each morning
to green walls, sepia photographs and white wax forget-me-nots.
Strange not to lie in the lumpy feather bed, listening to Irish shouts
from the middle landing, and estimating when things on the ground
floor were sufficiently under control for him to go down to breakfast.

Grandma Bassill stood in the front hall, watching him take the final
armfuls out to his car. As ever in mid-afternoon, with her hairnet,
apron and pompom slippers, she wore full make-up, earrings and a
double row of pearls.

"Grandad's going to miss you," she said. "He's liked having you here
to talk to of an evening."

Louis leaned down to put an arm round her shoulders.

"And you'll miss me like anything, won't you, Gran?"

"You've been a little devil sometimes, tying me apron-strings to the
back of me chair." She gave him one of her brusque, lipsticky kisses.
"But on the whole, I'm not complaining. It'll be funny not to have
someone to make a Wall's wafer for after tea."

Grandad was in his usual place, wheelchair pushed up to kitchen
table, dealing himself yet another hand of Patience. The snowy hair
was neatly combed, the pullover and collarless shirt both freshly
ironed. The thin face studied the value of each card with unfailing stoic
cheerfulness.

"I'm off, then, Grandad."

Grandad raised a slender arm to shake hands. "Ta-ta, boy."

"I'm really sorry to be going. You've both been really great to me.
But at least there won't be so much extra work for Gran in future."

"I've told Lou you're going to miss him," Grandma said. "You've enjoyed talking all about the old days, haven't you? And now you'll only
'ave me to thrash you at shove-ha'penny."

". . . It's just that, when I get this new job on the paper, I'll need to be
much nearer the centre of everything. I'll probably be out late most
nights, at the theatre or at parties . . ."

Grandad checked him with an upraised finger.

"You know there's only one way I'm not going to be pleased with
you, don't you? That's if you don't make the most of everything that's
coming to you in your career. Of course you need a place of your own.
You don't want to be stuck away over here with a couple of old-
timers."

"But I know I wouldn't be in London at all if it wasn't for you . . ." Louis felt a lump come into his throat. "And, Gran, you will be careful when I'm not around, won't you? No more standing stepladders on ice. Or falling backwards onto your head."

"Oh, rats!" she smiled, aiming a clip at his ear.

He looked for one last time at the little kitchen, the scullery beyond, and the overlooked back garden with its outside W.C. where you sat enthroned between piled seedboxes, a shovel, a rake and a set of pruning shears. "Be good, then, both of you. I'll pop over and see you every week."

But even as he said it, he knew he was lying.

# 14

During the first weeks of the new era, far from rushing to cash in on their long intimacy, Louis deliberately stayed out of Shildrick's way, avoiding the sixth floor's executive corridor, refraining from fraternal or congratulatory memos, even ducking round corners or into doorways rather than meet him face-to-face and fall under the faintest suspicion of being pushy. He would obviously get around to the Cicero question as soon as humanly possible. Meanwhile, there would be more than enough other people competing for his attention. It was up to his real friends not to add to the huge new pressures that must be upon him.

That resolution was sometimes difficult to maintain. For a tingle of excitement and expectation, well-remembered from the Stockton Evening Telegraph's grimy Gothic pile, now permeated every copper-faced floor of McIntyre House. Shildrick's very first week in the chair had shown how different was to be his regime from that of the remote and inaccessible Mowforth. Prowling the Newsroom early on Tuesday, the first day of the paper's working week, he came upon a telex machine spewing out lists of Civil Service examination results. When the first subs arrived, they found their new Editor hard at work, and the downtable drudge's job already half finished.

Louis could not help but smile at the familiar note in most of the Shildrick stories that were now whizzing around. How the editorial conferences, which Mowforth had been wont to conduct with donnish solemnity, now sat up straight with heads turning back and forth like a crowd at Wimbledon's Centre Court as the high-speed chair ricocheted from one side of the room to the other. How reporters rejoiced in new, uncorseted freedom, and printers tore their hair with fond exasperation at the lateness and constant unmaking and remaking of pages. How, during the final Saturday hours before press-time, instead of adjourning to the Garrick Club like his predecessor, Shildrick sat shirt-sleeved on the Back Bench between the Chief Sub and the Copytaster, debating page layout, writing headlines, rewriting copy; how long after the print-run had started he would still be there, palpably longing for some late-breaking story to give him the excuse to rejig page one all over again.

As might be expected, there was an immediate improvement in the look of the paper, which became simultaneously more direct and dramatic in its headlines and more tasteful and elegant of layout. With this came a marked increase in the decorative blocks and white-on-black flashes which marked long-running Shildrick features or crusades: "THE SALAMANDER SCANDAL," "THESE FLASKS CAN MAIM," "THE BLAKE FIASCO," "THE UDI DEBACLE," "SOUTH AFRICA'S TORMENT," "WHY FLORENCE IS DROWNING," "INSIDE GEMINI 12," "CLEAN UP OUR COAL TIPS" and, of course, "SIGNALS FROM A SEA-DOG."

Somehow Louis continued to suppress his impatience as a wave of staff changes were announced, touching almost every department in Shildrick's vast new domain. The supercilious Nick Fenton, for example, was elevated from Close-up to a new post called Managing Editor (News). The Dispatch's correspondent in Jerusalem was transferred to Tokyo, its Tokyo correspondent to Bonn and its Bonn correspondent to Cape Town. The dramatic critic Cyril Stanniford, after thirty years' service, was displaced by an epicene youth who did facetious play previews on BBC2's *Late Night Line-up.* A new Fashion Editor was poached from The Sunday Times, a new Business News Editor from the Financial Times and a new Travel Editor from the Sunday Telegraph.

He felt unease and vague resentment that so many other than himself could now claim to be Shildrick protégés, recipients of inspirational encouragement to surpass themselves and heart-lifting praise when they did so. Early in November, word percolated down from the Steam Section that Hugo Kennie was, as long rumoured, to give up Cicero at the year's end, but that so far no decision had been made concerning his successor. Every fibre in Louis clamoured to reiterate how ready, willing and able he was to step into Kennie's shoes. Yet he still held back, knowing in his heart that Shildrick would realise and appreciate his consideration.

There was at least the distraction of the new flat, the excitement of a half-share in his very first front door and living at long last near if not precisely at Swinging London's very hub: just round the corner from Biba and Bus Stop, within walking-distance—at a pinch—from Portobello Market, six Underground stops (change at Notting Hill Gate) from Carnaby Street and only a three-shilling taxi-ride away from the King's Road.

Despite his coruscating public rudeness, Brenda Brown proved a congenial flatmate, good-humoured and tolerant; as keen as was Louis on the fantasy of their being two young Edwardian men-about-town, and the poky, musty gas-reeking basement some elegant, Turkey-carpeted set of "chambers" in Half Moon Street. Neither found any hardship in sharing the big rear bedroom; on the contrary, it was fun to lie awake into the small hours, running through their combined back catalogue of obscene jokes, discussing every possible topic from the efficacy of the U.N. and the morality of blood sports to the funniest Dud and Pete routine, the brilliance of Dirk Bogarde in *The Servant* and the perfection of Jane Fonda's behind. When Louis brought home a shirt that was a mistake, Brenda knew how to refold it with pins and cardboard so artfully that the shop would unquestioningly take it back again. In the mornings, Louis tactfully looked away as Brenda sat on the edge of his bed, rubbing a thick green substance into his bald head to encourage the faint golden gossamer that hung on there.

A Tesco supermarket at the corner largely provided their diet of beer, red wine, Vimto, steaks and Welsh rarebits smothered in mustard pickle. On nights when Louis had drawn a fresh advance in expenses, they'd go for huge biryanis at the Curry Inn in Earl's Court Road, or have Spanish omelettes and Mateus rosé at a place called the Sombrero in High Street Ken whose basement discothèque attracted an exclusively male clientele, many wearing minidresses, back-combed wigs and false eyelashes.

The early threat of their landlady did not materialise. Apart from the occasional "Umph, umph" down the connecting staircase, Mrs. Atyeo remained sequestered in her ground-floor den with her books, her decanters and her bastard of a deceased husband. The one inconvenience was that Louis's and Brenda's mail was put through her front door; at night, they would find letters flung from above as if in wild, impetuous fury. This and the periodic scuffles through their ceiling inspired Brenda to go from room to room, calling out like a medium to an unruly poltergeist: "Can you hear me, Blue Feather? Knock once for 'yes,' twice for 'no' . . ." The famous BBC son-in-law was made manifest only once, during an electricity black-out, when Mrs. Atyeo sent him down to investigate the fusebox above the kitchen arch. It was strange to have the ruthless inquisitor of prime ministers and potentates standing on a stool in their sitting room, his ridden-up jacket-hem revealing buttocks of a neatness that would not have shamed Nureyev.

An elaborate code of signals was agreed whereby one bedroom-sharer would warn the other that he was engaged in wild fornication and must not be disturbed for trivial reasons like clean clothes or sleep. But for both, thus far, the code had been purely theoretical. Despite his M.G.B. and sizeable private income, Brenda had no regular girl-friend. Apart from China Lee (Playboy's Pet of the Month for December 1965) his great love was the wife of Crichtons' chief auctioneer, a sensitive, cultivated woman—as he told Louis—throwing herself away on a mindless brute scarcely able to tell Sheraton from Hepplewhite.

"She's got the most beautiful straight back," his voice would sigh wistfully through the darkness. "If I had her here now, you know, I don't think I'd even try it on. I'd just want to talk . . . and fondle her . . ."

The state of Louis's heart remained secret, however, even on the Sunday, half-way through November, when Fran Dyson's honey head and crossed arms could be seen in stacks on every newsagent's counter and street vendor's table. He meant to give the whole Dispatch a miss that weekend, but unfortunately Brenda brought home a copy and stood in the kitchenette innocently ogling it while saddle-soaping a new pair of hunting boots.

"Pleasant little tits, aren't they? I've always liked nipples that cover the whole end like that."

"OK, I suppose." Louis shrugged, affecting to study a Business News exposé of a fraudulent pension fund.

"Oh, come on! You mean you wouldn't like to wake up in the middle of the night and find one of those brushing against your cheek? Who's the bint, by the way? Not one of your usual cover models, is she?"

"I've no idea," Louis said brusquely.

The New Eve issue was a monster success, selling out the Dispatch's entire 1.6 million print-run in a few hours, creating such a demand for the Magazine that used copies were reportedly changing hands at two or three times the paper's full cover price throughout the following week. Nor did anyone seriously believe the phenomenon derived from its exhaustive, rather learned survey of female anatomy throughout history, illustrated by the Venus de Milo, Chaucer's Wife of Bath, Goya's Naked Maja, Lillie Langtry, Diana Dors and Twiggy. The cover picture naturally aroused some disfavour, from the embattled forces of conservatism within Fleet Street as well as outside it. But the general re-action, as always, was envious admiration of the Dispatch's nerve, and a gadarene rush to capitalise on it. The following month's issues of Nova and Town magazines had a cover model flashing an airbrushed millimetre or two of nipple above a black lacy basque and a waist-tied peasant blouse respectively. In the Sunday tabloids' traditional pin-up shots, bikini tops instantly plunged to the same forbidden area, though the murk of their newsprint hid the sensation from all but the most eagle-eyed. The Telegraph's Saturday magazine risked the apoplexy of colonels and bishops in the shires by running fashion pictures of female undergarments that were a breathtaking departure from knee-length bloomers and liberty bodices. Even The Times relaxed its immemorial ban on the use of the word "bra." Few could doubt that British journalism had taken arguably its greatest leap forward since front pages abandoned small-ads in favour of news.

The identity of the Dispatch's cover girl was not made public, despite several hundred entreating letters from male readers, a few enclosing keepsakes which had to be disposed of in thick black plastic bags. Within the Magazine's large social circle, however, she was the sensation of the hour. Several times each day, some visiting writer, literary agent or couture luminary could be seen whispering interrogatively to Jessamyn or Val Lewis, then gazing at the demure honey-gold head beyond Terry Bracegirdle's office glass with that now familiar expression of gloating incredulity. Enquiries about the unknown cover girl had come to the Picture Desk from several leading model agencies; in addition, two or three of the eminent photographers under contract to the Magazine begged to use her again, in sessions for book-jackets or advertisements. But it emerged she was not interested in a modelling career, even when the supplicant was David Bailey himself.

"Sorry, David, I can't give her to you for your seraglio," Bracegirdle told him, laughing. "She only did that for us as a one-off. Anyway, she's much too bright for the borin' life of a model girl."

Bailey nodded sardonically. "I see, Terry. She's 'bright,' is she? Say no more, I get it. You bloody lecherous old sod!"

At this same time, paradoxically, Louis's long night of failure on the Magazine was beginning to show faint glimmers of dawn. Thanks to David Kausman's patronage—a force simultaneously stiffening Toby Godwin's backbone and defeating the malign inertia of Cedric Scurr's felt-tip marker—the Tolkien and Yoko Ono profiles (though not yet "Whither the Sixties Servant?") were finally making their way through the production process. At least now he had an answer when schoolfriends at the pub asked whether he'd died, and when his mother's voice said plaintively down the telephone line from East Anglia: "I couldn't find anything again this Sunday . . ."

Kausman continued to encourage him, though in a style very different from Jack Shildrick's. With Kausman, praise took the form of reproach, the constant intimation that he wasn't making enough use of his abilities, not pushing himself hard enough to attain the quality that lay within his grasp. Before the two profiles went to Margaret Cole for subbing, Kausman took each of them apart, identifying weaknesses of construction and infelicities of expression, working over individual adjectives as ruthlessly as a drill sergeant with a flabby recruit. He also composed their headlines: for Tolkien, "THE HOBBIT HABIT," for Yoko Ono, "BOTTOM ENOUGH TO BEWITCH A BEATLE."

From the casual overflow of Kausman's prodigiously stocked mind, Louis acquired knowledge far beyond any available at his Neanderthal private school, let alone in the cheerfully philistine life of the provincial reporter. It was like discovering a parallel twentieth century, peopled by entities whose names he would hitherto scarcely have known how to pronounce—Dadaism, Alma Tadema, Ferlinghetti, Bauhaus, Duchamp, Fischer Dieskau, Mies van der Rohe, George Grosz. He now knew how to distinguish Monet from Manet; that W. C. Fields was not the same as Sid Field, that Francis Bacon could be someone other than an alternative author of Shakespeare's plays, that Man Ray was not a kind of fish nor Le Corbusier a brand of Cognac.

Kausman also taught him how to make lunch in Soho stretch from one to four or even five o'clock, moving on from Wheeler's or Leoni's Quo Vadis to Patisserie Valerie for dessert, Bar Italia for espresso, the French pub for liqueurs and finally Colman Cohen's tobacconist's in Old Compton Street to buy a cigar and light it at their brassbound eternal flame. He introduced Louis to Chinese garlic dumplings, Indian tandoori chicken, Japanese teriyaki and Mexican guacamole; to the writing of Maupassant, Rex Stout, Willa Cather, O. Henry and Talbot Baines Reed and the films of Eisenstein, Buñuel, King Vidor and George Stevens; to Bolívar cigars, Dr. Bustani Egyptian cigarettes, Crème de Menthe frappé, Kendal mint cake and the words "kif" and "charge" rather than "pot" or "hash."

Yet even while lifting another garlic dumpling between chopsticks he could now use with ease, or lighting his second Bolívar number 3 of the day, Louis still felt, along with Buddy Holly, that it was raining in his heart. His upbringing in the public glare of bars and cafés had made him intensely secretive, and Fran was a secret so tinged with self-disgust that he could not confess it even to Brenda in their talks after lights-out. He fixed his features in an expressionless blank each time he happened to see her getting into Bracegirdle's yellow E-Type outside McIntyre House at night, and when they arrived for work the next morning, separated by a careful but unconvincing few minutes, and Freya Broadbent and Margaret watched the door close behind them, then leaned close to share the latest "vignette."

"Apparently," Mrs. Broadbent said in the reverent murmur of a vicar's wife during Sung Eucharist, "last Thursday they checked into a suite at the Cumberland, and spent the whole night licking one another all over.''

"He's got her officially promoted to researcher now, surprise surprise,'' Margaret said. "This week she was talking to some big Hollywood producer for the Liz Taylor profile. She's doing all the captions for the 'What Is Scotland?' issue—and, if you can believe, getting her name in the same type-size as Magnus Magnusson's.''

"What I can't understand is how someone so woebegone-looking should turn out to be such a siren.''

"The quiet ones are often like that. They go around all day as if they wouldn't say boo to a goose. But as soon as that bedroom door closes . . .'' Margaret mimed a bead-swinging, hand-rotating twenties flapper.

"By the way, Mags, did you know that when poor old Venetia got the heave-ho, she was with-it enough to nick Terry's private contacts book? Evidently it's proving jolly useful in her new job at the Weekend Telegraph.''

"What I'll never know is why none of these little dollies he screws and then dumps has ever resorted to the ultimate revenge. I mean, Stephanie Bracegirdle must already have some inkling of what goes on.''

"I gather Stephanie's rather fatalistic about the whole thing,'' Mrs. Broadbent said.

"She's probably decided that half an oaf is better than no bread at all.''

---

The editorial car waiting outside McIntyre House had a familiar bull neck and Teddy-boy haircut behind the wheel. It was Shildrick's sometime driver, Les. "So where we off to today?'' he asked

"Weybridge. St. George's Hill estate.''

"What—to interview the Beatles?''

"No,'' Louis said gloomily. "Elizabeth Taylor's mother.''

He had meant to use the journey for background research. Beside him lay seven bulky cuttings envelopes, only a small portion of those available from the Library: TAYLOR, Elizabeth (career as child star); TAYLOR, Elizabeth (previous marriages to N. Hilton, M. Wilding, E. Fisher, M. Todd); TAYLOR, Elizabeth (affair with and marriage to R. Burton); TAYLOR, Elizabeth (children, natural and adopted); TAYLOR, Elizabeth (troubles during filming of *Cleopatra*); BURTON, Richard (theatrical and film career); BURTON, Richard (affair with and marriage to E. Taylor). But unfortunately Les was in a chatty mood.

"Course, now he's Editor he's got a nice Rover three-litre, not these clapped-out Fords any more. My mate Geoff drives him mostly, but I still get asked to fill in now and again. Bloody pleasure to do it. That kind of bloke you'd go through hell for, wouldn't you? 'Ere, you ever seen his wife?''

"Yes. A couple of times.''

"What'd you think of her, then? More like his mum than his old lady, isn't she? I'll tell you something. I had both of 'em in the back of the Riley one day, and you've never heard anything like it! Givin' him a real ruckin', she was. 'Why can't you come home when you're sup- posed to . . . the kids are forgettin' who you are' sort of thing. I'll tell you, without a word of a lie, I've run him up to Hampstead sometimes, he's gone in the front door, then come straight back out again. 'Take me back to the paper, Les,' he goes. 'It's too bloody much with it all in there.' So I don't reckon things on the home front are all that merry and bright, know what I mean?''

They turned off the main road, into a hushed preserve of mock-Tudor mansions, sculpted hedges and fanciful topiary work. "That's Ringo Starr's place," said Les as they passed a pair of vehemently shut iron gates. "And John Lennon's we're just comin' up to now. See the girls waitin' outside? And the Rolls with coloured squiggles all over it?''

Mrs. Sara Taylor received Louis in a small chintz drawing room with French windows bolted against the winter expanse of lawn and swim- ming pool. She was a bird-like woman with receding curly hair and the same deep violet eyes that (he now knew from cuttings) were among her daughter's most striking features. Her husband, who appeared partly disabled, sat near the log-fire in American golfing clothes, inter- jecting a gruff word now and then.

"Of course, our real home is Bel Air," Mrs. Taylor said. "But Eliza- beth and Richard insisted on renting this place for us because Daddy here has been ordered to have complete rest and quiet after his stroke. And we do so love to catch up with our family and old friends.''

With an effort Louis recollected that Hollywood's greatest modern screen goddess had been born a British subject. He stopped his mind from telerecording the room and strove to elicit the kind of quotes that could be dropped as disembodied pearls into Toby Godwin's definitive profile.

"Are you, would you say, a close family?''

"Oh, goodness, yes," Mrs. Taylor said. "And even more so since Richard has been one of us. Wherever both of them may be in the world, they call us all the time, don't they, Daddy? And we have our Christmases together, and holidays at their house at Cap Ferrat. We do the simple family things. Like picnics . . . barbecues.''

7 faithfully.

"Elizabeth is crazy about hot-dogs," Mr. Taylor put in. "With bacon, cheese, relish, everything. She can eat five of those straight off."

Louis felt a kindling of interest as he scribbled.

"Has . . . your daughter changed much since she . . . ?"

"Married Richard? Oh, yes, wouldn't you say so, Daddy? For one thing she's gotten a whole lot tidier. When she was a little girl, she hated to clean up her room. Clothes would be left scattered just everywhere. But Richard's very neat. He goes round emptying ash-trays all the time. Just lately I've noticed Elizabeth doing that, too."

"You get on well with him, do you?"

"Oh, yes, he has a wonderful rapport with us both. Just look at what a dear thing he wrote." Mrs. Taylor reached out and took a silver-framed photograph from the piano-top. It showed Elizabeth Taylor in tweed suit and dark fishnet stockings seated in an armchair with Richard Burton perched beside her. Behind them was an expanse of bookshelves. Up the picture's right-hand side was an extravagantly scrawled dual inscription.

"What does it say?" Louis asked, reopening his notebook.

"Richard has written, 'Wait till you see the library we're going to have in Switzerland.' And Elizabeth has written, 'From Elizabeth, with more love than all the books in the world.' "

---

"There was a call for you while you were out," Margaret said. "From Jack Shildrick's office. He wants you as soon as possible."

So the moment had finally come! Louis raced to the fifth floor, torn between exaltation and wild panic. What if—knowing Shildrick—he was expected to make his debut as Cicero-to-be this coming weekend? He had long planned his first lead item, a mock-reverential survey of old-fashioned funny men like Nat Jackley and Arthur English. The problem would be finding humorous fillers as droll as that one about Kenneth Kaunda's trousers.

But the summons turned out to be merely from Shildrick's middle-aged secretary, Enid. In her outer office, the door stood wide open on the panoramic corner sanctum that Shildrick had inherited from Dudley Mowforth. The white desk was swept clean, the padded chair motionless, the lectern bare of papers and layout sheets.

"Oh, yes," Enid said, glancing down a list on her desk. "Could you go along and see Desmond Follett?"

Louis stared at her. "Are you sure?"

"Yes, Desmond Follett. The Literary Editor. You just go out of here . . . past the Newsroom. He's in room 516."

"But I think there's been some mistake. Is Jack not around?"

"No, he's gone to New York with the Chairman. This was one of the things he left on his dictating machine." She held up the list. "See? 'L. Brennan to see Literary Editor.' "

Desmond Follett was a frowstily elegant man of about fifty with back-swept silver hair and a handkerchief pushed up one pinstripe jacket-sleeve. He inhabited a cramped cubbyhole with two facing desks and a wall of shelves filled with shiny new books of every size.

"Has the Editor not spoken to you about any of this?" he enquired, looking at Louis with no great enthusiasm down a long, aristocratic nose.

"No, not at all."

"Dear me, that's strange." Follett pulled the handkerchief from his sleeve like a conjurer, wiped his nose and stuffed it back. "Well, the vacancy is as my deputy here. You'd be largely responsible for subbing and making up two, sometimes three books pages. I take it you know all about proofreading and working on the stone?"

"Yes," Louis said numbly.

"And you have some skill at packing up parcels?"

"Yes."

"That's very important. We send out an average of thirty books a week. For salary, I fear I'm constrained to offer only the N.U.J. minimum. But there is a small extra emolument, which we would divide, from sale of review copies."

"Would I be writing anything?" Louis asked.

"As a general rule, no. I try not to trespass on the space of our regular critics. But, should the spirit move you, you might from time to time do the odd unsigned short notice."

"I see."

"Pardon my saying so, but you do seem rather nonplussed by all this?"

"It's just that . . . I thought I was going to be offered something a bit different."

"And what would that be?"

"The Cicero column."

Follett gave a snorting laugh. "Aha! Another one! *Cicero filio dedit.*"

"I'm sorry?"

"Forgive me," Follett said, without humility, "but you're about the fourth person I've met to whom our esteemed new Editor has faithfully and unequivocally promised the Cicero column. When in fact the appointment was decided some months since."

Louis felt as if the entire contents of the bookcase had toppled out and buried him.

"Decided?" he managed to say.

"Yes. Basil Hamilton's coming from The Observer to do it. A witty and pointful writer, many aver. Though a little vulgar for my taste."

# 15

By the second week of November, Freya Broadbent and Margaret Cole had begun animated discussions about Christmas.

"Festus has invited Tarquin to stay at his villa in Marrakesh," Mrs. Broadbent said. "I'm probably going to be in Spain the previous week on my General de Gaulle research, so I thought I might give them a look-in. Morocco's hot in December, isn't it?"

"Freya, are you serious? You're going to gate-crash Festus?"

"Hardly gate-crash," Mrs. Broadbent said. "He's still my husband, at least technically. I daresay he'll have masses of his boy-friends there, but I shan't intrude. I'll be quite happy visiting archaeological sites. And I've decided I'm really going to make an effort with the language." She held up a small book entitled *Getting to Grips with Arabic.*

"People are already starting to ask me about our Christmas party," Margaret said.

"Mm, ditto here. I met Laurence Harvey and Paulene Stone at Gaia Mostyn-Owen's drinks the other night, and they were most perturbed. Apparently there's a rumour going round that we're not having one this year."

"After what happened last year I'm not surprised."

Louis looked up from typing the testament of a minor co-star in *Elephant Walk* that, despite her beauty and wealth, Elizabeth Taylor was "an earth mother at heart."

"What did happen last year?" he asked.

"It was just that the numbers got completely out of hand," Mrs. Broadbent said. "The trouble with inviting people from the fashion and pop world is that they always bring along huge entourages of their own. Sandie Shaw I remember arriving with a party of about twenty."

"And it did get rather wild," Margaret said.

"Yes, I agree, that bottle-throwing incident was a bit beyond the pale. And if people want to have it off, I think they should choose somewhere a bit more discreet than the floor of the photocopier-room."

"According to Jim, even our nice security men have put their foot down and said never again in the office. So God's talking about having it at his house this year."

"It won't be the same," Mrs. Broadbent said. "For me, an office Christmas party isn't complete without the spectacle of God dancing on top of a desk."

"And I can't see Monica Godwin going a bundle on the idea, can you? You know how neurotic she is about that collection of antique harpsichords."

In Louis's previous journalistic jobs, Christmas had signalled little beyond an increase of normal panic and overwork. At The Sunday Dispatch Magazine, it proved to be a long-drawn-out season of Dickensian jollification under the aegis of an Editor whose natural attire might have been a bushy white beard and a red suit trimmed with ermine.

Its official inauguration came in the first week of December, when Toby Godwin took all the Magazine's male "young rips" to see the Oxford versus Cambridge University rugby match at Twickenham. Beforehand in the car park they ate cold grouse, gulls' eggs and mince pies from a Fortnum and Mason hamper, and drank vintage Pol Roger whose breathtaking chill matched the early dusting of snow on the grass.

Godwin himself was patriarchally magnificent in a Russian hat and an ankle-length fur coat whose yellowish striations suggested wholesale massacre of many small animals, possibly hamsters, but in an era too far distant to feel pity or outrage now. As their chief's mirthful and girthful figure swaggered ahead of them into the grandstand, Terry Bracegirdle grinned and nudged Cedric Scurr. "Get a load of God. He looks just like some old queen, out with all his young men . . ."

Louis was seated at the extreme left of the party, next to Jim Deaves. As Godwin passed a box of outsize Romeo y Julietas along the row, Deaves said something to Bracegirdle about "when I was on the Express."

"I didn't know you were on the Express, Jim," said Louis.

Deaves sheltered a match in nicotine-stained fingers to light his cigar. "Oh, not 'arf. In the palmy days of Arthur Christiansen."

"What did you do there?"

"Visiting fireman. I used to be 'Express man James Deaves flies in to riot-torn Penang.' "

He smiled at the question which died, unspoken, on Louis's lips.

"Quite so. You're wondering how such a glorious career could end up in a backwater of McIntyre House, costing issues and signing expenses. Tell me, have you ever read *Black Beauty?*"

"A long time ago."

"Well, you remember how some of *Black Beauty*'s masters were horrible, cruel men who beat and starved and overworked him, but others were kind, and gave him easy jobs, a lovely warm stall with lots of bran mash to eat. I've never found a better description of working in Fleet Street."

A bottle of Remy Martin now made its way along the row from Toby Godwin. Deaves took a deep swig and handed it on to Louis with a wink. "Take it from me, old chum," he said, "God runs the warmest stall in town."

In the game that followed, Toby Godwin cheered the dark blue of the university whose debating society and dining clubs he had once adorned. Louis cheered the light blue of the university he would longingly glimpse when collecting Portia Bolton-Phelps from secretarial college. "Cambridge!" he cried, wreathed in Havana smoke and brandy fumes, as plausible a product of dreaming spires and May Week as anyone in the grandstand. Even this greatest of his life's regrets had finally ceased to matter.

Another Yuletide event with the status of ancient tradition was the secretaries' lunch, when the half-dozen girls with the arduous job of typing the young rips' letters, serving their coffee and Alka-Seltzer, sending off cheques for their household gas and electricity bills and lying to their wives were rewarded with a special seasonal taste of the restaurant high life which they themselves enjoyed daily throughout the year. The occasion was almost medieval in its condescending democracy as well as its implication that this lordly head-patting might well be a prelude to more serious varieties of droit du seigneur.

A private upstairs room was booked at one of Godwin's favourite lunching-spots, the Gay Hussar Hungarian restaurant in Greek Street. The menu—chosen with concern for palates soon to be fatigued by Christmas fare—was wild cherry soup, cold pike mayonnaise, roast duck with red cabbage, and Esterhazy chocolate and fresh raspberry torte, accompanied by schnapps, Bull's Blood, Armagnac and plum-flavoured slivovitz.

Compounding the medieval atmosphere, two tables had been laid in a T-shape. As the party took their places after preliminary drinks, it somehow fell out that Fran Dyson ended up at the top table, between Godwin and Terry Bracegirdle. She was wearing a faintly patterned pink shift dress with long, trailing sleeves. Her hair, which she had flicked off her shoulders to hang straight down her back, seemed to Louis more seamlessly pale than usual, less honey than white gold.

He himself was seated far down the stem of the T, between Val Lewis and Godwin's secretary, Tessa Burland. The latter had freed her chestnut hair from its usual severe bun and discarded her tortoiseshell spectacles. As the meal progressed, her normally impenetrable calm and discretion showed signs of going the same way.

"Is God always so happy?" Louis asked her as gales of scarlet-faced "hooh hooh hooh!" blew from the top table.

"Oh, Lordy, no!" Tessa held out her glass to be refilled with Bull's Blood. "Do you mean you've never seen him pout?"

"I can't say I have."

"Well, believe me, you haven't seen a pout until you've seen God pout."

He stole another look at Fran, who was eating cold pike with the care her trailing sleeves demanded and listening in black-eyed rapture as Toby Godwin told a long and uproarious story about the M.C.C.'s seven-year waiting-list. "Butter wouldn't melt in her mouth, would it?" Tessa commented drily.

"Don't you just know the type?" Val Lewis said.

"Hmmm, don't we just!" Jessamyn O'Shaughnessy interrupted from across the table. "It's the deadly Little Me Syndrome. She goes round accidentally tripping men up and just happening to fall directly underneath them."

The Magazine's leisurely production schedule had been manipulated to allow everyone a ten-day break beginning on the day before Christmas Eve. Not since leaving school had Louis contemplated a Christmas holiday of such magnitude, and he was somewhat at a loss about where among the far-flung remnants of his family to spend it. Grandma and Grandad Bassill would be going away, as usual, to her sister Aunt Flo in Streatham. Staying with his mother and Aubrey at Hedloe Manor Farm, as he usually did, would mean log-fires and Land Rovers on the credit side but on the debit side endless talk about pheasant-rearing and Brussels sprouts, not to mention the threat of social encounters with Portia and her mother.

"You're welcome to come down to the Island with me," Brenda said.

"Thanks, but I think I'll see if I can go to my father's in Berkshire."

"I thought you said he takes absolutely no interest in you."

"He doesn't."

"And your stepmother's a nightmare."

"That's right."

"And they live in squalor."

"They do."

"And are more or less permanently pissed."

"Right."

"Are you by any chance what's called a masochist?"

"No—it's just that I've been thinking I ought to make one last effort to get through to him. And Christmas seems as good a time as any."

---

The summons he'd been dreading came on the Magazine's final working day before Christmas. This time, Enid waved him past her desk and through the wide-open inner door. Shildrick was back under the white Anglepoise lamp, hammering away at his portable typewriter balanced on the familiar strew of papers, books and proofs. With Sunday falling on December 27, the paper would be working until late on Christmas Eve, then reassembling for a climactically busy Boxing Day.

At the sight of Louis, he swung his padded chair around, got up and stared moodily through his panoramic window at the chill pink sky around the G.P.O. Tower. "So you think you're too good for the Literary Department, do you, Poet?"

Guilty as Louis had felt since electing not to become Desmond Follett's sub-editor and parcel-packer, this tone of bleak disillusionment took him aback. "Not at all . . ." he stammered.

"It would have been perfect for you. Desmond's a first-rate Literary Editor, perhaps the finest in Fleet Street. He'd have given you a superb grounding in subbing and production . . . you'd have been dealing with some of the Leviathans of the book-reviewing world. I don't understand how you could pass up such an opportunity."

Put in that way, it did sound infinitely privileged and promising. "I'm sorry . . ." Louis said lamely. "I just didn't want to give up writing."

"No one said you had to stop writing," Shildrick almost snapped. "It was just a way to give you an entrée into the paper. I know you wanted Cicero . . . you've been badgering me about it long enough. But you're obviously not ready for a major slot like that. I'd be doing you a disservice as much as anyone by letting you loose in it. Besides, there was pressure from other people up here to bring in an established name. And Basil Hamilton's a brilliant writer, you know."

"Yes, I know he is."

"Who, anyway, probably won't want to stay more than a couple of years at the most. My idea was for you to widen your experience, become an important member of staff up here, so that when Cicero came vacant again you'd be an obvious front-runner."

An additional wave of remorse broke over Louis for having thought, however briefly, that Shildrick had not dealt totally honestly with him. How could he not have guessed this wise, far-sighted plan for his ultimate advancement? And now, with his childish petulance and impatience, he'd ruined everything.

"Anyway, it's not as if you were doing so wonderfully well on the Colour Mag. You've been there . . . what? Six months? And how many of your things have they run?"

Shildrick strode to his lectern and shuffled some papers on it, growing visibly angry as he did so. One caught Louis's eye, a memo in the familiar electric typeface of Toby Godwin's office."It's no place for you, Poet . . . or for any serious journalist. If you ask me, they're out of bloody control down there, thanks to this ridiculous carte-blanche they get from Lord M. They've lost all regard for what the ordinary reader wants. And talk about arrogant! If you send them an idea, you hardly even get a civil reply."

Nearby, half-concealed by *Burke's Peerage,* lay a copy of the Magazine's New Eve issue. Shildrick pulled it out and glared at Fran's golden head and shyly-crossed arms. "As for this . . . didn't you think it was an utter disgrace? I tried my best to get it killed. I mean, are we The Sunday Dispatch or bloody Tit-Bits?"

It was the first time Louis had ever known him to be on the side of censorship and repression: not battling in the front line to start something but intriguing on the back-stairs to stop it.

"You tried to get the New Eve cover killed?"

Shildrick nodded grimly. "Too true I did. But it craftily wasn't sent up to Dudley until colour-proof stage, when changing it would have cost fortunes."

He glanced up, mistaking Louis's expression for a fresh paroxysm of remorse. With a sigh he took off his glasses and polished them with the tail of his tie. The feminine eyes were no longer accusing, even though still sadly disappointed. "All right, Poet . . . we won't rub it in any more, being Christmas and all. It's your future. But I think you're making a mistake. It's obvious the Colour Mag's never going to give you a halfway decent crack of the whip."

"I do want to stick it out there," Louis said.

"Aye, of course you do. It's a life of bloody Riley." Shildrick replaced his glasses and tucked the tie-tail inside his shirt with a brusque movement. "Just don't think it'll necessarily go on like that for ever."

---

Toby Godwin's house was an imposing semi-detached residence halfway along a white Regency avenue in Belgravia. When Louis arrived just after 9 P.M., the gold-lit drawing-room window displayed a packed and murmurous crowd. The road was choked by large cars double-parked to left and right, many with uniformed chauffeurs waiting behind their wheels.

The holly-wreathed front door was opened by a teenage girl with an unmistakable blobby face, although set in an expression that was patient and rueful rather than happy and bonhomous. Behind her stood an angular woman in a sleeveless black dress, her greying hair pinned up in a haphazard style that proclaimed both "intellectual" and "too good for all this." In one hand she held a new yellow duster, in the other a tin of lacquer polish.

"Ah, Louis! Excellent!" Godwin himself, massively pink-pullovered, lurched into view, one arm encircling Val Lewis, the other a girl of unknown identity.

"Welcome and well met, dear boy. Can I present my wife, Monica?" The grey-haired woman paused from reading the instructions on the polish long enough to nod grimly. "And this is my daughter, Joan. Named in honour of the greatest poem in the English language, whose opening lines I'm sure you cannot fail to remember. 'Miss Joan Hunter Dunn, Miss Joan Hunter Dunn . . . furnished and burnished by Aldershot sun . . .' " Judging by the look of glum stoicism on the girl's face as she took Louis's coat and scarf, it was not the first time this booming recitation had been delivered.

There was not space to advance more than a few inches into the packed drawing room. At one end was a gaudily-lit Christmas tree with a pile of obese-looking presents beneath. At the other, the crowd lapped around the mottled curves of a baby grand piano, a spinet and two harpsichords. Just inside the door stood Cedric Scurr, dressed in a pale orange paisley shirt and matching cravat, and chewing on one of the thin Dutch cheroots that gave his breath an habitual odour of decayed liquorice. He betrayed no sign of ever having set eyes on Louis before.

"Now, good people, *attention s'il vous plaît* . . . allow me to introduce Louis Brennan, one of our most able young writers on the Magazine . . . Tony Crosland . . . George Weidenfeld . . . Gaia Mostyn-Owen . . . Clement Freud . . . Peter Cook . . ."

"I like your tie," said a man in a bottle-green velvet Beau Brummel jacket, with the fuzzy hair and colliding eyebrows of a satyr in an erotic frieze.

"Thanks very much," Louis said, taking a glass of champagne from the tray of an immobilised waitress.

"Goes awfully well with that khaki suit and yellow shirt. I'm Arden Sinclair, by the way. I once sent you a postcard. Do you remember?"

The almost unbearable exquisiteness of the voice was suddenly familiar from far-off days last summer. "Of course . . . the publisher. And you
rang me up, too."

"That's right. In Middlesborough, wasn't it?"

"Stockton."

"You were going to write a novel, remember?"

"Have you seen the diamond yet?" asked someone in the group
around Toby Godwin.

"I'll say I have—all two million quidsworth of it! And the rather nice
thing is that when you admire it, there's no pretence at false modesty.
'Yeah,' she says, 'ain't that a lovely load of ice!' "

"We're putting together the definitive profile of Elizabeth Taylor,"
Scurr elucidated. "God's spent the last week interviewing her at this
fantastic house on Cap Ferrat."

At this Louis saw a shifty expression—what might, indeed, almost be
called a pout—cloud the benignity of Godwin's face. "Not quite accurate, dear boy. I haven't actually interviewed her yet."

Scurr grinned. "So what were you doing when you drove around
Antibes with her, drinking bourbon out of silver goblets?"

"These were . . . harumph . . . exploratory conversations prior to an
interview. A feasibility study, if you like . . ."

"Well, don't forget we need the words by early Jan."

A waitress proffered a tray of hot hors d'oeuvres. Arden Sinclair took
a bursting vol-au-vent with what, surprisingly, proved not to be a cloven hoof. The shaggy-ridged eyes appraised Louis as if he were another
succulent nibble. "And are you?"

"Pardon?"

"Writing a novel?"

"I meant to. The trouble is finding the time to settle down to it."

Sinclair nodded sagely. "I know . . . The Blue Bugloss."

"Pardon?"

"Have you never read Connolly's *Enemies of Promise?* About the
blighting effect of journalism on true literary endeavour. I'll send you a
copy."

David Kausman materialised between them, brown-suited and yellow-shirted, eating a chipolata on a stick like Henry VIII attacking a leg
of mutton. "I was just telling this young man that he should write a
novel," Sinclair said.

Kausman put the chipolata stick into his breast pocket and glared at
Louis. "I know he should. And I wish he'd pull his finger out of his arse
and get on with it."

Sinclair drifted away. Kausman and Louis discovered a minute pocket of space beside a corner alcove displaying antique teapots. "What's happening with you at the moment?" Kausman demanded.

"Still doing legwork for God's profile of Elizabeth Taylor. And wondering if I shouldn't have taken that job as Desmond Follett's deputy."

"Are you insane?" Kausman spluttered. "Being stuck away behind a desk . . . marking up other people's pissy copy? It would be stultifyingly tedious!" They paused as Monica Godwin darted from the crowd with a face of thunder, whisked Louis's glass off the harpsichord and resentfully rubbed away its damp circle with the cloth in her hand.

". . . But Shildrick had specially earmarked it for me. I sort of feel I'm letting him down."

"Oh, balls! He's just an Editor with a slot to fill, who wants to fill it in the easiest way possible. When are you going to wipe these idiotic stars from your eyes?"

Kausman's one great blind spot was remaining as stubbornly immune to the wonder of Shildrick as the most envious snobs and cavillers on the Magazine. Louis took another draught of champagne, suddenly engulfed by gloom. The prospect of seeing his father and stepmother tomorrow afternoon materially assisted this.

"At least on the paper I might feel I belonged a bit more than I do now."

Kausman smote the shelf, making the precious teapots rattle. "You're a writer! You don't have to 'belong' anywhere! Never mind the backstabbing! Never mind the politics, the ghouls and the faggots! You've got a toehold in the place where you ought to be. Don't let anybody prise you loose."

Margaret Cole, Freya Broadbent and Jim Deaves were standing together beside one of the antique harpsichords. Beneath were piles of music with titles in German and French.

Mrs. Broadbent wore a chocolate-coloured Foale and Tuffin minidress with a lacy bib front and exaggerated leg o'mutton sleeves. Idly Louis wondered if this might be the long-delayed night when he and she ended up in bed together.

"I just don't know how I'm going to fit it all in," she was complaining. "I'm flying to Marbella first thing tomorrow, then on to Marrakesh to surprise Festus. On the twenty-eighth, I'm supposed to be in Dijon, but I honestly think I'm going to have to scrub that if I'm to make it to Berne on the thirtieth. By the by, Jim, I've got a pink slip in my bag which I wish you'd be an angel and sign before we're all too squiffy to see."

Deaves set down his champagne glass on the polished harpsichord top, looking bewildered. "This is your General de Gaulle story, is it, Freya?"

"Yes, and I must say it's proving ab-so-lute-ly fascinating. God has said I can have five thousand words, but I think I may well need more."

"But . . . have I got this right? You're reconstructing General de Gaulle's wartime stay in a village in Kent."

"Yes, Petts Wood."

"But you need to research it in Marbella, Dijon and Berne?"

"And quite a few other places," Mrs. Broadbent nodded. "Because obviously lots of the people who knew the de Gaulles in Kent during the War have since scattered to the four winds. The postmistress is widowed and living on the Costa del Sol. The people who owned the teashop where Madame de Gaulle had scones every afternoon now run a shooting lodge in Corsica. Several key people in the story have emigrated to America. The Catholic priest who used to give them confession is now in the West Indies . . ."

Margaret Cole was wearing a white silk dress with a square embroidered collar, vaguely Egyptian in character. It was the first time Louis had ever seen her in make-up—lots of black around the eyes and almost flesh-pale lipstick. For all these months he had regarded her as an elder sister; someone to sympathise with his complaints and laugh at his sillier puns. Tonight, so transformed was the rather severe, high-cheekboned face that he fleetingly wondered if she might be the one he ended up in bed with.

"Have you seen the Standard tonight?" she asked.

"No. Why?"

"There's a huge piece by Ray Connolly, confirming that the Beatles have given up concert tours. From now on they're going to concentrate on making records and pursuing individual projects."

Louis clutched his forehead. "Christ, I don't believe it! I told Terry about that weeks ago."

Bracegirdle, it happened, was now visible in the front hall, taking off a fun-fur coat and a Tiny Tim–style multicoloured knitted scarf, and being welcomed by his Editor with a grizzly bear-hug. He wore a bright yellow tunic in the new Indian style, with a gold medallion dangling from a long chain around his neck, and white trousers and shoes. There was also a glimpse of Fran's pale, straight hair, tumbling down a blouse of turquoise sateen. As another drinks waitress fought her way past, Louis grabbed a fresh glass of champagne and took a despairing swig.

"I don't know," he sighed. "What have I got to do to get through to that bloke?"

"Be fifteen years older," Margaret said with a wry, pale pink smile.

"Sorry?"

"The trouble with Terry, as David Kausman once said, is that he doesn't like anybody to be younger than he is. Why do you think he

only ever commissions these heavyweight older writers like Mailer and
Capote? Before you came, he was the Magazine's marvellous boy. He
thinks you're out to usurp God's affections from him."

"But that's ridiculous."

"Not to Terry. Don't you know what he calls you? 'Babe Brennan.'
And 'The son God never had.' "

Louis glanced across the room at Bracegirdle, who looked even more
than usually incapable of mean or malicious behaviour, talking and
laughing with Val Lewis and Scurr with one arm hooked around Fran's
neck as if they were two working-class lads out on the piss together. He
felt no resentment—indeed, paradoxically found himself liking and admiring Bracegirdle even more, and wishing even more to be liked and
admired by him in return.

"He is my Features Editor, though. I'd like to feel he was behind me."

Margaret flicked one corner of her hair with a patient smile. "You
mean like he used to be behind Venetia, and like he's now behind Miss
Charcoal-Eyes Dyson? Don't you understand that he has to be on top of
someone before he's behind them?"

---

Supper was served in a downstairs room whose Christmassy red glow
gave the three huge cold turkeys on the labyrinthine buffet a fleeting
look of naked amputees suffering the torments of purgatory.

Jessamyn O'Shaughnessy lurched hilariously against Louis, her diaphanous indigo-and-gold Liberty gown richly contrasting with the
hectic flush of her cheeks. "Bear witness, everyone, I'm starting a diet
as soon as Christmas is over. The only thing I wonder is, can one still go
down on people if one's slimming? I've never seen any analysis of the
calorific content of sperm."

"Don't worry, Jessamyn," Margaret's voice replied. "I seem to remember reading that a pint, if you should be so lucky, would equal
something like point 008 of a small lettuce leaf."

"Oh, look, it's EVELYN!" Jessamyn cried rapturously as a bulky, coquettish figure appeared in the doorway.

"I'm surprised he's not already out on Cap Ferrat with Elizabeth Taylor," Mrs. Broadbent remarked. "I mean, it's quite obvious God has no
intention of buckling down to write this profile. Poor Evelyn's been
standing by for weeks to go in and salvage it."

Beside Strachey stood a man with the slightly stiff and wary posture
of someone brought along rather than invited. Aged about forty, he
wore an old-fashioned Italian suit, high-buttoned to a pin-collar and
Slim Jim tie. The black cockade of brilliantined hair, the puffy mouth

and close-set, staring eyes were as well known in their way as the features of any pop star.

"Is that who I think it is?" Louis murmured to David Kausman.

Kausman turned and looked.

"If you think it's one of the Kray twins, you're absolutely right."

"Which one?"

"It's Ronnie."

Louis peeped round Kausman's bulk again, wondering at this era which could bring into the same social orbit a Labour Cabinet minister and the most spectacularly ruthless and cold-blooded of all East End hoodlums.

"Ronnie's the mad Kray twin, isn't he? And the queer one."

"I really would keep your voice down," Kausman said. "Unless you want to end up inside a concrete flyover on the M4."

Nor was Ronnie Kray the only unofficial guest to have been imported by Evelyn Strachey. With them also stood a man and a woman, both of late middle age and in conspicuously non-festive attire. The man wore a dowdy sports jacket and pale grey trousers, the woman a drab floral frock and shabby flat shoes. Though welcomed with impartial expansiveness by Toby Godwin, they looked about them with faces noticeably lacking in yuletide hilarity. Offered champagne, both shook their heads, whereat Kray said something to them in a plainly encouraging undertone. Each then hurriedly took a glass and sipped with as much pleasure as if it were castor oil.

"More underworld colour?" Louis murmured to Kausman, who merely shrugged in mystification.

Later, there was dancing at the non-harpsichord end of the upstairs drawing room. Louis found himself partnering Margaret, whose preferred step was a cautious but not inelegant jive. Beside them the pink-woolly, scarlet-faced bulk of their Editor did the Frug on legs as surprisingly nimble as a Russian circus bear's, and with a patrician bellow of "Ba-Ba-Ba Ba-Barbara Ann" against the Beach Boys' multi-harmonic refrain. Half-way through "Good Vibrations," Jessamyn came into view, cleaving through the dancers on a long, staggering trajectory as if the polished floor were the deck of a liner in a mid-Atlantic gale. "Oh . . . *très* hip!" she jeered thickly, and Louis received a whack on the buttocks from a flailing hand.

During the next interlude, Kausman beckoned him aside.

"You know you were wondering about that odd-looking couple with Ronnie Kray? Well, Evelyn's just told me who they are. Apparently, earlier this evening Kray called at one of the Bethnal Green pubs where he regularly collects protection, and the landlord couldn't pay him. So as a punishment he made this unfortunate man and his wife drop everything and come on with him here. Can you imagine a more exquisite form of sadism?"

The couple were now wedged in the teapot-alcove, listening to Freya Broadbent's vivacious account of General de Gaulle's lost Kentish years with faces which, indeed, might have been enduring some ultra-refined and intensified form of the Chinese water torture.

Later, as celebrities departed and the dancers thinned, there was a longish period when Terry Bracegirdle and Fran were the only couple on the floor. To Louis's gloomy mind, it was like a scene in a Hollywood film when everyone falls back for the big number by Fred Astaire and Ginger Rogers. Fran danced a Shake of sinuous nonchalance, honey hair drifting against her face, while Bracegirdle, in his Buddhist-yellow tunic and white cricketer's trousers, leapt around and flailed his arms exaggeratedly to stress with what youthfully unaffected exuberance he threw himself into everything.

"What do you think of this modern dancing, then?" a refined Cockney voice said from the shadows a few yards away. Ronnie Kray was standing and watching with a benign, elderly-statesman air, and his two hostages tense and ghastly-faced beside him.

He met Louis's glance and smiled with his puffy mouth but not his small, hooded eyes. It felt like being lazily sized up by a king cobra.

"Very pleasant party, isn't it?" he said. "I like to get out and about . . . see how the with-it set enjoys theirselves. Pity there's no one to get on one of these old joannas and give us a nice tune, eh?" he added, turning to his captives.

"Please, Mr. Kray," the man almost sobbed, "we'll get it by tomorrow, first thing . . . without fail . . ."

Kray shook his head sorrowfully.

"Dear oh dear, Frostie. How long we known each another?"

Frostie essayed a ghastly smile.

"Ooh . . ."

"Go back a lot of years, don't we? Wasn't your cousin Joe sparring partner to brother Reg and me in the old Hoxton days? Didn't I stand godfather to your Dolly's boy . . . wossis name? Kenneth?"

"You did, Mr. Kray . . . and I want you to know she . . ."

"So wossall this Mr. Kray stuff? Since when did I stop being Uncle Ronnie?"

It was now almost 1:30. David Kausman, Margaret, Mrs. Broadbent and Jim Deaves had gone. Toby Godwin, all Ba-Barbara-Anning spent, lay in a stranded-whale posture on a Regency-striped Chesterfield. Near the larger, paler harpsichord, Mrs. Godwin knelt with a pint tankard of water and a cloth, sponging at a red wine stain on the cream shag-pile rug.

From the overworked tail of his eye, Louis saw that Fran, too, was ready to leave. She disappeared for some time, presumably to the ladies', and returned, bringing her black velvet coat and Bracegirdle's shortie fun fur. In the intervening few minutes, however, Bracegirdle had launched into the party-piece for which he was famous. His back elaborately crooked, his Geordie accent flutingly precise, he was being Laurence Olivier as Richard III for the amusement of the few survivors around the door.

> I that am rudely stamped, and want love's majesty
> To strut before a wanton ambling nymph;
> I, that am curtail'd of this fair proportion . . .

Fran said something to him and touched his arm, but he shook her off with schoolboyish high spirits. "Oh, leave me be, girl. I'm just gettin' into me stride. How does the next bit goa? Oh, aye . . .

> Cheated of feature by dissembling Nature,
> Sent into this breathing world scarce half made up . . .

An indulgent general chuckle caused Richard III's accent to become that of the Queen as mimicked by the more outrageous current satirists.

" 'People keep asking One why One refused to make a Christmas broadcast to the nation this year. Basically, it's because One got totally pissed orf with the whole thing . . . My husband and I' . . . Surely, in this day and age, she should make it 'My bloke and I . . .' "

"Hooh hooh hooh!" came a sudden bellow from the supine pink shape on the Chesterfield. "Not exactly what you might call an ardent monarchist, our Terry."

"I'll say I'm not!" Bracegirdle fended off yet another effort by Fran to help him into his coat. "Parasites and bloodsuckers, the whole lot of 'em. But never fear," he went on, now in the accent of Long John Silver as portrayed by Robert Newton. "All of 'em'll swing, come the Revolution. Aaar, Jim lad! Them as dies'll be the lucky ones!"

"Excuse me," a quiet voice interjected.

Ronnie Kray had materialised from the shadows midway down the room. The podgy face above the high-buttoned jacket wore a pained expression.

"I don't think you ought to say things like that," he said mildly.

Bracegirdle grinned in delighted disbelief. It was apparent that,

whether through drunkenness or the greater intoxication of performance, he had not the faintest idea who this was.

"Oh, ye doan't, do you?"

Kray shook his glossy head. "No, I don't. And I think it's very bad
manners to go around in public denigrating our Sovereign Lady, Queen
Elizabeth, who's done a wonderful job ruling this country. If you ask
me, the country wouldn't be in the state it is if there was a bit more respect for institutions like the monarchy."

Bracegirdle had been listening in an exaggerated impersonation of
Rodin's *Thinker*.

"Well, thank you for those very plangent observations. I'm sure we
all feel very moved and enlightened."

There was a sharp intake of breath from the mesmerised onlookers.
But Kray seemed deaf to the over-larded satire. "Not at all," he said in
the same mild tone.

Bracegirdle glanced round with a bright-eyed smile. "And I wonder if
there's something else you could tell us?"

"Certainly, if I can."

"That's where you get your suits? I mean, I thought John Collier
stopped doin' bronze lovat in about 1958."

Initially believing the question a serious one, Kray had turned back
one of his jacket lapels to look at the name on its lining. The words
"John Collier," however, caused the same flickering change of expression as might a new note on the snake-charmer's pipe. In a swift, economical movement, he walked over to Bracegirdle, took one of the
Deputy Editor's wrists lightly between a finger and thumb, and began
to speak softly into his ear. He seemed to be outlining some plan or
strategy in exhaustive detail, yet with huge indifference, not even looking into the face barely an inch from his own but staring away as if at
something mildly deplorable half-way down the room. Bracegirdle's
features, meanwhile, had crumpled, like one of his own long shirt-
collars with the bone-stiffener taken out.

"Now then," Kray said at length, withdrawing from Bracegirdle's ear
and dropping his wrist. "Why not admit you was talking out of turn?"

"I was talkin' out of turn," Bracegirdle agreed with an impassioned
nod.

Kray turned to Fran, who was still waiting with the two coats over
her arm. "I wouldn't bother with him, love, if I was you. I think when
he was born, they threw away the baby and kept the afterbirth."

The hooded eyes moved round the room as if savouring afresh its
taste and elegance, then settled on Louis, who had been watching while
seated among the piles of antique music between the legs of the nearest
harpsichord.

"Now, there's a much nicer young man of the moment. Nice clothes. Nice attitude. Talks decent. Acts decent. That's the kind of young man I'd be with if I was in your very pretty shoes, not some arsehole who looks like he's borrowed his mother's maternity smock."

Fran did not reply or even look at Louis, merely gripping Bracegirdle's arm preparatory to guiding him from the danger area as soon as this should be permitted. By an almost imperceptible sign, Kray indicated that it now was. The white-faced Deputy Editor was fun-furred, Tiny Tim–scarved and steered towards the door. Kray gave Louis another of the lazy-lidded approving smiles that, somehow, were even more frightening than his animosity.

"I mean, I know I'm the one talking out of turn . . . But if I was in your shoes, that young man under the harmonium is the kind of young man I'd prefer to be seeing me home."

Clouded as that much nicer young man's senses were, he realised there was one thing about the New Year, 1967, which could be predicted with some certainty. Joining Terry Bracegirdle's gang was going to be harder than ever.

# 16

It was late in the afternoon of Christmas Eve. Louis's father sat four feet from the television set with a face of tragic absorption, his fingertips pressed together, occasionally flicking at his lower lip with his joined thumbs, as if *The Dick Van Dyke Show* were some problem in advanced calculus. Opposite him sat his second wife, a woman fifteen years younger, with a resigned, flinty face, wearing her usual too-short plaid skirt and fluffy marabou mules. From across the High Street outside could already be heard a hiss of deep-fat fryers, punctuated by noises of pop music, cars and souped-up motorbikes. As a well-known vinegary stench began to seep through the leaded window, Louis pondered yet again on his father's peculiar ingenuity. Who else could have come to rural Berkshire seeking refuge from seaside squalor and noise, and settled directly opposite a busy fish-and-chip shop?

The idyll of the cottage where they sat had likewise proved less than perfect. True, it was one of Hungerford's oldest buildings, pebble-fronted and thatched, with fishing and pasturage rights granted by charter from John of Gaunt. But it also now served as a service-centre for the amusements with which Louis's father supplied pubs and clubs in the district. In every oak-beamed room, cheek by jowl with grandfather clocks and wheelback chairs, stood a Wurlitzer or Bal-Ami jukebox or a garish slot machine, intact or under repair. To the patina of seven centuries had somehow been added the dank, seaweedy, depressing ambience of Seaview Pier Pavilion.

Whatever changes might have befallen Louis elsewhere, the ground rules for watching television with his father remained the same. He must never touch the controls of the set nor the copy of TV Times which lay ceremonially open at the relevant day's schedule. He must not talk during the programmes nor even in the commercial breaks. He must never attempt to sit in his father's large, overstuffed armchair nor, even more emphatically, in his stepmother's smaller facing one. To do so would be "not fair," a paternal expression still weighted with near-paranoiac chivalry. So—even while she was absent at her hairdressing business, "Madame Desirée"—Louis made do with a small wooden-armed chair or a stool once used for supporting coffins.

Since his arrival the previous afternoon, his father had not given any indication of having seen, let alone read, his four nationally published pieces of journalism. He, conversely, had heard much about the heroic struggle of a small-time impresario against a Fate apparently motivated by personal vindictiveness.

"Remember all those Victorian penny-in-the-slot machines, like the Caley and the Allwyne de Luxe, we used to have at the Pavilion? When we got out in 'sixty-two, I virtually gave them away for scrap. Now I hear they're being sold in antique markets for hundreds of pounds each . . .

"When I got into gaming machines, I thought all our troubles were over. Then the Government goes and brings in a law limiting jackpot payouts to five shillings. Of course, it's put the kibosh on the whole business . . ." These melancholy reflections were spurred by a fresh burst of noise from the fish-and-chip shop across the road.

"We always said, didn't we, that whatever happened we'd never be reduced to selling fish and chips?" Louis's father glanced across at his helpmeet, whose response, as ever, was a nod of bovine acquiescence over her bright purple knitting. "Just our luck, wasn't it, that one season we tried it? The only year this century when there was a national potato-famine . . ."

They were to have Christmas lunch with the landlady of a riverside pub where Louis's father maintained a gaming machine called Mad Money. "I think it may be a bit of a free-for-all," he remarked gloomily as they drove there.

His forecast, if anything, proved an understatement. By one o'clock, both the landlady and her man friend, a pink-trousered chef, were in an almost Neanderthal state of drunkenness. By four o'clock—no lunch having yet appeared—the landlady had acquired a black eye, and she and the chef were hurling their presents at each other across the rosily lit bar. Rescue came then with an S.O.S. service call to Louis's father, necessitating a cross-country drive to Reading. At five o'clock, Louis stood in the darkened, freezing bar of a workingmen's club, helping to mend a slot machine called Viva Las Vegas.

Evening found them back watching television, in the heightened atmosphere between Louis's father and stepmother that alcohol invariably produced. After numerous gins, wine, brandy and port, her usual mute aquiescence had changed to subtle but dogged defiance; his chivalrous over-protectiveness to barely supportable claustrophobic disgust.

The BBC's Nine O'Clock News began. Louis's father raised bleary eyes to it from a plate of wet walnuts, then glanced at the purple knitting and fluffy mules in palpable anguish. "God, you're so dumb, aren't you? . . . Got no conception what's going on inna' world . . ."

The lead item was Singapore Charlie Small, who—heaven alone knew how—had made his landfall in Australia within the tea clippers' 100 days. There was special satellite film of *Lady Patricia* entering Sydney Harbour, an intrepid, baseball-capped figure standing on her prow. A later sequence showed the unfortunate moment when she rammed a launch full of photographers, and then a cutaway to Mrs. Bunty Small, watching with an expression that might have prompted some mariners to go for non-stop circumnavigation.

Almost equal footage was devoted to a small, bedraggled shape perched on the rim of the wheelhouse where the Sunday Dispatch Magazine's correspondent had once scrambled in murderously tight Chelsea boots. ". . . And there's news of a somewhat smaller intrepid seafarer," the newsreader, Robert Dougall, continued archly. "Pidgy the pigeon is reportedly doing fine and looking forward to getting on cooing terms with his cousins down under . . ."

"This is a won'erful, won'erful story," Louis's father mumbled. "But you don't give a damn about it, do you?" His eyes swivelled around to include Louis, and confirm his own inattentiveness as a Sunday Dispatch reader.

"Here's this won'erful man . . . who's sailed round the world all on his own . . . with just a poor li'l bird to keep him company . . . He's one of the great heroes of our time . . . And neither of you gives a tuppenny damn . . ."

On the morning after Boxing Day, a phone call for Louis was put through to the cottage from his stepmother's hair salon. To his surprise he heard Val Lewis's impersonally sultry voice.

"Louis? I'm sorry to break in on your Christmas . . ."

"Don't worry."

"You're taking over the Elizabeth Taylor profile from God. He's decided he can't face writing it after all . . . surprise, surprise. So you're going to have to finish interviewing her, and then pull the whole piece together."

Sick terror seized him simultaneously by the throat and the scrotum. "Me? Are you sure?"

"Yes, it's all down to you. The problem is, all the colour pages press on January second and we need the words less than a week later, so you'll have to move like greased lightning. Can you fly to Salzburg tonight?"

"Salzburg?"

"Actually, you fly to Munich, then go to Salzburg by car. It would have been Cap Ferrat, where God saw her, but she's now upped sticks and gone off to be with Richard Burton while he's making some kind of war movie."

"But . . . I thought Evelyn Strachey was standing by to take over."

"That was the original plan. But then word filtered through from La Taylor herself that she'd rather have you. Apparently, you went down very well when you interviewed her mum."

The sick terror—the compulsion to run and hide his head, shouting, "No, I can't! I can't possibly!"—had vanished. Now he was standing on the wings of the lead biplane in a Busby Berkeley aerial finale.

"I've managed to get you into the hotel where the Burtons are staying . . . the Österreichischer Hof," Val said. "You leave on BEA Flight 792 from Heathrow at six-thirty. Have you got your passport with you?"

"I can get it."

"OK. If you go to the information desk at West London Air Terminal, your ticket and traveller's cheques and God's research file will be waiting for you."

---

It was the first time Louis had travelled by air. To intense excitement and novelty was added the sumptuous luxury of a first-class cabin where he was the only passenger. Two hostesses and a male steward were provided to welcome him orgiastically, instal him like a boy rajah in a throne-like padded seat and hover nearby, almost fighting for the privilege of gratifying his smallest whim.

As he sipped his third champagne cocktail and gazed lightheadedly down at London's receding glow, the steward came up with a silver-wrapped package. "Excuse me, Mr. Brennan . . . I've been asked to give you this."

Inside was a box of twenty-five Romeo y Julieta cigars and a card: "Good hunting and best of luck! God."

Between eating smoked salmon, filet mignon, baked Alaska and After Eight mints and drinking Veuve Clicquot, Château Lafitte and

Remy Martin, he studied the fat folder of background research on Elizabeth Taylor that had accumulated over the past two months. There were extensive interviews by Evelyn Strachey and Jessamyn O'Shaughnessy with former husbands, close friends, film studio bosses, producers, directors, lawyers and business advisers. There was the detailed account which Godwin had evidently dictated off the cuff to Tessa Burland—in itself enough and more to sustain a full profile—of staying at the Burton-Taylor mansion on Cap Ferrat and lunching and dining with them at various sumptuous restaurants in Nice and Antibes, whither they would invariably drive in a chauffeur-driven Cadillac, sipping bourbon and Perrier water from silver goblets.

Near the bottom he found his own reports on Mrs. Sara Taylor and marginally interesting film co-stars like Victor Spinetti and Michael Hordern. There was also a single sheet recording Fran's encounter with the Hollywood producer Pandro S. Berman. He recognised the typeface of her poems and Eskimo short story and, with a woozy surge of fondness, noticed that she'd misspelt "adolescent."

On arrival at Munich, the ordinary passengers were held back while Louis disembarked at his leisure. Through the open cabin door came a glimmer of ice and a gust of breathtaking cold. "Did you have an overcoat, Mr. Brennan?" the steward asked.

"No," he replied, buttoning his epauletted corduroy jacket up to the neck.

In the arrivals hall he was met by a man in a leather Lenin cap, holding up a piece of cardboard lettered "HERR BRENNAN." Ten minutes later he was in the well-heated rear of a Mercedes station wagon, cruising through a Christmas-card landscape of neon-lit white.

The driver's eyes regarded him curiously in the interior mirror. "You do not bring overcoat?"

"No."

"Is necessary here. Much snow and ice we are having."

Austria proved, if anything, even snowier and more prettily illuminated than West Germany. An hour after crossing the imperceptible frontier, the Mercedes slushed round a floodlit town square and stopped outside an encrusted Gothic façade. "Sere you are!" the driver announced proudly. "The Österreichischer Hof!"

Two scarlet-uniformed footmen bore Louis's holdall and cigars ahead of him through a revolving door, into a foyer of Mozartian magnificence. An ornately carved staircase led to galleries of bedrooms, rising in concentric squares to a distant stained-glass roof. On the left was an expansive open-plan drawing room filled with groups of high-backed brocade armchairs.

He approached the polished reception desk and rang a brass bell. From an inner office emerged a man of wrestler build, wearing mutton-chop whiskers and a black tail-coat. "My name's Brennan . . . London Sunday Dispatch."

"Yes, of course, Mr. Brennan," the man said in almost accentless English. "Welcome to the Österreichischer Hof. Kindly register. And there is a cablegram for you." He reached inside a pigeonhole and handed Louis an embossed envelope containing a single folded sheet:

TAYLOR NOW INSISTING ON EDITORIAL APPROVAL OUR PIX OF HER. SOMEONE EXOFFICE BRINGING COLOUR TRANNIES TOMOR-ROW FOR YOU TO CLEAR WITH HER DURING YOUR INTERVIEW.

REGARDS VAL LEWIS

With a brisk creak, the revolving doors turned again. Into the foyer came two men dressed in the steep-peaked caps, greatcoats and boots of World War II German officers. As each removed his cap, Louis's jaw dropped. For these were the two ultimate Nazi villains from every black-and-white war picture in his fifties youth. One, blond and icy-faced, numbered among many atrocities the cold-blooded shooting of Robert Beatty in *Albert RN;* the other, with bushy brows and black-ringed eyes, had personally tortured John Mills and innumerable other fine British servicemen in *The Colditz Story.*

As they passed en route to the drawing room, the black-eyed one was saying, in that familiar cold, mad accent which had so often warned captured R.A.F. officers or girl Resistance fighters: "Ve haf vays of mak-ing you talk":

". . . nought to a hundred and ten in forty-five seconds. I promise you, its acceleration is absolutely marvellous . . ."

The concierge followed Louis's gaze and smiled. "Some people from the movie. They're all staying here."

Two different scarlet-clad footmen conducted him up to the second gallery, into a lofty room with a row of shuttered windows overlooking the floodlit square. The huge wooden double bed did not have sheets and blankets but a puffy white quilt. As the footmen withdrew, an eerie single peal came from the bedside telephone.

"Mr. Brennan?" said a calm American voice.

"Speaking."

"My name is Bob Wilson. I'm with the Burtons. Did you want to go out to the location tomorrow?"

"Yes . . . please."

"That's fine. I'll meet you in the lobby at nine-thirty."

As he came downstairs next morning, the side-whiskered concierge beckoned to him. "Mr. Brennan . . . you have a colleague checking in today?"

"Yes. I believe so."

"Do you know at what time?"

"I'm afraid not."

"And the party's name?"

"I'm sorry, I don't know. I think it may be a Miss Lewis."

"OK. We will hold a room until ten tonight."

"Hi, Mr. Brennan," said a quiet voice at his elbow. "I'm Bob Wilson. Are you all set?"

It had never even occurred to Louis that Mr. Wilson might be black. Elderly and light-skinned, he wore an anorak with a fur-trimmed hood and carried a sheaf of papers and magazines from the lobby newsstand.

Outside waited a chauffeur-driven black Mercedes with chains attached to its wheels. As footmen lunged to open both rear doors, Mr. Wilson glanced curiously at Louis's cord battledress jacket, thin brown trousers and already freezing gloveless hands. "Aren't you bringing an overcoat?" he asked.

"No."

"You might want to reconsider that. It can get pretty cool up in those mountains."

"Really, I'm fine."

The car swished out of the square and through beamed and gabled thoroughfares like illustrations for Grimm's Fairy Tales. Louis fumbled for the notebook in his back pocket.

"Do you mind if I start by interviewing you?"

Mr. Wilson inclined his bald head. "Go on."

"You work for Miss Taylor, do you?"

"No. I work for Mr. Burton."

"May I ask in what capacity?"

"I used to be his dresser. Now I'm more a secretary-type thing."

"And this film he's making . . . can you tell me something about it?"

Mr. Wilson shrugged. "It's a war picture. He's the good guy. What can I tell you?"

Within a very few minutes, the journey became spectacular and terrifying. They were ascending an almost vertical, icy road of continuous hairpin bends, with sheer rock on one side and a sheer drop on the other. Away in the distance stood white-pelted mountains with sharp peaks. Snow began driving horizontally at the windscreen. The speed-

ometer needle seldom dropped below 80. There was some comfort in remembering that meant only kilometres per hour.

It was nearly an hour before they slithered to a halt on an icebound
promontory with breathtaking peak and chasm views. In the centre
stood a long-fronted café, surrounded by cars, Dormobiles and a silver
van into which hooded figures were loading camera equipment.

Blowing on his fingers, Louis followed Mr. Wilson through the café's
swing doors. The interior was cramped and steamy. Of the ten or so
gimcrack wooden booths, two-thirds had been commandeered by the
film unit. Groups of men and women in expensive ski-wear were eating
hot cheesy snacks, drinking mulled wine from glasses with metal han-
dles, and loudly laughing and talking, watched with envious wonder
by a scattering of ordinary customers.

In the centre of the enclave sat Richard Burton, dressed in a Nazi officer's field-grey tunic half-unbuttoned on a bright red undervest. The familiar craggy and rather pockmarked face was pallid with thickly
applied make-up. On the bench beside him lay an officer's cap with a
gold-wreathed peak and a pair of grey woollen gloves. On his jodhpured
knee was The Times, folded open at the crossword.

Louis scanned the room, then turned to Bob Wilson in consternation.
"I thought Miss Taylor would be here," he whispered.

"She'll be by later. Just have a seat right here."

"Right here" was on the furthermost side of the booth adjoining Burton's. Since, clearly, no introduction was to be made, it would be up to
Louis to find a conversational opening. But the look of irritated absorption on the rugged face did not bode well for this.

After a moment or two, Burton sighed and threw down his paper. In
the voice whose bardic precision never varied, be it playing Jimmy Porter or Mark Antony, he said: "Twenty-three across is an absolute bitch.
'Newt-loving visitor to mansions where nightingale sang.' Ten letters."

His companions in the booth looked blankly at one another. Burton
scowled. "C'mon, c'mon," he said, now with an impatient American
inflection. "Doesn't anyone around here have even a smattering of general knowledge? 'Newt-loving visitor . . .' "

"Fink-Nottle," said Louis.

Burton glanced round. "I beg your pardon?" he said in a tone colder
than the glacier outside the panoramic window.

"It's P. G. Wodehouse . . . Bertie Wooster's flat was in Berkeley Mansions. The nightingale sang in Berkeley Square. And Gussie Fink-Nottle
was Bertie's friend who kept newts."

"Gussie Fink-Nottle. Of course." Burton computed the letters on his
fingers, then triumphantly inked them in. He glared across at Louis, be-

nignly now, and raised a beckoning finger. "Young man . . . come here
and sit by me."

They had just worked out the final clue ("Could be arranged for arranging the rice in Bengal"—currycomb) when there was a loud com-
motion outside. Two or three people from the film unit jumped up to
pull open the folding doors. With the gust of cold air appeared a small,
hook-nosed man in Basque beret, carrying two white Pekinese dogs,
and after him, Elizabeth Taylor.

There was little outward sign of the sex goddess who had bewitched
George Sanders in *Ivanhoe*, taunted Paul Newman in *Cat on a Hot Tin
Roof* and been unrolled semi-nude from a rug in *Cleopatra*. She wore a
shapeless mink coat, a purple mohair sweater with a large roll collar,
pale blue Lycra ski-pants and white moon boots. Her face was obscured
by outsize sunglasses, her black, curly pompadour dragged down by a
pink chiffon scarf tied under her chin. With a schoolgirlish squeal she
rushed over to Burton, who had chivalrously risen, and threw both
arms round his neck, kicking up one leg behind her. "Hi, Boofy!" she
cried.

Burton tactfully disengaged himself and scooped up one of the Pekes.
"Did you have a good sleep?"

"Uh-huh, but I got so thirsty. I haven't been able to stop eating tan-
gerines."

Louis had also risen awkwardly to his feet. "This is the new fellow
from the Sunday Dispatch," Burton said. "Got a bit better figure than
his predecessor, hasn't he?"

She took off her sunglasses, and Louis met the gaze of dark violet eyes
with double black lashes that made his knees almost buckle under him.
"Hi," she said with a friendly grin. "You're the one my mom liked so
much." For all its fluting American accent, her voice still had an un-
definable Englishness.

". . . Only the stupid fool thinks he can come to the Alps in December
without a proper overcoat. I've already told him he's raving mad."

A plump little hand, frosty with diamonds, tested the thinness of
Louis's jacket lapel, then instinctively flattened back its chronic outward curl. "Honey, you'll freeze. Especially if you come with us to the
schloss later on."

"He's a Wodehouse buff, so we'd better look after him," Burton said.
"I've sent Bob over to Wardrobe to see if they can't lend him something
a bit more suitable."

———————————

That afternoon the film unit moved to a medieval castle situated even
higher in the mountains. Burton was portraying a commando officer,

dispatched on an heroic mission disguised as a Nazi *obergruppenführer*. The scene now being shot required him to ride a motorcycle combination at top speed round the castle courtyard while enemy sentries blazed down with machine guns, mortars and grenades from every tower and battlement.

Louis spent the afternoon with Mrs. Richard Burton in a turret room directly above the ring of cameras, lights and trodden snow. Wearing the red-tabbed greatcoat of a Wehrmacht field marshal, he sat in a high-backed carved chair, usually with one or other of her pet Pekes, O Fie and E'en So, on his lap.

Conducting any kind of formal question-and-answer session was next to impossible owing to the constant comings and goings of aides, secretaries, hairdressers, make-up artists, the film's director, producer and associate producer, plus privileged groups of rubicund cadets from the police academy also housed at the castle, flourishing autograph books and cameras. Between takes, as Burton conferred with his director and his stand-in for the more dangerous motorcycle sequences, his wife would rush to the window, lean far out and squeal "Hi, Boofy!," frantically waving a mink-rippled arm. He would usually respond with the same slightly long-suffering Roman salute that Antony had given Cleopatra in Hollywood's most prodigal epic of all time.

On the carved sideboard stood an electric coffee pot, a jumble of wine and spirits bottles, cold chickens, sausage, cheeses, pickled cucumbers, giant bars of chocolate and tins of opulent Teutonic wafer biscuits. The World's Greatest Sex Goddess ate almost continuously, improvising snacks with equal generosity for whomever else happened to be there. Louis noticed how perfectly in character were the diamond-studded hands, shiny with chicken fat or folding rye bread around a slice of Gruyère.

In the act of passing him a four-triangle wedge of Toblerone, she smiled sympathetically. "I'm sorry . . . It's been crazy here today. But you can ride back to the hotel with me if you like, and then we'll all have dinner. OK?"

Daylight was fading fast and snow blizzarding again when they left the castle keep to return to the convoy of limousines parked on the road far below. Half-way down an immense flight of icy steps, with a Peke cuddled into his coat and the World's Greatest Sex Goddess gripping his arm for support, Louis let out an involuntary giggle.

"What?" she asked.

"I was just thinking—this time tomorrow, I'll be back in bedsitter land."

For almost an hour then she was at his exclusive disposal, returning to Salzburg in the rear of a Cadillac as long as an L.C.C. ambulance.

Even Gaston, her Basque chauffeur-cum-bodyguard, was shut out by a wall of green-tinted glass. The only interloper was O Fie, the Pekinese, stretched across their combined laps and snoring gently.

Alas, so powerful was the car's heater, so smooth its suspension as it took each downward hairpin bend, and so quintessentially dog-like the odour of O Fie, that Louis almost immediately began to feel travel-sick. From experience dating back to childhood he knew the only succour from that fatal dry patch in the throat; that sensation of one's eyes being inexorably drawn into a squint. If he could not put his head through an open window, he must at all costs look nowhere but directly forward. While attempting to frame sequential questions about *Lassie Come Home,* the studio boss, Jack L. Warner, and the challenge of playing Helen of Troy in *Doctor Faustus,* he kept his gaze tenaciously riveted on the snowy road unreeling beyond Gaston's black beret.

"Please don't think me rude, facing the front like this," he said, "but I'm afraid that if I look at you, I'll feel sick."

In the instant of horrified realisation, he could not help but look at her again. After a brief double-take, the World's Greatest Sex Goddess threw back her head and laughed.

"I'm sorry . . . I didn't mean . . . it's just car sickness . . ."

"The best thing is to suck some candy," she said, opening her bag. "I don't think I have any Life Savers."

"I may have a Polo mint." Groping in his back trousers-pocket, he found two in a grimy silver twist, many weeks old. "Would you like one?"

"Thank you," she said, picking out the first greyish mothball shape and popping it into her mouth.

---

Back at the Österreichischer Hof, he was just emerging from a ferociously efficient shower when his bedside telephone pealed. "Mr. Brennan?" the concierge's voice said. "Your colleague from London is waiting for you at the front desk."

Amid the day's distractions, Louis had scarcely thought about the photograph-courier from London. He had vaguely expected either Val Lewis or her assistant, Carol. Curiously enough, as he traversed the final gallery before the carved staircase, he had a sudden premonition of who it would be.

She was standing at the reception desk, looking lost and forlorn, honey hair tumbling over a garish black-and-white PVC raincoat. The side-whiskered concierge bent down like a kindly bear, almost guiding her hand with the pen on the registration card.

There was just time to rehearse a voice of quizzical amusement. "Hi."

"And your passport, please," the concierge added.

"Oh, yes . . . sorry." Fran groped in her shoulder-bag, producing both her passport and one of the yellow plastic boxes used for storing colour transparencies. The latter she held out brusquely to Louis, like a present she was half-embarrassed to give.

"Why you here?" he asked in jokey cable-ese.

She reflapped her bag with a shrug. "Search me. I just got a call first thing this morning, telling me to go to the Kodak labs, then straight to London airport."

"Well . . . it's extremely nice to see you."

She ignored this. "How's the piece going?"

"Great."

"Have you actually talked to her yet?"

"Good God, yes. Spent almost the whole day with her."

The black centipede eyes narrowed gratifyingly.

". . . and I'm just about to have dinner with Burton and her."

"Christ, you lucky thing."

He was back on his lordly eminence once more. "I'll probably be with them till fairly late. But, if you're still around, maybe we can have a mulled wine together afterwards . . ."

At that moment there was a bump of revolving doors and Richard Burton came into the lobby, accompanied by Bob Wilson. "Louis!" Burton shouted. "Settle an argument. Is Mrs. Spenser Gregson Bertie Wooster's Aunt Agatha or his Aunt Dahlia?"

"His Aunt Agatha. Aunt Dahlia's surname is Travers."

Burton removed his field-grey forage cap, nodding sagely. "And she's the one with Anatole the chef, right?"

"Right."

"Elizabeth did ask you to put on the nosebag with us, didn't she? We shall be a small but select party . . . The director was supposed to join us, but now there's some problem with the second unit."

His glance settled on Fran, whose honey head had been humbly bowed throughout this exchange. "And can one enquire if this very attractive young lady is with you?"

"Yes," Louis began. "She . . ."

"Bring her along then. We'll see you in the Terrace Restaurant in fifteen minutes."

# 17

"Did I ever tell you how I almost lost the bloody diamond? Along with most of the rest of her jewel collection?" Burton drained his glass of Gewürztraminer and held it up to be refilled by the green-aproned sommelier.

"It was outside Geneva railway station, when we were arriving home from Paris, the Christmas before last. I'd put the diamond . . . and what else, Bessie? Your ruby pendant? And the sapphires Nicky Hilton gave you? . . . Just shoved them all in an ordinary brown paper-bag, thinking no thief would ever twig they were there. While we were loading up the car, I put this bag down just under the running-board—and then clean forgot about it! We were almost at the house when I realised what I'd done. Back we went like a bat out of hell and there it was, still lying in the gutter . . ."

The restaurant, a lofty salon frescoed with plump cherubim and lit by huge chandeliers, was otherwise empty of diners. Only the wonder-struck eyes of half a dozen attentive waiters were bent on the exotic assembly at a secluded banquette table.

It was, indeed, a sight to awaken keen nostalgia in many an Austrian breast. Of the six males present, three others apart from Burton still wore German officers' uniforms from the day's filming. Both the blond and the black-eyed ultimate Nazi fiend had been invited to join the party, as had a thickset, balding Welsh actor named Brook Williams who played one of Burton's fellow commandos in disguise. Interspersed among the field-grey tunics, black-tabbed collars and Iron Crosses sat Mrs. Richard Burton, Louis, Fran and an assistant director from the film unit, a thin, cheesy-faced youth deputising for his absent boss in watching over their production's number-one asset.

Louis was seated with his back to the restaurant, between the blond

Nazi fiend and the assistant director and opposite the subject of his still-unfinished interview. She, too, still wore her daytime garb of purple rollneck sweater and Lycra ski-pants, with her mink loosely draped around her shoulders. Beside her plate stood the plastic box containing the work of the world's leading glamour photographers, from Art Kane to Otto Storch. Each transparency was picked up in slightly grubby diamond-studded fingers and briefly inspected against the chandelier light. The few that found favour were replaced in the box. The many that did not were neatly bisected by a pair of silver nail-scissors.

"What's the matter with that one?" Burton said as a cardboard mount stamped "IRVING PENN" joined the heap of casualties.

"Yuk! He's got me wearing a headscarf, like some kind of ghastly fishwife."

"I like you in a headscarf," he protested.

"Tough titty, buster." She paused in her editing as a waiter brought her a thick slice of chocolate torte studded with fresh black cherries and ruched with Chantilly cream. Otherwise, the table had been cleared but for coffee cups and wine, brandy and liqueur glasses.

"I never knew anyone as handy with a knife and fork as Elizabeth," Burton remarked tolerantly. "This is a woman, I promise you, who can eat four hot-dogs on the trot and still be ready for dessert."

"Five," his wife contradicted calmly. "I had five that day at Bennie Thau's."

Burton held up his glass to be refilled again. "When I first met her on the set of *Cleopatra,* you know, I nicknamed her Ocean because she seemed to me to embody all the strength and dark passion of the Atlantic, the lulling warmth and radiance of the Pacific. But I'm thinking of changing that now . . . to Tubby."

The World's Greatest Sex Goddess's only rejoinder was a spirited V-sign.

To the untrained observer, it might have seemed pure accident that Fran had ended up seated next to Burton on the curve of the red plush banquette, where there was otherwise no rivalry for his attention but the visits of sommeliers, silver trolleys and serving tables. Though still in her travelling outfit of navy polka-dot dress, she looked as glossily fresh as if the unit's Wardrobe and Hairstyling departments had been buffing and grooming her all afternoon. Ostensibly reticent and agog, she nonetheless managed to give an impression that Burton and she were somehow apart from the company, sharing the intimate seclusion of a love-seat.

Flicking strands of honey hair earnestly from her mouth, she would occasionally interrupt his monologue with a question of seemingly reckless impertinence: ". . . In *Who's Afraid of Virginia Woolf?* you had those terrible rows . . . you even had to spit at each other. Did you find it affected your relationship off-camera?" Burton, who had seemed merely amused at the beginning, now seemed utterly captivated, lighting her cigarettes, refilling her glass, even resting one field-grey arm on the ledge behind her in a way hardly calculated to promote marital harmony. And to be sure, accustomed though Cleopatra might be to Mark Antony's dalliances with slave girls, a look of decided grimness had appeared in the double-lashed violet eyes.

Louis himself was finding it increasingly difficult to keep a grip on his senses. The stress of interviewing without a notebook—replaying each answer continually in his mind with all its twists of vocabulary and construction until he could get away to scribble in the Gents'—had left virtually no opportunity for eating. At one point, he remembered being served a creamy-pink wedge of pâté de foie gras; some time later, he felt a waiter remove it, still untasted. Drinking, on the other hand, presented no problem: thus far, as accompaniment to some breadsticks and a few mouthfuls of blanched veal, he had consumed two Negronis, three glasses of Château Lafitte, four of Gewürztraminer and a Sambuca liqueur, circled by more wavery blue flame than most Christmas puddings back in England this past festive season.

His neighbour, the blond Nazi fiend, turned to him with a face of mindless sadism that seemed to visualise him strapped to a chair and with his toenails being slowly pulled out with rusty pliers.

"Whereabouts in London do you live, Louis?"

Though required under the Geneva Convention to give only his name, rank and serial number, he admitted it was off High Street Ken.

"Oh, really? I'm up in Campden Hill Square. Nice little garden flat . . . I've been there for years. We must get together for a jar one evening at that nice pub, the Windsor Castle."

―――――

The party seemed to reach a natural and peaceable end shortly before 1 o'clock. On his way through the lobby, however, Burton did a kind of sideways parachute roll into one of its high-backed brocade armchairs. His wife, already half-way upstairs, turned back with a look of exasperation. "Come on, Dickon. You know you have an eight-thirty call tomorrow."

"One last Remy. Then I'll be with you." A wave of his arm simultaneously called a waiter and beckoned Brook Williams, the young assistant director and Louis into surrounding chairs. Fran, who had just collected her room-key, made as if to join them, but after some palpable inner conflict Burton smiled regretfully and shook his head.

"Sorry, angel . . . it's really more than my life's worth. Why not go up and rest that pretty head?"

They watched her ascend the staircase and walk along the first gallery. "Nice girl," Burton commented to no one in particular. "Who's fucking her?"

For another hour or so, between relays of Remy Martin, Armagnac and schnapps, the bardic voice rose majestically up through the many-galleried vault to the stained-glass roof.

"I first met Noël Coward when I was on Broadway, playing Hamlet. He walked into my dressing-room and kissed me full on the lips. 'You may not think much of that, dear boy,' he said, 'but I can assure you it was absolutely rrrriddled with sex . . .'

"Brook and I have this great idea for a musical based on Christie, the murderer who papered up all those women behind his kitchen wall. For the finale, all the headless torsos would come out and do an ensemble number called 'Cupboard Love' . . .

"Have you heard the latest Aberfan joke? You remember that Princess Margaret started a fund to send toys to the children who survived? Well, they're playing underneath this huge heap of toys, and it suddenly collapses and buries the whole lot of them . . ."

It was during the Aberfan story that Louis realised the group had acquired an additional listener. On the brocade stool next to Burton's armchair now sat a heavy-faced man with slicked-back hair and owlish horn-rimmed spectacles. Bundled in his arms were a white raincoat and a badge-studded Alpine hat.

"Erm, excuse me," the young assistant director protested. *"Bitte, mein herr . . . österrisch?"*

"Naw," was the gruff reply. *"Amerikanisch."*

Seemingly unaware of the freezing disapproval all around him, the newcomer leaned up to Burton and proffered a fleshy white hand. "Mr. Burton . . . I'm Fritz R. Hoenigsman . . . Stateside-born, but living right here in Salzburg. When I heard that voice, I just had to come over and say . . . how much I've really enjoyed you."

"Thank you," Burton said coldly. "And now . . . would you mind very much? This is a private party."

The man sat back, cuddling his raincoat protectively. "Not very friendly, are you?" he said in an aggrieved tone.

"I'm not in the least unfriendly," Burton replied. "It's just that I'm having a quiet drink with a few friends, and I'd appreciate a little privacy."

"You could be polite," the man said.

"I'm being perfectly polite."

"I'd better call the manager," said the assistant director, levering himself up in his chair. But the concierge's desk—like the rest of the lobby—was deserted.

"I didn't wanna promulgate anything," the man said. "Like I said, I just heard your voice, and had to come over to tell you how much I've really enjoyed you . . ."

"And I said 'Thank you,'" Burton replied with greatly increased tartness. "I appreciate it. Now would you please be so kind as to go away?"

The man doggedly stayed put, clutching his raincoat and Alpine hat. Burton turned back to Brook Williams and Louis. "Where was I? Oh, yes . . . Gielgud's tactlessness. I remember one night. . . ."

"Nice way to treat a relation, I don't think," the man said.

Burton gazed incredulously at him, "What?"

"You and me. We're family."

"I've never seen you before in my life."

"I mean family . . . like family," the man insisted. "My great-grandfather came from the Vale of Neath, in dear old Bonnie Wales. That makes me just as much a Selt as you are."

The first glint of amusement showed on Burton's pockmarked face. "No," he replied. "I am a Selt. You are a Sunt."

Comprehension took a moment to dawn behind the owlish spectacles. But when finally it had done so, the result was spectacular. Casting aside his raincoat and Alpine hat, the man rose, ducked around behind Brook Williams, who was laughing ostentatiously, and locked one arm under his chin in a grip clearly intended to cause death. Burton shouted angrily and started to struggle to his feet. The man stood away from Williams, opened his jacket, plunged a hand into his trousers-waistband and produced a black object which looked preposterously like—because indeed it was—a heavy short-barrelled revolver.

In the ensuing moment of general stupefaction, Louis happened to glance at the young assistant director, entrusted with the care of his company's multimillion-dollar star for this evening only. On his face was a look which made Munch's *The Scream* by contrast appear mild pique.

Burton had sunk back into his armchair and was looking at the snouted black shape with almost dispassionate interest. "What'd you want to go and pull a gun for?" he asked.

The man waved the revolver indecisively. "I just wanted to show you . . . that I'm armed."

"Everyone can see perfectly well that you're armed," Burton retorted.

"Please . . ." gasped the assistant director, starting to rise. The man turned the barrel to include him.

"Siddown!"

"Sure." The assistant director subsided, nodding eagerly. "Anything you want. But please . . . just put the gun away."

The man glanced right and left, seeming to take stock of his situation. In the whole twilit expanse of lobby and drawing room there was still not another soul. "OK." He indicated a brocaded stool, about four feet in length. "All of you . . . sit in a line over here. And I'm warning you . . . don't do anything stoopid."

To Louis, drunk as he was, the scene had the unreality of a slowed-down film, with figures congealing and soundtrack grinding to an inarticulate blur. He sat on the end of the stool with the assistant director next to him, then Brook Williams and Burton in their half-unbuttoned field-grey tunics and visible thermal vests. The man was now flourishing the revolver directly under Burton's nose. "Not so tough now, eh?" he said with an unpleasant leer.

The assistant director slid forward onto his knees, holding out both arms. "Please . . ." he entreated. "Please . . . just put the gun away . . ."

The man nodded sagely.

"You think you're plenty tough. You'd really love to slug me now, wouldn't you, like they have you doing it in all the papers. Well, c'mon, try it. Just try it."

"Please . . ." the assistant director almost wept from the carpet. "Please put the gun away . . ."

Changing the revolver to his left hand, the man reached down and cuffed Burton lightly on the side of the face. Burton, however, continued to gaze down at his own jackboots as if engrossed in memorising a part. "Doesn't matter what you do, love, I won't hit you," he said quietly.

Then, by a process Louis had not been able to follow, the galleried vault was echoing with furious shouts. Burton was on his feet being restrained by Brook Williams, with the assistant director down among their legs, still grovelling and pleading. The air rang no longer with the accent of Hamlet or Jimmy Porter but with that of an enraged Bowery cab driver.

"Don't mess with me, baby," Burton snarled. "Either use that rod or put it away . . . Or are you too dam' yellow . . . ?"

For some time, in his state of dreamy detachment, Louis had been watching a figure make its way down from the third gallery to the second and from the second to the first. Not until the last broad descent, however, did his numbed senses finally identify Mrs. Richard Burton, barefoot and dishevelled, clad in a black leather overcoat clutched around a long nightdress of flame-coloured chiffon.

Glaring at the scene below, though clearly not taking in more than the smallest fraction of its significance, she addressed Burton in a hissing undertone. "Richard! Will you come upstairs this minute! Your voice is ricocheting all over this hotel!"

A look of poleaxed astonishment had appeared on the gunman's face. He pushed the revolver back into his waistband, rebuttoned his jacket and stepped forward with outstretched hand and a smile of sickly ingratiation. "I'm so sorry . . ." he stammered. "I had no idea. . . ."

The violet eyes blazed at him. "Well, now you do!"

"This is a real pleasure . . . I want you to know . . . how much I've enjoyed you . . ."

"Elizabeth . . ." Burton began, "I don't think you quite understand what's been going on here . . ."

"You bet I do. And I'm telling you . . . come to bed now, this minute, or don't bother, ever!"

"Don't you give me orders!" Burton roared.

"Yes, I will give you orders!"

Burton's response was an angry stream of Welsh, which his wife answered in kind and with equally passionate fluency.

"Aah, hoppit!" he said, waving a field-grey arm.

"Hoppit yourself!" hissed the World's Greatest Sex Goddess. And, clutching her leather coat tighter around her nightdress, she stomped furiously up the stairs again.

---

Fran's room was three heavy oak doors away from Louis's on the second gallery. She answered his agitated pounding wearing her long granny nightdress but still in full make-up. "I must talk to you," he mumbled, lurching past her. "There's just been the most incredible scene downstairs."

Her room had the same four-poster bed, puffy white quilt and heavy wooden shutters as his. Her dress and striped PVC raincoat were thrown together over a tapestry chaise-longue. The bedside lamp shone on a packet of Peter Stuyvesant, her French lighter and an open paperback by Anya Seton.

"Christ, how amazing!" she said when he had described the encounter with Fritz R. Hoenigsman.

"I know. It's terrible to admit, but half of me was wishing the gun would go off, just to see what'd happen . . ."

"Where's the man now?"

"No idea. After Liz Taylor went upstairs again, he kept us sitting in a row for about another twenty minutes. Then he said, 'I have to take a piss . . . don't anybody move.' As soon as his back was turned, we all scattered for the lifts."

"You must write about it," Fran said.

"God, I know! What an intro for the profile!"

"No, I mean file a separate story for this Sunday's newspaper."

Louis sat down on the edge of the bed, attempting to collect his spinning senses. "I could. But that would defuse the effect of the Magazine piece."

"You must do it for the paper," she said vehemently. "Richard Burton held at gunpoint! That's really big news."

"I know. But no one else was there. It'll still be news when the Magazine comes out. Why should the Steam Section have the best of it?"

"But supposing some Austrian journalist finds out about it? You said there were lots of them sniffing round."

"I'll take that chance. No one with Burton's going to give out the story, are they? And the man with the gun certainly isn't. So how can anyone find out?"

"I think you're taking a crazy risk."

"Crazy" was said with the slightly softened *r* that always made Louis's heart melt. With a superior smile, he patted the honey head. "I do know what I'm doing. It'll have far more impact as intro to a Magazine cover story." A sudden throb between the eyes made him wince. "The only trouble is, Burton's got me so pissed, I may not remember everything that happened by tomorrow."

"If you like, you can dictate it to me," Fran said. "I'll take it down in shorthand, then type it up for you when we get back."

He stared at her, unable to credit her goodness and kindness. "You'd really do that?"

In answer she pushed him back on to the pillow, picked up his legs and laid them on the puffy white quilt. Fetching a bulky office shorthand pad and a pen from her shoulder-bag, she sat down beside him, demurely but almost in the curve of his body.

"Are you really sure?" he protested feebly.

"Of course."

"It's so incredibly nice of you."

"I know . . . I'm a little saint. Now, how do you want to begin it?"

"Oh . . . anything. It's just rough notes." He strove to focus his thoughts. "Put something like 'World War Two movie melodrama changed to real-life suspense for Burton as he drank with cronies in the lobby of the Österreichischer Hof . . .' "

When he had filled half a dozen pages, Fran closed the notebook, but stayed seated where she was. "Can I tell you something?" Louis asked.

"Yes."

"It's what I've been thinking about all evening. And it's a bit rude."

"Tell me."

"I want to kiss your breasts."

Without a word, she turned to him and, as if humouring a child, unbuttoned her nightdress at the front. The warm, moist cones smelled of baby powder and a kind of limey scent. He was aware of her great blackened eyes wide open and watching him from above.

"Will you come to bed?" he whispered.

"All right. Just give me two minutes to take my make-up off."

But in less than a minute he was unconscious.

He awoke to find sun glinting around the heavy window-shutters. The striped PVC raincoat, the polka-dot dress, the shoulder-bag, the cigarettes, the lighter and the Anya Seton paperback had all gone.

Down in the lobby, the brocade armchairs and footstools had been restored to symmetric circles. The side-whiskered concierge was back on duty.

"Excuse me," Louis said. "Has Miss Dyson checked out?"

"Yes, sir. Early this morning."

"Did she leave any message?"

"No, sir."

At that moment, the lift doors opened and the Burtons appeared with their full retinue of chauffeurs, secretaries, dressers, hair-stylists and Pekes. As they passed Louis, Mrs. Burton gave a motherly "Aah!," darted over and planted a kiss on his cheek. Burton, in a navy-blue overcoat, looking as wrecked as a man could and still live, gave him a conspiratorial wink behind her back.

"It was real," he murmured. "It was a Webley four-eighty."

18

For three days, including New Year's Day, Louis sat in the empty Magazine concourse, weaving his observations from Salzburg and the research files of his senior colleagues into first, second and third drafts. It felt like being alone at the controls of a huge, empty spaceship. Apart from his typing, the only sound was a periodic gush from the central heating vent overhead. Parties and women were all very well, he occasionally thought to himself, but no pleasure quite equalled that of settling down in peace to do copy.

On the third day, as he polished his fourth and final 7,000-word version, a handful of people had returned—Gilda, from the Art Department, Val Lewis, Tessa Burland. At noon, Margaret Cole appeared in a new shaggy Afghan coat, red-nosed and wan, having spent the whole ten-day break in her Finsbury Park bedsitter prostrated with 'flu.

There was also a reverse-charge call from Freya Broadbent at a hotel in Berne.

"I've struck the motherlode!" her voice yipped so stridently that Louis had to hold the receiver away from his ear. "Yesterday, I interviewed a woman who used to give Madame de Gaulle English lessons in Petts Wood. And she's now put me on to an old school-friend of hers who often entertained the de Gaulles when they lived there . . . even helped them hire staff and choose fabrics for their rented house. The snag is, this older woman now runs an au pair employment agency in Corfu. Could you tell Jim Deaves when he comes in that I'll need an air-ticket and about another couple of hundred . . . ?"

Next morning, Evelyn Strachey and Jessamyn O'Shaughnessy arrived back together. As they passed Louis's desk, he looked up with a smile meant to convey rueful apology for his impossible good fortune.

Jessamyn gave a disdainful sniff while Strachey twisted his hips and tossed his hairless head.

"Both of them must have been spitting with fury because you got the Taylor profile," Margaret remarked. "And now, to add insult to injury, seeing the quotes they collected go into your copy . . . I bet they'll be screeching and bitching in that office all day like the Ugly Sisters when Cinderella marries the Prince."

Just after lunch Val Lewis came over, a look of puzzlement on her puggy face. "Louis," she said, "did you know the Steam Section's running something about the Burtons this Sunday? Steve Huckle, the paper's Picture Editor, has just rung me, trying to cadge a black-and-white print. Something about Burton being held at gunpoint . . . dressed as a Nazi officer?"

"How could they have got hold of your story?" asked Margaret.

Louis shook his head numbly. "I've got absolutely no idea."

"You'd better find out what they're doing, to make sure it doesn't jeopardise your piece."

"What should I do? Ask their Newsdesk?"

"I'll tell you what'd be quicker. Today's Thursday, so it's probably been set by now. You could sneak up the back stairs to the composing room and sneak a look at it in galley."

For a Magazine person to enter the newspaper's composing room was like crossing from West to East Berlin. Breathing the half-forgotten inky reek, expecting to be challenged and marched off at any moment, Louis skirted a bank of clattering linotype machines. Just beyond was the metal table where the unarranged type was laid and, next to it, a revolving rack of spiked galley-proofs.

Third from the top on the spike marked "News," he found what he sought:

"NAZI" BURTON AND WIFE
FACE DOWN ARMED INTRUDER

*From Fran Dyson, Salzburg*

World War Two movie melodrama changed to real-life suspense for Richard Burton here last week as he drank with friends in the lobby of the luxurious Österreichischer Hof Hotel . . .

It ran to half a column, in almost the exact words of his off-the-cuff dictation, albeit crudely rendered down to newspaper-ese and two-sentence paragraphs, and with a heavily-doctored climax.

After a time, the sound of angry shouting brought Elizabeth Taylor herself down from her fourth-floor suite. Seeing that her husband was in danger, she displayed extraordinary lack of concern for her own safety, interposing herself between Burton and the gunman and talking calmly and quietly to him until he agreed to give up the weapon.

Twenty yards away, Jack Shildrick was bending over a page in metal, with Nick Fenton and an aproned compositor. " 'Ullo, Poet," he called out in a brisk but friendly tone, indicating he bore no grudge over the Assistant Literary Editorship. Thank heaven for one person in the world, at least, who was always honest, straightforward and dependable.

Downstairs, Fran had just arrived and was alone in Terry Bracegirdle's office, hanging up her striped PVC mac. For some few seconds, she didn't realise Louis was standing in the doorway. She had on the pink shift dress with wide sleeves that always gave her a look of willowy grace.

At long last, she turned and noticed him there. "Oh . . . hi," she said casually.

"How could you do a thing like that?" He expected some kind of denial, or at least excuse, but she merely shrugged and sat down on the spare chair to change her shoes. "How could you play such a dirty, lowdown trick?"

"Oh, please," she protested with a wince.

"What do you mean 'Oh, please'? You get me to dictate my copy to you, then calmly go off and file it under your name!"

"It was a wonderful news story. You were just going to waste it."

"It was my story. What I did with it was my affair. And to make up the whole ending like that . . ."

She shrugged again, pulling a flat shoe around her heel in the way which still made Louis long to be in every part of her life. "When did you write it?" he couldn't help asking.

"On the flight back from Munich. Then phoned it in from Heathrow."

He shook his head, almost smiling. "God . . . the deceit. The absolute, utter duplicity . . ."

"Oh, come on," Fran said briskly. "A bit in the paper's hardly going to affect your full-colour extravaganza. Anyway, they told me it'd probably have to be cut right back."

"So what do you want me to do? Sympathise? . . ." He broke off as a woman he did not recognise appeared in the open doorway. Aged about thirty, she had an elfin, pretty face, haloed by auburn curls that were probably a wig. She wore a shortie grey suede coat, trimmed with black fur, and long zip-sided boots. "Are you Miss Dyson?" she asked Fran in a shy undertone.

"Yes."

"I'm Stephanie Bracegirdle."

Fran's black eyes flickered at Louis with—he was interested to see— genuine consternation. "Oh, dear," she said tonelessly.

Mrs. Bracegirdle plunged a hand into her bag and brought out a long blue envelope.

"I found the tickets, you see! Nice little trip you were planning, weren't you . . . first class to Ibiza!"

"Oh, dear," Fran repeated, now with compassionate softness.

" 'Oh, dear' is right! The silly bastard only goes and leaves them inside a library book, doesn't he? Lovely bed-time reading for me, isn't it, with my Horlicks and plain chocolate digestive!"

"Look, we must talk." Fran said. "It really isn't as you think."

"Don't treat me like a fool." Mrs. Bracegirdle's voice, almost apologetic a moment ago, had risen to a harsh, curdled shout. "Do you think I don't know what goes on on Thursday nights . . . and on those business trips when he's supposed to be with Norman Mailer in Washington? 'Cos you don't think you're the first, do you, dear? You couldn't think that. Not unless you've just come down off the top of a Christmas tree!"

She looked around her with the rapid, appraising glance of one seeking a weapon. On her wayward spouse's desk, epitomising what old-world traditionalism coexisted with his trendiness, lay a brass-and-green-onyx inkstand. Surprisingly, however, Mrs. Bracegirdle ignored this in favour of an expenses-sheet with numerous supporting receipts attached by paper-clip.

"Leave us alone!" she cried, hitting Fran with the expenses-sheet in rhythm with her words. "Leave us alone! Leave us alone! Leave us alone! Leave us ALONE!" White bills from the Terrazza and pale blue ones from the Ritz American Bar scattered like confetti.

Her full pink sleeves crossed defensively before her face, Fran dodged behind the desk, then made for the doorway, which by now had become crowded with fascinated onlookers. Pushing her way between Tessa Burland and Margaret, she ran off down the concourse in the direction of the lifts.

"Sorry." Mrs. Bracegirdle smiled at the assembled faces, then shut her eyes and gave a howl so loud, long and eerily full-throated, it made her cough, choke, retch and finally start to vomit copiously over her spouse's cherished rectangle of executive red carpet.

# SECTION
# THREE

# Arts

# 19

The figure in the red spotlight looked like some fugitive from a slave plantation who'd first become a Quaker elder, then got mixed up with the Charge of the Light Brigade.

Slung about his skinny frame was the gold-epauletted tunic of a Crimean War hussar or dragoon, its braided halves revealing a ragged frilled blouse, a multicoloured scarf and scarlet buccaneer sash. On his head was a high-crowned, broad-brimmed black hat, festooned with silver badges and amulets and the tail feathers of rare game birds. His patched knee-breeches were tucked into high-heeled boots of costly dark suede. Against the tangle of chains and thongs on his chest, he hugged a sky-blue Fender Stratocaster.

He was singing a song called "Hey, Joe" in a soft, almost shy bluesey voice while playing lead guitar to his own vocal, a feat of dexterity and co-ordination which none but Chuck Berry had attempted before. This was not the "pop" of last year with its Chelsea-booted, mop-topped innocence. This was new-look '67 "rock," jagged and unbridled, no longer content with mere hand-holding, kissing and saying good-night. Especially in the hands of this young American import, its riffs had a searing fluidity that was almost human; a banshee wail that buzzed against the wax in Louis's ears and grated on the fillings in his teeth. For all its multifarious clamour these past three or four years, the electric guitar had never come near such eloquence before.

The lighting changed from soft red to garish white that flickered with a frenzy more extreme than the most primitive silent film. Like a Chaplin possessed by demons, the tall-hatted figure had now dropped to his stripey knees and was playing the Stratocaster behind his head, now upright between his thighs like a shark-headed phallus, now sidelong under his chin, pulling at its strings with his teeth and—judging by the thunderous slurps issuing from the main amplifier—even lapping them with his tongue.

The P.R. man leaned over the candlelit table to Louis and bellowed something. "What?" he shouted back.

"Another Scotch and Coke?"

"No, thanks."

"Something else? Brandy Alexander? Cuba Libre? Tequila Sunrise?"

On the stage, the lighting had returned to normal. The flickering fellator was once again a shy young Quaker dragoon, bowing to the applause with conventional politeness in front of his two-man white backing group. An unseen compere bellowed, "Yeah! All right! Let's hear it for the Jimi Hendrix Experience . . ."

Louis peered at his watch with an exasperated sigh. Seven months on the Sunday Dispatch Magazine had taught him that P.R.'s needed to be shown the whip at regular intervals. "Look, I've been waiting almost half an hour. Is it on or isn't it?"

"Let me just go and check," the P.R. said, rising hurriedly.

After about five minutes, he reappeared.

"OK, it's cool. Brian seems to have wandered off somewhere. But Mick and Keith say come on over anyway."

Louis followed him through the camouflaging darkness that was de rigueur at all such trendy clubs. Huddled around discreetly lit tables he could distinguish Roger Daltrey of The Who, Chas Chandler of the Animals, Ray Davis of the Kinks, Mike Nesmith and Davey Jones of the Monkees.

In the darkest corner, Mick Jagger and Keith Richard sat in a semicircular booth among half a dozen unrecognisable faces. The table before them was densely forested with Scotch, vodka, Bacardi, Southern Comfort, tequila and Coca-Cola bottles, plates containing half-eaten steaks and toyed-with desserts, and a plundered 500-carton of Marlboro Kingsize.

At close quarters, both notorious Rolling Stones proved disappointingly small and puny. Jagger, in particular, was scarcely recognisable as the scourge of every parent and policeman in Britain. The infamous long hair was combed vertically down into his paisley shirt-collar. The sagging wet lips were drawn inward. The strutting, flaunting body was discreetly buttoned into an Edwardian velvet jacket.

"Mick," the P.R. murmured reverently. "This is Louis, from the Dispatch supplement."

Jagger nodded his oversized head. " 'Ello, Lewey," he said in the accent that mysteriously combined lisping public-school choirboy with raucous East End tough.

". . . like I said, they want to do a major feature on the band. Probably a cover story . . ."

Louis sat down on the end of the bench, his back firmly to the P.R. "We've met before actually. I interviewed you backstage at the Middlesborough ABC when you were on tour with Little Richard. But I'm sure you wouldn't remember."

Mockery glimmered in Jagger's wide-set eyes. " 'Ow could I ever forget the Middlesborough ABC?"

It was not an easy interview, partly because of the darkness and noise and numerous listeners, but principally because Jagger had an air of exclusivity and abstraction more suited to some Bourbon monarch than the vocalist with a rock group. Especially at questions about the Stones' chequered past, the narrow eyes would film with boredom, the choirboy-Cockney voice slur into inarticulateness. Now and then he tilted a Coke bottle against his lips in a parody of some grog-swilling pirate.

"I read about what happened on *The Ed Sullivan Show*. Were you angry that they made you change the words of 'Let's Spend the Night Together'?"

Jagger shrugged. "Nah. We're used to all that shit."

"But 'Let's spend some time together' was so banal. Surely even Ed Sullivan knows that boys and girls today have moved on from the Bobby Vinton era."

" 'F you say so." Jagger glanced around restively and sucked from the Coke bottle again. "Quoite honestly, it's a drag talkin' about it . . ."

Overtures to Keith Richard, surprisingly, proved much more fruitful. For all his physiognomical resemblance to Count Dracula on a bad morning, he was friendly, articulate and plain-spoken. Most surprising was the voice, one never heard either on stage or at press conferences, which had the fruity, sentimental rasp of some old-time actor-manager.

"Do the American police still give you as hard a time as ever?" Louis asked him.

"Not quite," Keith replied. "Now while they're roughing us up, they ask for autographs. It's 'Sign this, ya limey faggot or I'll bust ya goddammed head open!' "

They were seated at one end of the leather bench, with an empty place to Keith's right. Into this, from the encircling darkness, now slid a ferrety individual in an outsize shirt-collar, with greasy hair curtaining his forehead. Despite his rodent-like ugliness, Keith greeted him affably. "Hey, Toulouse! What's happenin', man?"

For answer the newcomer glanced furtively around him, groped in his jacket pocket and produced an object wrapped in a patterned scarf.

Laying it reverently on the table, he flipped the folds away from a small, dried-up lump rather like a petrified cowpat.

"The real thing?" asked Keith.

"Beautiful," Toulouse assured him in a rapt whisper. "Bought in Tangier yesterday morning. Best dealer in the Grand Socco."

Keith leaned forward and sniffed the lump appreciatively. "Quanta costa?"

"Fifty."

Across the table, Mick Jagger's pale face was aghast. "For Chrissake man, put it away, will you!" he hissed. "You gone crazy or summink?"

Keith grinned at the vendor apologetically. "Sorry, man. Some other time. It's makin' my compadre over there a bit too uptight."

Toulouse stared at Jagger, then back at Keith. "Are you kidding me?"

"Nah, this is the original Mister Clean. His dad used to be a P.E. instructor. He's been brought up not to do anything that might spoil his hockey."

Toulouse shrugged, rewrapped the lump of hashish and put it carefully back in his pocket. "By the way," he said, "did you know Brian was freakin' out?"

Keith glanced at Jagger and pulled a long-suffering face. "Oh, Gawd—where? The men's bog?"

"No. The birds' bog."

The P.R. man having vanished, there was no one to prevent Louis from joining the hurried exodus through a nearby door marked "Chicks." Beyond was a long mirror outlined in white fairground bulbs where two or three girls had paused in the act of back-combing and false-eyelash-fixing to stare at the tableau in the corner.

On the glossy grey carpet was what seemed at first glance to be merely a heap of Afghan fur, silks, jewellery and embroidery. It took a moment to distinguish the golden fringe and eyeless, pale face of the Rolling Stones' founding musical genius.

A girl with cropped blond hair and long racehorse legs was crouching beside him, shaking him gently. "Brian," she said in a faintly foreign accent. "Come on, there's a good boy . . ."

Keith went over and squatted on the worn-down heels of his scarlet boots. "Tripping?" he asked sympathetically. The girl nodded.

"What's he on?"

"S.T.P."

Keith gave a low whistle. "Shit! That stuff can keep you poppin' for up to seventy-two hours. Where'd he score it?"

"I think Jimi must have given it to him."

A piteous moan came from the gold-fringed face. Keith leaned closer. "What say, Brian? I can't hear you, mate."

"Do you see them?"

Keith glanced round, mystified. "See what, man?"

Brian Jones shrank back into his furs, covering his face with ring-studded fingers. "Can't you see 'em? Horrible great black insects . . . all over the wall!" He clung to the blond girl and began to sob. "Don't let them get me, Anita! Please don't let them get me!"

Louis glanced at Jagger, who was still hovering indecisively at the threshold. The face that publicly reflected only shameless arrogance was twitching with unease. "Leave him, Keith. Anita can handle it OK."

"We can't leave him, man. Cat's on a really bad trip."

Jagger withdrew, murmuring distractedly to himself. "It's all gettin' really heavy . . . I dunno where it's gonna end . . . If he goes on like this, he's bound to get busted . . . then that's our American tours right up the spout . . ."

---

"Oh, my GOD! The ghastly, *creepy* little cow!"

Jessamyn O'Shaughnessy's voice shattered the noontide peace of the Magazine, thickened with chain-smoker's outrage. She had been in her usual conspiratorial huddle with Evelyn Strachey around Cedric Scurr and his flat-plan when an interdepartmental messenger had appeared and handed her a large manila envelope. It was the seemingly innocent contents of this which had unleashed her contemptuous wrath—a note and a box of Black Magic chocolates.

For the remaining forty-five minutes before Toby Godwin's Ideas Lunch she could be heard from different parts of the concourse, unburdening herself to incredulously sympathetic colleagues.

"I was outside the front entrance last night, trying to get a taxi home in the *pouring* rain, remember how it was *bucketing* down? I saw one come round Ludgate Circus with his For Hire sign on . . . I'd got my arm up in the air like the Statue of Liberty . . . he even flashed his lights to show he'd seen me. And then that bloody *pushy* little Fran Dyson comes out and steals it from under my very *nose!* I mean, that was bad enough, but now she's sent me this *creepy* little note of apology—and the most *mingy* little box of Black Magic you can buy. I mean, I don't think it's even *half* a pound! Did you *ever* in all your life!"

As the story ricocheted at him from various angles, Louis pondered the contradictory nature it revealed. The taxi-stealing part, admittedly, was quite in character. But having brought off that coup in what sounded a particularly stylish fashion, wherefore these subsequent curious stirrings of conscience? And, especially, wherefore this clumsy attempt to secure the goodwill of one whom the P.R. industry could barely sweeten with magnums of Dom Pérignon, haute-couture clothing and first-class air-tickets to Bali?

Though more than a month had passed since Fran's departure from the Magazine, her name continued to echo through its inner councils, almost daily testing Louis's firm resolve never even to think about her again. It was not just that she had broken the unwritten but sacred code of dolly-bird "bits on the side" by refusing to remain on the side, and thereby reducing the marriage of the Deputy Editor to barely retrievable chaos. Even worse, she had been responsible for rupturing the surface sheen of sunny bonhomie that constituted office life under Toby Godwin. Indeed, on that day when Terry Bracegirdle's wife had materialised in the concourse, shrieking, weeping and vomiting, the agonised discomfiture of the Editor had been terrible to behold. As Margaret Cole remarked, "He reminded me of an embarrassed old panda I once saw at the Zoo, standing on its head, cuddling a sheaf of bamboo and wishing everything would just go away."

Godwin had, of course, acted with gallant loyalty to his principal young rip, instructing Jim Deaves to rid the Magazine of Fran as soon as could be diplomatically engineered with her secretarial union, N.A.T.S.O.P.A. But this had been pre-empted, literally, from above. Impressed with the exclusive story she had filed on her own initiative, the newspaper had offered her a six-month trial as a general reporter.

Though only one floor separated her from Louis, the mutually fierce apartheid of Magazine and newspaper spared him all but the most fleeting encounters. Occasionally, as he waited for a lift, the doors of an upward-bound car would open and there she would be in her bullseye-striped PVC mac, holding a sandwich in a bag and a lidded plastic coffee cup, the news reporter's insignia of desk-hugging keenness. Once or twice she had given him a hint of her dimply-devilish smile; he, for his part, affected total blindness and preoccupation.

In the deep bottom drawer of his desk he still had her background interview with the Hollywood mogul Pandro S. Berman. Sometimes, despite all his best resolutions, he would covertly move aside the notebooks piled on top of it and look at the pale grey characters of her typewriter, the amendments in her neat, schoolgirlish hand and the way she'd misspelt "adolescent."

The young rips found Tessa Burland sliding the silver foil covers from cold sea trout with fennel, and their Editor chuckling fatly as he wound the cork from a bottle of Muscadet.

"Here's a go, chums! BBC2 want to make a film on me for their *One Man's Week* series. Chap name of . . . what's his name, dear heart?"

"Tancred Philpott," said Tessa.

"You've seen these things, I'm sure . . . following Joe Blow through a typical week at work and play and so forth. According to this Philpott cove, they've never had a Sunday magazine editor before."

"Are you going to do it?" asked Val Lewis.

Godwin chuckled again, spooning lobster mayonnaise. "I really don't see why not. Though what having a camera crew dogging one's every footstep is like I can't begin to imagine."

"Easy job for them," Cedric Scurr remarked. "For God's typical week, all they need do is set up their cameras at the Savoy Grill . . ."

"And Rules," Evelyn Strachey said.

"—And Boulestin."

"—And the Gay Hussar."

"Hooh hooh hooh! . . . 'Set up their cameras at Rules and Boulestin!' . . . Impudent young scallywags!"

Beside the Editor's plate lay a two-page memorandum whose closely spaced typing, the work of no secretary, was instantly recognisable to at least one person present.

"I must tell you that we're in receipt of yet another suggestion from Mighty Jack Shildrick, who is nothing if not persistent." Godwin picked up the memo and read aloud in his booming parody of Shildrick's ever-urgent enthusiasm and passion:

" 'I've joost seen some horrifying statistics on the state of Britain's teeth. Did you know that one in three children under ten suffers from chronic tooth decay, that forty percent of adults over thirty have lost between twenty-two and thirty-seven percent of their teeth to gum disease and that the proportion of denture wearers has risen from twenty-five percent in 1946 to fifty-one percent last year? I think there's scope for a major Colour Mag survey called something like "The ABC of Teeth"—the perils, the myths and how to safeguard them, especially from the child angle. This is a major crisis in the nation's health you ought to be looking at.' "

There was a bemused silence, then Jessamyn softly exclaimed, "Yuk!"

"Great scope for visuals, Cedric," Jim Deaves said. "How about famous denture-wearers without their top sets?"

"Yes . . . or gingivitis in full colour?"

"So the answer to Mighty Jack, I take it, is as usual: 'Thanks but no thanks.' " Godwin passed the memo to Tessa for consignment to the file now bulging with rejected Shildrick ideas, and snipped the foreskin of a Bolivar number 1.

"Right then, boys and girls, to more germane matters. I understand we're well forward with 'What Did Christ Really Look Like?' Perhaps, Val dear, you'd be kind enough to bring us up to date."

Val Lewis opened the orange folder on her pointed brown knees. "We've got two researchers out in Nazareth, combing the place for thirty-three-year-old carpenters. When they've lined up a good enough selection, we fly the country's leading pre-Renaissance art expert to Tel Aviv to choose the most likely candidate, and then get him photographed by Bailey, probably on the Mount of Olives."

"Sound good to you, Terry, dear boy?"

Bracegirdle swept back his quiff in the manner signifying creative turmoil. "Ah feel we should be thinking a bit more modern," he said. "Why not make it a real whodunnit? We could photograph all the carpenters together like a police identity parade."

He expanded his idea, growing visibly more cheerful. The past month was well-known to have been an arduous one chez Bracegirdle, with all "late work at the office" strictly curtailed and no outings other than escorting wife, child and bassett hound to suburban department stores.

". . . We could give the whole portfolio to Scotland Yard and ask them to make up an Identikit picture. The cover could be like a wanted poster . . . 'Have YOU seen this Redeemer of Mankind?' "

By now Louis had learned that the best moment to suggest anything was right at the meeting's end, when his colleagues were heavy with food, muzzy with wine and fatigued with supercilious mirth. Today, therefore, he bided his time until almost 3 o'clock, speaking up suddenly and rapidly amid the plate-piling, yawning and preliminary scrape of chairs.

"I'm still looking into the Rolling Stones as a profile idea. Mick Jagger's a bit boring but Keith Richard's really good value . . . and, anyway, it's his guitar-playing as much as Jagger's voice that makes the band. They're really starting to open up to me, so can I stay with it?"

Godwin raised questioning eyebrows at Bracegirdle and Strachey, who both shrugged apathetically.

"OK, dear boy. Perhaps you'll let us know the strength of it in due course."

It was a Sunday-morning scene only partially successful in evoking Algernon Moncrieff or Bertie Wooster. Louis, wearing orange Marks and Spencer pyjamas, lay on the musty carpet of the basement living room with sections of the Sunday Dispatch littered far and wide around him. Brenda lolled in the undersized armchair, wearing a frogged black Tunisian kaftan and socks with suspenders, smoking a pink Sobranie cocktail cigarette and studying the News of the World.

Every part of the Dispatch, outside the Magazine, now bore Shildrick's unmistakable imprint. On page 1 of the news section was a triumphant banner headline, "GAG BY AUTO GIANT FAILS." Three Sundays ago, the Close-up team had revealed that in a leading British-made luxury car the dashboard cigar-lighter was in such dangerous proximity to electrical wiring that using it could make the vehicle spontaneously combust. The manufacturer's response had been to cancel their multimillion-pound advertising account with the Dispatch and threaten a High Court injunction preventing publication of any further revelations about the cigar-lighter. Lord McIntyre, as ever, had backed his Editor against both the commercial and legal sanctions. In subsequent weeks, under the heading "DEATH IN YOUR DASH," Close-up had unearthed half a dozen case histories of vehicles turning into somersaulting fireballs at their drivers' attempts to light a cheroot. Today's splash announced that the manufacturers had totally backed down, conceding "a major design fault" in the car and agreeing to the Dispatch's demand for the recall of all models fitted with the lethal accessory.

It was not merely that, in the space of barely two months, Shildrick had transformed and galvanised the paper in all its labyrinthine departments. He also had broken the immemorial tradition that Editors of "quality" Sundays were lofty, amorphous beings whose names were barely known to journalists outside Fleet Street, let alone the wider public. During the furor over "Death in Your Dash," he had appeared on the BBC's *24 Hours* programme, facing spokesmen from the car manufacturers with the relaxed intensity Louis remembered from many television appearances in the Teesside area. That night, as much as the issue at hand, Shildrick himself became news by declaring that, even were the story to be successfully injuncted, he would risk imprisonment for contempt of court rather than drop an investigation so clearly in the public interest. Seven million viewers had heard him memorably define the purpose of the Sunday Dispatch under his editorship: "to stand up for ordinary folk against the playground bullies of this world."

His gregarious, inquisitive nature and unquenchable energy made him a public figure in a way that the reclusive Dudley Mowforth had never been. His passionate involvement with all aspects of the paper did not preclude a packed social calendar. Queen, the only magazine to retain Society pages in these egalitarian times, recorded his presence at superior dinner-tables, fashionable receptions, theatrical first nights and film premières—but always, one felt, in a spirit of objective investigation, trying to find out what made these people really tick and whether it could be turned to the Dispatch's advantage. Jean Shildrick standing firm in her dislike of parties, his only companion as a rule would be the driver poised to whisk him back to any late-breaking drama at the office.

The strain on Louis's loyalties was now acute. When his colleagues at the Ideas Lunch belittled and lampooned Shildrick, he still felt bewildered outrage, as of old. But he was uncomfortably aware that the ideas with which Shildrick bombarded Toby Godwin deserved their cool rebuff as often as not. The energy and originality which crackled from every page of the newspaper seemed to fail him whenever he tried thinking in colour. His view, repeatedly stated, was that the Magazine should develop its vestigial role as a "service" to its readers, concentrating less on keeping them at the cutting-edge of fashion and more on the décor of their homes, the seeding of their window-boxes, the education of their children and the routes of their weekend rambles. Rather than running uncaptioned spreads by the world's great photographers, he urged greater use of helpful diagrams, sketch maps, "fact boxes," charts and graphs. It was curious how one so inspired in the use of newspaper photographs, so stylish in monotone layout and typography, could appear so blind, if not actively hostile, to the Magazine's pioneering aesthetic. As Cedric Scurr scornfully remarked, "His idea of good visuals is a mouthful of rotten teeth."

Besides, Louis now owed an understandable allegiance to that determinedly Shildrick-proof outpost of the Sunday Dispatch which maintained him on a diet of champagne, game pie, sea trout, kedgeree and hothouse strawberries, and kept his wallet stuffed with five-pound notes; which housed and clothed and buffered him from life's unpleasantness rather as he'd once read that medieval monasteries used to feed, clothe and accoutre their monks. How could his principal loyalty not be to the jovial Chief to whom he owed this existence at the zenith of prestige and fashion, punctuated by extravagant treats, free of fear, unburdened by routine or responsibility, altogether so continuously exciting and enjoyable that he positively rushed to be at his desk by 10:30 each morning?

Nevertheless, at bottom he felt himself still Shildrick's man; still responded to the tingle of excitement that percolated down from the fifth floor; still believed—for all his own clumsy short-sightedness over the Assistant Literary Editorship—that Shildrick had incalculably thrilling things in store for him. Large as might be the divide between, he had no doubt that Shildrick kept a close eye on everything he did. Indeed, when his Elizabeth Taylor profile appeared in mid-January, a vintage Herogram had come winging down, praising his "masterly ordering of rich material" and his "delicious touch."

He leafed backwards through the news section, filming over his eyes like some tropical toad as he passed the Romanesque white-on-black heading CICERO, the wide-set columns, smartly punning subheads and elegantly understated italic signature *Basil Hamilton*.

Near the bottom of page 4, the Steam Section's repository for routine home news, his eye was caught by a single-column heading in lower case:

NO INCREASE YET IN
PRICE OF CHEESE

*By Fran Dyson*

Brenda Brown bought the News of the World in an ironical spirit, imbibing each Sabbath's feast of randy vicars and disgraced scoutmasters with the quizzically pursed lips of a hairless David Frost. This morning, however, he had been reading in silence for some time. Now, at last, he threw down the paper and said: "Your friend Mick Jagger's been and gone and done it."

"What's he been up to now? Trying to get into the Savoy without a tie again?"

"Rather worse. Exposed as a rampant dope fiend."

"What?" Louis yelled.

"He's been bragging to the News of the Screws that he uses speed . . . hash . . . even L.S.D."

"It's not possible!"

"It's here in black-and-white." Brenda retrieved the paper and read out: " 'During the time our investigators talked to him at Blases Club, Jagger took about six benzedrine tablets . . .' "

"I don't believe it."

" 'Later on at Blases, while our investigators were still present, Jagger showed a companion and two girls a piece of hashish and invited them back to his flat for a quote smoke unquote.' "

"I just don't believe it! He's petrified of drugs. Or, rather, of being busted for drugs. I told you how scared shitless he was the other night at the Speakeasy."

"Hm, well I think he may well have quite a hard time convincing Mr. Plod."

That evening, coincidentally, Jagger was among the guests on Eamonn Andrews's new television "talk show." Once again, he was the very opposite of his surly, demonic public image. Beside him sat his girlfriend Marianne Faithfull, that fragilely perfect blond English rose.

"Now," Eamonn Andrews began hesitantly, "there's been a lot of talk of drugs flying around in the press today. Do you have any reaction to that?"

"Yes, I do," Jagger replied in his choirboy lisp. "It's all a pack of lies. And I'm suin' the News of the World for libel . . ."

"Will Michelin Man be coming round later?" Brenda enquired.

"You're very rude, but yes."

"So you'll be wanting the bedroom."

"Yes."

Louis had become glancingly involved with a girl named Antonia Napier, a temporary appointment at the Magazine to help Erica Kirk, the Cookery Editor, with research into London's best Continental bakeries. Vertiginously upper-class, with a voice of the same foghorn timbre as Peggy Mount's, she had attracted him with a figure aptly described by Margaret as "Junoesque." But that was before her five-day-a-week schedule of intrepidly sampling croissants, brioches and *petits pains au chocolat.* Now one would not have looked for her on Olympus so much as on a flag outside the famous French tyre factory in Fulham Road.

This evening, bedroom activity was limited by what Louis felt more than ready to recategorise as the Blessing. Good sport that she was, however, and loath to see anything go to waste, Antonia knelt between his legs, hooked reddish hair purposefully behind one ear and did something which—thanks to intrusive mental pictures of jolly men constructed from motortyres—had lost much of its initial riveting novelty. While uttering the sounds of lowering steer-like appreciation that good manners demanded, Louis glanced from his hung-up dark green velvet suit across to Brenda's framed hunting prints, pewter spirit measures and electric trouser-press. The sound effects on Antonia's part, once more exciting even than "big, cruel nurse," now seemed merely distracting; it was as if she were evaluating flavour and crispness in yet another variety of croissant.

He awoke alone in his bed with a jolt, to a repeated shrilling of the front door-bell. The luminous dial of his new Rolex Oyster (bought on expenses) said 1:28. On the other side of the room Brenda turned over and murmured, "Who is that barbarian?"

With the living-room light Louis also switched on the thick bulb outside the glass-paned front door. Through its security bars he glimpsed tumbling honey-coloured hair.

Fran was standing on the doormat, clutching the collar of a dark-

coloured coat and shivering perceptibly. The black centipedes looked at
him with mute entreaty like some poor little orphan arriving at a foster
home.

Louis had opened the door only about an eighth. "Well?" he said
icily.

"I was passing. I wanted to see you. Is that allowed?"

"And why should you want to do that?"

"Please can I come in? I promise I'll only stay a minute."

The coat she wore was of severe, almost funereal cut, save that it terminated some eight inches above her knees and there was no sign of a
skirt underneath it. In one hand she held a pale object, only slowly
identifiable as a thick damask table napkin. As Louis stood aside, she
thrust this into his hand. 'There you are . . . a peace offering.''

Wrapped in the napkin was a slice of fresh pineapple. It had been
carefully, even artfully prepared with no trace of green scales on the
outside, the hard middle bit cut away. He struggled with a vision of her
trimming and paring meticulously in that kitchen full of scummy pots
and dead-rat teabags.

"You do like it, do you?" she asked anxiously.

"Oh yes. Love it. Thanks."

"Can I sit down? Just for a minute? I promise I won't stay long."

With barely subdued exasperation, he nodded at the single small
armchair. Fran sat down on the very edge of it, her heavenly legs closed
up and heels together, manifestly taking up as little room as possible.
Sections of The Sunday Dispatch were still strewn about the carpet.
"Saw your piece today," Louis said.

She clutched her coat around her and pulled a shivering face. "Yeah
. . . big deal."

"It was OK."

"Not exactly in your league, though, was it?"

He felt slightly less riven with glacial resentment. "Oh, I don't
know," he demurred without notable conviction.

"By the way, your Liz Taylor thing was wonderful. I meant to write
to you about it."

"The Ugly Sisters shafted me in the end, though."

"Sorry?"

"Evelyn and Jessamyn. They were spitting with rage that neither of
them had been asked to write it. Their revenge was getting Cedric Scurr
to put so many photographers' credits under the headline that my
name was just about buried."

"You should still be pleased," Fran said. "It was a marvellous show. I
saw the TV ad for it, too."

A giant wave of fatigue washed through Louis. He fetched one of the nasty wooden chairs from the unpleasant table near the window and sat down facing her. "Why you here?" he asked.

She smiled wanly at the cable-ese joke. "I don't know. Perhaps I shouldn't have come. I'm only disturbing you." She bent her head, showing him her back-combed golden crown.

"What's the matter?" he asked, though still not warmly.

"Everything."

"Surely not everything?"

"Almost everything."

"But you're on the paper. You've made that leap." He gave a short, bitter laugh. "Never mind how."

"Yes," she agreed bleakly. "I'm on the paper."

"Don't tell me you don't like it."

"Oh, I love it! Junior of juniors in the Newsroom! Getting all the junk no one else can be bothered to do. 'No increase in price of cheese!' Weren't you just dying to know that?"

This came out with a humorous twist that melted another glacier. "Mm," Louis said, smiling despite himself. "I'd have thought Jack Shildrick would have found you something a bit more . . ."

Fran shook her head. "Not Shildrick. He doesn't even know me."

"But he's everywhere!"

"But much too preoccupied to bother with some poor little dogsbody on six months' probation."

"I thought it was Shildrick who took you on?"

"No, it was Nick Fenton."

"Well . . . however much Shildrick seems to bomb around, believe me, he's incredibly approachable. If you had an idea for a piece and took it to him, I know he'd give it a fair hearing."

This last was spoken with extreme unevenness since Fran, with no prior warning, had left the chair, pushed his pyjamaed legs apart and knelt deep inside the resultant gap, wrapping both arms around his waist. Her hair smelt of Silvikrin shampoo. She seemed to be weeping quietly.

"Just stick it in a memo . . . you'd get an answer straight back . . ."

Her only reply was to cling to him still tighter, as if fearing to be torn loose by some freak whirlwind.

"What is it?" Louis demanded testily, stroking the spun-gold crown.

She murmured something inaudible.

"Come again?"

"I want to be with you."

"What—like your big brother?"

"Don't be horrid to me."

"You were fairly horrid to me."

"I didn't mean to be," she whispered, turning her face up to his. The kiss, though brief and light, was still enough to bring the Ice Age to an unscheduled end.

"Damn," he murmured.

"What?"

"You feel too nice."

She smiled with all her devilish dimples. The black centipedes moved in, out of focus again.

"Damn!" he said after a few moments more. "Damn, damn, damn!"

"You sound like Professor Higgins."

"Who?"

"Professor Higgins. In *My Fair Lady.*"

He slumped back in the chair and looked at her, unable to stop himself stroking her cheek. She took his hand and kissed it, then laid her face against it again. They might have been sitting before a roaring log-fire in some cabin in the heart of the Canadian Rockies.

"All right," he said testily. "All right, all right, all right. If you're really straight up this time."

"I am really straight up this time."

"All right. We'll start again."

"Can we?" she said in a small voice.

"Yes."

She murmured something else inaudible.

"Sorry?"

"I said, 'Can we have a quick one to seal the bargain?' "

"What?" he said dazedly, remembering his bout with Michelin Man not two hours since, and the consequent firm set of his petrol gauge to "Empty."

Fran knelt back, slipped off her coat and felt amongst her hair for the rear fastening of her polka-dot dress.

"What?" she repeated with her dimply-devilish smile. "Who? Where? When?"

# 20

The following Wednesday morning a party of men trooped through the Magazine concourse, clad in heavy boots and fur-lined anoraks and carrying bulky metal boxes, tripods, a multi-dial tape recorder and an elongated microphone cocooned in dingy-looking felt. To add to the sense of occasion, Freya Broadbent had returned to her desk after a two-week absence, sporting coral earrings, a turquoise bandanna and a suntan the colour of butterscotch.

"How was Antigua?" Margaret asked her.

"Fascinating! I had a lovely long talk with Father McDermott, who used to cycle from Topsfield over to Petts Wood every Sunday to hear the de Gaulles' confession, and usually stayed to lunch afterwards. What's really amazing, though, is that he's still in touch with Madame de Gaulle's old dressmaker, a wonderful character by all accounts, who actually made the coat she wore for their return to Paris after the Liberation."

"And who, presumably, isn't in Kent any more either?"

"No, after the war she went out to live with her daughter in Australia, and is now in an old people's home just outside Brisbane. I'd have flown straight on there if I hadn't promised faithfully to be at the launch of Elizabeth David's new cookware shop."

As she spoke Mrs. Broadbent freed one arm, then the other from the long, shapeless jersey she wore over her brown Foale and Tuffin minidress. Pulling the jersey over her head, she accidentally took the dress half-way with it, revealing what Louis had always suspected would be a neat little bust in a purple half-cup bra, and knickers not oppressively sensible under dark-seamed tights.

"Oh, Louis, I'm so sorry!" she said with her attractive giggle, slithering the dress into place again.

"That'd be a nice moment for the documentary," Margaret re-marked.

"They haven't started yet, surely."

"No—the producer's still in with God, trying to find out what makes up his typical week. I don't think he's going to find exactly an abundance of material."

From the office that Jessamyn O'Shaughnessy shared with Evelyn Strachey came a shout of almost deranged laughter. A moment later Jessamyn emerged, brandishing a familiar slender periodical. "Have you lot seen today's Private Eye?" she demanded.

"No," said Margaret. "Which poor devil's being eviscerated this time?"

"Just listen to this. It's absolutely won-der-ful!" As Jessamyn found the place and began reading aloud, Strachey appeared in the doorway behind her and Cedric Scurr hung his hairy forearms over the glass partition of the Art Department.

"The pampered gentleman hacks at Lord Muckintyre's moneyspinning Sunday Dispatch are growing alarmed at the ee-bai-goom philistinism of their new Editor, 'Mighty' Jack Shildrick. Recently, on hearing that Shildrick was scheduled to lunch with a leading politician at the White Tower Greek restaurant, smoothie Old Etonian Deputy Editor James Way urged him not to miss the establishment's famous moussaka. 'I'll try it,' Mighty Jack replied, 'but only 'alf a glass, mind, 'cos I don't really like drinking at dinnertime.' "

" 'Dinnertime'! Oh, my God!"

"Eh, oop, lad, what do you want on your batter pudding? Jam or gravy?"

"I don't believe it," Mrs. Broadbent interjected crisply. "Not even Shildrick could be that ignorant."

"But you know he is," Evelyn Strachey said. "Don't you remember when he thought that Leni Riefenstahl was a man . . . like Lenny Bruce?"

"And Alma-Tadema was a woman," grinned Scurr, "like Alma Cogan."

During these exchanges Louis had been seated with head bent, studying the Library clips on Mick Jagger and feeling himself go alternately hot and cold like a faulty ring on an electric stove. Part of him wanted to rise up, especially against the Ugly Sisters, and cast their snobbish calumnies back in their teeth. But another part of him uncomfortably conceded they had at least half a point. As well as the Riefenstahl and Alma-Tadema incidents, he remembered a memo from

Shildrick objecting (in vain) to a proposed piece on George Eliot's love life "even though he may be a major nineteenth-century writer."

Relief came with a buzz of the phone, and Tessa Burland's efficient voice: "Louis, could you come in and see God for a minute, please?"

Godwin sat at bay behind his pristine desk, facing an unattended film camera on a low tripod and a ring of darkened arc-lamps. On the polished work-top sat a small, elderly man whose wizened brown face and protruding eyes reminded Louis of concert-party comedians in his seaside youth.

"Hullo, dear boy, thanks for dropping by. Can I introduce Tancred Philpott, producer of the *One Man's Week* series, who's putting together this little slice of cinéma-not-too-vérité, I trust, hooh hooh! And which, to my surprise, I find is to be filmed in colour. As an exercise for when the Beeb goes over to full colour transmission. Is that right, Tancred?"

"Right!" the wizened man assented in a clipped BBC announcer voice bizarrely at odds with this ultra-contemporary usage. He smiled at Louis, his features collapsing into a death mask of vertical grooves and nicotine-yellow teeth.

"This is Louis Brennan, the young writer we keep on staff here—indeed, for such eventualities as the one I'm about to explain to him. You don't mind, do you, if we, ah, hold a short editorial meeting?"

Philpott shook his gnarled head and waved wrinkly, blue-veined hands.

"Hey . . . like I said!" he intoned as precisely as if reading the Home Service weather forecast. "This is your thing, man! We're here to get hip to your thing. I don't wanna, like, foul up your groove in any way, you dig?"

Godwin turned back to Louis with manifest relief. "A slight emergency, dear boy. A black hole has suddenly appeared in our issue for April twenty-third. What Cedric had schemed as a double-page colour ad has suddenly now reverted to editorial, leaving us in dire need of a piece at short notice. Let me see, you're currently engaged in profiling the Searchers, is that right?"

"The Rolling Stones," Louis said.

"And are you totally over your head with that?"

"It's still just a feasibility study, really. I'm spending this weekend at Keith Richard's cottage in Sussex. After that I should know if it's worth going ahead."

"Well, I wonder if you might knock off something for us meantime, in your enviably instantaneous style? We've been offered an interview with Robert Greenham—a name more than familiar to you, I trow."

"Of course."

"Of course . . . great theatrical knight . . . creator of definitive Shake-spearian roles second only to Olivier . . . tireless worker for charity . . . all-round doer of extremely decent things . . . The peg is that, after forty years before the footlights, he's making his first essay as a director." Godwin glanced at a piece of paper. "He's doing *Oedipus Rex* at the Duke of York's with Albert Finney and Peggy Ashcroft . . . all in boxes."

"Boxes?"

"Apparently it's an entirely original concept and interpretation. So, dear boy, do you think you can ride to our rescue on this one? It's a quick interview at his flat in Albany, then two thousand words by early afternoon Friday. "Grandee of British stage makes revolutionary new departure," you know the sort of thing. We're getting Duffy to photo-graph him with the cast . . . and their boxes, too, presumably."

Tancred Philpott, meanwhile, had begun jiggling about convulsively on the work-top. "Hey! This is, like, peachy stuff, man!" he exclaimed. "Is it cool with you if I, like, wop it in the can?"

Godwin glanced at Louis in bewilderment. "You mean . . . film it?"

"Right! Great piece for the top of the show! You fill in your guy . . . make him hip to the jive . . . he grooves off. You dig?"

"Then do go ahead, dear boy, if you think it helpful."

An urgent summons was relayed to the waiting crew of bearded cameraman, absurdly well-muscled sound-recordist, electrician, elec-trician's mate and T-shirted youth bearing film-canisters, sticky tape and miniature black-and-white clapperboard. After a few moments of intense squeezing past and stumbling over leads in the confined space, all was ready. The ring of arc-lights clicked on with hideous force.

"OK, man," Philpott's cut-glass voice said from somewhere to the left. "Just groove through it like before. Nice and easy, you dig? Mark it!"

The T-shirted youth passed the clapperboard before the camera lens and in a voice heavy with boredom—though nowhere near as much as it would be—intoned: "*One Man's Week* . . . Toby Godwin. Take one! Action!"

---

Fran's desk was in a remote corner of the Newsroom, next to the glass divide with a passage containing men's and women's lavatories. Unlike other reporters, she had no colleague at the steel desk facing hers, which was littered with dog-eared telephone books, old copy on spikes and a yellowing pile of Hansard Parliamentary reports.

"Grotty, isn't it?" she said, wrinkling up her nose.

Louis firmly put aside insistent mental comparisons with the Stockton Evening Telegraph. "Oh, I don't know. At least you're not behind a pillar."

"Sorry?"

"The newsrooms at some of the dailies have enormous thick pillars in them. People whose faces don't fit get put behind the pillar. Some subs at the Express apparently haven't been seen for years."

He glanced round uneasily. This, after all, was East Berlin and his papers were far from in order. "And do you really never run across Jack Shildrick?"

Fran shrugged. "I see him bounding along this corridor sometimes. He's got his own private bathroom next to the gents' loo."

The notion was curiously at odds both with Shildrick's democratic style and his personal modesty and austerity.

"It's quite nice actually," she added.

Louis stared at her. "How do you know?"

"How do I know? I use it."

"To do what?"

"Have a bath. His Tuesday conference always lasts at least two hours, same on Friday. And I've usually got nothing much to do. What could be nicer than a long soak with a good book . . . maybe a few grapes. Mmm!"

Her dimply-devilish smile vanished as if wiped clean by a blackboard cloth, and a look of forlorn resignation took its place.

Glancing round, Louis saw Nick Fenton approaching from the far-off Newsdesk with the vaguely effeminate flip-flop gait peculiar to Oxford and Cambridge graduates. He wore a purple shirt and turquoise-and-white tie, and sipped from a mug decorated with Victorian calligraphy. "How's it going?" he asked Fran curtly.

"All right," she muttered.

Fenton glanced at Louis, or rather through him, and sipped more coffee with an upper-class slurp. "When you've finished, if I'm not here, give it to Merrick. All right?"

"Yes, all right."

"Super!" Fenton said with witheringly ironic emphasis.

Louis scowled at his departing back pleat. "Toffee-nosed sod, isn't he?"

"He can't stand me," Fran said. "Who do you think gives me all the junk to do?"

"So what's he nagging you about?"

"Just a drear little piece for News Digest on the Decimal Currency Board. But I can't seem to get it in the right order."

"Shall I look at it for you?"

"No. Don't worry."

"It's no worry."

"I don't want to waste your time."

"Oh, come off it." He picked up the sheets of copy beside her type-writer. "We're past that stage, aren't we?"

The constructional problem was as simple to Louis as arranging chairs around a table. "Look . . . you're fine down to here . . . then knock out this boring quote about the Japanese yen . . . Go straight from 'Britain the fiscal odd man out of Europe' to phased introduction in 'seventy-one or 'seventy-two. See?" He paused and glanced at Fran's hairline, wondering if what had happened the other night in his gas-leaky living room really and truly had happened, whether there was the remotest chance of its happening again and why, while it was hap-pening, he hadn't taken more care to appreciate every second.

"So you mean leave in the bit about the deutschemark?"

"Yes. That bit's fine . . ."

" 'Ullo, Poet. Slumming it among the black-and-white set?"

Shildrick had come up at a noiseless run, evidently from the Picture Desk since he held a sheaf of glossy black-and-white prints in addition to galley-proofs, a book annotated with long strips of paper and a pris-tine new Hansard. There was something strange but not immediately diagnosable about his face.

" 'Ullo, Miss . . ." he added, glancing at Fran with a polite but vague smile. It was obviously true that he hadn't noticed this humblest and most temporary member of his reporting staff. And she, for her part, seemed perversely bent on keeping it that way, nodding back almost brusquely, then dropping her glance to the copy in her typewriter.

Louis had belatedly realised what was different. Shildrick was minus his glasses. The hooded, feminine eyes were not only exposed but en-dowed with a new directness and keenness. "Contact lenses," he ex-plained, clearly not for the first time. "I've been meaning to give them a go for years, but only just got up the courage. What do you think?"

"Great," Louis said. "What do they feel like?"

"A bit odd at first, but you get used to it. Like having an eyelash in your eye."

With the dexterity of a Mississippi card sharp, Shildrick spread the glossy prints over the empty desk facing Fran's. In one, slim Oriental women with their hair elegantly pinned up ran shrieking from a village of burning straw huts. In another, helicopters hovered over a forest margin, dealing out sheets of fire as mistily diaphanous as crop spray. In several more, black-clad figures lay half-submerged in a brimming rice paddy. He beckoned Louis to look and, by implication, his illicit bathroom-borrower too if she wished. But she remained seated, her gaze steadfastly averted.

"Did you hear what George Brown called us in the Commons the other night when he was half-pissed? A traitor! How dare we criticise the Government for being America's poodle! Supporting this bloodbath in Vietnam, even though it's murderously misconceived, and the Americans themselves don't want it. Well, I'll give him treachery this Sunday, even if it knocks the Special Relationship back to the shelling of the White House." Shildrick stabbed the paddy-field view with a passionate forefinger. "Who do you think those dead bodies are, Poet?"

"Vietcong," Louis said.

"Vietcong suspects, so-called. But from an altitude of two hundred feet, how can anyone be sure? We've got this marvellous piece about a Texan general who takes off from Saigon every Friday in his personal helicopter, with his personal MI6 carbine, mows down a couple of hundred peasants and goes back as toned up as if he's just done nine rounds of golf. I'm running this one or—maybe this—one over eight columns with a strapline all across the top, 'This is what three-star General Hiram T. Rolnick calls a turkey-shoot.' "

He scooped up the prints, gave Fran a perfunctory smile and drew Louis on with him a few paces. "How are you, Poet, anyway? I've not seen you since that marvellous spread on Liz Taylor. Did you get my note about it?"

"Yes. Thank you."

"You're really coming to the peak of your powers. I hope Toby Godwin realises that. Who've they got you doing now?"

"Sir Robert Greenham."

"Oh, that's a good idea!" Shildrick's newly exposed eyes kindled with ever-dependable enthusiasm. "He's such a marvellous actor! I've met him, you know."

"Really? What's he like?"

"I sat next to him at the party Tony Richardson gave for Vanessa . . . Vanessa Redgrave, that is. And he was absolutely charming! I mean, not a bit stagey and gushy . . . a funny, intelligent, nice man. And he does wonderful work for charity. Loves children, even though he's none of his own. In fact he's asked me to be on this committee he's chairing, to redevelop Aberfan as a tourist attraction. You must be sure and ask him about that. When are you seeing him?"

"This afternoon."

"He's got the most magnificent flat, like something out of one of his own plays. I was there for drinks the other night. John Mills dropped in with his wife—and Hayley, too, which was quite a thrill. Well, it's a wonderful subject for you, Poet. I'll look forward to your piece."

Louis walked back to Fran and frowned at her with tender exasperation. "You're bonkers."

"What?" she said dully.

"Shildrick was right here. Why didn't you talk to him? Suggest a few ideas?"

"He wasn't here to see me."

This, of course, was gratifyingly true. "But you could have made a bit of an effort. Anyway, now he knows your face at least drop him a note. I'm sure he'll respond immediately."

---

The white-and-gold front door was answered by a Chinese, or possibly Malay, Thai or Filipino youth, wearing a pink-and-white candy-striped apron with heart-shaped pockets, and holding a long-handled feather duster. His face, very far from inscrutable, wore a look of almost manic eagerness.

"Good afternoon. Louis Brennan, Sunday Dispatch Magazine."

"Yes, yes, yes, yes," the whatever and whoever he was replied in an Orientally inflected public-school accent. "You want Pookie, don't you? This way, my dear chap."

Louis followed him down a curved corridor lined with framed playbills, and into an immense pastel sitting room with a domed glass roof and a book-lined gallery running two-thirds of its length. At one end of the gallery a door opened and a brown figure wrapped in a pale blue bath-towel was briefly visible.

"Do take a pew, my dear fellow. Pookie will be with you as soon as he's decent. Would you care for coffee? Brazilian, Blue Mountain or Mincing Lane?"

Seated among the numerous cushions of a salmon-coloured sofa, Louis studied the framed photographs on an adjacent grand piano, attesting to the twin streams of Sir Robert Greenham's life. Here he was on the one hand, in black or white tie and laughing uproariously with Noël Coward, Laurence Olivier, Rex Harrison, James Robertson Justice and Lionel Bart. Here he was on the other bowing to the Queen Mother, genuflecting before the Pope, having a medal pinned on him by General de Gaulle, enjoying a joke with Dr. Adenauer and receiving an evidently heartfelt handshake on behalf of the United Nations from the Secretary General, U Thant.

Behind him, he realised, was a cushion less yieldingly comfortable than the others. Pulling it clear, he saw it was royal blue, rather than silver or lime-green, and embroidered with the gold initials E.R.

"Ah, you've found my Coronation cushion!" boomed a voice of familiar staccato cadence. The great theatrical knight himself descended from the gallery, surprisingly attired in a beachcomber-like outfit of décolleté yellow shirt, white bell-bottom trousers and open-toed espadrilles. The classically handsome face had jowls more pendulous than any picture had ever disclosed, and wore a patina of thick—and, in some sectors, crumbly—orange make-up. With him came powerful gusts of bath salts and aftershave lotion. He held out a hand whose nails shone as if varnished.

"All of us in the Abbey were allowed to keep our cushions afterwards, so that's a very special souvenir of a wonderful day, even though, of course, it poured with rain the whole time. I don't know why, but they gave me the most heavenly seat in the south transept, where I could see everything, only a couple of rows behind darling Dickie Mountbatten."

"Pookie, don't be a such a silly ass!" the Oriental person chided, setting down a laden coffee tray. "You know very well why it was."

"Well, yes, one had rendered some small service in coaching the young couple in projection, which was extra important, you see, since it was all to be on telly for the very first time. The dear Queen was such a pro, I told her I could get her on in the West End any time she liked. Whenever I lunch at the Palace now, we still have a little giggle about it."

Coaxing the knight to talk was in no sense arduous. He poured coffee for Louis and then took a facing armchair, cradling one knee, twiddling his exposed toes and beaming as if upon an emissary from Littlewoods bearing a First Dividend cheque.

"I love The Sunday Dispatch!" he sighed. "Though there's so much to read, it usually takes me all week to get through it. I always save the coloured supplement for last, though. It's my special treat to read in bed on Wednesday or Thursday night."

"And I believe you know our Editor?"

"Joe Shadrach? Oh, goodness, yes! An absolute sweetie!"

With heart already sinking fast, Louis opened his notebook. "*Oedipus*, I gather, is the first play you've ever directed. Could you tell me how that came about?"

"One has been very fortunate in that, over the years, productions in which one has had some small say have met with approval from kind friends. Just before Christmas I was at Kenny More's, talking to Albie Finney and Johnny Gielgud, when it just hit me! I turned to Albie and I said, 'Albie, darling, tell me if you think I'm completely crazy' . . . but darling Albie, when I told him, said, 'Bobby, dearest! I'm on for this whenever you want to do it! Wherever I may be in the world, darling, call me and I'll drop everything . . .' "

"And it's played all in boxes?"

"Not so much in boxes as on plinths. The symbol of the hollow square, you see. Characters in the ascendant stand on plinths and those in the descendant crouch under them. Johnny Gielgud, when he came to rehearsals, had a wonderful line about that. 'Darling!' he said. 'How could I ever have thought of doing *Hamlet* without the plinths?'"

"What was Jack Shildrick thinking of, saying he isn't gushy?" Louis spluttered to David Kausman. "He was awful! Why do actors always insist on using these lovey-dovey names? Surely, 'Albie' Finney is more trouble to say than 'Albert.' It's a wonder he didn't call Peggy Ashcroft 'Peggy-y.'"

"Did you get nothing out of him?"

"He talked for three hours, but it was all so bloody boring! This marvellous, clipped voice, spilling out one horrible cliché after another."

"I always think we're unfair to actors," Kausman said. "Because they speak great lines, we expect them to think great lines as well. Their skill isn't intellectual at all, it's instinctive. They're readers of the tea-leaves of personality. You should make that point in your piece."

"But what am I going to do? I can only use about four of the quotes."

Kausman reflected for a moment, stroking his piratical beard. "Treat it like a *Candide*. Just write completely simply everything that happened from the moment that majordomo or catamite or whatever let you in. All those monstrous details you described to me will tell the story better than any quotes."

"You mean the china camel with flowers coming out of its back?"

"The music-stand holding the book of Erté illustrations."

"The gilt palm tree?"

"And the Chinese figures along the mantelpiece. What was your nice line?"

" 'Like jaded bus queues.' "

"You've got your piece, boy. Write it!"

Doing it that way required only one draft, finished and delivered in barely an hour. It was, after all, only 2,000 words to fill a hole.

# 21

The bedroom in which Louis awoke next morning was that of a classic olde-worlde English cottage, oak-beamed, slanty-floored and slope-ceilinged. Its contents, however, were less perfectly in character. In one corner—so loomingly lifelike that it caused him a momentary start of terror—stood a stuffed grizzly bear, wearing sunglasses, a gunbelt and a broad-brimmed grey hat inscribed "Oklahoma Highway Patrol." Scattered at random over the historic floorboards were a palm tree in a copper urn, a twelve-string acoustic guitar, a cardboard carton with the Heinz 57 trademark and a single ski-boot. Apart from the stripped-pine double bed, the only other furniture was a section of three aircraft seats that had evidently been removed from their rightful setting with some violence.

The wall above Louis's pillow was a yellowing collage of newspaper cuttings about the group whose profile-worthiness for The Sunday Dispatch Magazine he had not yet quite assessed. Most were familiar, though here and there he found a wave of Establishment revulsion that had passed him by: "MP SLAMS 'UGLIEST GROUP IN BRITAIN'"; "STONES CONCERT MAYHEM INJURES 13"; "CRUDE, RUDE ROLLING STONES HURL INSULTS AT POLICE"; "STONES LYRIC OUTLAWED BY BBC"; "3 STONES FINED FOR 'DISGUSTING CONDUCT' AT SERVICE STATION"; "ALBERT HALL JOINS STONES BAN"; "STONES LP COVER 'INCITES VIOLENCE AGAINST BLIND' "; "ROLLING STONE HELD AFTER 'INSULTING' U.S. FLAG."

There was a faint tap, as by some deferential domestic, at the ironbound door. "Come in," he called.

The man who appeared had the demeanour of a butler, and carried a tray that included tea, but there the resemblance ended. Broadly built and swarthy, dressed in a floor-length embroidered robe, he looked more like some colourful character from the world of all-in-wrestling. Round his forehead he wore a band embroidered with astrological signs; on his barrel chest hung a three-strand amber necklace and a chain supporting a small gold razor-blade. "Cuppa char?" he enquired in a homely voice.

"Oh . . . thanks very much."

"There you go." The man set an earthenware mug on the floor beside Louis, then held out his tray with a flourish. On it were four saucers of capsules in various sizes and colours: some blue, some purple, some yellow, some orange.

"Howsabout a little sparkle? Just to start the day off right?" He indicated each saucer in turn. "Purple hearts . . . blue bombers . . . yellow submarines . . . Sunshine. I can recommend the Sunshine."

Louis had been warned by David Kausman that in circles such as these, refusing anything one was offered constituted the height of bad manners. But, for the present at least, he must try to keep his wits about him. "I won't, thanks," he said, composing his face into a leer of polite regret.

The man nodded understandingly. "Hey, I know where you're coming from. Worried it could be a bad trip, right? But this is really sweet and mellow. You'll feel like you're being rubbed all over with golden guineas . . . being bathed in ass's milk by Persian houris . . . lying in a sunlit cornfield, talking to the Archbishop of Canterbury."

"No . . . really," Louis said. "Not for the moment."

"Hey . . . it's on the house, you know?"

"Maybe later."

When the latch had clicked after his visitor, he got out of bed and padded past the grizzly bear to the tiny dormer window. Beyond the gravel drive, with its parked Aston Martins and Mini-Coopers, stretched a wide lawn with an ornamental lake, at the edge of which gambolled a grey wolfhound the size of a Shetland pony. Through the encircling woodland could be seen patches of sea and shingle beach.

In the foreground, a slight figure in yellow trousers, striped matelot sweater and gymshoes performed an energetic sequence of press-ups, sit-ups and running on the spot. Mick Jagger, yet again, was failing to live down to his image.

---

At midday Louis found his way to a long pine kitchen whose comprehensive squalor might have impressed even Fran. A frilly-shirted man with a Zapata moustache and a blond girl in a print kaftan were eating cereal at the long refectory table. The only other occupant was a dark-skinned boy in a fez and striped djellabah, making coffee in a copper pot on the psychedelic purple Aga.

Only as Louis sat down did he recognise the moustachioed man as

George Harrison. So that was the next implausible fashion the Beatles had decided to start. "Morning," he said with elaborate nonchalance, tipping Sugar Puffs into a bowl commemorating the Coronation of Edward VII.

The blond girl looked up with a white-lipped, rather melancholy smile.

"Hi."

"Hi. I'm Louis."

"I'm Pattie. This is George."

"Hi," Louis said.

Harrison nodded briefly and returned to his Weetabix. Behind the raffish Mexican bandit whiskers, his face was chalk-pale, gaunt and—were such a thing conceivable in one of the world's four most God-gifted beings—unhappy and hunted-looking. Louis noticed the almost parodic good manners with which he tipped the bowl away from him and spooned up milk with regular, careful outward motions.

There was a murmur of voices in the passageway, followed by a gurgling laugh. In the doorway stood Marianne Faithfull, talking to a dark man whose short haircut, navy-blue blazer and cravat looked more suited to some yacht club than the house party of a pop renegade. At his appearance, the boy in the djellabah and fez called out a question in a guttural tongue. The blazered man replied affirmatively in the same language.

Louis, meanwhile, was staring at the girl whose liaison with the chief Rolling Stone, not long since revealed, had excited much the same general horror as seeing a Vestal Virgin carried off on the pommel of Attila the Hun.

In person she was even more chastely lovely than on camera, her long fair hair and huge, misty eyes set off by a cream silk shift and gold slippers. Her voice, however, was not quiet and meek, as in TV interviews, but rich and cigarette-throaty, her laugh vaguely foreign in timbre and full of mockery and mischief.

She had the air of a *grande-dame* hostess, demanding of Louis who he was, then introducing him to a rubicund man in a brocade waistcoat who was digging Marmite from an outsize jar. "This is Christopher Gibbs. I expect you know his antique shop in Chelsea." She grabbed the arm of the yacht-club-looking man. "And this is Robert Fraser. You *must* know the Robert Fraser Gallery."

To that, at least, Louis could assent. He'd been there with David Kausman only the week before, looking at the work of American pop artists like Andy Warhol and Jim Dine and hearing how (along with Kausman himself) Fraser had been their earliest British champion.

The boy in the fez—now identified as Fraser's Moroccan servant, Ali—offered his master a tray bearing a cup of syrupy black coffee and a small engraved box. From this Fraser took an aspirin-sized white tablet, holding it up as though admiring the tints in a glass of claret before placing it carefully on his tongue. "Jesus, Robert, you're starting early," Marianne complained.

"It isn't smack," Fraser told her.

"Oh, no?"

"No—it's what they call a speedball . . . smack cut fifty-fifty with coke."

"Sounds heaven. Who can I get to give me some?"

"Spanish Tony. Who else?"

"Hey, Keith," Marianne said as their host made a belated entry, the wolfhound ambling at his heels. He wore a black shirt, a red-and-gold leather waistcoat and white hipsters that had been clumsily patched with floral material in and all around the crotch. Taking a bottle of bourbon from the Welsh dresser, he yanked the cork out with his teeth, spat it on to the floor and took a leisurely swig.

"Where's my old compadre?" he asked.

"Off for a run through the woods," Marianne replied.

"Did he see the lawyer on Friday?"

"Oh, yeah. This big-time Q.C., who looked at us like we were something the cat had brought in. But even he had to admit we've got a cast-iron case."

Louis's mental tape recorder noiselessly switched itself on. "What was behind that exposé, so-called?" he asked. "It obviously wasn't in any way accurate."

Marianne gave her foreign-sounding laugh. "Accurate! Mick Jagger talking to the News of the World . . . let alone bragging how many bennies he could take, then inviting them back to his place for a smoke!"

"So what really happened?"

Keith took another swig from his bottle. "What happened was the News of the fuckin' Screws decides it wants to nail a beastly, drug-crazed Rolling Stone. So two of their cats go along to Blases and wait for a Rolling Stone to show up. Only it isn't Mick who shows up, it's Brian. And these two News of the Screws guys are so square, they can't tell the difference."

"You mean all those quotes were from Brian Jones?"

"Right. Who loves talking to the press and shocking people. And who was so pissed and spaced out that night, he'd have admitted to buggering Princess Anne on top of the G.P.O. Tower."

Louis gave a low whistle. "My God! That's really going to cost them."

Jagger himself appeared at this moment, glowing with wholesome exertion. Ignoring the company, he opened the wardrobe-size fridge, took out a bottle of milk and drank deeply. As he did so, the butler-like —or unlike—individual who had dispensed early-morning tea and tablets came in with a tray of empty mugs and almost empty saucers, whistling cheerily.

"Morning, campers!" he said, setting the tray down on the cluttered draining board, where Ali was now slicing up tomatoes, aubergines and courgettes.

"Good morning, Doctor Daydream," Marianne, Fraser and Gibbs replied in kindergarten chorus.

"Is everybody happy?"

"Yes, Doctor Daydream."

"That's the stuff to give 'em!"

Jagger watched him bustle out again, then turned to Keith in agitation. "That guy knocked on our door this morning, before fuckin' ten o'clock. Offerin' us all kinds of shit."

"Yeah." Keith nodded. "He went round the whole house."

"What you doin' with a fuckin' pusher in the gaff, man?"

"He ain't no pusher. He's a real quack—Harley Street, so Robert here says—who makes up all these groovy little pills as a sideline. And he's a bit of a giggle, too, you got to admit."

It was clear that Jagger failed to see the humour. The narrow eyes were filled with something like panic; the overstuffed lips looked suddenly thin and drained of blood.

"Jesus, man, are you crazy, invitin' someone like that? Don't you realise what I got goin' on at the moment? How careful I gotta be?"

"He thinks the News of the Screws are watching us," Marianne said.

"Yeah . . . well, I know bloody well our phone was tapped this week."

"And you thought those two men outside in that van were spying on you? When the poor chaps were only repairing a gas-pipe."

She took Jagger's arm, laughing throatily at the expression on his face.

"Oh, come on, Mick. You don't have to do anything you don't want to. Just look on it as a nice, relaxing Sunday in the country."

---

So it was to prove, at least until darkness fell. After the leisurely breakfast of cereals, coffee and bourbon, Keith and his Irish wolfhound, which answered to the name "Syphilis," led everyone but Ali and Doctor Daydream on a straggly walk down through the woods to the pebble beach. Both the two Rolling Stones and their women wore creamy Afghan coats and embroidered, fur-topped boots which, with their flowing hair, gave them the look of ancient Saxons mobilising against Norse invaders. The sea was sunlit and silk-smooth. Pink carnelians glinted here and there among the pigeon-grey shingle.

Louis walked alone, with Marianne and Christopher Gibbs behind him and George and Pattie Harrison in front. The Beatle moved with a wavery unassertive gait, not unlike that of royalty. He spoke not a word to his wife, the one-time sparky fashion cover girl whose golden head for most of the expedition remained dejectedly bowed. Marianne was talking about them to Gibbs in an intermittently audible undertone.

". . . my dear, they all treat their women the same . . . like tyrannical northern workingmen. Poor Cynthia Lennon has the worst time. Whenever they go to a party, she runs straight upstairs and locks herself in the bog . . ."

Louis stopped and waited for them to catch up. Marianne gave him one of her misty-eyed smiles. "So, Mister Sunday Dispatch . . . what do you make of all this?"

He nodded at the Harrisons. "That's the biggest surprise so far."

"What do you mean, the moustache?"

"The moustache. And the fact of a Beatle socialising with a Stone. They're supposed to be such deadly rivals."

"Like Montague and Capulet, you mean? No, that's all balls, isn't it, Chris? They're really the most incredible close mates. Don't forget that John and Paul wrote the Stones' first hit. They're always getting together to bitch about contracts and managers."

At Marianne's insistence, the walk was extended to a nearby Victorian folly, said to belong to the Surrealist collector Edward James. It had a silent, untenanted air, but through the garden French windows could just be distinguished one of James's most celebrated possessions, a scarlet sofa shaped like a pair of pursed lips.

"Look, Mick!" Marianne said, pulling her reluctant consort up to the glass.

"We shouldn't be 'ere," he protested. "It's private property."

"See? They're lips exactly like yours!"

"Oh yeah. They are, aren't they?" Jagger's spirits seemed to revive at this mirror-image of himself, however distant and indistinct.

They returned to the cottage just as a long-case clock next to the Vox amplifier in the front hall was chiming 6 o'clock. In the vaulted, oak-beamed living room, a smiling Ali waited behind a buffet table covered with salads, dips and baskets of flat Eastern bread. In an adjacent inglenook sat the burly figure of Doctor Daydream, now minus his astrological headband but augmented by a large and indubitably medical-looking leather attaché case.

Before Ali could begin serving, Marianne entered and clapped her hands. *"Malheureusement,"* she said, drawing out the word in such a way as to suggest its opposite, *"les 'Arrisons vont partir"* . . . The Beatle's melancholy, moustachioed face also appeared, jerking once by way of summons to his wife, who was about to help herself to salad. "I'm bored," he explained with the childlike simplicity permitted only in the very great.

As the roar of their Aston Martin died away, Marianne grimaced sympathetically. "Poor Pattie! Another long night of sitar-practice in Esher. Now, if you gentlemen will excuse me, I'm going up to have a nice hot bath."

There was nowhere to sit but on a circle of outsize Moroccan cushions. Keith passed round smouldering joss-sticks, tuned the television to a soundless image of hymn-singing Anglicans, put Bob Dylan's "Subterranean Homesick Blues" on the hi-fi at cannonading volume, then crossed to the door and flicked a switch. A glass ball suspended from the ceiling began to turn, sending patterns of flecked silver and gold into every corner of the room.

When Marianne rejoined them half an hour later, she was wearing what seemed like the pelt of some large, dark orange animal wound around her and secured somehow under her armpits. "I couldn't be fagged to get dressed again, so I pulled this off one of the spare beds," she explained. "Is that OK, Keith?"

"Sure, darlin'. Whatever you want."

"I mean, it's not a valuable heirloom, is it?"

"Nah, I got it in Portobello Road."

"Nobody minds, do they?" Marianne looked round with insincere anxiety; the bedspread in fact covered her from just below the breastbone to just above the knees. "After all, this is 1967. And if they're going to allow nudity in the theatre, I'd better get used to it, hadn't I?"

With the company complete, Doctor Daydream left his inglenook and began moving from cushion to cushion with his open briefcase like some surreal kind of commercial traveller. Not everyone succumbed to the multi-coloured tablets once more on offer. Christopher Gibbs shook his head and reached out to a dish of Turkish delight; Robert Fraser held up his own carved box. Even so, Louis realised that in his case protocol could not be offended a second time. He began to evaluate possible hiding-places for the doctor's mellow vision-makers among the beaten copper pots that lined the hearth.

"No, man." Jagger's familiar protest, by now almost a whine, came from a neighbouring cushion. "I told you . . . I don't do any of that."

"Oh, come on," Doctor Daydream chided. "Why not let go and live a little?"

Beside him Marianne laughed throatily. "I told you, you're wasting your time. He even gets uptight when he takes an Anadin."

"Don't think of it as drugs," Doctor Daydream urged. "Think of it as expanding your consciousness. In the ordinary way, we use only about a tenth of our brains. This can be the key to unlocking the other nine-tenths."

"It's just that I 'ate losing command of my faculties."

"But you don't understand! This is dimethyl triptomyne! It enhances your faculties. It'll make you feel like you've been wandering round the Antarctic for weeks, and suddenly a nursie with a lovely kind face has rescued you, tucked you up in bed and started reading you *Winnie-the-Pooh.*"

Glancing up for no particular reason, Louis saw a face peep in through the leaded bay window. It was female in gender and seemed pale and craggy, like a witch in a children's book; having glanced quickly around the room, it faded into darkness again. So brief was the moment, he wondered if it really had been a face or just another trick of the labyrinthine twilight.

"Erm, Keith," he called out. "I think there might be someone out in the drive."

"Probably another of those bloody fans. They're always hanging round, after autographs."

A loud knocking suddenly became audible from the direction of the front door. "Oh, shit, what did I tell you?" Keith sighed.

"Fuckin' leave it," Jagger said. "They'll soon get fed up and go."

The knocking ceased abruptly; there was the rattle of an iron latch and a murmur of voices which even at that remove did not suggest Rolling Stones fans. Then the door from the passage opened and Ali the Moroccan stood there, ghastly-faced, his mouth opening and closing. Before he could speak, a tall silhouette strode past him into the middle of the room. Gold and silver flecks from the mirror ball danced over a many-buttoned uniform, complex shoulder insignia and a white-braided peaked cap.

"Is Mr. Keith Richard here?" the silhouette demanded in tones of chilling sobriety.

"Yeah, man . . . over here."

"Mr. Richard, good evening. My name is Chief Superintendent Dineley. I have a warrant to search these premises pursuant to the Dangerous Drugs Act 1964."

With brutal suddenness the overhead lights were switched on. Policemen came crowding through the door in almost farcical quantity, wearing Roman-crested helmets, long raincoats and carrying rubber torches of baton-like thickness and length. As well as the dozen or so in uniform there were three plain-clothes detectives in old-fashioned shortie overcoats and winklepicker shoes, and two policewomen with hair coiled in buns under the new "swinging" bowler-type hats.

A long moment of mutual appraisal took place, in which the invaders seemed hardly less dumbfounded than the invaded. Louis noticed the almost virginal horror with which each officer surveyed the empty bottles, full ash-trays, foreign tapestries, and reclining figures. All in addition repeatedly sniffed the incense-heavy air, some with frowns of concentration, others with knowing smirks.

The sight of Jagger, lying on a cushion with the rug-wrapped Marianne beside him, caused a palpable stir. A rosy-cheeked uniformed sergeant murmured his name to one of the plain-clothes men, who nudged a companion and mouthed the same syllables with eyes suggestively bulging.

Chief Superintendent Dineley, an oddly reassuring figure, struck his flank lightly with the baton in his black-gloved hand. "Now, gentlemen—sorry, and lady—this need not take very long if you're all sensible and co-operative. Gentlemen, please line up over there to be searched. The lady, please accompany one of my female officers to another room."

The burlier of the two W.P.C.'s advanced on Marianne to assist her in rising from her cushion. The face under the jaunty headgear wore a look of grim piety, perhaps expressing compassion for whatever manner of wild animal the fur rug had formerly been. The male officers watched intently, to put it no higher, as Marianne was led off to be searched—or, given her unclothed state, scanned—in decorous private. As she and her escort reached the doorway, the rug slipped a couple of inches off her shoulders and she raised a hand to catch it. The W.P.C. scowled and intensified the punitive grip of finger and thumb under her elbow.

The seven males had been herded into line on the small uncluttered area of floor next to the window, through which numerous black official vehicles could now, too late, be seen glinting in the darkness. Louis found himself with Doctor Daydream on his left and on his right Robert Fraser, murmuring reassurances in Arabic to the terrified Ali. It was clear that in the official mind Fraser's clothes, accent and haircut set him apart from rock 'n' roll riffraff. He had not been assisted across the room, as had some others, by pushes and shoves, and the P.C. who asked him to empty his pockets did so with obvious embarrassment. "Sorry about this, sir," he murmured. "Anyone can see you're a gentleman."

The two plain-clothes men, meanwhile, were turning over cushions, rummaging through drawers, peering behind tapestries, pulling apart the stack of L.P.'s next to the hi-fi and subjecting each overloaded ash-tray in turn to a lingering, connoisseurish sniff. Chief Superintendent Dineley watched them benignly, occasionally slapping his side with his baton.

"Do you mind telling me what this is about?" Keith called to him from the end of the line.

"Certainly, sir. We have reason to believe that illegal substances may be being used on these premises. I must caution you that, should any illegal substances be found, you as householder will be held responsible in addition to any other charges that may result."

"I get it," Keith said drily. "You pin everything on me, do you?"

"Yes, sir. We pin everything on you."

Impersonal hands patted Louis's armpits and inner thighs and traced the high contours of his boots inside his trouser-legs. Emptying his pockets yielded nothing but a comb, half a packet of Polo mints and a compressed clump of Sunday Dispatch five-pound notes. It all felt oddly like an incident at his boarding-school, when his whole dormitory had been got out of bed and interrogated about a misdemeanour of which he was glowingly innocent. As for the culprit then, he felt fascinated trepidation on behalf of Doctor Daydream, whose briefcase full of mani-festly illegal substances—still gaping open after the last "sparkle" it had dispensed—stood in horrifyingly plain view next to the coffee-table.

Robert Fraser's P.C. had by now found the engraved box, and tipped four white tablets from it into his palm.

"I wonder if you'd mind telling me what these are, sir?"

"They're insulin tablets," Fraser replied.

"And are you diabetic, sir?"

"Yes, I am."

"I see." The policeman slid the tablets back into the box, held it out to Fraser, then paused with an apologetic smile. "Perhaps we'd better keep just one back for analysis, hadn't we?"

Like proud gundogs, wagging tails almost visible, the two plain-clothes men rejoined Chief Superintendent Dineley with the fruits of their search. One held a carved pipe of vaguely Red Indian aspect, the other a small china pudding basin which had been deputising as an ash-tray. The Chief Superintendent raised each critically to his nose, then handed it to his sergeant, who slipped it into a labelled polythene bag. Meanwhile one of the uniformed P.C.'s, gifted with keener eyesight than his colleagues, had at long last descried the looming bulk of Doctor Daydream's briefcase. As he bent to examine it the Doctor's voice rang out, cosy and insinuating no longer, but curtly authoritative, as if it had suddenly leapfrogged an entire social class:

"Please don't touch that bag! It's full of exposed film." The P.C. withdrew his hand as hurriedly as if he'd touched fire.

There was no disguising a sense of anticlimax, even disappointment, among the raiders. It was plain they had expected to stumble on outlandish forms of decadence and perversion rather than this admittedly colourful but essentially domestic Sunday-evening scene. Nor had they been met with the Rolling Stone insolence and rebellion which their large numbers clearly were meant to contain. After the initial shock, the atmosphere was calm, civilised, even friendly. Keith Richard and Chief Superintendent Dineley in particular were on increasingly cordial terms. Most seriously deflating were the responses of one whom, above all, officialdom might have expected to behave like some cornered wild beast. For Jagger, throughout the whole search, had been the very picture of meek submissiveness, frozen in the knock-kneed stance of a discomfited child, answering questions in his chorister's lisp, raising his arms so high to be frisked that he revealed a schoolgirlish strip of bare midriff.

"Sorry about this, sir," the sergeant said, handing back the small mirror that was all Jagger's pockets had proved to contain.

The sullen face creased into a smile of undeniable charm. " 'S all right."

"Just doing our job, you know."

"Yeah, sure."

"My daughter loves your music actually." The sergeant took out his official notebook. "If I rip a page out of here, would you mind signing it for her?"

"Sure."

An echoing footfall on wooden stairs announced the return of other officers charged with searching the bedrooms. One of them, holding a green velvet jacket on a hanger, came and murmured to Chief Superintendent Dineley.

"Mr. Jagger," Dineley said politely, raising a sleeve of the jacket. "Can you identify this garment?"

Jagger turned and looked. "Yeah, it's mine."

"These were found in the inside pocket, so presumably they're yours as well." The Chief Superintendent held out a glass tube containing a small residue of pale blue pills.

"They'll be sent for scientific analysis, but I have reason from my colleague here to believe they may be amphetamines of an illegal nature."

Jagger stared at the tube with a curious look in his slanted eyes. His tongue appeared and moistened the overstuffed lips.

"I asked if these tablets belong to you, Mr. Jagger?"

"Yeah," Jagger nodded. "They're mine."

# 22

"What was their reaction afterwards?" David Kausman asked.

"Quite calm and philosophical. In a funny way, almost relieved. Like they'd been expecting it for a long time and were glad to get it over with at last."

"What a good thing George Harrison left when he did. I shudder to contemplate the public outrage if a Beatle had been busted. It'd be tantamount to defacing a national monument."

"I still can't understand the Jagger business, though. He was meant to be terrified of drugs. If anyone even showed him anything, he reacted like Dracula to a crucifix."

"Maybe that was just a P.R. number for your benefit," Kausman suggested.

"And it was such a weird, lopsided kind of search. The fuzz even opened up a plastic sachet of mustard that Keith had kept from some American airline meal. But all the time there was a briefcase bulging with Black Bombers and Yellow Submarines standing right in the middle of the room that they hardly even bothered to look at."

"Did you never find out any more about this Doctor Daydream character?"

"No . . . he disappeared straight afterwards. I think the fuzz may even have given him a lift."

"Curious," Kausman mused. "Well, it all adds colour to a splendid yarn."

"Which, unfortunately, he can't write," Margaret said.

"He can't? Why can't he?"

"If there are charges pending, which sounds pretty likely, the whole thing becomes sub judice. Publishing anything before they came to trial would lay us open to massive proceedings for contempt."

"What!" Louis clutched his forehead in anguish. "That way, all my best stuff would already have come out in open court! I'd have no real piece left!'"

Margaret shrugged. "It's a bind. But even we couldn't take a legal risk of that magnitude. I somehow can't see God taking to bread and water in Pentonville, can you?"

Louis's telephone buzzed. "Of course, Fraser's the one who's really going to cop it . . ." he began, picking up the receiver. "Hello, Louis Brennan."

"Enid here. Could you come up and see the Editor, please?"

He ran up to the sixth floor with customary excitement and expectation. Maybe Shildrick had already heard of his adventure and wanted full details. Or maybe Basil Hamilton had already had enough, and Cicero was to be his at last.

"Poet . . . how could you?"

Shildrick was standing behind his wide, littered desk, wearing the look of incredulous horror usually reserved for manufacturers of self-combusting cars and genocidal Texan generals. In one hand he held a buff-coloured Magazine page-proof, something which as a rule was carefully not circulated to him.

"This piece of yours on Robert Greenham is vicious . . . petty . . . snobbish . . . small-minded. I'm amazed that a writer of your calibre could put his name to this. In fact I'm flabbergasted."

He glanced over the proof again, seemingly close to nausea. " 'Pendulous wattles' . . . 'A dewdrop suspended from one magisterial nostril' . . . 'Trying on poses like a C & A shopper trying on hats . . .' What kind of stuck-up little prig are they turning you into?"

Louis could only stand there and gape, transfixed by these first-ever hard words from Shildrick but, even more, astonished by the reason for them.

"It's nasty . . . it's petty . . . it's offensive. And what's this headline supposed to mean? 'Oedipus, Darling.' "

The headline was in fact none of Louis's doing, but had been composed by Toby Godwin, a rare example of direct input from the Editor's office, repeated four or five times thereafter for the benefit of the *One Man's Week* film crew. Margaret's original suggestion—neatly encapsulating the presumed home life of the great thespian, the play he was directing and its geometrically arresting stage design—had been "Cocks and Box."

To Shildrick's expression of puzzled revulsion was suddenly added a rapid, disconcerting blink of the left eye. With a grimace he cupped the palm of one hand close under the eye, dragging its lid downward with his other forefinger. A poke of the finger was followed by several more rapid blinks. The new contact lenses clearly were taking time to settle down.

"So what does it mean? Are you suggesting he's a woofter? If so, that's even lower and nastier."

"Not at all," Louis stammered untruthfully. "It's just to give the flavour of a theatrical personality. You know . . . effusive . . . a bit over the top."

"What does that mean?" Shildrick snapped. "He's a great actor who's given untold pleasure to millions and whose good works are admired all over the world. If he should be a bit extravagant in his manner, is that any reason to beat him black-and-blue? Because this will give pain, you know, Poet. And I always thought you had such subtlety and sensitivity. Did it never occur to you how someone would feel, reading things like this about himself?"

There suddenly flashed on Louis's inner eye a vision of almost a year ago—Shildrick's office at the Stockton Evening Telegraph; factory chimneys, not St. Paul's, through the window; an Editor smiling at his theatre critic's irreverence and ready to take his part against any outside pressure or attack.

"Well, I'm sorry . . ."

"Yes, you should be, Poet."

"I mean, sorry you feel like that about it. I certainly never meant to write anything hurtful. Or embarrass you in a social way . . ."

"My knowing him socially has got nothing whatever to do with it. I'm shocked you should even suggest such a thing. Your prerogative as reporter is to write what you see. But make it fair. Make the insights true. Don't descend to this cheap music-hall sneering and sniggering." Shildrick's voice had by now regained its usual tone of crisp, irrefutable reason. He glanced at the proof again with a wince. 'A cravat of the warring hues of a toasted cheese nightmare!' I mean, Poet . . . really!"

"I'm sorry," Louis said, unequivocally this time.

Shildrick was blinking his left eye again, the troublesome contact lens adding a suggestion of manly tears that the world could be thus.

"You've got to like people. It's the most important thing in this job. And the most important, above all, for anyone who aspires to a column like Cicero. I can tell you, Poet, I'm shocked and disappointed, and that if you carry on in this sort of way, I may have seriously to reconsider the plans I was making for you."

How like him, even at such a moment, not to split the infinitive.

In a stupor of dismay, Louis returned to his desk and dialled Fran's extension.

"Newsroom," she said in the dull, resigned voice of which he was trying to cure her. He'd told her that a first step to better assignments could be answering brightly with her full name.

"I've just had the most incredible rocket from Shildrick over the Robert Greenham piece."

"What about it?"

"He says it's vicious . . . offensive . . . unfair. Christ knows how he got his hands on a proof . . . I hate to say so, but I think it may be because he goes to dinner parties at Greenham's. God! The Shildrick I used to know would never dream of . . ."

"Just hold on two secs," Fran interrupted. Rather more than two secs passed while she conversed, in tones not at all meek or resigned, with a distant voice that could have been Nick Fenton's. "OK . . . yeah. Yeah, Caldrose . . . It's the main R.A.F. station down that way . . . Sorry," she said, returning to Louis. "One of these massive new oil tanker's run aground off Land's End, and spilled virtually its whole cargo. Wilson's called it the biggest threat to Britain since the Blitz."

"Oh." He paused for the requisite half-beat. "So will we be getting together later?"

"Sorry, not tonight. I'm booked on a sleeper from Paddington at six-fifty."

"Paddington!"

"The R.A.F. are going to try to disperse the oil slick with napalm bombs before it reaches the Cornish coast. I'm going up with a photographer in one of the planes tomorrow morning."

Louis gaped at the dots inside the mouthpiece. "Blimey! That's an improvement on the price of cheese!"

Later that afternoon, Toby Godwin was summoned to the sixth floor. He returned half an hour later with a wry smile and called his young rips around him. Observing this, Tancred Philpott jumped up from the couch in the reception area, beckoning with claw-like hand to cameraman, sound-recordist, electricians and clapperboard-operator.

"I'm so sorry, dear boy," Godwin told him. "This is in the nature of private family business. Would it break your heart if I asked you not to film just for the present?"

"Sure, man, that's cool. Like I told you, we're here to find your groove. You want we should split, right?"

"Just for five minutes. If you'd be so good."

"Sure, I can relate to that. You know?"

Godwin smoothed the wrappers away from a new box of Romeo y

Julietas, chose one and passed the box around. "Do any of you kids have any idea how one of our page-proofs might have fallen into the clutches of Mighty Jack Shildrick?"

"Not the foggiest," Cedric Scurr said, glancing at Bracegirdle.

"Jim—we couldn't conceivably have sent one to him in mistake for Dudley Mowforth or the ad boys?"

"I can't see how. The Production department knows your strict instructions."

"Well, he's got hold of one, somehow or other. And he's raising absolute Cain about the piece young Louis there has done on Robert Greenham. I've just had to spend half an hour convincing Lord M. not to kill it."

"He went to Lord M.!" Jessamyn yelled. "About a profile of a boring actor!"

"I agree it seems ludicrous. But Mighty Jack seems to be making it the beachhead for a concerted full-frontal assault. For those who haven't read Louis's piece, it contains the odd lively physical detail and the suggestion that Greenham's discourse might occasionally be somewhat less than riveting. To Mighty Jack, this typifies the morass of triviality and self-indulgence in which we're enmired, and the way we've lost all touch with the ordinary reader."

"God, the cheek!"

"The awful bourgeois little prick!"

"And what was Lord M.'s reaction?"

"Since he's only ever heard vaguely of Robert Greenham, somewhat nonplussed. It weighed rather more when I explained the cost of dropping a colour spread at this late stage. I said twenty thousand—was that about right, Cedric?"

Scurr nodded. "Twenty to twenty-five."

"So it's still in?" Jessamyn asked.

"It's still in. Lord M. reiterated our editorial prerogative as the senior profit-making arm of the Sunday Dispatch. But there's no doubt that Mighty Jack's dour northern eloquence made an impression. In a somewhat chilling little postscript, our Proprietor suggested that in future maybe we should take a quote less special unquote line on things."

" 'Less special'?" Bracegirdle repeated. "What do you suppose that means?"

Godwin gave a wry smile. "It means, I fear, that Mighty Jack's beachhead may be better established than we'd like to think. We must look out for Panzer tanks with foliage on their turrets."

He slid back the glass panel beside him. "Tessa, dear heart, could you tell the BBC boys that if they like to come back in now and do a spot of filming, they're more than welcome."

———————

Going steady, for Louis, had always involved a set of private jokes, sayings and catchphrases, initiated by himself and adopted by his partner as proof of her admiration and devotion. His brain held an extensive archive of these, nearly all now too hideously embarrassing to remember, like pretending he was Popeye the Sailor to the girl's Olive Oyl, or speaking in mock-Chaucerian, or putting "Harry" in front of every other word, so that "off" for instance became "Harry-offers" and "indigestion" "Harry-indijaggers." Or calling her "my dear" with a courtly, old-gentlemanly flourish, or seizing her to dance wild impromptu polkas, or singing her Tom Lehrer songs or his part as the Captain in a school production of *HMS Pinafore*, or thinking up quaint terms for sexual activity, like "tweaking" or "china" or "what Tiggers like for breakfast."

With Fran, the first of these potential private jokes had been the horse. It stood in a gilt frame hanging from a stall in Portobello Market, a chestnut silhouette, classically magnificent until you reached the eyes, which were set in a manic squint. They laughed a lot over it, then Fran volunteered the surprising statement that she liked riding and was "basically a country girl."

"A country girl? You?" he said, looking at her carefully hollowed honey hair, chalk-white face, piebald fun fur and Alice in Wonderland crocheted stockings.

"Of course. Growing up in the New Forest, what else could I be? I more or less lived on a horse from about the age of eight."

Louis tried to imagine her doing the things he knew from Brenda Brown that horse-enthusiasts did: tightening girths, saddle-soaping saddles, plaiting tails, shovelling shit. It was not easy.

"And do you still ride?"

"Not so much. It's so difficult in London, unless you want to take one of those poor old hacks around Hyde Park. Or flog all the way out to somewhere like Richmond . . ."

Moving on to the next stall, they suddenly came face to face with a young man in a grey polo-neck with a row of beads around it. Seeing Fran, his rather beaky features hardened, he ducked forward and said something inaudible into her ear.

"Who was that?" Louis asked, despite already having a fairly good idea of the answer.

"No one," she said, forging on resolutely. The polo-necked young man had stopped and was staring after them, his face contorted with fury, or possibly anguish.

"It was just someone I used to go out with," she admitted when Louis raised the subject again later, in a coffee bar called The Days and Nights of the Chimera. "When I broke it off, he got rather bitter and twisted."

"When was that? Before you joined the Dispatch?"

Her black eyes might really have been centipedes for all the expression in them.

"I'd prefer not to talk about it if you don't mind."

There was a very great deal that Fran preferred not to talk about, if he didn't mind, as of course he pretended he didn't. For instance, about her recent, dramatically terminated relationship with Terry Bracegirdle, concerning which Louis could have stood quite a bit of close narrative detail. And why she had removed her clothes so coolly for Patrick Prince, but then been overcome by virginal modesty when some of London's top photographers clamoured to make her a star. And why she had sent chocolates in clumsy contrition for brazenly stealing that taxi from Jessamyn O'Shaughnessy. And what could have possessed her to risk her tenuous position on the Dispatch reporting staff by using the Editor's private bathroom. And why, oh why, given that fortuitous encounter with Shildrick, she had almost sullenly refused to take advantage of it?

Mystery shrouded even such commonplace elements in her life as her home and family. He knew that both her parents were living, and that she had an older brother from whom derived her ideal of a chaste night's sleep. On one occasion in the Newsroom, Louis had heard her mother talking to her on the phone, in an evidently upper-crust contralto, using her curiously Italianate full name, "Francesca." But from what kind of house, cottage or manor, urban or actually in among the New Forest's trees and shaggy ponies, he still had no idea.

"Going steady" in any case was hardly the term for what went on, these weeks of late February and early March. All his working life until now, Louis had comfortably used the excuse of being a journalist for dilatory or unreliable behaviour. Now for the first time he found himself on the receiving end of this. If he suggested going anywhere, even early in the week when there was no pressure on the Dispatch's news staff, Fran was never sure that she could make it. And if he attempted a meeting on Thursday or Friday he could virtually count on her being stupendously late, if indeed she turned up at all. Once when they were due to see Lelouch's *Un Homme et une femme* at the Curzon, he spent two hours in The Days and Nights of the Chimera, raving soundlessly at the astrological designs on the wall.

His Magazine colleagues had no idea he was now dating this legendary figure from the recent past; not that Louis cared whether they knew or not. But though he might be unmarried, with no small son and bassett hound to put at risk, Fran insisted on total secrecy, refusing to leave McIntyre House at the same time he did or meet him anywhere where they might be seen by Sunday Dispatch people, a prohibition which ruled out most pubs and restaurants east of Marble Arch. In all previous incarnations of "going steady," Louis had hated his partner to be too much all over him in public. But now he was the one who wanted to kiss, canoodle and hold hands in pub and restaurant alcoves and Fran was the one dodging and recoiling as if from a hovering wasp.

At her top-floor flat in Marloes Road, his position was not much less ambiguous. She still shared the place with another person, or other people: that much was indicated by unfamiliar garments among the jumble of clothes over its outer banister-rail, and alien spoors in the unbelievable squalor of its kitchen and bathroom. But Louis never saw this flatmate or these flatmates—indeed, on his twice-weekly overnight stays, he was conscious of being kept carefully out of her, or their, way. During sex, if he uttered any noise above a whisper Fran would press a warning forefinger to his lips. Once, when he so far forgot himself as to say "I love you," he heard an unknown voice outside the door reply, "I love you, too."

He was forbidden to call at the flat except on appointed nights out (usually Wednesday and Sunday) or by elaborate advance arrangement. The point had been painfully underlined by a non-date evening when he'd bumped into her in Ludgate Circus, found her a taxi home and then in a spontaneously masterful gesture jumped in next to her. Fran's response had been to crumple up with exasperation, almost despair, in a way he'd never seen before. "No, please . . ." she almost wept. "Please . . . PLEASE. . . ."

The same mysterious rules held her apart from Louis's social circle, where once he'd looked forward to lording it with her hanging submissively on his arm. After that first dramatic late-night visit, he managed to inveigle her to his flat only once more. Brenda Brown cooked dinner for the three of them (steak fondue), addressing Fran with grave courtesy that, his flatmate knew, camouflaged serious lust. The two of them talked horses, Fran from the fence-jumping, Brenda from the fox-killing, viewpoint, and she asked him, with perhaps too much reporter's assiduity, about a sale of Fabergé snuffboxes he was currently organising. At the end of the evening, she kissed him good-night on both cheeks. Things like that did not often happen to Brenda.

"He should get a hairpiece," she said firmly in the taxi back to her flat. "It's no disgrace these days. Everyone's wearing them."

"He's tried," Louis said. "But he never really got the hang of all the sticky-taping you have to do with a wig. It kept slipping down over one eye. We ended up using it as a duster."

"And is he?"

"Is he what?"

"You know . . . a queer . . . an arse bandit . . . a cream bun."

He laughed incredulously. "Brenda? You can't be serious."

"But he hasn't got a girl-friend, has he?"

"It's not for want of trying. He proposes to the same person in his office about every other week."

"Can he whistle?"

"I'm sorry?"

"I read somewhere that queers can never whistle. And they never eat beetroot. Does . . . your friend eat beetroot?"

"It's one of his more revolting habits actually. He likes it in sandwiches with Heinz salad cream."

Later, making love was the same as usual. She lay impassively underneath him, her black eyes sometimes glancing round to check the starfish spread of her hair on the pillow. "Come on," she encouraged from time to time, as if he were a timid New Forest pony on a leading-rein. Then, several minutes of silent pushing and shoving, his wonderment at her softness and slimness gradually overwhelmed by the suffocating weight of the blankets on his back. "Go on . . . be happy," she finally said, as usual. And that was it. Or rather, wasn't.

He rolled back onto the pillow, sighed and glanced round the now familiar room. On the wall just inside the door was a poster of the Eiffel Tower. On the Habitat bedside locker stood a travelling clock in an open leatherette oyster, a programme from the Royal Court theatre's production of *U.S.* (she'd joined him in time for act two) and a small cube of Cheddar cheese, as luminous with sweat as if it had just done ten rounds with Henry Cooper. Under the bed could routinely be found mugs half-full of cold coffee and, sometimes, eggcups containing yellow-smeared shells. Amazing how someone so fresh and fragrant, inside and out, could be so perfectly happy in such surroundings.

She pulled on her skimpy blue bath-robe and began peeling off her false eyelashes at a mirror inside the wardrobe door. He noticed how, leaning close to dab, she rubbed one bare foot against the back of her other leg. He clung to such things as signs that she was revealing herself to him as no one else before.

"I'm sorry," she said dully over her shoulder.

"Why are you sorry?"

"To be a disappointment."

"It doesn't matter. I get too excited. Or, as my Grandma Bassill says,
' 'et up.' "

"It's not your fault . . . It's just that it almost never works out for me."

"Don't worry," he said. "Come over here and I'll cuddle you?"

"Like my big brother?"

"All right, all right, if you insist . . ."

What could have gone on at that house in the New Forest?

---

The fatal portent, if he had only seen it, was the spray-lashed hulk of
the tanker *Torrey Canyon*, her back broken on the Seven Stones Reef,
her cargo of crude oil slithering towards the West Country's golden
beaches. It was, to be sure, mainly a picture story, its aerial drama typically spread across the whole top of the Dispatch's front page. But
Fran's story on the effort to break up the slick with explosives ran directly under it in double-column blackface, with her photograph inset
in a strapline, "Dispatch girl flies in with R.A.F. Tornados."

At the time, Louis attributed this merely to the caprice of the Dispatch's news sub-editors. However, it proved only the start of an amazing upswing in Fran's reportorial fortunes, and a corresponding further
decline in her need to be with him. She could not see him for the whole
of the following week either, having been assigned to the student dem-
onstration, or "demo," or "sit-in," at the London School of Economics.
Her account of political grievance and anti–Vietnam War sentiment
differed little from what the dailies had been saying ad nauseam. But
this, too, ran on page 1, and again the subs were unaccountably benefi-
cent: not only a byline and photograph but also billing in bold type underneath as "The new girl around the Dispatch."

It was that same Sunday evening at her flat that the first definitely
suspicious circumstance manifested itself. As Louis sat under the pink
paper dragonfly waiting for her to change, the telephone on the floor in
the passage began to ring. Violating all protocol, he went out, picked up
the receiver and said "Hello." At the other end there was silence, followed by a hurried click.

His initial thought was that it must be Nick Fenton. True, Fenton
seemed as curtly offhand with her as ever—but that might just be lethal
upper-class Oxbridge charm. And who else but the Managing Editor
(News) could procure her advancement from inside-page obscurity to
"the new girl around the Dispatch"? Unless it was the Chief Sub. Or the
Chief Home News Sub. Or the Splash Sub. Or the Copytaster.

His suspicion seemed proved one morning when he was talking to
her at her desk (all contact or intimate gesture naturally prohibited)

and Fenton walked up carrying a single long-stemmed red rose. But the arrogant Oxbridge features were impersonally harsh, and he slammed the rose down with no more delicacy than if it had been a dead halibut.

"That's the third one this week!" he snarled. "Can you kindly tell your ardent suitor, whoever he is, that I am not bloody Interflora!"

On the Tuesday after "Oedipus, Darling" appeared, Louis received his first-ever McIntyre House inter-office memo containing neither praise nor invitation to a meal:

> From: the Editor
>
> Robert Greenham was in tears when I spoke to him this morning. Such a cruel and snobbish hatchet-job does the Dispatch no good and it does you no good. I am thoroughly disillusioned that a writer whom I had always thought insightful and wise could descend to such triviality and spite.
>
> JS

"So an old ham's in tears," David Kausman commented drily. "So what's new?" He threw back the memo dog-eared by the impatient pressure of an outsize thumb.

"You don't think I was too cruel, then?"

"Oh, for pity's sake, man, be your age! That sort of incorrigible old pro bursts into hysterics when his egg isn't boiled the way he likes it. I'm surprised our great, crusading Editor should be so naïve."

Louis read through the reproachful words again, lingering on the curt "JS" where there had always been a fraternally scribbled "Jack."

"I feel like resigning," he said flatly.

Jim Deaves, who was passing, sucked in Senior Service smoke with a vehement shake of the head. "Never resign. It's the first rule of Fleet Street. If you think they want to get rid of you, always wait for them to pay you off."

"In any case," Kausman added, "it's completely wrong of Shildrick to be bollocking you at this stage, as he knows full well. Once the piece was accepted and printed, it became God's responsibility."

But if "Oedipus, Darling" had lost Louis his most dependable admirer, it also had won him a clutch of wholly unexpected new ones.

"Hey, I loved your piece on Greenham," Terry Bracegirdle said, joining him on the urinal-step and untrousering what he strove not to see as a fleshly version of one of Godwin's cigars before trimming.

"Really?"

"Aye, it was just the job. Wonderfully well-observed. I laughed like a drain at the bit about the cravat."

When he returned to his desk, Evelyn Strachey was conferring over a proof with Margaret. The heavy Hapsburg face, in which he normally read only chill indifference, gave him a coquettish beam. "Awfully good piece on Greenham last weekend."

"It was good, wasn't it?" Margaret agreed.

"Awfully good. Jessamyn thought so, too."

"I'll say!" Jessamyn called from her desk. "He's had something like that coming for years, the awful, pasty little troll."

Life in the Magazine's sheltered preserves for all these months had virtually removed the concept of blame and retribution from Louis's life. But one, if not the other, was indubitably happening now, and prolonging itself to an extraordinary degree. Later that day, Toby Godwin was again called up to the sixth floor. When he reappeared half an hour later, Bracegirdle, Strachey and Jessamyn all came from their offices to learn the result. The BBC2 film crew also hurried forward.

"Tancred, dear boy, I'm so sorry but would you mind desperately if we left this bit out as well? I promise it's nothing that would add significantly to what you're about."

Tancred Philpott's lizard-like lips moved briefly as if in silent prayer. "Sure, man. No sweat."

"So tell us what Mighty Jack said," Jessamyn urged.

"He's still in the most fearful bait. Apparently, all Greenham's friends in the theatre and film world, the likes of Gielgud, Dickie Attenborough and the Boulting brothers, are up in arms on his behalf. While I was there, Dame Sybil Thorndike rang in personally to cancel her subscription to the paper. And he's also saying it's an extremely bad thing for Louis's career. I told him with all the politeness I could muster that we'd be the judges of what's best for Louis's career."

There was a murmur of defiant concurrence from Louis's new-found allies. Together with his guilt, dismay and disbelief, he felt a surge of unholy exhilaration at being the centre of such controversy.

"Mighty Jack has adopted what I can only call a petty and vengeful way both of dissociating himself from the piece and getting at us as an institution. Half the Steam Section's Letters Page on Sunday is to be given over to actors, producers, charity bigwigs and whatnot, denouncing our piece and personally attacking young Louis there."

"Is there nothing you can do?" Bracegirdle asked.

"Unfortunately not. Autonomy cuts both ways. We've handed it out, so we've got to sit and take it."

"You mean, Louis has," Margaret said.

Godwin gave him a graceful, suety smile. "I'm sure Louis's shoulders are broad enough. We'll think of him as that boy sailor, what's 'is face, standing alone against the might of the German Fleet."

"Jack Cornwall," Kausman supplied.

"I'm sorry?"

"You mean boy seaman Jack Cornwall. Hero of the Battle of Jutland."

At this most inopportune moment, the boy sailor's telephone buzzed. "Hi," a husky voice said in his ear. "It's Marianne Faithfull. Am I interrupting the creative muse?"

"No, it's OK."

"Look, we need your help. Mick and Keith are being done for drugs. I suppose you guessed."

"I thought it was pretty much on the cards."

"Mick's got a favour to ask you, though he's too much of a star to ask you himself. Could you meet us on Thursday night? We're going to be at Abbey Road."

"The studios?"

"Yeah, Studio One. About ten."

"You mean P.M.?"

"*Mais, naturellement.*"

By the time he hung up, the impromptu meeting had dissolved and Tancred Philpott's film crew were gearing up to shoot Toby Godwin giving dictation. Kausman had sat down at Mrs. Broadbent's vacant desk and was threading a sheet of paper into her typewriter.

Louis's euphoria at becoming a cause célèbre had faded. All that remained in his mind, apart from a fleeting, irrelevant vision of Fran's breasts, was the certainty that he'd thrown away for good and all any hope of becoming Cicero.

"I still can't believe this," he heard his own voice say numbly to Kausman. "I've always looked on Shildrick as a tower of strength."

"Well, now you see him being a tower of Jell-O."

"But remember how he stood up to National Motors when they threatened to injunct that Close-up story? And told George Brown to get stuffed when the Foreign Office tried to change his line on Vietnam?"

Kausman paused in staccato one-finger typing. "It's the same highly selective form of courage most Editors have. Against corporations and governments, he's a man of steel. But a man of straw if anything threatens to louse up his social life."

"What's that you're writing?" Louis asked.

"A letter to the paper in support of you. Saying that you're an accu-

rate reporter who doesn't deserve to be traduced by toadies and lickspit-
tles. I can guarantee in advance that they won't use it, but it's time we
showed a little solidarity here."

Fran's direct line had been engaged the four or five times today that
Louis had tried to call her. Now, at last, the ringing-tone sounded and
the fatalistic voice said, "Hello, Newsroom."

"The shit's still hitting the fan over Greenham. All sorts of theatre
and showbiz types have complained to Shildrick. So they're now going
to be given space on the Letters Page to say what a monster I am."

"Well, I suppose they do deserve right of reply," Fran said.

Louis stared into the receiver. "What?"

"You had your say, so it's only fair they should have theirs."

"Whose side are you on?" He was to recall this question later, with
amusement.

"It's not a question of sides. But you can be a bit gratuitous on the
Magazine. Don't forget, I used to work there."

"How could I have forgotten!"

As something like their first row seemed to be building up, he hastily
changed tack. "So are they shooting you off again this week?"

"Yes, Toulon."

"Toulon! What for?"

"The launch of France's first nuclear submarine."

"Any idea when you'll be back?"

"No. Sorry."

"Had any more single red roses hand-delivered?" he asked, feigning
amused unconcern.

"No," she replied in her most colourless tone.

"And you've really no idea who might have been sending them?"

"No. No idea at all."

In his preoccupation it had never occurred to Louis that the event at
Abbey Road Studios, their spiritual home, might involve the Beatles.
But here they were, all four eerily small, wearing turned-down Mexican
moustaches and befrogged Ruritanian uniforms of brilliant coloured
sateen, John's yellow, Paul's sky-blue, George's orange and Ringo's violet. Here were their manager, Brian Epstein, and their producer, George
Martin, and, in a forest of music-stands, a full symphony orchestra in
full evening dress, embellished by carnival hats, false beards, joke red
noses and black hairy King Kong paws.

Jagger, Richard and Marianne stood at the requisite sumptuous bar
and buffet with the crowd of other pop and style notables invited along

to witness whatever was to be recorded with these surprising elements. Louis recognised Mike Nesmith from the Monkees and Donovan, Britain's answer to Bob Dylan, in the most hideously tapestried version of the new "hippy" style he had yet seen. All, in their non-drinking and -smoking hands, held tambourines, burning joss-sticks, balloons, blow-out squeakers or flowers.

Marianne wore a man's suit of tails and top-hat, tilted like Marlene Dietrich's in *The Blue Angel*. She thrust a glass of Dom Perignon and a white carnation at Louis and pulled him behind a harp festively hung with pink and silver balloons.

"We thought it was all going to be straightened out," she said. "Keith's friend, Spanish Tony Sanchez, said he knew somebody at the police labs who'd lose the samples if we paid seven grand in a brown bag. We paid the seven grand, but the fuckers are still doing us."

"On what charges?"

"Mick for possession of illegal amphetamines, even though they're only just outside the legal limit. Christ, you can buy them in France and Italy to stop little kids being travel-sick. They couldn't pin anything on Keith directly, but the pipe they took away had some grains of hash in it, so he gets done for allowing use on his premises. And poor Bobby Fraser, of course, for the smack."

"It was a set-up, man." Keith ambled over to join them, still in his floral-crotched white trousers, Bourbon bottle in hand.

"Do you remember that weird guy in the kaftan?" Marianne said. "The one that looked as if it'd been made out of the curtains from a Wimpy Bar?"

"Doctor Daydream?"

"Doctor Daydream, *oui*. No one seems to remember now exactly where the good *docteur* came from or who invited him to join us. And the boys in blue did seem amazingly uninterested in his briefcase full of goodies."

"You think he might have been the one who tipped them off?"

Marianne ran her fingers lightly over the harp strings. "That's where we thought you might be able to help. You could find out through your paper if he really was a Harley Street doctor, like he said. Or an under-cover rozzer . . ."

"Or a spy for the News of the Screws, like I reckon he was," Keith added.

"Knowing all the shit that went down could really help Mick and Keith's case." Marianne refilled Louis's glass and gazed into his face with eyes of virginal supplication. "Oh, do, please, won't you? Please!"

"Okay, I'll try. But I can't promise anything."

On the studio floor, something finally seemed to be happening. The four Ruritanian Beatles took their places behind music-stands, not with their usual guitars, bass and drums but with brass band instruments. George Martin, surprisingly elegant and genteel, conferred with a conductor resembling Paganini but for his plastic bald pate, red nose and hooked-on plastic female breasts. Around them drifted errant balloons and flights of soap bubbles.

"Those are my only instructions," Martin said with a shrug. "John wants you to make a sound 'like the end of the world.' "

As Louis went out he passed Brian Epstein, slumped in a chair, jacketless and tieless and looking strangely at odds with the carnival atmosphere. The snub face glanced up, half-recognising the footman who'd once served him a Scotch.

---

The St. John's Wood night was balmily warm and scented with premature spring blossom. A taxi with an obliging yellow light appeared almost instantly. Restless and low-spirited as he felt, as well as more than a little drunk, Louis was in no mood for keeping rules. "Marloes Road, please," he said.

When he arrived, as luck would have it, two people were coming out of the front door, which one of them held open for him. As he climbed the first flights, he could hear music floating down. It was her favourite single of the moment, Cat Stevens's "Matthew and Son." So she had returned from France without letting him know. Unless—please God— she let her ghostly flatmate or flatmates borrow her records.

The top landing light was on and, as he neared the palisade of dresses and coats, tumbling bathwater grew audible under the music. He realised now this was probably the worst idea he'd ever had, but nonetheless took a final Sherpa's gulp of oxygen and carried on to the summit, passing a small table with a passport and some foreign money on it, a familiar shoulder-bag with a B.E.A. label tied to the strap, and a dark blue overcoat folded neatly on a slim executive valise.

"Matthew and Son, the work's never done, there's always something new-woo-woo-woo . . ."

Fran's pink shift dress, her shoes with the low gold-backed heels, her tights and chronically off-white brassiere lay strewn in their usual trail along the passage to the bathroom. Through the open door of the living room, the Habitat paper globe shone on an enormous spray of red roses, two dozen at the very least. On the saggy sofa, beneath the pink paper dragonfly, sat Jack Shildrick, wearing a black-and-white patterned bath-robe and reading a newspaper.

In the instant that Louis froze and—too late—took a giant granny's footstep backwards out of sight, he had time to notice three things. That the bath-robe was of big-sleeved Japanese design, possibly more accurately described as a happi coat. That Shildrick's bare legs, although crossed with unfailing elegance, were hairless and spindly. And that the paper in his hands was the Evening News.

# 23

The call came a few minutes after he'd arrived at his desk next morning. Not via Enid but—for the very first time, he realised—Shildrick personally getting in touch with him.

" 'Ullo, Poet." The voice was as usual, grittily urgent, hinting at councils of war, vital deadlines and top secret scoops, but nowhere at paper dragonflies, spindly legs or happi coats. "We'd best have a word, hadn't we? Can you come now?"

Margaret looked up from her layouts and pulled a sympathetic face. "He surely can't still be banging on about Greenham. Just tell him to take it up with your head of department."

"Don't stand any crap," Terry Bracegirdle called encouragingly over the Art Department screen. "Remember Able Seaman Cornwall."

"And on no account resign," Jim Deaves added.

Shildrick was perched on his window-ledge, looking out at the panorama of St. Paul's, Tower Bridge and the river. No portrait painter or photographer could have arranged the scene to more symbolic effect. Down there, the City with all its ancient secrets, dark corruptions and glib plots against ordinary folk. Up here, the one man with valour, dedication and audacity enough to expose and defeat them.

He turned and gave Louis his fragile Brontë sister smile, tinged with gently amused reproach. "There was no call for you to rush off like that, you know."

"I didn't . . ."

"You did! One minute you were there, the next you were half-way down the stairs. I haven't seen a quicker exit since de Gaulle walked out of the Common Market talks."

"I mean, I didn't want to intrude."

"Don't talk so daft, you weren't intruding. You'd have been more than welcome to stop and have a cup of tea."

At this Louis could only gape. Of all the possible reactions he'd been steeling himself against, the very last one he expected was bluff northern hospitality.

Shildrick stared at him, so keenly that he found himself colouring and dropping his gaze. He felt much as he had at the age of ten when, straying to a remote pierhead sun-deck, he'd come upon his father lying full length on a woman with bright red hair. The fault was his, for being somewhere he had no business to be.

"Well, I must say . . . I never thought we'd be having this sort of confab, Poet."

"No."

"I'd no idea, you know."

"Sorry?"

"I mean that I was getting in your light or anything. She said the two of you . . . I mean, it was . . . you were just friends."

"Did she?"

"That's really all it was, is it? Because I wouldn't dream of . . . you know . . . a takeover bid."

"No," Louis found himself saying. "It was . . . we were just friends."

"Good," said Shildrick. "That's the most important thing to get straightened out." Rather contradicting this, he went and shut his door, then returned to his desk and pressed a switch on the intercom. "Enid—no calls for about fifteen minutes, please, unless it's the Chairman or Number Ten. And tell James to start the features conference in his room. I'll be there directly."

He sat back in his padded chair, swung it around and, as always going for the crystal clear, pile-driving intro, said: "I love my wife very much, you know."

Louis nodded, recollecting that steely-haired, impatient woman, and frozen peas rattling in bitter cascade.

"I remember the first booklet on journalism I got from the Careers Officer at Accrington Grammar. 'The successful newspaperman needs two things,' it said. 'A strong digestion and an understanding wife.' Well, Jean's been always been that. A wonderful wife who's stuck by me through thick and thin, and as a mother you couldn't fault her. And she's not a well woman, Poet. Only last year, she had to go into hospital and have her tummy all cut open."

"I'm sorry," Louis said, feeling his own vitals crinkle up in sympathy.

"Thank you. She's quite all right now, but she's always going to need tender, loving care. As for my kids . . . well, you've met them . . . Warwick and Seth and little Rosalind. I'm devoted to them, even though I can't always spend the time with them I'd like. I'm determined to give them the advantages I never had. No getting up at dawn for them, the way I used to, to mug up Horace and Virgil for my scholarship exam, before starting a two-hour paper-round. If anything keeps me going, day and night, every hour God sends in this crazy, wonderful world of print, it's that one thought."

He flicked himself round to stare through the window as if the faces of Warwick, Seth and Rosalind had become superimposed as a triptych around St. Paul's dome. "They're wonderful kids, Poet. Warwick's playing table-tennis very nearly to junior league standard. Seth's top of his class in everything but chemistry—takes after his Dad there, I've got to admit. And little Dozzie, you know, is an angel. Childhood's such a world of golden innocence . . . so easy to rend asunder."

Louis, who had got his drift some half a column back, stammered, "Of course . . . I wouldn't dream . . . I mean, I won't breathe a word . . ."

Shildrick smiled proudly at him. "Thank you, Poet. Not that it crossed my mind for a second that you'd be other than totally discreet. I don't have to spell out the damage that kind of cheap tittle-tattle could do . . . and not just to innocent little ones. That Street out there is such an envious, mean-spirited place. Our rivals would make hay with any excuse they could find to undermine us. It just so happens we're on the point of establishing that one of this country's leading pharmaceutical companies has rushed a new contraceptive Pill onto the market with such indecent haste that thousands of women all over the United Kingdom are passing blood. Just think how those poor lasses' interests might be jeopardised if some nasty, mischief-making little par was to find its way into Private Eye."

"Absolutely," Louis mumbled.

"It'll be just between us, then?"

"Of course."

"Good lad." Shildrick visibly relaxed, sighed and shook his head. On his face appeared a look which to Louis was somehow more distressing than his most virulent reprimand: a rosy, bright-eyed leer, reminiscent of Terry Bracegirdle in the rutting season.

"I must say, it's all happened so fast, my head's still spinning. She's a marvellous girl, isn't she? Or bird, as they say these days."

"Yes."

"Sort of lonely and forlorn in a way. You feel you want to pick her up and look after her, know what I mean?"

"Yes, I do."

"But by 'eck, you can't tell a book by its cover!" Shildrick's distressing smile intensified. He leaned forward, speaking from one side of his mouth. "Strewth, what a little goer! I've never been with anyone like that . . . you know, in the bed department. Jean was never . . . Jean was always . . . I can tell you, it's made me feel fifteen years younger."

Louis nodded blankly, riven by anguish and embarrassment yet also, at the phrase "bed department," unable to suppress a vision of serried mattresses at Selfridges or Harrods. Clearly mistaking his silence for further evidence of loyal discretion, Shildrick extended a small, cool hand.

"Put it there, Poet. I know I can always rely on you as a blade-straight, steel-true friend. I'm sorry relations have been a bit strained over the Robert Greenham business, but I hoped you knew I was acting fundamentally with your interests at heart. Yours is a very special talent, you see. I want to see it put to the best possible use."

Louis perceived the first glimmering of personal advantage in all this. "So will you drop the page of letters attacking me?" he asked.

Shildrick winced as if lashed to wild mustangs pulling him in contrary directions.

"I'd truly like to, as a quid pro quo. But I'm afraid they've all gone through now, been subbed, headed and set. Neil Hobman in Letters would have my head on a pike if I unmade his layout at this stage. And they are very good, cogent arguments . . . especially the one from Tony Richardson. And anyway, it's only half a page. An old Evening Telegraph man like you should have shoulders broad enough for that."

———————

Fran waylaid him half an hour later, in the white-tiled passage to the Library. "Don't worry," he said before she could speak, "I've already been got at. My lips are sealed."

The black centipedes misted over in the look that had not come his way in a very long time, followed up by another, equally much-missed old friend: "Thank you."

She was wearing her good-girl outfit of cream silk blouse, black skirt and flat-heeled shoes. A black velvet Alice band exposed the white-gold hairline he always longed to press his lips against. She put out a hand as if to touch his shoulder. He raised his armful of cuttings envelopes like a protection against vampires.

"I'm sorry. You've got every right to be cross with me."

"Cross? How can I be cross?" His voice, bitterly harsh and with too much spit in it, seemed to belong to someone else. "I knew you'd be onwards and upwards sooner or later. I just never thought . . ." He made a feeble gesture, symbolising Shildrick's presence in the very air.

"I know," Fran said meekly. "I'm sorry."

"Tell me . . . just for curiosity's sake. How long's it been going on?"

She made the familiar resigned wince of her pale lips. "I dunno. Couple of weeks."

"So that was him on the phone when I picked it up?"

"Yes."

"And sending you roses every day?"

"Yes."

"And getting you the best news stories to do each week. And a photo-byline."

Fran said nothing.

"Oh, well . . ." He gave an arid laugh. "I've served my purpose, haven't I?"

"How do you mean?"

"I mean putting Shildrick right in your path. Lining him up nicely in your sights for you. Giving you a bit of company and some help with your copy while you were getting the trap ready to spring. God, how could I have been such a born bloody fool?"

"It wasn't like that." She almost whispered.

"Oh, don't let's kid ourselves. It was exactly like that. Just friends is what you said we were, isn't it? Just swapping comics and going out for bike-rides!"

With immaculate timing he spun on his Cuban heel to stalk away, then turned back. "By the way, put my mind at rest about something. I did leave a page-proof of the Robert Greenham piece lying around at your place, didn't I?"

"A page-proof?" Fran repeated as if it were some phrase in Aztec. Louis gave a laugh a little closer to genuine humour.

"Oh, dear! Quite reminiscent of magic nights in Salzburg, isn't it? OK, well, that takes care of everything I reckon. See you around, as they say."

Half-way along the passage, he turned. Fran was still standing with head bowed, showing her Alice band. Bloody good acting, he thought through a sudden, helpless blur of tears.

———

What with display ads and a four-column headline ("ROBERT GREENHAM: IN FRIENDSHIP'S NAME") the paper's half-page of letters denouncing Louis boiled down to only about a third of a page. The choicer specimens were read aloud by Paul Rich and My Cunt that Sunday evening in the back bar of the Feathers.

" 'From Sir Donald Wolfit. Sir—I was astonished last weekend on opening my Sunday Dispatch, a paper whose probity and fairness I had always believed beyond reproach, to read in your coloured supplement . . .' " Part of Shildrick's revenge had been to leave uncorrected every misrepresentation of the Magazine's title: "coloured supplement," "colour section," even "colour comic."

" '. . . protest in the strongest possible terms at this vile, scurrilous and inaccurate portrayal of my old friend Bobbie Greenham . . .' "

"... 'Such vitriolic cruelty says more about your Mr. Brennan than about a man who has been decorated by most of the governments of the free world ...' "

"... 'It is sad to see the Sunday Dispatch colour section reduced to poisonous ravings that would bring a blush to the cheek of Julius Streicher.' " My Cunt lowered the paper, looking puzzled. "Who's Julius Streicher?"

"Was," Brenda corrected. "The chief pornographer of the Third Reich."

"I've always thought I'd like to go in for pornography," My Cunt remarked, "but I didn't have a pornograph." He belched gaseously, turning the sound into "Uttoxeter."

"All right, that's enough," said Brenda, crumpling the Letters page into a ball and shying it at the open log-fire. "We've got to go easy on poor old Julius here. Don't forget his bird's just given him the cold haddock."

"Aaah!" the others chorused sentimentally.

"Never mind, Lou," My Cunt said. "If you're hard up, there's always me." He proffered a pimply chin. "Give us a kiss."

"Poor old Brennan," Paul said. "Back to hand-shandies again, eh? Would you like us to get Stubbington for you?"

"No, thank you," Louis said firmly.

When they returned home from the Curry Inn, Brenda sat up in bed with a Schimmelpenninck cheroot and the beagling notes in Horse and Hound, while Louis had a further silent sob under the covers. Through the ceiling came the habitual faint scuffle from their landlady's quarters.

"Are you there, Blue Feather?" Brenda murmured. "Rap once for yes, twice for no."

"Brenda—why am I such a complete and utter pig's fundament? You can be quite frank."

"It's called thinking with your dick, old lad. That little gentleman in the purple helmet has never been best known for logical reasoning."

"You never really liked her, did you?"

Brenda removed the amber cigar-holder from his mouth.

"I thought she was sly, manipulative, amoral, with some elements of authentic evil. But it didn't tot up to actual dislike, no."

Louis turned and belaboured his pillow with low, impassioned cries of "Fuck, fuck, fuck, fuckety-fuck fuck fuck!"

"At any rate, you can congratulate yourself on a flawless career move. You found you were dipping your wick in the same place as your Editor. You backed off. As a manoeuvre, it has a chaste, unimprovable perfection."

"Yes. I made way for an older man."

There was silence for some moments, during which the heartsick one felt sufficiently restored by his own witticism to reach for the copy of Playboy under his bed.

"Anyway," Brenda added, "if she came knocking on that area door tonight, don't pretend you wouldn't take her back like a dose of shakes."

"What?" Louis dissolved into melodramatic splutters. "Are you serious? Do me a favour! I should bloody well cocoa!"

"Hmmm."

"What?"

"I just said 'Hmmm.' "

"Well, please don't. It's extremely annoying."

"Hmmm!"

---

Reverberations from the Greenham affair continued into the following week, as surprising in their positive results as their negative ones. On Monday, Louis picked up his office phone to hear the original of the nose-pinched voice used by himself, all his friends—indeed, everyone in Britain—wherever farcical comedy was to be conveyed.

"Louis? Spike Milligan here. I'm sorry they're giving you grief over that Robert Greenham article, which was good and true. I wrote a letter backing you up, but they told me there was no space for it."

This casual call from the longest-lived of all his heroes rendered Louis virtually speechless.

"Oh . . . thanks . . ."

"I remember, a few years ago, I was at one of these horrible white-tie premières that Greenham so revels in. He came over, gripped my left bicep and just said, 'Darling! . . .' I replied, 'If you think I'm so wonderful, then why don't you ever fucking give me a job?' No, you got the beastly bum-gas to the very life!"

"Well . . . it's really nice of you to ring . . ."

"It's just to say, don't let the buggers get to you. And if you ever want to drop in and hear more about the old fraud I'm always here, Orme Court, Bayswater. The name's on the bell: Spine Millington. Or you can meet me in Kensington Gardens, by the Pixie Oak. I'll be naked and wearing a reincarnation."

There was also a call from an exquisitely modulated voice, invoking visions of bushy eyebrows, cloven hooves, horns and a lashing tail.

"Louis? Arden Sinclair. I'm calling to praise you immoderately for your piece on Robert Greenham. And to ask when you're going to write that novel for me?"

Another, longer-standing guilt welled up. "I know . . . I keep meaning to get on with it."

"I so wish you would. I'm aching to get you between hard covers."

"The trouble is, I can never seem to get interested in my characters."

"Generally the best raw material for a first novelist is himself. I seem to remember you come from rather a colourful background. Weren't you telling me at God's party that your father ran a skating rink on a pier?"

"Yes, among other things."

"That's immediately compelling. And your mother helped?"

"No, she left . . . after he eloped with a bronze medallist. In fact, our family more or less broke up on roller-skates."

An odd, strangled sound came down the line. "And you're just sitting on stuff like that!"

"I will try again," Louis said. "I promise."

"When?"

"This summer . . . if I can find time."

"Make time," Arden Sinclair said, "or I'll have no alternative but to slash my wrists."

---

How the Shildrick-Fran business could continue undetected by anyone else at McIntyre House caused Louis intermittent bafflement. Admittedly, such a development was the very last one would have expected in a man whose aura had always been of monastic single-mindedness; whose only known infatuations up to this point had been for pictures, layout and the chattering orgasms of the teletype machine. It was still strange that, in so vast a hive of inquisitive journalists and with so many signs to be read, Shildrick's surrender to the Swinging Sixties should apparently not have raised a single interrogative eyebrow.

To the insider, as much as the outsider, the spectacle was merely one to be remarked on many another Fleet Street paper. A female reporter was proving she could compete with men on almost any type of hard news story. The following Sunday, the photo-byline of "the new girl around the Dispatch" reappeared on page 1, reporting on the introduction of breath tests for suspected drunk drivers. The next week her name figured in a team byline, covering the fall of the Greek government to a cabal of right-wing army colonels. Louis could imagine the right-wing colonels standing round her in a solicitous group, vying to explain the situation in terms she could understand.

The Sunday after that her photo-byline made its first appearance on the leader page, annexing space usually filled by the Political Editor or some noted academic, with "THE SAD TRUTH ABOUT FUN FURS." It was written in a style rather different from hers, two-fistedly energetic and forthright and (for the one person knowing enough to make the comparison) uncannily similar to Shildrick's adjacent editorial on that week's bloodless coup in Sierra Leone.

At times Louis felt like some Indian scout or buckskin-clad backwoodsman, nodding sagely over signals and portents which only he could distinguish and interpret. There was, for instance, the sudden change in Shildrick's dress-style from its clerical simplicity; his adoption of suits with nipped-in waists and high side vents, of shirts in darker, trendier colours like purple and lilac, with deeper, longer collars and brighter and broader ties. There was, even more tellingly, the metamorphosis of his hair from its old '65-ish flat-top to a sculpted cockade, bushy thickets above the ears and surreptitiously lengthening sideburns.

Further clues—indeed, what amounted to a coded map of the liaison—could be found in his ideas for the Magazine, which now were noticeably less preoccupied with window-boxes and tooth decay than with fashion, pop music and other constituents of a "scene" which hitherto had never seemed remotely interesting to him. The suggestions were read aloud to Godwin's young rips with satirical contempt, yet no inkling whose tastes and opinions they actually reflected. "A boutique on the King's Road called Just Men would make a marvellous men's fashion spread for you . . ." "I think there's a heck of a good story to be done on the bistro phenomenon. You could get wonderful pictures at places like Bistro du Vin in Kensington, where all the with-it set go . . ." "How about a piece on Cat Stevens, who's just hit the top of the charts with 'Matthew & Son' . . ."

In any case, Shildrick's public profile was currently at such a high, his newly-coiffed head seen so often on television, his no-nonsense voice such a staple of the Home Service's *Today* programme, it seemed inconceivable even he could find time for anything outside this rich harvest of his foresight, imagination, stamina and audacity.

Ever since Singapore Charlie Small's departure from Australia on the homeward leg of his world-circumnavigation—an occasion somewhat marred by his collision with a packed Press launch in Sydney Harbour—he had been followed by a gathering tempest of publicity, by no means all helpful to his puppet masters in London. For, if the world now hailed Singapore Charlie's courage and resilience, it had also become aware of his age, frailty and seeming inability to traverse the deck of *Lady Patricia* without falling over. He had proved himself and his tiny craft magnificently in half his enterprise, but could his luck hold? Might it not be wiser to quit now, while he was ahead? Another famous solo yachtsman, "Fiji" Bob Bluett, confided to the Daily Express that matching *Lady Patricia* against Cape Horn's ninety-foot waves would be "nothing short of suicidal." Envious Fleet Street rivals gleefully rushed to exploit this theme of Singapore Charlie as sacrificial victim on the altar of Sunday Dispatch hubris. The R.S.P.C.A. also stepped forward to condemn the enterprise for the "physical and mental stress" it would undoubtedly inflict on Pidgy the pigeon.

Shildrick had vigorously countered these Jeremiahs—or were they Jonahs?—by publishing assertions from the mariner himself that he'd never felt fitter nor fuller of confidence since his great aviation triumphs in the twenties and thirties. Further to calm the national disquiet, a leading ornithologist wrote an article on the adaptability and stoicism of pigeons, concluding that Pidgy might even "quite enjoy the lively motion." While maintaining undiminished confidence in Singapore Charlie's seamanship and self-sufficiency, the Dispatch announced that a complex organisation for shadowing and monitoring *Lady Patricia* had now been put in place, involving the Royal Navy, the British Antarctic Survey base and the armed forces of two Latin American countries, as well as ham radio enthusiasts throughout the Southern hemisphere.

Singapore Charlie rounded Cape Horn on 23rd March, a day when conditions were at their spring-time worst for twenty years. Visibility was so bad that the Dispatch's Santiago correspondent, flying with a local freelance photographer in a Chilean Air Force plane, could bring back only the vaguest of images. A tiny grey hull leaned almost flush to the water, with what seemed to be a pair of legs waving from a hatchway on its deck.

This last great hurdle surmounted and *Lady Patricia's* bows turned towards home, drama suddenly struck. On 3rd April, Singapore Charlie inexplicably broke off all radio contact. For ten days the scientists and radio hams, avidly listening from Patagonia to Darwin, heard no single "Oh, lumme!" over his frequency. Opinion was divided as to whether King Neptune had claimed another victim, whether the mariner's mind, such as it was, had cracked, or whether this might not be just Shildrick giving his global scoop a final, expert twist. At any rate, the possibility that Singapore Charlie had perished or gone insane confirmed his status as a world hero. Special prayers for his deliverence were spoken by the Archbishop of Canterbury. The Queen sent a message of sympathetic concern to Mrs. Small. Schoolchildren throughout the country held candellit vigils for Pidgy.

Then on Saturday 14th April—fortuitously, at the hour of optimum convenience for the Dispatch's printing schedule—contact was re-established. Next morning, under the splash headline "FOUND!," Singapore Charlie apologised for causing anxiety, explaining with familiar insouciance that "four months alone out here can send a chap a bit doolally."

It was obvious that when *Lady Patricia* entered the Western Approaches in mid-May, every news organisation in the world would be waiting to mob her. To preserve the Dispatch's exclusivity, a pre-emptive air–sea photocall was arranged to take place at a point some 200 miles west of the Azores. The mission teamed the paper's top action photographer with its rising star reporter, flying in a chartered DC-3 specially equipped with a dark-room and a machine for wiring the prints directly to London.

On 26th April, a triumphant eight-column picture showed *Lady Patricia* lunging for home under full sail, baseball-capped sea-dog at her prow, befeathered stowaway still huddled on her deckhouse. "STORMING TO GLORY," ran the strapline that could have come from only one pen. "NOW IT'S 'ARISE SIR CHARLIE'!"

And underneath: "World Exclusive by Fran Dyson. The new girl around the Dispatch wins her spurs."

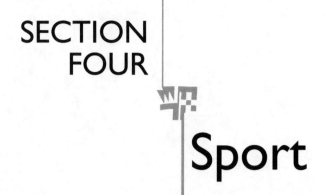

# SECTION FOUR

# Sport

# 24

Outside in sun-drenched Piccadilly, hippies were marching against the Vietnam War, hungrily photographed by tourists of all nations. Inside Fortnum and Mason, men in black tail-coats glided over the scarlet carpet, assisting with the purchase of Beluga caviar, apricots in brandy or chocolate-covered bumble-bees. At the turquoise-and-gold Fountain, crowded with tweedy countrywomen up in town for a day's shopping and a matinée, Louis and his mother met for tea.

His metamorphosis during the eight months since their last meeting seemed to have put her into a mild state of shock. Now and again, like some incredulous Asiatic owl, her head would draw back and her eyes re-focus to take in both his neck-length sideburns at once as well as his curtained brow, floppy-collared emerald sateen shirt and pale blue seersucker Beau Brummel suit. Her lack of outright comment thus far did not betoken acquiescence, however; it was simply deciding where to begin.

"How's Aubrey?" he asked, doggedly not meeting her horrorstruck gaze. "Just the same?"

"Yes, as mad as ever. You know how he's always up and around the farm by about five every morning . . . and now, with the weather so hot, he hardly bothers to dress. Just strolls around in a pair of muddy shoes, his underpants and Old Harrovian cap. He frightened the life out of a gang of gypsy women who were pea-picking last week. They thought he was an escaped gorilla."

She paused to light a Player's No. 6 and inhale with her unique sound, as if the smoke were almost too hot to bear. Thanks to The Sunday Dispatch Magazine, they had been given one of the premium booths along the raised rear section. Down at the counter a girl wriggled up onto a stool, twitching a tiny purple skirt over flawless knees and shaking back pale gold hair. But, thank God, it wasn't Fran. Oh, God, if it only had been!

"I watched your friend Singapore Charlie being knighted," his mother said. She spoke as of a private indoor event rather than a public outdoor one which had won the BBC more viewers than any live transmission since Princess Margaret's wedding. "The Chief Cosmetics Buyer at Fowler's hired a set so that we consultants could see it. I must say, I was rather surprised at what happened. The Queen wasn't really hurt, was she?"

"No . . . just thrown a bit off-balance, I think. Poor old Charlie never has been very steady on his feet. And I don't think he's got his land legs properly back yet."

"We were all looking out for you among the V.I.P.'s. But you weren't there, were you?"

"No."

"I thought . . . you know, as you'd done the original write-up . . ."

"It's purely a newspaper thing. I happen to be on the Magazine."

"But that Editor, Shildrick, was always such a friend of yours. I assumed he would have . . ."

"Look, I've explained about a dozen times," Louis snapped, grabbing off the teapot-lid. "It's a newspaper thing. I'm on the Magazine. We're completely separate entities." He prodded the single visible teabag with savagery.

"I just wonder if you think it's quite wise . . ." his mother began.

So here it came at last.

"What?"

Her eyes made another rapid tour of his head and face. "I mean . . . the hair quite so long . . . and the sideburns . . . I could have them off in seconds, you know, with some of my leg-wax."

"No, thank you," he said glacially.

"I'm only thinking of what's best for your career."

"My career is fine, thank you very much."

"It's only that all the really well-dressed young men I know . . ."

"All the well-dressed young men you know are bloody deodorant salesmen!"

She made the downcast face that had always mortified him, even as a toddler. Not intimate enough with her to apologise, he grasped for the one subject they had in common.

"How's Gran?"

"Full of beans as usual. I gave her a full facial last night, and took off her moustache, which pleased her. Grandad's gums have been playing up, so they've had him on baby food for a couple of weeks. Living on stewed apple can't be much fun. But you know how cheerful he always is."

"Yes, I know."

"I keep saying they should send some of his old legs back to Roehampton instead of just hoarding them. You can hardly open a wardrobe upstairs without three or four toppling out."

For all his seeping guilt, Louis could not repress a smile. "Have you found the one with the mudguard shoe? And the maroon sock?"

"Ugh, don't! It gives me the willies!"

"God, I really must get over there. It's just that it's all been so . . ."

So? So anything but busy or hectic. But, nevertheless, so totally impossible to find a single evening to take the Northern Line out to Clapham South; to waste even a minute that might be spent posing and preening himself somewhere trendy.

"They understand you've got a lot on. Don't forget Grandad was in much the same line, always dashing about everywhere for Gaumont-British. He's very proud to think you've taken after him."

"I'll go this weekend," Louis said, knowing that he lied.

"He keeps up with everything you write, you know. And Grandma always saves it to read to Aunt Flo when she comes over on Thursdays . . ."

Their booth faced the small revolving side door from Duke Street St. James's, which at this moment turned with a discreet "bump" to admit a totally naked man. He was tall and well-muscled, with shoulder-length brown hair, the aquiline, bearded face of an Apostle, and a penis about nine inches long. He surveyed Fortnum's Fountain for a pensive moment, then set off around it at a trot, swan-necked member rhythmically flopping; up the steps, along and down again, past the counter with its pastries and bridge rolls, then for a short distance inward, weaving among the tables of countrywomen with their tweeds and sensible shoes and D. H. Evans carrier-bags, before finally exiting through the door to Jermyn Street.

There was a moment of stunned silence. Then the entire place, including Louis—and, to do her credit, his mother—broke into applause.

———

He entered the flat to hear a blast of the Beatles, unmistakable yet more different and ambitious than even they had ever managed to be before. In the cavernous bedroom, the French windows stood wide open; Brenda Brown was out on the sunless patio in a bottle-green smoking jacket, jigging up and down and waving his bald head with eyes screwed up like one in a trance. Under his retroussé nose was what at first glance looked like a bad shaving-cut but on closer inspection proved to be a paper moustache in the Victorian walrus style that everyone nowadays found so amusing.

The sound from the adjacent Dansette was instantly hypnotic. Louis sat down on the step and picked up the L.P. sleeve from the floor. Out of it dropped another paper moustache, a set of chevrons and a badge saying "Sgt. Pepper's Lonely Hearts Club Band" in ironic carnival script.

"Isn't it magnificent?" Brenda shouted, holding his moustache in place with an agate-ringed forefinger.

"Absolutely. And I can't believe this cover." It was a collage of every possible figure in the pantheon of Pop Art pseudo-worship—W. C. Fields, Karl Marx, Bob Dylan, Aleister Crowley, Diana Dors, Tom Mix, the young Marlon Brando, all shaded in the reddish sepia of some old music hall ensemble. The Beatles themselves featured as little more than extras, in their Mexican moustaches and fluorescent hussar suits, standing beside their long-outdated moptop effigies from Madame Tussaud's.

"Brilliant, isn't it?"

"God, and no wonder! It's only designed by Peter Blake."

"Look inside. They give you all the words, too."

Louis opened out the sleeve and scanned the tiny black-on-red print. " 'Picture yourself in a boat on a river,' " he read. " 'With tangerine trees and marmalade skies . . .' "

They listened to it four more times, from cheery vaudeville opening to the chill valediction by John Lennon alone in that demented symphony orchestra of red clown-noses and King Kong paws. From neighbouring houses could be heard the same album, also played, as if disbelievingly, over and over again. As the strings built up yet again to the "sound like the end of the world"—awakening in Louis a corresponding cacophony of pain, betrayal, fallen heroes, spindly white legs and happi coats—Mrs. Atyeo appeared at the window above and shut it with a disgusted crash.

"I think they may have gone too far this time, though," Brenda said.

"How do you mean?"

"Can you imagine the Light Programme playing much of that? The whole thing's riddled with references to drugs. 'Lucy in the Sky with Diamonds' is obviously about L.S.D. Then there's 'fixing a hole' . . . 'get high with a little help from my friends' . . . 'I'd love to turn you on.' They've even got marijuana plants on the cover."

Louis peered at the innocent-looking garden that formed the cover's lower half. "Are you sure?"

"Perfectly. They're identical to the ones My Cunt grows in his window-box."

Later, as they drove to the Feathers with the top of Brenda's M.G.B. down, the same music still poured from every window. Children on the street were wearing the chevrons and holding paper moustaches under their noses.

"You've never written anything about the Beatles, have you?" Brenda yelled above a ruthless double-declutch.

"No, I haven't."

"Why is that?"

"Too many others at it."

"Like?"

"Oh, everybody. Ray Connolly . . . Maureen Cleave . . ."

"Have you never entertained the thought that you might conceivably do it better than other people?"

He shook his head firmly, at the core still pessimistic and self-deprecating.

"No, waste of time. The whole story's so well-known. And I've left it much too late to get on the band-wagon."

---

"Oh, I'm sorry," Shildrick said. "Am I intruding?"

The answer might have seemed amply provided, if not by the array of plundered salads, quiches, pies, cheeses and fruits, the empty and half-empty bottles, the brilliant light and crouching television technicians, then by the sudden silence where uproarious laughter had been a moment ago, and the circle of scandalised faces amid blue Havana cigar-smoke. For insouciant flouting of solemn tradition, it was a moment fit to join H. M. Bateman's famous cartoon series of the 1920s: "The Newspaper Editor Who Walked In on a Magazine Ideas Lunch."

Still seemingly oblivious of what he had done, Shildrick gave the young rips an amiable nod. "Sorry," he repeated, but with no particle of contrition. "I just wanted a word with Toby there . . ." Having initially just popped his head around the door, he now swung it open to its fullest extent. A pace or two behind him stood Fran, wearing what Louis recognised as a new buttercup-yellow frill-fronted shirt, her skin tanned like liqueur honey, her hair gorgeous, the mole on her neck still where it had been when he used to kiss it, her blackened eyes as firmly downcast as a funeral mute's.

The BBC2 cameraman, at his low-level tripod between Deaves and Val Lewis, switched off and glanced questioningly at Tancred Philpott, who was perched in the attitude of an Indian street beggar, gnarled bare arms hugging ancient knees, at the work-top's extreme inner end. Philpott's response was manifest avoidance of Toby Godwin's eye, accompanied by a firm switch-pressing motion of the thumb. The camera turned over again; the new scene went ahead, unchecked.

Godwin had sorrowfully lowered the half nectarine he was about to put into his mouth. "At your service as always, Jack, dear boy. Can we tempt you to a mouthful to eat?"

Shildrick glanced indifferently at the collation. "Not for me, thanks. Knowing you lot, I'll bet it's all stiff with garlic. Anyway, I've just had me All-bran."

"A drink, then?"

"I never drink at dinnertime."

A muffled snort came from behind Jessamyn O'Shaughnessy's raised wine glass. Shildrick turned to her with an expression of polite enquiry. "Perhaps I should explain," Godwin said hastily. "These TV chaps are making a documentary on me. Do you know the series *One Man's Week?*"

"Ah, of course. Very good." Shildrick gave the pointing camera friendly acknowledgement. "So I'm going to be a star at last, am I?" The point was made, clearly yet somehow with no taint of self-regard. To the man who had escorted Singapore Charlie Small to the royal dais on Plymouth Hoe under the ogling eyes of every television network in the world, this was small beer indeed.

He seemed to have completely forgotten Fran, who'd dropped back through the doorway almost out of Louis's sightline and was looking towards the Magazine's lunch-deserted concourse like some awestruck newcomer to an ancient college or exclusive gentleman's club.

"Did you really think my teeth idea was such a non-starter?" Shildrick went on in the same light, agreeable tone. The camera returned to Toby Godwin, whose countenance, as if independently functioning in slow motion, assumed a look of anguished puzzlement.

"I'm sorry? Teeth?"

"I sent you a note suggesting you do an ABC of Teeth—a reader-service guide to better oral hygiene. But you didn't like it."

Godwin exhaled a sound of barely endurable regret. "We appreciated the suggestion. It was just that Cedric here couldn't quite realise it visually."

"Could you really not?" Shildrick glanced down at Cedric Scurr's black-stranded pate with what seemed the mildest surprise. "I'd have thought it cried out for visuals." Beyond the oscillation of his brown button eyes, Scurr made no reply. It was the first time Louis had seen his authority questioned in any way.

The camera-lens revolved and settled on Shildrick again. By scarcely perceptible means, never departing from his tone of apologetic deference, he was now in charge of the meeting.

"So tell me then . . . if you can afford to pass up things like that. What momentous projects are you planning to unleash over the next few months?"

The faintest spectre of a pout formed on Godwin's doughy face. "They are all set out in our usual schedule to Lord M., dear boy."

"Aye, of course," Shildrick nodded. "I could get a copy from him. Or ask him to tell you to give me a copy. But it'd be friendlier to hear first-hand. We really must stop thinking of ourselves as competitors, you know."

The ensuing long moment reminded Louis of a scene in Dickens's *Our Mutual Friend* where a feeble and wavering soul had been pulled back from the brink by the combined effort of other, stronger souls. In this case, however, the psychic battle was quickly over. To the silent anguish of those around him, Toby Godwin shrugged and flipped open the blue cardboard folder beside his plate.

"Well . . . let me see. We've got the Good Screws Guide. That's a directory of the most and least luxurious British prisons, done in the style of the Good Food Guide. Terry, dear boy, as it's your brain-child, perhaps you'd care to elucidate."

"We're assessing them under different headings," Bracegirdle explained, his rosy face as stiff with unfelt geniality as a corpse's injected with formaldehyde. "Cuisine, of course . . . hours of recreation compared to hours banged-up . . . sanitary facilities. We thought of doing it with little symbols just like the Good Food Guide . . . crossed knives and forks . . . barred doors . . . chamberpots . . ."

"For whose benefit?" Shildrick interrupted. "The professional criminal?"

"Noah . . ." Bracegirdle began.

"To let criminals know, before they commit some act of violence or social mayhem, where they can expect the softest treatment?"

"Not that, we hope," Godwin demurred.

"What, then?"

"Just a bit of harmless, knockabout fun, dear boy."

"A bit of harmless, knockabout fun," Shildrick repeated tonelessly. "I see. Anything else?" Momentarily robbed of his usual poise, Godwin coughed and shuffled papers. The camera zeroed in pitilessly to savour it.

"Harumph . . . Ah, yes . . . Evelyn here has come up with a rather nice twist on the old party game . . . you know, if the human race were to be destroyed by nuclear holocaust, which ten world figures should be saved for the optimum propagation of the species? Only we plan to do it as 'Whose Sperm Would You Freeze?' "

Shildrick gazed down the room at Strachey, whom it was possible he had never laid eyes on before. Then the subject of the Magazine's forward plan seemed to disappear from his thoughts. Not troubling to turn, he flicked a forefinger like a little white hunter calling up some trusty native bearer. Fran advanced level with him, eyes still humbly fixed on the carpet.

"By the way, I'd like to recommend Fran Dyson, this talented young lady we've been grooming on the paper. She's about to start a column for me, but she's full of ideas and I'm sure could turn out belting Colour Mag stuff, given the chance." His tone was the impersonal, slightly abstracted one of a school head with hundreds of other pupils to think of. "I know how you've got a thing about outsiders, but that doesn't apply since she tells me she started off here."

Louis secretly locked his fingers together and squeezed them until the blood fled into their tips. He was trying not to picture the circumstances in which Fran might have imparted that information.

"She did indeed," Godwin assented heavily. Terry Bracegirdle's face, now completely finished by the mortician, stared off towards the G.P.O. Tower. "Hello, Francesca," Jim Deaves said in a friendly, ex-boss way.

"Hello," she murmured.

"Coom on, don't be shy, lass," Shildrick urged in a sudden access of northern friendliness and down-to-earthiness, perfectly pitched to camera. "They won't eat you. Tell 'em the idea you just told me."

"I'd like to interview Cat Stevens," Fran said tonelessly, still not quite looking up.

"Cat Stevens!" Shildrick repeated admiringly. "Absolutely super idea! Biggest thing in the charts! Rare example of solo singer-songwriter in an era dominated by groups, am I right?" He turned to Fran, though still not looking directly at her. "And didn't you say he's got a new L.P. about to come out?"

"Yes," she nodded. "Next month."

"There you are, then! Perfect timing!" Shildrick smiled blandly from Scurr to Jessamyn as if daring their bottled-up normal reactions to come forth. "You can get scrummy colour pictures done by one of your big star names. And you needn't pay her either, not if she's working on company time. The accounts department will like you for a change."

Perhaps in response to another silent clamour of souls, Toby Godwin made one last effort to take back the reins. "Well . . . young Louis there is our authority on pop music. What's your view about this, dear boy?"

Louis saw the recumbent cameraman turn the guide-handle again, and found himself looking directly into the whirring lens. Shildrick's and Fran's eyes were also fixed on him, their combined force more intense than the arc-light overhead. Moistening lips suddenly dust-dry, he said, or rather croaked:

"Mmm . . . I think it could be quite good."

Godwin gave a shrug of capitulation. "OK, then, why not let her have a go?" He looked at his secretary, Tessa, but, carefully, nowhere else. "Stick it on the list, will you, darling? 'Pat Stevens.' "

"Who shall I put down as handling editor?" Tessa asked.

"Put Louis," instructed Shildrick.

---

"I know—don't tell me, Poet. You're hopping mad with me." Shildrick jumped up and came half-way across the room to meet him, dabbing at what might have been a tear of manly remorse. Or perhaps it was a contact lens still giving trouble.

"You've every right to be annoyed. Of course you should have been there, having done that original very good piece for the Review Front and started the whole ball rolling. If I'd had my way, you'd have been sitting next to the Lord Mayor of Plymouth." Louis opened his mouth and closed it, his hopping madness—if that was the term—completely defused. This was an apology for something he'd already decided to swallow and forget.

"Hey, I like your tie!" Shildrick added unexpectedly, putting out a delicate hand to feel it. "Where'd it come from? Just Men?"

"Lord John."

"Just Men have got some smashing ones, too. We must go and have a rummage through them together some time."

He linked arms with Louis and propelled him towards the newspaper-lectern, continuing in a murmur, as if there might be eaves-droppers all around. "I knew you'd understand it was out of my hands. There were only a limited number of seats on the dais, and the Palace was getting very sticky about our quota, you know what they're like. It was really just the Chairman, Dudley, me—and Fran, of course, as she got us that wonderful scoop in the Azores. I could have fought your cor-ner harder if all this stuff on the dangerous Pill hadn't been going through, and the Middle East not looking good either." The hooded feminine eyes looked earnestly up into Louis's face. "But there's no ex-cuse. You should have been there, Poet, and I'm truly sorry."

"It's really OK."

"You're not totally disgusted with me?"

"No, not at all." He had anyway assumed the snub must have been someone else's fault. "I watched it on the box. It was a wonderful occa-sion."

"A proud affair, wasn't it?" Shildrick gave his sudden, luminous smile. "Our old sea-dog, honoured in the very place where Good Queen Bess knighted Sir Francis Drake. I always knew in my bones he could be the hero this country was waiting for. And it's all still happening, you know. *Lady Patricia*'s going on permanent exhibition at Portsmouth, alongside Nelson's *Victory*. And Pidgy's on a nationwide tour. Did I tell you the Royal Marines are making him an honorary colonel?"

"I was sorry about the Private Eye story," Louis said.

Shildrick released his arm and sighed deeply. "Can you tell me why they always have to be so vicious? I can bear it, goodness knows, but to besmirch an occasion of splendour and pageantry with such schoolboy smut just beggars belief! You were watching, Poet. You saw what happened."

"Yes . . . as he knelt on the footstool, he sort of stumbled."

"Exactly! Stumbled for a second, that's all. How can they twist that into him bumping the Queen on the tits?"

Spread across the lectern was a layout sheet with the Dispatch's Weekly Review logo pencilled in at the top, and a photostat picture of the newly-ennobled Sir Charles Small occupying its entire upper half. With his famous baseball cap, he now wore a brass-buttoned blazer and a tie bearing the stripes of some exclusive yacht club. Perched on one outstretched sleeve was his past year's shipmate, drab of plumage, curved of beak and blank of tiny eye.

"We start running his memoirs on the twenty-fourth," Shildrick said. "Wonderful stuff it is, too. Did you know he was an aviator as well, back in the twenties and thirties? Flying all round the world in these tiny biplanes built of not much more than twigs and string . . . navigating by the stars . . . landing on sixpences in the middle of nowhere. What a man! You can help me, actually, Poet. I thought I'd headline this first instalment 'Pidgy and Me'—or do you think it should be 'Pidgy 'n' Me'?"

" 'And' in full."

"You're right!" Shildrick pencilled the words in his neat, illegible hand. "Trust you to go for the more elegant alternative. Incidentally, I know I took a bit of a liberty, roping you in as Fran's éminence grise on the Colour Mag."

With some effort Louis remembered he'd come up to protest that very thing. "It's OK. The only thing is . . ."

"Thanks, Poet. I always know I can count on you. She needs a friendly face to work to. They're such a load of snobs down there. With you involved, I know her stuff won't just get bunged in the Overmatter and forgotten."

"But I'm not really an editor."

Shildrick gave him a playful punch. "Go on, you're a born editor.

Fran's told me how you've helped her with copy before. She thinks incredibly highly of your talents."

This sudden superimposition of Fran-style flattery onto Shildrick-style flattery was overwhelming. "Well, of course," he stammered, blushing. "If you really think . . ."

"I was going to ring you anyway," Shildrick went on. "Are you busy this Friday night?"

"Um, no, I don't think so."

"There's some fashion show on a Thames riverboat she's mad keen to go to. And I wouldn't mind. But you realise how careful we've got to be. I thought maybe you could pick her up and take her and I'd join you later, barring any eleventh-hour panics here."

Louis gazed at him. "You mean you want me to go along as camouflage?"

Shildrick crossed to his desk and picked up a gold-embossed white card. "There's a fashion show . . . champagne . . . a barbecue . . . fireworks. All manner of trendy folk guaranteed to be there. You leave from Charing Cross Pier at seven-thirty." He flipped the card across with a smile of the very mildest reproof. "Not 'camouflage,' Poet. How could you say that? We'd really love to have your company."

---

Beside the vertical row of shabby named door-bells had appeared a matt steel entryphone, its illuminated panel bearing the palpably more cautious and equivocal printed legend "Top Flat." Shildrick clearly had not wasted any time in beefing up the security and early-warning system at his new love-nest.

Pressing the buzzer, which caused its faint gold light to go off then on again, Louis speculated on the other characteristic improvements which doubtless had been made up there. He imagined the unnamed flatmates and passers-through winnowed out like split infinitives from a galley-proof; the squalid kitchen and bathroom made neat and logical as Sunday Dispatch page layout; the bedroom's crumpled tissues, week-old coffee cups and lumps of sweaty cheese all vigorously consigned to the spike; the toilet seat now infused with pride and self-confidence enough to stay up on its own.

"Hello," Fran's voice answered at length, blurrily harsh.

"Hi, it's me."

"Oh . . . hi."

"Are you fit then?"

"Did you come in a taxi?"

"Yes, it's waiting."

"Well, let it go. I'll drive us."

"In whose car?"

"Mine."

"My, my, things are looking up."

"Sorry?"

"It's all right. Forget it."

After a few minutes she opened the door, looking beautiful beyond his worst fears. Her dress was a skimpy beige suede bodice, its only skirt the buckskin fringes from a zigzagged pelmet just under the bust. Her hair was looped into thin braids around a Red Indian headband.

"This is incredibly nice of you," she said.

"Yeah, well, that's me, isn't it? Mister Nice." As she came out, she made as if to kiss him on the cheek. He dodged like a rugby forward, though too late to avoid a heartbreaking shaft of her perfume. It was the limey one, from the bottle shaped like a heart.

"Jack just phoned to say he's going to be a lot later than he thought. War's broken out in the Middle East."

She said this in an unexpected way, not with awe and excitement at the thought of how Shildrick would rise to the challenge, but a faint shrug and a twist of her pale-painted mouth, like wasn't it just typical.

A few yards down the street stood a brand-new turquoise Mini-Cooper with a hefty silver exhaust pipe slanting from its rear. Fran got in and leaned over to unclick the passenger door, buckskin fringes streaming away from both her legs. The black leather interior was already strewn with old newspapers and cigarette packets. On the back ledge lay the embossed programme from the knighting of Singapore Charlie Small.

She drove as young people in Mini-Coopers were expected to, zooming in and out among buses and taxis and a trotting detachment of Life Guards. From Knightsbridge to Birdcage Walk, groups of foreign tourists gaped as they passed, often too wonderstruck even to level cameras. Louis gripped his bucket seat with both hands, trying not to feel carsick, nor notice her fringed legs as they pumped one pedal, then the other.

"So you're doing a column now, are you?" he shouted.

"Sorry?"

"Didn't Jack say he was giving you a column?"

Visible brain-cudgelling was required before this came back to her. "Oh . . . yes. In his new Trend section."

"His new what section?"

"Trend. It's taking the place of the old Fashion and Home pages . . . a younger angle on today's swinging society . . ."

Louis could guess only too well who had successfully promulgated that younger angle, to the cost of the paper's middle-aged Fashion and Home Editors. But at least the lurching fear he'd harboured since the Ideas Meeting proved groundless. Shildrick hadn't given her Cicero.

"So what's your column on?" he asked.

"Fashion . . . pop . . . design . . . everything trendy. It's going to be called The Cool Look."

Moored at Charing Cross Pier was a white river cruiser, its two decks outlined in coloured lights. A frilled and feathered throng was filing aboard, handing invitation cards to white-gloved butlers. On the Embankment nearby was an Evening Standard newsbill: "ISRAEL'S BLITZ-KRIEG."

Louis bought a copy and glanced through the screaming lead story as they queued for the gangplank. In what was called "a pre-emptive strike," Israel had attacked the air forces of its three belligerent neighbours, Egypt, Syria and Jordan, and swept over the Jordanian border with the object of capturing Jerusalem. Within barely three hours this afternoon, 374 Arab planes had been shot down or destroyed on the ground. It was all described with the breathless euphoria of some specially exciting horse race.

Exactly who was giving the riverboat party and for what reason never did become clear. On embarking, they were handed silver tankards of Bucks Fizz and shown to red plush chairs around a catwalk on the covered upper deck. As the cruiser chugged past the Houses of Parliament and Battersea Power Station, contemptuous models flicked up and down in high-necked Victorian blouses and lace-trimmed bloomers, Ukrainian peasant frocks, bare-midriffed hippy gowns, hip-high, wet-look boots and bra-less sheaths of transparent chiffon. Somewhere past Kingston they rendezvoused with another cruiser, identical save that in its stern half a dozen tall-hatted chefs presided over a buffet and smoking barbecue. As the two craft lay broadside together, revellers swarming over gangplanks between them, a third boat appeared, hove to some thirty yards away and began to let off fireworks.

"Doesn't look as if he's going to make it," a much less spiky (if he wasn't careful, almost mellow) Louis said, three-quarters of an hour later. Fran and he were back on the original cruiser, sipping coffee and vintage brandy with David Hockney to their left and Nyree Dawn Porter to their right. At their feet were the expensive Liberty print carpet bags that had been a free gift to every guest. All around them were willows, reeds and meadows of foaming cow parsley. Swans glided on pink-dappled, glass-still water. Every possible embarkation point seemed to have been passed; indeed, it couldn't be long before they turned back.

Fran gave her resigned little wince, pulling at one of the golden squaw braids.

"What is it?" he asked.

"I know what you think of me. You didn't have to make it so clear."

He gave what he hoped was a hippy-like philosophical shrug. "Look . . . it's fine. It's cool. You've scored a terrific coup. I'm really glad."

"It wasn't like that. I know you don't believe me, but it wasn't."

"I told you. It's all right. It's . . ."

"Don't pretend you know all about it. You know nothing about it." She took a swig of brandy with such passion that a tiny rivulet leaked down her chin. For some reason, this moved Louis inexpressibly. He pulled his vermilion silk kipper tie from the top of his jacket and offered her the outer fold as a handkerchief. She accepted it without comment.

"I can only say how it looked to me," he said.

"Well, how it looked to you may not have been the way it was."

"OK, so tell me the real way it was."

She gave him a look of patient grimness, or it might have been grim patience.

"Look . . . I'm a chick, right? A dolly-bird in a big man's world. Trying to get on in my job . . . putting up with all their slimy remarks and innuendoes . . . hanging on with every finger and toe. Then the Editor starts ringing me up . . . sending me roses . . . what am I supposed to say? 'No, thanks very much, sod off, and what's my next assignment please?' If you think that, you're more naïve than you look."

Louis felt a sudden gust of wild, silly hope. "Are you saying it was all Shildrick's fault? You didn't encourage him?"

Fran winced again, now looping the braid round and round her forefinger. "I'm just saying . . . you know what he's like."

"Yes. I know what he's like."

As if on cue, the cruiser suddenly cut its speed and people crowded over to the left-hand rail amid an excited hubbub. Up ahead, two men were standing on the stone parapet of a lock, waving and pointing to the adjacent landing-stage. One, judging from his peaked cap, was the lock-keeper; the other wore a shortie raincoat and a greasy Teddy-boy quiff. It was Shildrick's driver, Les.

With swashbuckling drama worthy of Robert Louis Stevenson, Shildrick himself appeared in the doorway of the lock-keeper's cottage, hurried down the steps to the landing-stage, was helped on board, then vanished among the crowd in the lower saloon. Not for another twenty minutes or so did he find his way to Louis and Fran on the upper deck forward. So many people had waylaid him to offer congratulations on one or other aspect of the Sunday Dispatch, or solicit news of the evening's parallel excitement in the Middle East.

He wore a new pale grey chalk-stripe suit whose deep-vented jacket and flared trouser cuffs accentuated his small stature as none of his former, non-trendy clothes had ever done. Nor was it the happiest match with a turquoise-and-white psychedelic tie and a yellow button-down shirt whose deep, rolling collar had somewhat the appearance of a surgical neck-brace.

He greeted Louis with elaborate bonhomie, giving Fran only an amiable but impersonal nod. "Leading stoker Shildrick reporting on board, Cap'n Brennan, sir, with apologies. But it's been an evening and a bloody half, as you might expect. In fact, till an hour ago I wasn't sure if I'd be spending tonight in London or Tel Aviv."

"What's the situation now?" Louis asked.

"The Israelis will be in Jerusalem by tomorrow . . . probably at the Suez Canal by the day after. The poor bloody Arab alliance has been knocked for six on every front. Marvellous timing for us, anyway, as the dailies tomorrow won't have time for any background to speak of. For Sunday's paper I'm doing a twenty-eight-page pull-out-and-keep briefing on the whole seething cauldron of Middle East politics. We've got marvellous eyewitness stuff with Moshe Dayan's tanks and the Jordanian Desert Legion . . . profiles of Golda Meir, Nasser and King Hussein . . . Close-up on the diplomatic finagling back to T. E. Lawrence and the Balfour Declaration . . . If the U.N. doesn't force a ceasefire too soon, we may even be looking at an instant paperback."

For the rest of the outward journey and the entire homeward one, even though no one seemed remotely inquisitive about them as a unit, Shildrick kept up this same masquerade. Louis and Fran were the young couple out on a date, being democratically chatted to by their journalistic lord and master. He stood or sat with them for only a few minutes at a time, speaking exclusively to Louis, acknowledging Fran merely by nods and vague smiles, even though every word he uttered was manifestly for her benefit. Then he would dart off again to renew his cover by talking to some celebrity—Jimmy Tarbuck, Peter Hall, Anthony Newley and Joan Collins—always with an ostentatiously paternalistic exit-line for the benefit of possible eavesdroppers: "Just talk amongst yourselves for a bit" or "I'll leave you young people together."

He came back again as the cruiser was nearing Hampton Court, in the last glimmings of daylight. Fran, it happened, had gone below to the Ladies'. On a high branch over the water sat a heron with an expression of fastidious hauteur recalling Evelyn Strachey.

Shildrick leaned over the rail with a sigh. "Beautiful in this light, isn't it, Poet?"

"Beautiful," Louis agreed.

"Such a pity people don't talk about 'the gloaming' any more. It's such an expressive noun, don't you agree?"

"Yes, it is."

"No other press here tonight, were there? I mean barring Queen and the society mags."

"Just an old soak from the Evening News who was drunk by the time we passed Big Ben."

"But no one who could be a sneak for Private Eye?"

"I'm pretty sure not."

"Thank God there are no more gossip columns to speak of. In the bad old days of Hickey on the Express, we'd have been rumbled in five minutes. Where is she by the way? Gone to the little girls' room?"

"Yes," Louis said, wishing his teeth did not grate quite so keenly at things Shildrick was saying tonight.

They passed a line of river-front bungalows, shanty-like affairs seemingly knocked up from odd pieces of driftwood. The picture windows were blank, the gardens overgrown, the jetties peeling and derelict. Shildrick sighed again, but this time with barely governable excitement. "Dark deeds, Poet," he murmured.

"Sorry?"

Shildrick moved closer, so that Louis could smell the powerful Guerlain aftershave he now wore. "I'll tell you why I really left the paper tonight, even though all the telex machines were spewing out like a tickertape parade. Because I'm onto a yarn that leaves even a Middle Eastern war at the starting-gate. A bobbydazzler of a yarn, Poet! And the key to it is a place on the Thames, just a mile or two from here."

Louis glanced up river and down, at the bungalows, moored cabin-cruisers called *Dipsy Doodle*, the beer-gardens and landing-stages of crowded waterside pubs. "This isn't your one about the unsafe Pill?"

"No." Shildrick gave his short laugh. "I can't say any more, even to a trusted friend like you. Just I'm that much away"—he held up forefinger and thumb separated by a millimetre—"just *that* much away from breaking the story every investigative journalist in Fleet Street would give his right arm for."

He broke off as Fran reappeared at the top of the steps, and readjusted his face into its former kindly indifference.

"Eh up, here she comes!" he murmured, ventriloquist-style. "Super gear she wears, doesn't she? And isn't that a champion little pair of knockers?"

# 25

The thing is," Mrs. Atyeo continued in her nervous gobble, fingering the brooch that secured her rather elegantly draped scarf, "as I'm sure you, umph, both realise, keeping up a house of this age and size costs a veddy great deal of, umph, money; in fact my daughter and, umph, umph, son-in-law are constantly saying, 'Mother, it's too much for you. Why don't you sell it and move to one of those new mansion flats in Duchess of Bedford Walk, which would be far more convenient?' But my answer is 'No, this is my, umph, home and I shall stay here as long as I'm able,' but, of course, you appreciate, it is all veddy expensive to maintain when one is, as one is, on a, umph, on a, umph, on a, umph, fixed income . . ."

In the split second before these last two words were uttered, Louis saw Brenda Brown stiffen and narrow his eyes like a hunter who sees the game break cover at last.

"The thing is, you see, Mr. Brown and Mr., umph, Brennan, there's some work that badly needs doing, a new damp-proof course at the back, for example, and repairs to the roof, and other jobs which my, umph, builder says ought to be got on with in the summer months to take advantage of the, umph, good weather, and what I've called you both up here to ask, umph, umph, umph, umph, umph, since you are my tenants and share the house, is whether, if I put these works in hand as I'm advised I really must, both of you would be willing to help?"

It was plain enough that their landlady was not soliciting volunteers to strip to the waist and help instal a damp-proof course or repair the roof. Nevertheless, Brenda put down his minuscule glass of sweet sherry with a look of agonised mystification.

"I'm sorry? I'm afraid I don't quite follow."

"Umph, what I'd like to know is if I do put these various works in hand, as I'm advised I really must, whether both of you as my tenants would be willing to, umph, umph, umph, to help?"

Brenda glanced at Louis, who had been studying the portrait in oils of the late Mr. Atyeo above the mantelpiece. Monocle on ribbon, striped cravat, camel overcoat slung around shoulders: bastards didn't get much more obvious. "Are you saying you want to put up the rent?" Louis asked.

Mrs. Atyeo was still not to be enticed into such brutal candour. She touched her scarf-brooch again, dewlaps quivering like Droopy the Bloodhound. Why had they never thought of nicknaming her that? "What I'm saying, or rather asking, umph, is whether, as my tenants, naturally standing to benefit from the good order and upkeep of the property, if I do put these veddy expensive works in, umph, hand, you'd both be willing to help?"

But the two formerly nice young men, for diverse reasons, were in no such helpful frame of mind. In their subterranean bathroom, parti-coloured toadstools now furled behind the lavatory cistern and along the skirting board, suggesting the advance guard of some fungoid monster bent on ultimately devouring the whole of Campden Hill. The front right-hand ring of their electric cooker did not work and the front left-hand one could not be shut off. The odour of leaking gas still hung about their musty sitting room like incense in a church. When it rained (admittedly, an infrequent occurrence) water gushed down the sloping rear patio to seep under the French windows of their shared bedroom. Yet despite repeated complaints—on an ever dwindling scale of old-world courtesy—no remedy had been offered beyond inconclusive surveys by the famous BBC son-in-law with his cruel inquisitor's glasses, too-short jacket and pert little chorus-boy's behind.

In addition, as might be expected from almost seven months' close cohabitation, the formerly nice young men had begun getting on each other's nerves somewhat. Brenda's nerves were got on by the noise that Louis made when biting into an apple. Louis's nerves were got on by Brenda's deadpan comment of "My! That *is* a noisy apple!" every time he ate a Worcester or Granny Smith. Brenda's nerves were got on by Louis's habit, when coming to bed later than he, of turning on the bright rather than the soft overhead Habitat globe. Louis's nerves were got on when, after a specially frustrating day in the auction world, Brenda strode from room to room, blowing his silver hunting-horn with an ear-splitting "Weeee! Heeee! Heee! Heee!" Both their nerves were got on by using the bathroom after the other and finding the shaving-mirror all foggy.

As a further complication, after years of worshipping females from afar and counterproductively insulting them at close quarters, Brenda had finally struck the elusive synthesis of a girl he wanted to go out with who also was willing to be taken out by him. A Rear Admiral's daughter named Katinka (did the Rear Admiral serve with the Swedish Navy? Or the Indonesian?) she had the straw-coloured pigtails and squat, muscular build of a wardress in a concentration camp. Returning late one night, Louis had found her seated before the gas-fire in one of her swain's Aquascutum smoking jackets, ruefully picking at a piece of haddock with a fork. The traumatic preceding business was another strike against the flat, according to Brenda.

"She's incredibly highly strung, you see," he explained in a voice which, although not loud, was almost certainly within Katinka's earshot. "And also quite abnormally small Down There. The slightest noise from Blue Feather through that ceiling and she'd shut up like a clam. One could never get any proper rhythm going." He made it sound like, as indeed possibly it had been, some ill-executed, frilly-shouldered and arm-weaving Latin-American dance.

This evening, having promised to think over their landlady's request, threat, entreaty or whatever it had been, the two formerly nice young men drained their sweet sherry and returned down the stone staircase to what neither any longer had the spirit to call their "chambers."

"I for one have no intention of paying the disgusting old bat a single brass farthing more for this . . . this open privy," Brenda said. "In fact, if she tries to put it up, I shall just leave. At least she didn't manage to screw a deposit out of us."

"No, we only agreed that if we did any damage, umph, umph, we'd be sure to make it good. Remind me to buy a lump-hammer tomorrow."

That next weekend, it fatefully happened, both formerly nice young men had reason to go out of town. Brenda took Katinka to meet his parents on the Isle of Wight, and perhaps see what after-dark rumbas and congas could be achieved there. Louis joined a press trip to the Loire vineyards that would have been commandeered by Mrs. Freya Broadbent were she not currently somewhere in America.

Arriving back before Brenda on Sunday evening, laden with complimentary wine, Armagnac, cheeses and hothouse strawberries, he found London, unusually, in the aftermath of rain. Its full extent was not revealed, however, until he'd paid off his taxi and let himself into the flat. Something clearly like a rehearsal for Judgement Day had gushed down the patio to unite with an overflowing drain against the doors of his and Brenda's bedroom. Their two beds and Brenda's jacket

rack–cum–trouser-press stood in three or four inches of stagnant water
scattered with dirty leaves and sodden flakes of someone else's (umph,
umph) salmon-pink toilet-paper.

———————

"And you write for The Sunday Dispatch, do you?" Mr. Mulholland
said, leading the way up the maroon, black and white–tiled front steps
of number 8 Inkerman Terrace. With an effort Louis desisted from ritual study of his putative new landlord's bottom as revealed by the double rear-vents of a Prince of Wales check jacket. Why was it that
middle-aged Englishmen of this particular rubicund and bald-headed
type so invariably combined suede Hush Puppies, bow-ties and yellow
knitted waistcoats with the pertly upraised posteriors of lithe African
warriors?

"Yes. The Colour Magazine."

Mr. Mulholland made the reverent face that people always did, and
took out a large bunch of keys on a ring with an M.G. tag. He had the
slightly harassed and distracted air of a junior school headmaster on
some chaotic sports day. But the M.G. key-ring was a promising sign,
hinting at racier and more soulful predilections. More promising still
was this sign that Mr. Mulholland himself did not reside in the house
where he had a bed-sitting room to let.

"Perhaps you could do an article on landlords in London," he suggested. "The problems we have to contend with . . . the oppressive Socialist legislation. I can give you all the details if you wish."

In the front hall he fumbled for another key and unlocked the first
door on the left. The room had a floor-length bay window overlooking
an identical terrace of white mid-Victorian houses, and was clad in
mock-Tudor wood panelling from floor almost to ceiling. On the right of
the window stood a dark wooden desk with ornately carved drawers
and legs. Facing the door was a single bed with a scarlet candlewick
coverlet. The message all this sent to Louis could be expressed in one
word. Heaven.

"Before I bought it, the house used to be a private hotel," Mr. Mulholland explained. "This was the cocktail bar. The two . . . ahem . . . chaps
next door have got what used to be the restaurant."

He swung open a section of panelling on the left of the window. "This
is the wardrobe . . . and wash-basin . . ." An adjacent waist-high panel
revealed a sink with a mirror above it and a small, string-operated neon
tube.

"It's all . . . very handy," Louis said, trying to control the tremor of
ecstasy in his voice. His first foreboding dip into London's bedsitter subcontinent, and what had he found? The college study of his dreams!

"Telephone at the end of the hall," Mr. Mulholland continued. "Gas fire with usual meter. Bathroom at the top of the stairs. Of course, you're very well situated here . . . Park five minutes away, Gloucester Road tube just around the corner. . . ." He paused, clearly reluctant to offend a personification of the Sunday Dispatch. "Tell me, Mr. Brennan, this, er, flood at your last accommodation, I presume was not caused by your goodself?"

"No. Not at all."

"Pardon the question. A landlord has to know these things."

"Of course." Louis glanced deliriously round the panelled walls again. Inset at intervals near the top were gilt Tudor roses. And the aching invitation of that carved old desk! "I'd really love to take it," he said. "I feel I could . . ."

Mr. Mulholland nodded, seeming to pick up what he meant. "Yes. It would suit someone like you—of literary prognostications, so to speak. It's two-ten a week, in advance. That includes electricity and daily servicing."

"That's fine."

"I probably shouldn't say this . . . but the last person who was here used to come in and out via the bay window. You can easily hop from that little balcony over to the front steps. And it's quite safe to leave it on the catch."

"Two-ten, you said . . ." At the sight of multiple Sunday Dispatch fivers, Mr. Mulholland's headmasterly geniality waxed still further. Louis felt as if he'd won the egg-and-spoon race and come top in spelling.

"Your key, Mr. Brennan. Welcome to Eight Inkerman Terrace. I shall look out for your things in the Dispatch supplement. And if you ever want to write that article on landlords in London, do let me know . . ."

His first act of tenancy in his mock-Tudor Paradise was to perform wild, exultant Nureyev leaps all around it. Then, before even starting to unpack, he sat down at the dark old desk, unzipped his typewriter, threaded a quarto sheet of Sunday Dispatch white bond into it and typed:

THE END OF THE PIER

*A novel by*
LOUIS BRENNAN

---

"I got the most wonderful stuff in Arizona," Freya Broadbent said. Her suntan was richer than ever and she wore earrings and a bracelet of pale turquoise and silver which, her listeners already knew, had been made by Navajo Indians.

"The War Office official who arranged for the de Gaulles to settle in Petts Wood turns out to have been an American Air Force colonel on secondment who now, of all bizarre things, runs a rattlesnake farm just outside Flagstaff," she continued, hammering each word home like a tin-tack. "You see these signs all along the highway, 'Skunks and rattlers, fifteen miles' . . . And by an even more amazing coincidence my source in Flagstaff was still in touch with the Petts Wood G.P. who treated Madame de Gaulle for phlebitis, and, for reasons too complicated to go into, has ended up in a retirement home in Reno, Nevada. While I was down there, I happened to see this sign saying, 'Drive-in divorces' and I thought, 'Golly! There's an opportunity! I've been meaning to divorce Festus for all these yonks, but never gotten—as they say over there—around to it. So why not?' "

Margaret gazed at her, open-mouthed. "Freya, are you serious? You divorced Festus while you were away on assignment? On expenses!"

"Well, of course, I shan't claim for the actual divorce," Mrs. Broadbent said with dignity. "But the chance did seem too good to miss. And I can't tell you . . . it was so easy. You drove in married and drove out five minutes later, single. The judge was rather charming, actually. He took me to dinner afterwards at the International House of Pancakes."

She glanced round the Magazine concourse, evidently finding its tempo hard to adjust to after her eventful 10,000-mile journey. The only visible activity was the bridge school that Evelyn Strachey and Jessamyn O'Shaughnessy conducted each afternoon with a circle of their more exclusive fashion friends. Play alternated with a quiz about Hollywood in the twenties, thirties and forties.

". . . Which director went so far over budget on his greatest film that the amount was put up in lights on Hollywood Boulevard?"

". . . Whose real name was Archie Leach?"

". . . Who said, 'Kid, if you look like you're working hard, you ain't working hard enough . . .'?"

"So what's been going on round here?" Mrs. Broadbent asked, raising her voice slightly above the bridge-players' shrieks of laughter.

"Skunks and rattlers of a slightly less obvious kind," Margaret said. "Mighty Jack Shildrick's got so bold and pushy, he gate-crashed one of God's Ideas Lunches and virtually forced him to commission a profile by our old friend Miss Charcoal-Eyes Dyson. And, if you can believe it, instead of saying 'Push off and leave us alone,' God just rolled over and showed his tummy."

"There wasn't much he could do," Louis said. "Not with the film crew there."

"Film crew!" Mrs. Broadbent exclaimed. "They're not still around, surely!"

"Oh, yes, they are! That poor producer, Philpott, is almost climbing the wall. Six weeks' filming and they still haven't got enough to represent one working week in a half-hour documentary."

"Someone should have told them," Mrs. Broadbent said. "This is one man whose working week consists of nothing but smoking cigars and having lunch."

Margaret smiled pityingly. "They've tried every trick in the book to make him look like a busy, involved, decisive Editor. Faked high-powered conferences with Terry over features and with Cedric in the Art Department . . . showed him at the printers, where, of course, no one had the faintest idea who he was . . . filmed him playing croquet with Brigid Brophy and John Mortimer . . . picnicking at Glyndebourne . . . in a punt on the river at Cambridge, reminiscing about his great days as President of the Union. The specially reinforced punt they had to build apparently cost a fortune."

The subject of the BBC2 documentary emerged from his office at that moment and waddled towards them, cigar in hand. "Ah, God!" Mrs. Broadbent greeted him briskly. "The trip to the States was a great success, you'll be pleased to hear. I'll be putting the results down in a long progress report."

"Excellent," Godwin said, with something less than his usual brio. "And, er . . . what's this one on, dear heart?"

"De Gaulle in Kent."

"De Gaulle in Kent?" Godwin repeated blankly.

"God . . . don't tell me you've forgotten! Early in the last War, General de Gaulle and his wife spent several months living in a Kent village called Petts Wood. You assigned me to put together a day-by-day reconstruction of his life there. I've already been to Switzerland, Spain, the West Indies and Australia, talking to people. As well as Kent, of course."

"Harumph . . . well, that sounds excellent, dear heart. Quite excellent." Godwin drew on his cigar and glanced over his shoulder like a hunted man. Through his office glass could be seen the lizard-like head of Tancred Philpott, these days wearing the expression of an accusing and reproachful lizard.

"Hey . . . listen, kids." He beckoned Jessamyn and Strachey from their office and Scurr to the low partition of the Art Department. "I've suggested to the BBC chaps that my box at Lord's might be a fruitful field of observation. But our friend Tancred wonders if we couldn't make it more an editorial event . . . you know, kicking the odd idea around between overs of England versus India. So would you all terri-

bly mind trickling along at one today?" Their Editor's tone was almost
pleading. "It's just lunch and a spot of champers. You needn't watch
the cricket if you don't want to."

A diplomatic pouch of page-proofs had just been couriered from the
printers. Margaret held one up for a final scan-through, then passed it
over to Louis. "This piece on Cat Stevens by Charcoal-Eyes Dyson isn't
as bad as one might expect. In fact, in one or two places it's quite read-
able."

Louis was glad to hear it. The original copy submitted by Fran having
been unusably chaotic and clumsy, he'd spent most of an evening at
the carved desk in his Tudor-panelled bedsit doing a total rewrite.

"It's still twenty-eight lines too long, though," Margaret said. "You'd
better take it up to Mighty Jack Shildrick."

"Shildrick? Why Shildrick?"

"Because under this new order that's mysteriously come into being,
any changes or cuts in Charcoal-Eyes's copy have to be cleared personally with him."

---

The conference area of Shildrick's office, though recently expanded and
refurbished, was crowded to capacity. Around the hollow square of off-
white sofas sat James Way, the Deputy and Foreign Editor; Nick Fenton;
the in-house lawyer, Angus McRory; two men in pinstripe suits who
could only have been outside solicitors, and a superior-looking, sandy-
haired man in a one-piece white wing-collar and cravat who could only
have been a Queen's Counsel. The paper's Health Correspondent, sallow-
faced and wheezing, perched on the edge of an adjacent chair. The exposé of the unsafe contraceptive Pill clearly had reached crisis point.

But still weightier things were on Shildrick's mind. Snatching the
proof of Fran's profile, he abandoned the meeting and strode off
towards his desk, reading hungrily. The Q.C., who had been speaking
when Louis came in, hooked his thumbs in his waistcoat-pockets,
leaned back and stared at the ceiling with a yawn. The two consultant
solicitors shuffled the pink-ribboned documents on their knees. Each
minute of their collective time would be costing Lord McIntyre hundreds of pounds—or rather, guineas. One could almost hear the terrifying taximeter clock up and up.

"This isn't right, Poet," Shildrick said, beckoning. His expression was
troubled in a way that the legal threats of Britain's largest pharmaceutical giant could not make it.

"How do you mean?" Louis asked.

"It's not the piece she wrote."

"It had to be played around with a bit."

Shildrick looked mystified. "Why? She got some really good stuff out of him."

"But the shape wasn't quite right. And it was a bit . . ." Louis searched for the right tactful word but couldn't find it.

"And all this in Overmatter?"

"Yes. There are twenty-eight lines to cut."

Shildrick drew in his breath sharply. "Can't you fiddle the layout around to get it in?"

"It's a Terence Donovan picture. It's already gone to press at that size."

"All right," Shildrick conceded. "But at least put back some of the good stuff she had in her original version. Wasn't there a part about the lyric of 'Matthew and Son'? How does it go? 'There's a five-minute break and that's all you take . . .' " He turned to the assembled legal brains. "Do any of you know the words to 'Matthew and Son'?"

Angus McRory stared disbelievingly down his long nose. "I'm sorry?" the Q.C. queried.

" 'Matthew and Son,' Shildrick repeated. "It's a pop song. By Cat Stevens. Been at the top of the charts for weeks now." He snapped his fingers in triumph. "Oh, aye . . . what am I thinking of? 'It's a five-minute break and that's all you take. For a cup of cold coffee and a piece of cake . . .' "

He wrote the words painstakingly in the margin, also inserting a quotation from an earlier chart success, "I Love My Dog," and the fact that Stevens recorded on the Deram label, while the Q.C. examined his fingernails, the two solicitors fidgeted and glanced around, the well-being of menstrual cycles all over Britain hung in the balance, and another horrifying digit of legal costs notched up almost audibly.

"Thanks, Poet," he said in a ventriloquial murmur. "This is important to her. Her first piece in the Magazine. You understand?"

Louis nodded. That much at least he understood.

"Have we said that Stevens's parents are Greek?"

"Yes."

"And that he enjoys painting in his spare time?"

Louis nodded again.

"Right. Champion." Shildrick handed the proof back. "By the way, are you very tied up at the beginning of next month?"

"No. Not very."

"Basil Hamilton's off on holiday for two weeks. You can stand in for him as Cicero if you like."

So the great reward had come at last, when least expected, and with the curiously flat feeling that always seemed to accompany impossible dreams come true. For Louis knew that what was being rewarded was not his writing ability.

---

"He's found himself a bird! I know he has!" Jessamyn O'Shaughnessy said, adding slices of rare beef to the half-lobster, king prawns, smoked salmon, broccoli quiche and honeydew melon already on her plate. As an authentic M.C.C. member as well as entertainer on an heroic scale, Toby Godwin leased one of the highest and best-situated private boxes in the Lord's grandstand. Today its indoor dining room, containing the buffet lunch and bar, was crowded to capacity. The outdoor balcony, offering an unrivalled view of England's match against the Indian touring team, was deserted.

"Who's found himself a bird?" Terry Bracegirdle asked, wresting the cork from a bottle of Chablis Grand Cru.

"Who? Mighty Jack Shildrick, that's who!"

"What?" Cedric Scurr yelled with an involuntary dribble of mayonnaise down his swarthy chin.

"I've suspected it for months," Jessamyn continued, spooning up couscous, "ever since he dropped those ghastly Happy Heppy suits of his and started getting his hair done at Crimpers. But I didn't know for certain until yesterday. On my way back from lunch with Donyale and Penny Tree, my taxi pulled up at lights in Oxford Street next to a turquoise Mini-Cooper. Some little dolly whose face I couldn't see was driving and Mighty Jack was in the front passenger seat."

"That's no proof," Evelyn Strachey scoffed. "It was probably some girl researcher with the Close-up team. You know how he likes to be all democratic with the rank and file."

"That's what I first thought, too," Jessamyn said. "But then, just as the lights were about to change, I saw him take her hand off the steering-wheel and kiss it."

The faces around her showed more delight than could have been accomplished by the most artistic play on the sunlit greensward below. "Well, well, well, whoever'd have thought it?" Bracegirdle said. "Fleet Street's most boringly married man gets his busy little leg over at last!"

"You didn't see who it was?" Val Lewis asked.

"No—only her arm. And a pink fluffy mini up to here. But I'll find out her name! I will, I will!"

Looking into Jessamyn's bloodshot eyes, Louis marvelled that, even with a clue like the fluffy pink minidress, such an elementary deduction should still elude supposedly top-rank journalists. His clear duty now was to find a telephone with all possible speed and warn Shildrick the bloodhounds were unleashed and baying. Then a thought came into his head, so simple and radical it momentarily took his breath away. It ran as follows: "Why the hell should I?" He turned it over several times in his mind, liking it more and more, as he helped himself to walnut-and-grape salad and held out his glass to a napkin-wrapped bottle of Dom Pérignon.

"Boys and girls!" Toby Godwin shouted amidst the foreground clash of cutlery and the muted background ripple of cricket-lovers' applause. "Could I have the tiniest bit of 'oosh just for the moment?" He smiled apologetically in the direction of the television camera, whose soft whirr no one noticed by now. "Tancred, dear boy, I'm sorry to do this to you again, but would you mind dreadfully cutting it for the next moment or two?"

The producer said nothing, merely nodding and burying his face in his skinny hands like one taking refuge in private prayer. His cameraman, lighting-man and sound-man switched off their respective instruments with enthusiasm and returned to the brimming plates and full glasses beside them. These weeks of filming Godwin in his natural habitat had seen all the BBC2 crew go up at least a size inside their custard-yellow polo shirts and frontally-pressed jeans. The clapperboard-boy in particular, gorged on duck pâté and profiteroles, could not perform his simple office without a grunt of effort. Admittedly they had now reached "*One Man's Week*, Toby Godwin—take 46."

"As you know," Godwin resumed, "this morning I had my regular chinwag over coffee and a brioche at Claridges with Tim Mandeville, our Advertising Director. And he told me something which rather spoiled the conviviality of the occasion. For the current quarter, that is the three months ending August thirty-first, our ad bookings are down on the same period last year."

"Down?" Scurr repeated blankly. "By how much?"

"Sixteen percent. It's clearly just a blip," Godwin continued hastily amid the murmur of consternation. "Midsummer is a notoriously lean time for advertising, and made no better by the jiggery-pokery our good Harold and his chums are practising on the economy."

"What does Lord M. say?" Bracegirdle asked.

"Lord M. says nothing for the present. Since our record until this point has been one of continuously ascending profits, I feel confident that he too will accept it as the merest blip. But I'm sure you all agree it behoves us to give that extra bit of zing to our autumn schedule, so that Tim can go back to the bigger agencies and say, 'Come on, you fellows! Can you really afford not to be in on this?' "

"We've got 'What Did Christ Really Look Like?' Bracegirdle said. "And we could probably get 'The Steins' done in time as well."

" 'The Steins'? " Godwin said, mystified.

"It's based on a theory of David Kausman's that every important person in Western civilisation has or had a name ending with 'stein.' We're doing an illustrated portrait gallery from Wittgenstein through Helena Rubenstein to Brian Epstein."

"Obvious audience-pleasers, both," Godwin nodded. "But I'm thinking now of a mild change of tack towards the reader-service area—which, as we all know, has long been pressingly advocated by Jack Shildrick."

"Shildrick?" Scurr said with a bilious grimace. "You mean we've got to start doing what Shildrick wants?"

"Not at all, dear boy, not in the broader perspective. But at this present, rather embarrassing fiscal juncture, with Mighty Jack as palsy-walsy with Lord M. as he is, it might be politically prudent to consider something like . . ." Godwin cast around him for inspiration. "Well, let's say, for the sake of argument, a home-improvement series."

The young rips stared at one another in fathomless dismay. "A home-improvement series?" Bracegirdle said weakly.

"A subject, I'm sure, very close to many of our readers' hearts. We could do advice on painting. . . . er . . . improving . . . all that sort of thing. It could well bring in appreciable new advertisement revenue from builders . . . double-glazers. Or should it be 'glaziers'? What do you think, Jim? Could you conceivably get that off the ground for us to run in mid-August?"

"But, God . . . I know nothing about home improvement," Deaves protested.

"You've got a home. That ought to be sufficient basis to commission a few features in the relevant areas. And Cedric I know, if he puts his mind to it, can make the visual side of even something like this attractive as well as . . . harumph . . . instructive . . ."

A white-bloused Lord's waitress had appeared in the doorway and was waiting for a gap in the conversation. General contemplation of the home-improvement series amply provided this. "Is there a Mr. Brennan here?" she asked.

"Yes," Louis said.

"Telephone call for you."

Standing in a room whose walls were lined with sepia Test teams and historic cricket bats, the last voice in the world he expected to hear was Grandma Bassill's.

"Lou? Your office told me you were there."

"Hello, Gran," he said, making an effort to sound sober and sensible. "How are you both? Look, I'm really sorry I haven't . . ."

"Grandad's gone," she interrupted.

"Gone? Gone where? Back to Roehampton for a fitting?"

"No . . . gone. Died. He's dead, Lou. Grandad's dead. He went at half-past eight this morning."

---

He pressed the bell that went "brring!" and, from immemorial habit, poked in the stiff letter-flap and peeped through. Though the absent person could by no stretch of imagination have been called noisy, an unnatural stillness seemed to hang in the front hall with its terracotta-coloured lino, its steep stairs, its coat-stand crowded with pin-bearing hats and umbrellas known as "gamps." The first door to the left, that of the "best" sitting room, was vehemently closed.

Grandma came tripping to let him in as always, wearing pompom slippers, an apron and the lipstick, earrings and double-strand pearl necklace she'd never failed to put on at this time of day to please her man. On the left upper arm of her pale blue cardigan was a band of black crêpe. As Louis bent to hug her, he felt an urge to scoop her close, but knew she'd have hated that. "What a do isn't it, eh?" she said in a voice betraying only gentle bemusement.

His mother had already arrived, as had Grandma's younger sister, Aunt Flo, a woman equally tiny but less svelte, and with several large facial bumps, some of them sprouting long grey hairs. Pushed back against the larder door was a wheelchair containing two short legs with rockers instead of feet. On the green baize tablecloth lay a pack of playing cards, its box discoloured and crumbling with years of careful use.

Grandad's exit, it transpired, had been as unostentatious as every-thing else about him. " 'E was quite all right last night," Grandma said. "We 'ad our Bourn-Vita as usual, and a last game of shove-ha'penny. When I took his tea in first thing this morning, he was in an awful tem-per, really snapped at me, which isn't like Dad, as you know. Then he says, 'You won't leave me, Mum, will you?' I says, 'Don't be a silly fool, why would I leave you?' Then I turned round to pick up his bottle, and when I turned back . . ."

Her voice was still faintly bemused, her only sign of emotion the hands twisting in her aproned lap. "He's still here," she murmured to Louis. "In the front room. Do you want to see him?"

How much Louis didn't want to see that frail, depleted personage lying in state with the Magicoal fire, the hand-coloured wartime wedding photographs and scallop-fronted cocktail cabinet, he could not begin to conjure. Fortunately, his mother broke in on his behalf: "Oh, no, Mum, of course he doesn't . . ."

"But he was always very fond of his grandad."

"I know. But the young people don't do that these days . . ."

While arrangements were discussed, he sat and stared through the scullery window to the tiny back garden, where Grandad's roses were out in full glory. He remembered an indomitable figure leaning down from the wheelchair, trowel in hand. Over the river it might be Swinging London, hippies, Mini-Mokes, love, peace and floppy hats. Here, it was still the world of H. G. Wells, Kipps and Mr. Polly.

"We should send out bereavement cards," Grandma said. "Black-bordered shows respect. Like Mother and Father did when poor Harry died of his appendix."

"They don't do that any more, Mum. Just a notice in the South London Press will be enough."

Grandma suddenly reached over and took Louis's hand. "You know, Lou, he was always so proud of you for following in his footsteps. Specially that article you wrote in the paper about him. Thought the world of that, he did."

"We ought to contact Tommy Scales and his other old colleagues from Gaumont-British. They're all bound to want to come to the funeral."

"I'll see to the wreaths," Aunt Flo said. "You can get beautiful ones these days, spelling out 'Dad' in flowers. I thought Ted and me could send one in the shape of a whisky bottle. 'Cos Gus always did like his little nip of Johnnie Walker, didn't he?"

Picturing a memorial Johnnie Walker bottle sculpted in flowers, Louis felt the beginnings of a supercilious Ideas Lunch snigger. Then he checked himself. Hollow and unfamiliar though it seemed without its central inhabitant, the little kitchen solved the conundrum of his identity as instantly as always. The old iron grate; the wooden-armed easy chair with Woman's Own under its cushion; the salmon-and-pale-blue knitted tea-cosy with ribbons on top and singe marks round the spout-hole—all told him exactly who he was and where he came from.

# 26

And what was the young lady wearing?"

"She was wearing a fur rug, sir," the police sergeant replied. He was the one with the rosy-cheeked, jolly face of a Toby jug. Louis remembered the rubberised reek of his macintosh and the elastic band he'd stretched and twirled between his fingers.

"A fur rug?" prosecuting counsel repeated in a tone itself as silkily strokable as sable or mink. "Did you say a fur rug?"

"Yes, sir. I believe it was some sort of bedcover."

"I see. And what else?"

"Nothing, sir."

"Nothing?"

"No, sir. Underneath she was completely naked."

"So what you're saying in other words is that, apart from this fur rug, the young lady was nude."

"Yes, sir."

"The only female in the company of . . . how many men?"

The sergeant glanced at his notebook and briefly computed. "Eight, sir. Including the Moroccan servant."

"Including the Moroccan servant," prosecuting counsel repeated to give the jury the full benefit of the phrase. "And how would you describe the young lady's comportment at this time?"

"Her what, sir?"

"How did she behave?"

The sergeant cast around briefly for the *mot juste.* "She was in a merry mood, sir."

"A merry mood! Not at all concerned by the fact that a large number of police officers had just entered the premises?"

"No, sir."

"A mood, in short, which might well have been consistent with the smoking of cannabis?"

"Yes, sir."

"And, having been discovered nude but for a fur rug and alone with eight men—including the Moroccan servant—did the young lady comport herself with the modesty one might expect during investigation by police officers?"

"No, sir. As she was being led away for search by my female colleague, D.C. Rosemary Slade, she deliberately let the rug fall."

"Disclosing parts of her nude body?"

"Yes, sir. Disclosing parts of her nude body."

To the left and right of Louis, behind and in front of him, reporters from every national were scribbling frantically. Despite his growing anger and incredulity at the proceedings, he could not repress a feeling of wonderful superiority over these poor devils, still tied to diaries and deadlines and scrambling for telephones. Now and again he would make a leisurely note on a Sunday Dispatch memo pad with his (bought on expenses) Sheaffer ballpoint.

The courtroom was packed to capacity and stifling hot. High-set leaded windows kept out all but faint hints of the brilliant sunshine and raging pandemonium outside on Chichester Market Square. The three defendants sat in the dock in a row, closely—in the case of Mick Jagger, perhaps rather hopefully—watched by a cordon of burly police warders. On the left was Robert Fraser, short-haired, dark-suited, clearly regretting his choice of weekend associates with every fibre of his being. In the middle was Keith Richard, wearing a scruffy black frock-coat and white silk cravat, his demeanour as well as clothes recalling some seedy tap-room character in a Dickens story. Jagger by contrast had clearly done his utmost to discipline his shampoo-shiny hair and to dress in a restrained and respectful manner. Not that the majesty of the law remotely understood that a leaf-green blazer, olive-coloured hipsters, a frilled shirt and multi-striped tie were the Mick Jagger version of extreme conservatism. It showed as much on the faces of counsel, with their gowns and starched bibs and little pigtailed perruques, as on that of the Judge himself with his cascade of ratty grey curls, his fur-trimmed red tea-gown and scarlet sash. The hairstyles and clothes of modern pop musicians really were impossibly outlandish, extravagant and effeminate!

The Judge stopped writing and gazed up, a look of annoyance on his not very benign face. In the public gallery above the dock, thirty or so teenage girls with uniform black eyes, centre-parted hair and psychedelic dolly dresses leaned perilously over the rail, jostling and elbowing for the restricted view of their darlings. To the legal drone below they added a constant excited rustle, as if someone were opening an outsize box of chocolates.

"As I already have had occasion to point out before," the Judge snapped, "this is not a bear garden. It is a court of Quarter Sessions. If this noise does not cease, I shall have no hesitation in taking the appropriate measures."

". . . And so, Sergeant," prosecuting counsel resumed, "it is your belief that the young lady deliberately let the rug fall, disclosing parts of her nude body?"

"I would say so, sir. Yes."

"In order to incite or provoke you and your officers in the execution of their duty?"

"Yes, sir."

Louis remembered the moment well, and by now was not surprised at the vast chasm between his memory of it and the official one. All morning he had listened to the silkily polite questions of prosecuting counsel and the slow, stilted replies of police witnesses—often with recourse to notes made at the time—somehow transform that rather cosy domestic Sunday evening in Keith Richard's living room into a nameless sexual orgy in which the most reprehensible party was not Richard nor even Jagger, but Marianne Faithfull. Since Marianne faced no criminal charges, the Judge had magnanimously ruled that her name could not be used in open court. But who did not know which once-perfect English rose now shared the disgusting lifestyle of Jagger and his circle? Since Marianne herself was in court, seated next to the Stones' P.R., Les Perrin, prosecuting counsel could scarcely make his innuendoes about "the young lady" without looking her straight in the face. With every gloatingly scandalised word, scores of eyes undressed her all over again.

On Louis's right sat the Daily Mirror man, bald and beetle-browed, with the wheezing respiration of the chain-smoker. As Jagger himself was called to the witness-box, Louis felt a nudge.

"Were you really there?" the Mirror man husked.

"Yes, I was."

"So is it true about the Mars bar?"

"I'm sorry?"

"There's a story going round that when the cops burst in, Marianne had a Mars bar stuck up her quim and Jagger was licking it."

"Mr. Jagger," his counsel said, "do you take drugs?"

"No, sir." The voice was educated and choirboy-soft.

"Did you go to Mr. Richard's house that weekend for the purpose of taking drugs?"

"No, sir."

"In fact, I believe that when this person—ah—Doctor Daydream attempted to persuade you to take L.S.D., you vehemently . . ."

"Mr. Petherbridge!" the Judge interrupted. "I have already given you my ruling on this."

"Yes, my lord. But it is the defence's contention that Doctor Daydream was an agent provocateur, deliberately insinuated into the weekend party, possibly by a Sunday newspaper whom Mr. Jagger was suing for a gross defamation . . ."

"And I have said, Mr. Petherbridge, that this line of argument cannot be pursued so long as your Doctor what-you-call-him faces no criminal charges and is not in court."

"Quite, my lord. But if further time could be given for him to be found . . ."

"He has not been found so far, Mr. Petherbridge." The Judge turned to the jury, a stolid double row of local bourgeoisie without a young face or a splash of modern colour among them. As always in these asides, judicial testiness was replaced by a smile of almost overweening geniality. "As to whether he ever existed at all," the Judge added, "I'm sure that the ladies and gentlemen of this good Sussex jury will have no difficulty in forming their own opinion."

With a faint shrug, defence counsel turned back to Jagger. "Now, Mr. Jagger . . . these four amphetamine tablets that were found in your jacket pocket. You don't deny that they were yours?"

"No, sir."

"In fact, you bought them in Italy, where I believe they're quite legal and freely available at any chemist's shop."

"Yes, sir."

"Did you know that in Britain they came under the heading of an illegal drug? That is, illegal unless specifically prescribed by a doctor?"

"No, sir."

"What did you do when you found out?"

"I rang my G.P.," Jagger said in a voice so fragile, one could barely imagine him having strength enough to pick up the telephone. "I said I needed summink to help me stay awake while we were working in the studio . . ."

"The recording studio?"

"Yeah. And he said I could take 'em as long as it was only in an emergency."

"So in other words you had a perfectly valid doctor's prescription."

"I thought so, yeah."

While the daily men plunged to their telephones, Louis hurried through the dark vestibule and out into the brilliant sun. Already, by some near-psychic process, news of the verdict and sentence had reached the besieging multitude. Hundreds of screaming, weeping girls were being held back by a double line of police, some with helmets quite badly knocked askew. At the distant margins of the crowd vans were selling hot-dogs, ice cream and T-shirts saying "I LOVE MICK" or "THE STONES ARE INNOCENT." From transistor radios everywhere could be heard the new Beatles single that seemed woven into the very breeze:

"All yuh need is loov! Loov! Loov is allyuhneed!"

Two police Black Marias drew into the kerb, with motorcycle outriders before and behind. A distressed Marianne was led down the steps of the Court building, to be swallowed up in the mêlée of photographers at the bottom. A moment later, two plain-clothes detectives brought out Jagger and Robert Fraser close together and, it first seemed, fraternally holding hands. Then Fraser moved his arm, taking Jagger's with it, and sunlight flashed on silver handcuffs, no different in 1967 from in 1667. Jagger's face wore a look of stupefied dismay, the overstuffed lips sagging and bloodless, the once-cool, narrow eyes wet with tears.

A dry-eyed Keith Richard followed, similarly linked to a uniformed warder. On his way down the shrieking avenue towards the second Black Maria, he noticed Louis standing there, and raised a manacled hand in salute.

"You know what they're calling this?" he shouted. "The Summer of Love! Good, eh?"

As Louis approached the swing doors to the Magazine concourse, they were brusquely pushed open from the other side. Towards him strode a familiar yet still unbelievable figure, white-haired, rubicund and wearing a black double-breasted suit tailored some time before the Second World War. It was Lord McIntyre of Ludgate Hill, completely alone and with the unmistakable air of one intent on investigating or verifying something for himself. As he passed, the faded blue eyes swept over Louis with what might have been a glimmer of World Cup remembrance. Then he was gone, leaving behind that faint, inexplicable fragrance of pepper.

The half-dozen people to be found scattered through the concourse at this somnolent fag-end of a Friday afternoon all wore expressions of profound shock. "He just materialised out of nowhere," Margaret was saying to Val Lewis. "Usually you get at least a four-minute warning,

with commissionaires pinning back doors and standing to attention
. . . I don't think anyone had any idea he was even in the building."

"What did he do?" Val asked.

"Just walked in and stood gazing around, as if he could hardly believe his eyes. Because we're not exactly a hive of fruitful endeavour
today, even for us. God's still at Lord's with the BBC crew. Terry Bracegirdle and his new secretary haven't been seen since before lunch. Jessamyn, Evelyn and their little clique were playing bridge and drinking
Scotch. Cedric was the only executive you could say was actually working . . . and that was designing a book-jacket as a freelance job."

"He asked me what I was doing at present," Mrs. Broadbent piped
up. "I told him all about General de Gaulle in Petts Wood, but I must
say he didn't seem terribly interested."

"Anyway," Margaret said, "it's a deeply sinister development."

"Sinister? Why sinister?"

"It was obviously some kind of spot check, wasn't it? When have we
known Lord M. ever do anything like that before? And do you think it's
pure coincidence we've just been told that our ad bookings are down
for the first time ever? If you ask me, some little skunk or rattler whispered in our Chairman's ear that if he happened to drop in on us unan-
nounced, he'd find all the stories about our being a bunch of useless,
shiftless layabouts proved beyond any question."

"By skunk or rattler, you mean Mighty Jack Shildrick."

"Yes, I mean Mighty Jack Shildrick."

Louis was only half-listening to all this as he took off his jacket and
hung it over the back of his chair. The single box pleat had been badly
crushed by hours of sitting at West Sussex Quarter Sessions. "How did
it go with the Stones?" Margaret asked.

"Both found guilty. Keith Richard got a year, Jagger three months."

"You're joking!"

"Nope. And Robert Fraser got six months. At least he can comfort
himself that he pleaded guilty."

"I thought Jagger was supposed to have had a doctor's prescription
for those tablets," Mrs. Broadbent said.

"The Judge directed the jury that a doctor's verbal say-so didn't
count as a prescription. So Jagger had no defence."

Margaret gave a low whistle. "My God! Will they really bung him in
chokey for a trivial offence like that?"

"They already have. I've just seen him driven off to Wormwood
Scrubs in handcuffs. Can you imagine the fun they're going to have
with him in there?"

"A wonderful payoff for your piece, though."

Louis's telephone rang. He picked it up and covered the mouthpiece, glumly shaking his head. "Both Jagger's and Richard's counsel have given notice of appeal, so it's all still sub judice. We can't run anything until after after the appeal's heard, which could be weeks from now . . . Hello, Louis Brennan."

"Hello, Editor's secretary here," Enid's brisk voice said. "Mr. Shildrick asked me to confirm that you'll be doing the Cicero column for two Sundays, July the fifth and the twelfth."

"Yes, I've cleared it with Toby Godwin. That's fine."

"And he'd appreciate your advice about something, if you can spare a few minutes."

"OK. I'll come right up."

"No, not here. He asks if you could join him where he is now . . . the Lord John boutique in Carnaby Street."

———

Shildrick was standing before a full-length mirror, wearing a body-hugging shirt of crinkly lime-green voile, open half-way to the waist, and a pair of butcher-striped hipsters about five inches too long for his legs. But for that impediment, he could convincingly have climbed a rope with a cutlass between his teeth in some silent Hollywood epic of Caribbean life. A pink-vested teenage assistant hovered nearby chewing gum and grooving to the Four Tops' "This Ol' Heart of Mine."

" 'Ullo, Poet," the gruesome reflection said into the mirror, as cheerily as if Louis had come upon him sketching layout or formulating a front-page splash. "She's put her foot down and said I've got to be trendier . . . is that the proper word? At least, when we're at these with-it places like Sybilla's and the Speakeasy. You're the Colour Mag's number-one snappy dresser, so I had to have you to arbitrate. What do you think of the shirt?"

The word that occurred to Louis was "cloacal." "It's fine," he said.

"They are worn open at the front like this, aren't they?"

"They can be."

Shildrick twisted doubtfully to left and right, smoothing hips and shallow buttocks of disconcerting girlishness. "These slacks are the rage, I know," he shouted to the assistant. "But by gum, they're hard on the goolies. I don't think I could sit down without defenestrating myself. Anyway, they're much too long."

"Get them altered for you in ten minutes."

On top of an adjacent shirt-carousel lay a black felt hat with a high, concave crown and hugely wide, unstiffened brim. Shildrick picked it up with both hands and gingerly set it on his head at the dead straight set of a Quaker elder. The assistant tutted impatiently and tweaked the enormous brim to an acute angle over his right eye.

"Looks great on you. Reelly fantastic."

"What do you reckon, Poet?"

The hat made Shildrick look like a mixture of Hoss Cartwright from *Bonanza* and Cesar Bombski, the Beano comic's resident anarchist. But the eyes under the tilted brim had a vulnerability Louis had never seen in them before. "All right, isn't it?" he added almost pleadingly.

"Yes. It's fine."

Along one flimsy grotto wall hung an array of leather and suede jackets, chained together in the now familiar anti-shoplifter precaution. Their metal-linked sleeves and collars brought back to Louis the spectacle he'd witnessed in Chichester earlier today. He turned to a multi-coloured shirt-rack and sent its impacted puffed sleeves angrily spinning.

Shildrick's unobscured right eye glanced curiously at him in the mirror. "What's wrong with you? You look like a wet Monday in Salford."

"What's wrong?" Louis echoed bitterly. "I've just watched a show trial we'd condemn to the skies if happened in Russia or . . . or McCarthyite America. What's even wronger is I've been sitting on an exclusive for months that I still can't write because of this country's damned stupid, restrictive laws of contempt . . ."

"Hold up a second." Shildrick removed the hat and handed it to the assistant with an apologetic smile. "A bit too *Mark of Zorro* for me, I'm afraid. But I'll take this shirt and the gold one, and the slacks, if you wouldn't mind pinning 'em up." He turned back to Louis. "OK, Poet, tell me the whole thing. Omitting no detail however trivial, as Holmes said to Watson."

While the assistant knelt between them with pins, Louis described the unfolding monstrosities of the Rolling Stones' drug raid, trial and conviction. Shildrick nodded his head, saying "Mm, mm" in the rapid, almost hungry way he had when absorbing large quantities of fact.

"But surely Jagger's been asking for all this," he said at length. "If you deliberately set out to offend Society's mores, you shouldn't complain when Society turns on you."

"All right, so he's been provocative. He wears his hair too long. He recorded a song called 'Let's Spend the Night Together,' which is only what popular music's been saying in not so many words for the last fifty years. Is that any reason to parade him in handcuffs like an eighteenth-century sheepstealer and bait him with the rabble's curse?"

Shildrick's eyes brightened, as if powerful electric bulbs had been switched on behind each of them. "That's a tremendous line. Where's it from?"

It had popped out so spontaneously that Louis had to think for a moment. "Oh, yes . . . *Macbeth*, last act. 'I will not live to kiss the ground before young Duncan's feet and be baited with the rabble's curse.' "

"So you're saying Jagger's been made the scapegoat for all Society's unease about pop music's connection with drugs and juvenile delinquency?"

Louis gave the shirt-rack another impassioned twirl. "Absolutely."

"And he's really not a drug-crazed, decadent, unhygienic lout?"

"Absolutely not."

"All right, you've sold me." Shildrick prised his left leg free and smiled down at the Lord John assistant, encouraging even in the marginally creative context of pinning up trousers. "Just do this side the same as the other one and I'm sure it'll be champion. I'll get my driver to pick everything up tomorrow."

He opened the louvred changing-room door, already half out of the terrible voile shirt and showing an almost as regrettable cellular vest underneath. "Just give me two minutes to change, Shakespeare, then you and I have got an appointment with a typewriter."

At six-thirty the following evening, a compositor slotted the last line of type into the design, hammered it all over with a mallet, pushed its trolley across the composing room, slid the bound-in metal page through a roller of blank paper and unfurled the first smudgy "pull" of tomorrow's splash story.

The splash was a Shildrick tour de force, pile-drivingly dramatic yet utterly simple. The quotation from *Macbeth* in the face of Nemesis, "BAITED BY THE RABBLE'S CURSE" ran across ten columns above its quintessential image in modern times. A grainy wire-service photograph, deliberately not cropped or retouched, to emphasise its crude intrusiveness, showed Mick Jagger through the open rear door of the police car that had brought him to court, holding up his and Robert Fraser's manacled hands in a vain attempt to shield his face from the flash.

The accompanying story took the form of extended editorial comment, Louis having willingly sacrificed his byline to throw the paper's whole weight and gravitas behind it. To be fair, he doubted whether he could have written it as Shildrick had with his help, pounding out quietly furious phrases on the battered portable, probing and ferreting for extra facts he'd all but forgotten, weaving them expertly into a seamless narrative of official paranoia, myopia and vindictiveness. There was swingeing criticism of the police, both for the D-Day-like scale and drama of the original raid, and for still refusing to say whether they had been tipped off by the Sunday scandal sheet which Jagger happened to be suing for libel. There was a stinging denunciation of the prosecution for its tactic of proving Keith Richard had allowed drug-taking in his house by the implication that he'd simultaneously been presiding over a sex-orgy. The Judge was roundly condemned for allowing irrelevant lurid detail about "the girl in the fur rug" yet prohibiting all reference to the agent provocateur who might or might not have been planted among the weekend guests. A separate single-column story, "THE FORGOTTEN MAN," railed against the unfairness of placing Robert Fraser in the dock alongside two defendants whose notoriety could only rebound disastrously on him.

"Granted, the sentences handed down are wholly right and proper under the law as it stands," the piece ended. "We have no doubt that, if the law still permitted it, these two hapless minstrels would even now be in the tumbril for Tyburn or in some stinking slave galley en route for Botany Bay."

The whole operation had been carried through at an intoxicating speed and with a decisiveness and dynamic energy that Louis had long since ceased to look for in an editorial superior. Still more heady was the appearance of his words in type, albeit unsigned, less than an hour after finishing them rather than five weeks if one was lucky. He was in Shildrick's office, marking literals on the second proof, when Angus McRory, the legal adviser, appeared in the doorway with the one just sent down to his office. The legal adviser's usual look of long-nosed disdain had been replaced by one of perplexity. On the galley in his hand, a red ballpoint line had been drawn through the story from top to bottom. "Jack . . . you know what I'm going to say, don't you?"

"Yes," Shildrick replied calmly.

"The Jagger-Richard case still has to go to appeal, so remains technically sub judice. This lead story of yours constitutes deliberate and flagrant contempt of court."

Shildrick's telephone buzzed softly at that moment. He perched on his desk, turning away slightly and speaking with a murmurous economy that told Louis the caller could only be Fran. His face striped by late-evening sun through a Venetian blind, he had never looked more romantically slender and youthful. For another fleeting moment Louis wondered whether to warn him that *Macbeth* was not the only one pursued by Nemesis; that Birnam Wood, in the shaggy shape of Jessamyn O'Shaughnessy, was already on the march. But as he was now, undiminished by lime-green voile—or, for that matter, cellular undervest—it felt presumptuous to think anyone or anything could harm him. The castle keep seemed utterly impregnable with its vast, cluttered desk and shaded lamp, its hundreds of loyal shirt-sleeved soldiers all around, its great war engines in the basement, awaiting the boy thane's signal.

With a concluding murmured endearment, Shildrick rang off and turned back to McRory. "What I'm saying, Angus, is that this is an occasion when public interest rates higher than any literal interpretation of the law. I hold no brief for Jagger or . . . his friend. My concern, the concern of any paper in a democracy deserving the name, is to prevent the law we all hold dear being manipulated to harass and incarcerate two pop musicians on marginal offences merely because officialdom doesn't like the length of their hair."

"I must warn you that contempt of court with no mitigating factor carries heavy penalties. The paper could face a punitive fine."

"I've spoken to Lord M. already. He's bullish."

"You personally could be fined. Even receive a custodial sentence yourself."

"You mean join Mr. Jagger in chokey." Shildrick grinned. "I know that, and I'm prepared to take the chance. In fact, when the first edition's out, I'm sending a copy straight round to the Director of Public Prosecutions with a personal note saying that if anyone wants me, like for example a government law officer, they can find me here, helping to sub the late sports results."

McRory shrugged. "It's your neck. Oh, and there's another point, on copyright. This quotation in the headline . . . is the author going to object to its appearing without acknowledgement?"

# 27

Cicero had his own airy glass-walled office overlooking the plebeian expanse of the Newsroom. He also had his own secretary, Lydia, who had served every incumbent of the column since the pre-McIntyre late fifties. Early as Louis was on his first morning, he found her already there, opening a pile of mail even higher than Freya Broadbent's daily one. She was slight and earnest-looking, with the kind of voice that would pronounce "Mummy" as "Mummie" and the kind of fifties hairdo that still needed bobby pins.

He half-expected her to resent so great an institution falling to one so young and inexperienced, never mind a detested "Magazine person." But she proved amiable enough, dispensing coffee, then laying before him the black Morocco folder containing his possible engagements for the next two weeks.

"The opening of a new play, *There's a Girl in My Soup*, with Donald Sinden. You're invited to the first-night party at the Ivy afterwards . . . A lunch for the President of the Seychelles at Les Ambassadeurs . . . United Artists pictures are offering an exclusive interview with a new young star, Dustin Hoffman. They can arrange a screening of his film, *The Graduate*, for you if you're interested."

"OK." He tilted back in Cicero's opulent chair, enjoying the thought of Steam Section plebs out there, wondering who the hell this upstart in a black shirt and leather coat thought he was.

"And there's this, too, if you dare," Lydia added. She passed across an invitation card, plainer than the rest and decorated with a familiar self-parodying coat-of-arms:

> *Lord Gnome*
> *Invites you to the*
> *Private Eye Lunch*

*The Coach & Horses, Greek St. W.1*
*Thursday, July 13, 1967*

It was news to Louis that Lord Gnome's vitriolic organ had any such ge-
nial, socialising side. He examined the card with a little thrill of dread,
as if it might be poisoned like the Bible in *The Duchess of Malfi*.

"Who else will be there?"

"Anyone who can provide a bit of scurrilous gossip . . . other journalists . . . publishers . . . literary agents . . . even the odd M.P. Michael Foot
often goes. Tom Driberg's there nearly every fortnight."

"The very people the magazine always sends up rotten?"

"Of course. They all love it really."

"What . . . being called 'flabby-faced cowards' and 'boring old farts'?
And cartooned by William Rushton sitting on the lavatory? They must
be born masochists."

"No, they just love publicity. And any publicity's better than none at
all."

Through the glass wall to the right was an office newly refurbished,
with touches of luxury and individuality not even granted to Cicero.
Rather than standard-issue grey steel, its desk was Habitat white;
there was a matching low coffee-table with two egg-shaped chairs on
stems. When Louis enquired about its occupant—still not visible at almost 11:30—Lydia's protruding eyes rolled heavenward in a familiar
way.

"It belongs to our latest star writer, Fran Dyson. Have you read her
column in the Trend section?"

"The Cool Look? Yes, I've seen it."

"Don't you think it's quite appalling?"

"It's . . . well, it does try a bit hard."

"The whole thing has to be totally rewritten by the subs every week.
No one can understand how she gets away with it."

He silently digested this further proof that journalists are among the
world's most unperspicacious creatures. "Doesn't she come in on Tues-
days?"

"She's in Amman," Lydia said with another eloquent eye-roll.

"Amman? Jordan?"

"Doing the first interview with King Hussein after the Six-Day War.
Ed Roper, the Diplomatic Editor, is absolutely hopping mad . . ."

She lowered her gaze as the door opened and Shildrick peeped round
it with the conspiratorial jollity of an uncle interrupting a children's
party. "Well, well, well," he said. "Here beginneth the new order, eh?"
He was wearing a suit of thick black chalk-stripe with a matching sher-

bet-pink shirt, tie and breast-pocket handkerchief. He looked round the office, then at Louis, smiling proudly as if it had been a long, hard climb but they'd finally battled through together.

"You're an independent kingdom here, you know, Poet. You choose your own pictures, do your own layout, sub your own copy and mark it up . . . how's that for power? You'll find all sorts of people will come around, badgering you to do puffs on friends of theirs. But just fend 'em all off. I'll back you up if need be. By the way, have you seen this morning's Times?"

"No. I haven't had a . . ."

Shildrick flipped open the copy that lay uppermost in Lydia's IN tray. "Half the letters page still on about the Jagger case. And almost every one mentioning us by name. Pretty good, eh?"

"I know," Louis said. "It just keeps rolling on."

To be sure, no previous Shildrick crusade—not even his succour of unnumbered motorists from incineration via their dashboard cigar-lighters—had raised his public profile to its current dizzy high. His being manifestly no Rolling Stones fan gave still greater weight to his indignation at the treatment of Mick Jagger and Keith Richard, and the awesome professional and personal risk he had been prepared to run, simply for the principles of justice and fair play. It was already a Fleet Street legend; how a still-damp first edition of "BAITED WITH THE RABBLE'S CURSE" had been messengered to the home of the Director of Public Prosecutions while Shildrick sat insouciantly sub-editing late athletics results with his jacket off, almost daring the hand of authority to descend on his unprotected shoulder.

But no such retribution was to come: not that night, nor next day when the Dispatch sold out its entire 1.7 million print-run, nor the following Monday after every other national (save only the Daily Telegraph) followed the Dispatch's lead in ignoring the sub judice law and concurring that the judge at Chichester Quarter Sessions had gone preposterously over the top. The concerted voices of Fleet Street—allied to mass demonstrations, marches and vigils by Rolling Stones supporters throughout the land—had brought immediate response from a Government keen to repair its dented popularity by any not too troublesome means. Within barely forty-eight hours had come an announcement from the Attorney General's office that Jagger and Richard would be released from prison on bail pending their appeal in the High Court.

Admittedly, such was the nature of the great moral stand, Shildrick's primary source and collaborator could receive no public share in its glory. But he was content. He had his reward. For whatever non-journalistic virtues. For two weeks, anyway.

"Telly's still going wild about it and all," Shildrick went on. "I've just had David Frost on the blower. He's doing the whole of this week's show on soft drugs, whether they should be legalised, whether the penalties are draconian, whether pop musicians bear any responsibilities for encouraging young kids to try them. I'm to be on with the Home Secretary . . . John Osborne . . . Paul McCartney . . . and the Archbishop of either Canterbury or York."

Hitching up one bullseye-striped trouser-leg, he perched on the edge of Lydia's desk and gave her one of his unaffected, boyish smiles. "I suppose you couldn't rustle us up a cup of char, could you, love?"

She struggled to her feet, blushing furiously. "Of course. I'll just have to wash out some cups . . ."

"Two sugars for me. And a nice chocolate suggestive wouldn't go amiss if you could find one." He waited for the door to close, then jerked his head at the adjoining office with its Habitat white. "You know who's next door, don't you, Poet?"

"Yes," Louis said.

"You don't mind, I hope?"

"Not at all," he lied.

"She's off in Jordan at the moment. Talking to King Hussein."

"Yes, so I heard. How's it going?"

"Very well, I gather. She sounded pretty chuffed in the cable I got last night. And The Cool Look is shaping up nicely, don't you think?"

Louis opened his mouth, then closed it again.

"I know, I know . . . there are still one or two few rough edges," Shildrick said. "It takes time for any new columnist to find their voice. Speaking of which, what's our locum Cicero planning for his maiden address to the Senate?"

"I'd like to do a piece on The Who. When it looked like Jagger and Richard were going to be inside for months, The Who took out a whole-page ad in the music papers to protest. And Pete Townshend, I believe, is quite a . . ." Louis's voice tailed off as he realised Shildrick had stopped listening.

"Aye, that's all right for down-page, but I'll tell you what'd make a belting lead. We're starting Sir Charles Small's memoirs on the Review Front this Sunday, and I've got the old sea-dog himself coming in on Thursday night to start the printing-run. Pidgy'll be there as well, so lots more humble-pie from the competition. A nice, amusing piece for Cicero, and as you've met the Smalls already, a pleasant reunion for you."

It was more than fifteen months since Louis had worked directly for Shildrick. Down on the Magazine, when you didn't want to do something, you had only to make noises of the most perfunctory regret.

"If you don't mind," he said with a Terry Bracegirdle–ish grimace,

"I'd really much rather do Pete Townshend. You'll get plenty of cover-age in other papers anyway. And I'd hate to start off my stint with something people will think is just an in-house puff."

Shildrick slid off the desk with an expression Louis had never seen before, certainly not in those dear old democratic days back in Stockton. The soulful face was suddenly freezing cold, the voice clipped almost to expressionlessness.

"I've told you what I want as your lead. Do it or get out."

---

The official party made their way gingerly down an iron stairway into the long, vaulted basement filled with giant machines in dull green housings, and peering, crawling, shouting men. After Shildrick's pin-striped and pink figure came Sir Charles and Lady Small, then three or four of the paper's advertising and promotions executives and finally two Royal Marine colour sergeants in cockaded red berets, one of them holding a large and luxurious wooden birdcage decorated with almost as many badges and as much gold leaf as its guardian's battledress. The climactic honour bestowed on Pidgy the pigeon had been to become the Marines' official mascot at their depot in Portsmouth. There he now lived a high-profile life of parades, royal inspections and visits by parties of schoolchildren from all over the world.

Sir Charles Small wore the baseball cap which symbolised his great voyage and, to a worldwide public, was now as instantly recognisable as Hopalong Cassidy's Stetson or Charlie Chaplin's bowler. Under its elongated brim, the nut-brown face had the benignly vague expression of one accustomed to perpetual limelight. His nautically cut blue suit was Savile Row–sleek, his striped tie clearly that of the most exclusive yacht club in the universe. But old shipboard habits died hard. Half-way down the staircase, for no perceptible reason, he stumbled, grabbed the rail for support and momentarily swung out underneath it, only prevented by the help of several hands from plunging onto the very press now being readied to print his reminiscences. There was a faint "Oh, lumme!," accompanied by an equally familiar basilisk glare from his lady.

Louis was standing beside the first machine in the line, in company with the Dispatch photographer who was to provide Cicero's main pic-ture. Nearby waited a gaggle of photographers from rival titles, the Mir-ror, the Express, the Mail and the Sun. There was not a Fleet Street picture editor who could resist another crack at the year's two great heroes, notwithstanding the Dispatch's sky-high syndication rates, ob-ligation to credit McIntyre Newspapers Ltd. in every caption and an embargo on publication until after Sunday, enforced by punitive legal action if need be.

Sir Charles reached the bottom of the stairs in safety and stood there like some docile trained animal, crinkling his eyes in that well-known misty, far-horizon look as camera-shutters buzzed and whizzed all around. Even the machine-minders and overseers, men as a rule notoriously lacking heart or soul, crowded round for a sight of the great circumnavigator. Louis hung back, assuming there was not the smallest chance the old sea-dog would remember him. But, to his amazement, he received a broad, gap-toothed smile and found his hand sought and gripped by a brown, horny one.

"I'm so sorry I never got a chance to thank you for that first article you did on me," the sea-dog shouted. "It was easily the best one of all. Got a real kick out of it, I did."

"Oh . . . thanks." With an effort he cast his mind back to that first-ever Sunday Dispatch assignment in the long ago of '66—Patrick Prince's Lotus Elan, Newman's Hard Marina, the numbing shock of his Magazine colleagues' duplicity and Shildrick's miraculous rescue with the Review Front.

"Re-read it most days while I was at sea," Sir Charles continued amid a fresh volley of Nikon-shutters. "Whenever I got a bit down-in-the-mouth, your lovely wordies always gave me a lift. Bunty didn't care much for the joke about the body of a thirty-year-old . . . but I must admit I laughed like a drain."

"I'm really glad to hear it."

"Only wish I could've had you to help me write these dam' memoirs. I did ask for you. The chap they sent really was a bit clueless . . ."

Louis stared at him. "You asked for me?"

"Too right! Same as I said I'd like you to be the one who met me at that rendezvous in the Azores. But both times Jack said you weren't available."

"Thank you now! This way," Shildrick interrupted, ushering his charge firmly away. "Did I tell you we're almost doubling the print-order for these next four weeks? And the TV ads go out at peak time on the Friday and Saturday nights before each episode—that's the plan, isn't it, Jeremy? I hope you're ready for literary fame, Sir Charles. Because we're going to make this the biggest publishing event since Churchill's *History of the English-Speaking Peoples* . . ."

A boiler-suited machine-hand fitted the last curved plate, foundry-cast from type and photographic blocks, onto the fifth and final press in the line. Other hands had almost finished feeding taut streamers of blank paper through successive pairs of rollers that would speed them from machine to machine, printing page after page of the Review section in the order that they'd be read, at the speed of a hurtling car.

Even in this troglodyte region, Shildrick knew everyone by name, from the Chief Overseer to the youngest apprentice. The very fact that such an event was permitted—the presses operated, however symbolically, by someone not in the fiercely demarcated and volatile print union—showed the exceptional regard in which he was held. He seemed as much in his element here as in the paper's cerebral power-house, proudly explaining the miracles of high-speed rotogravure to the Smalls, now and then sniffing the hot, inky air as blissfully as if it were ozone.

". . . You see those long strips of newsprint that look a bit like toilet-paper? They're what's called the web . . . Threading them through the rollers at the right tension is a highly skilled job . . . The worst thing that can happen, once the presses are running, is for the web to be broken. It can be caused by the smallest thing . . . even spitting on it . . ."

"Something I've always wondered," Sir Charles Small shouted, "is how you fold all the pages into a finished paper once they're printed."

Shildrick smiled indulgently. "On the folder."

"Oh, you have a special machine that folds them?"

"Yes, we do."

Sir Charles turned to his wife with a look of enchantment. "Isn't that interesting? They're got a special machine that folds them!"

Shildrick and the Chief Overseer together conducted him to the pale green console bearing the crucial large silver master-switch. Possibly bearing in mind his exploits afloat, the activation of this switch at a given signal, from up to down, was explained several times in exhaustive detail. But, the signal received and understood, Sir Charles brought off his task with unqualified success. A red light flashed on the console, an archaic Klaxon brayed and, with a low throb, very slowly at first, the streams of blank paper began moving through the serried rollers.

As the presses gathered speed, an entreating shout came from the group of outside photographers.

"Can we 'ave the bird out now?"

"Can we 'ave Pidgy out?"

Shildrick glanced at the two Marine sergeants, who had set Pidgy's cage down on the stone floor near the foot of the staircase, and were ostentatiously mounting guard at either side of it. "Sorry, lads. He belongs to the Marines now. And they've asked that he shouldn't be let out."

There was a wail of protest.

"Aw, come on! Just one on Charlie's shoulder!"

"Or eatin' out of his 'and. Like they did on the boat."

Shildrick shook his head regretfully. "I'm afraid it's not possible. They're terrified of anything happening to him . . . it was tricky enough even to borrow him for the day like this. Remember, this is a national celebrity. He's meeting Princess Margaret tomorrow . . . setting off on a goodwill tour of the Middle East by aircraft-carrier next week. So we can't take any chances. You're welcome to photograph him through the bars if you like. Or I think maybe our Red Beret friends there might even stretch a point and let Sir Charles hold up the cage."

Sir Charles himself, seasoned performer that he now was, listened with a look of disappointment rapidly shading to petulance. "Oh, come on, Jack," he protested. "One picture on my shoulder can't possibly hurt, can it? The creature knows me well enough, after all."

"I'm sorry. I gave a written promise to the Captain-General . . ."

"Oh, Charles, do stop making a fuss!" Lady Small interposed in a voice easily audible above the accelerating presses.

"I'm an old corvette man myself," Sir Charles remarked and, fired by this non-sequitur, with a swiftness and co-ordination seldom seen aboard *Lady Patricia*, he stooped and unlatched the frontal grille of the cage.

Even by the modest aesthetic standards of the kind, Pidgy was not a prepossessing bird. His plumage was dull battleship-grey, still ingrained with the dirt of City monuments where he had once congregated with 10,000 friends. A few streaks of black and white adorned his folded wings, a dab of iridescent green his ignoble head. His tail feathers in particular had an unpleasant, matted look as if, rather than just being indifferent to personal hygiene, he actively repudiated it.

Initially he seemed to show no alarm, merely walking forth with a wobbling, top-heavy gait and pecking with sublime pointlessness at the oily stone floor. All might have been well had not the larger of the Marine sergeants made a heavy-booted, maladroit lunge to recapture him. At this an appalled look came into Pidgy's candy-pink eye, and he lumbered into flight, landing on the sill of a wire-covered window, twenty feet above.

The ceremonial party gazed upward in horror, all excepting Lady Small, who favoured her spouse with a look that might have chilled the blood of Jack the Ripper. The outside photographers hurried forward, groping in canvas bags for longer-range lenses.

"Oh, lumme!"

For a moment Shildrick, too, looked as if he had no dearer wish than to hammer the sea-dog into the ground with a mallet. Then typical cool commandingness supervened. "Keep calm, everyone. This is a sealed room . . . and that window doesn't open. He can't possibly get out. Can I ask our guests from other papers to stand back? Please, lads! We don't want to get him more rattled than he already is."

The two Marine sergeants had advanced and were attempting to lure back the fugitive with entreating cries, whistles and clucks. But, against the roar of the presses, these could hardly be heard even at ground level. The distant grey profile gazed down at them with fathomless apathy. By some means little short of magical, white excrement was already splashed on the upper part of the wall.

"Maybe we should get some food!' the Chief Overseer shouted to Shildrick.

"Sorry?"

"I said, 'We should get some food!' That'll bring him down all right."

"He's very fond of crisps," the bigger sergeant said.

"It's worth a try." Shildrick plunged a hand into his trousers-pocket, brought out a handful of change and beckoned to Louis. "Poet . . . be a trouper. Run up to the Canteen and get us a couple of bags of crisps."

"What flavour?"

"Plain's what he likes best," the sergeant said. "He don't mind cheese and onion. Not smoky bacon . . ."

But at that moment, Pidgy tired of his eyrie and took flight again. His wings formed a grey arc that was almost graceful as he followed a trajectory apparently designed to end back at his open cage-door. Unfortunately, it took him close over the head of a machine-hand supervising the rush of the paper web through the first tumultuous rotary press. With a phobic wince, the man ducked and flailed both arms. Veering right, the grey crescent flew straight into the teeth of roaring rollers more lethal than any to be found off Cape Horn.

The sundered web produced another fifty or so Sunday Dispatch Review Fronts, headlined "PIDGY AND ME," and smeared with entrails and grey feathers, before a dozen wild voices and a frenzied Klaxon brought the machinery gradually to a stop.

# 28

Louis's novel was now making rapid strides. He had begun it with blithe disregard of almost all existing examples, fired only by the journalist's primal urge to get it "out"—i.e. typed—as soon as possible. An average novel chapter, he calculated, ran at around 6,000 words, slightly shorter than his profile of Elizabeth Taylor. He need produce only twelve Elizabeth Taylors, or twenty-four Oedipus Darlings or thirty-two Pincher Bassills, and there would be a book.

He worked on it for five or six hours each day, using the unlimited free time—and free stationery—of McIntyre House, topped and tailed by an early-morning and an evening session in his new bed-sitting room. Further to speed the task, he had bought a second-hand Smith-Corona electric typewriter whose keys pressed effortlessly and with a faint "puff" like the percussion cap of a flintlock musket. On good days, he could produce fifteen to twenty finished pages, which usually meant fifty to sixty rejected ones drifting around his feet. He'd become so fastidious a typist with the Sunday Dispatch's superfine white cartridge paper that a single smudged letter made him wrench out the sheet and start another.

He told no one what he was doing, other than Margaret Cole, who directed him to her own special, surprising passion, D. H. Lawrence, and David Kausman, who commented that it was about bloody time. Although Kausman himself had never written a novel, he seemed to have discussed its theory and problems with most of the modern masters. "F. Scott Fitzgerald used to say it was like swimming underwater ... Kingsley Amis says you should always break off half-way through a sentence. Then when you take it up again, you know exactly where you are ... Elizabeth Bowen always compares it to reclaiming an overgrown garden. For the first hundred pages, you're hacking away brambles. Then you can settle down to enjoy laying the paths and planting flower-beds."

What you mainly had to do was not do other things, and in this Louis found little hardship. Ceasing to share the flat with Brenda Brown had brought a natural end to the carousing among old school-friends which up to now had been the main obstacle to serious literary endeavour. Apart from bistro meals alone, he found he seldom went out at night any more, and often carried on typing through the whole of Saturday and Sunday. In this wood-panelled ground-floor hermitage, the root-less, under-educated reporter could become what he'd always hank-ered to be: a stay-at-home and a "swot."

His pleasantest working hours were late at night, from 10 to 1:30 or even later, seated at the big carved desk in a blossom-scented breeze from the open French windows, with Radio City, "the Tower of Power," playing softly on his stained and trusty old Philips "3-Transistor." Ink-erman Terrace had no pubs to create disruptive noise or music, and at that hour there were few passing cars or even pedestrians. The only sound was an occasional murmur of voices from the adjoining room— an even more unusual apartment than Louis's, long and half-timbered like an old-fashioned teashop—where two tight-trousered older men carried on a domestic life of muffled tempestuousness. Now and again, the door would open and a choking sob be heard as the swarthier and more muscular of his two neighbours enacted a regular *Wuthering Heights*–ish pantomime of rushing wildly forth into the night.

Such was the musket-volleying impetus he'd built up on the Smith-Corona that even deputising as Cicero did not seriously hinder his work schedule. That Friday, the day after Pidgy's death, he wrote the last of the column's 2,000-odd words, had dinner at the Lee Yuan in Earl's Court Road, then returned to 8 Inkerman Terrace to make a start on Chapter 6. This was to relate, in lightly fictionalised form, how his fa-ther had once tried to entice customers into Seaview Pier Pavilion by blowing forth the scent of fresh-percolated coffee with giant electric fans.

Around midnight he was just starting to feel hungry again when a peal came from the coinbox telephone at the end of the hall. With a dis-tracted sigh, balancing a half-finished sentence on his tongue, he stumped out in stockinged feet and snatched up the receiver. "Hello. Flaxman 2179."

"Poet, it's me. Have I woken you up?"

"No, it's OK," he said with a sinking heart. Surely to God his Cicero page wasn't to be tampered with yet again.

"I'm sorry to bother you so late." Shildrick's voice was strained and distracted, as though speaking from a mainline station with his train about to depart. "I wouldn't do if there was anybody else I could turn to . . . Fran got back from Amman this evening, and she's not well. In fact she's been taken quite ill."

The half-finished sentence was wiped from Louis's mind. "Taken ill? What with?"

"With what," Shildrick corrected instinctively. "It's her tummy . . . she's got these terrible griping pains. I hate to ask, but do you think you could come over? I'm really up a gum-tree here."

"Of course. I'll jump in a taxi now."

"You don't mind?"

"No, of course not."

"Oh, thanks, Poet. I can't tell you how I'd appreciate it. You know where the flat is, don't you?"

"Yes, I do."

He was there in less than twenty minutes. Though the front door stood ajar, he scrupulously pressed the "Top Flat" entryphone button. "Hello," said a voice, in its defensive neutrality hardly recognisable as Shildrick's.

"It's Louis."

"By, that was quick!" the voice said with something more like its normal tone. "From now on I shall call you the instant Englishman."

Louis ran up the five shabby flights as heedlessly as an athlete at the peak of training. The top banister-rail, he was surprised to see, still had dresses and coats all along it like cast-offs put out for a rummage sale. Shildrick was waiting for him at the top of the final flight, wearing an almost non-trendy dark blue suit, a pale blue shirt with a conventional collar and a tie more herring- than kipper-shaped. "Thank the Lord you're here, Poet," he said, glancing at his watch. "I've been almost going spare."

"Where is she?"

"In the bedroom . . . I can only think it's some bug she's picked up out there . . . First thing tomorrow morning I'm complaining most vigorously to the Jordanian Embassy . . ."

Fran was kneeling in the centre of the bed, both hands pressed to her stomach, honey-frost hair dangling forward over her face. She wore only a turquoise ruffle-fronted blouse and a pair of panties, familiarly off-white. The posture of doubled-up agony contrasted oddly with her rich suntan. Louis tried to avert his eyes from the rest of the room, as his thoughts from what now must happen here. But he couldn't help noticing that her bedside locker looked as unspeakable a mess as ever. On the wardrobe's open plywood door, with anomalous neatness, was a wire coat-hanger bearing Shildrick's new green voile shirt and butcher-striped hipsters.

He went over to her and gently touched her shoulder. She pushed a strand of hair aside and looked up with that familiar resigned wince.

"How are you feeling?"

"My tummy hurts," she said dully.

Shildrick took his elbow and drew him to one side. "I'm afraid I've got to go, Poet . . . I'm already hours late at home. Could I leave her in your very capable and caring hands?"

Louis glanced from the background figure on the bed to the foreground figure whose incorrigible need to be somewhere else at maximum velocity for the first time seemed less than flattering. Into his mind came a vision of a gloomy front hall in Hampstead, and a lurking figure with hair in curlers and rolling-pin at the ready. Despite the seriousness of the situation, he felt his mouth involuntarily twitch.

"It's all right, everything's arranged." Shildrick handed him a scrap of paper with a name and address scribbled on it. "This is a doctor we used as a consultant on the unsafe Pill story . . . very helpful chap, with consulting rooms at the best end of Harley Street. I've contacted him and he'll see her, even though he's got to drive in all the way from St. Albans. If you'd just be so kind as to take her and bring her back."

"OK," Louis said.

"Tell him to send the bill to me, of course. Care of the Dispatch." Shildrick went over to Fran and gave her what seemed no more than a friendly pat on the shoulder. "I must get off now, love. You understand, don't you?"

She nodded with a grimace that did not seem born entirely of abdominal discomfort.

"Our chivalrous friend here will take you and fetch you home. I'll ring you first chance I get tomorrow, all right?"

"All right. 'Bye."

"Oh, and, Poet . . . could I stress? The bill's to come to me at the Dispatch. It mustn't be sent to my home, for obvious reasons. You will make that very clear, won't you?"

"Yes, all right," Louis said almost impatiently—amazing himself that he could feel almost impatient with Shildrick.

The rapid descending footsteps died away and the front door distantly slammed. Louis sat down next to Fran, trying to notice as little of the bed as possible. "Feeling any better?" he asked.

She nodded, biting her lower lip.

"Shall we try and get to this quack then?"

He helped her into her white bell-bottoms—a process somehow more moving than helping her out of them ever had been—then fetched her black corduroy cloak from the banister-rail. "Is your Mini outside?" he asked, draping the cloak round her shoulders.

"Yes. If it hasn't been nicked."

"OK, we'll take that."

They slowly negotiated the five flights, Fran resting in the crook of his arm as if she were built to fit there. She still had the same limey perfume, overlaid with something muskily erotic. He thought it a pity the shabby stairs didn't carry right on to the centre of the Earth.

On the car journey she huddled in the cloak, rested her head against the passenger window and seemed to nod off. Now and then, Louis glanced at her face, lit by passing shop windows and red traffic-lights.

Thanks to a wrong turning in Marylebone, it was almost one by the time they reached Harley Street. Even so, a surprising number of lights still burned along the Georgian façades. They parked right outside the number Shildrick had given, and Fran was able to walk unaided up the steps to its broad front door. Louis found the appropriate brass plate and pressed the entryphone button next to it. After a moment, a crackly voice said, "Yes?"

"Dr. Porteous? I've brought Miss Dyson."

"For Jack Shildrick?"

"That's right."

"Please come in, go to the end of the corridor and take the lift to the third floor."

The door buzzed open and they entered a dark hallway, floored with checkered black and white. At the end was a modern lift, barely large enough for two people. Louis pressed the button and turned to Fran with a reassuring smile. "By the way, how was Jordan?"

"Fine," she said.

"And King Hussein?"

"Difficult."

The doors slid open and they stepped out into a twilit passage, opposite a door with a brass plate on it. This, however, proved to be firmly locked. As Louis was vainly twisting its white china handle, a door further down on the other side opened and a man's head looked out. "Yes? May I help you?" he asked in a voice that seemed oddly familiar.

"We're looking for Dr. Porteous's office."

"Porteous?" the man repeated, mystified, then his face cleared. It was a large face, with dark-shadowed cheeks that obviously could sprout into beard with the smallest encouragement. His hair was unnaturally long for a medical man, curling not far above the collar of a wrinkled beige cotton jacket. On his ample shirt-front, instead of a tie dangled a necklace of astrological signs. Through the doorway behind him could be seen an array of glass tubes, retorts and Bunsen burners. Evidently he was one of the dedicated band whose scientific experiments took no account of time.

"Ah, I think you want the third floor. This is the second floor."

The door closed again, and Louis stared at its pale green Georgian panels in stupefaction as he recognized that burly figure, albeit no longer kaftaned; that zodiacal necklace; above all, that cosy, persuasive voice. At long last, much too late to benefit anyone, he had tracked down Doctor Daydream.

———

"Did you know you had a grumbling appendix?"

Fran shook her head. He pushed the end of her cloak inside, shut her door, then walked round and slid behind the wheel.

"It sounds almost friendly, doesn't it? But you heard what he said. You'd better get it seen to."

She pulled the cloak around her with a shiver. The black centipede eyes stared bleakly as if contemplating the appendectomy operation which Dr. Porteous had said would have to happen sooner or later.

"Hey, come on, cheer up!" Louis said heartily, poking in the ignition key. "I believe there's very little to it these days. And at least you haven't copped some ghastly Middle Eastern lergy."

Before he could release the handbrake, Fran toppled sideways against him and began to sob with a quiet, coughing sound.

He put his arm round her shoulders—just to support her, he told himself firmly, trying not to notice the way her hair parted in shining streams from the nape of her neck.

"Hey . . . come on. What is it? You're not scared of a silly little op?"

"It's not that!" she mumbled almost testily.

Before he could stop them, his lips nuzzled the back-combed golden crown. "What, then?"

"You're so nice to me."

"Yes, I know. It's so-o difficult."

"You're the only decent one . . ."

"Am I? Oh, dear, what a bring-down." His lips were drawn to the top of her head again as though magnetised. "Do you want me to ring Jack and tell him it's nothing serious?"

"I shouldn't bother," she said in her dullest voice.

"But he'll obviously be worried about you."

He felt her stiffen against his arm. "Oh, yes, you saw tonight who he was 'worried' about. Directly you arrived, he was out of the door like a frightened rabbit."

This same not very original simile had already occurred to Louis, but defending Shildrick was almost a reflex. "Don't be too hard on him. He's got a hell of a lot on his plate at the moment. You heard about the pigeon, I suppose?"

"Yes," Fran said with a sniff.

"A national hero . . . killed by The Sunday Dispatch's printing press. All the dailies have had a field day with it, there have been questions in Parliament, the R.S.P.C.A.'s threatening a full-scale inquiry. Shildrick being investigated! You can imagine how that goes against the grain."

"Yes."

"And . . . he is a married man."

This last line was a bad miscalculation. Fran struggled up from his shoulder and turned to him. "My God, do you think I don't know that? Have you any idea what it means, being the Editor's little bit of fluff?"

Louis thought he had a pretty good idea. It meant photo-bylines, a column in the new Trend section, an office furnished by Habitat, over-seas assignments that really should be the Diplomatic Editor's. But the black centipede eyes had an affronted, almost ravaged look—though, oddly, not a single tear shone in them.

"I guess you have to be pretty careful . . ."

"Careful!" She laughed bitterly. "It's like living under the Gestapo! We can't go anywhere we might be seen . . . we can't even walk down the street together. I'm kept holed up in that flat like a little tart . . . waiting till he can make an excuse to sneak off and see me . . . counting the minutes till it's time to go back to the wife and kiddywinks."

She fumbled in her shoulder-bag and took out a packet of Peter Stuyvesant. Louis lit it for her with her latest French disposable lighter, a jade-green one. She nodded thanks and offered the pack to him; she never had been able to remember he didn't smoke cigarettes.

"Shall I tell you the most depressing part?" she continued, sounding a little less depressed. "It's never being able to give him anything."

"What . . . you mean like presents?"

She nodded. "That wife of his knows every last thing he's got. If he came home with a new tie or pair of cufflinks or even a hankie, she'd be onto it. I can't write to him in case she intercepts the letter. I can't even give him a passport photo of me for his wallet in case she finds it. Shall I tell you the only thing he's let me give him?"

"OK."

"Guess."

"An earring."

"No."

"A pen?"

"No."

"A button."

"No."

"I give up."

"One of my pubic hairs," Fran said.

Louis felt the corners of his mouth begin to twitch and strain. "Tricky thing to carry around," he commented.

For an instant she glared wildly at him, then her pale lips also began to tremble.

"I mean . . ." he continued, "I don't think Asprey's do leather cases for them yet."

"Shut up," she said, making as if to hit him on the forearm.

"But it's true that some relationships are hair today, gone tomorrow . . ."

They both burst into giggles. Fran's head sank back onto his shoulder, and she gave a wistful sigh. "God! It's so long since I had a really good laugh."

His lips shaped another helpless, covert kiss. "Shall I tell you what's always puzzled me?"

"What?"

"Why Jack's so willing to trust me with you. I mean like this . . . late at night."

The black centipedes flickered upward. "He thinks you're safe."

"What, like your big brother?"

"No, not in that way."

"What way then?"

"He thinks you're a woofter."

Louis leaned away and stared down at her.

"A what?"

"A woofter. A homo. A cream bun."

The charge was so absurd, so utterly opposite to all that had ever got him into hot water, so inconsistent with the most casual study of his habits and behaviour, he could only open and shut his mouth like a stranded guppy.

"Jack thinks that?" he managed at length.

"Yes."

"How . . . on what grounds?"

"Oh, various things . . . your clothes . . . the length of your hair . . . the fact that you lived with a bloke called Brenda . . ."

"He's actually said it to you, has he?"

"Oh, yes."

"When?"

"When I first told him I'd been out with you. 'Oh, no trouble there,' he said. 'Bit of a woofter on the quiet, that lad.' "

As a mimic she had no skill whatever. But, little as he wanted to believe it, and despite Fran's less than perfect record as a reporter, the quote had a horrible ring of authenticity.

"And your being on the Magazine has probably got something to do with it," she added. "He's always going on about 'Toby Godwin's nest of bloody woofters' and how he's going to fix you all one day."

———

Private Eye's lunches did not take place in surroundings of ostentatious glamour. The Coach and Horses proved to be a nondescript pub at the Shaftesbury Avenue end of Greek Street, a few doors away from Mario and Franco's Terrazza restaurant. Upon showing his invitation card from Lord Gnome, Louis was beckoned behind the bar counter and directed up a staircase edged in grey rubber, stacked with beer- and mineral-crates and rich with odours familiar from his early childhood.

On the first floor was a bare-boarded room with every window flung wide open on Soho's sun-drenched, sleazy bustle. A table with a red-and-white-checked cloth was laid with smallish crescents of melon and half a dozen bottles of gaudily labelled red wine. At the inner end, Peter Cook was smoking heavily and talking to Antony Crosland, the Minister of Education, and Barry Fantoni, the cartoonist. Beside a shabby mantelpiece stood John Wells, composer of Mrs. Wilson's Diary, Paul Foot, author of the Footnotes investigative column, and Arden Sinclair, the publisher, whose bog-brush hair was scattered with dewdrops of sweat. He gave Louis the smile which by rights should have had a tusk sticking up at either side of it.

"Hi, sweetie. Welcome to this convocation of London's dirtiest minds. Let me pour you a teeny-weeny tincture." He picked up a bottle from the closed lid of an upright piano and glanced at its label, knitting his satyr's eyebrows. "Ah, yes, charming little vineyard . . . know it well. Wonderful south-facing slopes in the most picturesque part of Acton."

Beside him stood a man of about thirty, with a pitted and flaking complexion, dressed like an impoverished schoolmaster. "Can I introduce the Editor of the Eye?" Sinclair said. "Louis Brennan . . . Richard Ingrams. Or Big Dick, as he's known on the magazine."

"Hullo, Cicero," Ingrams said in a nasal, parsonical voice.

"Yes, I liked your page on Sunday," Sinclair said, "especially the piece on The Who."

"The who?" Ingrams queried.

"The Who. Popular music group. Don't pretend you haven't heard of them, Big Dick."

"The only popular music group I know of are Spiggy Topes and the Turds."

As the company sought their name-cards round the table, a heavier-than-usual footfall sounded on the stairs. William Rushton entered, wearing a humorously unsummery tweed cap and Norfolk jacket and brandishing a midday edition of the Evening News. "Blessings on you all, my children," he boomed. "And glad tidings of great joy. Spiggy has got off!"

Paul Foot grabbed the paper and glanced through its screaming front-page lead. " 'Mick Jagger and Keith Richard have had their prison sentences quashed by the Lord Chief Justice,' " he read. " 'Both Richard's conviction and sentence have been overturned on the grounds of errors in the trial Judge's summing-up. Jagger's conviction was upheld, but the sentence was quashed in favour of a one-year conditional discharge.' "

Louis was placed with Barry Fantoni on his left, John Wells on his right, with the Minister of Education beyond and Arden Sinclair directly opposite. "You were there when they were busted, weren't you?" asked Fantoni.

"Yes, I was."

"So you can answer the question that's racked the whole nation. Did Inspector Knacker really find Spiggy licking a Mars bar pushed up Marijuana Faithfull?"

"No," Louis said.

"So were they really not engaged in nameless bacchanalian couplings?" Rushton said.

"No, they were watching children's television."

"Hear that, Big Dick? We'll have to kill our coverline."

"What coverline?"

" 'A Mars bar fills that gap.' "

The entrée was fatty steak, chips and peas, served with only marginal good grace by the pub's Irish barman. There was a babel of funny voices, Cook's E. L. Wisty vying with Wells's outraged archdeacon and Rushton's (admittedly rather outdated) Harold Macmillan, and names from Private Eye's inimitable bestiary—"Wilson," "The Grocer," Baillie Vass, Eric Buttock, Knacker of the Yard, Barry McKenzie, E. I. Addio. When the joke was against the Prime Minister or another member of his administration, none laughed with more abandon nor offered a follow-up jibe with more alacrity than the rubicund and tallow-haired Minister of Education. Louis waited for a chance to say something witty himself, but it was like trying to jump aboard a line of fast-moving boxcars. By the time he'd got his funny line ready, the opening had accelerated out of reach.

He realised that Arden Sinclair was asking him something across the table.

"Sorry?"

"I said, 'I suppose you haven't started that novel yet?' "

"As a matter of fact I'm half-way through chapter seven."

The publisher clasped his cloven hooves together. "I burn to read it. When may I?"

"Not until I'm quite sure it isn't just a load of old rubbish. I'm trying out the first three chapters on David Kausman first."

At the name Kausman, John Wells turned round with interest. "Where is David these days? Lucian Freud was saying in the French last night that he hadn't seen him for weeks."

"I heard he was in Leningrad," the Minister of Education said.

"Leningrad? Why?"

"Some kind of extraordinary commission from the Russian Government to rehang all the French Impressionists in the Hermitage."

"I thought he was supposed to be in analysis," Barry Fantoni said.

"No, he's given that up," said Wells. "He decided he couldn't continue when his analyst turned up wearing brown shoes with a blue suit."

A large cardboard square with a protective sheet of tissue paper was handed along the table to Arden Sinclair. "Pathetic infantile smut," he commented approvingly, passing it over to Louis. A cartoon in Rushton's familiar scratchy style, it showed George Brown seated on top of a lavatory cistern, his trousers around his ankles. A moustachioed Civil Servant type was looking round the door and saying, "Still haven't quite got the hang of it, have we, Foreign Secretary?" Louis passed it on to the Minister of Education, who laughed so much he succumbed to a fit of coughing and had to be plied with Perrier water.

At the end of the table Richard Ingrams, Rushton and Peter Cook were now sifting through recent news pictures of the great and the good and discussing what rude things could be shown issuing in bubbles from their mouths as a cover for the next issue. Ingrams held up an agency print of the Queen and the Duke of Edinburgh being greeted by an Asiatic dignitary in Nehru cap and white trousers. "Brenda and Phil the Greek on State visit to Nepal. Anyone?"

"Mount Everest's in Nepal, isn't it?" Rushton asked.

"People often ask me why I married Her Majesty the Queen," John Wells said with deadpan solemnity. "But all I can ever say is 'Because she was There.' "

"This is the one we should go for," Fantoni said. It was the most widely-reproduced image of two national heroes in happier times. On the left stood Sir Charles Small, in baseball cap and blazer, with Pidgy arranged Long John Silver–style on his shoulder. Beside him, with a smile rather blatantly proprietorial, stood Jack Shildrick.

"Poor Pidgy," Peter Cook said in the droning accent of E. L. Wisty. "And only next week he was due to take his seat in the House of Lords . . ."

"Got it!" Rushton boomed. "Singapore Charlie is saying, 'This little bird really has got guts.' And Mighty Jack's saying, 'I know. They're spread over half the first edition.' "

"Is that really the only feathered friend he's ever been mixed up with?" Ingrams asked amid the guffaws.

"Who?" Sinclair asked.

"Mighty Jack Shildrick. I mean, is there nothing we can tease him about, other than having procured the death of Britain's favourite shite-hawk?"

"You mean of the leg-over variety," Fantoni said.

"Precisely so."

"Nay, nay, lad, not Mighty Jack," John Wells protested, shaking his head. "Everyone knows he's always preferred a nice strong coop of tea to anything saucy."

"I'm not so sure he has the boringly blameless private life he's supposed to," Ingrams said. "Word has it around the Street of Shame that he's got a bit of crackling stashed away somewhere."

Every face at the table turned to Louis. "How about it, Cicero?" said Barry Fantoni. "Is your boss in a leg-over situation?"

"Cicero's rather a friend of his, I believe," Arden Sinclair put in with a malicious, tusky smile. "Weren't you together on the Muck-shire Journal or something oop north?"

"The Stockton Evening Telegraph." Not much of a witty line, he inwardly admitted to himself.

"Well, as another northern lad, you moost know. Is Mighty Jack really the little saint he cracks himself oop to be? Or is there a filly in the paddock?"

An expectant silence had fallen. Through the open windows Louis could hear distant Beatles music, mingled with unalluring invitations to "live shows" in Greek Street below. Woolly with wine as he was, he knew he should stop it here, change the subject, make a deflecting joke, say nothing at all, be thought poor value and struck off Lord Gnome's future guest list—anything but tumble into the trap yawning at his feet.

Then, with the high-speed clarity of semi-drunkenness, he realised three things all at once. First, even though some, himself included, might call her a dishonest, secretive and exploitative bitch, he was in

love with Fran, really and truly. Second, he was tired of helping someone else be in love with her. And third, almost more than he could express, he resented being called a "woofter."

Therefore, instead of buttoning, zipping and padlocking his lips and
then holding them shut with both hands to make sure, he sipped from
his glass, shook his head and gave an exaggerated sigh. "What are you
trying to do? Get me sacked?"

"Aha!" Ingrams said in triumph. "I knew it!"

"So tell us," Rushton urged. "Who's the lucky lass? His secretary?"

"I can say a definite no to that."

"Is it that red-headed girl in the Close-up team?" Fantoni asked.

"No in italics."

"Is it your Fashion Editor, what's her name? Jessamyn?"

"No in italics and underlined twice."

"Give us a clue," John Wells pleaded. "Just the tiniest little clue-let."

He opened his mouth and the company craned forward: London's
most celebrated wits—not to mention the Minister of Education—
hanging on his every word. It was irresistible.

"All I will say is . . . if I were you I'd take a Cool Look at the whole
subject."

## 29

The perils of being too clever had first been brought home to Louis when he was six years old. A group of his nursery-school coevals, male and female, were seated on a sports field making daisy chains, blowing fluff from dandelion clocks, shining buttercups against each other's throats and discussing what original and surprising things might be done with the silver-green burrs that floated from the hedge. Out of nowhere he had conceived a brilliant elaboration on Roger Sim's "I'd put one on my arm" and Clair Thomas's "I'd put one on my head."

"I'd put one up my nose," he said. "Then it'd be able to dance with all the bogeys."

He still remembered his companions' almost demented shriek of laughter and his own triumphant blush, quickly chilling to dismay as he realised just how far he had exceeded all permissible joke-telling limits—that so revolutionary a witticism could not possibly be contained within this small group, but was destined to ricochet through the entire school and in doing so inevitably reach the scandalised ears of authority. He remembered how desperately he'd wished words could be grabbed from the air and stuffed back into one's mouth; how for a time he'd deluded himself with the hope that everyone might forget all about it and life go on as before . . . And then opening his eyes in dread, knowing that if retribution was to come it would come this morning.

With exactly that same sensation, fifteen years on, the grown-up Louis lay contemplating his bed-sitting room ceiling on Private Eye's next publication day. Through the panelled wall, his two neighbours were already up and murmuring to each other in low, hysterical tones. He rolled over, covered his head with the pillow and attempted to reassure himself as he'd been doing with indifferent success for the past week and a half. After all, he'd done nothing but drop a tiny hint—so tiny, indeed, it had been lost on most of his fellow lunchers until Paul Foot reminded them The Cool Look was "a pisspoor column in that pisspoor new Trend section." To his relief, the conversation quickly moved on to some trouble Tom Driberg M.P. had recently had in a gentlemen's lavatory. He only wished he hadn't seen Richard Ingrams give a satisfied smirk and jot a note on the pad beside his plate.

The newsvendor outside Gloucester Road tube station had not yet received his consignment of Private Eye and the bookstall, being W. H. Smith's, refused to stock it. To make matters worse, someone in Louis's train compartment was already sniggering over a copy. Peering from his strap, he saw that on the orange-bordered cover at least Shildrick had been spared. After all they'd used the Queen in Nepal, with Prince Philip saying John Wells's words and a second, indecipherable balloon issuing from the mouth of the Asiatic dignitary.

In the tobacconist–cum–dirty bookshop a block from McIntyre House, he finally laid hands on a copy—almost the last one, he noticed, in what was usually a substantial pile. Breathless with foreboding, he opened it and flicked past Lord Gnome's editorial and the sarcastically-headed "Colour Section" to the page chronicling scandals, bungles and idiocies among the celebrities of Fleet Street.

For the first time the feature bore a formal heading, "STREET OF SHAME." Its lead item, in the minute black print only one step above typewriting, read:

> Pampered hacks at Lord Muckintyre's Sunday Dispatch are puzzling over the rapid rise of busty blond hackette Fran Dixon to star status on the moneyspinning rag. Despite a lack of talent little short of spectacular, it has taken "The New Girl Around the Dispatch" [sic] barely three months to progress from Agricultural Correspondent to foreign troubleshooter, featured columnist on the ludicrous Trend section and, latterly, interviewer of world figures like King Hussein of Jordan (who was reportedly so incensed by the crassness of the hackette's questions that he has lodged a formal complaint via his Ministry of Information to the Foreign Office).
>
> For all her journalistic shortcomings, La Dixon has gained the ear of the Dispatch's diminutive Northern whizzkid Editor, "Mighty" Jack Shildrick, on whose orders she is being relentlessly promoted as the paper's next hot property after Sir Charles ("Oops, sorry, Your Majesty!") Small and Pidgy (RIP). Even loyal Shildrick henchmen like Managing Editor Nick "The Prick" Fenton have lately been heard to wonder how their tiny chief, an alleged champion of newspaper craft, can favour a writer whose copy is so bad, in one insider's words, "it has to be subbed before the subs will deal with it."

The answer, of course, is that Mighty Jack's ear is not the only organ over which the pouting hackette now enjoys influence. His wife, Joan, and four children may be intrigued to learn that he and La Dixon have become such close colleagues that he has rented her a luxury pad near the West London Air Terminal, and frequently calls there, no doubt to hold editorial discussions of a confidential nature.

In the Magazine concourse, even such work as would normally be happening at 10:45 had been suspended in favour of rapturous Private Eye–reading. Margaret had a copy propped on her typewriter, with Jessamyn O'Shaughnessy grinning down at it over her shoulder. Even Cedric Scurr, that devout non–words man, was poring over one beyond his glass screen. From Toby Godwin's office, where Bracegirdle and Deaves could be seen lounging with beatific smiles, came a prolonged and uproarious "Hooh hooh hooh hooh hooh hooh!"

"It was always obvious to me she must be knocking someone off," Freya Broadbent commented, "but I always assumed it was just one of the section editors."

"This girl aims high," Margaret said.

"I told you all, didn't I, but you wouldn't believe me!" Jessamyn exulted. "She must have been the one he was with that day in the Mini-Cooper. I ought to have recognised the legs."

Mrs. Broadbent spread the small, neat hand whose nails she had been leisurely painting purple. "What I can't understand is why no one on the Steam Section realised what was going on right under their noses."

"Maybe they all did, but just kept quiet about it," said Margaret.

"What . . . like with Edward the Eighth and Mrs. Simpson?"

"Why not? Shildrick is quite popular up there, you know."

"So who do you think can possibly have let it out?" Mrs. Broadbent asked.

"Someone who hates his guts, obviously."

"What about James Way?"

"No . . . Jamie's too much of a pukka gent for anything like that. More likely it was someone Miss Charcoal-Eyes has been allowed to pre-empt. Like Deirdre Rees-Millington, the Fashion Editor."

"Or Marcus Forman, the Chief Reporter . . ."

"Or Ed Roper, the Diplomatic Editor . . ."

Margaret glanced across at Louis, who had assumed the pious look of one above trivial sexual gossip and was rolling a sheet of paper into his typewriter.

"Hey, young Brennan . . . didn't you say you were going to a Private Eye lunch with your Cicero hat on?"

He affected to search deep within the recesses of memory. "Oh . . . yes. It was pretty boring actually."

"Didn't they say anything about this?" Jessamyn demanded.

"What?"

"Don't act dumb! About Holier-Than-Thou Mighty Jack being a big dipper on the sly."

"No. I don't think so."

He sat in a trance of guilt and remorse, typing one gibberish sentence after another, as the revelation continued to be savoured, discussed on telephones, shared with visiting photographers, illustrators, photographic stylists and fashion models. It was not long before Jessamyn O'Shaughnessy, the self-appointed bloodhound-in-chief—displaying an industry and application seldom devoted to her fashion copy—emerged from her office with the follow-up.

"You'll never guess how she nabbed him! I've just heard it from my friend Liz Goldsworthy on Business News. Apparently Shildrick's got some sort of private bathroom that no one's supposed to know about. Late one Saturday night, he pops in for a wash and brush-up, and who do you think he finds sitting in his bath?"

"My golly!" Freya Broadbent said. "You have to give it to her. The girl's certainly got bags of nerve."

"Can't you just see it?" Margaret said. "That woebegone expression of hers . . ."

"And those pretty little tits!"

"Which he objected to so violently when they were on our New Eve cover," Mrs. Broadbent put in.

"And and and and and," Louis typed resolutely. "And and and and but but but but but but but 123456789@%!?*."

Not until past midday did his telephone give the expected, heart-sinking buzz. "Editor's secretary here," Enid's brisk voice said. "Mr. Shildrick says could you come up in about fifteen minutes?"

He realised it might be advisable to make what plans he could for imminent unemployment. "Do you know if David Kausman will be around today?" he asked Freya Broadbent.

"No, he rang in this morning and left a message. He's going to be lecturing at the Courtauld Institute all this week."

"He didn't mention my novel, did he?"

"No. Should he have?"

"I left him the first three chapters to look through, days ago. I just thought he'd have responded by now."

"If I were you I'd send them straight to a good literary agent," Mrs. Broadbent suggested. "Graham Watson at Curtis Brown. Or Michael Sissons at A. D. Peters."

"What's the point?" Louis said dully. "If Kausman doesn't like them, they're obviously dross."

Margaret had been talking on her phone for some minutes in the low, calming voice she reserved for the printers when pages were behind schedule or contributors whose copy had been cut. But as the conversation proceeded, even her formidable cool seemed to waver. "Are you sure?" she said a number of times, and "Oh dear" an even greater number of times. Mostly, she listened to what was evidently an impassioned monologue. "Well, I'm extremely sorry," she said at length. "Perhaps I could . . . Yes, I'm sure you're very upset . . . Yes, I can imagine . . . If I can just take your name and address, I'll pass that information to the relevant person."

She hung up and sat back, blowing out her cheeks. "Mags!" Mrs. Broadbent said in concern. "Whatever's wrong? Who was that?"

"A reader."

"Complaining about something?"

"One might say so. You know the home-improvement feature we ran on Sunday? The one that was meant to be a sop to Jack Shildrick?"

"Yes. I must say that, boring or not, Cedric made it look absolutely marvellous."

"I thought so, too. Especially that double-page spread on how to build a conservatory extension to your house. The only problem is, our directions apparently included the knocking down of the retaining wall."

"What? The main structural support?"

Margaret nodded. "Like an obedient Sunday Dispatch Magazine reader, this man did exactly what we said. And now two-thirds of his house has collapsed."

---

Shildrick was perched on his window-ledge, gazing out at his matchless view of St. Paul's and the City. " 'Ullo, Poet," he said quietly, scarcely bothering to turn round. In contrast with the furl and swagger of the awful green voile shirt, he looked tired, dispirited—and something else Louis had never thought him before. The word, no getting around it, was "little."

The penitent advanced on leaden feet and stood before the wide white desk with its ever-burning Anglepoise lamp. On the usual heap of copy, proofs and reference books lay a Private Eye, open at the relevant page.

"Atrociously written, isn't it?" Shildrick remarked in the same neutral undertone. "I hate this modern trick of tacking adjectives in front of nouns without a definite article. And why do people think that saying 'intrigued' rather than 'interested' adds some kind of ironic literary flourish?"

He picked up the Eye, glanced through it apathetically and let it fall again.

"Every other fact wrong, as usual. Don't they ever check anything? Her surname's not 'Dixon.' She was never Agricultural Correspondent. I've not bought her a pad . . . she had it ages beforehand. And it's not 'just behind the West London Air Terminal,' it's about a quarter of a mile from it."

A confusion of questions, not all strictly germane, jostled in Louis's mind. Was Shildrick deliberately delaying the moment of confronting him with his treachery, or giving him the chance to own up to it like a man? Why was it bad style to say "intrigued" rather than "interested"? Had the manifold activities at this desk ever included the covert removal from a wallet, nostalgic contemplation—possibly even surreptitious sniffing—of a treasured single feminine pubic hair?

". . . And vicious, too, all this about the King Hussein piece. There were no complaints about her questions. In fact, His Majesty's let us know via his embassy how pleased he was with the interview."

Louis took a breath, as if diving from the topmost board. "Jack, I . . ."

Shildrick's sultry eyes settled on him, filled with such sadness and disillusionment that he could cheerfully have gone downstairs and followed Pidgy the pigeon straight into the rollers of the rotary press.

"You don't have to say anything, Poet. I know it was nothing to do with you. You've been a wonderful, discreet friend to us both all these weeks. I know you'd cut off your right arm sooner than be a party to anything like this." Fortunately he had turned to the window again, and so did not see the violent blush which his tribute produced.

"In fact, I don't believe it even originated in this building," he continued. "Someone from the competition must have spotted us somewhere, and put two and two together, is all I can think. Someone who resents my achievements with the paper and was determined to bring me down, no matter what heartbreak and emotional chaos their poisonous mischief might cause."

The loyal, discreet friend, still dazed at being off the hook, cast around for the right note of sympathetic objectivity.

"But . . . after all, it's only Private Eye. Most people don't believe a word they read in it. You could deny the whole thing."

"People know there's always a grain of truth. And, anyway, it's not my style to lie. Even if my family life is about to come crashing round my ears." Shildrick glanced at Louis's face and managed a wan smile.

"What an ally you are, Poet! I think you're feeling this even worse than I am, aren't you?"

"But . . . surely it couldn't come to that?"

"I just don't know. Jean hasn't seen it yet. In the normal way, she'd probably not see it at all. But with this sort of thing, you know there are always a dozen kind, thoughtful friends to get straight on the telephone."

He sat in his black leather chair and tilted it back, leaning wearily against the padded head-rest. "I'm not concerned for myself so much as for Fran. It's monstrous that she should have to go through this when the whole thing was my fault and she's been the completely innocent party."

"Umph," Louis said indistinctly.

"She's going to have to leave the Dispatch, of course. She could hardly stay on, not now. However brilliant the copy she turned in, there'd always be someone to say she was getting preferential treatment." The dark eyes suddenly flickered with indecision. "I'm right, aren't I? She can't stay? It'd not be fair on her."

"No. Yes. I mean, I suppose so."

"She says she's always fancied TV more than print journalism. I've got a few good friends over at the BBC. Peter Pagnamenta's always romancing me to be on his *24 Hours* programme. Maybe if I asked him, he'd give her a try-out there. She's got the looks, after all. And the kind of classless voice they go for nowadays."

During these latter reflections, Louis had felt his heart sink even below the nadir of buying Private Eye this morning.

"So . . . does that mean . . . ?"

"Does that mean what?" Shildrick demanded.

"You're still . . ."

"Still what?"

"Staying together. You and Fran."

"Staying together? Fran and I? Not 'Fran and me.' Of course. What else could I do? You see, I love her, Poet. It's that simple."

The desk intercom buzzed discordantly. With no change of expression Shildrick leaned over and pressed the switch.

"Yes, Enid?"

"Your wife is downstairs in Reception."

For the first time in many weeks, the Magazine's Ideas Lunch did not convene under sweltering arc-lamps. On this aspect of Toby Godwin's average week, at least, the BBC2 crew had more material "in the can" than they could ever hope to use. Instead, they adjourned to the pub across the road, leaving their equipment piled in the small foyer area and Tancred Philpott slumped on a nearby couch. The producer's reptilian face wore a preoccupied look, as if weighing the merits of merely pointing a revolver at his temple or actually inserting it into his mouth.

The young rips attacked Whitstable oysters, asparagus, Scotch salmon mayonnaise, langoustines, Westphalian ham, grape-and-walnut salad, Roquefort, Brie, crème brûlée, tarte au citron, summer pudding, Mouton Cadet, Pouilly Fuissé and Rosé d'Anjou with zest made still keener by Jessamyn O'Shaughnessy's update on the topic of the hour.

"She's thrown him out of their house neck and crop. Told him never to speak to the kids again. Threatened to take every penny he's got. Cut the flies out of all his trousers . . ."

"What?" yelled Deaves and Val Lewis together.

"I kid you not! When she found out, the first thing she did was to go through his whole wardrobe, all those ghastly trendy suits, and cut the zips out of every pair of trousers. Then she went round the house, collecting everything else of his she could find, and made a bonfire of it all in the garden. Apparently he had framed awards and testimonials to himself all over every wall. Well, Mrs. S. has now torched the lot!"

There was a shriek of merriment from everyone except Louis and Terry Bracegirdle, across whose handsome face passed a wince of sympathetic fellow-feeling.

"And what about the deadly Miss Charcoal-Eyes?" Cedric Scurr asked.

"Gone!" Jessamyn said.

"Gone?"

"With a huge payoff in lieu of notice. And straight into a plum job at the BBC. She's going to be a reporter on the *24 Hours* programme."

Evelyn Strachey coquettishly cuddled naked white arms. "Well, all I can say is . . . Hugh Greene, the Director General, had better watch out for his cherry with her around!"

During the past week, with ever more delectable revelations drifting down from the newspaper floor, there had been times when Toby Godwin's purple-faced, spluttering bellows of mirth had aroused genuine concern about the stress on an already overtaxed heart. But now, as he drew on an outsize Montecristo and poured himself a third glass of vintage port, his face was its normal suet colour and unwontedly solemn.

"Hey, listen, boys and girls—draggy news, I'm sorry to say. Tim Mandeville has just sent me the schedule of our ad bookings for the autumn. And it turns out that the drop in revenues for June and July wasn't the seasonal blip we'd all hoped. We're also going to be down in August and September, and forward projections until Christmas don't look any too wonderful either."

Jim Deaves broke the shocked silence. "Down by how much, God?"

Godwin picked up the memorandum that lay on his otherwise virginal desk-top. "Seventeen percent in August, twenty-three percent in September—though that second figure's not quite set in stone. Tim's mounting a special push with some discount rates to the big supermarkets like Safeway and Tesco."

"I can remember a time when, if Tesco tried to buy space, we just laughed at them," Jessamyn said bleakly.

"I must emphasise that none of this is any adverse reflection on us. All our competitors in the glossy field are looking at precisely the same loss of income. The unpalatable fact is that the boom we've enjoyed these past two or three years seems to be over. There's hardly a big-name advertiser, from cars to Scotch whisky and after-dinner mints, that hasn't got the wind up about the economic situation and cut its advertising budget drastically. What money there is to spend is now being concentrated on the new colour TV, another factor over which we had no control. Our reps are chasing a dwindling market."

"The economic situation?" Bracegirdle echoed. "What's up with the economic situation?"

"I thought this country was supposed to be riding the crest of a great wave," Jessamyn said. "British pop . . . British fashion . . . British design. The world can't get enough of bloody Britain."

"All the merest surface froth, I'm afraid, darling. It's now become clear that Harold, with the help of his trade union buddies, has made the most almighty bog of the economy. Tony Callaway, the Editor of Business News, told me yesterday he reckons we're heading for the worst financial crisis in twenty years. He thinks Harold will be forced to devalue the pound by Christmas, perhaps even earlier. There'll be a massive credit-squeeze, tax increases, inflation . . . In short, if I may be pardoned the vulgarity, the Swinging Sixties turn out to have been nothing more nor less than Shit Creek."

The question in every mind was voiced by Cedric Scurr. "What about Lord M.?"

Godwin's surprisingly slim little finger coaxed a chunk of ash from the end of his cigar on to his dessert-plate.

"Lord M., given the imperatives which regulate his existence, has been understanding to a quite remarkable degree. But, human nature being what it is, I can't say how long that forbearance will continue. Especially not with Mighty Jack Shildrick, his blue-eyed boy, whispering in his ear that the Magazine's produced by elitist snobs for elitist snobs, and he, Mighty Jack, should be given dominion over us to run features on window-boxes, DIY and dentistry."

"So what can we do?" Bracegirdle asked.

"As I see it, we have two alternatives," Godwin said. "The first, much favoured by Jim here, is to make some internal economies that will please our accounts people and might slightly reassure Lord M. in the short term—use up the Overmatter instead of commissioning new pieces, cut expenditure on foreign stories, go easy on expenses, that kind of thing. But I must say, I'm agin it. You never really do any good by saving halfpennies."

Deaves blew out cigarette-smoke with a splutter somewhere between exasperation and admiration. "I wouldn't call a hundred grand's worth of Overmatter 'halfpennies,' God. Or sending Bailey to the Great Barrier Reef to photograph the definitive sea urchin. Or nearly two thousand a month for champagne . . ."

"My own view," Godwin interrupted firmly, "is that this is no time to get the collywobbles. After all, boldness and decisiveness—to the point of intellectual arrogance, if you like—have always been our strongest suit. We should go all out to reaffirm ourselves as the pre-eminent title in our field, prove yet again, for those with short memories, that we have more style, originality and panache than all our competitors put together. We've tried Mighty Jack's more populist approach, and it hasn't worked." He glanced at Tessa, his secretary. "How many readers now have notified us that they've knocked down the retaining walls of their houses?"

"Five."

"Harumph. Well, more fools us for straying out of our proper milieu. Between now and Christmas, let's go all out to give our readers the most meaty, action-packed smasheroos they've ever had, even from us."

Bracegirdle glanced through the list on his lap. "We've got Anthony Burgess on Mickey Mouse . . . V. S. Naipaul on the hard-up princes of Rajasthan . . . Cartier-Bresson in Bali . . . Evelyn Strachey on drag clubs in East Berlin . . . our theme issue on culture-shapers whose surnames end with 'stein.' "

"This Steins idea is exactly what I mean—us at our adventurous, eclectic best," Godwin said. "We should rush it into production for mid-September or even earlier. I may add that we shall be facing especially stiff competition from the Steam Section in this next quarter. Mighty Jack has bought several major books for serialisation in the Review, and there's also a huge Close-up exposé in the works."

"Any idea what about?" Cedric Scurr asked. Beside him, Louis gave a start, remembering Shildrick's portentous hints on the evening of the river cruise. He wondered afresh how the scoop to end all scoops was to be conjured from Thames-side pubs, beer-gardens and landing-stages.

"No knowledge, dear boy. It's been going on in conditions of secrecy that would do credit to MI5. But the overall strategy is obvious—to prove to our Chairman once and for all that we are no longer the principal reason why one point seven million people each week buy the Sunday Dispatch."

The Editor refilled his port glass and held it up to the light as if its ruby tint might possess the properties of a crystal ball.

"What I'm wondering is if there might not be some purely visual idea we could throw into the mix. Something like the New Eve and 'What Did Christ Look Like?' showing off our strengths of photography and layout at their best, and proving to our readers beyond any question that, even when the Steam Section pulls out all the stops, it's still fundamentally only good for wrapping up fish and chips."

Bracegirdle consulted his list again. "There's always 'Three Men in a Boat,'" he suggested.

"Ah, yes," Godwin said with a reminiscent smile. "We've long had this idea of re-creating the journey from Jerome K. Jerome's scrumptious book to discover how the Thames has changed over three-quarters of a century. I was going to be one of the men and David Kausman was to be another. The main problem when we looked into it was finding a boat of sufficient strength to bear our combined weight, hooh hooh hooh!"

"Hold on, though," Bracegirdle said. "Maybe there's something there if we try thinking modern. Why not turn it into a fashion feature? Victorian gear's all the rage just now. We could do some scrummy spreads of girls lying in punts in long dresses and straw hats."

"Three Men in a Boat—to say nothing of the birds, eh?" Godwin chuckled. "What do you think, Cedric?"

Scurr gave his minimal enthusiastic nod. "Yeah, not bad. I could get Patrick Prince to photograph it."

"Shrimpton would love to do it," Jessamyn added. "And I could ask Penny Tree . . . maybe even Twiggy if she's around."

"We could do a separate spread on Victorian picnics," Val Lewis suggested.

"And maybe something on the difficulties of courting in those days," Jessamyn put in. "I mean, with all the constricting corsets and things they used to wear, was it really possible in an open boat . . . ?"

"Hooh hooh hooh hooh!"

"Who's going to take the parts of the three men, though?" Louis asked.

"You can be one if you care to, dear boy," Godwin replied. "In fact, I think all we blokes should all appear as extras in the appropriate costume . . . helping the ladies in and out of their river craft, serenading them on the banjo and sharing a glass of bubbly as the need may arise."

He glanced with a hint of compassion at the slumped, disconsolate figure of Tancred Philpott out in the foyer.

"As well as a nice little jolly for us, it also may be a way to help our BBC2 chums achieve what I believe is called 'a wrap.' "

# 30

The man who presented *24 Hours* bore little resemblance to the starchy figures who had dispensed BBC television news and current affairs throughout Louis's childhood. Instead of brilliantine and black tie, he wore a Beatle fringe, a high-buttoned Carnaby suit and flowing kipper tie. The studio graphics, too, were quintessentially modern—in other words a shameless steal from The Sunday Dispatch Magazine. Behind the anchorman's desk was a huge "24" with "hours" written minutely sideways on the upright of the 4, a creation which both in extravagance and unhelpfulness to the eye might have come straight from the desk of Cedric Scurr. Positioned asymmetrically round it were grainy blow-ups of the characters in tonight's news drama: Lyndon Johnson, President of the United States; Dr. Martin Luther King, leader of the American Civil Rights movement; Tony Blackburn, the disc jockey.

"G'devening," the presenter said with the gritty faint northernness Jack Shildrick had made almost obligatory for serious masscommunicators. "Five American cities including Washington, the nation's capital, are tonight in the grip of racial turmoil." His left eyebrow raised itself a fraction in acknowledgement of that comfortably far-off place where almost everything unpleasant, as well as bizarre and risible, could still be relied on to happen.

"Appeals for calm by Dr. Martin Luther King and other Civil Rights leaders have been unable to prevent a wave of looting and arson across the continent, from New York to Los Angeles. President Johnson has declared a state of emergency and warned that the severest measures will be taken to restore law and order. Nowhere was the violence greater than in the car-manufacturing city of Detroit, from where Fran Dyson now reports."

There followed scenes from an August night very different from this peaceful, blossom-scented, pub-murmuring one in London. Buildings blazed, outsize cars lay overturned and gutted, looters smashed shop windows and made off with outsize refrigerators and television sets, tear-gas eddied, fleeing figures, male and female, were pursued by police and, now and then, clubbed to the ground. Through billowing black smoke rolled a convoy of tanks, followed by open-top trucks full of steel-helmeted troops.

The voice-over was undeniably suited to television reporting, Louis thought, especially after obvious education in pacing and stress. Its slightly toneless, resigned quality if anything enhanced the sombreness of the images. The fractionally softened *r* was noticeable only now and then.

"Following an estimated thirty-eight deaths and millions of dollars' worth of damage to property, a state of martial law now exists in this industrial centre, once known only for its Ford and Chrysler automobile plants and the records of Diana Ross and the Supremes. The Governor of Michigan ordered in units of the National Guard after the police admitted they had lost control of the situation . . ."

Now here was Fran herself, microphone in hand, standing in the centre of a wide street littered with police cars and fire engines. Her pale hair tumbled around a military-style shirt of which the top four buttons, at least, were unfastened. On either side of her, like some ceremonial guard, stood a soldier with dangling chinstraps, flourishing a stubby machine gun.

" 'Baby, baby, where did our love go?' may indeed be the question Detroit will ask itself tomorrow morning as the full cost of these riots is counted." The blackened eyes narrowed with an indignation that seemed wholly genuine. "The answer is . . . in poverty . . . in unemployment . . . in slum housing . . . in the obligation of American Negroes to go to war on behalf of a society by which they still feel enslaved. So long as these evils remain, there will be no help for America's exploding cities."

"Fran Dyson, reporting from Detroit," the studio presenter said. He shuffled his papers, intensifying the severity of his expression. "Now . . . from revolution in the air to revolution in the airwaves. The BBC has announced the creation of a new pop music radio network to take the place of the offshore so-called pirate stations. Called Radio One, it will begin transmitting next month, with programmes hosted by former pirate disc jockeys Tony Blackburn, Stuart Henry and Kenny Everett . . ."

"I'm sure Brian won't keep you waiting very much longer," the receptionist said.

She was a handsome, debby type with ash-blond hair tied back in a velvet ribbon and pendulous earrings. The entire wall behind her was a grainy black-and-white blow-up of the four Beatles as the world still preferred to visualise them—mop-topped, Cardin-suited, happy and uncomplicated. Louis remembered those Beatlemania days of '63, dreary ones for him on the Whittlesey Advertiser, when he'd watched them clowning on *Juke-Box Jury* and enviously imagined the parties and girls that must be waiting for them afterwards.

On the glass coffee-table in front of him lay copies of all the national papers, the music weeklies and trade magazines like Variety, Billboard and Cashbox. He picked up the Daily Express and looked again at the picture which showed the Beatles of today, unalike in clothes, hair and physiognomy, no longer smiling, happy or fulfilled by the straightforward fruits of global stardom. With them was an exotic personage over whom even they towered, a tiny Asiatic gentleman with shoulder-length hair and a straggly piebald beard.

Beyond the receptionist was a firmly shut office door through which could be heard a murmur of voices, one light and educated, the other brusque and plaintive, with an intonation Louis was almost sure he recognised. He was just exchanging Variety for Billboard when the voices grew suddenly louder, the door was flung open and John Lennon stormed out into the small foyer. Hair cropped almost to prison length, Oriental moustache dribbling to his chin, close-set eyes ringed by wiry National Health glasses, here was the least recognisable carefree mop-top of them all.

"You've always tried to put us in your bag, haven't you?" he shouted back through the open door. "Buttoning us up in your little monkey suits! Combing our hair and straightening our ties! Trying to make us loovable!" It was infinitely strange to hear that watchword of the hour, not sung via satellite link to a worldwide audience of 600 million but spoken in tones of withering irony and contempt.

"You know it's true," he continued, interrupting a faint demurral from within, "but you'll just never accept it, will you, Brian? We were never loovable! Not even Paul! The only way we got through all this shit was by being the biggest bastards in the world!"

Turning away, he met Louis's eye and, surprisingly, gave him a brusque nod before scooping up a pile of letters, packets and record albums from the reception desk and banging through the swing doors that led to Stafford Street.

There was a brief pause, during which Louis saw the debby receptionist look down and gnaw at her lip as if such scenes were familiar as well as upsetting. Then Brian Epstein appeared in the doorway. Despite the extreme heat—not to mention the prevalence of loose kaftans, billowy trousers and open-toed sandals—he was dressed as for a board meeting in a dark blue suit, white shirt and muted red silk tie. Since that night at Abbey Road studios, the wavy hair had grown just perceptibly longer. The snub, rather shy face was expressionlessly urbane.

"Mr. Brennan?" he said in his slightly actorish voice. "I'm so sorry to have kept you. Please do come in."

The inner office was airy and tastefully furnished, more like some society hostess's drawing-room than the operations centre of Britain's most phenomenally successful pop manager. The only giveaways were the framed Golden Discs around the walls, and the photographs of his principal protégés on their unstoppable ascent—here shaking hands with Princess Margaret, here posing outside Buckingham Palace as Members of the Most Excellent Order of the British Empire, here sparring with the World Heavyweight Champion when he'd still been called Cassius Clay. Oddly, there appeared to be no mementoes of the many others, both groups and solo performers, whom the same Diaghilev touch had magicked into the charts these past four years. All you saw, wherever you looked, were Beatles.

Louis became aware that Epstein was regarding him quizzically.

"Have we met before by any chance?"

He decided it would take too long to explain about impersonating a footman. "I was at Abbey Road when you recorded 'A Day in the Life.' "

"With Mick and Marianne, was it?"

"Sort of."

"And how can I help The Sunday Dispatch?"

As well as he was able, Louis summarised the theme of the issue now being rushed into production to entice laggardly advertisers. "It seems to be a fact that almost every influential figure in twentieth-century culture has had a name ending in 'stein.' We'd like you to be interviewed and photographed as part of our Steins portrait gallery."

"And who else is in it?"

"Oh . . . Wittgenstein, the philosopher . . . Eisenstein, the film director . . . Helena Rubenstein, the cosmetician . . . Jock Stein, the manager of Celtic football club."

Epstein lounged back behind a large, immaculately ordered desk whose red leather surface also was covered with photographs of the Beatles.

"I'm really not that interesting, you know. Just a furniture salesman from Liverpool who got lucky." He nodded at the fringed faces all around them. "Are you sure you wouldn't rather talk to the boys?"

Louis shook his head, remembering the painfully inculcated wisdom of Terry Bracegirdle. "I'd love to talk to them. But I don't think the Magazine would let me do a piece about it."

"Oh, really? Why not?"

"They've been done so many times already, haven't they?"

"Not properly. Not the way the Dispatch Magazine would do it. They're all such fascinating characters, you know—especially John. And they're doing wonderful things in the recording studio at the moment. I could arrange for you to sit in on one of their sessions. Or when John and Paul are putting a new song together. You could talk to George Martin, their producer . . . Dick James, their publisher . . . Neil Aspinall, their roadie, who's been with them from the very beginning."

For the first time in many months, Louis wondered whether Bracegirdle might be not totally infallible on this particular subject.

"Well . . . it does sound fascinating. Could I get back to you about it?"

"You know they're into transcendental meditation now, don't you?" Epstein said.

"Yes, so I read. But I thought it was only George who was mystical."

"They've always been like that. If one takes up something, the others do it as well, for solidarity. But they do seem genuinely taken with this Maharishi person. Personally, I think it all sounds a bit dotty. Still, they aren't children any more. I suppose they must be allowed their own sweet way."

The words unccountably brought a tremor into Epstein's cultivated voice. He took the white handkerchief from his breast pocket and dabbed at a corner of one eye. Louis looked hurriedly off at a picture of them riding bicycles in the well-remembered scene from Help!

"They're off on a jaunt with him this Bank Holiday weekend . . . some initiation course he's running at a teacher-training college." Epstein replaced the handkerchief with fastidious care, and managed a wan smile. "In Bangor, North Wales, if you can believe it. Their wives are going as well, and Jane Asher, and Mick and Marianne. If you like, I could arrange for you to travel with them."

"I'm afraid I'm going to be tied up on Bank Holiday Saturday."

"Well, how about Sunday? I'm driving down early in the morning to check up on things, so I could offer you a lift."

Epstein took a pen from a gold-and-onyx holder, scribbled something on a card and held it out. Louis had a sudden odd feeling that the world's most envied entrepreneur was lonely, even isolated. But how could that possibly be?

"This is my home address . . . Chapel Street, Belgravia. Do come. At the very least, we can discuss what part my being called 'stein' has played in my success."

---

"Aiv-rey liddle breeze seems to wees-pair Louise," Toby Godwin sang in a fruity baritone, tilting his straw boater roguishly over one eye. There was, indeed, a fleeting resemblance to Maurice Chevalier, if a Chevalier herded into a windowless stall, denied all movement and force-fed on cream buns, doughnuts and Yorkshire pudding for twenty years.

In the centre of Godwin's office carpet stood a large wicker hamper just delivered from Bermans, the theatrical costumiers. Other male participants in "Three Birds in a Boat," as the River Thames fashion extravaganza had been renamed, were rummaging through it and trying on straw hats, striped blazers, white flannels and canvas shoes. Val Lewis and Tessa Burland stood by with lists on clipboards, reporting on organisational strategy to date.

"Turk's boatyard at Kingston can provide an authentic period camping skiff, that's the type with hoops for a canvas cover," Tessa said. "I've asked Harrods' menagerie for a dog to play Montmorency, as near as possible to the illustrations in the book. And Fortnum and Mason are all lined up to do the food."

"Excellent! No reason why we should mortify the flesh, is there? Val dear, do we know yet where it's all going to happen?"

"Patrick Prince wants to shoot on an island a couple of miles from Bray," Val said. "It's a bit of a problem, what with all the vehicles we'll we using. Luckily there's a pub called the Boat and Bottle just downriver, that can rent us space in its car park."

"How many spaces will we need?" Jim Deaves asked.

"Let's see . . . there's hire cars for the models . . . the stylist . . . hairdressing and make-up people . . . Mappin and Webb's van, bringing the silverware . . . Fortnum's van . . . the BBC2 crew's Dormobile . . ."

"You'd better book the whole dining room at this Boat and Bottle as well," Terry Bracegirdle said, tying a striped cravat over his turquoise psychedelic tie.

"And a few bedrooms, I thought, in case the shoot goes on very late."

"Might as well collar 'em all, darling." Godwin squinted at his boulevardier reflection in the window. "Sank 'eaven for leedle gairls," he warbled pensively. "For leedle gairls get beegair aivrey day . . ."

"I'm sorry it's got to be on Bank Holiday Saturday," Val said. "That's the only time Shrimpton's got free before she goes to Milan."

Jessamyn O'Shaughnessy joined the spectators in the doorway, nurs-

ing her mid-afternoon tumbler of Scotch. "Did you see your former secretary on the box last night?" she asked Deaves.

"No. Any good?"

" 'Exploding cities!' " Jessamyn snorted. "Exploding titties more like!
I mean, have you ever seen anything *like* it?"

Reluctant as he was to think about Fran's breasts, Louis could not
help reflecting on the almost mythical quality they had assumed since
Private Eye's designation of her as a "busty hackette." In fact, the unbuttoned shirt had displayed barely even a hint of cleavage. From Jessamyn's rolling eyes, and hand gestures eloquent of helpless spilling
forth, one would have thought a topless Jayne Mansfield had materialised amid Detroit's racial unrest.

"I hear she's already causing chaos at *24 Hours*," Val Lewis said.
"She's only been there five minutes, and she's pinching all these amazing overseas assignments from people like Julian Pettifer . . . All the men
reporters are up in arms about it."

"There are about eight producers to every programme like that," Jim
Deaves remarked. "I wonder which one she's managed to knock off."

"Probably all of them, knowing her," said Jessamyn.

The topic still had enough fascination even to reclaim Toby Godwin
from his Maurice Chevalier impersonation. "So tell us, darling, what's
the posish as of now between Miss Exploding Titties and Mighty Jack
Shildrick?"

"Haven't you heard? They're living together."

"So it's really serious, is it?" Jim Deaves said.

"Seems to be. Mighty Jack's bought a flat somewhere in Chelsea. He's
supposed to be divorcing his wife . . . the whole schmear . . ."

Margaret Cole had appeared among the spectators in the doorway.
"Louis," she called. "Michael Sissons of A. D. Peters on the phone for
you."

He picked up the receiver, unable to imagine what the youthful dy-
namo of an illustrious literary agency could possibly want with him.

"Hallo," a laid-back voice said. "Is that Louis Brennan?"

"Yes."

"Michael Sissons here. I've just finished the opening chapters of *The
End of the Pier*."

Louis goggled into the mouthpiece. "You have?"

"Yes . . . and I'd like you to come in and see me. How are you fixed
next week?"

"Er . . . could I ask where you got them?"

"Where I got them? David Kausman sent them to me."

"He did?"

"Yes. Didn't you know?"

"No."

"With a typical Kausman covering note, saying that if I didn't take you on as a client, I'd need my head examined. And I have to say, I think he doesn't overstate the case. Even with a hangover, they made me laugh out loud."

---

"So what's the deal?" David Kausman asked. He and Louis were at Bentley's Oyster Bar, side-by-side at the counter while a smiling old man in a white mess-jacket opened oysters almost as fast as Kausman could swallow them.

Louis took out Michael Sisson's letter and passed it over. He still felt slightly dazed and unreal, as if lunch-time noise and clash, the flushed-pink lobster shells, the misty yellow wine bottles in their beds of crushed ice, were part of a dream that wouldn't stop.

"Arden Sinclair's accepted it on the basis of the seven chapters I've done and an outline of the rest of the story. He'll pay an advance against royalties of three hundred pounds."

"Not a bad advance for a first novel, not bad at all. And with Sinclair you can bet you'll get an eye-catching jacket and a first-class launch."

"I didn't even realise you liked it," said Louis.

"Liked it?" Kausman threw back his head and tipped another sea-smelling, living mollusc between the black halves of his beard. "I thought it went without saying that I liked it. If I hadn't thought it funny, quirky and original, do you seriously think I'd have sent it to London's beadiest-eyed literary agent, threatening to gouge out his vitals with a blunt cheese-knife if he didn't agree to represent you?"

"I don't know how to thank you, David . . ."

"Oh, shut up!" Kausman said, almost savagely. He scanned the letter again, squeezing lemon juice over his last surviving victim. "I see that Sinclair wants the complete manuscript by December."

"Yes, to publish next spring. I'm wondering if I can do it."

"Of course you can do it! Get up every day at dawn, if you have to! Work all night with a wet towel round your head!"

"But what about the Magazine?"

"Leave the Magazine."

A grilled sole overlapping its plate was set before Kausman and he applied himself to exposing its backbone as deftly and lovingly as if cleaning off some Old Master. Louis gazed at him with an eye hardly less blankly incredulous than the sole's.

"Leave? Are you serious?"

"Absolutely."

"But . . ." He couldn't help laughing. "I'd be crazy. I've got a marvellous job. I couldn't have a better one."

"I know—you're spoiled rotten. And it's had the worst possible effect on you. When you first came from your provincial paper last year, you were a whirlwind. You'd sit and rattle out a piece in a couple of hours . . . then be raring to go for the next one. I've watched you over the months getting slower, more complacent and arrogant."

Kausman reached for the second of the two Chablis bottles in their ice bucket and brusquely refilled Louis's glass to the brim. This was reproach decidedly lacking its usual subtext of praise.

"For God's sake, do something that journalists almost never do! Think ahead! What do you want to be at the age of thirty? And forty? Another Evelyn Strachey, writing the same piece over and over again? In journalism—I should know!—the years fly by. And nothing ever changes! The same backstabbing and intriguing goes on over the same meaningless titles and squalid little offices. The same battles to the death are fought over who controls the same pathetic plots of space. If you're not careful, you could still be at the Magazine twenty years from now. And heaven knows what barbarians will be running it then!"

Louis took a long-delayed swig from his glass. "I don't know . . . Maybe you're right. I'd better talk it over with Jack Shildrick."

"Jack Shildrick!" Kausman flipped over the sole to its uneaten side, a gesture redolent with impatience and derision.

"He is a friend."

"Oh, yes, he's been a great friend to you, I must say! Tried to turn you into a parcel-packer for the Literary Department. Sold you up the river when you offended one of his showbiz friends. Kept you endlessly dangling on a string for the Cicero column. Pinched your exclusive on the Rolling Stones. I've watched it happen time and again. He dazzles you first, then he screws you."

Louis said nothing. It was all too horribly like what he himself had lately been struggling not to think.

"You'd feel the pinch financially, of course," Kausman went on. "No nice pink slips to cash in every other lunch-time. What do you have in the way of savings to keep you going?"

He pictured what remained of this last year's blizzards of ready money—almost entirely to be found hanging in his Tudor-panelled wardrobe at 8 Inkerman Terrace. "Not a hell of a lot," he admitted.

"The other thing would be to get Sissons to make you a deal for a non-fiction book as well. One that would pay you a whopping advance you could live on while you finished the novel."

"I don't even know that I can write a fiction book, let alone a factual one."

"Please don't talk bloody horseshit. Anyway, there's a perfect subject that's been right under your nose for months if you'd only realise it."

Louis picked up his knife and fork to address the scallop-and-bacon kebab he hadn't yet started. "Oh, really? What's that?"

"The Beatles. And please don't instantly pull that face."

"But, David—they've been done and done so *many* times!"

"So you've been brainwashed into parroting by knuckleheads like Terry Bracegirdle. But think . . . in all those millions of words, what have you ever read other than fanzine stuff about cuddly moptops? *Sergeant Pepper* was a work of art! It's about as much to do with the Top 20 as *The Waste Land* has with 'Pop Goes the Weasel.' And they're still only at the beginning."

As Louis chewed the orange gentilia of a scallop, he felt words abruptly knock for admission to his mind. He grabbed a paper napkin and scribbled: "Adoration of young men unprecedented since pharaohs of Ancient Egypt . . ."

"You've already touched on it by happenstance at so many points. You saw Brian Epstein almost in tears after they'd quit live concerts. You were with Harrison before the Stones' drug bust . . . at Abbey Road when they recorded 'A Day in the Life.' And aren't you already talking to Epstein for the Steins issue?"

"Yes. Oh, did I mention—he's offered to drive me to North Wales this Bank Holiday Monday, to watch them meditating with their Maharishi."

"God Almighty!" Kausman exclaimed with such fervour that a shower of fishbones assailed Louis like a fusillade from tiny longbowmen. "The story's being dropped into your lap! What more do you need to convince you? One of them to kick the bucket?"

---

Since the rejig of his domestic circumstances, Shildrick's working hours had drastically altered. No longer was he the first person at work on the newspaper floor each day, the hungry 9 A.M. scanner of rival headlines and overnight agency copy. Gone, too, were those legendary Saturday nights when dynamite would hardly have prised him from the shirt-sleeved camaraderie of the Newsroom and subs' table. Save on exceptional occasions, the paper in its climactic hours was now left to James Way or its "number three," Jeremy Hart. Anyone requiring the Editor's definitive judgement must seek him out dining at the latest trendy bistro or dancing, among people considerably younger than himself, at Blases, Sybilla's or The Speakeasy.

Likewise, it would once have been unthinkable to meet him leaving McIntyre House like any Magazine person at barely six on a Friday evening. Yet here he was, darting from Lord McIntyre's private lift at the side of the commissionaires' desk. Any notion that he might be bound for private talks with the Prime Minister at 10 Downing Street, or perhaps the Chancellor at Number 11, was dispelled by the bulging Tesco shopping bag he gripped in the same hand as his executive briefcase.

He stopped and waited for Louis, switching the Tesco bag to his unoccupied hand. The sensitive face looked pale and drawn, though whether that came from recent domestic traumas or too much all-night raving was impossible to say.

" 'Ullo, Poet. You're quite a stranger nowadays. Where you been hiding yourself?"

It occurred to Louis that the Chelsea boot had been somewhat on the other foot. However, he merely smiled and said, "I've been working at home quite a lot."

"What are you up to now?"

"I'm writing a novel."

Shildrick's eyes lit up with their instant, passionate absorption. "Really! That's wonderful! Just what I've always thought you should do. What's the subject?"

"Oh, it's sort of autobiographical. All about my early life and my father's various . . ."

But the interest had faded from Shildrick's face. With the elbow of the hand holding the Tesco bag—whose contents could now be seen to include a bottle of red wine and a large bunch of parsley—he motioned Louis through the automatic glass doors. Outside, his company Rover was at the kerb, with Les's Teddy-boy silhouette behind the wheel.

"I'm so glad I've run into you," he murmured, as if there were eavesdroppers all round (which nowadays there very well could be). "She's flying back from the States this evening, and I'm as nervous as a kitten up a tree, like the song says. Could you come and keep me company? Please? Just for half an hour?"

Deciding one had had enough of being exploited by Shildrick in the abstract was one thing, but resisting Shildrick in person was a very different proposition. Without knowing quite how, Louis found himself in the back of the Rover, rounding Ludgate Circus and heading along Fleet Street. For all his stern recent resolutions, he felt his heart beating uncomfortably inside his new seersucker jacket. So tonight he and she would be in the same city once again. Against all logic, that made him want to wind down the window, stick out his head and give three cheers.

Despite the arresting simile, Shildrick's resemblance to a kitten up a tree was minimal. He lounged back in his seat, studying the office-fronts of his main daily and Sunday rivals with eyes reflectively half-closed. For the first time, Louis noticed the inordinate length of his lashes. Ridiculous to imagine one could ever have competed with such a man!

"Tell me something, Poet," he said as the Daily Telegraph's neoclassical façade passed on their left. "What would you say was the biggest story to have broken in this country in the last twenty years? A story just as big to the Belly-laugh there as to the News of the World up its alley in Bouverie Street. I'll give you a clue," he went on before Louis could answer. "Burgess and Maclean . . . George Blake . . . Whatever-he-was-called Vassal . . . Kim Philby."

"Spies?"

"Aye . . . spies. The men who've sold this country's and NATO's defence secrets to the Russians as casually as you and I would ring up our Aunt Mabel in Manchester."

In sudden disquiet Shildrick leaned forward to check something in the Tesco shopping bag, satisfied himself that it was there, then sat back again.

"This is the age of shattered illusions, Poet. All these years, the Hot-spur and Boys' Own Paper taught us that a spy was a man with a beard in a black hat and cloak, holding a fizzling bomb. Now we know he's more likely to be an ex–public schoolboy . . . an Oxford rowing Blue . . . the sort of pukka English gent who was always thought the soul of honour and patriotism. It's quite unbelievable how top-drawer the worst ones were, you know! Burgess and Maclean were Foreign Office diplomats. Philby sat on high-level liaison committees at the heart of bloody NATO, initialling top secret documents one day, sending 'em off to his masters in Moscow the next."

Louis struggled to reprise headlines which at the time had had rather less impact on him than Merseybeat's dominance of the Top 20. "I agree, it was an incredible story. But it's run its course now, surely. When Philby defected, wasn't that the finish of it?"

"That's what we were told, of course," Shildrick nodded. "The Philby affair exposed such disgraceful flaws in our security services, the Government's only get-out was to say they'd smashed the whole ring. But it's always been rumoured that as well as Maclean, Burgess and Philby, there was a fourth man. Someone maybe at an even higher level in the F.O. or Secret Service, who was in a position to know when Burgess and

Maclean's cover was about to be blown, tipped them off just in time to defect in 'fifty-one, kept Philby in place and protected him until he got out in 'sixty-three, but for some reason was never exposed himself.''

Shildrick gripped Louis's elbow and glanced through the window, as if some eavesdropper might be clinging to the outside of the car.

"The Fourth Man, Poet! It's the story that beats Graham Greene's Third Man into a cocked hat . . . the one every other editor on that Street back there would do murders for! And I've got it! Well, as near as, dammit!''

So this was Shildrick's secret weapon in the McIntyre House Cold War. Compared to some colour photographs of Jean Shrimpton and Twiggy in Victorian costume, seated in a boat, it did seem fairly strong.

"Close-up have been all out on it for over a year,'' he continued. "We've established beyond a doubt that there was a fourth man, that he was an even more senior and respected member of the Establishment than Philby, that the security services nabbed him at about the same time, but promised him immunity from prosecution in return for everything he could tell them about his bosses in the K.G.B. We're fairly sure he's still in some senior public position, his pension rights secure, while smaller fish like Vassal and Blake are doing life in Parkhurst. So it's not only the spy yarn to end all spy yarns, you see! It's the ultimate story of collusion and cover-up in Whitehall . . . how morality is bent for the sake of expediency . . . how our so-called democracy is still hamstrung by the gentleman's club and the old school tie.''

Louis could only nod raptly. It was not only the quintessential scoop, but the quintessential Shildrick scoop. The vision in his mind was one to which only a nineteenth-century Punch cartoonist could have done full justice—the Boy Editor, wielding a broadsword inscribed "TRUTH,'' delivering the coup-de-grâce to a writhing serpent inscribed "OFFICIAL COVER-UP.''

"The problem is, how to flush him out? We've interviewed scores of ex-Service and Whitehall people who obviously know his identity, but are too scared witless by the Official Secrets Act to let on. We only know the code-name MI6 gave him while they were debriefing him—which, to save his precious face, went on in the most bloody farcical circumstances you can imagine. When MI6 wanted a meeting, they'd put a small ad with this code-name, 'Maurice,' in the Personal Column of The Times. And Maurice, of course, didn't have to do anything so demeaning as go into their office. He and his interrogator used to meet at a pub up the Thames called the Boat and Bottle.''

For a moment, Louis wondered why the name rang a bell. Then he remembered. The Magazine's operations base for its Bank Holiday Sunday photo-shoot also happened to be called the Boat and Bottle. Wiser to say nothing about that, of course. He felt like a double agent at least the equal of Close-up's elusive quarry.

"Time after time, we found ourselves running into the same wall of silence," Shildrick went on. "Then Nick Fenton came up with a brilliant idea. Why not try putting our own small ad in The Times, using the 'Maurice' code-name, as if we were MI6, calling him back for further interrogation? We knew how he made the journey each time—by motor cruiser from Turk's boatyard in Kingston. When he stepped on to the Boat and Bottle's landing-stage, there we'd be, waiting with a photographer like a lovely variant on the old Lobby Lud idea. 'You are the Fourth Man and I claim my scoop of the century!' "

"God!" Louis breathed. "How marvellous!"

Shildrick gave a wry smile. "If it works. We've placed the ad and named a date and a time . . . which I can't reveal even to a friend as loyal and discreet as you. It's the very longest of long shots. Maybe he won't believe he could be wanted again after all this time. Maybe there's some other code-word apart from 'Maurice' that we should have used, and he'll smell a rat. Maybe he doesn't read The Times. But maybe, just maybe, he'll swallow the bait, hire his little motorboat and come chugging along the Thames. By gum, Poet . . . think of it!"

They stopped in one of the towering orange streets off Sloane Square. Shildrick groped for the Tesco bag and got out, motioning Louis to follow. With a little thrill he realised he was to be shown the secret love-nest.

Here it was a climb only to the first floor, up a well-decorated staircase carpeted in new glossy grey. "I really ought to go," he protested as Shildrick unlocked a front door strangely like that of a suburban semi-detached house.

"You can stop five minutes for a cuppa, can't you? Then Les'll run you anywhere you want to go. I know she'll be delighted to see you."

Inside, a narrow hall stretched straight ahead, also smartly grey-carpeted. Along it, in a trail no backwoods trapper was needed to identify, lay various discarded garments and possessions—a leather coat, a single silver-heeled shoe, a wide-brimmed hat in fawn suède, an open suitcase spilling forth underwear, cosmetics bottles and cartons of unfamiliar cigarettes.

"Fran!" Shildrick called. "Are you about?" He put down his briefcase and carrier-bag and, with a little cluck of exasperation, began to pick up the fallen clothes. "Franny! Are you there?" But the flat was resoundingly silent.

"She must have popped out for a minute," Louis volunteered.

"Aye, to do a bit of shopping or something . . . you know what they're like. Anyway, come in here, Poet, and I'll get the kettle on. You can talk to me while I do the vegetables."

"I didn't know you cooked."

Shildrick's eyes rolled briefly heavenward.

"I didn't."

He led the way into a small kitchen, evidently maintained with a pristine neatness which someone had recently made a brief but vigorous attempt to undo. On the stripped-pine table stood two mugs half-full of cold tea and an ash-tray of spent filter-tips. A dirty frying-pan lay next to the sink with an egg-smeared plate and a tablespoon cradling not one but two dead-rat teabags.

The spectacle caused a brief but noticeable spasm to cross Shildrick's face. He swept the dirty mugs from the table to the sink, then seized a J-cloth and rubbed away the brown rings they had left behind. "Dear, oh dear," he murmured under his breath. "These girls of today . . ."

"Perhaps I had better go," Louis said.

"Nonsense! Just sit down there a minute while I get things shipshape. I'm sure she'll be back any second."

But there was no sign of Fran—not while Louis and Shildrick drank two mugs of tea each, nor while Shildrick scraped potatoes, trimmed broccoli, positioned blobs of butter and garlic all over two veal escalopes and washed lettuce in readiness for the welcome-home dinner. At 9:15, when she still had not returned, he abandoned the idea of cooking and prevailed on Louis to go out for a Chinese meal, leaving Fran directions where she could find them. But from the garlic dumplings—which Shildrick pointedly refused—to the tinned lychees, she did not materialise, and when they climbed back to the flat at 10:45 it was still empty.

"I can't understand it," Shildrick said for the umpteenth time. "I just hope nothing's happened to her. If she's not here by eleven-thirty, I'm definitely ringing the police."

At 11:57 a key scraped in the front door and Louis felt the whole underneath of himself bunch like a fist. Shildrick put down his coffee mug and slid from his kitchen stool, his face torn between annoyance and relief. "We're in here, love," he shouted.

It was, however, a full two minutes more before Fran appeared in the doorway, looking as little as was possible like someone just off a plane from America. Her honey hair was swept back by a black velvet Alice band, showing silver pendant earrings. She wore a long black velvet dress with a high lace collar, and lipstick that was either black or the darkest conceivable purple. In one hand she held an evening bag and what seemed to be a scarlet theatre programme.

The black centipedes moved from Shildrick to Louis as if with faint amusement.

"Oh . . . hi."

" 'El-lo, pet!" Shildrick said vibrantly, starting towards her with open arms. Louis, to his amazement, saw her flinch momentarily, as if garlic dumplings had after all been indulged in. At that moment a man in a dark green velvet suit, frilled yellow shirt and black butterfly bow-tie appeared in the doorway behind her.

"This is Alex Lycett," Fran announced in her familiar toneless way. "My producer on the Detroit race riot story. Alex . . . this is Jack . . . and Louis."

Lycett was about thirty, with the sort of civilised, intelligent, superior, unbearable face that could only belong to someone from the BBC. Louis loathed him on sight, though clearly not a millionth as much as did Shildrick. "Hi," he said with lazy condescension—or rather, "Hiyee."

"Hi," Louis muttered.

Fran seemed unaware of the crackling tension in the room. "Like a coffee, Alex?" she asked.

"Mm, please! What a very civilised thought!"

She went to a cupboard and began taking down cups and saucers. Shildrick followed her, speaking in his ventriloquial murmur. "Whatever happened to you, love? I've been sitting here, worried half to death. I was going to cook us a special dinner as well. I'd got everything ready."

"Didn't you find my note?"

"Note? What note?"

"Saying I was going to be a bit late. Alex had tickets for *Don Giovanni* at Covent Garden. It was a seven o'clock start, so there was only just time to rush from the airport and change."

Shildrick gaped at her. "You mean that's where you were all this time? Sitting at the opera?"

Fran opened the fridge, took out a carton of milk and shut the door carefully, only then deigning to turn the black centipedes on him in a look that managed to be both icily challenging and blankly indifferent.

"Yes," she said in her dullest voice. "What's the matter? Did I do the wrong thing again?"

# 31

How's your friend?" Fran asked.

"Which friend?"

"That you shared the flat with. The one with all the waistcoats."

"Brenda? Oh yes . . . you never did like using his name, did you? He's fine. He's bought a maisonette in Holland Park and is about to get engaged."

"Engaged? Who to?"

" 'To whom?' I'm surprised anyone with Jack Shildrick could make that mistake. To a girl called Katinka."

"Is that the one he used to propose to every week?"

"No, that was his boss's wife. Actually, I believe Katinka was the one who popped the question."

It was just after 8 A.M. on the Friday before August Bank Holiday weekend. At Fran's suggestion, Louis had joined her for breakfast in the staff cafeteria at BBC Television Centre. A huge penthouse space, with panoramic views over Shepherd's Bush, it offered star entertainers and scene-shifters alike an array of hot and cold dishes recalling the great days of the Edwardian country house weekend. As a nod to the prevailing theme of drama and documentary output on both channels, there was even northern black pudding, cut into dainty slices.

Breathing the heavy, cosseted BBC atmosphere, Louis remembered a time when to work here had been his own ultimate dream of status combined with security. Despite the shortness of her sojourn, Fran seemed to have been totally absorbed by a world if possible even more rarefied than McIntyre House. Her conversation teemed with jargon terms like "TX date" and "Steenbeck," and references to internal politics of a complexity that made the Dispatch by contrast seem positively rustic. For all the ton-up girl wildness of her hair and open-necked safari shirt, she was tense and self-conscious in a way he'd never seen her before. Even during this brief memoir of Brenda Brown, the black centipedes constantly fluttered right and left to check who of importance was at neighbouring tables or queueing in the self-service line. At roughly one-minute intervals, she broke off what she—or he—was saying to smile, nod or mime a vivacious "Hello" to someone in the middle distance.

"It's wonderful news about your novel," she went on, as if referring to the death of a near relative. "Congratulations."

"As long as I can finish it."

"Don't be mad, of course you'll finish it."

"I could never have written as much as I have while Brenda was still blowing hunting-horns in my ear. Honestly, this place I've got now is so-o wonderfully quiet. And safe, too. I can leave the French window unlocked and come and go that way. Every time I walk in I feel like saying 'Anyone for tennis?' "

The punchline was hardly out when her eyes wandered off again to acknowledge a smile from Kenneth Kendall, the newsreader, three tables away. As they returned to Louis, he gave an ostentatious chuckle. There was no point any more in trying to win her with niceness.

"I've heard of BBC Canteen eyes. But yours must be the worst case on record."

"You'll be sorry you were so foul to me," Fran said. Reaching down beside her, she brought up an outsize brown paper carrier-bag and plonked it on the table in front of him.

"What's this?"

"Open it and see."

Mystified, he pulled the bag apart at the neck and peered inside. Wadded in tissue paper was a pair of black cowboy boots, their pointed toes tipped with silver.

"For me?"

She nodded.

"But why . . . whatever made you do a thing like that?"

"I know you like boots."

He took one of them from its wrappings and ran a finger over its soft, tooled upper, thinking of her going into the shop, choosing this pair in preference to others, fumbling in her shoulder-bag to pay; himself in the forefront of her thoughts for all that time.

"Are they all right?" she asked with a touch of her old deferential anxiety.

" 'All right'? They're sensational!"

"They are your size." He had no idea she ever knew it. "They should fit you."

"I'm sure they will. It's really sweet of you!"

Her face dulled. "I'm not sweet. I thought you realised that by now." She slumped back on the beige plastic and stirred her coffee, unconscious that Michael Parkinson was wrinkling his face at her in a friendly manner while paying at the cashier's desk.

"I could tell what you were thinking the other night. You thought I was foul to him, didn't you?"

"It was a bit like seeing a Vietnamese village sprayed with napalm," Louis admitted.

"But he had no right to be that way to Alex Lycett, who's my main producer on the programme, and incredibly good. Without Alex, we'd never have got half that stuff in Detroit."

"He had gone to quite a lot of trouble over dinner, though."

"You don't understand . . . he's the same with any other man who comes within ten feet of me." She took another cigarette from the packet on the table, American-bought Winstons. "If we're out at a club, and some young guy comes up and asks me to dance, he practically goes berserk."

A piquant thought occurred to Louis. "Does he know you're meeting me here?"

"No."

"But didn't he ask where you were going at seven-thirty in the morning?"

"I haven't seen him for days . . . that's another thing that happens. He, Nick Fenton and the Close-up team are off together on some caper. I've been told—by his secretary—not to expect him until after Sunday."

"It's not the Fourth Man, is it?"

The black centipedes showed no glimmer. "Sorry?"

"Hasn't he told you? He's on the point of exposing the Fourth Man in the Burgess-Maclean-Philby spy ring. It could be the biggest coup of his career."

But Fran was staring vacantly off at the West Kensington rooftops. "I hate England. It seems so small and shabby and provincial. In America, you can really breathe." She shook a symbolic deep drag on her Winston. "That's really why I asked you to meet me here. To tell you I'm probably going over there to work."

The clash and bustle of the cafeteria receded, as if his ears had become unaccountably stopped up with wax. "Oh, yes?" he heard a voice say from somewhere inside his own head.

"I had an offer from the ABC network while I was in New York. It's incredibly easy for an English person to get into television over there. They think we all know the Beatles."

Louis pretended to be meticulously concerned with re-wrapping the cowboy boot in tissue and sliding it back into the bag. "When would you be going?" the voice inside his head enquired.

"Quite soon."

"How soon is 'quite soon'?"

"End of September. Depends how soon I can get a work permit."

"What does Jack think about it?"

"He doesn't know yet."

"What do you think he'll think when he does know?"

She shrugged.

"You know he's incredibly in love with you, don't you?"

She shrugged again.

"He's burnt his boats . . . left his wife and children . . . let himself be laughed at up and down Fleet Street . . . pilloried in Private Eye. All for you."

She shrugged yet again.

"Tell me something," Louis said. "I'm really curious."

"What?"

"Have you ever loved anyone? Really loved them, I mean?"

"Yes, I have as a matter of fact." She blew out a plume of smoke and looked him so squarely in the eye that for a tremendous moment he thought she might be going to say . . .

"When I was twelve, I used to go with my friend Hazel Slarke every night to watch this skiffle group called the Devils practising. I was so naïve, I had no idea what a skiffle group was. I thought it was called a 'striffle droof.' But Hazel Slarke and I used to sit in this scout hut all evening, watching them play, and in some numbers their singer kept time by hitting me on the top of the head with a tambourine. He never even spoke to me, only hit me with a tambourine. But I've never loved anybody so much in my entire life."

---

Three hours later, he was standing on Platform 2 at Paddington, watching scenes not visited on a British Railways mainline station since the filming of *A Hard Day's Night*.

The entire concourse, from Platform 1 to the internal roadway, was a multi-coloured wall of teenage girls, kept in check by metal crash barriers and a supplementary line of shirt-sleeved police. The glassed-over vault rang with that familiar, hardly human shriek, all the more frantic for the recent inaccessibility and distressing nonconformity of its objects. Every so often, a section of the barrier would buckle under the pressure and be roughly shoved back into place, or a fainting figure in a cheap dolly dress be passed over the top for resuscitation by attendant medical teams. High on his plinth, the bronze Tommy in the Great War memorial gazed down with a philosophical air, as if he'd seen all this before at Mons and Passchendaele. The very last theme to be divined in the occasion was a turning aside from the world's clamour, and a quest for the healing spiritual power of meditation and solitude.

Beside the waiting train stood a group of British Railways officials, among them the Stationmaster himself in ceremonial top-hat and frock-coat. Nearby were massed reporters from all the daily and Sunday papers, and the set-up cameras of a dozen television news teams, not only BBC and ITV but also American, French, West German, Dutch and Japanese. From the carriage windows stared the wondering faces of other passengers, coincidentally bound for the obscure North Wales town which, overnight, had become the world's most celebrated destination. As an earnest of the pilgrims' devout intent they were to travel not in their own private Pullman, but on an ordinary stopping train, crowded, old and none too clean.

Louis apart, all the British reporters were specialists who had been covering this same story in a pack since its straightforward early days of "Yeah yeah" lyrics and hailing jellybeans. With a sinking heart he recognised the Evening Standard's Ray Connolly, whose Pop Around column had been first to announce virtually every new, implausible twist in the saga. There, too, were David Wigg of The Express, Vincent Mulchrone of The Mail, Bob Hart of the Mirror, not to mention all the trade press, Melody Maker, Disc, The New Musical Express. On a bandwagon so overcrowded, how could there possibly be room for even one more?

The police cordon at the platform entrance now parted to admit the first and most unlikely of today's pilgrims. It was Mick Jagger of the Rolling Stones, dressed with almost monastic simplicity in a square-necked gold smock, white trousers and open-toe sandals, and flanked by two hefty bodyguards in dark glasses and Italian suits. After him came the Stones' P.R. man, Les Perrin, and Marianne Faithfull, wearing haute couture's most diaphanously extravagant version of the earth mother look.

As the TV microphones clustered around Jagger, Marianne saw Louis and gave him her misty-eyed, mischievous smile. "Hello, Mister Dispatch supplement. What brings you to this thoroughly mystical event?"

"The same as everyone else. Total disbelief."

She gripped his sleeve in her *grande-dame* fashion and steered him beside a trolley of milk-churns also ready to embark on the transcendental journey to Bangor. "You don't have a cigarette on you, do you?"

"Sorry, I don't smoke them."

"Or the teeniest whiff of hash?"

He shook his head.

"Fuck! I just don't know how I'm going to get through a whole weekend in North-bloody-Wales! Look . . . when we get there, would you be a sport and smuggle me in a couple of bottles of Stolichnaya vodka?"

"I'm not coming on the train," Louis said.

"But, my dear—you must! It'll be the hoot of a lifetime! Can you picture it—the Beatles staying in a hall of residence at a teacher-training college! We're not even sure they've been warned to bring some money with them. They never carry it, you know . . . just like royalty."

"I'll be there on Bank Holiday Monday. Brian Epstein's offered me a lift with him."

Marianne's face clouded. "Poor Brian," she murmured.

"Why 'poor Brian'?"

"Surely you must know? They're going to dump him—either when he goes down on Monday, or soon afterwards. All the love and peace in the world can't alter that."

"Dump him? You mean fire him?"

"Yes, I mean fire him."

Louis glanced quickly around to see if any of the Beatles Reporting Corps might be listening. But they were all besieging Mick Jagger along with BBC and ITV, quizzing him on how many hours each day he expected to meditate, and whether the Rolling Stones' new single, "We Love You," could really possibly mean what it said.

"But why on earth would they do that? Epstein was the making of them."

Marianne shrugged. "They think they've got too grown-up—they don't need that kind of old-fashioned manager to look after them and wipe their bottoms any more."

"Maybe they're right," said Louis.

"Are you crazy? They need him now more than they ever did! Even Mick, who as you know is no sentimentalist, has done his best to talk them out of it. But now they've got their own guru to put them straight about everything."

Amid redoubled shrieks from outside, five diminutive figures were ushered through the platform gate and beside the train to a carriage door, held open by a red-jacketed steward. Four of the figures were Beatles, all wearing Genghis Khan moustaches, embroidered Indian tunics and garlands of bright orange flowers. The fifth and most diminutive was Maharishi Mahesh Yogi, lank-haired and piebald-bearded, clad in a shapeless cream silk garment rather like a 1920s tea-gown in some need of laundering. Even at this time of haste and urgency, the holy man was clearly deep in some kind of sermon or homily, punctuated by expansive gestures of his voluminous sleeves and curiously shrill giggles. At one point, he turned and gave a cheery last wave to the screamers on the concourse, evidently supposing their salutations to be all for him.

A train guard had also appeared, holding a green flag and glancing ominously at a silver pocket-watch. "You'd better get on board," Louis told Marianne. "This guy's beginning to look a bit serious."

"Walk me to the door then. It'll be nice to be treated like a lady for a change."

"By the way, I did eventually run in to Doctor Daydream—at least, someone I was almost sure must be him. But I didn't have the nerve to ask if he really did put those four pills in Mick's jacket pocket."

Marianne shut the carriage-door after her, pulled down the window, leaned out and beckoned him close. "I'll tell you who really did put them there if you swear never to write it. Swear!"

"OK."

"*Moi.*"

There was a shrilling of whistles, and the train began noiselessly to move. Louis walked alongside, staring up at her.

"You?"

"It was just an accident. I got a whole lot of them from a disc jockey we know in St. Tropez. Mick always went ape-shit whenever he saw them around the house, so I had to hide them somewhere he'd never think of looking."

He accelerated to keep up with her. "Are you really on the level?"

"*Absolument.* He took the whole of that ghastly rap for me. He said his career as a wicked Stone could stand a drugs bust, but mine couldn't. He wasn't going to let my name be dragged through the mud. But don't dare even whisper it to a living soul. He'd kill me if the awful truth ever came out."

Louis stopped and let the rest of the train slide by on its journey to inner peace and wisdom, and the seaside resorts of North Wales.

"What awful truth?" he shouted.

"That underneath . . ." the husky voice floated back, "Mick Jagger is an old-fashioned, chivalrous English gentleman."

---

Patrick Prince's assistant, the former New York policeman, picked up the dog, descended gingerly to the water's edge holding it at arms' length and placed it in Jean Shrimpton's lap. A Yorkshire terrier little larger than a whiskered cockroach, it went on barking demoniacally.

Patrick himself ducked behind his tripod-mounted Nikon, calling out exhortations to the moored punt's human occupants. "OK . . . super! Penny, darling, hold the parasol up a bit. Yeah, that's cool. That's groovy! Right. Twigs, babe, to me. Oh, yeah! YEAH! Now, Penny, this way, pussycat! Jean! Head right a bit, love! Bit more! Super! Oh, give it to me! Yeah! And again! Again! Super! Super!"

Further up the bank, the BBC sound recordist took off his headphones and gave a shrug of despair. From behind the camera arose the reptilian physiognomy of Tancred Philpott. "Hey, man?" he called to Patrick.

"Yeah, baby?"

"Can you, like, do something about that dog? It's barking, like, all the time, man! Our soundtrack is gonna be nowheresville!"

Shrimpton bent her head in its outsize Victorian picture hat and murmured endearments to the hairy, featureless face. But it continued to bark, or rather yelp, with regular, almost rhythmic flashes of white teeth.

"Maybe the poor little bugger's 'ungry," Twiggy suggested, twirling her own Japanese parasol behind her long-ribboned sailor hat.

The shoot had already been in progress some two and a half hours. At the top of the bank, on the hummocky grass that largely constituted the island, extensive back-up forces waited with crowded trestle-tables and sun umbrellas rigged over folding chairs. Each model had her own make-up artist, her own hair-stylist, her own dresser to help her into the variety of Victorian costumes that hung from metal racks in thick plastic shrouds. Nearby, under a spreading willow tree, tail-coated waiters were laying a snowy tablecloth with heavy silverware, including candelabra, and unpacking bottles and foil-wrapped foodstuffs from refrigerated boxes. Beside the punt and a period hooped camping skiff were moored the half-dozen cruisers and motorboats which had ferried the party from its cars and vans at the Boat and Bottle pub, a quarter of a mile upstream.

Further along the bank, where a makeshift champagne bar dispensed a choice of Bollinger or Pol Roger, other figures in Victorian dress strolled or reclined, sipping from the glasses in their hands. It had been decided that, as well as Toby Godwin, Bracegirdle, Jim Deaves and Louis, some female extras were needed for the Victorian picnic shot. Here, accordingly, was Mrs. Freya Broadbent in a saucy apple-green ensemble with black satin frogged jacket and matching straw hat. Here were Val Lewis in a peach silk blouse and hobble-skirt, and Jessamyn O'Shaughnessy in frothy high-necked beige, only slightly spoiled by the Gitane dangling from one corner of her mouth. The only young rips absent from the frolic were Cedric Scurr and Evelyn Strachey.

Bank Holiday Saturday, with its infallibly brilliant weather, had brought out river traffic at least as dense as in Jerome K. Jerome's 1880s. The island was not the Thames's usual midstream variety, but lay to the side of a broad curve, with a busy lock and the rim of a weir away to its right. Along the green-gold, glinting highway came a ceaseless two-way stream of dinghies, punts, canoes, launches, cabin-cruisers and tourist-packed riverboats. But—except among tourists—scarcely a glance was given to the exotic sideshow. These were the sixties, after all.

As Patrick Prince tried for his shot yet again, the Yorkshire terrier leapt from Jean Shrimpton's arms and strained over the rim of the punt, its frenzy inexplicably redoubled. Hired from Harrods to impersonate Montmorency, Jerome's immortal cur, it rejoiced in the pedigree name Mabli Makepeace of Luton Hoo. Though warranted to have previous experience of modelling, it had proved resolutely unphotogenic, lunging and snapping homicidally at anyone who tried to integrate it into the riverside idyll. Its bark, which had operated since 10:30 that morning virtually without pause, was not the expressive monosyllable of normal-sized dogs, but a continuous sound, both manic and dreary, like a small engine that would not work but was still being revved time after time by someone incredibly stupid.

Once more, the BBC2 sound man grimaced in anguish for his ruined soundtrack and waved his arms to signal "cut." "Jeez, man!" Tancred Philpott called in the voice of a man very near tears. "What *is* its problem?"

"I think I know what it is," Patrick said. "It doesn't like white boats."

The director looked wildly out at the congested midstream. "But . . . they're *all* white, man!"

The most ambitious shot required the three models to be rowed a short way up river in the hooped camping skiff, hands dreamily trailing the water. For still greater visual effect, Toby Godwin agreed to ply one set of oars, with Louis acting as a highly necessary counterweight at the other. The dog sat in Jean Shrimpton's arms, still barking dementedly at every white boat it saw. A few yards behind followed two launches, one containing Patrick and his wide-angle Nikon, the other with the BBC2 camera rigged precariously on its bows and the clapper-board boy in the cockpit signalling, *"One Man's Week*—Toby Godwin. Take seventy-four."

Godwin, on stroke oar, was indeed a magnificent sight. His generous girth encased in a blue, red and yellow striped blazer, with all four buttons fastened, he could as well have been setting forth to plunder the study cupboards of his classmates in the Greyfriars Remove. Rather than a straw boater, he wore a gold-tasselled school cap which shielded only minimal areas of his Napoleonic pate from the hot sun. Innumerable glasses of champagne and Kir Royale had enriched his complexion to almost luminous pink. "Now then, dear boy," he chuckled as they pushed off from the bank. "Having been brought up among seafaring folk, I trust you remember how to feather. And, girls, what about a chorus of the 'Eton Boating Song'?"

They had gone barely a hundred yards when a crowded, noisy two-deck river cruiser, painted a provocative brilliant white, came swishing the other way. With a climactic howl, Mabli Makepeace of Luton Hoo leapt to engage it, not remembering until too late that it is not given to Yorkshire terriers to walk upon water. For the first time that day his eyes became visible, bulging like those of an old-fashioned minstrel singer as four tiny paddling paws fought what was evidently a losing battle for buoyancy. The skiff and the two launches circled him for a few ineffectual moments, amid shrieks and entreaties from Britain's three top models, until Joe, the ex–New York policeman, leaned out and managed to grab the scruff of his neck, pushed him far enough under water to get a proper grip, then hauled his dripping form to safety.

Lunch under the willow tree took a further three and a half hours. It began as a Victorian picnic, styled and photographed after the Magazine's characteristic assumption that all Victorians picnicked on lobster, salmon and sea trout supplied by Fortnum and Mason, with wines by Grants of St. James and silverware from Mappin and Webb. Towards the end, at no very clear signal, it turned into a food fight à la Mack Sennett. As the film camera zeroed in for a close-up of Toby Godwin's guffawing face, with Twiggy squashing a fresh raspberry gâteau into one side of it and Jessamyn an individual summer pudding into the other, Louis wondered how much the sequence might merely reinforce the preconception of BBC2 views concerning a Sunday colour magazine editor's average working week. Amid the splattering cream and meringue, he felt a sudden odd premonition, indefinable and very slight, which he would afterwards liken to that first oh-so-gentle bump against the impregnable bulkheads of the *Titanic*.

By 4:30, all pretence at journalistic activity had been abandoned. Jessamyn, Mrs. Broadbent and the former New York policeman were splashing about in the shallows in their underwear. Jean Shrimpton was feeding left-over pâté de foie gras to the swans. Jim Deaves was asleep under the tilted brim of his straw boater. Terry Bracegirdle had apparently gone for a stroll. Even the dog's dementia had subsided to a low growl as it crouched under the table, gnawing the blubbery remains of a York ham.

"Not going already, dear boy!" Toby Godwin protested. He lay under the willow, smoking an outsize Montecristo, with his head in Val Lewis's hobble-skirted lap. His sideburns and eyebrows still had bits of cream sticking to them. He puffed his cigar and switched to the accent of Charles Laughton in *Mutiny on the Bounty*. "Is this treachery, Mr. Christian? If so, you shall swing from the highest yard-arm!"

"I must, I'm afraid," Louis said. "I'm joining the Beatles and the Maharishi down in Wales tomorrow. I ought to read up a bit on this transcendental meditation crap first."

"Swot!" Mrs. Broadbent cried accusingly from the water.

He took off his boater and removed a strawberry that had lodged in its scarlet ribbon. "God knows what Bermans are going to say when they see the state of these clothes."

"Luckily, we anticipated wear and tear somewhat above the average," Godwin said, "so we bought the lot outright. They're yours to keep, dear boy, if you care to have them among your souvenirs."

Down by the boats, Patrick Prince was consulting his light-metre, then glancing up at a sky grown unaccountably overcast.

"You splitting, man?"

"Bursting, more like."

Patrick grinned and jerked his head towards a wooded promontory a little further along the bank. "Before you go, cop a look over there?"

"Why?"

"It's Terry Bracegirdle and one of the hairdressers. Having a right old dingdong, they are. Wish I'd brought me Polaroid along."

Louis approached the knot of waiting boatmen, and signalled that he required ferrying back to the minicab fleet on standby in the Boat and Bottle car park. As the launch *Haywire* carried him over the broad thoroughfare, grey and even black clouds had begun massing thickly above the Victorian tableau. "Reckon we may have a drop of rain soon," his boatman said.

Had he not been quite drunk, and his mind not been full of Fran and her possible disappearance to New York, and Brian Epstein and the Beatles, and how an opening chapter about them might be put together, not to mention what still remained to be done to *The End of the Pier*, he doubtless would have made much more than he did of two vignettes which presented themselves during this barely fifteen-minute journey.

As his launch neared the left-hand bank, a few yards from the Boat and Bottle's landing-stage, he saw a man up a tree. The tree was small and the man was quite large, straddling a fork in its branches no more than six feet above the path, to the amusement or bemusement of passers-by beneath. He wore a short-sleeved white shirt and clutched what looked like a camera with a built-in flash. All Louis could be bothered to think at the time was that it must be some kind of boat fanatic, poised to snap unusual craft as they passed to and fro. And also how grotesquely unfashionable short sleeves on shirts had become.

The second vignette, even more quickly forgotten, came as he climbed out of the launch, brushing at his river-slimy, summer pudding–stained flannels, and happened to glance up the grassy slope to the Boat and Bottle's crowded family beer-garden. Under a yellow sunshade marked "DOUBLE DIAMOND," he fancied he saw the bull neck and Teddy-boy cowlick of Shildrick's driver, Les.

———————

Louis awoke at 7:30 the next morning, surprised as well as thankful to find almost no trace of hangover. The freakish overnight rain squalls had blown themselves out and there was already the promise of another brilliantly sunny day. A gentle breeze came through the open French windows beyond his writing-desk. He lay still for a few moments, enjoying an impossible daydream. Suppose he were to look up now and see Fran climbing from the front steps, over the balustrade onto the little balcony, pushing aside the muslin curtains with both hands as she stepped into the room?

An hour later he was spinning along Birdcage Walk, looking out at a city as empty and silent as if the Bomb had fallen and vapourised everyone but himself and his plaid-shirted cabbie. Even Buckingham Palace's front railings were deserted. " 'Ere," the cabbie shouted back. "J'you see the Beatles going off on Friday? With that Indian geezer?"

"Yes."

"Whadda they think they're up to, eh?" Only last week, the Queen herself had reportedly asked that same thing.

Twenty-seven Chapel Street was a white Georgian house in the bulkily elegant Belgravia style. Outside the porticoed front door stood a mineral-blue Bentley Continental coupé, soft top lowered to reveal its pristine beige leather trim. Travelling in that would be enjoyable, even to North Wales.

His ring was answered by a pleasant-looking black-haired man, wearing a white shirt and an unbuttoned red waistcoat. In the luxurious hall, a dark-haired woman in a nylon overall was using a vacuum cleaner. "The Spanish couple," alluding to that unpublished classic "Whither the Sixties Servant?," was evidently still a fashionable domestic accoutrement.

"My name's Brennan. To see Mr. Epstein."

An odd look—not quite worry, but definitely concern—flitted across the sunburned face. "Mr. Epstein is still asleep, sir."

"He asked me to meet him here at nine."

The news seemed reassuring, to both the Spanish butler and his wife. "Please come this way, Mr. Brennan. I'll let Mr. Epstein know you're here."

He was shown into a large drawing room just off the front hall. Through the open door he saw the butler pick up a white telephone, dial a single digit on what must be an internal system, wait for some moments, then replace the receiver with a perplexed frown.

Minutes ticked by. The room was a dream of tasteful contemporary design with creamy overstuffed couches and pastel grey and blue drapes. Yet it had a curiously unused feel, like "best parlours" where Louis had often waited in the north. On the white grand piano stood a cluster of silver-framed photographs which he at first presumed must be family. But all were of the Beatles, so young as to be barely recognisable, with hair swept off their faces and wearing leather jerkins with the collars turned up. In place of Ringo Starr was an unknown boy whose saturnine good looks were more magnetic even than Paul McCartney's.

After a quarter of an hour, he heard the telephone ring and went over to the door. The Spanish butler was speaking in an agitated undertone while his wife stood by, holding a can of Brasso. ". . . yes, Mr. Ellis . . . No, sir, not at all . . . Yes, sir, many times . . . And there is a gentleman from the newspaper here, waiting to see him. Yes, of course, Mr. Ellis. I will, sir, of course. Good-bye."

"No sign yet?" Louis asked.

"No, sir." With a glance at his wife, the butler relaxed his official manner. "The truth is, we are getting rather worried. Mr. Epstein has been in his room since late on Friday night. He does not answer our knock, or the house-phone. We are afraid he may be ill."

"Oh, dear," Louis said perfunctorily. Perhaps this would turn out to be a day of novel-writing after all.

"That was his business associate, Mr. Ellis, on the phone. I have told Mr. Ellis we are both very concerned."

For want of anything more helpful, Louis wandered back into the sepulchral drawing room. Five minutes later, he heard a car screech to a stop outside, and then a forceful peal of the front door-bell. Looking into the hall, he saw a man in a T-shirt and jeans, carrying a small black leather bag, running up the curved staircase, followed by the Spanish couple.

"Geoffrey Ellis just rang me," the man said over his shoulder. "Why on earth wasn't I told before this, Antonio?"

"Yes, doctor. I am sorry."

"How long has he been in there?"

"Since late on Friday night. He came back from his house in the country, and left a note for Maria that he was not to be disturbed."

Louis went to the foot of the stairs and watched. At the top, the doctor put down his bag in front of a cream-and-gold door, hammered loudly on it with the flat of one hand, then put his ear against it and listened. Fumbling in his pocket, he produced a coin, rapped on the door with the edge of that and listened again.

"We'd better break it down," he said tersely.

At that moment, the telephone on the hall table rang again and Louis picked it up. "Who's that?" an educated voice demanded.

"Louis Brennan. Sunday Dispatch Magazine."

"Can you tell me what's going on?"

"I think they're about to force the door."

"I'll hold," the voice said.

He laid the receiver on the table and ran upstairs, reaching the top just as the doctor put a T-shirted shoulder against the door and gave it a hefty shove. "I am not happy about it, sir," the butler protested. "He was so angry when we did it before . . . and he was just asleep . . ."

Louis stepped forward and squared up beside the doctor, who made room for him without comment. At the third charge of their combined weight, the door splintered from its frame. As he followed the doctor in, he saw the butler's wife already shrink back and bury her face in her husband's shoulder.

Before the bedroom itself came a small lobby, lined with fitted wardrobes, clothes-drawers and shelves of expensive toiletries in bottles and flasks. On both walls were pictures of the Beatles as they used to be, arranged in a laughing bouquet of moptops or leaping joyously into the air.

In the high-ceilinged chamber beyond, a solid bank of velvet curtains kept out every particle of sun. Not for some seconds could Louis's eyes distinguish the kingsize bed with its quilted head and satin coverlet, and the figure that lay in a polka-dot dressing-gown among strewn papers and photographs, its face turned to the wall.

From the dressing-room behind him came the sound of weeping and soft wailing in Spanish. The doctor picked up the bedside telephone, on which the business associate still awaited information. For a moment, even medical training yielded to the spirit of the sixties, where things like this—especially to people like this—simply couldn't happen.

"Geoffrey? It's all right . . . don't worry . . . it's all right . . ."

# 32

Quite a weekend," said Margaret Cole. "Britain's biggest pop manager found dead. And the Sunday Dispatch loses the Fourth Man."

There was no question which story the Magazine had found the more fascinating. Those who had not been on the river expedition crowded round to listen to Mrs. Broadbent's eyewitness account. Louis eavesdropped as best he could between phone calls to the police, Brian Epstein's company, Nems Enterprises, and the Westminster Coroner's office.

"It was just terribly unfortunate that Mighty Jack and the Close-up team had laid their trap at the very same pub where all our cars and vans and whatnot were parked. Apparently they had photographers hiding all along the bank . . . in trees . . . everywhere. We wouldn't have known anything about it if at about a quarter to six there hadn't been this most awful downpour of rain. Naturally we all scattered for our launches and raced back from the island to the Boat and Bottle as fast as we could. And, alas and alack, that happened to be at precisely the same moment that the Fourth Man hove into sight. Well, of course, one look at Patrick Prince and his cameras, and the BBC television crew, was quite enough for him!"

"God singing the 'Eton Boating Song' through a megaphone didn't help much either," Jim Deaves put in.

"No, nor that frightful little dog barking fit to wake the dead."

"So what did the Fourth Man do?" Cedric Scurr asked.

"What did he do? Turned his boat right around, put the throttle wide open and went straight back the way he'd come."

"Did you get any sort of a look at him?"

"I suppose we should have," Mrs. Broadbent admitted, "since we all went plunging right across his bows. I have to admit, I was too busy trying to protect my hat from the rain to notice very much else. Val saw him, though, or thinks she did, but couldn't make out much beyond the fact that he was wearing a light-coloured raincoat."

"How *wonderful!*" Evelyn Strachey exclaimed, cuddling his bare arms. "Just like a Keystone comedy! And what did Mighty Jack say?"

"I can't even begin to convey to you what Mighty Jack said. The whole of the Steam Section's front page was being kept open for the story; it was going to be the biggest scoop of his career. He'd even signed a contract with George Weidenfeld to write the book on How We Did It. The only word for Mighty Jack, as he saw the Fourth Man speeding away, and then all of us piling ashore in our Victorian blazers and bonnets, was incandescent!"

"Didn't the Close-up boys go after him?" Margaret asked.

"They tried. But with all the Bank Holiday crowds out on the river it was easy for him to give them the slip. They eventually found his launch abandoned near Richmond Bridge."

"What I can't understand," said Scurr, "is why this pub, the Boat and whatsit, didn't twig that two different Sunday Dispatch operations were going on on its premises. I mean, when we rang up to book the parking-spaces, didn't it occur to them to say, 'Oh yeah . . . some more of your blokes are going to be camped in our bedrooms that day, with binoculars and telephoto lenses'?"

"They obviously thought you were all involved in the same project," Margaret said. "After all, it's a perfectly normal assumption for an outsider to make—that departments of a newspaper work in co-operation with each other."

The group was joined by Toby Godwin, richly sun-kissed about the face and pate, his usual guffaw noticeably muted. "It's all highly unfortunate," he said, "but I really can't see that any scintilla of blame can be laid at our door. There was no possible way we could have known Mighty Jack and his boyos were playing cops and robbers on that same stretch of the Thames. The whole thing was simply the most bizarre coincidence."

"Which could have been avoided if the Magazine talked to the paper and the paper talked to the Magazine," Margaret said sweetly.

Godwin was still framing a reply to this when Tessa, his secretary, appeared at his elbow and spoke discreetly into his ear. The young rips still heard what she said clearly enough: "Could you please see the Chairman in his suite right away?"

"It might not be anything at all," Mrs. Broadbent said as they watched their Editor waddle stately from the concourse. "After all, God goes up to talk to Lord M. almost every day."

"But this time he put on his jacket first," Margaret said, "and put out his cigar. Somehow, I get the idea he's not expecting the usual cosy little chat."

He was back in less than half an hour. Immediately, Terry Bracegirdle was called in to see him; ten minutes afterwards, the young rips were summoned en masse. Bracegirdle was seated on his hands on the worktop, his aquiline features even more boyishly rubicund than usual. A still larger portent of something terribly wrong was the total absence of any form of refreshment.

Godwin met the questioning stares with a rueful smile.

"Well, boys and girls . . . that's it, I'm sorry to say."

" 'It'?" Cedric Scurr repeated.

"I'm out as Editor."

"Out?" said Jessamyn blankly.

"As of tomorrow noon. Terry B., too, as Features Editor, I'm afraid."

There was a gasp of unplumbable dismay. "You're joking!" Jim Deaves said.

"Would that I were, dear boy!"

"Not . . . because of that farcical business over the weekend!"

Godwin smiled again and shrugged, the gesture of an English sportsman graciously conceding defeat.

"As ever, you underestimate the oratorical gifts of Mighty Jack Shildrick. I may add that the quarter of an hour I've just sat through was a virtuoso performance, even by Mighty Jack standards. He managed to convince Lord M., not only that the Steam Section has lost the greatest scoop in its history, but that we down here somehow deliberately conspired to sabotage it, if you can believe this—" here Godwin launched boomingly into Shildrick-speak—" 'as part of a campaign to ridicule and oondermine the paper and all it stands for in the pooblic perception . . .' At one point, he even floated the amazing allegation that Private Eye's piece on his recent domestic vicissitudes originated in a leak from someone in this office."

Louis, feeling himself blush scarlet, tried to hunch down inconspicuously behind Evelyn Strachey. "You said that was absolute bollocks, I hope," said Deaves.

"Our Chairman, fortunately, is above the petty details of interdepartmental rivalry. But I'm sorry to say that the loss of potential sales with the Fourth Man exposé, added to the decline in our advertising revenue, have given Mighty Jack his trump card. Lord M. now sides with him in the view that we here have become complacent, arrogant and out of touch with the ordinary reader, and that the only way to win back advertisers to the Magazine is a complete re-vamp and re-launch under a new Editor."

"Appointed by Shildrick?" Deaves asked.

"Yes."

"Fucking little wanker," Jessamyn murmured with customary verbal imprecision.

"You're not leaving the company, are you, God?" Val Lewis asked.

"Lord bless you, no, darling! McIntyre Newspapers aren't the sort of outfit to just sling you into the street. I'm being given a new post—Director of Graduate Training. And Terry here's also moving to the fifth floor."

"I'm goin' to be number three on the Newsdesk," said Bracegirdle with a valiant pretence at brightness.

"It's not total wipeout," Godwin continued. "Even Mighty Jack realises the Magazine has to be kept running by those experienced in doing so. So he wants Cedric to stay on as Art Director." Scurr's goldfishy bifocals registered the joyous news without a flicker. "No other staff changes are planned at present, but no doubt some of you will feel impelled to consider your position here. I'm sure I need not spell out the implications of the phrase 'complete re-launch.' "

Each face around him showed full appreciation of what the phrase implied. It implied the end of 6,000-word pieces on the far-off and obscure, photographic essays rivalling any in Life or Stern, and first-class air-tickets around the world. It implied short, useful features on home and family-related topics, illustrated with maps, graphs and "fact boxes." Scores of laughable ideas, read aloud in funny northern voices and comfortably banished to limbo, seemed now to rise up, gibbering and rattling their chains: "Choosing Your Child's Comprehensive," "Ramblers' Britain," "The Year-round Window-box," "A Beginner's Guide to the European Economic Community," "The ABC of Teeth." Behind Evelyn Strachey's blue Aertex back, Louis remembered how many times he had sat here, secretly rooting for Shildrick and raging at his colleagues' disdainful disrespect. Now he felt his heart plummet in the same free fall as everyone else's.

The question no one could bear to articulate finally came from Jim Deaves. "Any idea who's going to be taking over from you?"

Godwin shook his head.

"Mighty Jack claims not to have quite decided yet. There are obviously several vociferous contenders on the Steam Section as well as those who, I now learn, have been secretly canvassed among our rivals. I was able to convince him that, as a courtesy to you all, he should announce it in person rather than coldly pinning it up on a notice-board. This he's undertaken to do at five tomorrow afternoon."

In Tessa Burland's outer office, a telephone started ringing. It seemed to Louis that it did so with unaccustomed harshness, reflecting this new era of evil news. A palpably intimidated hush fell on the meeting as Tessa answered it, then slid back the glass panel that connected her with Godwin.

"Granada Television for you," she said.

With a grimace of apology, Godwin picked up his extension "Hullo. Yes . . . speaking. Ah, hullo." He listened for some moments in mystification gradually turning to incredulity. "You don't say so!" he said at length. "Well, well, well, that's extremely handsome of them! Yes, of course, I shall be delighted. And the lunch is on the twenty-seventh, you say? Well, thank you so much for letting me know . . . See you then. Absolutely. Tinkerty-tonk." He replaced the receiver and turned back to his young rips with yet another wry smile.

"Here's a rum thing to happen on the same day one is axed as Editor of a colour magazine. That was Granada TV's *What the Papers Say* programme. In their annual Press awards, I've been voted Colour Magazine Editor of the Year!"

---

For the rest of that day, even the Magazine's mild semblance of activity came to a full stop. All through the concourse people huddled together in shellshocked groups, as if seeking comfort from physical closeness; old rivalries and disagreements were forgotten in the common shock, disbelief, outrage and trepidation. Nor was it long before rumours about Godwin's successor began crackling through the susceptible air like forked lightning around some old stylised radio mast. Half a dozen different names were mentioned, and discussed with varying degrees of horror, from John Anstey, Editor of the Telegraph's Saturday magazine, to David Frost.

"Please, don't let it be Nick Fenton!" Jessamyn entreated heaven, rolling her bloodshot eyes. "Please, please, PLEASE!"

"I still think it'll be someone from outside," Mrs. Broadbent said. "Dennis Hackett at Nova is supposed to be looking for a change. And he's a north country lad, just like Shildrick. Or, Cedric thinks, they might even bring some whizzkid over from New York, like Clay Felker of Esquire. After all, this is one of the world's great magazines."

"*Was* one of the world's great magazines," Margaret corrected. "From now on, it's going to be just another department of the Steam Section. Whoever takes the job is going to have to be prepared to do exactly what Mighty Jack tells them. So how can it possibly be anyone any good?"

In the course of the afternoon, Louis was called away from various mourning groups to take three telephone calls. The first was from the Westminster Coroner's office, informing him that the inquest on Brian Epstein would be opened the following day. The second was from Michael Sissons at A. D. Peters, relaying Arden Sinclair's offer of a £3,000 advance against royalties for a biography of the Beatles. The third was from Shildrick's secretary, Enid, asking him to come up right away.

Shildrick was standing at his lectern, studying a galley-proof with a Bic pen in his hand as if this anonymous, selfless aspect of editorship were the only one that really interested him. He wore his luminous grey striped Carnaby hipsters and a ruffle-fronted cerise satin shirt with huge leg o'mutton sleeves that might have made even Tom Jones think twice.

Victory became him rather less than defeat had become Toby Godwin. As he turned round, Louis saw that his eyes were unnaturally bright and each of his cheeks had a livid red patch near the top. "Well . . . I knew they'd go too far one day, and now they have," he said, twisting the Bic from north to south and east to west with a hand that visibly trembled. "It just goes to prove what I've always said. Give people enough rope, and they'll hang themselves in the end." His blouselike shirt and over-long hair augmented the impression of some tight-lipped northern harridan, as mimicked by Al Read, folding her arms and bridling a triumphant "I told you so."

"That whole episode at the weekend was an utter disgrace," he went on before Louis could speak. "A criminal waste of money and resources that should be called to account, even if it hadn't boogered up one of the great journalistic enterprises of all times. I'm not concerned for myself so much as for Nick and the Close-up boys after all their months of dedicated work. I'm only glad you weren't involved, Poet."

"I was. It's just that I happened to leave before the end. I even saw one of your blokes hiding in a tree."

"Oh, you did, did you?" Shildrick said in an even tone. "In that case, after what I'd told you and with your celebrated X-ray vision, I'm amazed you didn't put two and two together."

There was no answer to this; at least, none that could be summoned at the moment.

"Anyroad, I take it you've heard the news."

"Yes."

Shildrick glanced at him curiously. "You're pleased about it, aren't you? I know you never approved of the daft way they went on down there. You've sat on that settee over there and griped to me about Tony Godwin enough times."

"I know, but he was the one who gave me my first chance here. And I have worked for him for over a year."

"More than," Shildrick said.

"Pardon?"

"Not 'over a year,' 'more than a year.' It's amazing how many otherwise very literate people always get that wrong."

Louis experienced a fleeting but powerful urge to seek out the nearest copy of Fowler's *Modern English Usage* and ram it forcibly somewhere that the luminous grey hipsters made not so very inaccessible.

"I just think it's atrocious he should be unstuck at a moment's notice like that. And I'm kind of surprised at you, behaving like the worst kind of old-fashioned Fleet Street butcher. The Dispatch is always the first to condemn that kind of treatment of senior executives when it happens in the City or in industry."

The flush had gone from Shildrick's face and the triumphant tremor from his hand. He looked up, soulful eyes brimming with their customary appeal to reason, common sense and simple humanity. "I know you feel loyalty to Godwin—and Bracegirdle—and it does you great credit. Don't suppose for one second that I enjoy this kind of thing. When you sit in the chair of a great newspaper, there are often hard decisions to be made. Brutal decisions, even. But, if you're to stay on top of the job, they have to be made. Personal feelings, however strong, must be sacrificed to the greater good. I know you're enough of a professional to understand that."

Louis gazed at him, suddenly uncertain. Perhaps he really and truly didn't enjoy this kind of thing. Perhaps "the greater good" really was involved here rather than, as had first seemed, pent-up vindictive fury over the snubbing of "The ABC of Teeth."

"Besides," Shildrick added lightly, "you yourself could do rather well out of all this."

"Sorry?"

"That's why I wanted to talk to you." Shildrick took his elbow and guided him towards the windows, glancing round cautiously for eavesdroppers. "I know how much you love writing," he murmured, "and you do it superlatively well. But have you ever thought of moving up from that?"

"Up?"

"To more of an executive role. Writers in the long run don't do so well, you know. However senior, they can only be paid up to a certain level, whereas as a key figure in the command structure here you could be on three thousand a year, maybe even more."

Louis felt his innards give the sort of crazy downward lurch they had not done since long-ago days on the Stockton Evening Telegraph.

"You mean . . . edit?"

"Yes, I do." Shildrick's voice had the terse calm it always assumed when proposing a leap beyond one's craziest dreams. And there was only one such impossible leap he could possibly be referring to. All at once, Louis could visualise himself so easily . . . sitting at Toby Godwin's desk before the view of the G.P.O. Tower, cigar in mouth . . . having phone numbers dialled for him by the end of Tessa's pencil . . . initialling pages passed through to him by Margaret . . . presiding at the Ideas Lunch . . . throwing back Jessamyn's copy for the umpteenth rewrite . . . telling Evelyn Strachey to get up off his arse or else . . .

"But," the old, silly, diffident part of him couldn't help saying, "I've had no experience . . ."

Shildrick batted the object away. "You've got all the qualities a first-rate editor needs. You've got a marvellous nose for a story. You care passionately about good writing. And you work like a trouper. I know you always wanted Cicero, but in a way you've gone past that. What I have in mind would be a far greater challenge. And challenge is our life-blood, isn't it, in this crazy, wonderful world of Print? Not that I've any doubt that you'd do a wonderful job, and justify the high hopes I've always had for you. So what do you say, Poet? Are you game?"

Now Louis's eyes were the shining ones, and his cheeks the ones showing a hectic flush.

"Yes, I'm game," he said.

That evening, he took a break from Chapter 7 to look through the archive of Grandad Bassill's newsreel career that had been given into his keeping. It included a passport issued in the reign of Edward VII which opened out like a road-map; a crumbling accreditation to the 1911 Delhi Durbar; a typed letter of authority from George VI's Private Secretary to go on board the royal Yacht *Victoria and Albert* during the 1937 Coronation Fleet Review; and a temporary membership of the Washington Press Club, dated December 1942. There were also miscellaneous antiquated camera-lenses, booklets of regulations for the Grand Order of Freemasons (Streatham Hill lodge) and three dark khaki albums filled with sepia stills from the Great War, captioned in familiar tiny handwriting and with familiar understatement. A panoramic shot of heads in pillbox hats bore the inscription "A few Jerries."

He was kneeling beside his desk, with the albums and documents spread around him on the red cocktail bar carpet. Evening sun poured into the room, only slightly diffused by the net curtains of the open

French windows. In his absorption he did not hear the footfall on the front steps of the house, nor even the sound of someone taking the unofficial short cut from there across to his balcony. It was for no particular reason that he looked up to see a perennial early-morning and late-night fantasy come true. Two hands parted the billowing net, and there stood Fran.

She wore a long, hippy-like dress of a diaphanous pink floral stuff, its curly edges furled over and tied round the waist. In her hand was an outsize straw hat with a floppy brim. The light behind her made the honey hair sparkle like a mirage and showed the outline of her legs up to her waist.

"Can I come in?" she asked.

Without waiting for his reply, she stepped down into the room, revealing that she was also barefoot. The black centipedes took in the panelling and Tudor roses with a flicker of amusement. "My word! This is all very baronial."

The softened *r* made Louis's heart melt as always. But, tearing his gaze from the effect of the light on her dress, he spoke in the sternest possible cable-ese.

"Why you here?"

"I wanted to see you. Is that allowed?"

He laughed, not very pleasantly. "I don't think I'm the one you'd better ask that question."

"Can I sit down for a minute? I promise I won't stay long."

He shrugged with an impressive simulation of indifference, and motioned her to the carved wooden chair that was turned around from his writing-desk. She curled herself in it like some little Victorian paying an awestruck visit to her stern father's study. Louis pretended to be still more interested in the memorabilia spread on the carpet.

"I hear you got a wonderful scoop?" she said.

"Sorry?"

"Brian Epstein."

"Oh . . . yes. By a sheer bloody fluke."

"Why on earth would he do something like that?"

"No one can say for sure that he killed himself. He was full of brandy and sleeping-pills, but that could have been what are called 'incautious self-overdoses.' The inquest verdict will probably be death by misadventure."

"But everyone assumes it was suicide, don't they?"

Her face wore an artlessly attentive look that Louis saw through at once, having used it to advantage many times himself. But the temptation to show off was irresistible.

"He certainly turns out to have had enough reason. He was a homosexual, an alcoholic, probably a drug addict. His emotional life was chaos . . . you know, road-menders and Guardsmen. And on top of everything else, he knew the Beatles were about to dump him."

"But he had so many other Liverpool acts . . . Gerry and the Pacemakers . . . Cilla Black . . . Billy J. . . . ."

"All of them together didn't mean as much to him as the Beatles. He was hopelessly in love with John Lennon, you see. If this wasn't suicide, he'd made at least two attempts in the past couple of months. He could stand not managing Paul, George and Ringo well enough; it was losing John he couldn't live with."

"Christ, what a story," Fran breathed.

"I know." He couldn't resist a triumphant smirk. "Not bad, is it?"

"Are you doing it for Jack this Sunday?"

"No."

"But you must! The Magazine won't be able to bring it out for ages!"

"I'm not doing it for anyone," Louis said firmly. "I mean, not for anyone except me. It's the prologue of my book on the Beatles. Nobody gets to read it until then."

She stared in a way that made him remember Salzburg, Richard Burton, blond Nazi fiends and fourposter beds with puffy white quilts. "You're not seriously going to sit on it for all that time?"

"Why not? No one else has got it. I can afford to keep my nerve. It's all there." He gestured at the pile of notebooks on the desk behind her and then, as she twisted around to look, suddenly realised how incredibly unwise that might have been.

"Anyway, how about you?" he continued, keeping his eye on both her hands. "Are you taking that job in New York?"

"I dunno," Fran replied as wearily as if the job in New York were freeing blocked toilets. To his infinite relief she turned away from his research notes, fished a packet of Winstons out of her shoulder-bag and lit one with a French disposable lighter, now psychedelic orange.

"Surely you're not going to pass up such an opportunity? You'd be crazy."

"You want me to go then, do you?"

"I don't see that it's anything to do with me."

"Don't you?" she said dully.

"Speaking of big opportunities, I'm having a bit of an inward battle here myself. I was all set to leave the Dispatch and live on my advance from Arden Sinclair. Then this afternoon Jack had me up and as good as offered me the Editorship of the Magazine."

A flicker of something—unease, even distress—showed in the black centipedes. She took a breath, thought better of it and turned away, smoking hard.

"What?" Louis said.

"Nothing."

"You were going to say something. What? That I shouldn't take it?"

"It's nothing," Fran said. "Forget it." She inhaled again and glanced round the room once more, unaware that he was still watching her hands in relation to his papers and her shoulder-bag with the intensity of a store detective. "Do you remember the horse in that painting in Portobello Market? The one with the terrible squint."

"Yes. I still sometimes wish I'd bought it."

"I still wish I'd bought it for you. It'd go rather well in here."

He laughed. She did, too. He remembered how often they laughed at the same things.

"Do you still go to the Curry Inn like we used to?" she asked.

He nodded.

"And to the Maze coffee shop at midnight for ham and eggs?"

"Yes."

"I miss it."

"Me, too."

For the first time she looked down at the carpet. "What are these?"

"Some things of my grandfather's."

She leaned down and picked up the photo that had started Louis off, all those months ago: Grandad in top-hat and morning coat, training his mouse-eared camera on the 1924 Wembley Exhibition.

"He's the image of you. Look at those eyes. He's even got a mole in the same place you have."

"Was," Louis said.

"Sorry?"

"*Was* the image of me. He died."

"Oh, no," she murmured. "When?"

"Last month. I meant to tell you the other day . . . but somehow the moment never came."

"I'm sorry. You were really close to him, weren't you?"

"Yep," Louis said lightly.

She knelt down on the carpet and put her arm round his shoulders. He flicked through the photograph albums, talking in the same steady, detached tone.

"He had an incredible funeral. Hundreds of people turned up. Even I never realised quite what a star he was in his day . . . all these old codgers on sticks and in wheelchairs, who used to be the crème de la crème of photo-journalism . . . Tommy Scales from Gaumont-British, Jack and Jock Gemmell from Movietone, Terry Cotter from Pathé. Can you believe someone could actually be called Terry Cotter? The lesson was read by the man who used to do Gaumont's commentaries. Terribly badly fitting grey toupée, he wore . . ."

Fran said nothing, merely tightened her grip round his shoulders as if the two of them were riding a switchback together.

"There he is in the First War with D. W. Griffith . . . his car after it had been cut in two by a shell . . . With the Duke of Windsor . . . Tallulah Bankhead . . . G. B. Shaw . . . lining up Churchill, Roosevelt and Stalin at the Yalta conference . . ."

It seemed entirely logical for the Yalta conference to lead on to turning Fran's face around, kissing her cool, fresh mouth for a brief eternity, then helping her up with both hands, loosening the drawstring of her pink forget-me-not robe, walking with her over to the narrow single bed in a calm, unhurried way, lying her on the red candlewick coverlet and looking down at her, unrolled from her dress like a pale butterfly released from its chrysalis. Churchill, Stalin and Roosevelt, oddly enough, were still there somewhere as everything that had been so problematic before became perfect now: position perfect, balance perfect, temperature perfect, concentration perfect, sound-effects perfect in tone and volume. Even at the endlessly perfect uttermost moment, those three great leaders of yesteryear seemed to watch from the sideline, one noble and tragic in his wheelchair, one with piggy eyes and thick Russian moustache, the third making a wholly suitable V-for-Victory sign.

"God!" Louis said at length, blinking up at panels and mock-Tudor roses that seemed to add their own felicitations. "It worked. It really worked. It did work, didn't it?"

"Mm hm," Fran replied softly.

"You were laughing at the end."

"So were you."

"Funnily enough, the Eskimos call having sex 'laughing with someone.' "

"What?"

"I was thinking of the story you once showed me. About the Eskimo."

He fell asleep for a few moments, then awoke in panic. But she was still there; his notes on Brian Epstein were still there. He laughed, leaned over and, as so often in dreams, kissed her sparkly hairline.

---

Toby Godwin vacated the chair of The Sunday Dispatch Magazine in the same stylish manner with which he had overflowingly filled it. On his last morning, his desk-top was as pristinely innocent as ever of mundane paper- and production-work. At eleven, Tessa served him his usual Mincing Lane coffee and Fortnum's brioche; at 11:45 he smoked his morning Bolivar number 2; at 12:15 he departed with Scurr, Brace-girdle, Strachey and Jessamyn, his oldest confederates, for a farewell lunch at L'Ecu de France. Soon afterwards, black-clad young men and women from Nick's Diner appeared carrying foil-wrapped platters and white boxes of Pol Roger and, with deftness born of long practice, began transforming the Magazine concourse into a place of celebration.

From 3 o'clock onward, any contributor who wished was invited to drop in, say good-bye and drink the outgoing Editor's health. In the event, it proved the biggest party even the Magazine had ever given, attracting a galaxy of stars that brought Godwin's regime into sudden impressive focus. Among the writers were Kingsley Amis, Anthony Burgess, V. S. Naipaul and Len Deighton; among the photographers, David Bailey, Terence Donovan, Patrick Prince and Brian Duffy; among the fashion models, Twiggy, Maudie James and Donyale Luna; among the artists and illustrators, David Hockney, R. B. Kitaj, Patrick Procktor, Alan Aldridge and Peter Blake. Round the walls had been pinned photographic blow-ups of memorable moments from the past six years—Godwin presiding over his young rips at lunch at the Terrazza, Boulestin, Chez Victor and the Gay Hussar, and at dinner at the White Elephant, Bertorelli's and the Garrick Club; Godwin at Royal Ascot, at Glyndebourne, in the members' marquee at Henley, in his private box at Lord's; most poignantly of all, perhaps, in the car park at the Boat and Bottle, guffawing uproariously in his tiny, tasselled school cap. Even that most recent scene of scenes already seemed to belong to a world as mistily far-off as the summer before the Great War.

The corporeal Godwin stood just inside the door, greeting his un-numbered protégés with emotional handshakes, arm-grips and slaps on the back. Not a few guests—and not only women—spontaneously wrapped their arms round his generous girth, burying their faces in his distorted frontal shirt-pleat like children taking leave of Santa Claus. He continued to take his overthrow with the grace of a much slimmer man, merely nodding philosophically as this or that new arrival murmured outraged commiserations into his ear, and striving to put the brightest possible face on his new post as Director of Graduate Training. "I'm looking forward to it," his voice could be heard booming resolutely. "Of course, it won't be as enjoyable as editing the Magazine. Nothing could be as enjoyable as that."

"What happened to the film they was doing on you?" David Bailey asked him.

"Ah, yes . . . *One Man's Week.* I'm afraid it's been rather knocked on the head."

"Poor old Tancred," said Jim Deaves. "All those weeks of work for nothing. And he must have been pretty pissed off to think he could have had the Fourth Man in the can as well."

Godwin chuckled sympathetically, detaching a grey wedge of cigar-ash.

"I believe he's now transferred to Religious Programmes."

In the case of Terry Bracegirdle, bound for the paper's Newsdesk and a life of all too horribly genuine "working late," valedictory sentiments were more qualified. Several guests when they arrived were surprisingly encumbered by office items which they claimed to have picked up on the pavement outside McIntyre House—orange and blue cardboard files, headed notepaper, pencils, expenses-sheets and at last, illuminatingly, components of a green onyx and brass executive desk-set. Through the glass partition of Bracegirdle's soon-to-be-vacated office, a curious spectacle then revealed itself. Various of the Magazine's senior female staff—Jessamyn O'Shaughnessy, Val Lewis, and Tessa Burland—had congregated there and were systematically throwing or tipping everything movable through the open casement window. The calmly zestful and co-operative way in which they worked suggested some long-suppressed grievance in common. This grievance being all too easy to guess at, it was a considerable shock when the ultra-cool and contained Margaret Cole also came into view, flinging Bracegirdle's plum-coloured jacket through the window with bitter relish, and following it up with the wooden hanger on which it had been arranged.

Louis's full enjoyment of the spectacle was hampered by a recurring thought that half an hour from now, perhaps even less, he would be the Sunday Dispatch Magazine's new Editor, a young prodigy remarkable even for these times, lounging with his Cuban heels on Toby Godwin's desk and lighting a Havana the size of a Graf Zeppelin. Bowels almost liquifying with excitement, he fought his way to the champagne bar, where David Kausman stood mountainously chocolate-suited and smoking his usual flat, aromatic cigarette. As always, like certain American Indian tribes, David Kausman eschewed formal greeting. "What time is this gruesome announcement scheduled for?"

"Five."

"And there's still no idea who it might be?"

For a moment, Louis thought of unburdening himself. But it was too noisy. Too many hostile ears might overhear. And Kausman would be almost sure to disapprove.

"Nope."

Kausman's brown eyes swept over him. "What's the matter? You're looking very uptight."

"I'm absolutely fine."

From a few yards away, an uproarious "Hooh hooh hooh hooh!" floated from a group comprising Terence Stamp, John Schlesinger, Terence Donovan and Mary Quant. Godwin had evidently just been handed his leaving-card, a skilful Art Department mock-up of Manet's *Déjeuner sur l'herbe*, with a familiar jolly countenance superimposed on the reclining nude.

Kausman mesmerised a passing waitress and took a square of pumpernickel thickly wadded with smoked salmon. "Well, this is the end of *déjeuner sur l'herbe*. From here on, I think, it'll be more like bread and dripping on the back fire-escape. I must say God is behaving like a true gent. If I were him, I'd be looking through the new Yellow Pages for my neighbourhood contract killer."

"Do you think he was a good Editor?" Louis asked.

Kausman inhaled noisily. "Don't be absurd! Of course he was a good Editor."

"But he was so incredibly lazy. And pusillanimous. You know what we always said around the office: 'The Editor's indecision is final.' "

"Just be glad you were lucky enough to work for someone like that," Kausman said. "God had the very best quality an Editor can have. He sat back and just let things happen."

"Some very bad things."

"Agreed. And some brilliant things. Never forget he let *you* happen."

"I don't," Louis said.

"God had two great gifts. He made life enjoyable for his staff, and he knew how to delegate. That's how the very best newspapers and magazines have always come about. It's how Dudley Mowforth made the Dispatch what it is, or was. Editors who interfere in everything, like your pin-up boy Shildrick, aren't in that same league."

"But you've always had a down on Shildrick, haven't you, David?"

"Yes," Kausman replied calmly. "Because he's second-rate. Because he's a hypocrite. Because he's a snob. And because he's an egomaniac that even the art world would be hard put to match. You think he's such a great altruist and humanitarian with all these campaigns and crusades, but they're all done for one reason only, the greater glory of Jack Shildrick. Oh, and I forgot to mention petty envy and destructiveness. He couldn't bear the thought that the Magazine was a success independent of him. He was like a child, coveting a shiny toy. And now he's got it, he can't wait to start pulling its wheels off."

It had naturally been expected that when Shildrick came down to take formal possession of the Magazine, he would do so with formal triumph, surrounded by a Praetorian Guard of henchmen from the Steam Section. In the event, he came alone, and so diffidently that most of the gathering did not realise he had arrived. His pale grey double-breasted suit, midnight-blue shirt and nearly-matching tie seemed to have been chosen deliberately not to offend or alarm. In one hand he held one of the penholders from the recently vandalised executive desk-set. "I think this is yours, Terry," he said, handing it to Bracegirdle. "One of the commissionaires picked it up on the pavement near the front entrance."

The company had by now realised who he was, and drawn back several paces on all sides as if from contagious disease or extreme body odour. Only Louis stood his ground, a few feet to the left, holding his champagne glass with conscious delicacy lest unbearably mounting excitement should cause him inadvertently to snap its stem.

As usual, there was no sense of formal speechmaking, no rapping and calling for silence, no "Ladies and gentlemen," no throat-clearing and awkward groping for notes. Shildrick did not even appear to be raising his voice, even though it was clearly audible in the remotest parts of the concourse.

"I know quite a lot of you won't be thrilled to see me stood standing here, as we used to say in Accrington. In fact, some of you are probably wishing that quaint old medieval practices like the thumbscrew and the Iron Maiden hadn't been done away with in the name of progress." There was a faint murmur of concurrence. Kingsley Amis could be seen shaking his head in a heartfelt way.

"You think I've behaved like the worst kind of old-style Fleet Street butcher. You think it's an utter disgrace that Toby and Terry here should have been unstuck from their jobs at a few hours' notice . . . something you might expect to happen at The Daily Mail or The Express, but not The Sunday Dispatch." The murmur of concurrence was louder and fiercer. "Well, you're right," Shildrick said. "There were reasons it had to be done the way it was, which I can't go into here, but the fact remains that two of our senior executives were treated in a way that we as a paper would be the first to condemn if it happened in industry or in the City. I take full responsibility and I apologise . . . to Toby and Terry, to their staff and to all of you."

He turned dark, entreating eyes to Toby Godwin, who nodded graciously and mouthed the words "Not at all, dear boy." In his audience, hostility palpably changed to astonishment. This was the very last tactic anyone had expected.

"I hope you'll believe me when I say I'd be the last person on earth to denigrate what Toby has done with the Magazine over these past six years. He's made it the epitome of everything trendy—have I got that word right, Toby? The faces I see around now me attest to the quality of its words and pictures. Jessamyn O'Shaughnessy's fashion coverage has been some of the freshest and most irreverent around. Valerie Lewis's picture editing is a byword throughout Fleet Street. Cedric's Scurr's audacious virtuosity in layout and typography have been imitated but never equalled. I can remember when I was just another struggling hack in the provinces, going out to buy it of a Sunday morning and thinking, 'Ooh, heck! What sort of underpants are they going to tell me I should wear this week? Polka-dots or stripes?' "

There was a rustle of laughter. Both Jessamyn and Val Lewis were simpering with pleasure at their name-checks. Even Scurr's bifocals, for once, did not look totally expressionless.

"But all of you know this crazy, wonderful world of Print! Nothing ever stands still. The Godwin Magazine was perfect for its time, but times change, and we must change with them if we're to keep the Dispatch in its position as the pre-eminent quality Sunday, if we're to justify the loyalty of our readers, do right by our shareholders—and, incidentally, maintain all of you, freelances as well as staff, in well-paid and secure employment. Clearly no one in their right senses likes to break up a happy team. If you sit in the chair of a great newspaper, there are sometimes hard decisions to be made. Brutal ones, even. They may be for the greater good of everyone. But, believe me, that doesn't make it owt easier."

He paused and brushed at the tail of one eye with a little finger, as though reflecting on the hard thing he had done for all their sakes almost induced manly tears. Throughout the concourse there was now total, captivated silence. Then David Kausman's voice, quietly but very clearly, called out, "Shame!"

For an instant, Shildrick's soulful features crumpled into a look of pure, venomous hatred. Otherwise he did not acknowledge the interpolation. "This is the start of an exciting new era for the Magazine," he continued, "and one which I believe will see it going on to even greater glory. The sixties are the time of the young, the vital, the energetic, and in the very difficult task of choosing Toby Godwin's successor, your Chairman and I have borne that fact very much in mind." For the first time he looked directly at Louis, who curled all ten toes agonisingly inside Anello and Davide elasticated boots and took an almost fainting sip of tepid champagne.

"So as the new Editor we've selected someone you may think young, and possibly inexperienced, but someone whose talents are beyond question and who, we're confident, is the right person to steer the Sunday Dispatch Magazine towards the very different challenges of the nineteen-seventies. Will you please give her a warm welcome?"

Turning towards the deserted inner end of the concourse, he raised an index finger and beckoned briefly. The strip-lights were not on down there, so it was a moment before the general vision adjusted to the figure who came walking down the aisle between the desks, honey hair tumbling onto a cream silk blouse, head humbly bowed and black centipede eyes downcast, as always looking as though the last thing she wished in the world was to be the centre of attention.

The poleaxed silence was finally broken by Jessamyn's slurry murmur of "Jesus wept!"

# 33

You'll stay on, will you, Margaret?" Louis asked her as he cleared his desk of fourteen months' accumulated papers and notebooks. In the grey metal waste-bin already lay such poignant mementoes as the first page-proof of "Pincher Bassill," an opulent booklet on the worldwide operations of Ocean-Dredged Aggregates, a 10,000-word first draft of the Elizabeth Taylor profile and all those misguidedly voluminous notes on the role of the domestic servant in the egalitarian sixties. He realised he was still essentially rootless in his desire to carry as little as possible from even this era to the next.

"Yes, I'll stay on," Margaret said. "Beggars can't be choosers. And the same goes for Chief Subs."

"It's disgraceful the way they treat you, you know. You're the most conscientious, hard-working person here. Without you, the whole place would fall apart."

She smiled, hooking the mousy curtain of hair behind her ear; she was wearing the same pink Nehru dress she had worn on Louis's first morning. He wished he dared ask what it was that had precipitated that ritual casting-out of Terry Bracegirdle's jacket and coat-hanger.

"Conscientiousness doesn't do you much good in this game," she said. "Nor competence either, for that matter. But at least I'm above, or below, all the machinations. And after the bloodletting's over, they always need people like me to straighten things out."

He held up a carbon copy of "Oedipus, Darling." "Remember how you told me at the time you thought this was disappointingly thin?"

"I know! Who could ever have known it was such dynamite?"

"What about Jim and Val Lewis?"

"They'll stay, too," Margaret said. "They're both pros. And Jim, at least, has seen this kind of thing happen masses of times before. It's only in the last couple of years that people have started regarding jobs in Fleet Street as cosy sinecures."

"And Evelyn Strachey really has resigned?"

"Nothing so dramatic. He just hasn't bothered to come in again. He's rich, anyway; he's got no need to work if he doesn't want to. A couple of book reviews a year for the New Statesman are all he needs to keep ticking over."

"I'm still sorry I didn't hit it off with him. I still think when he's on form, and not being stupidly camp and self-indulgent, he's the best there is."

"You've got no one to blame but yourself for not hitting it off with him. You should have been prettier."

"And I suppose Jessamyn will hang on somehow, whatever she may say. And Freya, too."

Margaret smiled wanly. "Where else could either of them go? They're both unique creations of this place. Their names are their only job-description. I can't see any other magazine having a vacancy for a Freya Broadbent."

Indeed Mrs. Broadbent, when she arrived, proved to be in a state of high exhilaration. "You'll never guess what happened to me at the party!" she said, unpicking the headscarf-knot on her chin. "Jack Shildrick got me in a corner—amazing bedroomy eyes he's got, hasn't he?—and started asking me what I did on the Magazine. I told him all about my reconstruction of General de Gaulle's life in Petts Wood, and, my dear, he went absolutely crazy about it! Said it was just the kind of thing he was looking for, and must go in as soon as possible, with lots of pictures, maps and fact boxes. I must say, his enthusiasm is jolly infectious after all these years of God's laissez-faire."

"I'd get the copy up to him today if I were you," Margaret said. "Remember he's supposed to have a memory-span of only about seven seconds."

Mrs. Broadbent nodded earnestly. "The trouble is, I haven't quite finished it."

"OK, send him what you've done and he can imagine the rest. How much have you got on paper?"

"Well . . . nothing actually," Mrs. Broadbent admitted.

"Nothing! But, Freya, you've been working on it the best part of a year!"

"You know what dreadful trouble I always have with thinking up intros . . ."

Everything that Louis wanted to preserve of his Magazine life, apart from cuttings, could be packed into a flat attaché case (bought on ex-

penses). As he locked the clasp, he wondered what some future grandson of his might make of the curious miscellany. There was the stub of
an admission ticket to Wembley Stadium's Royal Grandstand for the
1966 World Cup; a glossy white book of matches from the Österreichischer Hof, Salzburg; a fulsomely autographed copy of *Oceans of
Excitement* by Singapore Charlie Small ("as told to Nicholas Fenton"); a
sheet of anonymous research notes on Hollywood producer Pandro S.
Berman; a short story about Eskimos and a poem, both in the same diffidently faint typewriting:

> ... Outside my room
> The street-lamp dies with a
> Click
> I am alone ...

Through the Art Department's glass partition, Cedric Scurr could be
seen laying out the new "reader service" front section of the Magazine
to be inaugurated with, among other things, "The Year-round Window-box"; "Insulating Your Loft"; "Car Insurance—the Dangers"; and
"A Beginner's Guide to Orienteering." Across the aisle from the Picture
Desk came Val Lewis's impersonally sexy voice: "Hi—Patrick? Are you
free to do a studio shot for us next week? It's for the new Family First
section: we need a double-page colour spread of someone's teeth. Yes,
that's right . . . teeth. With lots of fillings, and preferably a fair bit of
decay as well . . ."

---

"Don't be such a born bloody fool, Poet," Shildrick said with the kind of
faint wince he might bestow on a split infinitive in otherwise exemplary
copy. He was perched on his window casement, looking out at St.
Paul's and the City as if impatient now for fresh worlds to conquer. On
his wildly cluttered and melodramatically lit desk lay Louis's four-line
memo of resignation.

"The book project's fine," he went on before Louis could speak. "I'm
perfectly happy for you to do that . . . I mean, if you're really convinced
you can dig up stuff on the Beatles that no one has before. But you
know as well as I do that doesn't mean you've got to leave here. You
can even take a sabbatical if you like, work on it on full pay, use the Library, get our overseas bureaux to check things out for you. A lot of
your sources are probably going to be tricky to approach, what with
having been asked the same questions so many times before. It'll be all
that easier if you can still say you're Sunday Dispatch."

"My mind's made up," said Louis.

Shildrick jumped down, took him by the elbow and propelled him across the office in that intimate, confiding saunter that always led nowhere.

"Look," he murmured, "I understand that you're upset. But don't, for pity's sake, do something in haste that you'll repent at leisure. Because once you're out of here, you know, that's it. There's a dozen bright young men from the Varsity, Honours and Double-Starred Firsts, just waiting to take your place."

"Yes, I'm sure," Louis said.

"And what about the financial side? I know you've got an advance, but how long is that going to last? It's a hard world out there, Poet. I think you've probably forgotten. No nice free pens, paper and envelopes to help yourself to ad lib. No nice friendly cashiers to shovel out fivers for a pink slip."

"I'll risk it."

The playfulness vanished from the sultry eyes, to be replaced by hurt mystification, this in turn quickly replaced by coldness. "In any case, you're doing me a grave injustice. I never offered the Magazine to you, and it was never my intention to do so. You obviously don't have anything like enough experience."

"Oh, no? And you're saying Fran does?"

At this, something odd happened on Shildrick's face. Louis was reminded of seeing Harold Wilson, at great public moments, switch on a kind of automated physiognomical mask, accompanied by what was not so much a voice as a pre-recorded tape of exhaustively rehearsed platitudes. What followed had clearly been said many times before, to Lord McIntyre, the Sunday Dispatch Board of Directors—had, indeed, appeared almost verbatim in rival papers that morning, quoting him on his revolutionary appointment of Fleet Street's first female Editor.

"She's an extremely well-known reporter and columnist who's won a tremendous public through her inspired work as a correspondent for the BBC. She's got a highly developed visual sense, and all sorts of tremendously creative ideas . . ."

"And she was about to take a job with ABC Television in New York," said Louis.

The Wilson glaze vanished from Shildrick's eyes. "How did you know that?" he inquired coldly.

"She told me."

"When did she tell you?"

"Just . . . in passing. But that's why you've given her the Magazine, isn't it? To keep her in London. Not because of her highly developed visual sense."

Shildrick's frostiness disappeared, to be replaced by something even less welcome, a shamefaced, rather helpless grin. "It was a wonderful offer they made her, you know, Poet," he said, returning to his locker-room murmur. "A massive salary, car, superb fringe-benefits. Compared to that, even the Colour Mag looked pretty small beer. In fact . . ." He shook his head with a reminiscent smile. "I'll tell you what she said to me when she finally agreed to take it, shall I? 'The only job in Fleet Street I'm really interested in is yours.' "

"Just don't imagine she was joking," Louis said.

Shildrick gripped his elbow again and resumed their stroll, apparently believing a thaw had set in. "I'd no intention of misleading you with what I said yesterday night, please believe me about that. It's not my fault you got the wrong end of the stick. Well, not totally the wrong end, because I do want you on the Colour Mag in a key executive role."

Despite himself, Louis felt a tremor of excitement. Not enough, however, to end a sentence with a preposition. "Oh yes? As what?"

"It's naturally going to be a bit strange for her at first. And, make no mistake, the knives will be out down there. That Cedric Scurr's a thoroughly nasty piece of work, but I can't have him out just yet, not till the re-design and re-launch are up and running. It'd put my mind at rest, knowing she had at least one friend and ally to help me watch her back. Someone to act as a buffer against all those peculiar Magazine folk. And, maybe, to take the production side off her shoulders so she can soar creatively."

Louis gazed down at him, realising as never before how hideous was that black chalk-stripe suit with its butterfly lapels, especially worn with that candy-pink shirt, salmon-coloured tie and matching breast-pocket handkerchief.

"Just let me get this straight. You want me to be Fran's nursemaid? And you want me to handle production?"

"Not 'nursemaid'! Don't always go for the melodramatic metaphor, Poet. Just give a helping hand to someone I know you care about. And be an extra pair of eyes and ears for me."

"Oh, so you don't mean 'nursemaid' then. You mean 'spy.' "

"You can have a snazzy title, if you like. Choose whichever one you want. Assistant Editor? Managing Editor? Executive Editor? Consulting Editor? Chief Assistant to the Editor? Chief Assistant Editor?"

"Do you really think I want to spend my life writing headlines and checking whether colour pages are on-register?" A happy phrase from David Kausman floated into memory. "It would be too stultifyingly tedious."

"I only mean for a month or two," Shildrick said hastily. "Till she finds her feet and I can get shot of Scurr and Jessamyn O'Shaughnessy.

Then, of course, I'd want you to join me up here on the paper. We've got tremendous things on the go this winter, you know. I've bought Truman Capote's new book, *Answered Prayers,* for the front of the Review. We're following up Singapore Charlie Small with a round-the-world race for solo yachtsmen—non-stop this time—where your seafaring background could be invaluable. And there's always Cicero."

Louis detached his elbow from the finger and thumb, and set off towards the door.

"Now, Poet . . . come back here and stop being such a big, soft Nellie!"

"Good-bye, Jack."

"All right, I'll give you Cicero. You can even have it in writing. How about that?"

"I said, 'Good-bye, Jack.' "

As Louis went through the outer office, where Nick Fenton and half a dozen others sat waiting, offers, promises and cast-iron guarantees floated in his wake. "You can run the Trend section . . . be our man in New York . . . do Parliament . . . have a column on the leader page . . . When's your book coming out? Maybe we can do a deal now on serialisation . . ."

---

Fran was alone in Toby Godwin's old office, a place now even barer of visible editorial activity than in her predecessor's time. Under the long work-top, the refrigerator door stood open on an interior defrosted and empty. The black leather chairs, where young rips had been wont to lounge, were pushed together in an orderly line. None would have guessed what slap-up feeds and fine wines had been consumed here, what choice cigars savoured, what hilarious northern accents put on amid mocking, exclusive, carefree laughter.

She was wearing another blouse he hadn't seen before, white silk this time, its demure neckline and short sleeves intended to announce executive gravitas. From the glossy sheen of her Alice-banded hair, and errant wisps around her neck, he could tell that she'd washed it this morning. Before her on Godwin's pristine desk lay a red leather-bound volume of back issues, evidently being dredged for ideas or inspiration. Next to her, beyond the sliding glass panel, her inherited secretary, Tessa Burland, sat with an almost audibly resonating air of irony.

As Louis appeared in the doorway, the black centipedes fluttered up with an unhappiness he could almost have believed.

"You're horribly cross with me, aren't you?" she said.

"Cross? That thoroughly inadequate adjective!" He came and leaned against the work-top, still finding it deeply strange not to see cold lobsters, game pies, chicken breasts in mayonnaise, and walnut-and-grape salad. Through the window behind her, the G.P.O. Tower sparkled in unabated sunshine. But that had long since ceased to be exciting.

"I wanted to tell you last night," she said.

"Yes, I remember you went sort of weird when I said I thought I might get it. So why didn't you? Instead of letting me make a total arsehole of myself."

"I still hadn't quite made up my mind."

"Oh, come on!" he snapped. "I've just been talking to Jack. I know the whole thing was cut and dried days ago."

"But then I started having second thoughts . . . and he was all over me . . . I felt I had to get away and talk to you."

"Oh, yes? Like your big brother? Though, of course, I'm assuming you and your big brother never did things quite like that."

She looked away with a twist of her whitened lips. "Don't make it a joke. It was really wonderful."

"Mm, yes, I thought so, too. Funny I didn't even feel the knife between my shoulderblades."

"I'm sorry," she said. "I felt really wretched about it."

"Yes, I'm sure you did. I've seen these funny little surges of conscience before. Luckily they never last very long, though, do they?"

He looked around him with that old standby, patronly pride.

"Well, you've sure come a long way from collating expenses-sheets, haven't you? I wouldn't like to be in Jessamyn's shoes now when she puts down 'Coca-Cola for brushing my teeth.' You must be feeling pretty good."

"I'm feeling totally petrified if you want to know," Fran said.

He laughed—or, rather, snorted. "Petrified? You?"

"Everything's so new . . . the flat-plan . . . costing issues . . . negotiating with agents. And having to think up ideas that'll be topical in the middle of next year." She turned a page of the bound volume with a listless hand. "I sometimes feel as if my head's going to burst."

It was hard to resist an inner avalanche of sympathy, a compulsion that surged up from his very bowels to put his arms round her and protect her, but Louis just about did.

"Oh, come off it . . . You'll be fine. You've got Jim Deaves to help you on all the admin stuff. You know he's a perfectly nice chap. Cedric, admittedly, isn't such a nice chap, but he realises he's got to play ball with Jack."

"I want you to be here," Fran said.

"What for? To deal with the printers for you? Be loyal and conscientious, and get kicked in the teeth, like all loyal, conscientious people in Fleet Street do?"

"No."

"What, then?"

"I don't want to lose you."

"But you don't want to lose Jack, either, do you? And you need Jack more, at least for the time being. So what's the master plan? Give me a little tumble every now and again to keep the flat-plan ticking over . . . or whenever Jack needs to be shown the whip?"

"It's not like that," Fran said softly.

"It's always been 'not like that.' And it's never going to be 'not like that' any more." He went to the door, opened it, then turned and managed a sardonic smile. "You can check the grammar with the Editor. You'll find it's completely OK."

---

Down in the cream-and-hessian front entrance hall, the commissionaires were on duty, with their medals and red sashes, behind the black-lacquered counter. From over the adjacent partition came the siren murmur of Mack's Tele-Ad Birds. Taxis drew up constantly outside, releasing their passengers in the invariable certainty that it was "on the Dispatch's account." Visitors waited, sunken in the deep black leather couches, gazing with envy at those with the right to come and go as they pleased.

As Louis approached the automatic glass doors, he wondered if this might not be the worst mistake even he had ever made. Before his foot touched the black rubber mat inscribed "SUNDAY DISPATCH," and the doors noiselessly drew apart, he decided that on the whole it probably was.

PHILIP NORMAN's *Shout*, a biography of The Beatles, was a bestseller here and in England. He has written ten other nonfiction books, including *Symphony for the Devil*, about The Rolling Stones, and five other novels. He lives in London with his wife and daughter.

ABOUT THE TYPE

This book was set in Photina, a typeface designed by José Mendoza in 1971. It is a very elegant design with high legibility, and its close character fit has made it a popular choice for use in quality magazines and art gallery publications.